MW01132898

Project Day Lily

Project Day Lily

An American Biological Warfare Tragedy

Garth L. Nicolson, Ph.D. and
Nancy L. Nicolson, Ph.D.

Library of Congress Number: 2005900895
ISBN: Hardcover   1-4134-8519-7
               Softcover   1-4134-8518-9

This is a work of fiction. Names, characters, places and incidents either are the product of the author's imagination or are used fictitiously, and any resemblance to any actual persons, living or dead, events, or locales is entirely coincidental.

This book was printed in the United States of America.

To order additional copies of this book, contact:
Xlibris Corporation
1-888-795-4274
www.Xlibris.com
Orders@Xlibris.com
27692

Contents

Dedication

This book is dedicated to the memory of Dr. Fred Conrad (Colonel, USAF, retired) and five other academic colleagues who died under mysterious circumstances while investigating aspects of the alleged illegal testing of Biological Weapons in Texas hospitals, nursing homes and prisons.

This book is also dedicated to the men and women of our Armed Services and their family members who were put in harm's way and were never properly warned about the dangers of Biological Weapons.

And to the Texas Department of Criminal Justice personnel and its prisoners and to the people of the Great State of Texas who were betrayed and lost their health and loved ones to a vicious agenda in the name of 'National Security.'

"Of course the people don't want war. But after all, it's the leaders of the country who determine the policy, and it's always a simple matter to drag the people along whether it's a democracy, a fascist dictatorship, or a parliament, or a communist dictatorship. Voice or no voice, the people can always be brought to the bidding of the leaders. That is easy. All you have to do is tell them they are being attacked, and denounce the pacifists for lack of patriotism, and exposing the country to greater danger."

Reichsmarshall Herman Goering
Nuremberg Trials, 18 April 1946

THE FOLLOWING IS BASED ON A TRUE STORY

The authors have written this book in order to shed light on a crisis facing our country and the world. They have chosen to use a fictional format to maximize dramatic impact. The events described are true, but fictitious names, places and composite characters have been used to develop the story. Dialogue between the characters was constructed from the recollections of various sources. The scientific principals and results discussed in this book are true and have been documented in the authors' publications, reports and sworn testimony to Presidential Commissions and committees of the United States Congress.

FORWARDS

Forward to the Book
by Michael McClay

As of today, the history books will show that the single most destructive act of war ever launched against the United States was on September 11, 2001.

As of today.

Now, four years later, the citizens of the United States have been waiting for the other shoe to drop—another act of terrorism on a massive scale. It hasn't happened, but when it does (and it will), we may not know about it when it happens, and by the time it's discovered, it will be too late. It's there every day, lurking in the shadows, never far away from our consciousness.

After 9/11 there has been a flurry of activity in response to the tragedy. The Homeland Security Act created a new Executive Federal Branch. Laundry lists of scenarios have underscored screaming headlines of another daily news item related to this certainty. The War . . . Homeland Security . . . election year political fallout . . . daily acts of terrorism around the world . . . the list goes on. At the top of this list is bioterrorism and when that hits, it will affect everyone.

The authors of this book have as much firsthand personal knowledge about the biological threat we all face as anyone on earth. This book is a road map on how they discovered and found a treatment for some of the very biotoxins that are in the hands of terrorists and rogue nations who have the capability to unleash such an attack on the United States.

And what's been done?

Our ability to respond to a biological crisis has been improved from virtually nothing to a modest ability to respond to the most obvious threats, such as anthrax. Although deadly if inhaled in moderate doses, anthrax is not contagious and cannot be passed to others.

On the other hand, there are a variety of other biological warfare agents that are highly contagious and will spread to unlimited numbers of people with only casual contact. Most of these agents will initially cause an innocuous flu-like disorder that doesn't appear life threatening, only to later progress to a fatal disease that cannot be stopped by available drugs and treatments. These agents are difficult to detect, and the diseases that they cause are difficult to diagnose.

This is not a problem limited to the United States, as the citizens of Spain and Russia know all too well. All nations under the Charter of the United Nations are under this threat, and there are those out there who do not want to have this message heard. Not just terrorists, but our own government officials who don't want the population to know how unprepared we really are or that there are scientists within our own government and academic institutions who have perpetuated the terrorism.

This is the first and only book that exposes the truth on how this threat began (During World War II), how it was actively developed in our own military labs and in other laboratories around the world (During the Cold War), how it came to fruition (During the Gulf War) and how it's threatening us now. Little has changed since the Nicolsons first exposed the infection behind much of the illnesses associated with the Gulf War. These infections are still slowly penetrating into our population and will continue to cause chronic illnesses.

Project Day Lily chronicles the events surrounding what the public knows as 'Gulf War Syndrome.' To this day there are over 150,000 veterans of the first Gulf War that suffer from chronic illnesses and tens of thousands have died without acknowledgment or proper assistance to keep secret the origin of their illnesses. Some of these illnesses were caused by infectious agents worked on by our own scientists, some of whom were trained by 'Operation Paperclip' scientists brought back from Germany after World War II. This is based on solid, scientific facts, backed by some of the most respected and well-known scientific minds and leading professionals in the world.

The story continues to this day, although the book itself largely ends when the Nicolsons leave their academic positions in Texas after discovering a massive cover-up of illegal biological testing in the Texas prison system. The scientific information is completely factual as is the truth regarding the way the principals uncovered the events and the efforts of those who went to extreme and deadly measures to keep this vast scientific-military-governmental conspiracy from becoming public knowledge.

Michael McClay
Ventura, California
September 2004

Forward by the Authors

On January 5, 1993 former President George Herbert W. Bush delivered a speech at the West Point Military Academy that would accurately predict and prophesize almost a decade later the post-9/11 world that we live in today. The former President would emphasize that the most important aspect of leadership of the nation's highest office was the role of Commander-in-Chief of the Armed Forces, for it was in this capacity that the President's decisions affected every person on the planet. "We risk the emergence of a world characterized by violence, characterized by chaos, one in which dictators and tyrants threaten their neighbors, build arsenals brimming with weapons of mass destruction, and ignore the welfare of their own men, women, and children." "We can not be passive or aloof . . . or we could see an increase in international terrorism with American citizens more at risk than ever before." How prophetic this statement would prove to be. The world after September 11, 2001 has become exactly what former President Bush feared when he made his speech at West Point.

Our former President possessed a clear understanding of our complex world, but he might not have known that a sinister group of rogue scientists, physicians, bureaucrats and government administrators with extremist and inhuman attitudes existed and were camouflaged within the academic, military, veterans' and intelligence organizations in the United States and abroad. This well-organized faction, steeped in Cold War philosophies and backed financially by organized crime and global syndicate special interests, has operated and continues to operate within our midst while arrogantly ignoring the basic dictates of human rights and dignity. They continue to conduct their reckless experiments to test biological weapons and other weapons of mass destruction on an unwitting public and Armed Forces personnel using incredibly underhanded and amoral tactics and strategies. This group has not been held accountable, nor have they accepted responsibility for their heinous acts against mankind that span decades of abusive conduct since World War II.

Unfortunately, the professional organizations of scientists and physicians around the world have done little to identify and stop this rogue group and have for the most part been too intimidated or apathetic to assist Congress and the Executive Branch of the U. S. Government and other governments around the world to stop this form of insidious scientific-medical terrorism. We consider this to be one of the greatest betrayals ever perpetuated on the people and the governments of the world.

As scientists and researchers whose foremost goal is to protect peoples' health, we are ashamed that this deadly faction has been allowed to commit their abominable crimes against humanity. This book, Project Day Lily, is based on our two decades' struggle to make this rogue faction accountable and to provide positive scientific and clinical solutions for citizens and military personnel, such as the thousands of veterans of the first Persian Gulf War and their family members that have contracted various chronic illnesses. To assist citizens, veterans and military personnel we established the nonprofit Institute for Molecular Medicine (www.immed.org). Its mission is to discover novel solutions and treatments for chronic illnesses, such as those caused by incapacitating biological weapons.

In the ultimate irony the book underscores the reality that the rogue group responsible for developing and testing deadly biological agents on our citizens were financed by the illegal use of various trusts left to one of us. The use of financial instruments that are part of an inheritance illegally held by others unfortunately paved the way for financing the development, testing and manufacture of unconventional weapons of mass destruction. Groups of unethical attorneys and trustees managed the trusts that are responsible for financing what we consider to be a loathsome agenda against humanity as well as orchestrating a horrific campaign against us to prevent one of us from assuming control of her family's financial legacy, which was to be used for humanitarian purposes.

Fortunately the Patriot Act has ensured that only the true owners of trusts, such as the ones left to one of us, can give permission for the utilization of the funds. This law will ultimately prevent further illegal use of the funds. At present, we are working with the U. S. Government to make certain that these trusts are used for the good of the people of the United States and our neighbors around the world.

Garth L. Nicolson, Ph.D. and Nancy L. Nicolson, Ph.D.
The Institute for Molecular Medicine (www.immed.org)
Huntington Beach, California
November 2004

PROLOGUE

Incidents at the beginning of the first Gulf War (1991)

Preparation for the first assault into Iraq, 101st Airborne Division (Air Assault)

The sky was dark as only darkness can be in a Saudi desert with few physical features and essentially no vegetation. At the front lines Coalition Forces were pulling back from the border, regrouping and readying for the assault that would come in a few hours. The focused assaults on the Southern borders of Iraq and Kuwait would be almost entirely mechanized, and the armored personnel carriers, tanks, trucks, transporters and other vehicles began to line up for the run to the border and the breaching of the Iraqi border positions. They would be led by special tanks and bulldozers equipped with anti-mine devices to clear the border area of the deadly landmines that lurk just below the surface of the sand. Engineering units would destroy any obstacles and bridge any trenches that the Iraqis have built to slow the Coalition Forces. They would also quell any possible oil fires started in the trenches by filling them with sand, and they would bury any unfortunate Iraqi soldiers who refused to surrender or stay in their bunkers. However, the Iraqis had a special weapon waiting for their enemies just under the surface of the sand. They had hidden thousands of chemical-biological landmines that won't destroy vehicles but will release deadly clouds of chemical and biological weapons. They had also deployed more than 60 chemical-biological weapons sprayers to contaminate large areas just inside the border. The mechanized units would unknowingly be contaminated as they silently passed through such areas.

As the flashes briefly illuminated the border area, the immediate objective could be clearly seen, if just for a second or so at a time. Near the border was an endless bream or long wall of sand several meters high built to slow an advance of mechanized vehicles and provide cover for defensive forces. Distant piercing white flashes illuminated the breams briefly, and the flashes were followed with a slight delay by deadening explosions that sounded like dull thuds instead of high-pitched explosions. Coalition 'arty' was softening up the staging areas to the rear of the border defenses. The dull reports increased gradually almost as a rolling thunder as more and more coalition artillery opened up and pounded Iraqi positions that faced the coalition forces behind the border between Saudi Arabia and Iraq and Kuwait. As the incoming shells passed overhead, they screamed as they traveled to their targets. The softening up of the border area had been underway for several weeks, and almost daily B-52 high altitude carpet bombing attacks with dumb bombs have left Iraqi soldiers shaken and disoriented. There was no food or water left on the Iraqi side of the border, and all the Iraqis could do was wait for the attack that seemed to never come.

Many miles south from the Iraqi border at a Coalition airbase near Al Bitan in Saudi Arabia shadowy figures in MOPP IV (Mission Oriented Protective Posture–Level IV) NBC (Nuclear, Biological, Chemical) protection gear and night vision goggles stood guard and surveyed the no man's land that separated the desert between Iraq and Saudi Arabia. There was tremendous noise as UH-60 Blackhawk, CH-47 Chinook and AH-64 Apache helicopters of the U.S. Army's 101st Airborne Division revved their engines in the dark, the fiery jet exhausts breaking the silence of the desert. They were waiting for air assault infantry to load into the Blackhawks and Chinooks and begin the deep insertions into Iraq before the Ground Offensive of Operation Desert Storm was officially underway. Last second instructions were given to air crews and soldiers awaiting the command to commence Operation "Clean Sweep" to destroy Iraqi Command & Control Centers, Chemical and Biological Warfare Centers, storage depots and SCUD missiles armed with Chemical and Biological Weapons before the Ground Offensive started. The most important part of the mission was to block retreating Iraqi forces and prevent a northwestern retreat of Iraqi Republican Guard armored divisions. They would do this by taking the bridges that cross the Euphrates River and deploying in a formation that would block the Iraqi forces from moving North-West and force them back into a killing zone where a combination of air and land forces could decimate them at will.

In the night it was usually difficult to see without night vision equipment; however, the burning jet fuel provided a little light when the engines were revved. Soldiers emerged in long lines with their gear and supplies, and aircraft crews helped load the air assault forces and their supplies, including NBC protective gear, in preparation for the long trip North.

Alarm Black at a support base near the 101ˢᵗ Airborne Division HQ at Al Bitan

At a support base near the Base Bravo airfield a siren sounded in the background. It went almost unnoticed with the noise of trucks and transporters gunning their engines and maneuvering into columns, but in the tents containing NBC detection equipment pandemonium broke loose. A young Chemical/Biological Weapons Specialist that was in his first action yelled to the NBC Officer in the COC (Combat Operations Center), "Captain! We've got hypersonic incoming, probably SCUD B targeting our area! We already have CBW reports 3 clicks to the east!" The NBC Officer replied, "What does Charley Company report?" The CBW Specialist replied, "Their M8A1 units were positive for chemical agents, and Baker Company reports they are under chemical attack. We are the next unit down wind!" The Duty Officer continued, "Make sure our RSCAALs (Remote Sensing Chemical Agent Alarms) are on. Don't panic the men, Lieutenant, just go to MOPP IV, and clear the area." The CBW Specialist answered, "Yes SIR!" Sir, Headquarters says to disregard the Chemical Alarms. Why in hell would they issue that order when we are under attack? The Duty Officer stated, "Just get us to MOPP IV. We'll worry about what HQ says later!" The CBW Specialist replied, "Yes, Sir!"

The young First Lieutenant ordered his sergeant to use the camp PA. A moment later the Specialist alerted the base, "SCUD incoming, I repeat, SCUD incoming! Alarm Black! Alarm Black! Gas! Gas! Gas! Go to MOPP

IV! Go to MOPP IV! . . . . This is no drill! Go to MOPP IV! I repeat, Go to MOPP IV!" A siren sounded, and an Iraqi SS-1 SCUD B warhead exploded high in the sky above the area leaving a cloud of bluish purple mist hanging in the area. About 30 seconds later, the first RSCAAL Chemical Alarms went off, and then another, one by one. Over the post PA could be heard, "Alarm Black! Gas! Gas! Gas! This is no drill! Go to MOPP IV! Go to MOPP IV!"

As the Chemical Alarms sounded, soldiers ran for cover, and the order to go to MOPP IV was repeated several times. Soldiers quickly donned their NBC suits and masks, but some were slow to get into their MOPP gear and were quickly exposed to the bluish purple mist that was settling into the area. These exposed soldiers immediately felt burning sensations on their skin and throat and then their lungs felt like they were on fire. They began scratching their skin, eyes and throat, and then they began vomiting. They vomited over and over again as if they were trying to turn their stomachs inside out and expel them through their throats. Other soldiers in full MOPP IV gear began to deploy as Chemical Agent alarms sounded and other dull detonations were heard nearby. The soldiers were unaware that the purple-blue material was Prussian Blue–specifically designed to destroy the filters in the MOPP protective suits. They were also unaware that the Iraqi Prussian Blue was actually manufactured in Boca Raton, Florida and exported to Iraq during the Iraq-Iran war with the blessings of the United States and its Commerce Department.

At a support base near Al Bitan all was suddenly quiet. Then the muffled sound of "Medic! Medic!" was heard but not at a distance. Much more audible were the screams of exposed soldiers who could not find their MOPP gear in time. Then their screams began to be drowned out by the roar of trucks preparing to depart for the Iraqi border. At the same airbase Special Forces trained for identifying and destroying unconventional weapons also loaded for the deep insertions into Iraq. They had their own specially outfitted helicopters, painted black for the 'Special Ops' nature of their mission. Their mission was to find and destroy Iraqi Chemical and Biological factories, storage depots and SCUD launchers. As the Air Assault and Special Forces units loaded for battle, they didn't look back; there was no time to contemplate, only react. In addition to the airborne infantry of the 101st Airborne Division (Air Assault), Field Artillery units were also preparing to depart. The artillery and supplies would be carried along with their crews by the large cargo helicopters. As they lifted off, last second instructions on Chemical/Biological Warfare were given over the intercom to the crews and their cargo of airborne warriors who prepared to face the dangers of a modern battlefield.

Officers' Staff Meeting: 101st Airborne Division (Air Assault)

Lieutenant Colonel David Smith, Division Chemical/Biological Officer, 101st Airborne Division, was speaking to his staff. Although LTC Smith had not ever been in an unconventional war, he tried to speak with the authority that was expected by his staff. A tall slender Texan with piercing blue eyes, LTC Smith spoke with a slight drawl, giving away his West Texas origins. He stood ramrod straight while addressing the assembled officers and noncoms. Schooled at Texas A & M University and a product of the proud Aggie 'Corps' and 11th Man on Kyle Field at College Station, LTC Smith was actually slightly out of place with the younger Academy-trained officers. He did not want to show his staff that college chemistry and microbiology were not his strong classes at A & M. Along the way he had learned what he had to learn at Fort Detrick and the Dugway Proving Ground. "Ladies and Gentleman, the NBC offensive threat is high, I repeat, the threat is high. G2 indicates Iraqis have full complement of Chemical and Biological Weapons, including 120 millimeter rockets and SCUD B missiles specially equipped for CBW use, and these have been moved within the last 72 hours to forward positions here, here and here." He gestured as he pointed to a map of Southern Iraq. "Intel indicates likely hostile first use of Chemical and Biological Agents. First, be sure that your troops are ready for CBW attacks, your MOPP gear is fully operational and that each soldier has extra filter units. Second, be sure that they *all* take their PB pills as ordered. Some units will have to take the white antibiotic pills as well. Third, remind your units of the six basic steps of NBC warfare: (1) Preparation, (2) Identification, (3) Protection, (4) Survival, (5) Decontamination, and (6) First Aid. We have gone through this before, and you should be ready. The Iraqis have blister agents, nerve agents, blood agents, and choking agents, such as sarin, tabun, lewisite and mustard.

They also have several kinds of Biological Agents, including anthrax, botulism, micotoxins and others" . . . He paused . . . As LTC Smith continued, "For the Chemical Agents we have deployed M8A1 and M256 Chemical Detection Units and Fox Mobile Detection units. But let me remind you, we don't have any detection equipment for Biological Agents, so be especially careful if you see dead animals and soldiers with no apparent wounds. Don't assume only Chemical, unless your NBC unit has confirmed. Intel indicates that Iraqi forces are operating under Soviet War Doctrine, so they will be mixing Chemical and Biological Agents in the same attack to confuse us. Let me remind you that the biggest threat that we face will come from Iraqi unconventional weapons."

A Junior Officer asked, "Sir, How do we detect the Biological Agents?" LTC Smith responded, "We don't! As I said before, we don't have any detection capability for Biological Agents in theater. For whatever reason, the brass stateside wouldn't let us deploy our Pace Biological Detection Systems to the Persian Gulf. We've asked the guys at Fort Baker to send us their detection units, but for some reason the higher ups have decided that we don't need them. If you encounter suspected Biological Agents and are possibly contaminated, you will have to identify the agent by the types of symptoms that casualties are displaying. Most signs and symptoms of rapidly acting Biological Agents, such as anthrax, won't show up for a day or so after exposure. But if you see troops showing breathing distress and coughing up blood, skin itching, vomiting, diarrhea, fever, chills and other problems soon after an attack, they were probably exposed to Chemicals. Remember rapid fluid loss is one of the biggest problems in the desert. Units that have been issued the white antibiotic pills should immediately begin taking two per day. We know that the Iraqis also have slow acting agents, but don't worry about these in the field. They are not expected to cause any problems that could jeopardize our mission. Any other questions?" A Junior Officer asked, "Sir, what do we know about these slow acting Biological Agents?" "And why weren't we *all* issued antibiotics in case of BW attack?"

LTC Smith thought about the question before responding. He then said, "We do not have much Intel on their slow-acting BW. They should only cause chronic illnesses, so don't worry about them. I repeat, since these should not interfere with our mission, you don't have to worry about the slow-acting Biologicals. We will sort that out after the operation."

A warning on the sand

Air Assault Forces from the 101st Airborne Division were now on the ground deep in Iraq after a long 'helo' ride. They deployed during the night and established a perimeter in advance of an Arty company that would be brought in with the second wave. The 101st Field Artillery, mostly 105-millimeter howitzers, were carried in by the 'heavy' CH-47 Chinooks as soon as the area was secure. As the sun began to rise, dead animals were seen in the distance, and occasionally a dead Iraqi soldier was seen. 101st infantry units regrouped in full MOPP IV gear and were ordered to inspect the area containing the dead animals and Iraqi soldiers. Graves units would be burying the dead Iraqis in large sand pits as soon as some equipment arrived to dig the trenches.

At the moment, there was nothing that could be done for the dead Iraqis. A recon team had searched the area and already reported back. The rest of the 'Screaming Eagles' finally arrived in a Humvee with a TOW missile launcher mounted on top that had been 'air delivered' during the night. They noticed that the faces of the Iraqi soldiers were contorted and were dark purple or black in color. Equipment was scattered everywhere, including gas masks and CBW protective gear. No one wanted to go near the dead animals or Iraqi soldiers, so they just kept their distance and maintained a routine perimeter.

'Incoming'

The distinctive sound of a Russian-made 120-millimeter rocket screamed overhead and broke the silence of the desert. Then another was heard. A soldier shouted, "Incoming! Incoming!" Soldiers dove for cover, and one lost his M46 NBC protective mask. He fell face-to-face next to a dead, bloated Iraqi soldier. The blue-green, bloated face of the dead Iraqi was unusually contorted. His tongue was sticking out, hanging over his beard. The American soldier was frozen for a moment in horror. No matter how many times he had practiced putting on his MOPP gear, panic caused him to hesitate. As he looked at his comrades who had automatically put on their MOPP gear, even the horror of seeing the dead Iraqi soldiers could not overcome the hours upon hours of training for just this moment. But to the soldier who hesitated, a sick expression came over his face. It was too late. The burning in his lungs made him gasp for air, and mucus and clear liquid were pouring out of his eyes and nose, an almost impossible response in the ultra-dry desert of Southern Iraq. Instead of completing his MOPP donning procedures, he rubbed his eyes to stop the intense burning and pain. He would pay a terrible price for his untimely hesitation. The incoming rounds hit and sounded like low-yield explosive warheads, and they landed with a 'thud' instead of a high explosive blast, suggesting that a CBW attack was underway. Purple clouds rose from impact sites, another sign of a CBW attack.

An older Sergeant yelled, "Incoming! Take cover! Take Cover!" No one dared to ask the Sergeant what or why, they just reacted. As another round hit with a 'thud,' the Sergeant didn't hesitate. He yelled though his M46 NBC mask, "Alarm Black! Gas! Gas! Gas! Make sure you're MOPP IV!" But only a few of the soldiers could hear him yell through the cumbersome masks. Clouds of blue-purple mist covered the area, making the scene surreal. Eventually soldiers appeared through the mist in their MOPP gear. As they headed for their helicopters and then disembarked from the area, they did a head count to make sure that no one was left behind. Two privates were carrying the hesitant soldier who was now twisting, shaking and writhing in pain. His comrades placed him into his MOPP gear but it was clearly too late. He was loaded onto a Blackhawk for the long trip back to a Saudi Medivac base. His sergeant shook his head to his platoon leader, a young officer who was facing his first ever engagement with enemy forces. The young officer's eyes were as big as silver dollars as he watched his men in the Blackhawk. They were just as afraid. As the sun slowly continued to rise, the signs of war unfolded, smoke, noise, discarded equipment, and everywhere death. As they left for safer ground, it was a scene that no one would ever forget.

CHAPTER 1

The magnificent flower (circa 1980)

The U. S. Army Biological Warfare Research Center, Fort Detrick, Maryland.

In the rolling hills of Northern Maryland in the County of Frederick was a sprawling U. S. Army base that became during World War II and the subsequent Cold War years the main center for U. S. Biological Warfare research. Fort Detrick was America's premiere laboratory for the development of Biological Warfare agents and their defense. Even though Fort Detrick was to be mainly decommissioned and turned into a cancer research facility administered by the National Institutes of Health by the passage of President Nixon's Plowshare Act, the military activities remained relatively untouched at the U. S. Army's Institute for Infectious Diseases headquartered at Fort Detrick. Although the classified part of Fort Detrick where Biological Warfare research has continued to this day was much smaller than in its Cold War heyday, it remained a potent force in a secret war to develop and test new biological agents under the guise of Biological Warfare Defense. It was here and in hundreds of other laboratories throughout America that immediately after World War II our former enemies' scientists were brought in under Operation Paperclip to continue their research and development of some of the most horrible weapons of mass destruction known to mankind.

In 1980 in one of the hundreds of nondescript windowless light yellow concrete block buildings at Fort Detrick Dr. James Deutschman, Dr. Ming Lon, and Brigadier General Richard Armwhite were intently assessing the structure of a previously uncharacterized microorganism found in weapons grade cultures of anthrax saved from our enemies at the end of World War II. Dr. Ming Lon, who was considered a brilliant Chinese scientist now working for the U. S. Army, was an anthrax expert, and it was in his laboratory that the new microorganism was found in an old culture obtained from one of the German SS units retreating back to Germany from Eastern Europe. The Germans had been developing biological warfare agents for use in their killing programs in Eastern Europe, but they had not attempted to identify all of the organisms in their most potent cultures. It seemed that the 'best' isolates were mixtures of microorganisms, and Dr. Ming Lon was assigned to determine just exactly what was in these deadly mixtures. Dr. Lon was old-school Chinese, and his dress, demeanor and polite conversation style were consistent with his Mainland Chinese training. These men came to the Electron Microscope Laboratory to view the potent new microorganism that Dr. Lon had found recently using an electron microscope.

It was indeed a very unusual microorganism. It was not related to anthrax, the potent biowarfare agent that looks under a microscope like lines of small boxcars and can kill within days if inhaled deep into the lungs at very low concentrations. The agent found by Dr. Lon was much smaller than anthrax, it contained much less genetic material, and it did not have the typical 'boxcar' bacterial structure of anthrax. The unknown bug that was to be examined could no longer be alive for this procedure; it must be killed and chemically fixed and heavy metal atoms bound to it, then dehydrated in alcohol and embedded in plastic in order to be cut into very, very thin slices so that it can be viewed in the electron microscope. The electron microscope could magnify images hundreds of thousands of times and allow scientists to see minute details in biological structure that cannot be seen with other methods. The instrument used an electron beam to bombard the specimen, and this beam can be focused similarly to what would happen with light as it went through a series of glass lenses, but in the electron microscope magnetic lenses focused an electron beam before and after it penetrated the specimen. Then an image could be created by the penetrating electrons, which are focused onto a fluorescing plate that can be viewed through thick glass portals. Alternatively the beam can be focused onto a film plate. The entire instrument must be operated under a high vacuum so that air molecules won't interfere with and scatter the electron beam.

The three individuals were in a small dark room with a technician and the electron microscope. No one seemed to notice that the microscope they were using was made in Germany. Both Dr. Armwhite, a Brigadier General in the U. S. Army Medical Corps, and Dr. Deutschman, a scientist from the Pentagon, were products of the Cold War era, and their manner and attitude reflected this. General Armwhite was a rather nondescript man of medium height with a kind looking face that hid his ruthlessness. He was more concerned with his own glory rather than the welfare of any soldiers under his command that might be called to battle. He regarded enlisted soldiers as totally expendable scientific subjects to be used to further his own career. He coveted the position of Surgeon General of the Army but he would never be promoted to this rank because he lacked the personality for a leadership position. It came with the three-star rank of a Lieutenant General and all of the privileges and stature accorded to the rank. Few general officers ever even got the chance to be considered for three stars. It would have been the crowning achievement of an already 'distinguished' career of this one star general. Who would have ever thought that a physician/scientist could hold such a rank? However, as a physician he knew that he must feign concern on the surface for his fellow man, especially those who were ill and in need of medical attention. He was a cruel political animal who used medicine as a tool to achieve his ambitions of glory and power. Dr. Deutschman, a civilian member of the Department of Defense, was an arrogant scientist, and his philosophy was embodied in his demeanor. He was a throwback to the fascist attitudes of the World War II era, and one might have confused him with the stereotype 'mad scientist' of Hollywood B-movies. From his slight accent one might also have concluded that Dr. Deutschman was a 'Paperclip' scientist, one of the thousands of Nazi scientists brought over by the U. S. Army and the OSS after World War II, but in fact, his family emigrated from Germany to the United States generations ago. Dr. Ming Lon, by far the most intelligent of the trio, was trained in both China and the United States. He was considered a scientific genius in China and one of the best of his scientific generation, but he was not as arrogant as the others. He did, however, have a central flaw that was unfortunately very common among scientists of his generation. He was incapable of resisting illegal or unethical orders from his superiors. It was true in Communist China, and it remained true in the capitalist United States. He was indebted to the U. S. Government for getting him out of China, and he was not about to make the mistake of biting the hand that fed him. Dr. Lon smiled a lot in the company of more senior personnel. It was a trait that he learned in China, and he could not seem to rid himself of this somewhat obvious response. But his superiors actually liked it, because it seemed that he was being subservient. In reality, however, Dr. Lon thought that his superiors were idiots, placed in their positions out of political concerns not because they were of superior intellect.

The glorious day lily has bloomed

Dr. Deutschman was enthusiastically looking at the electron microscope screen in the darkened room. "It's magnificent! Just like the delicate petals of a glorious day lily. So beautiful for such a short time, and then vanishing from its garden. The perfect silent assassin . . . . Silent and untraceable." His voice had a mocking, sinister quality as if he was eluding justice and getting away with it. General Armwhite said, "No one would ever think a little 'mycoplasma' could be so deadly. They won't be able to get a diagnosis on this one!"

The minute 'bug' or mycoplasma, whose image they were looking at in the electron microscope, was a primitive form of a bacterium. In fact, it was so primitive that it had lost its outer protective shield or cell wall, the thick coating of complex sugars that protects bacteria from the elements and gave bacteria their distinctive shape. The little mycoplasma had also lost some of its genetic information, such as the genes that encode the thick cell wall and other genes that code for certain enzymes in metabolic pathways. Thus it was smaller than the most common bacteria, and without the distinctive cell walls found in most bacteria it could take on a variety of morphologies. It must hide inside animal or human cells to survive, and although originally thought to be fairly fragile, the little mycoplasma was hardier than anyone had ever imagined. Although it was considered primitive by bacteriological standards, it actually evolved from bacteria that contained cell walls, but along the way it lost its ability to make its own cell wall, probably because it no longer needed it when hiding inside hosts' cells and tissues. But it made up for the loss of some of its genetic information by having evolved with other genetic sequences that allowed it to enter and colonize cells just like viruses.

Although the little mycoplasma was first identified as a virus by Dr. Lon, technically it was not a virus because it retained the genetic and biochemical remnants of bacteria. Like a virus, however, it damaged cells by interfering with some of the cells' biochemical cycles, and it encoded some nasty molecules that caused invaded cells to slowly self-destruct and die. It also released metabolic products that damaged important cellular structures. Important targets inside cells were the mitochondria, the little organelles that likely evolved from a primitive symbiotic microorganism millions of years ago and that were often called the 'batteries' of cells because they produced the energy that each cell needed to survive. Other targets of the mycoplasma metabolites were the DNA or genetic machinery found in each cell. Dr. Deutschman said to his colleagues, "This creature will hide inside cells and cause unbelievable havoc. It will destroy the mitochondria, eventually sending cells into an unrelenting death program, and in the process gene expression will go crazy and surrounding cells will become damaged. This bug will then escape from its dying host cell and go to other places to eventually colonize every organ. And because pieces of the cellular membrane are dislodged when this little mycoplasma leaves its cellular hiding places, its victims should also present with an array of autoimmune symptoms similar to those found in various degenerative illnesses. It may even mimic some neurodegenerative diseases. It's beautiful, because it should cause diseases such as multiple sclerosis and rheumatoid arthritis, but no one will ever guess that they are caused by an infection. Most physicians are so stupid that they will never figure this out, and if they do we'll just sic the CDC on them. What a delightful weapon!"

Dr. Ming Lon had been patiently listening to Dr. Deutschman, who he considered a scientific idiot and egotistical grandstander and General Armwhite, who he considered more intellectually capable but also potentially very dangerous to the human race. He thought to himself that if he were a sane person, he might even consider them arrogant criminals, fully capable of developing and releasing upon humanity biological weapons of mass destruction just to prove a point. In fact, in their zeal to prove the effectiveness of the weapons that they have developed, some very tragic incidents have occurred. Most all of these have been carefully and cleverly covered up, so that the American public knew nothing of these monsters and their creations.

Most of the victims of the Fort Detrick experiments were civilian conscientious objectors, military recruits or prisoners, 'subjects' that these esteemed individuals considered completely expendable. Dr. Deutschman continued his monologue, not even considering that his comments were unnecessary and even boring to the other participants, "I can hardly wait to see the field results. Nobody will ever guess what it is and how it works! They will never find out that it's a mycoplasma. Our little program with the CDC has convinced everyone that mycoplasmas are completely benign and don't even cause disease. As usual, the medical community has played right into our hands. We will just have to agree publicly with the CDC on this and make sure that they don't later change their minds. Mycoplasmas don't cause disease, do they?" He laughed and slapped Dr. Lon on the back.

Dr. Lon, who was still acting subdued, slowly turned and addressed his colleagues. "Yes, I believe that you can control the CDC and even the AMA. But you may not be able to control everyone. And I agree, it's beautiful, and it's dangerous, but can we control it? What effects will it have on its victims if they are exposed to other microorganisms at the same time? What will happen if they are exposed to Chemical Agents and the mycoplasma? The Germans respected this little flower. If this begins to slowly spread in the community, can we really stop it? Have we really thought out all the parameters?" Dr. Deutschman quipped, "We'll just have to field test it to find out . . . . I can hardly wait!"

Dr. Lon was hesitant. "But there could be numerous permutations and combinations of mutations and even genetic exchange in this particular species. I don't think we have enough knowledge about this to detect it on the battlefield, let alone accurately develop adequate diagnostic procedures if it infects our own soldiers. And what about civilians? What happens if soldiers return and spread this to their families?"

Dr. Richard Armwhite, the egocentric general officer, interrupted Dr. Lon. "Oh, come off it, Dr. Lon. Don't tell me you're going soft on us! Who in the hell cares about its potential mechanisms at the cellular level anyway, and so what if a few people become sick. Besides, it's not as if it's a virus that cannot be treated with antibiotics." Dr. Armwhite continued, "It's not

HIV, you know!" Dr. Lon sarcastically answered, "No, It's *worse!*" He paused again and then continued, "You've got to know that this is probably the true killer in HIV-AIDS! My lab has found this in over 80% of AIDS patients, and it is especially high in the late stages of the disease. This is what is *really* killing the HIV-infected people not the HIV virus. The virus may knock down the immune cells, but it can't cause the morbidity and foul up every organ and tissue like this mycoplasma can. And now what we've done is make it impossible to detect! And I would like to know how it got into the AIDS patients?"

General Armwhite looked at Dr. Lon and became highly irritated. "I am warning you, Dr. Lon! Let's not get off on tangents and suppositions! You know damn well that officially it is HIV-1 that causes AIDS, and that's how it's going to stay. And don't ask how our little creation got in with the HIV program, and don't go back and remind me of our MKNAOMI and P2 projects! It just got a little out of hand in Africa, you know, and no one cared about those fags in New York, anyway. They will never find out that the HIV-1 doesn't cause AIDS without the mycoplama co-infection. Look, there are thousands of scientists working on AIDS, and none of them suspects a thing."

General Armwhite paused and then frowned. "Ming, I am growing impatient with your sudden humanitarian inclinations! Dr. Lon, you know that we can control this mycoplasma with antibiotics." Dr. Lon quietly replied, "I'm not so sure." General Armwhite responded, "It's a *beautiful* weapon! It's the last thing anybody would expect with the broad spectrum of signs and symptoms that patients could display. You know damn well it is capable of producing a number of very interesting illnesses. It can give us an advantage in terms of long-term military objectives with certain hostile countries. Think of what this might do over the long run in a country like North Korea or Cuba. It could eventually bankrupt their economies if everyone is chronically sick and unproductive. Hell, it wouldn't take that much!"

Dr. Lon shook his head and tried to again get across his point to General Armwhite. "I repeat, sir, how do we prevent this 'flower' from coming back to target our own men . . . . and eventually their families . . . . and even ourselves? I do not think it is so controllable. I am not convinced antibiotics will always do the job." General Armwhite stated in an aggressive manner, "Dr. Lon, people like you and me are not ever going to get sick from this little thing. We are different . . . We are superior, and we have the inside track."

General Armwhite gazed intently at Dr. Ming Lon, who was dimly illuminated by the fluorescent electron microscope screen. "Dr. Lon, we will not be 'felled' by our own creation!" Dr. Lon responded, "But sir, we may even outsmart ourselves with the chameleon-like characteristics of this thing and its potential to produce so many different symptoms in patients. We may not even be able to tell who has been infected and who is carrying it on to others. And it may change so often that we may not be able to identify or treat it . . . . and then what?"

Dr. Lon realized that he was not getting his point across. "It may masquerade as so many unusual illnesses and even autoimmune diseases, and only a very good scientist will be able to find it." He waited to make his point again, "I have my doubts that we can control this microorganism if it's ever released." Dr. Deutschman glanced at Dr. Armwhite and turned to Dr. Lon, "Damn it, Ming, enough of your drivel! This has already been decided at the highest levels. It's out of our hands."

In accordance with the attitude of General Armwhite, Dr. Deutschman, who was a bit of a political hack, changed to a fatherly manner, "Don't be so noble, Dr. Lon, the earth is already overpopulated, and the elimination of some inferior stock can only help improve the situation on this planet. Look at Asia, Africa . . . Are we going to let the entire world go to hell just because we can't control the masses from their expansive ways? Besides, this mycoplasma fits in nicely with the Crystal Spring Harbor Directive, whose long-term objective, need I remind you, is to provide the means to select or create, if you will, a more limited global population of superior individuals. So, only the best of the best *need* survive. We already have too many inferior people on this planet. They just clutter all of our objectives for the next millennium. They cause an imbalance in the New World Order. Look, you must agree coming from Red China! What a disaster! Look at what could happen if you turned over the planet to a bunch of communist idiots. The whole world would be just like Red China!"

Dr. Ming Lon waited until Dr. Deutschman's passion died down. "But sir, not all people are both physically *and* mentally strong, and some of the greatest people in history had a variety of handicaps, and they might be the ones who are eliminated." Dr. Armwhite countered, "Who the hell needs them! The world would be a much better place if we could humanely eliminate them." Dr. Lon responded, "I say we do not know enough about this mycoplasma's etiology, its mode of action and the number of different ways that it causes disease. We need to know its mutation capability and its genetic exchange rate. It could change into something that we could not even control. Since it moves slowly through a population, by the time anyone knows something is terribly wrong, everyone will be infected." Dr. Deutschman firmly stated, "You're overreacting again, Dr. Lon! I have no doubt in your ability to manage this infection, and since when have you considered anyone else's welfare since you arrived from Mainland China. Just remember we got you out of that work camp and educated you, so now that you have a good life, you think that you can do what you want and lecture *us*! I strongly urge you to play ball if you want to maintain your present living standard, or do you want to go back to Red China? Think of your future . . . . your family's future."

Suddenly it was quiet. The men all looked at each other. Finally, Dr. Deutschman said, "Do you fully comprehend what I am saying Dr. Lon? I want you to continue this vital work, and I do not want any unnecessary delays." Dr. Deutschman then took on an abstracted countenance while Dr. Armwhite appeared agitated but tried to maintain his philosophical manner. After a few moments of silence Dr. Deutschman finally spoke. "There will be plenty of opportunities to test the little 'Day Lily.' Right now we have some preliminary results in Texas that look promising. Remember, we must be prepared to fight a Soviet-type war using conventional *and* unconventional munitions. In other words, we have to be ready in the event that our soldiers become exposed to Soviet cocktails of CBW agents. Christ, we're not going to let those commies have the advantage. They have been introducing their war doctrine to their Middle Eastern clients for years now. It's about time that we catch up and even take the lead. We have to keep this project, this magnificent creation of yours, Ming, our little secret. As far as the world is concerned," he spoke with a sarcastic tone, "this fragile little flower does not exist. Do you read me?"

Dr. Lon remained quiet, but it was quite clear what the objectives were, and he will have to do what is required to take the little 'flower' into new gardens to see its potential, no matter how many innocents were its victims.

After all, it could prove to be interesting, and he might be able to even publish some of the work if he was clever not to reveal the real agenda behind the 'Day Lily.' He will just have to keep the important points secret from his scientific colleagues. This was done all the time by military scientists, so it should not be a problem. He was rarely allowed to publish in China, and the thought of seeing his name in print thrilled him. Thoughts of how to hide the real agenda and truth about the 'Day Lily' mycoplasma while publishing on the more academic points of the microorganism enthralled him. He would control the academic chess game, because he will be the only one that knows all of the facts behind the little mycoplasma. Dr. Lon hesitated and then smiled and nodded his head in approval to the two men. He was weak and would do exactly what they wanted, even though he considered them of inferior intelligence and incapable of important decisions that could affect the future of mankind. *One does not have to be evil to do evil, because good men only have to say nothing and do nothing.*

Belford College of Medicine, Microbiology Department, Austin, Texas.

Belford College of Medicine was one of the most prestigious medical schools in the United States. Founded as a stand-alone institution in Austin, Texas by a famous heart surgeon, Belford prided itself as a beacon of light in an otherwise rather primitive Texas medical academic environment. In fact, Belford did have many famous or well-known members on its faculty, and it had been extremely successful in obtaining Federal funding for its clinical and basic research programs. It was organized around its associated hospitals, including a large general hospital, a heart center, a surgery center and a children's hospital. Each of these institutions provided faculty members for the Belford College of Medicine, and in turn they gained academic prestige by their association with Belford. Located in downtown Austin, the Belford campus occupied several city blocks along with its associated hospitals. Together they made an impressive team of institutions, both in terms of personnel and facilities. From the outside Belford looked impressive with its tall white buildings, but at the level of an entry faculty member in the basic sciences, it was not quite as impressive as its physical appearance.

It was the late 1980s, and a meeting was taking place between the famous Belford College of Medicine Microbiology Department Chairman, Dr. Virgil Rook and a very junior faculty member, Dr. Marie LeBon, in Dr. Rook's office. The meeting was called by Dr. Rook to discuss Marie's attitude toward basic research and her invitation to the prestigious Meyerhoff Conference in Israel. But in reality the meeting was called to discuss Marie's opinion on biological warfare, a topic that had never come up before Marie was recruited to join the faculty.

Dr. Rook's office was decorated in traditional academic decor. Some of Dr. Rook's cherished objects were tarantulas and snakeheads suspended in globe-like spheres. A mural on the wall depicted Dr. Rook's role in the Belford Influenza Program, and there were pictures of Dr. Rook with then Congressman George H. Bush on the wall as well as various pictures of his trips to third world countries such as Egypt and his work with the Texas Prison System.

Marie knocked firmly on Dr. Rook's door in accordance with her impassioned personality. She was very nervous but masked it well by often taking on an arrogant and somewhat condescending attitude towards her peers. Marie was in her early thirties and had long dark hair. Although she was slim and petite, she stood out in the academic environment because of her good looks *and* brains. She was graduated from a prestigious biophysics program, and she had been disappointed to find her colleagues so narrowly trained compared to her multidisciplinary background. Her specialty was the study of complex structures in the nucleus of mammalian cells, structures that contain DNA genetic information and protein complexes called nucleoproteins.

Dr. Rook, the fatherly chairman who had seen it all when it came to new, young faculty members welcomed Marie to his office, "Come in, Marie. Have a seat." He pointed to a chair. He then looked directly at her and asked, "Marie, I am going to get straight to the point. I am concerned with your career. I see that you have been sparing with senior faculty in the Department about your unconventional ideas on cell nuclear structure. But before we get into that, I have to ask you an important question. What do you think of Biological Warfare?"

Marie was completely taken aback by the question on Biological Warfare, and her countenance reflected this. She hesitated and then said,

"Sir, I consider it completely unethical, and if I may say so, incredibly stupid. We cannot really control biological organisms." Dr. Rook smiled slyly and asked, "Would you ever participate in Biological Warfare research?" Marie shook her head, "Absolutely not!" May I respectfully remind you, Dr. Rook, that you are an expert in virology and the study of prokaryotes." Dr. Rook answered with a slight sarcastic undertone that eluded Marie, "I know I am an expert on viruses and bacteria, so what are you getting at?" Marie replied, "With all due respect, sir, you know very little about eukaryotes, mammalian systems in particular, which happens to be my expertise."

Dr. Rook rubbed his head. He smiled but seemed disappointed, "If you knew of germ warfare research going on somewhere near you would you remain silent?" Marie thought a moment and then emphatically stated, "No . . . . I don't think I would." Dr. Rook now looked distressed and disappointingly stated, "Well, Marie, you definitely are not a team player, and you are too smart for your own good. Your ideas are not in line with the accepted paradigms. Furthermore, your whole attitude is not politically correct for this environment."

There was silence for a moment. Marie looked puzzled. She had never seen Dr. Rook so mad and frustrated. Dr. Rook continued, "Do you understand what I am saying?" Dr. Rook clearly did not appreciate Marie's comments, and his attitude conveyed an outlook of resentment towards Marie. Marie looked puzzled by Dr. Rook's remarks and behavior, and although she was bright, she was also very naïve politically, and she did not accurately fathom Dr. Rook's line of questioning. She had no idea why Dr. Rook was asking her questions about Biological Warfare. Marie had not taken the time to explore all the aspects of her environment, because she like many young faculty members was so tied up in her own world that she had not taken the time to look carefully around her. Everything was not as it seemed, but Marie was too naïve to notice.

Marie's entire world was shaken, because the very humanitarian Dr. Rook, the champion of the downtrodden and the savior of the prison health system, had suddenly revealed a different side of his personality. Taken in a different context, every gesture of Dr. Rook, however, now alluded to a more sinister and jaded agenda of purpose, in stark contrast to Marie's young idealism. Marie finally said, "Sir, I know that I am different, but I try very hard to see other peoples positions and attitudes. I don't think that I am politically incorrect, I just have somewhat different approaches to the problems that face us." It had not quite sunk in that Dr. Rook was quizzing her about her moral ideas on Biological Warfare to find out if she could be a team player. In other words, Dr. Rook wanted to find out if Marie could put aside her moral objections and do something she was morally against to save her job.

Marie didn't take the bait, and Dr. Rook looked very disappointed. Unfortunately, the damage had been done, and no matter what Marie said from now on, she would be painted as someone who was not a team player. In her department team effort was very important, and her chairman was adamant about scientists and physicians working together in teams on important problems. Marie was naïve about academic politics, and she didn't realize that she had sealed her fate in Dr. Rook's department by not going along with the program.

Dr. Rook looked out the window, "By the way, Marie, do you like people? I perceive that deep-down you are a sentimentalist." Taken aback again by the line of questioning and Dr. Rook's demeanor Marie stated calmly, "Dr. Rook, I decided to become a scientist when I decided that my purpose in life was to help those suffering from disease. I have dedicated myself to this goal through my experiments." Dr. Rook turned directly at Marie and asked, "Where did you get these silly notions, Marie?" Then he hastily added not giving Marie a chance to reply, "Never mind." He switched the subject yet again and stated sarcastically, "No doubt, Marie, a trip overseas should be very exciting for you. But before I forget, you need to have a series of immunizations before your trip, the usual flu shots, gamma-globulin, so on. There's nothing more unpleasant than being sick away from home. To save you the trouble, I have prepared all the shots myself, and you can come by later today to my office. And I want you to prepare a complete summary of the conference. Again, Marie, it's quite an honor for someone at your junior level to be invited to this type of conference, so please don't mess it up. Do you understand?" Marie nodded, but she still did not know why Dr. Rook was being so nice to her. He was a distinguished senior faculty member at Belford, and who was Marie to question his instructions.

Marie meets her match

Marie had her eye on a certain department chairman at the Cancer Center across the street from Belford College of Medicine in Austin. She ran into Professor Jared McNichol at a seminar at the Cancer Center and tried for weeks to make an appointment with him to discuss her scientific ideas. Jared was in his mid-40s, a rather young age for a department chairman at the Medical Center, and Marie was surprised to find out that he was recruited to this position several years earlier. Jared had built his reputation in California at the University of California and was personally recruited by the President of the Cancer Center, the distinguished Dr. Clement Masters, to be the head of a new department that was being formed around Dr. McNichol. The University Cancer Center, also called the D. O. Madison Cancer Center, was located in downtown Austin next to Belford College of Medicine, the State medical school and several large hospitals.

The Cancer Center was founded by an oil baron, Dwight O. Madison, in the 1930s, and it had grown into one of the largest cancer centers in the world under the direction of an esteemed and politically savvy surgeon who reluctantly turned over the helm of the center to Dr. Masters. Jared's specialty was basic research and the cellular structure of normal and cancer cells, but he also had a background in microbiology and cellular biochemistry. His laboratories were located on the 9th floor of the Research Building, which was linked to the main hospital of the cancer center by a footbridge over a small street.

Tall and athletic, Jared was considered a quality catch among the women of the medical center. He was the captain of his volleyball team, and his office was filled with sports trophies, an unusual interest for an academic. Marie, who had been studying Jared from afar, finally made her move. After being put off by Jared's secretary (she was told she would have to wait for 6 months for an appointment to see him), Marie took matters into her own hands and walked right into Jared's office, introduced herself and began a discussion on the role of water molecules in stabilizing the structure of DNA.

Although initially Jared was a bit taken aback by the aggressive nature of this young scientist who just walked into his office, he admired her spunk—and her intellect. Here was a woman who knew what she wanted.

Since Marie was one of the best looking young female scientists that Jared had ever seen, it didn't take long to win him over. And win him over she did. In fact, he didn't have a chance against the slim dark-eyed beauty from Belford College of Medicine. Jared was ten years senior to Marie and much further along in his career, which started very quickly in California where he was the youngest full professor in the University of California system. They shared so many common interests that within no time they were spending so much time together that some considered them engaged. However, Jared had been married before, and he wasn't interested in re-marrying, at least that's what he thought until he met Marie.

Jared had a nice home in an upscale new development on the outskirts of Austin called Queenswood. It was located in a wooded area with gentle rolling hills, and the lots were quite large. Jared had the house built on the lot even before he moved to Austin, and he didn't spare any expense in its construction. After all, he had made a killing on his home in California, and he needed to dump his profits into another home or be taxed on the profits. The house had an obvious California look to it, modern with many large windows facing the woods to the rear of the house. The lot ran steeply downhill to a greenbelt where a jogging trail was located; however, you couldn't see the trail from the house through the trees and bushes. It took Marie only a few months to convince Jared that she should move in ("to take care of his two black Singapore cats when he was out of town"). So move in she did, and they began to enjoy long many hours in front of the large fireplace during the cold nights of the Austin winter. Marie was especially taken in by Yin and Yang, and Jared's two oriental cats almost immediately fell in love with Marie.

Marie contracts an unusual illness

Marie attended her meeting in Israel and returned to find an invitation to move into Jared's Queenswood home. It was exciting for Marie to finally move out of her small apartment in the medical center area and move into a large house in the suburbs. It was a happy time for both of them and for the two black cats, and all was well for Jared and Marie for several months. In fact, they were so completely compatible with each other and in love that the last thing they expected were health problems. However, Marie was hit hard with an unusual illness that eventually required her to take medical leave from Belford. Actually her department chairman forced her to take long-term leave when none of the Belford staff could identify or diagnose her illness. At the time Marie was having a very difficult time maintaining her research efforts, and she was often at home too sick to come to work.

Marie's department had a well-known research faculty that conducted clinical and basic research on various medical problems, including immune deficiencies and infectious diseases. It specialized in conducting medical trials in the state prison system, and her department chairman, Dr. Virgil Rook, was widely known for his work on prison health problems. Marie thought at the time that Dr. Rook was a marvelous humanitarian. He seemed so fatherly to the faculty that Marie once thought that she would have liked Dr. Rook as a real father.

Marie did not work in the area of infectious diseases that consumed most of her colleagues in the Microbiology Department, and she stood out in her department because of her background and research interests in molecular biology. Although both Jared and Marie were Ph.D.s from well-known universities, they were not specialists in infectious diseases or internal medicine, although Jared taught in the internal medicine 'block' in the State medical school in Austin. Jared was recruited to Texas to start a new department at the D. O. Madison Cancer Center specializing in molecular and cellular biology, and Jared's own research interests were in the spread of cancer or metastasis.

One evening Jared was working quite late in his office at the D. O. Madison, and upon finally arriving home he found Marie in very poor condition. Unfortunately, her health had declined to the point where she was practically bedridden all of the time. On this night she pleaded with Jared not to take her to the emergency room at a local hospital. Jared finally relented but made Marie agree to seek the help of her old friend and father figure, Dr. Rook. So the next morning Marie called Dr. Rook to make an appointment to discuss her health problems. Marie had always looked up to Dr. Rook as an expert clinician who knew a tremendous amount about unusual diseases, and she certainly had an unusual disease.

When Marie was finally able to speak to Dr. Rook on the phone, he was not the sympathetic father figure that she had known and once worked with at Belford. He seemed disinterested in discussing her clinical problems and was aloof and distant. In fact, Dr. Rook told her that he would be canceling her contract to come back to Belford, even if she recovered from her illness. When Marie discussed the conversation with Jared, he did not understand the change in Dr. Rook's attitude toward Marie.

Dr. Rook seemed like such a marvelous person, and he was always very interested in the welfare of his patients and faculty members. However, in Marie's case, he seemed to have turned into a hard stone, and he now considered her nothing but dead weight in his department. Dr. Rook appeared to be cutting his losses, and he considered Marie a lost cause. He obviously wanted to recruit someone else to her position, and therefore he wanted Marie out of his department as soon as possible.

Marie was devastated by Dr. Rook's decision. He never told her directly that he wanted her gone, but it was obvious by the way he and the other faculty members treated her when she dared wander out of her laboratory. They never talked to her about their own research, but they always asked probing questions about her research. At first Marie was flattered that they took such an interest in her research, but eventually she felt that they were just questioning her to find out what she was doing and what she knew about the other projects in the department. Marie could tell that these casual conversations were not friendly; the faculty was following the lead of Dr. Rook in easing Marie out of the department, but they wanted to know exactly what she knew about the research conducted in the department.

Marie has a near death experience

Marie's health had been steadily deteriorating during the year that she moved to Queenswood. The most obvious symptom was severe fatigue, but this had now progressed to other signs and symptoms as well. At this point she was beginning to lose the mobility of her left arm and leg, and this deeply concerned Jared. It started out looking like rheumatoid arthritis, with painful joints and loss of joint mobility, but her illness had progressed to atrophy and actual paralysis or semi-paralysis of the left side of her body. Marie was bedridden and had severe headaches and short-term memory loss, problems that she never had before her illness. She had skin rashes, and she was losing her hair. She had kidney and urinary problems and suffered from bouts of diarrhea. Her eyes were deteriorating and she could barely read without assistance. Her sensitivity to light was extraordinary, and it was almost painful for her to be in direct sunlight. She woke up at night in pools of perspiration; sometimes she was very hot and sometimes chilled, suggesting that she had a low-grade fever. Her stomach was constantly on fire, and she vomited often.

During her illness Marie changed from a cheerful, bouncy person to one who was withdrawn, constantly depressed and always irritable. No one had been able to tell Marie or Jared what was wrong with her, even though the medical facilities in Austin were among the most prestigious in the world and had been at the cutting edge of medicine for the last several decades. The physicians at the medical center that Marie consulted did not have a clue as to what was wrong with her. Jared believed that Marie was suffering from some kind of infection, but they could not identify any infection in the numerous blood tests that Marie had taken at Belford. At this point, the clinical lab at Belford was refusing to do any more tests for Marie, unless Jared paid in advance for the tests.

One evening as Jared entered their bedroom where Marie spent most of her time, he found her clutching her little stuffed elephant from her childhood named 'Lucky Lucius.' Marie hardly ever gave Lucky Lucius a second thought, until she got sick. Now she couldn't be without her little elephant. Marie told Jared in a very weak voice, "Jared, the penicillin makes me even more sick. Each day I seem to get weaker, and now I'm having trouble moving my left leg and left arm. It's as if they are held down with hundred pound weights . . . . and every time I move them the pain is unbearable. I have so many problems with my eyes that I am afraid I'm losing my sight. I'm scared! I know that I won't ever get well! Am I dying? Do you think I am going to die?"

Jared wanted to tell Marie that something was very, very wrong, but he also did not want to scare her. So he tried to reassure that her illness would eventually pass. When she told him that she was dying, he would say, "That's nonsense!" But he would also admit to her that her treatment must take a new direction, "I'm convinced that we have not gone the right way with your treatment, Marie. We have to think of something else." He tried to look at the slight woman wasting away in his bed in a detached manner, but he found that he could not be detached when it came to Marie. She was not the young vibrant young lady that he first met in his office over a year ago. Her haggard look, matted hair and pale color seemed like death warmed over. Not one to shrink from what he knew was right, he looked at Marie and smiled, "Marie, I believe that you have an infection, but it's something that no one has ever seen around here, or at least they can't think of an explanation. Look at you! You must have more than twenty different signs and symptoms. You've lost over 40 pounds. I don't know what kind of bug can on one hand cause your memory loss, headaches, depression and other neurological problems and on the other hand cause fatigue, eye problems, skin rashes, diarrhea, stomach aches, hair loss and all kinds of other crazy problems. Whatever it is—it attacks everywhere but you can't find it."

Jared thought to himself about Marie's long-term prognosis, but he did not verbalize his thoughts to Marie. He thought that there must have been something that he missed, something critical to finding what was wrong with her. Finally he told her, "Now it looks like you may have some type of meningitis. You would think that what ever it is, we could find something in your blood tests." Marie replied in an anguished voice, "It hurts so much to move and even eat! . . . . I saw myself in the mirror, and I look like a skeleton! . . . . It hurts to move, and I can't stay on my left side. It's too painful, like someone took a hammer to my body, especially my back and my left arm . . . . I am in so much pain! . . . . Why can't you find out what's wrong with me?"

Jared would stand at the door to their bedroom and stare at Marie for some time without speaking. He usually waited until Marie noticed that he was there, if she noticed anything at all. When Marie was aware of his presence, he would finally speak to her. "O.K. Marie, I'm worried; your weight is down to about 70 pounds, and it looks like you've lost about 40% of your body weight during the last year." Marie stared back at Jared for what seemed to be almost a minute but was really just a few seconds and said, "Jared, we went over the list of antibiotics, and you agreed that I have some sort of infection. You've been studying this. You say doxycycline crosses the blood-brain barrier, and the penicillin made it worse . . . ." Marie's voice trailed off.

Jared was trying to cheer Marie up, but his comments probably made the situation worse. "I asked Rook, but he was completely noncommittal. It's as if he doesn't want to know about your illness. I think he has written you off, and he doesn't think that you'll ever return to your position." Jared then tried to be more cheerful and upbeat. He didn't want to scare Marie. "We can try to get you the doxycycline, but I don't understand it. All your blood tests are within normal range, but you obviously have some sort of infection that we can't find with the usual tests. An infection responsive to dox should show up in your lab tests." Marie slowly said, "Look, Jared a measurement is only as good as its sensitivity. I tell you, I have been infected with something." Jared realized that Marie had some fight left in her. "O.K., I'll get Rook to give you the dox. After all, most medicine is based on empirical approaches, at least initially. Your chairman has been a pain in the ass, but I think that he finally believes that you are really sick. I just don't understand how it could be meningitis and not be detectable. Anyway, when I last spoke to him he agreed to do what we want. He just wants this problem to go away." Marie said, "Stop being the professor, Jared . . . He just wants me to disappear . . . but I love you anyway."

Jared was relieved that Marie had not lost her sense of humor, but he was very concerned that he might come home one day to find Marie dead in his bedroom with his cats on each side of her protecting her body. A feeling of helplessness had come over him, and he had never felt this way before. He promised Marie that he would not abandon her–this seemed to be her most dreaded fear, even more than dying a slow, painful death.

The worst day in Marie's life came in a sea of pain, dizziness and nausea. By mid-morning she was too weak to call Jared at work, so she just lay in bed moaning and longing for relief that can only come with death. Marie clutched her little stuffed elephant to her side and slowly drifted off. Her dreams become as vivid as life, and she dreamed of dying and floating up from the bed–free of pain and nausea at last. She could even look down and actually see herself lying completely still in the bed, with Yin and Yang sleeping at her feet. She seemed to be able to see all around her in any direction at the same time, even behind her. It's as if she had panoramic vision. Then a bright light beckoned her to come, and she heard voices telling her that she would be all right. She couldn't recognize the voices, but they were very peaceful voices. But then she heard what appeared to be her dead grandmother who was also calling on to her to keep fighting. Off in the distance Marie could barely see her grandmother, and she motioned for Marie to go back. Marie tried to go to what she thought was her grandmother, but the lady still waved Marie back. The other voices told her that she will be all right but she must go back and help others who might have the same illness.

Marie did not want to go back to the pain and to the ridicule that had been heaped on her by her colleagues. She just wanted to go peacefully, floating off towards the bright light. It was so beautiful. But just as she began her journey, she was physically jolted, and the pain and nausea returned. She couldn't seem to continue on her journey to the light. What was happening to her! It was Jared! She could barely see him, as if he was off in the distance not standing over her. She closed her eyes again.

Marie was mad at Jared for waking her up from the first peaceful sleep that she had in months. Jared was still shaking Marie and saying, "Wake up Marie! Wake up! Don't you go South on me, Marie! Keep fighting baby! You're going to make it." Jared shook her again, and Marie slowly opened her eyes and stared at him for a moment. Finally she said, "What in the hell are you doing? Why did you wake me up?" Jared said, "I thought for a moment that I had lost you!" Marie responded, "Are you crazy? What are you doing?" Jared smiled and said, "Marie, please don't scare me like that again!"

The slow road to recovery

The year was 1987, and Marie had made a long and painful journey back from a near fatal illness. The choice of doxycycline treatment at a critical point in her illness probably saved her life. She slowly got better with each treatment, but getting Dr. Rook to provide the necessary antibiotics had become a nightmare in itself. Jared had also made some changes in her diet, and he had been giving her some supplements to boost her immune system. Marie was tough; she was a fighter. She and Jared had fought the undiagnosed disease that wrecked her health, and they were finally winning the battle but at a difficult price.

Marie ultimately lost her faculty position at Belford College of Medicine, and she did not know what to do about it. It happened one morning when she received a form letter from Dr. Rook. She tore up the letter without even reading it completely. She was angry at Dr. Rook for not doing more to help her during her hour of need.

Marie had been trying to put her anger aside and find a new course in her life. Her colleagues at Belford were completely unsympathetic about her illness, as if she was making up her case of meningitis! Even her department chairman, the famous Professor Virgil Rook, was unkind to her when she became sick and even suggested that she needed psychiatric help. He always seemed more interested in his own experiments and clinical trials in the prison system than anything that she was doing in the lab.

Marie tried to be a 'team player' and help Dr. Rook solve a particularly difficult problem that they were working on with some unknown illness in the State prison system. The prisoners were coming down with an unusual infection during one of his clinical trials. Even though Marie tried to help Rook, for the most part he avoided her. In fact, almost everyone was hostile towards her at Belford. Eventually Marie received an offer to go to MIT, but she wanted to stay in Austin with Jared and his two black Singapore cats. A decision must be made if she wanted to continue in an academic career. After long and passionate discussions with Jared, Marie decided to put off any major decisions about her career. Jared had tried to cheer her up whenever he could, but Marie slowly slipped into a state of depression. As an afterthought she finally agreed to go with Jared on a road trip to Utah. He had been pushing her to go outside more and exercise, even if it hurt.

The trip to Bryce Canyon National Park

Marie and Jared decided to take a brief vacation away from the unfriendly Texas atmosphere. They flew to Las Vegas, rented a car and drove to Bryce Canyon, Utah for a brief holiday. Jared felt that the vigorous outdoor hiking would help rehabilitate Marie, who had been suffering from a mysterious infection that started slowly but eventually became a full-blown case of meningitis. Marie had been partially paralyzed and in severe pain, but she had made a slow but remarkable recovery. She had begun to gain back some of the weight that she had lost during her illness, and her energy was returning. She could even take semi-vigorous walks on the paths in their hillside community of Queenswood. But this was her first real attempt at being normal again.

Jared finally convinced Marie that Bryce Canyon National Park was the perfect place for her to get out and around in a beautiful environment. It was an extraordinary place, and Jared and Marie marveled at the beauty of the red cliffs, and the canyons containing hundreds of slender, eroded red pillars now capped with a slight dusting of snow. It is as if the formations had been poured one by one from a huge sand pail like making sand castles at the beach. Jared stopped the car near the rim of the canyon so they could get out and marvel at the panoramic view before them. After a brief look, Jared ran to a lookout at the edge of the canyon. The canyon looked absolutely spectacular because a snowstorm had just blown through the night before, and the top of the canyon and the pillars in the canyon had been dusted with fresh snow in some places. The contrast between the white snow and the deep red formations made for a spectacular photograph. It was here that Jared decided to challenge Marie the following morning to hike down to the canyon floor and back to the rim.

Jared had found a motel where they could stay quite close to the Park. They were tired from the trip and quickly fell asleep in their cozy hotel room. In fact, they slept until the next morning. After a large breakfast, they returned to the canyon rim and prepared to hike down into Bryce Canyon. The trip down was fairly easy for Marie, and she enjoyed the sights and sounds of screeching hawks overhead soaring in a brilliant blue sky. Once in the canyon, Marie and Jared felt like they were on a different planet. The red walls of the canyon and the occasional pine tree set between the large red pillars were fantastic.

Marie's long illness had made her weaker than they both thought, and the hike back out of the canyon was very long and painful for Marie. Since Marie had no one to complain to but Jared, he became the brunt of her pain and the impatience at her slowly recovering health. Jared continued to take verbal abuse from Marie for some time as they slowly made their way up the canyon, but then he decided to go up ahead and 'blaze the trail' to the canyon rim. He had received enough abuse from Marie and was going to force her to exercise her body and metabolize the 'toxins' that had weakened her for so long. After nearly reaching the top of the trail, Jared turned and waited for Marie to catch up. She slowly continued her painful ascent with occasional supporting calls from Jared to keep her going. Marie was becoming mad at Jared for forcing her to keep climbing without much rest.

Marie continued climbing the path, and when she finally reached the summit, Jared urged her to smile. She trudged up to Jared and grabbed on to him, collapsing in his arms. He picked her up, swung her around and urged her to smile, "Smile, Marie!" Jared laughed, pulled out his camera and snapped a picture of Marie who was flushed but looking like she was finally on the road to health. Her demeanor reflected someone who was in a pique. Jared teased her with a great deal of joy and jubilation. "You did it, Marie!" Marie sarcastically answered, "So? Give me the camera!" Jared said impatiently, "No! Marie, I know rehabilitation is painful, but you're getting better all the time!" Marie replied in a voice that was a cross between weariness and sarcasm, "It's only been two years of exercise and rehabilitation! Not to mention the thirteen months of constant nausea." They looked at each other smiling and at the beautiful view for what seemed to be almost a minute. Jared was proud of Marie. "You made it Babe! You must be better." Marie then said sarcastically, "So-o-o!" She paused and with a sarcastic expression said, "Let's hear it for me!" Jared ignored Marie's sarcasm. "Marie, you're courageous, and you're not a quitter! I'm proud of you! Remember you came pretty close to checking out on me. You were so weak and wasted that I thought you would blow away. And now, just look at you! You're almost recovered, and you can now pick up your career where you left off." At that time they had absolutely no idea how difficult it would be to continue life as it was before Marie's illness.

Jared and Marie sat down and enjoyed the view from the canyon's edge. After scanning the canyon from the bottom to the horizon, Jared turned and finally said, "Isn't it more fun to rehabilitate in such a spectacular setting?" Marie still a bit impatient replied, "O.K. You're right. I know you're right." Jared and Marie held hands and took a long final look at the beautiful scene. They then began walking slowly back to the car. During their walk, they had one last look at the spectacular scenery. Marie then said, "Jared this is beautiful, but my career . . . . I doubt I will ever be successful." She sighed and Jared waited for a moment to answer her. "Stop being so negative!" Marie responded, "I know, I know! But with the likes of Geldter and Krappner going around the scientific community constantly character assassinating me, discrediting my work and saying how I faked my illness. I don't know if I can ever get back to where I was."

Drs. Isaac Geldter and Amy Krappner were senior science faculty members and department chairmen at the D. O. Madison Cancer Center that had crossed swords with Jared and Marie. Geldter and Krappner believed that they were true geniuses deserving of many, in fact, all of the awards and accolades that anyone could possibly receive. In reality they were very average to above average scientists with extra huge egos, some would say egos typical of the Great State of Texas. Although Amy was born and raised in Wyoming, Isaac claimed to be from Israel, but he was really born and raised in Morocco. They both received their academic training in the Mid-West at Southern Illinois and Kansas State, respectively, but they liked to be known as from the 'East Coast.' To make themselves seem more important they always pulled down all those around them, even their closest colleagues, but never to their faces, and they constantly reminded their co-workers of their own importance in the grand scheme of things. They were not particularly well-liked by most of the Madison faculty, but they were completely convinced the opposite was true, and they spent a tremendous amount of time and energy entertaining their colleagues with jokes and stories. Thus they were the life of the party, especially at scientific conferences.

Drs. Geldter and Krappner made sure that they were always at the very center of every important meeting or event, and they always went out of their way and did anything possible to win important and powerful friends. This required quite a bit of energy and expenditure of time, but they prided themselves on their important allies and contacts. In reality, they spent about 50% of their waking hours schmoozing one person or another, for it was a fast moving world, and they must be on the professional radar screen at any cost. If it can't be done on merit, so be it, because Isaac Geldter and Amy Krappner were the world's experts at hyping themselves. In reality, if they didn't maintain the hype, they would probably have fallen quickly by the wayside and melted into the crowd, and this would have been catastrophic to their egos.

Marie was angry at Geldter and Krappner for befriending her and then turning vicious behind her back, but she had no way of knowing that this was their usual behavior. Marie, a quick study, realized early on that Isaac and Amy were at best untrue friends. She once said to Jared, "They are without a doubt the biggest phonies that I have ever met. Not to mention that they are continually telling anyone who will listen that I faked my data—which is quite difficult if not impossible to do in my line of research. It makes it particularly hard to make any sort of start in my career. It's so unfair! I do not know what they have against me. I don't even know them that well! And they don't know anything about me personally or my research. They're not even in my field, and quite frankly, they are so poorly trained in the hard sciences that it's impossible for them to even fathom my research! Yet they are so politically powerful!" Jared finally continued the discussion. "If it makes you feel any better, they did exactly the same thing to me and anyone else around them that they consider a threat, and in my case, they've been doing it for years." He then turned around and pretended to raise his shirt to show the wounds in his back. Marie answered, "That's easy for you to say, since you were already internationally known and respected before you came to Texas. Jared, you know that the majority of scientists are not going to touch the slightest controversy, especially in these times! They have attacked me at such a vulnerable point in my career! And they are not the only ones attacking me. I tell you I am fighting some unknown but powerful force, and I think whatever force it is would like to destroy more than just my career." Jared patiently waited to reply to Marie. "Now Marie, don't get paranoid on me! And quit feeling sorry for yourself! Remember, other researchers are also being attacked by these two miserable people. They must be incredibly insecure of their own science if they have to get ahead by attacking everyone else. But it has happened to me before and to a lot of others. You'll just have to live with it and go on. That's just the way they operate."

After a few minutes Jared became a bit reflective and said to Marie, "When Fuller and I first presented the Fluid Mosaic Membrane model, we were initially eaten alive. I remember one meeting in particular . . . ." Jared's voice trailed off when he noticed that Marie had tuned him out. He tried again more forcibly. "You have to know, Marie, that new ideas threaten mediocre scientists like Geldter and Krappner, and your Nucleoprotein

Gene Tracking technique is one hell of a lot better than anything they have ever come up with, so you have to expect that it will be met with resistance and even scorn by the mediocre people in the scientific community. So don't expect any praise from your fellow scientists for anything novel! I can tell you that from first-hand experience—it's not going to happen!"

After a few moments Marie continued in a resigned tone, "You're right, I know . . . . I know! But Jared, it seems to me that there is more to this character assassination than just the science! Remember how vicious the faculty was to me. My God! They even organized their students to throw spitballs at me during my seminar right before I became ill. And their colleagues interrupted me at every other sentence! I would like to know why they harbor such hatred without even knowing me! I never did anything to these people. I realize I was a bit arrogant after I got my degree, and perhaps I was a bit too blunt in my criticism of their research, but you said lots of beginning scientists go through a phase like that! I tried to apologize for any offense these people may have construed from my behavior or comments. But it was to no avail! And besides, their science *is* shallow. It lacks any deep molecular approach and fails to explore any mechanisms. I am beginning to think that being trained in physics is more of a detriment than a boost to my career. It seems that all that counts these days is political "savoir faire" to succeed . . . with the exception of you, of course! But I don't care what you say, I still *hate* the D. O. Madison Cancer Center. I tell you, it's an evil place! You can cut the evil with a knife when you walk in the lobby! What's more, I tell you they are hiding something sinister!"

Jared tried to calm Marie down. It was obvious that she was becoming negative again. "You are in one of your negative thought loops again! I know you hate the place, but I don't think it's the entire Cancer Center that you hate, it's probably just the administration and a few of the faculty. Be reasonable, Marie. There are lots of very decent scientists and clinicians, even at the D. O. Madison. And this evil you speak about . . . the notion that the D. O. Madison administration is hiding something." Jared paused for a moment and thought about what Marie had said. "You know, I feel that you are probably right from the rumors that I hear about Geldter and Krappner and their experiments with Belford in the prison system . . . But one day I would really like to see some proof, some documents or something." Marie replied sarcastically, "By the time you have identified the enemy it will be too late. You will never get the absolute proof that you require. They're not going to sky write their underhanded and unethical dealings for all the world to see." Jared didn't ignore what Marie had been saying, but he had to be practical about it. "The institution has its problems but it has not failed me yet." Marie snapped back. "Just wait! I tell you, one day we will understand the irrational behavior and attitude of the administration." Jared became somewhat impatient with Marie. "O.K.! O.K.! You are like a moray eel when you get on the subject of the D. O. Madison. You get stuck on a subject and just won't quit! Let's think of something positive like the upcoming meetings in Europe and Honolulu!" After a moment, Jared smiled. "You are definitely well enough to go."

Marie's attitude quickly changed and her face brightened at the prospect of going to Hawaii with Jared. "You think so?" Jared said, "Definitely! How would you like to get married in Hawai'i? (Jared used to live in Hawai'i, and he knew the correct pronunciation) And we can take a honeymoon after the Cancer Research Meetings!" Marie began to light up, and she beamed. "Really?" Jared replied, "Really!" Marie began squealing. "Oh, Jared! Yes!" Marie then jumped into his arms, and they kissed and laughed. Jared then began to swing Marie around and around. Marie was quick to compliment Jared. "What a wonderful proposal!" In a minute or so Marie finally calmed down. "Do you think I should present a paper on my Nucleoprotein Gene Tracking at the meeting in Cambridge?" Jared replied, "Why not? Remember, in the end it will be your research and publications that count. The rest is really just window dressing." Marie enthusiastically, "You know what?" Jared smiled and looked directly at Marie, "What?" Marie replied, "I think I will look up Professor Clever while we are in Cambridge. After all, he is the senior statesman in my field." Jared then became more serious. "Good idea!" Marie then said, "Perhaps I can get his feedback on the Nucleoprotein Gene Tracking technique. And maybe I can find out if he is purposefully blocking the publication of some of my manuscripts." Jared laughed, "Now you're talking! Prove your critics wrong!" Jared continued impishly, "What about Hawai'i? Are we going to stir up some more scientific controversy?" Marie playfully teased and flirted with Jared, "I think not! In Hawaii I will be your wife, not a scientist! But in England . . ." Marie, still playful, began a parody of how she perceived a British dry-witted and stuffed-shirt academician. "I will take full advantage of my oh-so-proper East Coast training and be the hard-nosed scientist!" Jared stated, "You're incorrigible!" They both started laughing and enjoyed their brief digression before returning to a more serious atmosphere.

Jared was finally jolted back to the present, and he began to take on a more serious expression. "You know, Marie, we are still being followed by that odd French-speaking couple. Look! Over there!" Marie looked intently and spotted the couple. He had on a typical French Beret, and the woman had a European look about her. "They're talking in French again but I can't make it out." Both Jared and Marie barely heard the woman say, "Cette place! Elle est trés belle!" Marie turned to Jared, "Now, look who's being paranoid! So they're French. Big deal!" Jared was still suspicious, "I tell you they were following us yesterday." Marie, who often complained of being followed, said, "So they are using the same itinerary as us! It's not uncommon, you know." Jared remained suspicious, "I tell you, I have seen this couple before. Only I cannot place it." Marie then became slightly irritated. "So, you finally agree that my sense of being followed might have some basis to it?" Jared replied, "O.K., you win. But I would like to know why?" Marie responded, "I wonder if it's because I studied with top physicists who were on the Manhattan Project. I had to sign papers after I received my degree that stated that I would not take my special talents to a hostile government. There always seemed to be intrigue hovering in the background at the Institute where I did my Ph.D." Jared laughed, "No way! Don't be so naïve! It has to be something else!" Marie thought about Jared's comment. "But what!" Marie paused thoughtfully, "I told you I felt there was something odd associated with me, but I don't know what!" Jared continued, "I swear you are like a little mushroom hiding in a cave. One day we will get to the bottom of all this! I promise you that!" Marie was now able to take on Jared's normal role. "Now, you lighten up! Let's think only good thoughts, like about where we are going on our honeymoon!" Marie's expression had taken on a decidedly seductive and flirtatious tone. They laughed again after the brief interlude regarding the French couple that had interrupted their conversation. Jared finally succumbed to Marie's way of thinking. "You're right. It's probably nothing."

The Conference at the Diamond Head Hotel

Approximately one month later the time came for Marie and Jared to attend an international joint meeting between the Japanese and American Cancer Associations. They also decided at the same time to get married in Honolulu. They were both excited about the trip, Jared to be returning to a former home and Marie on her first visit. The flight over to Hawai'i was routine and uneventful. After stopping briefly in Los Angeles, they had a completely calm and routine flight across the Pacific to the Hawai'ian Islands. Landing at Honolulu, they immediately took in the sweet smells of exotic plants and flowers in the airport Japanese garden. After retrieving their luggage, Jared literally pulled Marie off to the airport pick-up where they caught a ride to a car rental lot. Since Jared used to live in Kaimuki on Oahu, he always rented a car so that he would be able to take Marie to some of the places that the tourists never see on Oahu. Taking the H-1 into Honolulu and finally turning off onto Kapiolani Boulevard and then right onto Kalakaua to Waikiki, they made their way to the Diamond Head Hotel. Although the hotel was aging a bit and was now surrounded by more modern and taller hotels on the beach at Waikiki, Marie thought it was wonderful. She always wanted to visit Hawai'i, and now she was there with the man that she loved. Life could not have been better for Marie.

Jared and Marie finally checked into their room after a mix-up in their reservations. It turned out to be a nice airy room with a spectacular view of the Pacific and its dark blue waves breaking on the coral reef several hundred meters off shore. They were tired from the trip and decided to take a nap with the large sliding doors completely open to let in a warm Pacific breeze. They only woke for a lovely evening meal on the lanai.

The next morning was a big day for Jared and Marie. They had an appointment at the Honolulu Courthouse. The county courthouse in Honolulu was a bit unusual for a courthouse with its Polynesian flavor and gardens. It even had a special room for civil marriages, and Jared and Marie arrived dressed in more formal attire than the other couples waiting their turn to be married. Most of the couples were not locals, but visitors like Jared and Marie. Marie stood out in the crowd wearing a beautiful, long blue Hawaiian dress with red and white printed flowers. Jared chose a more conservative light cream suit, but under the jacket he was wearing a green and dark blue Hawai'ian shirt. Friends in Honolulu made sure that they were both covered with maile and other flower leis. The traditional Hawai'ian wedding leis have a delightfully sweet odor. In the old days only the alii or royalty were allowed to wear maile. Jared's best man for the ceremony was Professor Toshi Yakamori, an old friend and colleague at the University of Hawai'i at Monoa. Dr. Yakamori and his tiny wife Yuriko stood with Jared and Marie before the judge, and after the ceremony took them for a special Japanese lunch at a lovely little restaurant that sat on pilings elevated over a Japanese garden and large pool with a small waterfall. It was a wonderful time that Marie and Jared would never forget.

Later on the same day of their civil marriage the McNichols decided to attend the opening reception of the conference at the hotel. The reception was on the lawn in front of the hotel facing the beach and the ocean. As the newlyweds arrived, it was just sundown and a local group was playing Hawai'ian slack-key at the side of the festivities. Flame torches outlined the view of the famous Diamond Head volcano. As the other participants arrived and found out that a marriage had taken place earlier that day, the McNichols were congratulated, especially by the Japanese scientists attending the meeting. The newly married McNichols were still wearing the traditional Hawai'ian wedding leis around their necks, and they were still wearing Hawai'ian shirts and dresses. Marie looked beautiful with her long, dark hair and a tightly fitting red and white flower Hawai'ian dress. Jared didn't believe in the usual his-and-hers shirts and dresses, so he wore a different looking dark blue-purple Hawai'ian flower shirt and white pants and shoes. He still had around his neck the traditional Hawai'ian maile leis. The leaves still smelled quite exotic, and to the Japanese who had never seen or smelled maile, it was an unusual sight.

Dr. Issac Geldter and his wife Dr. Amy Krappner were also attending the conference in Honolulu. Since they must always be the center of attention, they were irritated when they found out that Jared had just married Marie, and *they* were now the center of attention, especially among the Japanese scientists. Isaac and Amy decided to purposely come up to the newlyweds, smiling to seemingly congratulate them and wish them well. Since Isaac and Amy were fairly non-descript and an unlikely looking couple, they always arrived to any gathering in an overly arrogant and loud manner to generate attention. This evening they marched into the reception with their heads held very high—smiling, laughing and talking loudly to everyone they encountered. Dr. Geldter appeared to the McNichols as a slightly pudgy-looking individual of medium height with a fish-like face under a slightly balding big head with dyed black hair. He had a slight Middle Eastern accent. He was domineering, but charming, and he possessed a degree of charisma typical of the New York Borscht-belt comedians. On this occasion he was not wearing anything Hawai'ian, and instead he had on his usual dark blue blazer and conservative tie. His wife, Dr. Krappner, was also of medium height with short-cropped dirty blond hair, a rather small head for her frame and beady, dull blue eyes. She always wore rather large glasses for the small size of her face. She was overweight and looked completely ridiculous and out of place in her Hawai'ian missionary dress and high heel shoes. The couple always seemed to possess an air of arrogance that they lorded over the rest of the conferees at any meeting that they attended. Amy was the sort of person who wanted to emulate fine taste but always fell short.

The McNichols were engaged in small talk about Hawai'i with two Japanese scientists, Drs. Sugima and Kazuchi, when Isaac and Amy approached them. From the 'false' expressions on Drs. Geldter's and Krappner's faces, it was immediately apparent that they were not pleased to see the McNichols married and at the center of attention, and in fact, they were not pleased to see them at all. But they decided to come right up to the newlyweds, so they could put on their false act of sincerity. The two Japanese scientists were at the time in light conversation with the McNichols and were very subdued, respectful, and polite. They were also not dressed in Hawai'ian clothes but had on their usual dark suits and conservative ties. Jared at well over 6 feet tall towered over the crowd of mostly Japanese.

Dr. Krappner was the first to speak, and the tone of her voice had a saccharin lilt to it. The demeanor of Dr. Krappner was usually completely false; her smile never reached her eyes when she said, "Isaac and I want to be the first to offer our congratulations on your *belated* marriage." She then laughed and hesitated a moment before saying, "You must think that this is so romantic!" She let loose with another falsetto-like laugh that was so typical of her personality when she was being insincere. Dr. Geldter chimed in with a big smile and put his hand out to Jared. "Mazel tov!"

Dr. Geldter always tried to be very personable . . . to your face. But in fact, he was probably the most vicious academic in Austin. The problem was that only his close associates knew this. He was very, very good at hiding his true feelings about others, and he always took the time to convince his peers that he was such a wonderful, intelligent person. Isaac Geldter was not known for his scientific brilliance but he made up for it by his political savvy and viciousness. Now that the issue of the marriage had come up, Dr. Sugima and Dr. Kazuki were reminded that Jared and Marie had just been married, and they both decided to give a bow of honor to the newly married McNichols, who then returned it. Dr. Sugima asked Jared, "Will you be coming to the Sapporo meetings next spring? Both myself and Dr. Kazuki are anxious to hear from both of you." Dr. Krappner and Dr. Geldter exchanged glances to convey a message to each other that they were not pleased to hear this. They always considered that they were *the* scientists to be asked first to any meetings in their fields, not people like Jared and Marie whom they considered inferior, even though Jared had more publications than Isaac and Amy combined and served on more editorial boards of academic journals. Isaac, a few years older than Jared, had always considered Jared less important than himself.

It was obvious to everyone that Isaac Geldner and Amy Krappner considered themselves to be the most famous scientists at the conference, and they did not like to hear someone else receive any kudos that they felt should be given to themselves, especially someone who was a faculty member at their own institution. Jared said to the Japanese scientists, "We intend to come to Sapporo and are very honored that you have asked us to present our studies. But a lot will depend upon how Marie feels. You know we are lucky to have Marie with us at all. She had some sort of exotic infection that at one point ravaged her to such an extent that she weighed only 70 pounds and was paralyzed on one side of her body." Dr. Sugima asked, "Really? I did not know." He projected a concerned attitude unlike Drs. Geldter and Krappner, who acted completely skeptical and demonstrated it by throwing their heads around and then looking at each other and smiling as if to convey that it was all a bunch of lies. Marie responded first. "I still am not quite up to par, but I am much better, and there does not seem to be any lasting damage. My left side is still weak with some kind of neuralgia, so I am continually exercising to rehabilitate it."

The Japanese scientists looked concerned. Marie continued, "It has been very difficult for me, and I was unable to work for over a year."

At this time Isaac and Amy were still looking at each other and almost laughing at Marie who was still explaining to the Japanese scientists that it took a long time to overcome her illness. Jared finally interjected, "We think she had some infection that was responsive to doxycycline, but she got worse when she took penicillin." Marie continued, "I am convinced that I got this illness in my department at Belford College of Medicine. Drs. Geldter and Krappner exchanged a glance between themselves and could not be contained from laughing. They were clearly acting as if they did not believe that Marie had an illness or that an infection was involved.

Dr. Geldter was smiling and finally interrupted the group of scientists and said in a loud voice, "Marie, I think that you have a marvelous imagination!" Dr. Krappner laughed and turned to Marie and added, "Are you sure your illness was not a result of some negative reaction to the criticisms you received for your molecular biology experiments? Did you think that your science wasn't getting enough attention?" At this point everyone involved in this small conversation group looked uncomfortable at the attempt to paint Marie's illness as a psychiatric problem. Marie barely contained her disdain for Dr. Krappner and her attempt to paint her as psychologically unbalanced. Marie looked directly at Dr. Krappner with a very cold and pointed stare and said, "Dr. Krappner." Amy smiled and interrupted Marie, "Please call me Amy." Marie continued with a slightly sarcastic tone to her voice, "Amy, I would not wish the illness that I have endured on my worst enemy. I can think of far better ways to get attention than to be nauseated continuously for 13 months with excruciating pain throughout my body. Controversy and pressure have always agreed with me, and frankly, if you are familiar with the history of science, any idea or model that is new and novel is often met with extreme resistance, derision, and even ridicule by the scientific community." Amy smiled and answered Marie in a completely false manner. "I really don't think so, Marie, or should I now call you Mrs. McNichols, but I meant no offense." Marie growing more angry continued, "Oh yes you did!" Dr. Geldter then interjected in a charming, laughing manner that quickly changed, "Really, Marie! Amy meant no offense, and I think that you are way out of line, already." Isaac often slipped into poor

English with a heavier accent when becoming angry, which he usually hid quite well.

The Japanese scientists took in the exchange with frank curiosity. They didn't understand how colleagues from the same institution could be so outwardly hostile towards one another. Marie ignored Dr. Geldter and spoke directly to Dr. Krappner. "Amy, you may be able to fool and charm most people, but you will find that I am not so gullible." Jared who completely believed in what Marie had to say but still interceded, "Girls, girls! You are starting to act like cackling hens. Amy, please, could you be a bit more understanding. Marie is still recovering from her illness, which I assure you was quite real, and she is still a bit sensitive when anyone suggests that her illness was all in her head. I went through the illness with her, and I can tell you that it was horrific. And I, myself, seem to now have some of the same symptoms that Marie had, only in a milder form. We do feel that there is some sort of contagion involved, and sooner or later, we will identify it and get to the bottom of this entire episode."

Dr. Geldter decided to ignore the group but then became rather combative. He got in Jared's face and asked, "What evidence, if any, do you have for your wild speculations?" Jared spoke directly to Isaac, "Everything about this illness smacks of infection, including the cycling fevers and other symptoms, and it responded to doxycycline." Isaac Geldter was still as skeptical as ever—he showed this from his body language and smiling while shaking his head—indicating that he did not believe what Jared or Marie had to say on the subject. This was a typical public performance for Dr. Geldter, but in private he was quite worried that he might come down with Marie's illness, so he avoided the McNichols for the remainder of the conference.

For all his smiling and acting as if Marie was insane, Dr. Geldter always kept his distance from Marie, and he moved back quickly when Marie made any move in his direction. He also moved so as to position himself so that he was never directly facing Marie. Dr. Geldter usually came across as a bombastic, pompous ass, and he did not disappoint at the conference. He never publicly acknowledged that anyone could think other than himself, and he always coveted the center of attention. This was especially true at conferences where he could strut around like an all-knowing peacock with his chest and feathers out for all to see. His usual behavior was to flit about from one group of people to another looking for someone that might recognize him as the 'most' famous scientist at the conference, and he was always willing to tell everyone his corny second-hand jokes that he picked up from his brother who was in advertising in New York. But for some reason at this conference, instead of discussing everything about himself, he wanted to let everyone know in public that Marie's illness was all in her head, so he broke away from the small group with the McNichols and mixed with other small groups where he could discuss the 'crazy' Jared and Marie with anyone who would listen.

The McNichols were still with Amy Krappner and the two Japanese scientists until the end of the reception. Marie finally cooled down, and with Isaac Geldner away schmoozing other groups of conferees, she related to Amy, "I am sorry if I seemed to fly off the handle, but it truly has been an ordeal." Amy replied sarcastically back to Marie, "Apology accepted." At the end of the reception Isaac returned to the small group to maneuver Amy away from the McNichols. He wanted to avoid any close contact, and he had quickly realized that there were politically much more fertile grounds at the conference. The Japanese scientists had tried to change the subject of this highly charged, unpleasant encounter in a typically polite Japanese manner. They were a bit embarrassed that Geldter and Krappner would even bring up the subject of Marie's illness on the same day that Jared and Marie were wed, but they were too polite to acknowledge the academic in-fighting between the American scientists. In Japan this type of disagreement would have been much more subtle and polite. But in America, it seemed, anything was acceptable behavior. Dr. Sugimura nodded to Drs. Geldner and Krappner and politely asked Jared and Marie to accompany them while he softly held onto Jared's arm, "Will you all join us at the dais."

Dr. Kazuki was now smiling again. "Come! Come! They are about to serve the meal. And I must give a quick opening speech before the dinner begins." Everyone finally moved off from the grass and found their seat on a large porch or lanai in front of the hotel. Several scientists had been gathering at the main table as well as in the crowd, and Drs. Geldter and Krappner, who were pointedly looking at Marie and Jared with a mixture of disdain and derision, immediately returned to their schmoozing of some clinicians from the East Coast.

The evening gala was outdoors, and it was a typical beautiful Hawai'ian evening. Some scientists who were previously speaking to Geldter and Krappner and were now seated at a table whispered as Jared and Marie walked by to take their seats. The head of the Japanese Cancer Association then reported to the assembled crowd that Jared and Marie had just been married in Honolulu. The McNichols were then asked to briefly address the assembly. Jared and Marie holding hands before the group then made a low bow while holding hands in the Japanese style of newlyweds. Jared then went up to the microphone. "Marie and I want to thank the Japanese and American Cancer Associations for honoring us on this most lovely and important day in our lives. I only want to express my gratitude and introduce my lovely young bride, Marie." There was some polite applause from the crowd, and some of the Japanese were taking pictures. At the side of the gathering were Drs. Geldter and Krappner looking at each other and sneering. They turned and told their colleagues something, but Jared and Marie no longer cared what they had to say about anything. Some day the truth about these two would be known. It was not just academic rivalry—they had something much more sinister to hide, and some day justice would be served.

The Presidential suite at the Diamond Head Hotel

Marie and Jared were just married and spending the first night of their honeymoon in Honolulu in a suite on the top floor of the hotel. As they entered their suite, they found that it was well appointed, with a spectacular moonlight view of the Pacific Ocean and the reefs off Waikiki. The Cancer Associations donated a lovely congratulations floral arrangement that had already been placed on a table. The McNichols undressed, and Marie began to tease Jared with a sexy new negligee. They were finally completely happy, and they made love on the floor in front of the lanai. Some time later Jared had to get up and he told Marie, "I'm having a slight problem. I don't feel so good–my stomach. Jared went to the bathroom and vomited all over the floor. He did not want Marie to know, because he knew that she was scared of this more than anything else. He tried to reassure Marie while he cleaned up the bathroom, but when he returned to bed, it was obvious that he was in the initial stages of the same disease that almost killed Marie.

Sweating profusely Jared tried to reassure Marie, "It was really nice of them to donate this lovely room for the first night of our honeymoon." Marie seemed preoccupied, and she looked away before answering. "Right. It's the least that they could do." Jared tried to look at her in the dark, and he said, "Come on, Marie. Lighten up. This *is* our honeymoon." Marie looked back at Jared. "Did you see how some of those people looked at us? As if I was Attila the Hun or some kind of freak. Better yet, as if someone had poisoned their minds against us. And I don't even know them." Jared said, "You mean those slime-balls Geldter and Krappner? People know them for what they are. You're overreacting. Everyone knows them, Marie." Marie was still irritated. "No, I am not like that; I am not overreacting . . . . I have seen that look before. As if someone has said some horribly untrue things about me. As if I am some sort of monstrous criminal! I don't understand it!" Jared continued, "You are getting in a negative thought loop again. It's time to put this aside, at least for our honeymoon." Marie said after a sigh, "O.K. But one day I am going to find out why I get these intense negative reactions from people I do not even know. And I think it's not just my science." Jared added, "I know that it's not your science. I've seen it too. But don't be so sure that it has nothing to do with science." Marie quickly changed her attitude, "I don't want to talk about it!" Jared answered, "You're right. I think we have much better things to concentrate on for the next few days. Don't you?"

Marie then tried to give Jared a sensuous look. In the dim reflected light they embraced and then began to undress each other. When they were completely undressed, Jared removed an orchid from the arrangement and tickled Marie near her cleavage. As they moved to the bed Marie told Jared, "It hurts that I love you more than anything!" Jared not knowing how to answer his new wife said, "I'm crazy about you, too!" Marie in a husky voice, "You know, people call me the kiss of death. Does that scare you?" Jared answered, "I love danger." They both laughed at the attempt to act in a sexually explicit manner. For some reason scientists were not very good at acting sensuously. Marie and Jared fell into the bed and made love while listening to the draperies ruffled by the trade winds and the gentle clanging of the wind chimes on the lanai.

The following morning Marie and Jared had breakfast on the lanai. They were obviously happier than on the previous day as they discussed the rest of their honeymoon on Maui and the strenuousness of their upcoming travel schedule. Marie and Jared would have to fly home only to leave in a few weeks for Europe. Jared, however, was slowly becoming sicker, and it was beginning to be more and more obvious. He tried to hide his health from Marie, but she sensed that he didn't feel well. With the reoccurring fevers, night sweats, fatigue, aching joints and terrible headaches, just like the beginning of Marie's ordeal, Jared feared that he would suffer the same fate as Marie. He was hesitant to tell Marie about his symptoms. He didn't want to worry her, and he was not quite sure if he had the same illness that almost killed her. For the most part he had hidden his illness and especially the nausea. It was the nonstop nausea during the illness that drove most people to consider suicide. It did not abate for months. Although a honeymoon should be the most pleasant time in a person's life, Jared was miserable but he could not let Marie know about his illness. Eventually she found out, however, and she then began worrying all over again. For now there was not much that could be done, but when Marie and Jared returned to the mainland, Jared knew that he must go on doxycycline as soon as possible or perhaps face death in the same way that Marie had done six months earlier.

CHAPTER 2

Watching From England as War Rages (1991)

Jared and Marie had been busy since they returned from their honeymoon. Jared had to tend to his department and solve the many problems that accumulated during his absence, and Marie had been invigorated by a new position in Jared's department. Jared actually made Marie a part-time investigator on one of his grants, and this allowed her to do some research in Jared's lab. She had been delighted to return to the laboratory and actually perform some experiments that she could not complete in Dr. Rook's department at Belford. This time, however, she adapted her research to the interests of Jared's—cancer and the spread of cancer cells to distant sites. Jared was also pleased with the arrangement, because he could keep track of Marie and keep her out of trouble. Not everyone in Jared's department, however, was pleased with the arrangement, and this would ultimately come back to haunt the McNichols when Dr. Masters, the President of the D. O. Madison Cancer Center, found out that Marie was working in Jared's lab.

Although Jared had been sick on and off, his illness did not progress to anything near what Marie had suffered. The doxycycline saved him from the most severe complications of the unknown illness, and he actually started to feel better by the end of eight weeks of continuous antibiotics. His signs and symptoms began to slowly subside, although he still had some problems, especially after flying long distances or being at high altitude for more than a day. The recurrences of illness would be a continuing problem for Jared, because he had to travel from Austin to

England, which was just far enough to kick off a relapse of the unknown illness.

Watching the Gulf War from England

Jared had been made a visiting fellow of the British Society of Medicine, and he was to receive the Medal of the Society for his research on cancer. He had to travel to the Society's headquarters in London to receive his award as well as lecture around Great Britain. Jared was nominated for the award by his old friend and mentor at the Imperial Cancer Fund in London, Dr. Kenneth Hallman. Dr. Hallman had been an old-timer in the cancer research area. He was older than Jared by at least 20 years, and he was a very distinguished looking British academic with his tweed blazer and wavy white hair. He and Jared actually started a cancer research journal fifteen years prior, and as the editors of the journal, they had been close colleagues ever since. As a visiting fellow of the Society, Jared must lecture and visit various research and medical institutions in England and Wales and then present a formal lecture to the Society in London.

The lecture tour took place just before war started in the Persian Gulf in January of 1991. Jared and Marie were closely following the build-up to the war (Operation Desert Shield) and the operation to liberate Kuwait from Iraqi occupation (Operation Desert Storm) with personal interest. Jared's step-daughter Suzanne was serving with the 101st Airborne Division as a crew chief on a Blackhawk helicopter, and her regiment in the 101st was widely expected to be inserted deep into Iraq as ground forces attacked into Kuwait and Iraq. Suzanne had been deployed in the Saudi desert since September of 1990, and Jared occasionally received letters from her describing the boring nature of their deployment. Their main mission during Desert Shield was to be ready for an Iraqi attack on Saudi soil that never came. So they spent most of their time planning and maintaining their fleet of helicopters. Their mission was about to change in a dramatic way.

The British Society of Medicine

Jared and Marie had arrived at Heathrow, and they had to make their way to the historic British Society of Medicine headquarters. The Society owned a marvelous old building on Wimpole Street in downtown London. The very thought of staying on Wimpole Street stirred thoughts of Sherlock Holmes. Although historic, the building had been renovated and contained offices, meeting rooms, a reception room, a bar and tearoom and apartments upstairs for guests. The Society building was rich with history as were the other buildings on Wimpole Street. As a visiting fellow of the Society, Jared had been given one of the choice apartments upstairs for two weeks as a base of operations while lecturing and touring hospitals and research centers in England and Wales.

Tired from the long flight, Jared and Marie fell quickly asleep after their arrival at Wimpole Street. They actually slept until the morning, and they then decided to take in the local sights on foot. London was a marvelous place to explore but Marie tired quickly, so they stopped in a small tearoom for an afternoon tea. Finding their way back to the Society building, they decided to take a brief rest only to sleep until the next morning. After rising and then listening to complaints from Marie about the lack of room service at the Society, Jared and Marie showered kneeling in a tub with a European-style flexible hose and showerhead, dressed and prepared to go downstairs for breakfast. Since Jared was usually ready before Marie, he went down to the lobby area to inquire about breakfast and was told that it was served in the tearoom until nine. So Jared returned to the apartment upstairs to bring Marie down for breakfast. Unfortunately he found her still in the process of dressing at 8:45 AM. Jared tried to be diplomatic and hurry Marie along. "Aren't you ready *yet?*"

This was actually a rather standard question in the morning for Jared to ask, because Marie was not a 'morning person' and had to be pushed a bit to get ready in a timely manner. Marie resented being rushed, especially in the morning, and she snapped back at Jared. "I'm not ready, and I'm warning you, *don't* push me this morning!" Jared laughed and told Marie, "They have a TV on in the tearoom, and they even have CNN." Marie replied, "You just want to watch the TV to find out what your stepdaugher is doing." Jared smiled, "That did cross my mind. You know, everyone is predicting that today will be the start of the ground offensive, and you know what that means." Marie responded, "Yes, I know what it means, and if you have to go watch it on TV, go ahead, but come back for me in 10 minutes." Jared replied, "O.K., you made your point. I'll wait for you right here. You know that they close the kitchen in 15 minutes." Marie did not like to be rushed. "Stop pushing me!" Jared just shrugged his shoulder. Marie was definitely not a morning person. If he went down to watch CNN, Marie would likely miss breakfast, and he would hear about it for the remainder of the day.

As it turned out, Jared and Marie just made it to the end of breakfast in the Society's tearoom. Some of the other guests had finished eating and had been watching a TV that was set up in tearoom in anticipation of the beginning of the ground offensive of the Gulf War. The rest of the patrons were only interested in hearing about the 1st Armored Division, one of the British contributions to the war effort, and they didn't particularly like the extensive coverage of the American Forces, but that's CNN. If the British stations had nonstop coverage of the war, the TV would have been tuned to the BBC or SkyNews. Marie said, "Jared, you know, there is something very unreal about watching the war live on CNN." She continued, "It's almost as if we are watching a movie." Jared responded, "Only in this movie people are actually getting killed." Marie paused, "I have a gut feeling that there is something unseen going on. It's so surrealistic . . . ." Jared finally said, "But this *is* the real deal." Marie said sarcastically, "I know what you mean." Jared continued, "It's weird seeing the live antiaircraft artillery tracers going up at *our* planes." He paused and turned to Marie, "I hope Suzanne is all right. You know, her unit will probably be the first to go into Iraq. They have a long history of being dropped behind the lines before the real action starts. Look at what happened just before D-Day."

That comment raised the interest of the local patrons. Marie was trying to change the subject because she knew that Jared was worried. "Suzanne seemed bored in her last letter." Jared saw that Marie was trying to change the subject, "A continual diet of MREs and poor sanitation in the middle of miles and miles of nothing but sand has got to be a major downer." Marie added quickly, "I know, and to be honest, I couldn't stand being out in the dust and sand without a shower for three months. I wish she were home– far away from all this." Jared asked, "What did you mean by unseen dangers." Marie, "I don't know. But what if the Iraqi Republican Guard just lays down its weapons and does nothing." Jared replied, "I doubt if that's going to happen." Marie continued, "It's almost as if they know something we don't." Jared replied, "Our guys will be ready for anything that the Iraqis

n throw at them. I wouldn't worry about that, but there will be
asualties . . . . *just* like any other war."

Marie and Jared watched TV in the tearoom for what seemed like
minutes but in reality it was just 30 seconds or so when Marie turned to
Jared and said, "Remember, Saddam said he would use *all* of his weapons,
and that this will be the Mother of All Battles. He also said he would take
the war to America." Jared smirked, "A lot of that is pure bullshit, but in a
way you're right. It will only be a battle with conventional weapons if
things go well for the Iraqis. And it won't go well for them, you can bet on
that. It's going to be one-sided, and that's when it could be dangerous if the
Iraqis start using their unconventional weapons." Marie added, "Which is
why I think there will be something unseen in these battles. Those SCUD
attacks—could there be chemical and biological weapons loaded on those
monsters?" Jared replied, "That's certainly possible, and even the
commentators have been talking about this for weeks now. They even
trained the reporters to put on gas masks. Sooner or later we're going to
find out." Marie asked, "But how much later?" Jared replied, "People *will*
be getting sick. If it's chemical weapons, they will be sick *very* quickly. If it's
biological weapons, then we won't know for some time after exposure."
There was a pause and then Jared continued, "And it is pretty common
knowledge that Iraq has a huge chemical and biological weapons arsenal."
Marie added, "Not to mention the fact that Saddam has the right personality
to actually go through with the use of chemicals and biologicals!" Jared
replied, "For Suzanne's sake, I sure hope not! But they have a history of
using at least chemicals." Marie said emphatically, "If they use biologicals,
they are insane!" Jared responded, "I agree, but no one ever made the case
that Saddam was sane." Marie continued, "They can't control it. There *is*
no way to contain a biological agent!" Jared said, "If they use it—that *is* the
question."

Another guest at the tearoom heard the McNichols discussing the war
and interjected half-joking, "I don't know why you Yanks got us into this
bloody thing! Haven't you got enough oil?" Jared replied, "Apparently
not!" Marie smiled, "Let's never underestimate the barbarism and stupidity
of man." Jared continued half-heartedly, "It's about Kuwait not oil. Ask
BP!" The guest was not convinced. He shook his head and smiled when
Jared mentioned British Petroleum, and he turned to watch the scene on

TV as he said, "Lord help us understand this bloody conflict." Jared just shrugged, and they finished their breakfast without making another comment.

The train to the Northeast

One of the responsibilities of a visiting fellow of the British Society of Medicine was to travel to various institutions and lecture about current research or treatment. Of high priority were institutions that were usually out of the mainstream for most academic visitors. In this way, they will benefit from having a British Society of Medicine Fellow travel to their locations, rather than their having to travel to London. Thus the information gets disseminated to more professionals who could not have made the trip. At the end of the visit a major presentation was usually scheduled at the Society building in London. This was also an award ceremony where the Fellow received the Medal of the Society. Since Jared was a cancer researcher, his responsibility was to deliver research seminars at various universities and hospitals that work on cancer.

The first part of the trip was to visit institutions in the Northeast, so Jared and Marie must find their way from Wimpole Street to North Euston Station and catch a train North. Jared wanted to go via the Underground to North Euston Station, but Marie wanted him to order a cab instead. Although Jared argued that a cab would take much longer than the Tube, Marie was afraid of the Underground and the crowds. She was still unsure of herself and her strength after her long illness.

The night before terrorists had set up a remote car mortar near Wimpole Street to lob mortar shells at government buildings in the area. It was a VW bus converted to hold six homemade mortar tubes that were pre-aimed and controlled remotely or by a timer. The terrorists simply drove the 'special' van to a prearranged location, parked, opened the top and set a timer or pushed a button from a block away. The mortar shells from such homemade devices made a lot of noise but usually did not cause much damage. Their intended purpose was for the most part psychological. In this respect, it probably had the opposite of the desired effect. Londoners were not easily scared, because the older residents still remembered and talked about the Blitz during World War II when the German Luftwaffe pounded London on a daily basis and caused considerable damage to residential areas. If anything, the minor attacks and bomb scares just increased the resolve of the British, who assumed that Saddam had enlisted the IRA to do the Iraqis bidding in the United Kingdom. Of course, they were right, and in London there was little sympathy for the IRA or the Iraqis.

From Wimpole Street to Euston Station to Reading

Jared was up early and down in the tearoom watching CNN for news of the war in the Arabian Gulf or what we usually call the Persian Gulf. The news was good but sketchy, and the ground war would likely be over in days not weeks. Although there was little specific news of the 101st Airborne Division, what news there was indicated that they were far from most of the intense ground action. While the U. S. Marines and Arab mechanized armies were racing North towards Kuwait City, the main thrusts of the coalition armored units after they rolled over the Iraqi infantry units at the border were headed towards the Republican Guard divisions in Southern Iraq, the most dangerous forces that the coalition would face. The 101st was being used as a blocking force along with the natural barrier of the Euphrates River, preventing Iraqi armored units from escaping to the north. With most of the bridges down on the Euphrates, the only escape would be East to Basra. But before they made it to Basra, they would be encircled and trapped. However, a ceasefire in less than a week's ground action would ultimately save the Iraqi Army from total destruction.

While the war in Iraq and Kuwait raged, Jared and Marie arrived by cab at North Euston Station to make arrangements for their trip to the Northeast. As they were in line to purchase their tickets, a uniform policeman, a Bobby with a bright orange vest on, ran up to the line, pointed and yelled, "Everyone move to the gates! Straight on now! Step lively! Move on to the gates!" At the same time the ticket office windows slammed shut, and there was no explanation. Bobbies with police dogs were running around sniffing passenger luggage, and Jared and Marie joined the crowd from the ticket office now moving to the gates. Along the way Marie spotted a piece of luggage without a passenger, and she yelled to a policeman, "I think you're looking in the wrong place!" She pointed to the luggage, "Who does this belong to?" The policeman replied, "Thank you young lady, now move on!" The dogs were almost immediately on the bag. Marie asked, "What are we going to do?" Jared replied, "We're going to get the hell out of here and go where they tell us!" The police were directing passengers onto a platform where a train was loading.

Marie and Jared were told by a Bobby to immediately board the train. Before they boarded, however, police dogs got a good chance to check out their luggage. Marie asked a policeman, "What if we don't have our tickets?" The Bobby said, "Don't worry, young lady. Just board the train, and please mind the gap!" Jared said to Marie, "He means, watch your step, Babe, and don't get your clothes caught between the platform and the train! Let's get on!" Marie to Jared, "You're actually liking this, aren't you?" Jared replied, "This is fun, don't you think? Marie replied, "No, I don't think *this* is fun!" Jared pushed Marie onto the train, "Where is your sense of adventure?" Marie said as she was pushed onto the train, "I don't like this! Where's my bag?" Jared said, "Let me get my bag on, and then I'll get yours." Marie replied, "Jared, my bag! I don't like this one bit!" Jared answered as he lifted Marie's bag onto the train, "I know, I know!" Marie asked, "Where are we going?" Jared replied, "I have absolutely no idea." Marie angry, "You mean, you just pushed me onto a train, and you have no idea where it's going!" Jared said, "That's right! But I do know that they must have a good reason to put us on this train." A passenger then turned to Jared, "Bomb scare!" Marie squealed, "I knew it! That bag in the station!" Jared ignoring Marie asked, "Do you know where this train is headed?" Passenger to Jared, "To Reading, I suspect. That's where this train usually goes at this time of the day." Jared turned to Marie, "Well, you just heard it, we're likely going to Reading." Marie asked, "But we aren't going to the Gray Laboratories?" Jared replied, "Right now we are apparently on our way to Reading!" Marie asked, "What do we do? We don't even have tickets, and we don't have a place to stay in Reading!" Jared laughed, "We'll work something out." Marie continued, "I don't like this!" Marie was mad at Jared for taking the events of the day so lightly.

Jared and Marie moved forward to another car, found two seats, and Jared found some space for their luggage. Most of the other passengers in the coach did not have luggage, which made it a bit easier. Some of the male passengers had to stand, because there were not enough seats for everyone.

Jared thought about giving up his seat, but Marie wouldn't hear of it. She did not want to sit next to a stranger on this very stressful day. Jared started talking to one of the passengers, "Do you have any idea of the train schedules?" The passenger replied in a Welch accent, "No, but I know this train." Jared asked, "Can we go North on this line?" The passenger shook his head, "I think not. I expect that we will see Reading before anything else." Jared turned to Marie, "I don't think that this will help us that much if we can't get a train to the Northeast." Marie asked, "Why don't we just go to the coast?" Jared replied, "Well, we can do that, but I expect that we will be missed." Marie continued, "Who will miss us? We were to have the weekend off, weren't we?" Jared replied, "You're right. We probably won't be missed until Monday before my lecture . . . And I would guess that we could call them and tell them what happened." Jared asked the passenger, "Would you have a map?" The passenger smiled at Jared, "I do, but it's not a very good map." He then removed an old British Rail map from his case and handed it to Jared. Jared looked at the map and studied it for some time. On the back was an old intercity train schedule. Jared finally turned to Marie and asked, "It doesn't look like we can go to where we should be going without returning to London, and I don't think that we want to do that."

Jared smiled and said, "Let's see. How would you like to go to Wales?" Marie became excited and immediately said, "Yes!" Jared continued, "That didn't take long, did it? From Reading, we can go to Llyandidno on the sea." Marie excited, "How did you know that I wanted to go to Wales for the weekend?" Jared answered, "I obviously didn't, but we might as well enjoy ourselves. It's probably safer in Llyandidno than anywhere in England." The passenger smiled and nodded his head. He was Welch, however, and Jared considered that he favored this idea anyway. Jared handed the map back to the passenger and thanked him. The McNichols then settled down to enjoy the scenery for the remainder of the trip.

The countryside whipped by very quickly. Rural England was so different from what Jared and Marie were used to that they never seemed to tire of watching out the coach windows. To the other passengers, however, the view was probably boring. The only highlight for them was the teacart that came by occasionally to offer hot tea and biscuits or what we would call cookies. They also had small sandwiches, and Marie was adamant about having some sort of a sandwich with her tea. They decided to do both, and they shared their meal with cups of hot tea. Marie was finally calming down from the ordeal of the bomb scare at Euston Station.

To Llyandidno, Wales

Jared and Marie were amazed that no one asked them for their tickets when they arrived in Reading. It seemed that everyone that had been pushed onto the Reading train was given a free ride by British Rail. At Reading Jared went to the ticket booth and bought two round trip tickets to Llyandidno, Wales. As it turned out, a train for Wales and Llyandidno was on the tracks waiting to leave from Reading. Jared signaled to Marie, "Get your stuff, and let's get out to the tracks! Our train leaves in five minutes!" Marie stated indignantly, "I can't make it in five minutes!" Jared said, "Yes you can!" Marie insisted, "No, I can't!" Jared replied, "You're impossible! Give me your bag. You can make it. Get your ass moving." Marie was mad, but with a little coaching they made the train. As they ran out on the platform Marie said, "Jared, just get on the train!" Jared replied, "I will, just as soon as I find our car." At the same moment the Conductor blew his whistle indicating that the train was pulling out, and passengers had to board immediately. Marie yelled to Jared, "What do we do now?" Jared was not frazzled, "O.K., get in this car, and we'll sort it out later!" Marie said, "I can't make it!" Jared insisted, "Yes you can!" He threw the luggage onto the train, while Marie was helped onto the train by another passenger. Jared jumped onto the train just as it moved and began pulling out of the station. He smiled to Marie, "See, we made it!" Marie was not convinced, "So what are we going to do about accommodations, Mr. Smartass?" Jared smiled back, "We'll just have to wait and see." Marie said, "I hate this! Couldn't we have just made some arrangements at the train station?" Jared replied, "What, and miss the only train for the next three hours? I don't think so. We'll go to the station booking place, and they will find us a room." Marie was angry, "Why do you always do this? I hate not knowing where we are going to stay." Jared calmly said, "It will all work out. You'll see. I do this all the time. Trust me." Marie stuck out her tongue at Jared.

Jared showed his tickets to another passenger who told him that he was in the wrong coach. Of course, Jared knew this, but he asked for directions anyway. It seemed that they were only one coach off, so they just had to move forward to the next car and find their seats. Marie said, "I'm having a hard time with this, and dammnit Jared you know it!" Jared replied, "I know, but look at it as an adventure in traveling." Marie spit back, "I hate traveling with you!" Jared smiled, "Sure you do. Now shut-up and enjoy the view." This time Jared was right. They moved forward with some difficulty and rather quickly found their seats and settled in for the lovely trip to Wales. As the countryside rolled by, they had a chance to relax and actually enjoy the view.

They were on a local train that made all the stops. After what must have been over an hour and a half or so, they finally arrived at Llyandidno Station, and Marie was upset all over again. They didn't have any accommodations. Jared told Marie to calm down and let him find the visitors' booth at the train station. Once the booth was found, a young lady was very quick in finding a first class hotel for the night. She called, found a room, and Jared made the arrangements and paid the booking fee. After a short cab ride, they arrived at the Palace Hotel, a famous old Victorian style hotel located almost right in front of the even more famous Llyandidno Pier. In fact, from their room on the third floor, they had a marvelous view of the pier and the sea. Marie was now very happy to be out of London, especially when Jared turned on the TV only to find out that London was having a spate of bombing emergencies at many of the London railway stations. Marie did not want to hear about the bombings, and they would later find out from the BBC that it was likely her directions to the Bobby that located a bomb in Euston Station that fateful day when they were pushed onto a train to Reading.

An unintended weekend in Wales

Llyandidno was marvelous in the winter because of the lack of crowds. In the summer the popular seaside resort was usually full of vacationers. But the winters were relatively free of most visitors, except for some on the weekends. Marie hated crowds, and a brisk walk on the Llyandidno Pier with Jared, even in the cold Welch winter weather, was a nice way to get away from the ever-present crowds in London. The pier itself was a Victorian style marvel with its intricate ironwork and lovely lampposts. There were little shops on the pier, but they were closed for the winter. There was even a Ferris wheel. Marie and Jared marveled at the stoic Welchmen who didn't mind the cold wind at all. To them it was probably a very fine afternoon indeed, but to the couple from the scorching Texas Hill Country, it was anything but mild. They were obviously from overseas and not used to such cold weather, but they enjoyed the scenery with the dull blue-gray waves breaking against the old pier. Jared loved the old pier and said to Marie, "This is great! I really enjoy walking by the sea, but I can't understand how this could be considered a resort." Marie responded, "It must be grand during the summer, with all of the shops open." Jared looked at Marie with a question on his face. He was raised near the Southern Californian coast where warm, white sands and clear, blue waters invited visitors to relax and bask on the beach. Jared wondered how visitors could enjoy the stony, bleak and cold beach, even in summer. But this was Europe, and good beaches were hard to find in the northern latitudes.

After a brisk walk to the end of the pier and then along the beach, Marie regained her appetite, and Jared and Marie decided to try the dining room at the hotel. They were not disappointed. They arrived at high tea, and they decided to visit the tearoom. There they spent a lovely time enjoying the British scones and clotted cream and finger sandwiches. Marie rewarded the hostess with ample praise, "I love your scones. And the clotted cream is just delicious." The Hostess said to Marie, "We make them fresh here at the hotel each day. I will tell the pastry chef that you approve." Jared also responded, "I would say that she more than just approves–she loves them." Marie and Jared relaxed in comfortable chairs in the cozy tearoom. The décor was not quite as old as the outer appearance of the hotel, and it was tasteful and very comfortable. The pictures on the wall were of scenes from late in the nineteenth century to early in the twentieth century. Jared strained to look at the pictures while Marie was enjoying her tea with milk–quite British but they both completely enjoyed the custom. In fact, visiting various tearooms at high tea became some of the most memorable times during their visit to the U.K.

After almost an hour relaxing and enjoying their small sandwiches and scones with tea in the tearoom, Jared took Marie back to their room, whereupon he almost immediately turned on CNN to find out what was happening in the war. They were fortunate that they chose the Palace Hotel, because it was probably one of the only hotels in Llyandidno to offer TV in its rooms and CNN to its guests. Unfortunately, there was not much on CNN about the war beyond what was on TV the previous morning, so Jared turned it off. The Pentagon was managing the news again, and they were only letting out some news that they wanted the people to hear. The BBC was not much better but it was a different slant from CNN. Unfortunately, the BBC World News only appeared at certain times during the day, a problem that would be later rectified. The war news was agitating Marie, so it was just as well that Jared turned it off for the evening. They were both quite tired from the ordeals of the day, especially Marie. They both fell asleep knowing that they were quite safe and sound in their warm bed in Wales.

The following day Jared was up early to watch CNN, but there was no report on the 101st Airborne. After breakfast Jared contacted the porter about a rental car, and they checked out of the hotel and were driven by cab to a car rental lot. Jared finally chose an English Ford for the weekend. After a discussion with the clerk as to the best routes of travel, Jared studied the map and they were off. Fortunately, Jared had some experience driving on English and Scottish roads and was quite used to the large lorries that passed ever so close on the 'wrong' side of the car. In Scotland and Wales the stonewalls that often border the back roads presented a real challenge when a lorry came bearing down from the opposite direction. This usually scared Marie who was not used to passing so close to stonewalls on the left that almost took the side mirror off each time a lorry passed on the right. The main 'A' roads, however, were quite manageable and without much traffic.

Marie and Jared drove to Conway Castle, built during the time of Bonnie Prince Charles. The castle was a beautiful structure with high walls and towers. It seemed incredulous that they could be enjoying a trip to Wales, running through ancient castles while half way around the world their step-daughter was in command of a Blackhawk helicopter deployed in the stark desert near the Euphrates River. Jared and Marie tried not to think about the ongoing battle for Southern Iraq. There was not much they could do about it, even if they knew more about what was really going on in Iraq.

Their next stop was Snowdonia, considered one of the most beautiful places in Wales. Their trip took them to a picturesque valley with snow-rimmed mountains on both sides. They decided to stop at a small village just off the main road. Jared spotted a shop selling hand-made sweaters, and they decided to take a look. Naturally, Marie found a heavy wool hand-made sweater that just fit her. It was probably made for a large child, but Marie was so petite that she could wear child sizes. The price was right, so Jared purchased the sweater, and Marie insisted on wearing it during the rest of the trip in Wales. They almost felt guilty about the good time they were having sightseeing in Wales when their stepdaughter was likely in combat in Southern Iraq. Jared admitted that he was frustrated that he could do nothing but watch CNN, so they decided that they had to go on and not focus on the war. There was nothing that they could do about it, even if they wanted to do something.

Back to London and another bomb scare

Because of the train debacle, Jared missed his lecture at the Gray Laboratories, so the next stop on his schedule was Kent. His contact suggested that they return to London, because there was no way to go directly to Kent by rail from Wales. To get to Kent Jared and Marie must return to Euston Station, pick up the Underground to Victoria Station and catch a train South. The first part of the journey came off without a problem. After a lovely trip to Reading where they changed trains and then to Euston Station, Jared and Marie departed for Victoria Station via the Underground. Marie was mad at Jared for not taking a cab to Victoria Station, but Jared convinced her that the fastest route was by the Tube, and they were much less likely to miss their train.

There was a good reason why Marie hated the Underground. It was crowded and stuffy, even in the winter, and Marie hated to be in crowded places with people that she didn't know. Jared and Marie struggled with their bags. The natives seemed unfriendly, but in reality they all had places to go and probably not enough time to get there. Only the tourists took the time to look around and talk to one another. They were a mark, and one scruffy young lad tried to get into Marie's purse and steal her wallet. She yanked it away from him, and Jared gave him a stern look. He just shrugged and likely moved on to the next possibility. Jared would have jumped him, but then he would have had to leave Marie and the luggage alone. He decided that it wasn't worth it. The rest of the patrons seemed so used to the crime, noise and crowds that they were barely awake.

The London Underground, once the most modern subway system in the world, was showing its age and was not a baggage friendly place. The tunnels and stairs were narrow and old in many stations, and the platforms were relatively small by modern standards. The addition of new lines was not especially well thought out, probably because they were afterthoughts, and the tunnel connections between the various lines were often quite crude affairs. The trains themselves were old but serviceable, and there was not much room for baggage, except on the special Express cars to Heathrow Airport, making them a bit awkward for inter-city travelers trying to get from one rail station to another. For the most part, however, they were quite reliable for moving around London, and they were much faster than surface transport. Jared preferred the Tube to the overcrowded, slow-moving streets, but Marie did not like the rocking on some sections of old Underground track and the packing in of passengers on some lines, even during non-rush hour periods. Jared had been studying his map of the Underground. He and Marie were the only ones in sight that did not know where to get off. Jared said to Marie as the Underground made its way toward Victoria Station, "We are just about there—only one more stop and then to Victoria." Unbeknownst to Jared and Marie, the bombers had already planted a device in the Victoria Station. This time it would cause a fatality.

Arriving at Victoria Station

Marie and Jared had finally made it to Victoria Station in order to catch their train to Kent. Entering Victoria Station was like taking a trip back in time. Except for the modern shops, ticket booths and signs, Victoria Station was like a picture from the past. Looking up at the old Victorian style roof and ironworks, one could actually get a feel for how this grand station might have looked in the nineteenth century with steam engines pulling old coaches into the station. Now most of the trains were electric and much cleaner and quieter, except for the diesel trains on the intercity routes. During the day when commuters were not overwhelming the old station, it was quite comfortable with all the shops and restaurants, except that there were few places to sit down and wait for trains. With tickets in hand Marie and Jared waited under the big board that flashed the destinations, track numbers and times of various trains. The clickity-clack of the old schedule board was constantly heard as each letter and number flipped over and over until they stopped and a new destination, track number and time appeared. Each row then moved up one as each train departed.

There was something quite reassuring about the large schedule board. It seemed odd compared to the all-electronic airports where such mechanical boards had long since disappeared in favor of multiple TV monitors. One could also find train schedules on TV monitors at every station, but there was something about the big schedule board that attracted customers. Perhaps because it was so easy to see the various trains and their destinations, and also it probably reminded passengers of a change on the board by its clickity-clack sound. Marie spotted their train first and shook Jared into consciousness. She said, "Our train is on track eight. I want to board now." Jared to Marie, "You can't go until it flashes 'boarding'." As he said this the cards in the 'boarding' part of the sign began flipping and finally stopped at 'now boarding.' Jared finally responded, "O.K., You're right. Let's go!"

They grabbed their black, wheeled baggage and headed for track eight where a mass of train riders had converged. Marie said, "I hate this!" But Jared didn't bother to answer. The gates opened, and the riders converged on the gate. The McNichols finally moved slowly to the front of the line as passengers passed through the gate. Jared handed the tickets to the man at the gate who punched holes in them, and they made their way out to the platform to find their coach. To make Marie feel better Jared had purchased 1st class tickets, so they had to find the 1st class coach. Once inside their coach they found that there was much more space for their baggage and the chairs were more roomy and comfortable than in 2nd class. They finally relaxed while Jared read the London Times. After a few minutes, a whistle sounded, and they were off. Later that day they would find out that they missed the fatal Victoria Station bomb by about 15 minutes. Their luck was holding.

To Kent and beyond

Jared had to lecture in Kent and at other sites in Southern England before returning to London to give the evening Society Lecture at Wimpole Street in downtown London. It was their good fortune that they had been invited to stay with Dr. Kenneth Hallman and his wife, Janet, who was a practicing hematologist at one of the Kent hospitals. Their home was on a lovely estate in Eastern Kentshire amongst rolling hills, woods and farmland. Professor Hallman picked up the McNichols at the rail station, and they had a nice ride through the countryside to the Hallman's estate. As they arrived, they were pleasantly surprised. The house was a lovely old mansion on a hill with ample space and beautiful views of the English countryside. By the time Jared and Marie were picked up at the train station by Kenneth, they were completely exhausted from their near miss at Victoria and the rigors of travel from Wales. Thus the McNichols both took an afternoon nap, and later they found Kenneth walking about his berry bushes in the garden. Jared joined Kenneth for a long walk, and by five in the afternoon they were finally ready for dinner, which was a delightful event indeed.

Jared had not seen Kenneth for about one year, and they had much research and journal news to catch up on. They were also bound by a mutual dislike of the egomaniacs in their field, such as Drs. Isaac Geldter and Amy Krappner and their ilk, and somehow the conversation eventually turned to this pair as Kenneth jokingly asked how they were doing. Jared and Kenneth had great delight in mocking their importance in the grand scheme of things, but the conversation finally turned to more serious topics, including the war and the bombings in London.

The following morning as Janet was off to the hospital, Jared, Marie and Kenneth made the rounds at the estate. Although it was a cold morning, it was a rare almost clear winter day in Kent. Usually there were high clouds that gave England and most of Europe that gray winter appearance, which can last for months on end with the only interruption an occasional winter storm. Kenneth was very pleased at the lay of the land, and it was clear that he was enjoying his recent retirement and the blessing of not having to fight the commuters going off to London each day. From this lovely location, it was quite a trip by car, train and then Underground to reach his former office. Marie and Jared enjoyed their weekend in the countryside in Kent, and on the following day Jared had to travel to Kent to deliver one of his lectures. The McNichols were beginning to feel quite at home in England, and the Hallmans had done a marvelous job in making them feel comfortable.

Return to The British Society of Medicine

Jared and Marie had to return to the Society building on Wimpole Street, London, because it was time for Jared's lecture and award ceremony. This time Marie was lucky, as Kenneth and Janet were to bring them by auto to the Society. Because of the shortage of car parks in central London, Kenneth had to make prior arrangements for the car. At least in 1991 he could bring a car into central London without paying a nasty fee. However, just arriving in central London was only part of the problem, since they had to find a place to leave the car. All of this had been arranged in advance by the Society, and the Hallmans and McNichols were grateful that they didn't have to take the train and then the Underground to get to the Society headquarters.

That evening was the lecture and the award presentation. Since he was a close friend, Kenneth would be presenting the award to Jared on behalf of the Society. The lecture on Jared's recent research on the molecular mechanisms of homing of metastatic cancer cells to various organs in the body was presented after a course of sherry, a very civilized custom that Jared thoroughly enjoyed. But Marie who didn't drink at all just used the occasion to visit with Janet and the other participants. After the lecture, question period and award ceremony, everyone retired to the bar for a refreshment and toast to the Queen before heading home or departing for a late evening meal.

At the reception after the lecture the conversation turned to a British pathologist, Stephen Paget, who in the mid 19th century proposed the 'soil and seed hypothesis' that certain cancers ('seeds') spread to particular sites ('soil') based on their properties and the properties of the organ site. Jared had used this theory to show how correct Dr. Paget was by demonstrating that malignant tumor cells express particular molecules on their surfaces that allowed them to home to, invade and survive and grow at particular organ sites, explaining in molecular terms why certain blood-borne cancers metastasized preferentially to certain predictable distant sites in the body. Everyone seemed to be satisfied with the festivities, and the Hallmans and the McNichols retired to a private meal with the officers of the Society in a special room reserved for the occasion.

After a delicious meal of English Grill, the conversation turned on many subjects until the final Port toast to the Queen. The McNichols were lucky, since they and a few senior members of the Society had only to go upstairs to their accommodations after the festivities were over. Before taking their leave for the evening, Jared, Kenneth and Marie had their pictures taken in front of a large portrait of the Queen. It was only after their return to Texas that Jared and Marie noticed how similar Marie looked to the Queen, almost like a close relative.

On their way home to Texas

The following day Jared and Marie were making their way to Heathrow Airport when they learned of the ceasefire in Iraq. They were quite relieved, especially Jared, who had thought about Suzanne and her brothers in arms in the 101st almost every waking hour during the trip. It had been difficult not knowing what was happening on the ground in Iraq and Kuwait, a situation that would be rectified in future wars when reporters would be imbedded in combat units. For now they were relieved to know it was over, and the casualties were extremely light for an operation of this magnitude. It was only years later that the real truth finally surfaced and the delayed casualties would pile up to become one of the most costly conflicts in U. S. history. No one would know this, however, because the truth would be kept hidden from the American people.

As they boarded their plane for the trip directly to Houston from London, Jared and Marie reflected on their recent experiences. Even with the bomb scares, homemade mortars and changes in itineraries, they had a marvelous time indeed. And they would find out that Suzanne was safe, at least for the moment. The long trip home was uneventful but tiring. The McNichols were happy to finally see Yin and Yang, who ran around the living room again and again in celebration of their return to Queenswood.

CHAPTER 3

A New Casualty of War (1993)

Suzanne had been back from the Middle East for over a year when she related to Jared in a telephone conversation that many soldiers in her unit were sick, and she was leaving the military after a nine-year career as a decorated, non-commissioned officer. She had managed to make it through Warrant Officer School with some difficulty, but now she was having health problems. It was difficult enough for a female soldier to be accepted into Warrant Officer School, and she needed all of her strength to make it through. But to Suzanne the reason for Warrant Officer School was to eventually fly for the Army. But to be a pilot, she would have to accomplish this first. For a soldier who was once awarded the title of best soldier in her battalion, Warrant Officer School was the acme of achievement, the highest rank of service for a non-commissioned officer or noncom in the all-volunteer U. S. Army, and the mark of a true warrior.

Jared received a call from Suzanne one evening. She had failed her physical for flight school, and she was devastated. Suzanne had always been in top health and had little patience for those who were always ill or unable to perform, and now it had happened to her. She had always wanted to be a pilot since she was a child, and this would have been the culmination of her ambitions. Now, however, she was facing an uphill battle to retain her hard-fought upward mobility in the military. If she complained that she was ill with chronic problems like headaches, memory loss, joint and muscle pain, digestive and other problems, she would find like others in her unit that there was little understanding of their conditions, no treatments and absolutely no sympathy for their medical problems. Others too, were facing the same difficulties, even the medics and officers that served in the Gulf were having problems in the various services that were deployed to the Persian Gulf in 1990 to 1991, but there were no explanations offered as to what it might be, so everyone was sent to the unit psychiatrist for evaluation.

Just about the worse thing that can happen to a very proud soldier, airman, seaman or marine was to have someone tell you that you were not fit psychologically as an explanation for your medical problems. Since the military psychiatrists could not explain the signs and symptoms of the veterans returning from the Gulf, they assumed that the veterans were suffering from psychological problems from their service in the Gulf War. After all, this was what psychiatrists did–diagnose psychiatric problems– and they did not want to admit that they had no idea what was going on. Military psychiatrists and psychologists indignantly noted that historians had recorded high incidences of chronic illnesses in veterans after each war since the War of 1812, so the undiagnosed illnesses must be related to what was called 'shell shock' in World War I or 'combat fatigue' in World War II and Korea.

Thus by virtue of their service in the Gulf War it was assumed by psychiatrists (probably none of whom had ever seen combat) that the veterans must be suffering from the psychological effects of combat. The new catchy term for this was 'Post Traumatic Stress Disorder' or PTSD, and it became such a popular diagnosis that some units had frightfully high incidences of this purely psychological condition. Notwithstanding the fact that many of the individuals who were receiving this diagnosis had not even seen combat in the Gulf, ever fired a M16 or any other weapon for that matter at an Iraqi, and were never even near the front lines or combat in this basically 100-hour war. The unknown chronic condition was found in front-line combat units, but it was also found in supply and quartermaster units, command and control units and other services as well as those that were deployed far from the front lines in the war. Some of the more interesting cases would turn out to be sailors on ships in the Persian Gulf hundreds of miles from the battle zone and even soldiers, marines and sailors that were waiting to be deployed from bases in the U.S. when the war abruptly ended. One of the common features of all these Armed Forces personnel was that they received the multiple vaccines given before or during deployment.

Denial and stonewalling

Chronic illness casualties from the Gulf War started to appear after the war, but it was slow at first. By six months after the war, however, there were tens of thousands of soldiers, sailors, airmen and marines reporting chronic health problems. Since these problems did not seem to be life threatening, they were largely dismissed. Also, the health problems did not seem to fit the established diagnosis categories used by the military. At first there ware even denials from the Pentagon that there were any health problems associated with deployment to the Persian Gulf after or during the war. Jared and Marie remembered clearly the Pentagon's spokesperson, Roger Ham, on television dismissing reporters' questions about any illnesses in returning veterans. The possibility that any illnesses might be due to Chemical or Biological Weapons was disdainfully dismissed as pure science fiction. After the spin fell apart when the reports of health problems did not go away, the Pentagon came up with an explanation that they thought would please everyone. The illnesses were all caused by 'stress', meaning that they were psychological not medical causes for the illnesses.

As the number of cases grew from 25,000 to 50,000 to over 150,000, the most common cause basically remained the same–PTSD. Notwithstanding the unusual signs and symptoms in most of these veterans that could not possibly have been explained by a psychological disorder, such as bloody diarrhea, unusual skin rashes, severe muscle and joint pain, intermittent fevers, thyroid and other problems, the Pentagon still insisted it was PTSD. Since most of the ill Armed Forces personnel had to have a psychological evaluation, this was where most of them received their PTSD diagnosis. Although other diagnoses were possible and even used to varying degrees among the services, there was pressure, especially in the 'unexplained illness' cases, to make sure that these veterans' illnesses were listed as PTSD. In fact, there were even directives and guidelines from the Pentagon to make sure that the most likely diagnosis in chronic illness cases that could not be easily assigned to known diseases or unexplained conditions was PTSD. In disgust, many Armed Forces personnel tried to cover up their illnesses or did not bother to report them, because a psychological diagnosis of PTSD could be the end of their promotions and careers in the military.

How many able and brave men and women of our Armed Forces had their careers ruined or cut short by such Pentagon antics will never be known, but it would not matter. The Department of Defense (DoD) was in a down-sizing mode, and the mustering out of less desirable personnel seemed to fit nicely with their own plans. Unfortunately, Suzanne was caught in the middle of this, and it was time to leave the Army and a career that she had been planning for years. And Suzanne was not the only one from the 101st who was now calling and explaining about their health problems to Jared and Marie. Thus the McNichols got a feel for the magnitude of the problem. Eventually many veterans from the 101st and 82nd Airborne Divisions, famous for their daring exploits just before D-Day in Normandy in 1944 and now famous for their air assaults during the Gulf War, contacted the McNichols for assistance with their 'undiagnosed' illnesses. Also, many of the veterans who received a PTSD diagnosis and a handful of antidepressants from medical personnel eager to please their superiors would contact the McNichols. Not all physicians in the military were so easily persuaded by the PTSD rush to judgment. But just like any other chain of command in the military, physicians must follow orders that come down from above or be relieved of duty. This was a powerful way to control the situation and satisfy the Pentagon's quest to deny that a new type of chronic illness was associated with service in the Gulf War.

An attempt to rationalize Gulf War Syndrome

By the end of 1992 the American press had coined a new term, Gulf War Syndrome, to characterize the undiagnosed illnesses in veterans from the Gulf War, and they smelled a story. They also were beginning to smell something fishy about the DoD and their explanations of the war-associated illnesses as entirely or almost entirely due to stress-related illness or PTSD. Counterattacking the pesky American press from their lofty positions in the Pentagon were some high-level military physicians who were enlisted to convince the press that the military's liberal use of PTSD to explain what now appeared more and more to be unusual illnesses of unknown origin was genuine and appropriate.

Along with this strategy was an all out effort to belittle the efforts of the small number of civilian physicians and scientists who dared to challenge the Pentagon in their zeal to brand the veterans as psychological cases. These civilian researchers and clinicians were proposing that the Gulf War Syndrome was a real condition that was, in fact, due to exposures to toxic chemical and biological materials that resulted in chronic illnesses with nonspecific signs and symptoms. Unfortunately, because of infighting and egos, the civilian researchers and clinicians could not decide among themselves how to present a uniform front to the public and to Congress, and thus they were easy to vanquish by frontal assault. It was surprisingly easy to 'roll over' the few voices that were speaking out against the all powerful Pentagon and CIA.

The DoD even convened meetings on Gulf War Veterans' Illnesses and conveniently forgot to invite some of their key detractors, and they would enlist their grant and contract powers to reward those who would without hesitation go along with the entire PTSD program just to receive some Pentagon funding. Thus in the early years of 'Gulf War Syndrome' research over 80% of the grant and contract awards from the Federal Government were for psychiatric studies. These would, of course, support the notion that Gulf War Syndrome was just PTSD. After all, what else would one expect from psychiatrists and psychologists? Didn't they receive their grants to study PTSD in Gulf War veterans? The DoD and/or the CIA went so far as to hire freelance authors to write comical pieces for various magazines that ridiculed the veterans and belittled their illnesses, all in an attempt to deflect criticism of the Medical Corps and the fact that they could not explain or successfully treat Gulf War Syndrome. Eventually the McNichols would fall into this 'target' category and join a growing group of researchers that questioned the wisdom of the mighty Pentagon. They would even become the brunt of dark humor and other assaults on their intelligence, integrity and loyalty by the 'hired guns' sent to discredit anyone who dared disagree with the official stance that Gulf War Syndrome was caused by stress and was just PTSD. No one wanted to hear that our Armed Forces might not have been fully prepared for modern combat against a second rate power that possessed unconventional weapons of mass destruction or that their preparations themselves might have been part of the problem.

A new veterans' illness or is it similar to civilian illnesses?

From their work with the unknown chronic illnesses in the U. S. Army's Airborne Divisions, Jared and Marie began to work with other units, such as the U. S. Army Special Forces Units that were stationed at the same bases with the paratroopers in North Carolina and air assault forces in Kentucky and some of the Navy SEAL units at Fort Bragg in North Carolina. The casualties were piling up faster than anyone could imagine, and there was much to do but little in the way of funds to help the veterans. In some units almost every other soldier was sick, and they were leaving the military in droves, either on their own or after medical boards set up to evaluate their medical conditions made the decision for them. Since no one was keeping track of the personnel that left the military for medical reasons, it was convenient to just write these veterans off and forget about them. After all, they were now the VA's problem.

Jared and Marie realized that something must be done to avert a disaster in the making, so a fateful decision was made that would change their lives forever and seal their fates in academia. It didn't seem like a difficult decision at the time. The veterans needed help, and they felt that it was their duty as parents of a veteran and loyal Americans to do something, anything, to help those in need, especially since they were not receiving the assistance that they needed from the government.

Thus the McNichols would start on a long and miserable road that almost bankrupted them and cost them their jobs and their future. In the process their idealism and zeal to uncover the truth would be severely tested along with their unwavering loyalty to the Armed Forces personnel who were placed in harm's way in 1991. They would be vilified by the Pentagon's Medical Corps and the CIA and made academic lepers by their peers and associates in academia. If they had only known their futures at this point in time, they would have thought much more carefully about interfering with military affairs and 'National Security' issues. But to let the veterans suffer without proper assistance was also unacceptable to Jared and Marie, so they would just have to suck it up and take the consequences of their actions.

Beginning to amass the data on Gulf War Illnesses

At the end of 1993 Jared had devised and sent out a preliminary questionnaire or health survey form to sick members of the Special Forces and Airborne units that they had interacted with during the last year or so. The idea was to document just what kinds of health problems they were having. Jared was assisted in this effort by some detailed information sent to him and Marie from veterans with whom they had been in contact with over the years. The idea was to make a table of signs and symptoms so that they could be compared with other illnesses or conditions from the literature. At the time the so called 'Desert Storm Illness' in the military was not widely known by the American public, except for some complaints by veterans that were aired as individual accounts mostly in local newspapers.

The mainstream press was just beginning to suspect that there might be a problem from the Gulf War, but for the most part the national press never would dive very deep into the issue. They would be and still are heavily influenced by the VA and Pentagon spin-doctors who were masters at deception and deflecting any possible criticism of military policies. Away from the press, Jared had assembled a small group of interested physicians and technicians with Marie to go over the data that continued to come in from veterans and active duty military personnel. In his office in front of a table with the few interested colleagues from Austin Jared listed the various signs and symptoms complaints that had come in on a white board using a black erasable pen.

Jared addressed the assembled informal group. "Let's see now, thank you all for coming. I would like your opinions on the following data. I have listed the signs and symptoms that we have obtained from the veterans who became sick after their service in the Gulf War in the first column. In looking through the literature I have found some of the signs and symptoms of similar chronic illnesses using Chronic Fatigue Syndrome, and for comparison, I have listed these in the second column. I have listed the signs and symptoms from Marie's almost fatal illness in the third column."

Table 1

Comparison of signs and symptoms of Gulf War Syndrome,
Chronic Fatigue Syndrome and Marie's Illness.

Signs/ Symptoms	Gulf War Syndrome	Chronic Fatigue Syndrome	Marie's Illness
chronic fatigue	+	+	+
joint pain/mobility	+	+	+
night sweats	+	+	+
muscle pain	+	+ (not always)	+
fevers	+	+ (not always)	+
headaches	+	+	+
skin rashes	+	+ (not always)	+
memory loss	+	+	+
stomach pain	+ (not always)	+ (not always)	+
breathing problems	+ (not always)	+ (not always)	+
sleep problems	+	+	+
diarrhea	± (not always)	+ (not always)	±
heart palpitations	+ (not always)	+ (not always)	+
vision problems	+	+	+
depression	+ (not always)	+ (not always)	+
hair loss	+ (not always)	+ (not always)	+
nausea	+ (not always)	+ (not always)	+
sinus problems	+ (not always)	+ (not always)	+
vertigo	+ (not always)	+ (not always)	+

Jared continued, "From the list I can't see much of a difference between the groups." Dr. Herlyn, a German physician who was a visiting research associate with Jared spoke first. "It's difficult to assess such illnesses when the signs and symptoms are so nonspecific." Jared responded, "I agree completely. This is probably one of the main reasons that these illnesses have caused so much confusion. They can't be diagnosed from the complaints of veterans without further information."

Primary care physicians could not get a grip on the illnesses from the Gulf War because there was nothing unique about the symptoms presentation that would allow them to be easily assigned to diagnosis categories. "We'll know more when we design a new survey form and send it out to enough veterans and civilians," suggested Jared. "But at least for now, it appears that the Gulf War Syndrome is not likely to be a new syndrome—it most closely resembles Chronic Fatigue Syndrome in its signs and symptoms but it tends to be more severe from the reports that we have received, more like what Marie suffered from in the late 80s." Marie added, "The worst part for me was the nonstop nausea and muscle and joint pain. I could hardly move without pain that you can't imagine." Jared continued, "At the height of Marie's illness she could barely move, and I thought that she would become paralyzed and not ever be able to move her left arm and leg again. But with antibiotic treatment and physical therapy she made a complete recovery." Marie related to the group, "I had such severe headaches that I thought that my head was going to explode! I never thought that I would recover, but I did—it took over a year just to begin to feel normal again." Jared added, "At least you recovered, Marie. These veterans are not recovering for the most part. They are not being offered anything in the way of effective treatments, except for antidepressants and other mood-altering drugs to treat their 'psychological' problems. This is a disgrace. But there is not much that we can do about it, except gather more evidence and try to find out what is happening to these veterans."

The mood was somber in the group. It's difficult to work on something without official assistance, especially without financial support for the rather expensive lab tests and analyses that had to be performed. Jared knew from his experience that it would be difficult to move the Federal bureaucracy to even consider that something other than psychological problems might be causing some of the illnesses from the Gulf War. There seemed to be a stonewall when it came to this issue, and Jared and Marie wondered why there was such resistance to finding out what happened in the Persian Gulf.

CHAPTER 4

Finding a 'Cause' and a Treatment (1994)

As time went on Jared and Marie began to realize more and more that the veterans, at least a rather large subset of them, were suffering from biological exposures, such as chronic infections, and chemical exposures. The McNichols had been receiving blood from veterans of the Gulf War, and they had begun to analyze the blood samples for infections. Word had gotten around the Airborne and Special Forces units that a research group in Austin, Texas had helped some officers from the Gulf War with their 'undiagnosed illnesses.' Since the veterans didn't seem to be getting much help from the Medical Corps, as a last resort they began to contact the McNichols to get some possible help for their problems. For the most part these were professional soldiers, airmen, sailors and marines, not youngsters that had never seen combat before or saw it for the first time in the Gulf War. They had been there before and didn't have problems after the combat ended like they had now. For these combat-tested veterans their post-war illnesses were something new. And they were particularly disdainful of the liberal use of PTSD to describe their clinical problems. If they didn't have PTSD after other wars, why should they have it now? What was so different about the Gulf War? Had we become a nation of people who were prone to psychological problems? Or was something else involved, something that no one wanted to acknowledge or recognize?

Jared McNichols had been compiling a list of Gulf War veterans' health complaints and asking for their medical records, if they could get them. Since military medical records and especially shot records were disappearing or being classified at astonishing rates, these records would not be available for analysis. That in itself was very suspicious. The Gulf War was the first conflict in history where veterans' shot records were lost, hidden or classified, possibly to prevent scrutiny of the vaccines that were given during deployment. The rationale that the DoD was giving out to reporters who dared to question their wisdom on the classification of Gulf War era shot records was that they did not want our potential enemies to find out what vaccines were given to individuals before or during deployment so that they would not know what countermeasures were taken against biological weapons. Most veterans that contacted the McNichols, however, were sarcastic about this rationale and doubted if Saddam had access to or was even interested in their individual shot records. The McNichols were convinced more than ever that many if not most of these veterans had chronic infections that either caused their illnesses or at least exacerbated their illnesses, and one possible source for infections was the military vaccines that were so liberally given to personnel during deployment. When a small number of shot records surfaced, usually because the veteran made a copy or hid the records, there were unidentified vaccines listed on the records. Were these unidentified vaccines experimental vaccines? Why was the information on the Gulf War era shot records so important that these records had to be classified as secret and hidden away from public scrutiny, and why were so many lost, over 500,000 by some estimates? Unfortunately, the saga of the lost or classified shot records has never been resolved.

One of the well-known problems in the manufacturing of commercial vaccines was biological contamination, and this was usually contamination by bacteria that can enter the vaccines at a number of points in the manufacturing process. Usually such contamination can be identified before the vaccine lots are released, especially if the contamination was via rapidly growing, commonly found bacteria, the most common type of contamination in commercial biological preparations. Possible contamination of vaccine lots was usually ruled out by incubating samples from various vaccine lots at body temperatures for varying times to see if bacteria grow out in the samples. Alternatively, samples of the vaccines can be inoculated into broth cultures containing medium that support the growth of most bacteria. However, not all contaminating bacteria will grow under these conditions, especially slow-growing bacteria and other possible contaminants such as viruses. Also, low-levels of contamination may not be identifiable in such analyses.

Returning to the possibility that biological exposures were important in Gulf War Illnesses, as they were now calling the Gulf War Syndrome, Jared made a list of most commonly found chronic infections that could be causing much of the problem. The list of signs and symptoms that Jared compiled was mainly from bacterial infections and included: *Brucella* species, the bacteria that causes brucellosis, mainly a veterinary illness that is endemic in the Middle East and elsewhere; *Mycoplasma* species, the small bacteria that lack a rigid cell wall and are responsible for many if not most infection-based asthma, bronchitis and genitourinary cases; *Coxiella burnetti*, the bacteria that causes Q-Fever, a chronic disease marked by undulating fevers and respiratory distress; plague caused by *Yersinia pestis*, an insect-borne bacillus-type bacteria that causes high fevers and pneumonia; and tularemia caused by *Francisella tularensis*, a small bacillus-type bacteria that causes pneumonia and swollen lymph nodes. Other than bacteria, the list is short and includes: leishmaniasis, an insect-borne disease caused by a systemic parasite that causes fever, cough, stomach pain and distortion and diarrhea. Most of these infectious agents have also been developed as incapacitating Biological Warfare agents by various countries, and certainly by the United States in its Biodefense programs. Jared moved to the large white board in his office and made a new table.

Table 2

Comparison of signs and symptoms of various illnesses caused by chronic bacterial or parasite infections.

Signs/ symptoms	*Brucella*	*Mycoplasma*	*Coxiella*	*Y. pestis*	*F. tularensis*	Leish-mania
Onset (average)	months	months	15-40 d	2-7 days	3-10 d	months
Infectious route	airborne	airborne	airborne	insect	insect	insect
acute fevers				+	+	
intermit. fevers	+	+	+			+
night sweats	++	++	+	+		+
pneumonia	+(some)	+(some)	++	++	++	
cough	+	+(some)	+	++	+	
joint pain	+	+				
muscle pain	+	+	+	+	+	+
swollen nodes	+	+	+	+	+	+
headaches	+	+	+	+	+	
gastrointestinal	+	+		+(some)	+(some)	++
skin rashes	+	+			+(some)	++
vomiting	+	+		+(some)	+	+
diarrhea	+	+			+	+
nausea	+	+		+	+	
endocarditis	+	+				

Brucella=*B. melitensis* Mycoplasma=*M. fermentans*

The table was not complete, but a rough picture began to form. Since most of the veterans did not experience symptoms until 3-6 months to over a year after they returned, most of the more acute infectious diseases were unlikely but not ruled out entirely. For example, low-level exposures might require longer to present than acute exposures. Some of the veterans were diagnosed with leishmania, a parasitic infection usually spread by the bite of a sand fly. There was a test for this parasite, but less than 100 cases were found in the Gulf War veterans, according to the U. S. Army Institute of Pathology Research.

Thus the McNichols were left with two infections that fit the signs and symptom profiles better than the others. They were also more likely than the rest because their natural history or pathogenesis was more consistent with the time of onset of symptoms: *Brucella* species and *Mycoplasma* species. These types of infections were not well known by civilian physicians. In fact, one of the problems that Jared and Marie would later face was the almost complete lack of simple knowledge of the average physician about many types of chronic infections. And these types of infections would be difficult to find in clinical samples or even more difficult to find in commercial vaccines.

Most physicians have been trained to recognize the presence of acute bacterial infections, because such infections if they progress to systemic or system wide infections can cause sepsis if not diagnosed early on. In this condition the rapidly growing bacteria flood every organ and tissue with rapidly dividing microorganisms, and their release of bacterial toxins poisons virtually every tissue in the body, a situation that can be fatal. Our immune systems usually recognize these rapidly growing bacteria, but the rapid proliferation of a microorganism can outstrip the ability of our immune systems to identify and destroy the invaders. By sheer numbers alone the microorganism invaders can overwhelm the immune system and its ability to destroy them. However, the slow-growing *Brucella* and *Mycoplasma* species proliferate so slowly and hide inside cells and tissues that they are not so readily apparent as their fast-growing relatives. These slow-growing bacteria can be much more insidious. They hide from the immune system rather than attempting to overwhelm it by rapid proliferation, and they take their time to slowly destroy tissues and cells that they colonize, and almost like parasites, they slowly take over their host.

The slow-growing pathogenic bacteria usually begin their infectious invasion by gaining access to the tissues, entering cells and interfering with their metabolism. They can also slowly attack the energy systems of the cell, such as the mitochondria, the little batteries in our cells that provide most of the energy that our cells need to function. This was why infected patients experience chronic fatigue and loss of energy–their energy generating systems are slowly being destroyed. The slow-growing intracellular bacterial infections can also cause genetic changes in cells, because some of the substances that they release are toxic to our DNA and the genes that make up our genetic apparatus. Slowly our genes can be modified in subtle ways that eventually can cause problems, such as genetic deletions or mutations. Many of the symptoms caused by such infections occur when specific tissues and glands are invaded. For example, if the thyroid gland is colonized by the microorganisms, changes in the production of thyroid hormones can occur. Sometimes the production of thyroid hormones can be reduced, sometimes it can be elevated, or the overall levels of thyroid hormones can even remain within the normal range or slightly out of normal range while fluctuating or cycling. Other problems occur when our bodies attempt to circumvent the infection, and this can result in the release of chemical substances that mimic some of the steps that occur during an immune response, resulting in intermittent fevers and malaise.

Very simple in genetic terms, Brucellas and Mycoplasmas need the cellular metabolism of a host cell to provide them with the building blocks for their synthetic machinery. During their evolution they lost the ability to make many of the things that they need to survive and grow, so they had to evolve as cellular thieves that steal what they need from their colonized host cells. They also evolved as experts in circumventing our immune systems. In the process of infection they can release substances that slowly circumvent host responses that begin to identify them as foreign and react against them. For example, they are masters at fooling the immune systems into seeing their exteriors as normal host structures, and they can actually release chemical substances that paralyze host immune responses so they won't be stopped from their slow infection process. They can also remove host membrane structures and incorporate them into their own bacterial membranes. For example, this can happen when the intracellular bacteria leave cells to infect other cells. In the process of escaping from the host cell, they often pull out small pieces of host cell membranes and escape with the normal host structures incorporated in their own bacterial membrane. Although this sounds innocuous, it can set up an autoimmune response if the host incorrectly identifies its own antigens as belonging to the bacterial invader. Instead of mounting an immune response that neutralizes the bacteria, the host inadvertently mounts an immune response against itself, an autoimmune response, resulting in host cell and tissue destruction. Such inappropriate immune responses are important in rheumatic diseases, such as rheumatoid arthritis. Interestingly, one of the more common complaints of the veterans was joint pain and loss of joint mobility, similar to the most common symptoms of rheumatoid arthritis. Most rheumatoid arthritis patients have similar types of chronic intracellular infections in their synovium, the tissues in the joints that separate bone.

In the process of colonizing virtually every tissue and organ system, the slow-growing intracellular bacteria can cause multiple signs and symptoms. Unfortunately, none of these were distinctive enough to warn physicians as to what might be the cause. Not just any species of *Brucella* or *Mycoplasma* can cause all of the signs and symptoms that were seen in the veterans, but now the range of likely infections could be narrowed considerably. There were other infections that would have to be considered, such as Rickettsial and other slow-growing bacteria and some parasite infections, but this was a good place for the McNichols' laboratory to start looking.

Since Marie had suffered from a mycoplasmal infection that almost killed her, Jared decided that they should investigate the possibility of infection by Mycoplasmas before anything else. First, they needed to decide which species of Mycoplasmas that they should investigate. There were approximately 50 different species of *Mycoplasma* that had been identified and had appeared in one publication or another, and they wanted to do a general as well as a specific search. Narrowing the number to those species that had been identified in humans, the number dropped to about a dozen. Then narrowing the search even more to those species identified as pathogenic in humans or suspected of causing chronic illnesses similar to Gulf War Illnesses, the number dropped again to about six.

At this point the McNichols research team could focus on any type of bacteria, a specific class of bacteria or on a specific species of bacteria. They decided to concentrate on a class of Mycoplasmas first because that seemed to be a good place to start. In order to approach the problem they had to devise a general approach for detecting essentially all species of Mycoplasmas and a more specific approach to detect certain species of Mycoplasma that were already associated with chronic human illnesses. Since they did not expect every case of Gulf War Illness to be caused by chronic bacterial or other infections, they would have to link any laboratory findings with the signs and symptoms of individual patients.

If the McNichols research team did not find any evidence for Mycoplasmas in the veterans' blood, then they could go down the list starting next with *Brucella* species. Certain *Brucella* species were already known to produce a chronic disease in man, brucellosis, and the signs and symptoms of the veterans were also similar to brucellosis. Brucellosis is an endemic infectious disease caused by a known infection that was found in the Middle East and associated with domestic animal herds like cattle and sheep where the infection can be fatal. Moreover, in countries like Saudi Arabia and Kuwait brucellosis was not an uncommon disease. It was not present in epidemic proportions, but hundreds of cases had been reported each year in these countries. Since the veterans were exposed to a variety of environmental toxins, such as chemicals, smoke, among other contaminants, their immune systems may not have prevented them from being infected by natural bacterial invaders already present in the Middle East. On the other hand, they might be dealing with something much more sophisticated, such as Biological Warfare agents. The fear was that if they found evidence for Mycoplasma or Brucella species, that these would be modified microorganisms, not the usual fairly benign species associated with some isolated chronic infections or animal diseases. Since the microorganisms that the McNichols' laboratory were looking for were slow-growing bacteria that caused chronic illnesses, it was unlikely that they were dealing with anthrax or other more rapidly growing bacteria. If these turned out to be modified agents, then they were looking for 'incapacitating agents' not 'lethal agents' designed to quickly kill their host.

The data indicate an infection in the Gulf War veterans

Now that the Gulf War Illness Research Team, as Jared was calling it, had settled on an overall approach to rule in or rule out chronic infections in the Gulf War Illnesses, Jared searched the medical and scientific literature for anything that he could find on Mycoplasmas and human illnesses. He was struck by the research of the U. S. Army Institute for Pathology Research on *Mycoplasma fermentans incognitus* published by Dr. Ming Lon. Was Dr. Lon the same researcher that Marie had spoken to when she was dying of some unknown infection? The publications indicated that Dr. Lon first thought that the *Mycoplasma fermentans incognitus* was a virus because of its small size and small genetic content, but he later found that it was a very small bacterium that had invaded cells just like a virus.

What had confused Dr. Lon was that the *Mycoplasma fermentans incognitus* or Mfi did not have a rigid cell wall like most bacteria, and it had considerably less genetic information than common bacteria. In fact, when Dr. Lon reported on the structure of Mfi, the description was so devoid of notable features that no wonder it remained an elusive, 'silent' infection for so long. Usually one can use the techniques of immunology to determine if an infection has occurred, because most bacteria elicited a strong immune response in their host. But in the case of Mfi, there was little evidence to suggest that it stimulated a strong immune response. If they used the presence of antibodies against Mfi to find infections, they could be completely fooled. In fact, Dr. Lon had already indicated that he could not find antibodies against Mfi in Gulf War veterans, a result that indicated to Jared that there were others who were also thinking along the same lines that chronic bacterial infections might cause some of the illnesses in the veterans. Thus their idea may not be so far-fetched after all.

To get around the problem that Mycoplasmas like Mfi were not likely to elicit a strong immune response, Jared decided that they would have to use another approach to find out whether Mfi or other Mycoplasmas might be present in Gulf War Illness cases. One approach that was not dependent on host immune response or on finding unusual antigens on the surface of the bacteria was to use the unique genetics of the bacteria to find it. For this approach Jared and Marie would have to use the genetic information available in scientific publications—mainly from the Army and other civilian researchers to probe for Mfi and other Mycoplasmas in the veterans' blood. Because they wanted a fast, reproducible approach that could be adapted to other infectious agents as well, they decided on using the same type of genetic assay for any of the bacteria that they thought might be involved.

Since every living thing must have the appropriate genetic information to reproduce, survive and grow, or in the case of viruses the genetic information to reproduce and circumvent or usurp host metabolism to grow and be assembled, the presence of an infectious agent can be determined by finding its specific genetic or DNA signature. Each species of microorganism had unique DNA (or RNA) sequences that could be used to positively identify that particular species. Once the specific DNA sequence was known, one only had to look for this unique sequence in a sea of DNA sequences from the host genetic information and from the genetic sequences of other bacteria, parasites, fungi and viruses. The bad news was that it was extremely difficult to find small amounts of anything in a sea of similar molecules.

The first thing that Jared and Marie had to do was decide which unique genes or genetic sequences of the genes that they should look for in the clinical samples. Jared eventually settled on two types of target genes—the genes that had been found to be the same in all Mycoplasma species and the genes that were unique to different Mycoplasma species. Fortunately, bacteriologists had been researching the differences in genetics of various bacteria for decades, and some information was already available from the literature that pointed to certain genes as common and certain genes as unique. Also, the techniques of molecular biology had already been developed to probe for differences in the genes of bacteria in various types of infections, so the McNichols team would not have to start from scratch in their quest to determine if veterans had any type of disease-causing bacteria in their systems.

Jared scanned the genetic database available on-line at the NIH and found DNA sequence information on a few genes of interest to the group. First was a general group of genes found in all bacteria that had some genetic variations and differences, depending on the path of their evolution over millions of years. This would prove useful as a starting point, but it could not be used by itself to identify a particular species of bacteria. Other genes would have to be identified to positively tell if a particular species of bacteria was present. To identify the unique gene differences they were looking for, they settled on two approaches. First, they would use the Gene Tracking technique that Marie had developed at Belford College of Medicine. Using this technique the bacterial DNA bound to proteins called nucleoproteins would be isolated and the bound genes would be probed using complimentary DNA sequences, usually about 20 or more of the DNA building blocks arrayed in a specific sequence that will bind tightly to the target DNA sequences in the bacterial gene.

This is like a lock and key reaction, and the specific complimentary structure of DNA in each and every living organism makes this possible. Since the key or probe to be used to bind to the species-specific DNA sequence was radioactive, they would be able to find the gene they were looking for after separating the nucleoproteins from the remainder of the cells' components by its radioactive signal. Once the radioactive probe bound to the unique DNA sequence, the complex of lock and key emits a radioactive signal. Second, they would use a technique that actually amplifies a small segment of the target gene sequence and makes millions of DNA copies of the gene sequence that then can be probed or even sequenced to prove the identity of the gene segment. This technique is called Polymerase Chain Reaction or PCR because it uses an enzyme reaction to replicate the small pieces of unique genetic information or sequence of DNA that can then be identified. Because this technique is so powerful, the scientist that developed this technique won the Nobel Prize for his contribution.

Various controls would also have to be devised to control for contamination, reaction specificity, fidelity of the reaction product, presence of interfering materials and other controls for the assays that they would use to make sure of their results. This all took tremendous time, effort and funds for equipment, supplies and personnel. Funds for this effort were in short supply, and the only funds available that Jared could use were from his endowed chair. None of the grant and contract funding that Jared had in ample supply could be used. Even with the resources, it seemed a slow and laborious process that took months to accomplish, but finally they were ready to run the tests on the veterans' blood samples.

The first tests that Marie and Jared's technician Bob Sonan ran in the laboratory indicated the presence of bacteria in the blood in most of the samples, but they could not identify the particular species. This was very disappointing, because no one would believe their results unless they could identify a particular type or species of bacteria. And the type of bacteria that they identified would have to be a known pathogen; otherwise no one would believe that it was responsible for causing illness in the patients. In these preliminary tests the unknown bacteria was found in the cellular fraction of the blood not in the blood plasma, the cell-free portion of the blood. In the cellular fraction of the blood were the red blood cells that carry the oxygen to the tissues, various white blood cells that were primarily used to fight infections and the platelet fraction involved in blood clotting. The evidence for bacteria was only found in the white blood cell fraction. The bacteria were likely inside some of the white blood cells that were in the blood.

Finally they would make the adjustments in methodology so that Marie's Gene Tracking technique worked with the clinical samples. After months of labor and refining their procedures to meet the challenge of finding a few bacteria in the white blood cell fraction of patients' blood, they finally had a useful but still time-consuming laboratory technique. It would still take more time to get the polymerase chain reaction or PCR procedure to work, but it was a start. As a first step, a gene common to bacteria but with unique genus and species sequences differences was used to generate a 'general' and also some unique 'species-specific' probes to the common and unique DNA sequences in genes found in all species of Mycoplasmas or to specific species of Mycoplasmas, respectively. The first tests that were positive did not indicate that the veterans had the more common or usual types of Mycoplasmas, such as *Mycoplasma penumoniae*, a common respiratory infection that had been already found in military recruits suffering from a type of pneumonia.

The negative results were disappointing and unexpected, since it was actually reported in a military medical journal that military recruits came down with chronic illnesses like a type of 'community' or infectious pneumonia caused by *Mycoplasma pneumoniae*. This airborne infection can spread rapidly in over-crowded conditions. The McNichols group next decided to try for other Mycoplasma species, including the one that Dr. Lon had reported, *Mycoplasma fermentans incognitus* or Mfi, and for the first time they were able to identify a unique Mycoplasma species in the samples.

In fact, 80% of the preliminary tests revealed Mfi as the type of Mycoplasma found in the blood samples when they found any evidence for a bacterial infection. The next most common species found was even less expected, *Mycoplasma genitalium,* a mycoplasmal infection usually associated with urinary tract infections not system-wide infections that caused multiple signs and symptoms.

Not every blood sample examined showed evidence of a Mycoplasma or even bacteria of unknown type, but almost half did, indicating that there were other infections to consider or other potential causes of the Gulf War Illnesses. This was also reasonable, since Jared did not expect to see the same infection in every blood sample or even in a high percentage of samples, just as they did not expect to find the same cause of Gulf War Illness in each patient. These were obviously heterogeneous illnesses, and only the American press would expect everything to be explained by 'one' cause, such as PTSD, probably just to make their job easier and make their press reports more succinct. At this time very few researchers were looking for infections in the Desert Storm veterans, except for one physician in New Orleans who had found remnants of bacterial cell walls in the urine of veterans and possibly Dr. Lon at the U. S. Army Institute for Pathology Research.

Most researchers who were not psychiatrists assumed that complex chemical exposures were 'the cause' of the Gulf War Illnesses, and in fact Jared and Marie would face determined competition from a medical research group in Dallas who thought that the McNichols' research was completely wrong and that the veterans with Gulf War Illnesses had come down with their illnesses due solely to exposures to chemicals, such as organophosphates like insecticides and nerve agents. Jared in particular thought that this was quite narrow thinking, to imagine that it was solely chemical exposures that caused all the veterans' illnesses. The Dallas group did not identify any chemicals but they did find that the brain scans of the veterans were unusual in that they showed areas of damage that could have been caused by chemicals or other toxins. Unfortunately, this same type of damage could also have been caused by infectious agents that penetrated into the brain and released bacterial toxins that can cause the same kind of damage, but the Dallas group never considered this before attacking Jared and Marie for suggesting that many of the ill veterans may have system-wide or systemic infections, including brain infections.

Thus Jared and Marie would get their first taste of Gulf War Illness politics. Because they didn't use press releases or press agents to defend their unpublished research, they would be immediately attacked if they spoke out about their results, especially in public. No one wanted to hear that infections might be involved in Gulf War Illnesses, especially the military physicians who were trying to promote PTSD as 'the cause.' Actually it would turn out that both Texas research groups were probably correct, although they both had many detractors, especially at the Pentagon. The fact that the researchers were apparently fighting among themselves actually played into the hands of the Pentagon. Finally, a scientific gadfly in Oakland, California at a small for-profit biotechnology company claimed that the veteran's illness were due to chromosomal damage that he found in about one-half of a group of veterans' blood samples. Of course, Jared and Marie and even Dr. Lon knew that intracellular infections like Mfi caused the same type of chromosomal damage along with chemicals, so this result could also have been due to infections like Mfi, chemical exposures or both.

The elusive Mfi and how does it fit with Gulf War Illnesses?

Within one week Jared, Marie and Bob Sonan had some preliminary results that they obtained in Jared's laboratory at The D. O. Madison. They then met in Jared's office to discuss the data on about 70 patients who served in Desert Storm. Jared was now very curious about the conversations that Marie had years ago with Dr. Lon of the U. S. Army Institute of Pathology Research. The lab results on the veterans indicated that the type of Mycoplasma was not the one that Jared expected, it was a type that was considered at the time relatively uncommon, *Mycoplasma fermentans incognitus* or Mfi.

Marie filled in some information for Bob Sonan who was attending the meeting. "When I was sick, I think that I had the same type of mycoplasma infection that Dr. Lon reported on, and when I did speak to him, he also thought that I might have Mfi. He said that I was very lucky to be alive from his experience. At the time he indicated that he had found evidence for Mfi in the Gulf War veterans, but when I tried to talk to him later about his comments to me, he denied it completely and said all of the tests on the Gulf War veterans were negative. I found this a bit disconcerting." Jared was skeptical and said, "Why would he tell you that they were positive and then change the whole story later on? Did he say that his preliminary experiments had been wrong or that they had contamination or something else that could explain the mistake?" Marie responded, "No, not at all. In fact, he almost seemed reluctant to even discuss his experiments, as if he was instructed not to talk about it, and he said they were probably all false-positives." Jared was skeptical, "That's pretty fishy! You would think that a scientist like Dr. Lon would have gone into a detailed explanation on what went wrong and why they could not repeat their initial results."

The McNichols had been frustrated by the way other researchers acted when they discussed their results on Gulf War Illnesses. Bob Sonan related to them, "Now I know why you want us to look for mycoplasmas in the Gulf War veterans. But even if we find them, they don't want to admit it." Jared smiled, "It sure looks that way. They don't want to admit anything, except PTSD. The whole thing is very suspicious. As I recall the Army pathologist, Dr. Lon, told Marie that we couldn't use antibody-based assays to detect the Mfi, and he's right, you wouldn't expect Mfi to produce much of an antibody reaction because it's mostly inside cells." Marie added, "Actually, Dr. Lon told me that he couldn't detect Mfi by antibody tests but he could find it with other tests, but it was difficult." Jared asked, "By any chance did Lon say what those other tests were?" Marie answered, "He did say that he was having a hard time correlating his molecular biology testing for Mfi with his other results." Jared added, "It's also very hard to find any information on Mfi in the medical literature. There were only a few publications on Mfi, and almost all of them were from Dr. Lon, who now denies that the Gulf War veterans have any infections."

Jared thought for a moment and continued the conversation. "Incidentally, there are only a couple of experts on this type of infection here in the U. S., one at NIH and one in San Antonio. Also, there is a professor Ricin in Israel who is an expert, and the Iraqis also appear to have some experts in this area. One professor in Baghdad has a very large lab that has been working on Mycoplasmas for years now. Marie and I have been discussing this problem amongst ourselves, and we would like to concentrate on screening for Mycoplasmas in general and Mfi in particular in the blood of the veterans." Bob Sonan asked, "Are we going to use the antibody tests from the Army to confirm our results?" Jared smiled, "I don't think that we can get any help from this Dr. Lon. From what I hear from Marie, this guy seems to speak in riddles, so I don't know what to make of him. The whole thing is very suspicious." Marie added, "He's very smart and appears to know what he's doing, but we have to conclude that we probably can't trust him since he works for the Army." Jared added, "The Department of Defense has already decided on its official position, and it's not Mfi!" Bob Sonan asked, "That's it?" Jared answered, "That's it. The vets don't have any infections. They all have PTSD! This Dr. Lon even holds a just-issued U.S. patent on Mfi, and in the patent it states that Mfi is probably involved in various chronic illnesses. So I listed Chronic Fatigue Syndrome along with the veterans' and Marie's signs and symptoms, and I bet that we will find mycoplasmal infections in Chronic Fatigue Syndrome patients." Marie asked, "Do you think we can trust the Army at this point to give us any good reagents or blood samples?" Jared smiled, "No, I really don't trust them at all. Apparently they have too much to hide. Officially, they first said that Gulf War Syndrome didn't exist, now it's a psychological condition, so they might want to hide any results on some bacteria found in the veterans' blood. Think about it. If we find that the vets are infected with bacteria that could cause their illnesses, there goes their psycho-mumbo-jumbo post-traumatic stress as the cause. And what if we found that not only did they have some bacteria in their systems, they are infected with Mfi? How are they going to explain that the Army knew about this all along and that *they* hold the patent on Mfi?" The group just stood there and absorbed what Jared had told them.

Jared explained to Bob and Marie that the U. S. Army probably knew all about the Mfi infections in Gulf War Illnesses. The Army patent was applied for in 1987, years before the Gulf War. And the inventor of record was none other than Dr. Ming Lon. "No, I don't think we can realistically expect any help from the DoD or Dr. Lon." Bob Sonan asked, "If we find the Mfi in the white blood cells of the veterans, what can they do to treat the infection?" Jared smiled, "Probably the same thing that we used with Marie, the antibiotic doxycycline. And by the way, this is the same antibiotic that the military used to treat cases of Mfi in their troops, according to one of their own publications." Marie added, "Only in my case it took over a year to begin to recover. It was horrible." Jared said, "This will be the difficult part. Most physicians don't know anything about Mycoplasmas and will only prescribe an antibiotic to treat such an infection for a couple of weeks, but that would be unlikely to put a dent this bug. We never did get a straight answer from this Dr. Lon about treating Marie with doxy." Marie, "When I talked to Dr. Lon, he told me that I was lucky to be alive. He said that most people who get to my advanced state usually die. This was years before the Gulf War, and he was very interested in how we were going to treat the infection." Jared replied, "Yah, he knew all along how to treat the infection. He just didn't bother to tell you!"

Jared paced around and then pointed to the board that they were standing in front of. "Marie, Bob my best guess is that the signs and symptoms fit with the laboratory results on Mfi infections, but that does not prove that the Mfi is causing Gulf War Illnesses. The vets were exposed to a number of things in the war, especialy chemicals, and some of them may have been exposed to depleted uranium. The chemicals, such as organophosphates, could have caused some of the signs and symptoms that they're reporting to us, but I doubt that they can cause them all, especially the fevers, joint pain and diarrhea–these are usually caused by infections not chemicals. And not every veteran has the same constellation of signs and symptoms. So we need to concentrate on the vets that have the signs and symptoms that we'd expect from an infection." Marie added, "I don't think I was exposed to any chemicals, but I did become very chemically sensitive during the illness." Jared gestured, "That's the curious thing about this illness. We just don't know how the chemical exposures fit into the picture, unless some of the veterans have their illness primarily due to chemicals or even radiologicals, mainly depleted uranium, and some due to infections or combinations of two or all three types of exposures. Jared turned to the board and started making a new table.

Table 3

Comparison of signs and symptoms caused by chemicals (organophosphates), biologicals (infections) and radiologicals (depleted uranium).

Signs/Symptoms	Chemicals (OPs)	Biologicals (infections)	Radiologicals (DU)
chronic fatigue	+	+	+
joint pain/mobility		+	?
night sweats		+	
muscle pain	+	+	
fevers		+	
headaches	+	+	
skin rashes	+	+	+
memory loss	+	+	?
stomach pain		+	+
breathing problems	+	+	
sleep problems	+	+	
diarrhea	+	+	+
heart palpitations		+	
vision problems	+	+	+
depression	+	+	+
hair loss	+	+	+
nausea	+	+	+
sinus problems		+	+
vertigo	+	+	

"This is my best guess at the moment," stated Jared. "Biological exposures or infections seem to be the best fit, but this doesn't mean that the other exposures weren't involved or even the most important in some patients. I am not sure how something like radioactive depleted Uranium or DU fits with all of the problems mentioned by the veterans. But if you consider that DU could easily cause immune suppression by attacking the bone marrow, then opportunistic infections could occur as a secondary event. The same is true with chemical exposures. The most likely chemicals are organophosphates like insecticides, anti-nerve agents and nerve agents but also solvents and other stuff, even organophosphate herbicides. These exposures could also end up causing opportunistic infections, so the groups are probably not mutually exclusive. We should be able to sort this out eventually, but the problem is that it is now years after the war and any toxic exposures will be hard to trace."

The advantage of looking for infection(s) was that infectious agents were alive and should still be around if they were the culprits. Chemicals on the other hand, may have caused damage, and if they are still present they would probably be found in very low concentrations, and they would be hard to find. Jared continued, "In the case of DU, if they want to find it, they should be able to detect it, since it's radioactive. Basically we'll be looking for a subset of patients with chronic infections, and the illnesses of the other vets who don't have infections were probably caused by something else." Bob Sonan asked, "How did they get exposed to DU? Isn't that in the tank shells?" Jared, "Yes, Bob, during the Gulf War they used hundreds of tons of DU rounds on Iraqi tanks, bunkers and armored personnel carriers. The Abrams tanks and Bradley Fighting Vehicles had DU munitions, and the Air Force used DU 30-millimeter rounds in the A-10 Thunderbolt GAU-8A cannons." Bob Sonan asked, "What is it about DU that they would make it into weapons?" Jared explained, "DU can be made into an incredibly dense metal with tungsten, and when this metal hits a target at high velocity it actually vaporizes and burns its way through the armor. The problem is that when it vaporizes, it forms uranium oxide powder that settles all over everything. This dense powder can be inhaled deep into the lungs if the particles are small enough, and they usually are. Eventually it's absorbed in the lungs, but over the long term it ends up mostly in the bones where the DU can irradiate the bone marrow."

Bob then asked Jared pointing to the board, "Do chemicals cause all those problems?" Jared said, "They apparently could cause most of the signs and symptoms on the board, especially if you were exposed to low doses of chemical mixtures that by themselves don't cause much of a problem. We know that the exposures had to be low enough in concentration to have caused delayed effects. There is a group at Duke in North Carolina and a USDA scientist in Florida that are studying this and finding interesting results with certain low-dose combinations of organophosphates. Remember, there were not a lot of obvious immediate effects, or so we were told by the press and the DoD. If soldiers were exposed to nerve agents at lethal doses, they would not have made it back, but after the war munitions were blown up at places like Khamisiyah, and this could have resulted in a cloud of low levels of nerve agents and other chemicals that spread for hundreds of miles over Southern Iraq and Kuwait."

Jared continued the conversation, "The DoD claims that nerve agents were never used in the Gulf War. However, the truth is that over 14,000 chemical alarms sounded during but not before or after the war, indicating that it was very likely that there were chemical agents released during the war. Of course, the Pentagon claimed that all of these were false alarms!" Bob Sonan questioned, "They must really think that the American public is pretty stupid." Jared replied, "Indeed they do!" Marie added, "They've always taken the American public for big stupid dupes." Jared continued, "Unfortunately, not enough is known about the effects of multiple low-level chemical exposures, but this professor that I mentioned at Duke has done research on this and also the guy in Florida at an agriculture station who used mixtures of chemicals at low concentrations to cause all kinds of neurological effects in insects. When he started talking about his experiments in the context of Gulf War Syndrome, he was fired." Bob Sonan stated, "I hope that doesn't happen to you!" Jared smiled, "So do I! And I hope that it's not that obvious." But it was obvious that the McNichols had raised the anger of the D. O. Madison administration and its President, Dr. Masters, in particular.

Bob Sonan and Marie realized that Jared's position *was* in jeopardy. If the government came down on the D. O. Madison for the research on Gulf War Illnesses, they might just use that as an excuse to fire Jared, even though he was a tenured faculty member. Jared became more reflective, "I don't know if our D. O. Madison administration has enough moral fiber to withstand the pressure of the DoD, especially when the government starts to come down on them for our findings. And on that note, I don't expect that we are going to solve this problem today, but I do want to thank you all for participating in today's discussion. I think that this will be the first of many on the subject."

The Navy SEALs make contact

One of the more interesting groups to contact the McNichols were the U. S. Navy SEALs. Jared and Marie had been discussing the problem of chronic illnesses in the 101st and 82nd Airborne Divisions with their picture framer 'Rocko' DeJon, who was in the process of framing some pictures for Marie, when he related to them that his brother was one of the commanding officers in a Navy SEAL team that served in the Gulf War. He indicated that many of them were now sick from the war. In fact, his brother's SEAL Team had seen extensive combat in Panama and elsewhere, so the unit was mainly made up of war-tested veterans who had tasted combat before. By virtue of their selection, training and experience Navy SEALs are not prone to psychological problems from war experiences. Rocko had related to the McNichols that his brother who was a Lt. Commander was losing his vision, he had lost 60 pounds during the last few months and had severe headaches, stomach cramps, night sweats and joint pain. "When I discussed it with him, he had been to every physician possible in the Navy with what he said were 'zero answers and zero results'."

When Lt. Commander Dale DeJon made contact with the McNichols, they had not yet completed their laboratory studies with the veterans' blood samples. When Marie heard about Dale's symptoms, she told Dale to get some doxycycline because that is what they had used to overcome the infection in other veterans. Jared, however, was more conservative, as usual, and warned Dale of the consequences if they were wrong about the infection causing his problem.

Eventually Dale proved to be positive for Mfi, he took the doxycycline and made a complete recovery. This turned out to be fortuitous, because Dale was high enough in the command structure in the Joint Special Operations Units at Fort Bragg to have a major impact on how the other SEALs and Army Special Forces were treated. Also, the SEALs like other Special Forces units that the McNichols worked with had their own physicians who often went into combat with them. These physicians were not under the heavy thumb of the Navy Medical Corps, so they could do things that a Navy doctor could not hope to do without being brought up on charges of disobeying orders.

At the time the existence of Gulf War Illnesses was officially being denied, except for psychological disorders like PTSD that the SEALs were unlikely to have from their make-up, training and prior combat experience. SEAL candidates who might be prone to psychological problems were quickly identified and moved out of the SEAL units. Unit cohesiveness and effectiveness depended on the utmost in psychological stability under fire, and the SEAL units prided themselves for their mental toughness.

Eventually their work with the U. S. Army Special Forces and Navy SEALs proved important, and Jared and Marie would be made honorary full Colonels in the Special Forces, and the first honorary SEALs in the U. S. Navy. Both Jared and Marie were especially proud that they earned the honor of being the only honorary SEALs in the history of the U. S. Navy, but Marie would tell them that Jared was the diver in the family, and she could not stand to put on a facemask and even look underwater. Jared had earned his way through college as a professional diver, and he had previously worked for the U. S. Air Force training astronauts and performing experiments in mock space capsules underwater before the days of NASA, so Marie felt that he should be the SEAL, but the SEALs wouldn't hear of it. They wanted to adopt Marie as their mascot.

Title 50, Section 1520, U.S. Federal Annotated Code

The Administration at the D. O. Madison Cancer Center found out from Jared's faculty that Jared was still working on veterans' illnesses. In particular, one of Jared's faculty informed the Vice President for Research that Jared was working with his wife Marie, and they found that a subset of patients with Gulf War Illnesses were presenting with complaints that are more consistent with chronic infections than with chemical or radiological exposures, and they were even less consistent with psychological explanations for their illnesses. They also reported that the McNichols found infections in the veterans' blood, and in particular a very unusual infection called Mfi.

The Cancer Center was concerned with the McNichols work on chronic infections and, in particular, their work on mycoplasmal infections. The reason for this was that the D. O. Madison had something to hide concerning some questionable experiments with Belford College of Medicine in the Texas prison system. In one series of experiments in the prison system these esteemed institutions actually exposed prisoners to mycoplasmas and viruses in aerosols to test vaccines and treatment approaches against the infections. In order to do this, the prisoners had to be infected with very dangerous airborne agents that resulted in chronic diseases that could progress to terminal, lethal illnesses. In order to perform these questionable experiments special rooms, wards and even prison blocks were modified so that the air coming in could be specifically contaminated with viruses or bacteria. The prisoners would then be watched very carefully for the onset of illnesses. When the prisoners got ill, they were taken to the prison hospital or in more extreme cases to special wards in the Austin Medical Center run by Belford College of Medicine.

In the past, no one would have thought much about using prisoners for all kinds of dangerous experiments. The history of using American prisoners in horrific experiments, such as the Tuskegee prison experiments on syphilis, were more common place than the general public knew. In fact, during the Cold War the U. S. Congress passed a law that in the Federal Annotated Code was called Title 50, Section 1520. This section allowed experimentation on the American public without their specific knowledge or consent, all in the interests of 'National Security.' Such laws only required notification of an official in local government before experiments were conducted by government agencies on the general public.

The prison systems were a popular place to conduct dangerous experiments, because complaints were rare, even when fatalities occurred. Although hotly denied at the time, Belford College of Medicine and D. O. Madison Cancer Center were collaborating with the Federal Government on the prison experiments in Texas, and they weren't the only institutions involved. Various other state prison systems were also being used under Title 50 to conduct horrific experiments without appropriate review, oversight, or proper public or patient informed consent required for testing new procedures on human subjects. Few of the faculty or staff at Belford or D. O. Madison knew anything about the prison experiments, except for some of the faculty members of Marie's old department at Belford, the Microbiology Department, headed by Dr. Virgil Rook, an expert at using prisoners as experimental subjects to test new medical theories. In fact, Dr. Rook had even published journal reviews on the use of prisoners for experiments that would not pass the smell test if they attempted to do them in the community.

Prisoners were ideal subjects, because they rarely knew what the experiments were about or the risks and dangers involved in the experiments. In fact, most of the prisoners didn't even care. For their services, the prisoners were given some small amounts of money or special privileges. All they wanted was some money to buy cigarettes or candy, and they eagerly wanted extra privileges. For some prisoners, this was the only way that they could get certain things that they coveted, even if it meant cooperation with some nerds from the Medical Center. Most of these prisoners were poorly educated, so they didn't understand anything that was told to them by the scientist and physician nerds who only wanted willing subjects for their experiments. This also suited the institutions, because they did not want patients complaining if something went wrong. Of course, they would be offered complete medical care if anything went wrong, and it often did. In fact, that was part of the plan to get the maximum amount of information from the prisoners.

If prisoners got sick or even died, and many did during these experiments, so what? Who was going to care about some poor, uneducated prisoners who got deathly sick or died while in captivity? Dr. Rook took advantage of this situation to perform experiments that he could never do with medical students or civilian volunteers. Marie and Jared had no way of knowing that the experiments in the prison system mirrored the experiments that were being conducted on military recruits, the other large group of guinea pigs available for government research on chemical and biological weapons.

The only problem in using military recruits for experiments was that the some of the services complained bitterly that their recruit pool was being depleted by the zealots running the experiments. In fact, some of the services, such as the U. S. Air Force, would restrict the use of their recruits for such experiments. Of course, there were always the Army and Marine Corps, and eventually some of these ex-guinea pigs found their way to Marie and Jared for assistance with their health problems, usually years after they were medically discharged from the Armed Services.

The common thread in these government testing programs was that the subjects rarely knew anything about the experiments that they were involved in, especially any information on the possible medical risks and side effects of the experiments. They were usually denied further medical assistance for their medical conditions, just like the Tuskegee experiments, and they were almost always denied access to their medical records. Thus they continued to be guinea pigs long after their direct role in the experiments ended.

Departmental problems with the McNichols research

Since they were concerned about the loyalty of their own faculty, the D. O. Madison administration made secret arrangements for some of Jared's faculty members to monitor the research that the McNichols were conducting with the Gulf War Illness patients in his department on the ninth floor of the Research Building. The D. O. Madison administration was very interested in the McNichols' research, especially when one of Jared's faculty members reported to the Vice President for Research, Dr. Francis Belcher, that the McNichols were investigating the possibility that mycoplasmas might be involved in Gulf War Illnesses. Unknown to Marie and Jared at the time, the D. O. Madison had been conducting their own research on biowarfare agents with Belford College of Medicine and Dr. Rook. However, this research was conducted away from the main hospital complex in an isolated research facility called the M. K. Black Building. The director of the Black Building was none other than Dr. Isaac Geldter.

For years the D. O. Madison had been supplying immunological expertise for the Belford prison experiments, mainly at the Black Building using Issac Geldter and Amy Krappner, who already had experience with such kind of work while employed at the U. S. Army's Fort Detrick. In fact, their prior relationship with Fort Detrick was a positive selling point when they were both recruited to the D. O. Madison in Austin. Even though Drs. Geldter and Krappner were civilian scientists working on cancer research projects and were physically located in different sections at Fort Detrick, they were heavily involved in assisting the Army's biowarfare research program by providing immunological expertise to the Army infectious disease specialists. In fact, Issac Geldter was very proud of his theory to load immune suppressor molecules into biowarfare mixtures so that exposed victims could not mount immune responses against Biological Warfare agents. He openly bragged to some of the D. O. Madison staff about his role in Army Biological Warfare research while at Fort Detrick.

Just because Biowarfare research was not being conducted in Jared's department or, in fact, in most departments at the D. O. Madison, this did not mean that certain faculty members in Jared's department were not immune to being recruited to assist in the Belford-D. O. Madison germ warfare testing program. Obviously most recruits could not openly conduct biological warfare-type experimentation without drawing attention to themselves in Jared's department, but the administration had other plans for these recruits. They would be used to monitor other faculty and report back to the administration. Jared had heard about Geldter's work with Dr. Rook at Belford and about the classified section of Geldter's department, and he made it very clear that his own faculty would have nothing to do with what he considered the unethical behavior of some of his colleagues. His attitude and the mycoplasma tests on veterans would be reported back to the administration, and this would eventually make Jared a marked man at the D. O. Madison.

To help in the process of examining the McNichols' research to determine if it met the criteria or priority of research that was to be included in the future plans of the institution, certain faculty members were recruited to carefully monitor the McNichols as they slowly made their way through the minefield of Gulf War Illnesses. These faculty rats willingly spied on the McNichols to gain favor with the D. O. Madison administration and especially for promised future promotions, salary increases and other favors. Although in some cases these faculty members had known and worked with Jared for decades, this did not stop them from quickly turning on him to advance their own careers.

The two faculty members that were almost openly spying on Marie and Jared for the D. O. Madison Administration were Drs. Thomas Domasovitch and Dr. Judah Nosan. Jared expected Dr. Domasovitch, who in fact was Jared's deputy but only an average scientist with limited abilities, of being a rat for the administration, but he had no idea that Dr. Nosan would stoop that low. Dr. Nosan did not need to be a rat to get ahead at the institution. Dr. Nosan was born in Poland and educated in Russia, so he may have had a different perspective on the research that Jared and Marie were conducting. Dr. Nosan, however, coveted another job at the D. O. Madison, and it was in his best interests to monitor Jared for the administration. On the other hand, Dr. Domasovitch was in a dead end position, and he was unlikely to be promoted from his present position of Associate Professor. He actually came to the D. O. Madison as an Associate

Professor from Iowa State University, and he hadn't been able to climb any higher up the academic ladder. Therefore, he was always readily available for additional administrative assignments, but he was useful in department teaching and administration. Dr. Domasovitch was also quite fond of 'hanging around' the McNichols lab and was quite eager to speak to the technicians and students. Dr. Domasovitch with his light hair and thick glasses was a natural schmoozer. From his mid-Western farm background no one would have thought that he could have been so easily been manipulated to do unethical things by the administration, but Jared and Marie were to learn a bitter lesson, in that many of the people that they assumed had principles in reality did not. They were easily and cheaply recruited by the D. O. Madison administration, who in turn, were easily recruited by Las Vegas organized crime financial interests as well as their international armaments companies, to perform illegal and unethical acts against the McNichols.

Although relatively unknown to the general public, Las Vegas organized crime interests had long been involved in the financing of companies that manufactured unconventional weapons of mass destruction. It would take the McNichols nearly two decades to uncover this, a fact that directly impacted upon Marie and her inheritance and birth identity. The harshness of academic life under Dr. Masters' administration would turn out to be a smokescreen for the motivation behind the attacks on the McNichols, which would eventually surface as an ironic twist between Marie's research interests and her true identity as the heiress to the same Las Vegas empire that was funding the organizations that were attacking the McNichols.

One day a smiling Dr. Domasovitch met Marie in the hall just outside Jared's laboratories. Jared's laboratories were down the hall from the departmental offices, and Dr. Domasovitch often passed Jared's labs on his way to his own laboratory. On this occasion he stopped Marie coming out of the laboratory and said, "I hear that you are finding *Mycoplasma fermentans* in the Desert Storm veterans?" Marie, who had little time for such antics and considered Dr. Domasovitch little more than a lackey answered, "Yes, Dr. Domasovitch, we are finding it in about 45% of the veterans that we have tested. Dr. Domasovitch then asked in a sarcastic way, "How do you know that the results are not just false-positives?" At this point Jared came down the hall and saw what was happening, and he interrupted the conversation, "Well, for starters, Thomas, we have run controls on specificity and sensitivity to insure that the results are real." Dr. Domasovitch turned from Jared to face Marie and said, "That doesn't prove anything." Jared moved closer to Dr. Domasovitch until he was between him and Marie, "It's a good start. We aren't done yet, but I believe that we have an explanation as to why the veterans are still sick years after the war and why their spouses are now getting sick." Dr. Domasovitch was skeptical, "I don't believe it." Marie just looked back at Jared, shook her head, turned and entered the lab where she went back to work. It was a waste of time talking to Dr. Domasovitch, who Marie considered a complete hack who had never produced anything of note in his entire career. In fact, she would constantly ask Jared why he ever hired Domasovitch in the first place, and then why did he support his career for so many years. Jared received very little in return for his loyalty and support of faculty members like Dr. Domasovitch. It was a weakness of Jared's, and Marie hated it and reminded him often of it.

When the topic of Dr. Domasovitch came up in prior conversations, Jared had assured Marie that Dr. Domasovitch's initial research at the D. O. Madison was acceptable if not exceptional. From what she had seen, Marie did not believe the story, even though Dr. Domasovitch previously had a grant from the NIH. However, once he received tenure, he lost his NIH grant and his grant applications were no longer of high enough priority to be funded. His research was considered average at best, but his teaching ability was good and he took an active interest in the graduate courses taught through the graduate school. Jared had used Dr. Domasovitch to run the Department's educational programs and to help Jared administratively, and this was apparently where Thomas had kept himself useful. Now that he had a chance to further his career, even at Jared's expense, he did not hesitate to jump at the possibility of gaining some future favors from the D. O. Madison administration.

Marie was sure that Dr. Domasovitch along with Dr. Nosan were reporting what the McNichols found in the lab directly to Dr. Belcher. She did not like Thomas and made no bones about it. With Marie back at work in the lab, Jared continued the conversation in the hall with Dr. Domasovitch by saying, "We have looked at quite a few possible types of infections, and a mycoplasma is the one that keeps coming up positive. Dr. Domasovitch turned serious and told Jared, "I know you are a careful scientist, and I have always respected what you have done in your career, but I just don't understand why you are pursuing this line of research. It's just going to hurt you and the Department, and we are all going to pay for what you are doing." Jared just stared at Thomas but then Dr. Domasovitch continued, "I am really concerned about you." Jared sarcastically replied, "I am sure you are, Thomas . . ." Dr. Domasovitch lowered his voice and became very serious, "You have got to stop this line of investigation and start thinking more about your career and the Department." Jared knew that Dr. Domasovitch and some of the other faculty were just thinking of their own skins, so he politely told Thomas, "I will carefully consider your position, but you in particular, as a Vietnam veteran, should see the value in what we are doing and understand exactly why we are involved in helping the veterans. And please don't tell me again that you are concerned about me." Dr. Domasovitch replied, "I am concerned about you, and I think I understand why you feel that you need to do this. What I don't understand is why you continue along this line of investigation when you know that the administration does not want this research conducted at our institution." Jared finally told Dr. Domasovitch, "You know, Thomas, this comes down to a major difference between our philosophies. Marie and I are not involved with the veterans to advance our careers or make the newspapers; we don't give a damn about that. We are trying to assist the veterans because no one else will help them. Maybe you were lucky when you came back from Vietnam. You didn't have a problem with Agent Orange. If you had been exposed to Agent Orange and later became sick and no one would acknowledge your illness or help you, then you might be able to see our point of view." Jared turned quickly on his heal and left Dr. Domasovitch standing in the hall. He never looked back to see if Thomas was still standing outside his laboratory.

There would always be some that didn't care about anything but themselves and their own careers. But it was particularly saddening to see veterans who thought that just because they escaped war without a health problem, the rest of those suckers brought it upon themselves and were just out of luck. This type of thinking was actually more prevalent than anyone expected in the Armed Forces, and there was little sympathy around the Pentagon for the veterans who became sick after the war. With the active help of the DoD, the sick veterans were called malingerers, malcontents and psycho cases, and there was little room for their complaints in the New Armed Forces.

CHAPTER 5

The Prisons Have a Problem (1994)

The prison guards ask for help

Marie had just entered Jared's offices, which were also the Cancer Biology Department's offices, and she began talking to Jane South, Jared's secretary, about Jared's stepdaughter and her illness from the Gulf War and the interesting results they found with the veterans' blood samples. The office was a typical institutional office. There was one picture on the wall and lots of file cabinets. There were two secretaries and an office manager stationed in the main area. Jared's office was in the back behind Jane's desk.

Marie said as she walked up to Jane's desk, "Hi, Jane!" Jane South looked up at Marie puzzled. Marie continued, "If you haven't yet noticed, I'm in a bitchy mood today!" Jane answered, "Is it that time again?" Marie answered, "Almost!" The other office workers looked at Marie behind her back with a mixture of false smiles and trepidation. Dr. Judah Nosan, who had just entered the office, said to Marie in a friendly tone, "How's the Desert Storm project going?" Marie answered, "Slowly!" Dr. Nosan continued, "Well, I asked my relatives in Israel if anyone was sick, and they said no one seemed to be affected." Marie asked, "Does that mean you don't believe that there is a problem?" Dr. Nosan shrugged his shoulders. "Well, Dr. Nosan I predict that illnesses will crop up in Israel over the next couple of years, but it will be the Israelis' stoicism that will preclude any help with the problems. And I don't think they are going to talk about it or let anyone know if it happens." She continued, "By the way, how do you account for the unusual cases of meningitis going around in Israel?" Nosan answered, "Just a coincidence. I don't think that there is anything to it."

Marie, "I admire your skepticism, but there is no such thing as coincidence or randomness in our universe. There are always patterns. Recognizing the pattern is the key."

Dr. Nosan changed his demeanor, and he became a bit more sarcastic. He said, "Why do you continue to be a scientist? No one here understands or respects your research. Why would you and Jared go into this line of investigation, anyway? This is just going to hurt his career. There is already talk about this hurting our department. Furthermore, I hear that you are going to inherit a lot of money some day. Why would you care about some veterans?" Marie replied, "Dr. Nosan "I find your line of questioning to be most derogatory and intrusive. I continue to be a scientist, because I trained for years in the hard sciences, training which you seem to lack. Furthermore, I do not derive my happiness from other professional's opinions, and quite frankly, the extreme negativity towards me seems to be an opinion primarily concentrated in certain administrative circles at the D. O. Madison, which I believe is 20 years out of date in its direction of research. . . . And how do you know about my so-called inheritance. I don't ever remember discussing this with you."

Dr. Nosan then became defensive. He quickly stated, "That's not true! I don't know of anyone here that is 20 years behind, and I thought you told me about your inheritance." Marie continued, "Forget about the inheritance for one moment. I am sick and tired of everyone's resentment about some inheritance." She paused for a moment. "So you can dish it out, but you can't take it!" Dr. Nosan's face was beginning to redden, and he was obviously becoming mad at Marie. But Marie continued, "Dr. Nosan, with all due respect, treating cancer cells with vitamins or irradiating cancer cells in an attempt to induce the formation of tumor-specific antibodies has been shown to be ineffective ages ago, and heating tumors to make them go away just isn't working."

Dr. Nosan looked puzzled at Marie and still did not answer. He was not expecting such a strong response. Marie continued the discussion but she noticed that Dr. Nosan was not bothering to pay attention or answer her. "O.K. Let's take the unrelated donor program for the bone marrow transplant unit. This is just another form of human torture with stupidity as the basic logic behind the project. I can hear them saying–all we have to do is trick the body to recognize a foreign tissue as its own! They even admit that they can't get a complete donor match. When you go into the unit, all you see are dying patients. But now they can have a horrible death from graft-versus-host disease." Marie was referring to the disease caused when a cancer patient starts responding immunologically to itself and begins attacking its own tissues. This occurs after a course of lethal therapy to destroy cancer cells that is so toxic that it wipes out the patient's bone marrow, the source of the body's immune cells. The patient is then given a dose of precursor immune cells from a donor's bone marrow. If the donated bone marrow cells are not a complete immunological match with the patient's cells, as the donated bone marrow cells populate the patient and begin responding, they eventually could attack normal cells and tissues that they recognize as foreign. When this happens, the outcome is usually fatal.

Marie continued her sparring, "Dr. Nosan do you know that biochemistry is the chemistry of subtlety? It usually means that those proteins in low abundance, sometimes labeled as 'minor components,' are often the critical elements in one's metabolism." Dr. Nosan asked, "So what?" She continued, "The majority of scientists at this institution have no deep training in physics and chemistry, so they do not have the background to ask certain basic questions, and therefore they continue to repeat and derivatize each other's results. Hardly breakthrough thinking here! Finally, I do not know where all this hearsay about my inheriting a lot of money started in the illustrious D. O. Madison grapevine, but frankly I hardly think that my future financial status has any bearing on whether I should be a scientist or what I produce as a scientist. Do I ask you about your money?"

Dr. Nonsan looked dumbstruck; he was not expecting the barrage from Marie. He turned from her and did not answer. Marie continued, "You know Dr. Nosan, I am aware that I am disliked here at D. O. Madison, and at this point in time I am tired of having to prove myself to a bunch of people that I consider unwinables. I hope you never have to experience the horror of a whisper campaign about your integrity and whether or not you are entitled or not to inherit anything. It is not very pleasant!" Marie then said in a tone that indicated that she was dismissing him as he walked out of the office, "I have a great deal of work to do, and I am sure you do too." Dr. Nosan didn't hear her, as he was already in the hall and out of range. Marie then turned her attention to Jane, "Well Jane, let's do something

productive today. Sparring with Dr. Nosan is a lost cause. All he cares
about is his own paycheck, anyway. After all that Jared has done for him, he
would turn on Jared in a heartbeat." Jane commented, "I can't believe you
took on Dr. Nosan and actually stated that you are aware of how disliked
you are by some of the faculty in the Department. Does this have something
to do with the research you and Dr. McNichols are conducting on the
Desert Storm veterans?" Marie, "Believe it! They don't want to hear the
truth. They are afraid of retaliation from Washington. You know Jane, this
inheritance thing that keeps cropping up . . . . Sometimes I wonder if the
inheritance is connected somehow to our research. You know, what if the
inheritance is financing in some way the biological weapons program?"
Marie quickly dismissed the thought, but it would resurface years later and
turn out to be completely true.

Jane picked up a piece of chocolate to munch on. "You know there was
an article on the front page of the 'Wallsville News' about a mystery illness
that is affecting many of the employees at the Wallsville Correctional Facility.
The employees even formed a support group. I know about this because
we have a home in Wallsville, and I brought a copy of the local newspaper
back with me. I have the paper with me right now." Jane reached into her
purse and pulled out a newspaper. It was not a large paper, but more like
the kind you see given out free at the supermarket. "Here it is. 'Mystery
Illness Strikes Wallsville.' The support group leader, a Sandra Maitland,
describes a mystery illness that affected her entire family, particularly her
daughter." She continued as she scanned the paper, "This Sandra Maitland
says that over 300 families in Wallsville have some form of this mystery
illness, and they want some answers."

Jane pointed out the article as she read from it. "The article states that
some individuals are experiencing a wide array of symptoms, and there
have been 26 diagnosed cases of Lou Gehrig's Disease along with 63 cases
of Multiple Sclerosis in the community. Six of the Lou Gehrig's Disease
cases were in Sandy's neighborhood, and four of these were on one block
alone. Isn't that disease supposed to be kind of rare?" Marie answered,
"I'd say very rare." Jane then asked, "You know, I was cleaning up Dr.
McNichols' office, and I couldn't help but notice the list of symptoms of the
Gulf War veterans. It sure looked like what Sandy Maitland was describing
in the Wallsville News. Maybe they have the same kind of illness as the Gulf

War vets? Maybe you and Dr. McNichols could help them?" Marie looked at the article, "It would be virtually impossible to have so many people diagnosed with Lou Gehrig's disease in the same area. That's a rare genetic disease." Jane said, "I thought so!" Marie interjected, "And all these cases of Multiple Sclerosis! You don't have to be a genius to conclude that something is wrong for this unusual disease cluster to appear in this small town."

Marie thought for a moment and asked jokingly, "You know what, Jane? I'll bet my old mentor Dr. Virgil Rook had something to do with this. When I was at Belford in the Micro Department, they were actually conducting some sort of vaccine experiments at one of the prisons in Wallsville. I wonder if this is the result of some sort of testing program at the prison?" Marie chastised herself, "You know, I must have been some kind of idiot to have thought that Dr. Rook was going to the prison system to take care of the sick prisoners. I used to think he was so noble. I think we should get this Sandra Maitland on the phone and ask if she and her family would be willing to be tested. We could look for some of the unusual infections like we found in the Desert Storm veterans and their families. They are also showing an unusual array of symptoms. And you know, Jane, it sounds like these neurological illnesses that are in Wallsville are very similar to the illness I suffered several years ago. Sooner or later Jared and I are going to get to the bottom of this mess!"

Marie hesitated but then added, "I know that some colleagues of mine were not very happy to see me recover. And just like some of the people around here, they had strong feelings against me. Jane, am I that obnoxious?" Jane replied, "Only a little." Marie laughed, "At least you are honest. People really love me or they hate me, and at times I am ostracized for no apparent reason." Jane said, "Now, don't go paranoid on me, Marie." Marie replied, "You're right. But I tell you there must be some explanation. Everyone tells me that I am an heiress, but I have never benefited from it in any way. I have always worked very hard for everything." Marie sighed and continued, "And The D. O. Madison has treated me abominably! If Jared were not on the faculty here, I would have been long gone!"

Marie turned to leave and said, "I find it very difficult to pander to the egos of petty bureaucrats that have absolutely no talent. It's hard enough to be respectful to some of the scientists who are actually excellent in their fields but jerks as people. Do you know what it is like to suck up to a combination of a jerk and scientific idiot?" Jane answered, "You always said politics were not your strong suit." Marie answered back as she glanced at the newspaper article again, "Please call Mrs. Maitland. I think that she would be interested to talk to Jared and me about the Mystery Illness of Wallsville."

The phone call from Sandra Maitland

Jared and Marie were going over some laboratory data the next day in his office when a call came in from Sandra Maitland. Jane picked up the phone and signaled Jared that Mrs. Maitland was on the line. Jared answered the phone and placed it on the speakerphone so that Marie could hear as well. Jared said, "Good afternoon Mrs. Maitland, this is Professor Jared McNichols, and Dr. Marie McNichols is here with me. I want to thank you for returning our call." Sandy said, "Well, ya'all are so busy that I was very surprised when Jane called and said that you wanted to speak with us over here in Wallsville. We are in the middle of nowhere, East Texas, and it's a real pleasure to find someone in Austin that wants to help us. Usually they run the other way! And call me Sandy." Jared replied, "Which is exactly why we called, Sandy, to find out about the Mystery Illness in Wallsville and see if there was anything that we could do to help." Marie added, "Hi Sandy, this is Marie McNichols. Jane read me the article in the Wallsville News about the unusual cases of chronic and autoimmune illnesses that you are experiencing in your area. Can you tell us something about them?" Sandy replied, "It's also a pleasure to talk to Mrs. Dr. McNichols, if I can call you that, girl?" Marie laughed, "Yes, you can, but you can also call me Marie." Sandy, "That's a nice name—You both have such nice names—I think that I trust you already." Jared laughed, "Well, you shouldn't go that far until you find out if we can help you!" Sandy replied, "Hell, no one has ever tried to help us, so you have already made it into my heart."

Jared turned serious and stated, "Jane and Marie here think that the signs and symptoms of the Wallsville Mystery Illness are very similar to what we have found in the veterans with Gulf War Illnesses." Sandy replied, "I don't know about that, but I can sure give you an earful about our problems. Our friends and neighbors here are all sick with all kinds of problems, but we are worried most about the ones who have been diagnosed with Lou Gehrig's Disease and MS. These people, including our own daughter, are afraid that they are going to die, and many have already. A man down the block dropped dead last month, right in his house. They didn't find him right away. On one block alone there are four cases of ALS. My daughter who just turned eighteen was examined by the neurologists at Belford College of Medicine, and they said that she has Lou Gehrig's Disease and may not live to her 20th birthday. We are very afraid of the future in this community."

Jared thought about what Sandy had said, "There is something very wrong for there to be so many cases of ALS in your community. What is the population of Wallsville?" Sandy replied, "About 35,000." Jared said, "I thought so. That's an incidence rate way out of proportion to the size of your community. Tell me, was there anything unusual about any of these cases of ALS? Where there multiple cases in the same family?" Sandy answered, "Not that I know of." Jared asked, "Do you recall if any of the ALS cases were called 'atypical'?" Sandy thought, "That rings a bell. That's what they told us at Belford College of Medicine about Jenny, our daughter." Jared continued, "If any of the cases are atyptical ALS, then they might be a neurodegenerative disease caused by a central nervous system infection that mimics ALS by killing certain nerve cells in the central brain. Does your daughter have some of the same signs and symptoms that you and your husband had that were listed in the local newspaper, such as low-grade fevers, stomach pain, memory loss, skin rashes, diarrhea?" Sandy perked up, "Why, Yes! They never asked us about that when we took her to the Neurology Clinic at Belford." Marie added, "They never seem to think about other diseases, only neurological diseases. That's so typical of neurologists."

Jared asked Sandy, "I think that your daughter should come in for some tests here, or can we get a fresh sample of her blood sent over to us here in Austin?" Sandy replied, "Considering the number of times that she has been stuck with needles with no answers or even a by-ya-leave, I don't think that's asking too much." Jared continued, "At the same time I would also appreciate a sample of blood from you and your husband." Sandy replied, "I think that can be arranged. Our family doctor here is at his wits end. He doesn't know what to do about all the illnesses." Marie continued,

"Once we get the blood sample, we can test it to see if Jenny has an infection. We are particularly interested in an infection caused by mycoplasmas." Sandy asked, "O.K. What ever that is? What did you call it?" Marie replied, "A mycoplasma is a small bacteria that doesn't have a cell wall and lives inside our cells." Jared added, "The type of mycoplasma that we are going to test for is known to penetrate into the central nervous system, and it may cause nerve cell degeneration. If this occurs in the right area, it could mimic ALS." Sandy said, "This is getting interesting. The Health Department keeps telling us that there is nothing in the Trinity water system." Jared looked at Marie, "Why would they test the water system?" Sandy answered, "I don't know. They said it must be in the water if there is anything in the area, but the water tested out O.K., so they dismissed our problem." Marie asked, "Why would they just test the water system? And what did they test for?" Sandy answered, "I have no idea. They just told us that everything was just fine, A-O.K., but no one believes them."

Jared responded sarcastically, "I can see why no one has any confidence in the Health Department!" Marie asked, "They aren't doing anything about the autoimmune illnesses?" Sandy replied, No. They keep telling us that it's all within expected values, what ever that means." Jared was sarcastic, "Expected values–Who are they kidding?" Sandy added, "That's exactly what we thought!" Jared continued, "One last question, Mrs. Maitland, what kinds of work do you and your husband do?" Sandy said, "Why he is the Assistant Warden at the Wallsville State Prison. I'm just a housewife."

Jared looked at Marie and then returned to Sandy Maitland on the phone. "Were there any other 'Mystery Illness' patients who worked at the prison?" Sandy spoke up, "You betcha! Most of the people who died worked at the prison, and a lot of the people who were sick worked at the prison, or their family members were prison employees. In fact, it was so bad that we specifically asked the prison doctor if there was any relationship between the illnesses in the community and what was happening in the prison." Marie asked, "And what did he tell you?" Sandy said, "He wouldn't tell us anything! That made me very suspicious." Jared asked, "Can you tell us anything about the prison infirmary?" Sandy continued, "I can sure tell you from my husband that there are a hell of a lot of sick patients in there, and not all of them are walking out." Marie asked, "Do you mean that they are no longer sick or are they dying in the prison?" Sandy said sadly, "Lot's of them are dying. My husband told me that at one point they were losing a few inmates per week, and they were told to keep quiet about it. He has to be careful, because everyone has been warned not to discuss anything that is going on in the prison. They could all lose their jobs." Jared responded, "It sounds like they could lose much more than their jobs." Sandy replied in her East Texas accent, "You got that right, dear!"

Jared tried to reassure Sandy. "We want to help you and your family, but to be candid with you, we are under a lot of pressure to stop our studies in the area of chronic infections." Sandy stated, "That sounds familiar! Are you going to help us or run the other way?" Marie smiled, "Yes, we are going to help, but as Dr. McNichols said, he has to be careful. Me, on the other hand, I am in so much trouble that it probably doesn't matter." Jared said, "We are going to help you, but for the moment we have to keep this among ourselves." Sandy emphatically, "You got that straight! I think that one of the mistakes I made was going to the local government officials and trying to tell them something was wrong. All they did was call the police to have us investigated. But it turns out my husband works with the local police on a number of security issues, so that didn't work." Jared reminded Sandy, "We still need those blood samples. I can send you the information on how to draw and ship them to us." Sandy asked, "I would rather bring them to you, if that's O.K.?" Jared said, "Certainly. You can bring them on ice to us here in Austin or you can come here and we will have someone draw the blood." Basically the conversation was over, and the McNichols did not give it much thought until approximately one week later.

The Maitlands come back to Austin

At least a week had elapsed since Mrs. Maitland's call to Jared and Marie. Marie had asked Jane to make arrangements for lunch with Sandy Maitland and her family on the day that they arrived in Austin. The arrangements were made, and one week later the Maitlands came back to Austin.

Marie walked into Jared's department office on that morning, "Good morning, Jane!" Jane, "Have I imagined that, or did you just say good morning." Marie replied, "You know I'm a night owl! Mornings are not my best time of the day. Jared on the otherhand loves to get up early. I hate him!" Marie finally became serious and asked, "Well Jane, what do you have for me today?" Jane looked at her notes, "After your weekly lab meeting, you are scheduled to go to lunch with Jared and the Maitland family." Marie asked, "The victims of the 'Wallsville Mystery disease'?" Jane said, "That's right! They are desperate for some answers." Jane paused and then told Marie, "They're in the conference room now if you want to talk to them." Marie said, "Thanks, Jane. I believe I will."

Marie walked out of the office and headed for the small conference room adjoining the department office. She still had her lab coat on. Upon entry into the conference room Marie said, "Hi, In case you don't remember, I'm Dr. Marie McNichols." With her East Texas accent, Sandy was the first to speak, "I remember you, girl. I'm Sandy Maitland, and this is my husband Clayman and my daughter Jenny." Marie held out her hand, "I'm glad you could all come to Austin, and I hope we can help you."

The visitors all smiled, sat down and then Marie said softly to the Maitlands, "We are in the middle of a spiritual war here, and I believe that your family's illnesses and the Gulf War veterans' illnesses may be a manifestation of that war." Sandy broke out into a smile, "I can tell right now that you're my kind of girl, Marie!" Clayman said, "We would like to take you and Professor McNichols to lunch. The people in the lab were nice enough to take our blood, so I don't think we can help them any further. We filled out all of the illness forms for Professor McNichols." Clayton and Sandy handed the forms to Marie. Sandy said, "Come on, let's go to lunch and talk. Where's your husband, Dr. McNichols?" Marie responded, "We made arrangements for lunch, and we are going to meet my husband at the restaurant. He has been off campus at a meeting, and it's easier for him to join us there." Sandy stood up and said, "Lead the way!"

Marie led the Maitlands down the hallway with the various departmental laboratories on each side. As they walked Marie said, "I know just the place, and we can even talk there without someone looking over our shoulders." Bob Sonan came out of one of the laboratories, and Marie said, "Wait, I want you to meet Bob, my right-hand man. I couldn't do anything without him. We've worked together for years and have never had a fight . . ." Marie paused and chuckled, "which is a major achievement in view of my short-fused temper! When I was getting over my near-fatal illness, Bob would do things for me in the lab before I had a chance, because he realized better than I did that I was not up to doing anything."

They all stopped in the hall and greeted Bob Sonan. Marie introduced them, "Bob, these are the Maitlands from Wallsville. They are suffering from some peculiar illnesses involving neurological symptoms that Jared and I think might be related to the Desert Storm Illness and that killer illness I had several years ago. Everyone said "Hi!" to Bob, and Marie continued, "Bob does all the gene tracking and polymerase chain reaction studies on the veterans. This pilot study is just a small part of our research program. My husband Jared is the chairman of this Department, which he founded. He oversees the research of over 150 employees here." Sandy said, "I don't know what it all means, but it's impressive!" Marie asked Bob, "Could you please show the Maitlands what a gene tracking study looks like."

Bob retrieved his lab book and showed the Maitlands an autoradiogram, which was really an X-ray film. He then said, "We radiolabel a specific sequence of DNA to act as a probe." Marie added, "The probe is like a key, only in this case it is radioactive. If it matches a particular lock, which in this case is a DNA or gene sequence from an infectious agent called *Mycoplasma fermentans incognitus*, the probe will attach itself to the DNA that has been affixed to this special Nytran paper."

Bob then held up an autoradiogram. "We develop this film which we place on the special paper that contains the person's nuclear fractions that we have separated from his white blood cells." Marie then carefully pointed with her finger, "If we see a band, like this one, it means that the infectious agent's DNA is present!" Sandy said, "That's really interesting! You mean to tell me that you can tell from those little spots on the 'whatever you call it' that I might have some infection?" Marie responded, "Yes. The reason we are able to find these infections is that we do not discard the portion of the cell where the infectious agent attacks. Other techniques that are used routinely involve purification steps that may prevent the chance of picking up these DNA sequences. You can think of the DNA in this case as a hidden lock or target. There seems to be some controversy about the technique and these invasive microorganisms. However, "I have over 25 publications on the technique, and it is summarized in an article written by my husband and I that was published recently in *Methods in Molecular Genetics.*"

Sandy thought for a moment and then asked, "That's impressive work, but I have two questions. Can you use that technique with our blood samples? And why are people attacking you and Professor McNichols ?" Marie answered, "Ah, you've been talking to Jane in the office. In answer to your first question, yes, we can test you, but it will take some time as we are a small operation, and we are swamped with requests. In answer to your second question, I really do not have a reasonable explanation as to why we have been attacked. My husband is one of the most cited scientists in the world, and he is the co-discoverer of the cell membrane structure. He is in all the basic biology and medical school textbooks." Marie continued, "Perhaps we have stumbled upon something that a lot of powerful people want to keep secret for a variety of reasons."

Clayman then asked a very important question. "What's the real reason?" Marie smiled, "If you ask me, I believe we are fighting a spiritual battle involving evil forces that for reasons unclear to me loathe whatever we are doing and want to keep it secret." Sandy perked up, "Believe it or not, I *do* know what you mean." Clayman then turned to Bob, "Thanks Bob, for showing us the film, what did you call it, the autoradiogram?" Bob replied, "Yes, that's exactly what it is. It's my pleasure. I hope our tests will provide you with some answers." Clayman and Jenny also thanked Bob, and the group continued down the long hall to the elevator.

As Marie and the Maitlands walked down the hallway to the elevator, Marie gave cursory greetings to some of the individuals who passed her in the hall. Marie turned to the Maitlands while they were walking and asked, "Do you feel the undercurrents here?" Sandy responded, "Yes, I sure do!" Marie continued, "It has been like this for quite sometime, and it has escalated ever since we voiced our concerns about the possible involvement of a biological weapon in the Desert Storm veterans." Clayman then responded, "That's awful. These people don't even try to hide their animosity." Marie replied, "I know. We have to live with it. They have never cracked a smile to me in the several years that I have been here. I was pretty arrogant when I graduated from the Institute of Biophysics, but I don't think I was any worse than anyone else. It's just that these people and the scientific community in general are devoid of a minimal display of enthusiasm for their work. I think that my personality really favors that of the opera singer, which was my other choice of a profession, and yet I have the head of a physicist."

They took the elevator to the ground floor. Marie continued the conversation after a chuckle, "I believe my colleagues can't handle this combination, or as Jared says, he believes their hatred stems more from something in my background . . . . which I am trying to find out about!" Sandy asked, "Why do you continue?" Marie responded, "Because I have a direct order from the higher power!" Clayman then spoke out, "That's good enough for me!" Marie said, "Remember, scientists are the last people to admit to the spiritual." Marie continued talking to the guests as they walked outside the hospital past the rose garden and to the visitors' parking lot. "I believe they are all in for a rude awakening some day." Marie turned suddenly to the Maitlands and asked, "I hope you like Italian food?" Jenny then laughed, "Sure do!" Marie asked, "I hope that you don't mind if we all pile into your vehicle, a great little Italian restaurant is just down the street, and Jared is planning to meet us there. Then he can drive me back to the hospital." Sandy said, "Let's go!" Sandy drove a big Chevy Suburban to Austin, so there was ample room for the group. She liked to drive, and since Clayman hated to drive the Suburban, Sandy did most of long-range driving chores for the Maitland family.

Lunch at an Italian restaurant

It was only a few blocks to the little Italian restaurant, and before they could settle in, they were there. Marie with the Maitlands in tow entered the little ethnic restaurant to find Jared waiting for them in the corner. He was seated at a round table that the five of them could comfortably fit around. A single classical guitarist was strumming on the guitar and was playing 'Aldi la.' As the Maitlands and Marie were shown to the table, Jared stood to meet the Maitlands. The owner of the restaurant came over to give Marie and Jared a special greeting. "Bonjourno!" Marie turned and answered, "Bonjourno to you, too, Mario! I hope you have my favorite?" Mario replied, "We do!" He paused, "The chicken cuttoletta with marinara." Marie said to the Maitlands, "I highly recommend it. It's a true taste of

Sicily!" Even Jared agreed with Marie on this point, and they sat down and all ordered the same entrée.

As the waiter began to fill their glasses with water, Sandy said to Jared, "We've been having some strange incidents up in Wallsville." Jared asked, "What kind of incidents?" Sandy replied, "All of us believe that we have been human guinea pigs!" The guitarist started to play a tune as Jared spoke to the Maitlands, "You know, I don't doubt you from what I have seen in your local paper." Marie continued, "We have seen this before. When we suggested that some of the Desert Storm veterans might be suffering from invasive mycoplasmal infections, you wouldn't have believed the hostile treatment we have received from our administration." Sandy asked, "What's that again?" Jared answered this time, "Mycoplasma. It is a very small, primitive bacterium that has lost its outer covering or cell wall, and it must invade cells to survive and replicate. When it invades cells it starts interfering with the cell's metabolism, and in some cases it can cause the cells to go into programmed cell death and eventually die." Marie added, "When we found this type of bacteria in the Desert Storm veterans' blood, we suggested that the common antibiotic doxycycline should be useful." Jared said, "Although this was basically a pretty standard approach, it was still empirical, since we didn't have antibiotic sensitivity data." Marie continued, "What were we supposed to do? Let our stepdaughter remain sick? If you had an answer to ease the suffering of your family, wouldn't you try?" Sandy replied firmly, "You bet your boots, girl!"

Jared then began the story of his stepdaughter Suzanne. "My stepdaughter and her roommate who is also a veteran of the Gulf War have completely recovered from their illness that they developed after their return. They were in the 101st Airborne but were never as sick as most of the patients that contact us. But we now have more data from other units that served, including the Special Forces and Navy SEALs." Marie added, "I, myself, almost died from a similar disease that involved the central nervous system and appeared to be similar to the Desert Storm Illnesses. Without doxycycline, I don't think that I would have recovered." Jared continued, "We don't think that we have a permanent solution to the problem, but the treatment is effective in allowing the veterans to recover— at least those that have this particular infection. We certainly do not have the entire puzzle solved. Not by a long shot. But we're making progress."

Marie added, "In short, we have a lot more research to do. As I said, we came forward as concerned citizens first, not necessarily as scientists. Now, we have to prove or disprove our hypothesis or modify it to include other factors as well." Sandy stated, "I'm with the both of you!" Clayman now became agitated, "You know, I'm a veteran, and we're all real proud to know both of you folks." Jared responded, "Thanks for your support. It has not been easy, that's for sure."

Jared continued the discussion. "All we can tell you is every time we mention the term Mycoplasma, a wall comes up." Sandy asked, "What's so special about this Mycoplasma bug?" Jared answered, "Normally mycoplasmas do not affect healthy people, although sometimes they might cause a bronchial or urogenital tract infection; however, the type of Mycoplasma that we found in the veterans seems to be very invasive and opportunistic. It's what we call a highly pathogenic Mycoplasma, in that it can cause severe disease." Marie added, "It appears to attack an individual's weak points." Jared continued, "We think that one particular species, *Mycoplasma fermentans incognitus*, may have been modified or made more pathogenic. In the military this is called 'weaponizing.' This means that it may have been modified to make it more survivable, more resistant to the elements, such as heat and dryness, and more invasive and more capable of causing disease. As it turns out, the Army knows quite a bit about this particular bug, and they have published extensively on it but they have never admitted that it has been modified."

Jared then related to the Maitlands the political problems that they have encountered. "Finding this mycoplasma in the Gulf War veterans has really gotten us into a lot of trouble. Every time we even mention the term Mycoplasma, it's as if we hit upon some raw nerve." Marie joked, "You know, something that is worse than a root canal or an impacted wisdom tooth!" Clayman answered, "I know what you mean!" Marie continued, "I even had one VA scientist tell me that there was no such thing as mycoplasmas in the Middle East." Jared laughed and told the Maitlands, "That's so stupid that you can't even imagine! It's like saying that there are no bacteria in the Middle East." Marie laughed, "In short, the response of certain individuals has been completely out of whack." Sandy added, "You mean like 'thou protestest too much'!" Marie chuckled, "Precisely!"

Jared was about to continue the conversation, when the lunch arrived. "After lunch we can go back to the hospital, and I can have some blood drawn for the test." Clayman responded, "We had that done already." Jared said, "Good! Did you fill out the Illness Survey Forms?" Clayman answered, "We certainly did! That's a lot of information!" Marie added, "Jared assembled that Survey Form. Unfortunately, it will take us several weeks to get you a result on the tests." Jared continued, "I have to apologize. We are very jammed up at the moment, and I promised some Special Forces units that we would get out their results first." Clayman replied, "No apology necessary. That's fine with us. We have waited this long to get an answer, we can wait a little more." Marie continued, "But time is still of the utmost importance, particularly for Jenny." She looked at Jenny, "If I were you, I'd try to get a prescription for doxycycline, just in case." Sandy said, "I have a sympathetic doctor who has just thrown his hands up in the air saying he has no idea how to help Jenny. He might help." Clayman added, "If not, we'll just go down to Mexico and get the stuff." Sandy added, "The good Lord helps those who help themselves!" Marie concurred, "Amen to that!"

As they ate lunch Jared asked, "Let me know if you start the doxycycline, and above all else, if you do start Jenny on an antibiotic, let me know how it works, especially if she has problems. I am trying to keep a running log of patients and their progress on doxycycline. Most patients actually feel worse at first. This is due to what is called the Herxheimer Reaction." Sandy asked, "The what reaction?" Jared continued, "It's just a die-off reaction where the bacteria that are being killed or suppressed by the antibiotics release chemical substances that cause all sorts of short-term problems. Usually the signs and symptoms become temporarily worse for a while, then there is slow improvement. To be safe you might wait for the lab results." Marie added, "I know that this has been rough on you all, but we think that this antibiotic might help. It saved my life." Sandy said, "Girl, I just believe you two are the answer to our prayers!" Jared countered, "I don't think Washington or the Pentagon would agree with that assessment."

After lunch, Marie continued the conversation. "Oh, by the way I am giving a seminar here at The D. O. Madison in month or so. You are all welcome to come if you want." Sandy responded, "We'll bring Cassie Mayer, the eyewitness news reporter. She has been following our plight!" Marie said, "That would be great!" But Jared had to warn them about inviting a reporter to the Cancer Center. "I am afraid that we may have to think this over first, Marie. You could find yourself in a bind by inviting a reporter to your seminar." Sandy sarcastically, "Fun!" Marie said, "They're almost too anxious for me to do something so they can attack Jared. I say we do it anyway!" Sandy agreed, "I hear ya!" Clayman turned serious and said to Jared, "Depending on what you find in our blood, I have a long list of guards that need testing. Do you think that you can do it?" Jared replied, "I think that we can help you, but I don't know about the long run. I am under increasing pressure to stop what we are doing with the veterans. You are an employee of the State prison system, and I am not sure how the State is going to react if you turn up positive." Clayman said, "You don't have to say another word!" The group became silent for a moment while they finished their coffee, except for Marie and Jenny who don't drink coffee. The hardy lunch made everyone feel a bit better, even though the McNichols realized again that they were in for a rough time over the next few months.

The harassment of the McNichols begins

A meeting was called by Dr. Francis Belcher, the Vice President for Research, at his office with some of his underlings. They were plotting a strategy to disrupt Marie's upcoming seminar in the Cancer Biology Department and to publicly humiliate and demoralize Dr. Jared McNichols. Dr. Belcher was a rather short, thin man in his early 60s with a white goatee and gray-white hair. He had big eyes that bulged out as if he had a thyroid problem. He was a rather witty hematologist from the Bronx but he trained upstate in Buffalo. He liked to drop names and act very political, but his accent was strictly New York City, which did not go down well in Texas. He called upon his employees: Dr. Martin Italiano, a short, salt and pepper-haired molecular geneticist with course features and a small beard who was educated in Kentucky but was originally from Staten Island; Dr. Roland Auchenhower, a tall, thin microbiologist of non-descript appearance from Pennsylvania; Dr. Laura Graham, a young semi-cute immunologist from Florida who had an over-inflated ego; and her husband, Dr. James Ross, a rather passive-aggressive oral surgeon of small stature originally from

Missouri. Drs. Graham and Ross came to The D. O. Madison recently from faculty positions at the University of Virginia Medical School. Dr. Edwin Moore, a virologist, was also present. They were not very physically attractive people, except for Dr. Laura Graham, who thought that she was a very attractive queen bee like Amy Krappner. The assembled faculty members were carefully chosen, because they were easily manipulated by authority. Their common bond was that they would do just about anything and use just about anybody to get ahead of their colleagues on the promotion ladder, and although an outsider would never know it from their public pronouncements and image, they were known to be less concerned with ethics and moral principles than their faculty colleagues at the Medical Center.

The faculty members were seated at Dr. Belcher's conference table. Dr. Belcher was standing and opened the meeting with his usual superior demeanor. His tactic was to begin with an amusing monolog, almost like a late night comedy show. He usually stood during meetings in his office, because he was so short compared to some of the participants that he felt in a more superior position if he was standing while they were all seated. He paced back and forth in front of his conference table and finally opened the meeting by saying, "Dr. Italiano, Dr. Auchenhower, Dr. Ross, Dr. Moore and of course, Dr. Graham, thank you for attending this meeting on such short notice. If anyone would like a cup of coffee and a doughnut, just help yourself. I have just returned from Madrid, and you will be the first to know that I have been elected to the prestigious European Academy of Science. Madrid was delightful. The food in Spain was excellent, and I had some of the finest wines that I have ever tasted. I would like to say that I was treated like royalty. The culture of Madrid reminds me a bit of New York, and I could go on for hours about Spain, but unfortunately, we have other duties here this morning."

As Dr. Belcher was finishing his usual opening diatribe, people at the meeting were involved in a variety of activities of settling themselves down for the meeting with their coffee and doughnuts. They knew Dr. Belcher only too well for his egotistical opening monologs, and some of them were waiting for him to finish so that the real meeting could start. Dr. Belcher finally ended the introduction, "I have some urgent and critical business to discuss with you. Dr. Masters has asked me to speak to you personally, and what I am about to relate to you must not be mentioned outside this office. Nor is my office to ever be mentioned in the context of this discussion. As far as you are concerned, I never spoke to you, and this meeting never took place. Do you understand Dr. Italiano? You are not to talk about it to anyone." Dr. Italiano had been making faces but eventually became serious and asked, "Why the secrecy? I think I know what you are going to tell us, Dr. Belcher." Dr. Belcher ignored the comment and continued, "You have each been chosen by Dr. Masters for a special assignment. It's quite a simple assignment, but it involves the utmost secrecy and confidentiality." Dr. Belcher paused for effect, "And just so you all should know the seriousness of the matter, I'd like to volunteer to you that what we do has the blessing of none other than our government."

Dr. Italiano diplomatically tried to change the subject. "Dr. Belcher, I am very pleased that you enjoyed your trip to Spain but the memo about this meeting peaked my curiosity. What kind of project would involve the likes of us and be so important and confidential that Austin or Washington would request our help?" Dr. Belcher replied, "That is a good question, and I will address that in due time. It has to do with a certain problem that we have been entrusted with." Dr. Auchenhower, who could be just as arrogant as his boss, "Dr. Belcher, I apologize, but I have to lecture in a few minutes. Could you please get to the point of the meeting." Dr. Graham, who was a bit of an airhead that advanced in her career mainly because of whom she knew and could schmooze, and because she was a woman then said, "The suspense is getting to us Dr. Belcher." Still standing, Dr. Belcher waved his hand and said, "All right! Now be quiet and listen. And don't interrupt me!" Dr. Moore whispered quietly to his colleague Dr. Italiano, "God forbid anyone should get a word in edgewise." Dr. James Ross, a more serious surgeon who was invited to the meeting because of his contacts with a faction in the CIA was irritated and said, "Let's hear what Dr. Belcher has to say." Dr. Belcher continued, "Well, it seems we have a dangerous couple amongst us! By dangerous, I mean that the two of them have stumbled into some very dangerous research that may have to be restricted. And what's worse is they are clever enough to keep their work going, and they have been extremely resilient. In other words, they keep coming back like a bad penny, only in this case the use of the word penny hardly applies."

Dr. Italiano was the first to ask, "For heaven's sake, Dr. Belcher, who are we talking about and why is this so important?" Dr. Belcher leaned on the table and stated, "Marie and Jared McNichols." Dr. Moore who has seen this behavior before and knew what was coming spoke first, "You've got to be kidding, Francis. Jared is one of our most recognized faculty members. He is in all of the biology and medical textbooks for his work with the cell membrane. Hardly any problems there. I've known Marie since she came here from her physics Ph.D. program. She has never struck me as a problem or anyone from a threatening background. She arrived in a beat-up Ford Pinto that barely made the trip from Florida." Dr. Belcher continued, "Apparently, Marie comes from a very secretive, dangerous and shadowy European family. For reasons that are not at all clear, her true family has been anything but supportive of her in her current endeavors. In any event, our sources have disclosed that her wealthy family is not pleased about her academic interests, and this family is not looked upon favorably by our government." Dr. Moore interrupted again, "So what! Is this what the meeting is about? This is ridiculous! We should be courting these people." Dr. Belcher answered, "As I've already stated, nothing *appears* to make sense in this case. But when Dr. Masters gives me a direct order, I have to give him my utmost cooperation, and you should as well. And I must remind you that we all serve at *his* pleasure, including you Dr. Moore." Dr. Belcher stared at Dr. Moore, who now realized that the meeting was about to get serious. Dr. Belcher continued, "Dr. Masters has ordered me to organize a program, let's say, to convince Marie and Jared to leave us as quickly as possible." Dr. Ross asked, "Why would you want to get rid of someone who is one of the most cited scientists that we have on staff? Dr. Italiano quiped, "If Isaac Geldter was here, he would be interrupting and telling us that he is the most famous scientist on our staff." Everyone chuckled around the room, because they knew Dr. Geldter was a blowhard and egomaniac. They also wondered why Drs. Geldter and Krappner were not at the meeting. They were the obvious choices for Dr. Masters' little games with the faculty, because either one of them would slit their mother's neck to please Dr. Masters. Dr. Italiano said, "We could probably get rid of the McNichols, and hardly anyone might even complain, especially about Marie McNichols." Dr. Ross ignoring Dr. Italiano, "I don't think so. I really don't know much about Marie, but I think that she does have some science that looks interesting, and really that should be all that matters. Didn't she recover from a near fatal illness a few years back?" Dr. Belcher growing impatient, "Dr. Ross, that illness you refer to was probably the result of a highly unusual infection she contracted while attending a Meyerhoff conference. She was very lucky to have survived." The scientists all looked at Dr. Belcher with an incredulous expression. Dr. Italiano finally asked, "Are you suggesting that there have been actual attempts on Marie McNichols life?" Dr. Belcher growing irritated, "Martin, haven't you been listening to anything I've said?" Dr. Italiano responded, "You have to admit, Francis, this is difficult to comprehend in our normal environment."

Dr. Belcher started to become evasive to indicate that he had nothing to do with the incident. "In response to your question and to the best of my knowledge, I must answer in the affirmative." He paused, and Dr. Italiano asked again, "You mean . . ." Dr. Belcher interjected, "Yes, there have been attempts on her life, and I presume this was partly because of her heiress status but that may not be the only reason." Dr. Auchenhower who has been listening with interest complained, "I don't know, Francis, I did not become a scientist with the goal of becoming involved in some sort of questionable intrigue, let alone some illegal activities for the administration. The fact that we are discussing an attempted murder of another scientist is not something I am particularly proud of. Furthermore, I get the feeling that somehow you are going to ask us to participate in something unethical or illegal. And if this is true, I find this unconscionable! I don't like it one bit!"

Dr. Belcher was becoming nervous but he needed to quickly respond to Dr. Auchenhower. "Now, Roland! You're jumping to conclusions! Who mentioned anything about illegal activities? We'll leave that to the legal experts! We are only faculty members here. Your role is to raise certain character and professional questions about Jared and Marie McNichols and the research that they have been doing with the Gulf War veterans. I have been told that you, in particular, are to ridicule Marie personally and professionally with the object of driving her to despair. You are also to assist in the evaluation of the McNichols research on Gulf War Syndrome. As you may know, they are making statements that some type of infection is involved, and the Administration is not supportive of this type of research. It goes against everything that we stand for here in the Medical Center."

Dr. Belcher continued, "Dr. Masters has decided that the type of research being conducted in Jared McNichols' laboratory is not in the mission of our institution, and it must be stopped as soon as possible. Also, I am told by a faculty member in Jared's department that the research is questionable and not in the best interests of our institution, and others have also suggested that their research on the veterans is not being conducted in a careful and prudent manner." Dr. Italiano ignored the comments on Gulf War research in the McNichols' laboratory. In fact, most of the assembled faculty really didn't care about the kind of research the McNichols were involved in; they really only cared about their own research and their own careers. He said, "The fact is that there are some rumors to the effect that Marie has already had attempts on her life while she was on the faculty at Belford. This could put us in a situation where *we* could be suspected of being accessories to these acts. I don't know much about their work with the veterans, but I don't see how this could be so important to the Administration. In fact, if they come up with anything, it could be very positive for our public relations program. Isn't the institution trying to raise hundreds of millions of dollars for Dr. Masters' building program?" Dr. Belcher responded, "Don't question and over-extrapolate what Dr. Masters has asked you to do. He has not asked you to do anything illegal." Dr. Italiano quickly countered, "No! He is just asking us to do something unethical, and it might be illegal or at the very least against the University Regents' Rules and Regulations. Why doesn't he just do this himself? He certainly has the authority to just step in and fire Jared and shut down his laboratory."

But in fact, Dr. Masters did not have the authority to fire a tenured member of the faculty for conducting unpopular research that simply displeased or embarrassed the administration, unless he could show that the research was unsafe, unethical or fabricated. The lawyers on his staff always seemed to bring up issues that he felt were irrelevant to his authority. He must now use another approach. In fact, he was furious with the University attorneys when they prevented him last month from initiating termination proceedings against Dr. McNichols for conducting the Gulf War Illness research without his written permission. Dr. Masters had used this tactic before, however, and it had resulted in a multi-million dollar judgment against the University. There was nothing in the University Rules and Regulations that specified that the President had to approve research projects in writing before they were initiated.

Belcher was now a bit more nervous in bringing this subject up to his faculty, because it appeared to circumvent or even break the rules and regulations of the University. So he appealed to the faculty's sense of patriotism instead, and he would try to convince them that the University would be behind them in their efforts. "You will be acting in a patriotic sense with the blessing of the University Administration." Dr. Graham, who usually didn't have much to say smiled, "I don't feel completely right about this. You are asking us do things that we could be fired for, if anyone ever found out about it. Mind you, I really don't care about these people, but I do care about my job and my career!" Dr. Belcher responded quickly, "Let me put this to you another way. As Dr. Masters told me, if you do not participate and do as you are told, you might find that your positions are not in the strategic plans of the institution, and therefore expendable in our upcoming budget hearings." Dr. Italiano then became indignant, "You can't do that! That would be brought up to the Faculty Senate so fast it would make your head spin. You can't force us to do this by threatening us with losing our jobs, especially if it breaks University rules." He continued and in a self-righteous tone, "This is blackmail!"

Dr. Belcher quickly backtracked. "No, no! You have it all wrong." He thought for a moment for the correct spin. "Dr. Masters is not going to threaten you with termination if you don't perform this task for him. On the contrary, Dr. Masters is going to *reward* you for a job well done! I know each and every one of you will be enthusiastic about this duty that he has chosen for you. The rewards could be considerable, you see, promotions, salary increases, research space, and so on." Dr. Italiano smiled and looked at his colleagues, "That's more like what I wanted to hear. Now, what does Dr. Masters want us to do? And by the way, I won't do anything without something in writing that I am acting directly on behalf of you and Dr. Masters. I don't want to be left holding the bag if you or Dr. Masters decides in the future that you didn't order me to do this little task for you."

Dr. Belcher was now a bit more irritated and nervous. "My office is not to be involved in any way in this task. I am simply following the instructions of Dr. Masters and relating his wishes to you. But if you want, I will make a request to that effect to Dr. Masters. However, I must tell you that Dr.

Masters will not put anything in writing to me, and I am only acting on his behalf. Let me state very clearly that I must not be directly involved. I am simply relating to you Dr. Masters' wishes. I am not to be involved directly, and I am going to deny ever speaking to you about this. Dr. Masters has requested that I tell you to begin by making a concerted effort to question Marie's upcoming seminar and the way that Jared conducts research in his department." Dr. Auchenhower asked, "What about Jared's research? He's the Chairman of that department, and he built it from nothing. Do you think that he is going to sit back while we destroy his wife in front of his own department and then question his own research?" Dr. Belcher, "I think the first issue will take care of itself, and I want you to concentrate on the research conducted by the McNichols here at our institution. I am sure that you will find something if you look hard enough."

Dr. Masters has asked me to have a plan for Jared McNichols. If he had any brains he would divorce his wife and leave this institution." Dr. Italiano added, "Isaac Geldter and Amy Krappner have been telling everyone that she's nothing more than a mad woman, and their research on Gulf War Syndrome is nothing but bullshit." Dr. Belcher said, "That's a good start, but we all know that Isaac covets Jared's department, so it could be interpreted as a bit self-serving. This is why Dr. Masters wanted other faculty members to join Dr. Geldter in his efforts." Dr. Ross who had been listening intensely finally spoke out, "How can you, Geldter or Krappner conclude that Marie McNichols is completely mad or that their research is bullshit?" Dr. Moore added, "On the other hand, it is common knowledge that she does not fit the academic mold. In any respect, her thinking, her dress, her dramatic tendencies are not exactly politically correct. But I do not think she is mad, just different, perhaps. By the way, why don't you get Isaac Geldter and Amy Krappner to do this dirty little job? They do it all the time, anyway, and you don't even have to threaten them. They would love to do it for the rewards."

Dr. Belcher was now growing impatient. "You are not as clever as you think you are, Dr. Moore. The point is that we are to collectively make sure that *everyone* here thinks that Marie is of questionable sanity and that Jared has gone over the edge in his Gulf War Syndrome research. Since we all know that Isaac and Amy have been, shall I say, extremely critical of the McNichols, among others at our institution, it can't be seen as some sort of vendetta against the McNichols by Isaac to take over his department. Also, it will be easier for Dr. Masters to say that the entire faculty wants these individuals removed from their positions."

Still pacing back and forth, Dr. Belcher continued, "You all probably have heard that Dr. Geldter has made a formal request to Dr. Masters to take over Jared's department and merge it into his own department. We don't want it to appear that this is just about a little take-over by another department chairman. Everything must appear very natural, including our criticisms, and it must come from a variety of sources at our institution. Your job is to question their credibility, their integrity, their character. And you are to make it appear as if they are not being ethical with their data on the veterans. Furthermore, Dr. Masters wants you to all make a concerted effort to block their peer-reviewed publications, bar them from invitations to any prestigious conferences, make certain they are not invited to lecture at any significant places and block any pending grant support. The NIH peer-review system makes it very easy to insure that Jared's grants are not funded. You all know people on the review committees, and Dr. Masters expects you to use these contacts. We also have some people in Jared's department who will inform us when he submits papers for publication, grant applications, and so on. You will let my office know of anything significant; otherwise I don't want to hear about it."

Dr. Belcher finally stopped pacing the floor. He looked directly at the participants. "These are Dr. Masters' orders. He wants a full-court blackball. You are to exert so much pressure on them that they will gladly leave the Cancer Center." Dr. Auchenhower responded first, "I don't like this, Dr. Belcher. How do we know that what we are doing has the government's or the University's backing?" Dr. Belcher in a fatherly tone, "Do you want a meeting with Dr. Masters? I could check with Clement, and tell him that you have to meet with him, because you do not believe in his directives. Is that it? Do you think that this is just something personal, or some kind of stupid academic game? Come on, I don't think that this is really a problem with any of you. And don't try to tell me that any of you actually have a conscience and wouldn't be involved in such activities if there were certain advantages that would be provided to each one of you. Be realistic! There is a good reason why you were each asked to be here today. Do you really think that the reason that you are in your present positions is solely because of your academic talents. The fact of the matter is, none of you are exceptionally talented. But you are all very good at what you do, and that is exactly what Dr. Masters is asking of you, to use your best academic talents when he requests them."

Dr. Italiano swung his head around and was now indignant. "I didn't come here to be insulted!" Dr. Belcher responded, "Don't be so smug, Dr. Italiano. It's not like you haven't done this before for Dr. Masters. Why is it that each time Dr. Masters makes a simple request, you act this way. Remember, I know you each very well, and I want you all to get on with Dr. Master's program, as he requested. After all, you are just following Dr. Masters' directives. You can think of the McNichols as potential threats to our National Security." Dr. Italiano interrupted again, "I don't give a damn about this so called 'National Security' angle! National Security? The last time I looked at my paycheck it didn't say some federal agency involved in 'National Security.' You have got to give us a lot more than some phony 'National Security' crap before I'm going to be involved. This is a clear breach of ethics and University policy, and we could each be liable for being involved in protecting the interests of some quasi-legal, unethical programs that are being run by Dr. Geldter out of the Black Building. We have heard rumors about the secret, classified experiments he is conducting over there in the special locked area and his involvement with Belford in the prison experiments."

Dr. Belcher ignored the comments of Dr. Italiano. "O.K.! Consider this. Dr. Masters does not like to be told that you strongly disagree with him and his directives, and you are turning down his offer to receive adjustments to your salaries and future considerations for promotion within his administration." The assembled academics looked at each other without speaking until Dr. Italiano came forward, "All right. All right. Why didn't you say so in the first place? I could overlook a lot for an above scale adjustment in my salary and some more research space. And I need a larger office." Dr. Belcher, "That's more like the academicians that I know! Let's see. Our immediate agenda is to disrupt Marie's seminar tomorrow in the Cancer Biology Department. Dr. Masters has arranged for Jared McNichols to be away for the time period of the seminar. I want each of you to find out in your own way exactly what they are doing with the Gulf War Syndrome project they started. Dr. Masters wants to know exactly what we can do to quickly stop this from continuing to embarrass the institution.

Dr. Belcher rallied his troops. "Now what's it going to be? Are you going to follow the directives of Dr. Masters or not? If not, and if you ever speak about this meeting to anyone, I think you will find that the Administration will be very unforgiving." Dr. Belcher paused for effect, "And instead of Jared and Marie being in the hot seat, you may find yourself there instead!"

Exasperated sighs were heard around the room, but some of the participants nodded their heads in approval. Dr. Auchenhower finally said, "O.K., Dr. Belcher, I believe that you have made your point." Dr. Belcher responded, "You mean Dr. Masters' point. They are his directives, not mine. I am only following his orders. It's only my job to relate his concerns to you, and I cannot be involved in this project in any way. I want to be very clear about that, and I want your understanding as to where these directives come from. They are not my directives; they are Dr. Masters' directives." Dr. Italiano asked, "So you want us to do the dirty work for you, is that it?" Dr. Belcher answered, "Not at all. I am following my orders, and you're going to follow yours! I must not be directly involved." Dr. Italiano quipped sarcastically, "And we'll take the rap if anything goes wrong." Dr. Belcher tried to smooth over the ill feelings, "Wrong? Nothing is going to go wrong. You are simply going to follow Dr. Masters' directives. Is that clear?" Dr. Italiano said, "O.K., I'll do my part for Dr. Masters and his directives. But, I still would like to be briefed by Dr. Masters about the so-called National Security aspects of the directives." Dr. Auchenhower added, "I feel the same, Francis. This is not some stupid game." Dr. Ross finally decided to speak out, "So do I, Dr. Belcher. What you are asking us to do has important implications." Dr. Belcher looked at Dr. Graham, "What about you Laura?" Dr. Graham responded, "I have no problem with what Dr. Masters is asking, but I would like to hear it from him. I would also like to know more about the increases in salary and other benefits that the Administration would like to bestow on us." Dr. Belcher did not know how to respond to Dr. Graham, so he decided not to respond at all.

Dr. Belcher finally told the assembled faculty members, "I'll try to arrange a meeting with Dr. Masters so that you will be able to hear it directly from the source. And to show you just how cooperative the administration can be, I will make sure that each of you has a chance to talk with our distinguished visitor who is coming next month from Jerusalem, Dr. Schlomo Ricin, the scientist who is coordinating with Dr. Geldter." Dr. Auchenhower stated, "That would certainly help. You have to understand, Dr. Belcher, this whole thing would seem fantastic to an outsider." Dr. Belcher quipped, "I know, I know! And if worse comes to worse, all we are doing is simply discouraging one over-inflated young scientist from joining our ranks and suggesting that another leave our great institution. It's not like we haven't done things like this before. Dr. Geldter summed it up himself by stating that Marie McNichols is just another lightweight scientist. And he seems to think that Jared's department would be better off if he administered it from the Black Building." Dr. Auchenhower added, "I'm sorry, Dr. Belcher, I am not convinced of that. Marie really has not been given the opportunity to test her scientific mettle, and as far as stripping one of our senior faculty of his position, I have grave reservations about the procedures and approaches that you, correction, Dr. Masters has advanced to remove Jared McNichols. This could happen without recourse to any faculty member at our institution."

Dr. Belcher had not thought that the meeting would be this difficult. He responded, "Dr. Auchenhower, I didn't know that nobility of character was one of your attributes." Dr. Auchenhower acted a bit disgusted at the prospect of ruining a fellow faculty member's career. After all, the *same* thing could happen to him if he crossed Dr. Masters, and he knew it. But he would go along with the directives, if only because he had put quite a bit of time into building his research programs at the D. O. Madison, and he didn't want to to relocate or move to another institution where he might not have the same benefits.

Dr. Belcher continued his comments, "Marie McNichols is just one of many young scientists who are looking for positions, and so it will make little difference if her career does not mature at our institution. Jared and Marie can just take positions elsewhere." Dr. Italiano interjected sarcastically, "Come on guys, they are just targets. Not persons! Targets! Get it?" Dr. Belcher, who had been standing and pacing in front of the table in his office during the entire gathering, signaled the end of the meeting by waving his arms, "Remember, this is what Dr. Masters wants, and I for one do not want to be the one to tell him he can't have what he wants. Is that clear to all of you! I hope so. Now remember, I must not be directly involved in any way. My office will remain silent about this. As far as anyone is concerned, I know nothing about this, understand?"

The participants looked at each other as they left Dr. Belcher's office. Once they were out in the hall Dr. Italiano turned to Dr. Auchenhower, "I don't like this. They are asking us to do things that could get us into a lot of trouble. And what if the System Administration is not as hot for this as Dr. Belcher indicates. They could eventually come after our jobs!" Dr. Auchenhower added, "I have known Dr. Masters for some time, and I have never known him not to get what he wants. The man has an insatiable ego, and I for one would not want to be in his way once he has made up his mind. I will go along with what he wants, but I don't like it. We could be left holding the bag if it blows up, and he and that little pimp Francis Belcher could deny everything. I think that we're going to have to be very careful about this whole approach."

The aftermath of a disastrous seminar

The next day Marie delivered her seminar to the department with constant harassment from faculty members and even students. Drs. Auchenhower and Italiano were present from different departments, and they harassed Marie constantly during her presentation. It was unusual for other faculty members from outside a department to actually show up at another department's internal seminar and bring their students, unless they were invited by the seminar speaker. In this case, that was unlikely. Jared could not help Marie, because he was called away by the Administration to another meeting that he couldn't get out of. Marie could not determine who can attend the seminar and who cannot. She was trapped. In Jared's absence Marie was left to fend off the attacks of Drs. Auchenhower, Italiano and Nosan. These three faculty members constantly interrupted her seminar with aggressive and sometimes derogatory questions, and they didn't let her complete her presentation.

Some of Jared's faculty did come to Marie's defense, such as Dr. Hong, a brilliant young molecular biology faculty member originally from Taiwan that Jared believed could go far at the D. O. Madison and Dr. Gollman, a young faculty member that Jared had picked for early academic advancement, but they couldn't stop the constant sarcastic interruptions. The students in the audience were frightened; they had rarely seen this side of the faculty. Some of the outside participants even threw spitballs at Marie in an effort to humiliate her and cause her to lose her temper during the seminar. She did not lose her temper, but she was incredibly mad by the end of the hour.

After the seminar was over, Marie was waiting outside the seminar room for Jared to arrive. The members of Jared's department passed Marie on the way out of the seminar hall. Some were sympathetic but most were not. When faculty bothered to show up from other departments and heckle a speaker in a department seminar, it was a bad sign. It usually indicated that there was some official organization to the harassment. They were sending a message from the Administration to Marie and Jared, and it was received loud and clear.

Since Jared and Marie started working on subjects like veterans' and prison guards' health problems, they had not made many friends among the faculty. Most sensed that the Administration was dead against their research, or they had heard it directly from the Administration. Unfortunately most of the faculty at the Madison were morally weak and usually lined up to curry favor from their superiors. In fact, some may have felt that by openly opposing Jared and Marie they could move to the front of the line for promotions, more space and salary raises, and little was done to dissuade them from this illusion. The Administration could not simply call Dr. McNichols on the phone or send him a memo and tell him to stop conducting research in certain areas. That would have seemed astonishingly like censorship, and it could result in some bad press reports or even another lawsuit. If there was one thing that the D. O. Madison Administration had historically prided itself on, it was manipulating the local press to support them no matter what unethical or even illegal acts they were involved in. Instead, the Administration used more subtle approaches like the use of peer pressure and economics to get what they wanted. To thoroughly committed and ethical faculty members such tactics could make life difficult for the Administration. Thus the direct 'hammer them' approach was not especially practical in some situations.

To the McNichols' advantage, the D. O. Madison was already feeling the burden of too many faculty lawsuits and a press that was less under control than at any time in the recent past. And the institution had even been warned by the System Administration that it was not good public relations to have so many lawsuits in court at the same time. They also read the local Austin papers. Against this background the D. O. Madison Administration decided to use more stealth and less bluster in dealing with one of its professors and his wife that they now considered a threat. They would let their faculty surrogates do the job for them, while they stayed for the most part completely aloof and even quasi-supportive, at least to the press. In this way it would seem like an internal squabble, a matter of a difference in academic opinion among the faculty. Then the Administration could then sit back and wait for the desired results, or it could step in to mediate the differences between faculty members. If the faculty decided that certain sanctions were necessary, the Administration could act upon these recommendations from the faculty without it appearing like they were directly involved in the first place.

Jared arrives too late to help Marie

Jared finally arrived after Marie's seminar to find Marie mad and alone outside the seminar room. She was pacing back and forth. Marie was also mad at Jared and wanted to go home immediately, but Jared couldn't leave the institution just yet. He could tell from Marie's demeanor that things went badly at the seminar, and he did not want to ask her just yet about the details. Marie told Jared in an agitated voice bordering on anger, "Where were you, and why didn't you help me exercise even a modicum of control over your faculty? After all, it's your department!" Marie then rambled on, "I tell you, these people hate me. I do not even know them. I don't understand why." Jared asked, "I saw Italiano and Auchenhower going down the hall. What were they doing at our departmental seminar, anyway?" Marie not answering, "I had no choice but to stop the seminar early. It had degenerated to a point of absurdity . . . They actually threw spitballs at me!" Jared asked, "Who?" Marie answered, "One of Italiano's people!" Jared asked, "Why did they do that?" Marie said, "Why don't you ask *him*?" She continued, "And I am sure that I have no chance of a position here, nor would I want one. Part of me wants to go to the faculty club and show them that they will not break me. Stronger people have tried and failed. But part of me wants to get the hell out of here and never return. Life is too short to put up with this kind of shit. To hell with the goddamn Ph.D. and this stupid institution." Jared, "Now listen, Babe, I missed your presentation, but I am as devastated as you, and I really cannot believe what happened. In all my years, I have never heard of anything like this."

Jared told Marie, "Look, I know you want to get out of this place but I can't go home just yet. I have some important meetings this afternoon. Let's compromise and go offsite for lunch. I'll take you home later to recuperate from your obviously unpleasant experience." Marie snapped at Jared, "Thanks. I'm hungry!" Jared trying to make Marie lighten up, "You're always hungry!" Then Jared in a gentler tone, "Don't let them prevent you from doing your work. Remember, it is your published manuscripts in peer-reviewed journals that will be remembered. The rest is all bullshit." Marie said, "That's what you always say!"

The McNichols gathered Marie's seminar materials and slides as they conversed. Both were still in lab coats, as they walked through the hospital's hallways on their way out to the parking lot. Marie put on her sunglasses as they exited the building, and she was still trying to hold on to her emotions. The shock of the humiliating seminar experience was just sinking in, and she was on the verge of tears. They reached Jared's pick-up truck in the parking structure, and he helped her into the passenger side. Marie was a petite lady, and the big truck that Jared drove required her to practically jump up or mount it like a horse to get into the cab. Once Jared got behind the wheel, the 'dam of tears burst' just as they left the parking lot. Jared turned right onto the boulevard and was driving to a restaurant a mile or so from the Medical Center.

Marie was now free from holding her emotions in. She cried out loud and asked why so many people hated her and trashed her science. Her tears were flowing freely, and she was wiping her eyes. Jared softly told her, "Please don't cry, Marie, they're not worth it. Those people are just workmen scientists who are not very creative. They don't have your cross-disciplinary training, nor the depth of your scientific comprehension." Marie responded, "Well, you know what I think. It was a total waste of time for me to bust my ass to get that physics training. I thought it would distinguish me from the run-of-the-mill scientists. But instead it has been a damn curse." Jared tried to be supportive, "I will help you professionalize your slides and seminars so that even your complex physics analyses will be understandable to a scientific idiot." Marie responded between sobs, "That's all well and good. But you don't understand! This has been happening to me for years now. I know I am not imagining it! And I know that my illness was no accident. I feel someone wants me dead . . . . Perhaps more than one person wants me dead." Jared was pleading, "Please, Marie, stop! You're just very upset! Don't get paranoid on me!" Marie responded, "You do not have my instincts about subterfuge and people, Jared. My God, haven't you noticed that certain people, our so-called colleagues, look at me as if they have seen a ghost! Come on, you had to notice their looks. They are not happy to see me. It's as if they wanted me dead!" Jared responded, "O.K., I have noticed the strange behavior, but I don't really understand it. Now it's happening to me as well but not at the same scale."

Marie continued to explain the history of her torment. "I have always been singled out for ridicule and unusually cruel behavior by people around me throughout my life. It happened after my parents divorced when I was nine. The entire neighborhood ostracized me. I thought it was because they thought the divorce made me emotionally maladjusted and therefore a bad influence on their children. I went to every parent in the neighborhood to ask them if they would let me play with their children again. I told them that my parents' divorce did not make me emotionally unbalanced, and that I had played with their children for years. But they were unreasonable, and so I told them that if they continued in their behavior I would give them a reason to hate me. I would break the class curve and make it so their precious little children would never be number one as long as I was present." Jared responded, "Listen to me, Marie." But Marie impatiently interrupted, "No, you listen for once. When I was a sophomore in high school one day I walked into the cafeteria with 200 noisy kids and suddenly everyone went silent. You could hear a pin drop. I continued to walk in with my head held as high as I could. I could not understand it; I had done nothing. It was as if someone had spread some vicious rumors about me. I never did find out what the rumors were as I was abruptly moved to Florida my junior year. Then it happened again at college. The professors would mark me wrong on my tests, even though they knew that I had answered the questions correctly. When I confronted the professors, they said we know you answered the test questions correctly, but we just don't feel like marking a person of your background correctly. I would ask, 'What do you mean by a person of my background?' They would always be evasive, and when I appealed to the Honor Commission at the University, the answer would be invariably there is nothing that they could do. I even got accused of cheating when I had a perfect average in biochemistry. But I didn't cheat! I took the exams again and still got a perfect score with the professor sitting right next to me. It seems there has always been some secret kangaroo court against me. It happened in graduate school. One day I walked into the institute, and it was deserted! I went into my laboratory where my major professor, who truly was harassing me sexually and threatening that if I didn't go to bed with him he would withhold my Ph.D., and some administrator raked me over the coals for three hours. They accused me of all sorts of things; my major professor wanted everyone to believe I was having an affair with him! I guess it was some ego trip. They even tried to dissect my friendly behavior and put other connotations on it by interviewing all the men in my program and asking them if I flirted with them. I have always been an extrovert, and I was very enthusiastic about my work but not about my professor in any romantic sense. You know I might as well have had an affair with him, as everyone was convinced that I did." Marie sarcastically, "The way I handled the situation was to just stop talking to everyone, and eventually the Director of the Institute asked me why I refused to interact, and I explained that my major professor had mistaken my enthusiasm for science for him."

Marie continued her monolog. "Ultimately I got my Ph.D. because the director of the Institute ascertained from my exams that I *was* being graded unfairly. He even apologized to me, and said his faculty had failed me." Marie paused and looked pensive, "And then he said something that really did not make any sense at the time. He told me that I was the most talented young scientist that he had ever worked with in his 45 years in science. And he said that it just did not seem fair that after we worked you so much and you completed our special program that we would never be able to enjoy the fruits of all that hard work. So I asked him, "We? Who is we?" He ignored me and went on saying, "We had so hoped that you would be able to develop the new math system that would be a logical extension of some of the Dirac systems. And now that is not possible." I asked him, "Why not, sir? You just said I was a talented student, and I completed the program!"

He then said, "Marie, are you holding back from me?" And I replied, "What do you mean?" Then he said, "Who are you, Marie?" I was really taken aback, and I answered, "I'm me! I'm the same person." He then continued, "Well, we'll see, Marie. It's been an honor to teach you, but I guess we'll have to send you to the trenches with the ordinary scientists." He then said, "Who knows, maybe God will intervene, and this will all turn out well after all."

Marie looked at Jared who was beginning to slow down to enter a parking lot, "You know, I remember that scene as if it were yesterday. I looked at him and said, 'I promise you sir, I will not fail you. I will do what you ask and more!' He then just patted me on the shoulder and said he was throwing a small party in honor of the completion of my degree, and then I had to sign papers saying that I would not take my talents to a hostile government and that I promised to spend at least seven years in science." Jared remarked, "I've never heard of such papers. That's ridiculous." Marie continued as Jared parked the truck, "I thought all scientists signed papers like the ones I signed after their Ph.D. training." Jared turned to Marie, "No, that's not the case! I have trained over twenty doctoral students and none of them ever had to sign any papers, nor did I. Marie, very odd things always seem to happen to you!" Marie responded, "I know!"

Marie continued the discussion as they walked toward the restaurant. "The same weird stuff happened when I was hired for my first faculty position at Belford. I was getting along very well with the chairman of the department, and then all of a sudden he turned on me overnight. I asked a technician that I really respected if I had changed significantly in 24 hours, and he said no. But he then pointed out that he noticed the 180-degree turnaround of the Chairman and the other faculty members in the department. And from that time on the Chairman tried everything to publicly humiliate me. What was even more strange was that the Chairman's wife who taught me laboratory procedures suddenly sought me out with an attitude of extreme fear, and asked me if I was going to have her husband hurt. I thought she was bonkers and could not understand why she would ask me such a ridiculous question. I told her that the only one who would probably hurt her husband was her husband himself, because he was his own worst enemy. I then asked her why on earth she would even think I would hurt her husband?" She looked at me quizzically. I then answered her by saying that I did not understand her husband's change in attitude towards me, as I had the highest respect for his science and teaching excellence. I did add, however, that I felt her husband and I had similar personalities and we were prone to strong opinions and that this was why we probably clashed. She then just nodded her head."

They entered the restaurant and were immediately seated in a small booth. Marie paused for a moment as they settled in, "It's happening again! The whispers, people looking at me as if I am the worst criminal on the planet, accusing me of being a whore, and worse. They look at me as if I'm crazy, and they constantly gossip about me. And I do not even know these people. I can see it in their eyes, at the seminar too. It's as if there was some sort of a trial, and I was already tried and convicted of some unknown crime. The bottom line is I just don't fit with these people!" Jared said, "Don't go paranoid on me, Marie! I am sure your past bad experiences have nothing to do with the present situation." Marie replied, "Oh, no? I think they have everything to do with this continual character assassination and harassment that I have been going through for years now. And one day, I tell you, I *will* get to the bottom of it. I told you that I felt there was something weird associated with me. You know, I have tried to subdue that part of me that is more direct and gregarious than the average science personality. But I can't change my entire self to suit some personality profile that does well with my scientific peers."

Jared responded to Marie. "There is nothing wrong with you or your personality! You are not that much different than other young scientists at your level. But I must agree, someone or something is definitely tampering with your career and besmirching your integrity." Marie, "Let's not forget that the FBI called you when you started dating me and asked if you knew anything about my family." Jared replied, "That *was* weird." Marie asked, "Jared, why in the world would the FBI be interested in my family? My mother is a real estate broker and my grandfather is a retired small businessman. My grandmother is a homemaker, and my father is a retired physician whom I haven't seen for years. There is nothing abnormal about them." Jared asked, "Are you sure they're your real family?" Marie responding, "What do you mean? Of course they are my real family!" Jared stated, "From my observations you do not look or act like any of them." Marie asked, "Are you suggesting that I am adopted?" Jared continued, "I don't know. But something just does not add up. You told me about your experiences growing up. Ordinary people just do not have these kinds of unusual experiences. And you can't tell me that a 65 ct sapphire belongs to some ordinary person." Marie said, "But my family barely could make ends meet after my father flew the coop. But now that you mention it, there always seems to be unusual intrusions in my life by people that have some kind of background of wealth or power, but I never see it directly." Marie looked pensive, "Like the time I wound up with Prince Charles' suite at a hotel in London and everyone else wound up in the basement. I just thought I was unusually lucky! And by the way, I had no idea the sapphire was real. I used to wear it with my Halloween costumes. Jared agreed, "But that jeweler flipped out when he saw it." Marie added, "And I was just as shocked to find out it was real. So, you are ready to admit that someone or something is interfering in my life, and even today's disgusting episode may have been orchestrated for some unknown reason?"

Jared thought a moment and said, "Yes. Now I am certain that you are being interfered with. But I think it is more related to the work that we are doing with the veterans and prison guards and their families." Marie asked, "But you said I was just being paranoid." Jared responded, "You have to understand, I was frustrated. What with everything else that is going on, but I know that you are right, Baby, something is going on. My advice is to just be consistent in your behavior, but be persistent as you have always been." Marie said, "I guess it is pointless for me to meet with Augustus Blair about my application for a faculty appointment in the Pediatrics Division. No way will I get the appointment after today's debacle!" Jared advised her, "Marie, you have to keep that appointment just to prove to them that you are a professional." Marie agreed, "O.K., I know. But it's not going to be fun. And I have to face this meeting back-to-back with today's episode!" Jared was trying to reassure Marie, "It's not going to be that bad. You can do it!" Marie's mood lightened a bit, "You know what I hope? That my guardian angel will see me through this ordeal tomorrow." Jared asked, "What do you mean by your guardian angel?" He looked puzzled, "Like in the Bible?" Marie indicated, "Something like that, but not quite. It's funny, but I always told my mother that I feel as if someone or something is always there to bail me out of trouble at the last second." Jared agreed, "Yeah, like me!" Marie laughed and Jared wiped the tears from her cheek,

"I know, you're right. But I mean before I met you. There seemed to be a presence. Perhaps it's just my imagination."

Jared looked at Marie pensively. "I think, Marie, as strange as it seems, you may be on to something! Think? Did anyone ever use that term for you in your past? Was there anything that you might suspect may hold a key to your real identity?" Marie pondered a moment, "Jared, I just remembered it. Yes! A long time ago, a man gave me Lucky Lucius." Jared puzzled, "What?" Marie said, "You know, Jared, my lucky stuffed elephant that I held when I was sick. It's always been my good luck charm. I know you think it's silly for a scientist to be superstitious, but I've always had Lucky with me during every crisis in my life. When I asked my grandmother who the man was all those years ago in my bedroom at night, she said he was 'Charley', my guardian angel. At the time I was about four years old. My grandmother emphasized that I was his baby, and he was my special guardian angel." Jared asked, "Did you ever see Charley again?" Marie, "I can't remember, but when I told my mother that I always felt someone was watching over me, she said "One day he will reveal himself. I asked her how do you know it's a man?" She said, "I just know!"

Marie finally chuckled as they looked at the menu in the restaurant. "You know, I always felt I had a guardian angel. Lately, people in my family, particularly my long lost father whom I see occasionally, told me that I actually have a godfather who is mysterious and powerful. But I don't remember meeting such a person. Furthermore, I was raised Jewish, and we didn't have godfathers, or so I thought. It just does not make any sense!" Marie was now laughing slightly, "I sure hope that this godfather, the elusive guardian angel, will come and save me."

Jared looked at Marie. He was in deep thought. He was ready to say something but decided not to and instead shook his head. "That's the spirit! How 'bout we get a fabulous meal and plan what we are going to do after we finish our duties at the Cambridge meeting?" Marie now changed into a more positive attitude and excitedly asked, "Can we go to Stonehenge? Maybe Scotland?" Jared replied, "Why not?" He said this as he signaled the waiter at the restaurant that they were finally ready to order. He knew that they would both be in for a rough time over the next few weeks.

Jared thought to himself as Marie ordered that he will seek advise from one of the only senior administrators at the D. O. Madison that he could trust, Dr. Frank Cannon. Dr. Cannon had been a strong supporter of the McNichols' research on Gulf War Illnesses. He was a retired Air Force Colonel, and he was currently the chief physician of the hospital and the Vice President for Patient Care. Dr. Cannon knew that there was a major cover-up going on with the Gulf War veterans, and he did not believe in the DoD's explanation of PTSD. He also seemed to know quite a bit about some of the military's classified programs on Biological Weapons. Although he had not told Jared anything specific about what he thought may be causing Gulf War Illnesses, he had been urging Jared to continue on his and Marie's current line of investigation. Frank Cannon was an easy man to speak to. He was almost a father figure to some of the faculty, and he was very well-respected by the University system administration. Jared concluded that Dr. Cannon was the one person who could help him. In fact, he was probably the number one choice to eventually replace Dr. Masters when he retired. His advice would mean a lot to Jared in these troubled times.

CHAPTER 6

The Emperor Strikes Back (1995)

A murder in the house

On a fateful Thursday morning Jared was parking his pick-up truck on the ground floor in the parking structure that was almost directly in front of the D. O. Madison Cancer Center. As he got out of his truck a light-blue sporty Japanese coupe drove into the spot next to him. Quickly Dr. Frank Cannon jumped out of his car. He was somewhat agitated but he was a high-energy type individual, so Jared didn't think anything of it. It was just 6:00 AM and the parking lot was mostly empty, a very good time to arrive at work before parking became a major problem. This lot was reserved for faculty and administration of the D. O. Madison and the nearby Belford College of Medicine and its hospital. As was the case for almost every parking structure in the Medical Center, there were more subscribers than parking spaces due to some pinhead administrator's calculation that at any one time a few of the faculty and administrators would be out of town and not using their spaces. So additional cars could be assigned to the same area making for a messy scene later in the morning.

It was Dr. Cannon who always arrived at his office before 6:15 AM to get a start on the day's problems before the bulk of the morning shift arrived at about 7 AM. Dr. Cannon smiled and spoke first, "Good morning, Dr. McNichols." He wanted to have a word with Jared anyway, and this was good because they could talk privately while they both headed into the Cancer Center through a side door on the ground floor of the hospital. Jared smiled and returned the salutation, "Good morning, Dr. Cannon." Dr. Cannon said as he grabbed his briefcase and locked his car, "Jared, I need to have a brief word with you. Can you walk with me to my office?" Jared replied, "Certainly. I wanted to make an appointment to speak with you."

Dr. Cannon spoke first as they walked to the door of the building, "I need to talk to you about your work with the Gulf War veterans and find out what I can do to assist you in your efforts." Dr. Cannon did not have to explain to Jared his interest since as a retired U. S. Air Force Colonel, he was especially interested in the research that Jared and Marie were conducting on the Gulf War veterans. As it turned out, Dr. Cannon had friends and colleagues that were veterans of the War and came back with unknown illnesses, and although this was not his area as a hospital administrator in the Air Force, he knew the military and some of its secrets, and he was keenly interested in helping Jared and Marie in any way possible.

Frank Cannon also knew from the Pentagon's response to what the press was calling Gulf War Syndrome that something was very, very wrong. Dr. Cannon asked, "Jared, tell me what you found with the blood samples that you have been receiving from the Special Forces?" Jared stopped and looked at Dr. Cannon and replied, "How did you know about that?" Dr. Cannon smiled, "It's all over the Administration, and I have to say, it has caused quite a stir." Jared responded, "Why would the Administration care about one little pilot research project?" Dr. Cannon did not answer but asked, "Tell me what you have found, and then I'll tell you what I know." Jared replied back to Dr. Cannon, "O.K., we found that just under one-half of the blood samples show evidence of a blood infection that could explain the problem." Dr. Cannon, "Tell me exactly what you found." Jared replied, "We found *Mycoplasma fermentans incognitus*, an unusual intracellular bacterial infection in the blood samples. This is the same organism that the U. S. Army Institute for Pathology Research has done a lot of work on. They just had a patent issued titled 'Pathogenic Mycoplasma.'" At this point Dr. Cannon's eyebrows went up, and he stopped and looked directly at Jared for a moment. He then responded, "Do you have any idea where they could have gotten this infection?" Jared answered, "No. But there are a number of possibilities, including the multiple vaccines that were given during deployment."

Dr. Cannon sighed and then quietly told Jared in a rather fatherly way as they were walking, "Jared, I know that you and your wife are trying to do the right thing with this problem, and I fully support what you are doing, but there are some in the Administration that don't want you to find anything, especially Mfi. Do you understand?" Jared stopped and quickly responded, "You know about Mfi?" Dr. Cannon replied, "If you are high up enough in the military ladder like I was, you know about it but you don't talk about it. I really can't tell you that much because it's still classified, and I can't discuss it, but I want you to continue your work. For your own good, though, I don't want you to talk about it to anyone. If I can, I will help you publish what you have found and disseminate the information to the appropriate places. At the right time, please come to me. I may even be able to find some minor funds to help with some supplies, but this will have to be done through me personally. We will have to be fairly quiet about what we're doing and try not to aggravate the situation. I have been trying to cover for you upstairs but I have to be honest with you, this is going to be a war."

Jared was completely taken aback and almost shaken by Dr. Cannon's use of the term 'war.' The connotation was that there were going to be casualties, and Jared did not want to be the first one. This was an entirely new slant on their research. It was usually difficult enough actually doing the research and finding the money to support the research without one's own institution going to war against a faculty member for conducting research that should be considered a completely worthwhile project. How could the Administration know and care so much about this one little pilot project, and why would they even get so involved. They didn't care about any of the other projects that he and his department were involved in, even those that resulted in awards. They only seemed to care if they could use the research for PR or fund-raising events.

Jared decided to ask Frank Cannon for more information. "Dr. Cannon, have they been following my research on this for some time?" Dr. Cannon replied, "Yes they have, and to be honest with you, they are not particularly pleased with your results. You're going to have to be very careful from this point on. I would not speak openly on this subject to any of the faculty in your department." Jared asked, "Why, are *they* ratting on me to the Administration?" Dr. Cannon, "Some of them were told to find out what you are up to. The Administration knows just about everything that you are doing .... and who you're talking to." Jared asked, "Who in the

Administration?" Dr. Cannon just smiled, "This goes right to the top." Jared asked again, "Why don't they just ask me directly? I've got nothing to hide!" Dr. Cannon looked at Jared, "There is a lot that you don't know about what's going on in the Medical Center, and some of it is very bad. It's bad for the institutions, it's bad for the State and it's bad for the American public." Jared asked, "Can't you give me hint about what's going on?"

Dr. Cannon stopped, smiled and continued the conversation. "I just returned from the System Administration, and they are very concerned about what's going on in our institutions here in the Medical Center, from the moral, legal and public relations perspectives. I have to be honest with you, there are going to be some major changes in the Administration here at the Madison, and this may be occurring rather quickly." Jared stated, "That's interesting! And this has something to do with our research?" Dr. Cannon, "Not directly. But it has to do with a number of the classified research projects that the Medical Center has been involved in for several years. Many feel that these projects are not in the best interests of our Medical Center, even though they have brought in a significant amount of dollars into our research programs. Now that I am a civilian again, I don't want us to get involved in classified projects that do not have our Armed Forces best interests in mind. We need to be doing positive things that have a positive impact on society. That's about all I can really tell you at the moment, but I am sure that it will all be very clear to you when it happens."

Dr. Cannon's comments stimulated Jared's curiosity. "What I want you to do is continue your research, but keep it low key, and be sure to avoid the press for the moment. There is nothing that incites the Administration more than press reports that they can't control." Jared responded defensively, "We really have no control over the press and what they write, but I see your point. Some people have told us that the press may actually help protect what we are doing by bringing it out into the open." Dr. Cannon replied, "I understand what you say, but I have to warn you that the press has their own agenda, and they really don't give a damn about the consequences of what they write about you and your wife." Jared agreed, "I will keep that in mind, Dr. Cannon."

Jared reflected a moment about what Dr. Cannon had told him. "You know, when I took over the old Virology Department and merged it into my department, there were a lot of rumors about the research that was going on before the Chairman suddenly died. Many of the projects involved testing viral and bacterial isolates, and some of older employees suggested to me that this was done using human volunteers. Does some of this have to with the prison system?" Dr. Cannon smiled and said as he turned to go into his office, "You're on the right track. I'm sure you will figure it out." Jared just stood there as Dr. Cannon continued into his office. As he turned he told Jared, "Remember, Jared, be very careful and keep any new information to yourself. Keep me informed, and I will try to defuse this at the upper levels."

A fateful morning

As Dr. Cannon entered his outer office and said good morning to his secretary and other staff that always arrived just before him, he hesitated for a moment, checked his mail and went directly to his private office. Dr. Cannon always started his workday with military efficiency, probably just like he had for the last 25 years. Jared turned and continued through the building. From the ground floor he had to circumnavigate a maze of halls, go up one floor so that he could access the Research Building, and then take an elevator to the ninth floor. Meanwhile, back in Dr. Cannon's office a non-descript man in his mid–to late-thirties entered the office and told Dr. Cannon's secretary that he had an appointment with Dr. Cannon. The secretary looked at her daily calendar but by the time she looked up he had already entered Dr. Cannon's office.

Dr. Cannon often worked at a large table in the middle of his office in the morning. In this way he could spread out his work and organize it for the day's duties. The dark-haired man asked for Dr. Cannon as he entered the office. As Dr. Cannon began to turn around in his chair, he was immediately struck with the first bullet. It hit him right in the back of the neck. He was paralyzed from the impact, and before he could do anything the second, third, forth and fifth bullets hit him in the back of the head and shoulder. A sixth bullet wasn't necessary but exploded in the back of his head anyway. It didn't sound like much. In the case of Dr. Cannon's homicide, a 25-caliber automatic with half-loaded dum-dum bullets was used. They don't make much more sound than a pop because of the reduced loads, but at close range they were very lethal, in fact even more lethal than full loads because they don't just go through their intended target and out the other side. They did a maximum amount of internal damage.

The dark-haired professional was only a foot or two away from Dr. Cannon's head, and the bullets exploded inside his skull and neck. Dr. Frank Cannon was dead before his head hit his table. His blood covered the paperwork that Frank expected to complete that morning before the usual staff meetings at 7 AM. As he turned to leave, the dark-haired man dropped the weapon and then told the secretary in a calm voice, "I think you'd better call a doctor."

The perpetrator then continued out the office outer door, down the hall, around the corner and through the maze of halls into the cafeteria. From the cafeteria he entered the kitchen, walked calmly by the employees who thought nothing of the dark-haired, casually dressed man, and he exited out through a back loading dock. In the entire process from entry to exit, the dark-haired man avoided every security camera that had been placed on each and every entry and exit at the hospital to prevent theft. It was a well planned and executed professional assassination.

The homicide would never be solved, and it would not be the last unexplained death at the D. O. Madison. Jared had lost a good friend and strong ally in Dr. Cannon, and it was humbling, considering the last conversation that he had with Frank minutes before his murder. In fact, Jared would be the last person to speak at any length with Frank before his death. Since no one knew of the conversation, Jared reluctantly decided to keep their meeting that morning secret and not tell the police. He had a very bad feeling about going to the police, and to reveal what had taken place before Dr. Cannon entered his office would have probably just resulted in another murder at the Cancer Center–this time Jared's–and it would not have helped the police solve the crime. Besides, the University Police worked for Dr. Masters. They reported directly to him, and in this case Dr. Masters wanted to know everything that the police knew about the murder of his deputy right in Dr. Masters' own institution.

Jared had no way of proving who was behind the murder, but he had his suspicions, and contrary to the Administration that was quietly blaming an Iranian family who had a mother with terminal cancer that was not admitted to the hospital earlier that week by Dr. Cannon, Jared felt that the top 'perp' was Dr. Masters himself. After all, it was Dr. Cannon that said he

was just back from the System Administration and that there were going to
be some major changes at the top of The Madison.

The buck stopped with Dr. Clement Masters, the 'esteemed' President
of the Cancer Center. Jared would discuss his conversation with no one
except Marie, who completely agreed with him that it was probably Dr.
Masters who had Dr. Cannon killed because he was a direct threat to
Master's position. They had no proof whatsoever for their suspicions but
they were sure about who was behind the hit. This was all the motive that
Dr. Masters needed, and Jared and Marie would try not to give him a
motive to murder them as well. From that time on Jared had a completely
different feeling about the famous D. O. Madison Cancer Center. Marie
already hated the place, but now Jared would reluctantly come to the same
decision. The question was what to do about it while trying to survive at
the same time.

An anguished Administration

The outpouring of grief for Dr. Frank Cannon was truly genuine, at least
for most of the faculty and all of Frank's close colleagues, for Dr. Cannon
was very well liked, and in fact, he was much more liked by the faculty than
Dr. Masters himself. Dr. Masters would pull out all of the stops to
demonstrate his 'anguish' over the death of one of his top deputies, right in
the hospital on a day in which Dr. Masters was conveniently out of town.
There was extensive press coverage of the incident, and it brought so
much attention to the Cancer Center that the University System
Administration was concerned, especially in light of the meetings that Dr.
Cannon had just had with the System.

Although Dr. Masters acted like an emperor who had lost a valuable
underling, the System Administration actually came down hard on Dr.
Masters, which was actually good for Jared and Marie who were also at risk
to succumb to the same fate as Dr. Cannon. In response to the murder of
Dr. Frank Cannon, Dr. Masters directed The D. O. Madison to undergo a
series of very public but entirely cosmetic changes. After beefing up security,
something that Dr. Masters had wanted to do anyway, there were some
changes in procedures to make the Cancer Center 'safer' for faculty and
staff. There were even meetings with the faculty and separately with staff

on how to improve security and prevent anything like this from every happening again. However, behind the scenes Dr. Masters made sure that there was nothing done to continue the System Administration's movement to remove him and some of his key deputies. He had pulled it off with a minimum of collateral damage.

With his political pull, Dr. Masters had fought off the challenge from Dr. Cannon's supporters in the System Administration, and few would ever suspect at the Cancer Center that the real murderer was still among them and was just as dangerous as ever. Dr. Masters also used the murder of Dr. Cannon to increase the surveillance on certain faculty members who he considered a threat to the Administration, and among these were the McNichols. The McNichols were not the only employees on the 'hit list,' and there would be other 'unexplained deaths' at The D. O. Madison that would never be tied to Dr. Masters or his henchmen. They were very good at covering their tracks, and they knew the weaknesses of their targets. They also knew that no one would ever actually believe that anything like this could happen at a major academic institution in America. They were counting on that to deflect any suspicions that might arise from the families of the assassinated employees. The Madison had become a very dangerous place for certain faculty members, especially Jared and Marie, and as it turned out, some of their close colleagues.

The D. O. Madison Administration is on the attack

Now that a major detractor of Dr. Masters had been removed from the equation, he was free to continue consolidating his power and removing anyone else who might be a threat. However, Dr. Masters did not expect the outpouring of concern for Dr. Cannon or for the incident itself. He would have to be more careful in the future. A different approach would be absolutely necessary for any future threats.

After a brief respite to let the smoke settle, Dr. Masters decided to continue his program to remove Dr. Jared McNichols from his position and therefore Dr. Marie McNichols as well. In order to do this a meeting was called to discuss the McNichols problem in his office at the D. O. Madison Cancer Center administration building. As the participants arrived at the President's Office, Mrs. Broderick buzzed Dr. Masters, "Dr. Masters,

Drs. Belcher and Geldter are ready to meet with you now." Dr. Masters replied into the intercom, "Thank you, Carol, wait one minute and then send them in."

Dr. Masters' office was that of a top executive, with the furniture and artwork associated with his administrative rank, expensive but not opulent in appearance. There were pictures on the wall of Dr. Masters with former U. S. presidents and governors of Texas, and there was a case with various memorabilia, even a football from a championship State University team. The office also provided a beautiful view of Austin Park and the large Medical Center. Dr. Masters, a tall, painfully thin man with wavy gray hair and steel blue eyes had a somewhat withered look about him, but he was considered very distinguished in appearance. He had the air of someone who was accustomed to getting his way. He insisted at always being the center of attention, except when he was fund-raising, and he thrived on the adulation of his underlings and the general public.

Dr. Masters stood up and walked over to the large window at one end of his office. He stared out the window and began talking to himself. He was actually a closet sociopath who had a quiet disregard for his fellow man, and he was entirely used to getting his way. He did not like dissent or people who might have a different viewpoint from his. However, he was very, very good at hiding his real feelings as any good politician should. Dr. Masters said quietly to himself as he looked out of his window, "Well old-boy, you've come a long way from the back hills of Northern Mississippi. Imagine bullshitting those naive, but filthy rich Texas oil families into believing they had to give over their millions for my very own building program. I will have built the biggest Cancer hospital in the world by the time I retire. And you know what they say about Texas being the biggest and the best. What a legacy. Nobody has been able to do what I have done! I want the biggest cancer hospital in the world to be named after me."

Just then the door opened and Dr. Masters turned to greet his visitors. He was always impeccably dressed, and his gestures and movements were always choreographed to place visitors, colleagues and foes at ease at all times. Dr. Masters had always prided himself on his political savvy and ability to influence important people to his way of thinking. Almost all of his colleagues and even his superiors in the University administration felt that his ego was unbearable, but he was usually cleaver enough to hide it on most occasions by being very friendly and personal and seeming to be modest and soul searching. In fact, he was quite the opposite, and he prided himself on being able to con even his most ardent detractors and convince them that his way and methods were superior. Over the years this had placed him at odds with the University System Administration, and they had learned not to trust his smooth style. He was actually demoted to his current position from the head of a university system in another state because of charges of misappropriation and improper use of university funds, but the charges were covered-up to prevent the complete embarrassment of the university in the press. Dr. Masters used this to his advantage with subtle hints that he would expose the University to the press unless he was assisted in finding a suitable position instead of being dismissed on the spot as any other employee would have been. Thus Dr. Masters ended up in Austin, Texas, and although he was no longer the top administrator in the university system, he did manage to find a suitable job in the D. O. Madison Cancer Center. Even though the committee that was charged with recommending candidates to his current position passed him over, somehow Dr. Masters bypassed the committee and found support at the state and national level for his appointment. The rest was history.

Dr. Masters was a survivor, and he knew how to use people. He was always aware of how to act in each situation to please his guests, even if he loathed them, and he moved to the door to greet his visitors with a large smile on his face, "Good morning gentlemen." Dr. Geldter moved quickly to come in first, since he was a blowhard of a person who just couldn't wait to impress everyone. But his superiors knew him all too well. "Everything is just great Dr. Masters! Amy and I just got back from the cancer meetings, and it was quite a triumph for us as usual. Our presentations dominated the meeting." Dr. Masters smiled and cut Dr. Geldter off as he placed his hand on his shoulder and gently pushed him into his office. He had grown weary of Geldter's attitude, and he didn't like Jews. Once the participants were all in his office, he turned to Dr. Belcher, his Vice President for Research, who was a closet Jew with a witty smile on his face, "Francis, how about you?" Dr. Belcher responded, "Unfortunately, I had to miss the meeting. I had a conflict with my commitments involving our joint research ventures with the European Academy of Sciences. As you know I am going to be elected to the Academy for my superb work, and . . . ." Dr. Masters interrupted him abruptly, "Francis, Isaac–Please! Sit down."

Dr. Masters pointed to where he wanted his group to sit down, in this case around his coffee table. He must control the situation completely, and he didn't want blowhards like Belcher and Geldter taking the limelight. He actually hated his Vice President for Research almost as much as Dr. Geldter, but he needed Dr. Belcher in particular for East Coast credibility since Dr. Masters grew up and was educated in the back woods of Northern Mississippi, in what most people would describe as 'hillbilly' heaven. He obtained his M.D. degree from a Tennessee university, and Dr. Masters had almost no credibility with the East Coast academic snobs. "I have called you here, because I have some urgent business to discuss with you that is of a highly confidential nature." Dr. Masters continued in a very dictatorial and self-important manner. He signaled Drs. Belcher and Geldter, who were still milling around to sit down around the coffee table in his office.

Dr. Masters waited until everyone was arranged to his liking, and then he started his introduction. "I've just been talking with a very important former government official who is one of the owners of one of the Belford spin-off microbiology companies." Not to be outdone, Dr. Belcher interrupted in an incredulous manner, "Dr. Masters, are we going to know the identity of this 'important' former official? I don't know if we should involve ourselves with some questionable commercial ventures of Belford?" Dr. Masters flashed his eyes toward Dr. Belcher and stated in a superior and sarcastic tone without raising his voice, "That's not important, Francis. He has asked for our assistance on a critical mission. A mission that may impact on the very fabric of our society at the highest levels." Both Drs. Geldter and Belcher scoff at the thought that there might be anyone more important than themselves, but they listen with some intensity even though they know that Masters likes to make even mundane matters seem very dramatic. Dr. Masters continued, "We have a situation that calls for extreme measures. It involves one of our more senior staff members and his wife. It appears that they have stumbled on some of our more classified research programs with Belford and are now a threat to National Security . . . . so we have been entrusted with, let's say, 'correcting' the situation. Dr. Geldter asked immediately, "You mean, Dr.

Masters . . . . I think I know exactly what you mean, and are we 'correcting' the situation or the persons?"

The entire group became silent for a moment, when Dr. Belcher broke the silence in his whinny voice. "I don't know, Clement, I don't think I want to know about any such classified programs at Belford. I asked you not to involve me in any programs that do not appear in my job description!" Dr. Masters showed subtle signs of losing his patience by staring out his window with his customary blank stare, but he managed to keep a smile on his face, "Oh keep quiet Francis, or I will arrange for you to have a new job description! One that you won't like at all." Dr. Masters face was growing red, and he didn't like to have anyone see him lose his cool during a discussion, particularly one that he initiated. He quickly cooled down and continued with a smile, "It seems that several attempts to 'correct' these individuals have failed . . . . Even that Russian Doll cocktail that was given at the Meyerhoff Conference a few years ago by our colleagues at Belford."

Everyone in the room perked up at the mention of an attempted murder. Dr. Geldter who was suddenly less arrogant became defensive, gesturing to Dr. Masters, "I do not understand how that happened. I swear to God already; It's not my fault. They blew it. They didn't follow my instructions." Dr. Masters flashed back a look of distain and interjected, "Are you saying you were aware of this?" Dr. Geldter now realized that Dr. Masters may not have been aware how intimately involved he was in the failed plot, so his style changed completely, and he reverted back to his usual arrogant self, "Well, I know about some 'rumors' as well as the means."

Drs. Masters and Belcher didn't believe for a minute that Dr. Geldter was not involved in the failed plot, but they let him complain until Dr. Masters interrupted, "Continue, Isaac, but be more specific." Dr. Geldter who was now hoping to avoid this particular discussion, "Pardon, Dr. Masters?" Dr. Geldter suddenly became more polite. Dr. Masters was again on the offensive, "Why do you not understand what I am asking?" Dr. Geldter replied as if to explain why he had completely flip-flopped in his conversation, "Oh, yes. As I was going to say, Dr. Masters, I do not understand why that particular cocktail failed. Dr. Geldter flipped back to his previous style, one that couldn't be stopped when he started expounding on how important his science is to the grand scheme of the universe. "I developed the macrophage inhibitors myself to suppress the immune responses to the agent. It should have been foolproof. Even Shlomo Ricin told me my work was brilliant. He also said that it should have been foolproof."

Dr. Masters was becoming impatient because Dr. Geldter had not answered his question. "Who is this Shlomo Ricin?" Dr. Geldter answered, "My good friend and advisor on several projects at the Black Building. He is a professor at Massada University in Jerusalem and probably the leading expert in these things, except for me, of course. I am the leading authority in this and many other areas." Masters was becoming irritated, "Well, Isaac, stop day dreaming!" Dr. Geldter was taken aback at the rare criticism but responded in style, "I beg your pardon, Dr. Masters."

Dr. Masters was now irritated, and he was also becoming sarcastic. "The cocktail failed, didn't it? So much for your 'leading expert' theory." Dr. Geldter responded to the criticism as if he doesn't believe that it could ever happen to him, so he quickly dismissed the comment and went on the offensive with his usual chutzpah, "I strongly doubt that they used it correctly. According to my studies, it should have been a slam dunk. Who is our current target?" Dr. Masters answered, "Jared McNichols and someone in his department . . . a person named Marie." Dr. Masters was examining a file folder pretending that he did not know Marie, but everyone in his office knew otherwise. Dr. Geldter interrupting said provocatively, "Marie! You mean Marie McNichols." He paused and gesticulated with his arms while his face turned red, "The bitch that Jared McNichols married! Dr. Masters, she's a light-weight scientist who has an over-inflated opinion of herself. Why bother! I was hoping that you would let me go after Jared McNichols again. He has been a pain in my side for some time." Masters responded, "Well, Isaac your job is not to question me but to devise the means . . . . and preferably this time you'll get it right!"

Dr. Masters thought silently to himself—And I don't want to have to use some crude approach like the one that I had to use on Frank Cannon. Dr. Masters now continued, "We have had someone go to the System Administration with some unproven allegations that the D. O. Madison was involved with Belford in some illegal human experiments using the prison system and local biotechnology companies owned by some very prominent public figures. Now we have an embarrassing situation right in my own hospital. Another homicide may not go down well with the System

Administration." The obvious execution-style murder had brought tremendous pressure and public scrutiny of the D. O. Madison Cancer Center, but as usual Dr. Masters had deflected the entire incident as an outrage to humanity by some crazed Iranian terrorists.

Dr. Francis Belcher was looking at his two colleagues with a nervous and stunned expression. He covered his ears in a gesture and told them, "I didn't hear any of this! Don't involve me in any of these questionable activities! I want to go on record as not being for this approach to the problem." Dr. Belcher can easily see himself in the same situation as Dr. Frank Cannon, and he was very nervous but would go along with whatever Dr. Masters decides. After all, Dr. Belcher benefited from Frank Cannon's misfortune, since the rumors at Belford suggested that the System Administration was going to replace all of the top administrators at The Madison. However, the rumors stopped after the loss of Dr. Cannon. Suddenly there was no one at his level to rat on Dr. Masters and his henchmen.

Dr. Masters was growing wary of Dr. Belcher. "Francis, I told you before to watch what you say! You have been involved in this from the start!" Dr. Belcher who was now visibly shaking said, "I don't want to know the details! I was only involved in blocking Marie's and Jared's grant applications, presentations and publications and placing some doubt on their research! You said that you wanted them both out of here as soon as possible. I did exactly what you asked. I didn't question the wisdom of this before." Dr. Belcher did not want to bring up the Frank Cannon incident. He was still afraid that Dr. Masters might some day use that same approach on his Vice President for Research.

At this point in time Dr. Masters was becoming slightly angry with his colleagues. "All right, Francis, all right. Let me explain the intense desire of certain individuals to see a conclusion to this problem, and I am not just referring to their accelerated departure from the Cancer Center. Marie happens to be an heiress, and certain special interest groups in Las Vegas who are involved with major defense contractors through a variety of investments do not want to see her inherit. In addition, the McNichols have found out way too much about our projects with Belford and the prison system." Dr. Belcher suddenly gaped at Dr. Masters, "Are you serious? Marie an heiress? I heard the rumors but I didn't believe it." He then became very pensive and timidly asked Dr. Masters, "Is it Marie's inheritance that is funding certain . . . sensitive projects?" Dr. Masters shot back, "Goddamn it Francis, must I repeat myself?" Dr. Belcher asked, "Then shouldn't we be nice to her, and it wouldn't hurt for future donations . . . ." Dr. Masters interrupted Francis before he could finish. "Haven't you been listening to a word I've been saying Francis? There are some that do not view Marie or Jared McNichols as players on our field." Dr. Belcher asked, "With all due respect, sir, why is Marie viewed as such a threat? She doesn't have any power or position. And if she is this heiress as you say . . . ."

Dr. Masters impatiently continued his monolog and he muttered, "Not yet, if I have anything to say about it. It's not the concern of anyone here, but her family is a blight on this planet, and their knowledge of our prison research threatens National Security. The last person around here that threatened our 'National Security' interests had an untimely fate!" The others in the room were dumbfounded at Masters' maniacal diatribe, but they were also too weak and effete to do anything except stare at him. Dr. Belcher was thus quickly reminded of the fate of his colleague Dr. Cannon, but he decided to interject again anyway in his whiny voice, "I don't know, Dr. Masters, but I would not like to be a party to this no matter who made the request. No sir, not for some political agenda I do not understand, nor believe to be anywhere near the truth." Dr. Geldter, who knew much more than Dr. Belcher about the prison research programs, was also growing impatient with Francis. "Dr. Masters, if I may interject. Perhaps we need someone like me in a more commanding position here at The Madison. Dr. Masters, I sent you several memos on this subject, and . . . ." Dr. Masters replied scornfully, "This is not the time to discuss promotions, Isaac!" Dr. Belcher reminded them, "Jared is so well known around the world; this could cause a real PR problem coming after Frank's homicide."

At the word homicide, Dr. Masters smiled as if he knew something that the others didn't. In fact, it was Clement himself that arranged for Dr. Frank Cannon's murder to remove a direct challenge to his position. Dr. Belcher continued, "Marie did an excellent job teaching physical chemistry to our physicians, and her Gene Tracking technology is, in my opinion . . ." Dr. Geldter interrupted Dr. Belcher, "That bullshit approach! My graduate students can do better than that!" Dr. Belcher then stated, "Causing any harm to one of our top scientists could be hard to explain but to his wife at the same time . . . ." Dr. Geldter interrupted, "He is bullshit already, and his department should have been merged under my chairmanship years ago as I have suggested before to you Dr. Masters. In fact, I have sent you several memos . . . ."

Dr. Masters didn't let Isaac Geldter finish. He held up his hand to cut off Geldter. He was growing increasingly annoyed and turned to Dr. Belcher, "Listen to me carefully, Dr. Belcher, if you want to keep your job and your precious lifestyle, you should get with the program or to put it more bluntly, you're straining our administrative budget." Dr. Geldter interjected again, "Sir, I have no problem with this assignment. Especially since Jared is a competitor and I consider Marie an enemy of Israel. One slip of a little girl and one department chairman should not make a difference in the general scheme of things." Dr. Belcher then tentatively stated, "If she is such an enemy of Israel, why is she an honorary Lieutenant General in the IDF?" Dr. Geldter ignored Dr. Belcher's comment.

Dr. Masters was at first taken aback by Dr. Geldter's reference to Israel, because he hated Israelis and Jews, but he raised both hands, smiled, and addressed the gathering, "I knew I could count on you both." But Dr. Belcher in a whiny voice still disagreed with the plan. "I don't know, Clement, I don't make enough salary for this type of project." Dr. Masters gave a scathing look directly at Dr. Belcher in an attempt to shut him up. But Dr. Belcher asked again, this time more nervous than before, "Are you sure about Marie being an heiress? Let's look at this objectively Clement. If her family is so rich and powerful, why have we been able to successfully block any appointments at your request? And we have been able to do a rather thorough character assassination, again at your request?"

Dr. Masters was irritated again by the constant interruptions, and he turned again to Dr. Belcher. "Damn it Francis, that is none of your business. I have my reasons." Dr. Geldter interrupted again, "I have no problem with this assignment, Dr. Masters, but I should be compensated for my enhanced job description." Dr. Masters ignored Dr. Geldter, who he considered just another blow-hard Jew. But Dr. Masters hid his contempt for Isaac and Francis completely. After all, he needed people like Francis Belcher and Isaac Geldter. Dr. Belcher tentatively asked, "Your motives, Clement, are they entirely based on Marie's and Jared's threat? Clement, did she reject you?" Dr. Belcher was referring to the widely circulated rumor that Dr. Masters himself tried to seduce Marie before she married Jared McNichol.

Dr. Masters was now visibly irritated, and his face turned red. He rarely raised his voice, but this time he replied sharply with a red face. "Dr. Belcher, I have had enough of your disgusting innuendos. You are nothing more that a little prick who is on the verge of being replaced. Do you want to leave this office with Isaac in your position? Now, I will overlook your unbelievable insult only because you have demonstrated in the past your somewhat tarnished but nonetheless loyalty to my administration."

The assembled group was stunned. They had not seen this side of their president, and they didn't dare interrupt Dr. Masters, except for Dr. Geldter, who was now more confident than ever of his new position with Dr. Masters and with Dr. Belcher's future demise. "Sir, I am completely loyal to your administration, and I am ready to do whatever you decide is necessary." Masters said abruptly, "Let's get back on track with my directive and take care of this problem." Dr. Belcher was now more subdued but still combative. "I still don't know why we have to do something so extreme. Jared is an important asset to our research program, and what did his wife ever do to warrant this approach? If she is an heiress, perhaps someday she stands to gain a great deal if she is not out of the picture. Who knows?" Dr. Geldter interrupted laughing, "Who cares? I say, let's get rid of both of them, and good riddance to bad rubbish."

Dr. Masters was trying to regain control of *his* meeting. "The bottom line is that it is our patriotic duty." Dr. Masters was actually sarcastic when he said the word 'patriotic' because he and everyone in the room knew that this was not true. The only 'duty' that he had was to himself and his self-preservation and avoidance of a future prison sentence. "I am sure there will be monetary and other rewards for us all if we are successful." Dr. Geldter continued in his efforts, "Dr. Masters, I am completely ready for this assignment. Perhaps I should contact some of my friends in the Mossad. You know, I was a decorated Army sniper in the '67 War." Dr. Masters again skeptical, "Good idea, Isaac." But his mood immediately changed. "But you were *never* a sniper, and you *never* received any decorations. In fact, you *never* even served in the '67 War, if you served at all, and I don't believe that you did, so don't inflate your record with me. Remember, I have your file." Dr. Geldter was slightly embarrassed that any one knew the truth about his lack of service in the Israeli Defense Forces, but he ignored Dr. Masters' comments. He had managed to fool almost everyone when he inflated his past accomplishments, but he returned to the matter at hand without missing a beat, "I hate these people; they're light-weights, and nobody is going to miss them, already."

Dr. Masters wondered why Dr. Geldter had slipped into almost pigeon English. Was it because of the deflating comments on Dr. Geldter's inflation of his military service? Now he knew how to keep Geldter completely under his control. Dr. Geldter would do exactly what he wants, because he does not want the world to know the complete fabrication of his Israeli military record. He turned to Dr. Belcher. "Well, Francis? Are you a team player?" Dr. Belcher answered, "Apparently I am, Clement, but I cannot be a direct participant in this. However, I am willing to continue the character assassination and professional muggings, as before. As you know, I am now on the NIH Cancer Advisory Board, and I can make sure that Jared's NIH grants will never be funded."

Dr. Geldter had suddenly regained his composure and he interrupted Dr. Belcher. "You can count on me, Dr. Masters, all the way." Dr. Masters said to the group decisively, "Good!" He looked at each of the participants. "I must be assured that this little discussion never gets beyond this door." Drs. Geldter and Belcher in an unsynchronized manner, "You have my word." "O.K., Clement."

Dr. Masters returned to the instructions he intended to give each participant. "Now, let's get down to business. Secret accounts will be established in each of our names at a bank in the Cayman Islands." Dr. Geldter immediately asked, "I need to know what bank and how much will be deposited." Dr. Masters was irritated again, "Not now, Isaac! You both will be reporting directly to me on the progress of our assignment, but not on the details. I have to have complete deniability on this. I don't want to know how you do it or when you do it; I am only interested in the results. You will work out the details among yourselves without involving or contacting me in any way. Is that completely clear?"

Dr. Clement Masters was a master at covering his tracks. Even with the remote chance that someone was caught in the act, he could deny everything and remain completely untouchable. Dr. Masters continued, "Now that's settled. I know that I can count on your complete cooperation. I repeat, I don't want to know any of the details, because my office cannot be involved in any way. You can handle this little project and discuss strategies among yourselves. It would be best if any situations occur while the subjects are out of the country. And I suggest a less messy, less traceable, event that might even look like a suicide. If you are successful at the professional and character assassinations, it might even seem reasonable. You know the old story . . . . A young, talented scientist is driven to despair by the rejection of her peers, and then her new husband is completely distraught over her loss."

Dr. Belcher who was still uncomfortable about the discussion of harming one of his faculty members continued, "Clement, don't make this out to be some Shakespearian drama. We arranged for heckling and interruptions of Marie's departmental lecture. We can make sure that she does not give another presentation in Austin. They are both traveling to Cambridge to some meeting." Dr. Masters said, "Good." Dr. Geldter interjected, "I don't understand why Jared McNichols was asked to give some bullshit lecture at Cambridge. I should be giving that lecture." Dr. Masters decided, "We just might be able to use this trip to our advantage. You could arrange something at the conference." Dr. Geldter added, "I have found out that Marie goes into anaphylactic shock if she eats asparagus." Dr. Masters asked, "How do you know that?" Dr. Geldter replied, "When she and Jared had dinner with us once she actually volunteered the information." Dr. Masters smiled, "Continue, Isaac." Dr. Geldter, "Perhaps we can arrange something for her at one of the meeting banquets. Remember, I am an expert on asparaginase, and I suggest this as a good approach." Dr. Masters replied, "That sounds like a possibility." Dr. Geldter bragging, "I have several publications on the subject."

Asparaginase, an enzyme isolated from asparagus, had been used to fight cancer in laboratory animals, but the approach never panned out in the clinic and was dropped as just another over-hyped research project of Isaac's that had gone by the wayside without any tangible legacy. However, Dr. Masters did not know this, and the others did not want to offer their opinion. "Yes, continue Isaac, but remember I don't want to know any of the details. This office must not be directly involved in any way." Dr. Geldter smiled and became excited, "We could use a macrophage inhibitor to block her ability to fight infection and a combination of microorganisms that we are working on at the Black Building." Masters asked, "I thought that was tried, and it failed." Dr. Geldter said, "But Dr. Masters, we did not include the asapraginase, let alone the bitch's allergy to asparagus."

Dr. Belcher had been listening with his hands over his ears pretending not to hear. He couldn't believe what he was hearing. He finally responded in a whiny voice, "We do not know that this approach will work and that the asparaginase will be immunosuppressive in this case. In fact, it could do just the opposite. And I haven't heard that Jared has any allergies." Dr. Geldter ignored the comment and arrogantly replied, "That's ridiculous! Of course the asparaginase will work. Who is the expert on asparaginase here, anyway?" Dr. Belcher responded, "You are assuming that the asparaginase will promote an inflammatory response, and we simply do not know this to be a fact." Dr. Masters finally interjected, "Listen Francis, Isaac has a possible approach to the problem. I like it."

Dr. Masters had been thinking to himself, and he raised his hand to his head. "All right. You should proceed with this approach. But remember, it has to be completely untraceable." Dr. Geldter said, "It will be! I'll contact Dr. Ricin and some of my friends in industry and in the Mossad to get some additional advice on the mixture. But I think that Dr. Ricin must be let in on this operation. We can arrange for some kind of travel award. He has been immensely valuable in his advisory capacity for our classified Army experiments with mycoplasmas and macrophage inhibitors."

Dr. Masters interjected abruptly, "Dammit, Isaac! I told you never to mention our classified Black Building program. If this information ever gets out, we would stand to lose a considerable amount of financial support." Dr. Masters knew that the off-ledger budget that is used to fund unconventional projects at the CIA and DoD that usually involve illegal activities and methods was commonly referred to as the Black Budget. Programs like MKULTRA and Manhattan II, highly questionable groups of projects involving unconventional weapons of mass destruction, were funded by the Black Budget. Dr. Belcher interjected, "As Vice President for Research, I should know the complete information on this line of investigation. Why wasn't my office appraised of this?" Dr. Geldter condescendingly replied, "Remember, you said that you didn't want to know any of the details, Francis! Make up your mind!" Dr. Masters continued, "Don't take it so personal, Francis. I don't even know the details, and I don't want to know them! My office should not be directly involved, and absolute secrecy must be maintained at all costs. If you must know, Francis, this program has been in place since 1973, well before you or I were even at The D. O. Madison. We are now in Phase IV of the Russian Doll Cocktail project directed by Dr. Geldter and Dr. Reichsmann, and they have been in close contact with our colleagues at the Belford as well as pharmaceutical companies and people like Dr. Ricin."

Although Dr. Belcher did not want to involve himself in such programs, he couldn't resist finding out some of the details. Dr. Belcher interrupted, "Russian doll cocktails? Why wasn't I appraised of this sooner? All I knew was that Dr. Geldter was conducting research for the government under our special biologicals program." Dr. Masters admonished Dr. Belcher, "These biological cocktails are analogous to the nested Russian dolls." Dr. Geldter smiling and interrupting, "You know, the doll within a doll and so forth." Dr. Geldter couldn't hold back any longer, "What Dr. Masters is trying to tell you, Francis, is that there are hidden ingredients in the cocktail which only together result in a lethal combination, one that is impossible to detect. It's the hidden ingredients that are the key here, already. They're perfect agents because of their stealth properties."

Dr. Belcher really did not want to hear any more, but he replied in a loud sarcastic tone that Dr. Masters ignored, "How marvelous!" Dr. Masters continued bragging, "In any event, The Madison is now in phase IV of its Russian Doll weaponization program. This phase of the program is perhaps the most crucial of the project because it involves classified clinical trials in our nursing homes outside of San Antonio and in the prison units around Wallsville. This is where we have a problem because some of the Wallsville prison employees have been in contact with the subjects in question."

Dr. Belcher became more and more uncomfortable. "Who in their right mind would agree to such a program?" Dr. Masters turned directly to Dr. Belcher and smiled, "Why *you* did, Francis! Don't be such an idiot. I have your signature on it. The subjects in our trials have no knowledge that they are being used for 'National Security' purposes. And it is all perfectly legal under Title 50. This also means that we don't have to use placebos or informed consent or have that damned FDA sniffing around. Don't forget, these are extremely important matters, and secrecy must be vigorously protected. We cannot afford to let anyone have the edge over us."

Dr. Belcher thought for a brief moment that Dr. Masters knew much more about these Black Budget programs than he thought. Although he knew vaguely what was going on in the M. K. Black Building under Dr. Geldter, he stayed far away from Dr. Reichsmann and the nursing homes outside of San Antonio. He did not want to know the details of what went on there, because it was not his direct concern. He asked sheepishly, "Has anyone considered the ethics in any of this?" Dr. Geldter sneered, "Ethics? Since when have you ever considered ethics?" Dr. Geldter continued, "It was my family that was wiped out in the Holocaust, while you were protected in that bullshit New York Jewish circle of yours." Dr. Masters quickly interrupted, "Isaac, your family was not wiped out in the Holocaust, so don't pull your Jewish sympathy schtick with me." Dr. Masters, who had taken on a self-important demeanor, had a smirk on his mouth. "However, I do agree with Isaac. Dr. Belcher, we are making very tough decisions here in order to preserve the true America." Dr. Belcher stated rather self rightously, "We are not at war, Clement!" Dr. Masters responded forcefully, "Dr. Belcher, we've always been at war." Dr. Belcher asked, "With all due respect, sir, why am I necessary to the success of this operation?" Dr. Masters sneered at Dr. Belcher, "You are the Vice President for Research, Dr. Belcher . . . . at least for the moment." Dr. Geldter quickly interjected, "Sir, I believe that I am ready to take on added administrative responsibilities." Dr. Belcher regained his senses and snapped back, "Remember, Dr. Geldter, you are still under me, or have you forgotten? I have the feeling that The D. O. Madison Cancer Center may be in over its head on this one."

Dr. Masters became angry at his subordinates. "Francis! You are promoting a very negative attitude, and you're an idiot if you can't see that we're in a silent war and we have been for the last 50 years." Dr. Belcher asked sarcastically, "With whom may I ask?" Dr. Masters responded, "With everyone and anyone who ever wanted our power and influence." Dr. Masters' demeanor then changed abruptly, and he became reflective, "I believe that we've lost our focus for this meeting, and we are going off on tangents here. Now where were we?" Dr. Geldter continued, "I believe that I was suggesting that we bring Dr. Ricin into our operation as he has demonstrated his usefulness with the operations in our nursing home studies." Dr. Masters slightly confused answered, "Right! That project has been running very smoothly thanks to first-rate organization between you, Dr. Reichsmann and that Ricin chap. We should make an effort to fly him here immediately! But I don't want you to ever speak on the phone about any of this, even in code. And we should routinely have Chief Costa sweep all our offices for any suspicious surveillance." Dr. Geldter then said, "You know, sir, it would not be a bad idea to include Amy in this endeavor. She is excellent at situations that may arise in conjunction with our personnel objective, and she is believable and charming. She'd be very useful with Marie, and she has been helping immensely with the discrediting of Marie and Jared." Dr. Masters responded, "Good idea, Isaac. Let's wrap this up. We do not have much time." Dr. Geldter had a big smile on his face and was basking in his glory.

Then Dr. Belcher recalled an important item. "The McNichols leave for England in a few weeks. I just reluctantly signed Jared's travel papers." Dr. Geldter said, "O.K., I'll contact Ricin immediately and book him on a flight to Austin, but we are going to have to offer him a reward if we are successful. In fact, we should all receive big bonuses for this project. And I will need more contingency support, and by the way, I was going to ask you about my salary this year. I only make one-half of what some of the surgeons around here make, and I feel that my contributions . . . ." Dr. Masters waved his hand and interrupted Isaac loudly, "Not now, Dr. Geldter!" Dr. Belcher was finally getting with the program, "I will contact some of my friends who are going to the Cambridge meeting and give them excellent reasons for interfering with the McNichols' presentations. I'll present their work as unreliable and a threat to established dogma. I have already been using my position on the Cancer Advisory Board to make sure that Jared's grants will have a very difficult time ever being funded." Dr. Masters with a self-satisfied smile, "Good! I have the utmost confidence in you boys. Let's remember, we are on an important mission, and professionalism must be maintained. Understood?" Dr. Masters stood up from his chair signaling the end of the meeting, "Don't fail me again. A lot is riding on this." Drs. Belcher and Geldter had just risen from their chairs, and they each shook Dr. Masters' hand and left the office smiling. At least Dr. Geldter was smiling, but Dr. Belcher frowned as soon as he turned away to leave the office. Dr. Masters turned, rubbed his hands together and looked out of his window as Drs. Belcher and Geldter exited his office. He thought to himself that this should be all wrapped up in a few weeks.

A visitor to the Texas Hill Country

Dr. Schlomo Ricin had just arrived in Austin, when Drs. Geldter, Belcher and Krappner decided to have a leisurely meeting with Dr. Ricin at a ranch due West of Austin at the edge of the Texas Hill Country where Isaac and Amy boarded their horses. Dr. Ricin was a non-descript-looking man with a gray beard shaped into a rather stubby goatee and was about 5 and one-half feet tall. He was thick-boned and had a strong Israeli accent. A picnic lunch was arranged after an early morning ride. Amy Krappner had just finished a rigorous ride and was showing off her riding ability to the group by jumping her horse. She was a proficient rider and was demonstrating that she could control her horse to clear a moderately difficult jump. Drs. Geldter, Belcher and Ricin were just pacing their horses in a walk after having just completed a vigorous run. After Amy's jump, she directed her horse at a brisk pace to the area where the others were dismounting from their horses.

As they dismounted, the laughing riders were engaged in typical horsy-set mannerisms. Dr. Ricin was patting his horse as was Dr. Belcher, who appeared afraid to get too close, and Dr. Geldter was giving his horse a sugar treat. Everyone was fully enjoying the lovely setting. Dr. Geldter finally spoke, "There's nothing like a good early morning ride to clear the cobwebs." As he patted his horse, Dr. Geldter was admiring it, and he beseechingly said to Drs. Krappner and Ricin, "Isn't she a beauty?" The horse was black with a white star on its face. "She stands 17-hands high! You know she has the Rose of England blood in her! And to think that those stupid Texans with their Polo on the Plains fund raiser actually bought this for my personal use. I call her my veterinary laboratory assistant in my department budget!"

Dr. Belcher was not a natural with horses. He reminded Dr. Geldter, "Isaac, I wouldn't brag if I were you about your department accounting procedures. Some day, someone might just look more carefully into your books. And while I appreciate your infatuation with your equine friend, quite frankly, I am just not so horse-crazy." Dr. Geldter answered, "By the way, Francis, you have a lot more to hide than I do!" Dr. Belcher replied, "You know, Isaac, last week I had a difficult time hiding your special rosewood furniture from the press. It seems they got wind that you spent over $160,000 on your new custom office furniture, and I had to cover for you and pretend that it was all an accounting mistake. Then there was the condo that you placed on your department budget." Dr. Geldter angrily replied, "But we use that so that we can attend those bullshit Monday morning meetings of Dr. Masters. Do you know how long it takes us to drive in each morning? Besides, we use it for department visitors like Schlomo here." Dr. Belcher continued, "Well, it's pretty difficult defending your department budget, and there's the complete furnishing of a condo just for your convenience. However, I convinced them that the whole story was ridiculous, but you had better show me more respect or I just might tell them the truth next time."

Dr. Ricin changed the subject. "Dr. Belcher, it sounds like you didn't have much fun riding!" Dr. Belcher replied, "So-so! I am more the New York theater rather than the horsey type. This is different, but give me 5th Avenue any day. You know, I used to live on 5th Avenue." Dr. Geldter chuckled as if he didn't believe a word of it. "You mean Brooklyn! How about you Schlomo?" Dr. Ricin answered, "Me? I love horses! In Israel I take a brisk ride around the hills above Jerusalem, and there is something breathtaking about riding a horse through the desert around Eilat. It makes me feel like Lawrence of Arabia, minus the camels, of course. By the way, tell me again how do you manage to have your institution pay for these fine horses?" Dr. Geldter guffawed disdainfully, "Those stupid Texans actually raised the money for these horses and their upkeep from their idiotic cancer fund raising campaign, but they will never figure out how we got them to transfer the funding for this!" Dr. Belcher sternly, "I wouldn't go into that if I were you, Isaac!" Dr. Geldter turned to Dr. Belcher, "Dr. Ricin understands how important our work is and that we require certain special rewards. Well, Francis, it seems you are the only non-horse person amongst us." In a sarcastic manner Dr Belcher answered, "Well, bully-bully for me!" Dr. Geldter said, "Don't be so touchy, Francis! You seem to be a bit upset lately. Perhaps you need a long vacation in New York!"

Amy joined in as she rode up and squealed, "Did you see my jump? Did you see it?" Dr. Geldter smiling replied partly in Yiddish, "It was terrific, already, Boobalah!" He didn't see the jump. Dr. Krappner said to Dr. Belcher, "Well, how did you enjoy the ride Dr. Belcher?" Dr. Belcher sarcastically answered, "Immensely!" There was a pause in the conversation, and Dr. Geldter then continued, "We enjoyed the ride, except for Francis. I am afraid he likes New York better." Dr. Belcher replied, "I did not say I didn't enjoy it. It's just that I'm New York City bred, and I prefer the theater over riding horses all over the Texas countryside." Dr. Krappner smiled, "Well, at least you were game for it! Who knows, if you practice staying on your horse, you may actually begin to enjoy riding it." She then laughed. Dr. Belcher answered sharply, "Don't count on it!"

Dr. Krappner dismounted and announced to everyone, "I've brought a great picnic lunch. Pâté fois gras." Dr. Belcher interjected in his sarcastic manner, "You mean chopped liver?" Dr. Krappner in a very dry tone, "Ha-Ha!" She continued, "Caviar, Baluga, of course." Belcher, sarcastic again, "Of course." Dr. Ricin added, "It's not as if any of us is kosher." Dr. Krappner continued, "There's fresh fruit, a variety of cheeses, home-made French bread, Coq au vin salad, and for dessert, chilled Crème Brulee au Chocolate." Belcher replied sarcastically, "In other words, we're having yuppie chicken salad and gourmet chocolate pudding." Dr. Krappner giggled and in a slightly flirtatious manner said, "You're incorrigible, Francis."

Amy thought that she was very desirable to the opposite sex, but it was not true at all. In reality she was an ugly person, particularly her inner person but those around her didn't bother to ever tell her, because she wouldn't have believed it anyway. She said, "Oh, I almost forgot we also have an excellent Chablis Blanc and some mineral water to accompany this scrumptious meal." Dr. Ricin quipped sarcastically, "You Texans sure know how to live." Dr. Krappner laughed, "It helps when you're not bogged down by sentimental principles. "Dr. Ricin answered, "I know what you mean. Survival in a harsh world when you are at the top requires some extreme measures at times."

The picnic was laid out on a collapsible table set with silver and crystal right by the Guadalupe River that ran through some of the most picturesque countryside found in South Central Texas. The river had an unusual turquoise-green hue, and it was one of the only rivers in Texas that was not completely mud brown and ugly. Unusual rock formations were visible with a variety of cathedral-type trees situated near the shore. The group slowly sat down to the meal. It was obvious that Amy liked to be a Queen bee. They toasted each other. Dr. Krappner raised her glass, "Here's to our little project. May we all derive great fortune from the fruition of our patriotic mission." Dr. Geldter added, "Le Chayim. Here's to the elimination of Marie and Jared. They have been a pain in my ass for so long." Dr. Ricin now had his chance, "To financial success! May we all achieve what you have done here in Texas! I salute ya'all!" The group laughed at Dr. Ricin's attempt to add a little Texas-talk at the end of his salute.

Suddenly, Dr. Geldter acted like he had a revelation. He started waving his hands, "Wait a minute, already. I heard from my contacts that some Las Vegas organization is actually funding our projects through their defense companies. They own some large defense corporations, like the Cornelyus Group, and they have a lot of ex-Washington people on their boards. Is this some kind of Mafia thing? I heard that they've been trying to kill Marie for the last 25 years." Dr. Belcher was thinking of only himself and added, "Yes! That's apparently correct! I have it on good authority that Marie is the heir to a huge Las Vegas empire, and the local crime bosses never want her to receive a penny of it. But I have to be frank with you, if that's true, aren't we taking a risk? What if she survives?" Dr. Ricin interjected, "Of course there's always some risk with this type of operation. Anything worthwhile involves risk." Dr. Geldter piped in, "I think that Mafia stuff is a lot of horseshit, just some Hollywood bullshit, but I have another concern. I want to be paid a lot more for my efforts. Damnit, Francis, you never supported my salary position with Clement Masters at our last meeting. He can reward us with a lot more than we're taking home, and all he does is tell us they're going to set up some account on some Goddamned island that we can't even easily access. And I should have my salary doubled . . . immediately! I am worth a lot more than that bullshit surgeon that you brought in as a Vice President! You don't pay me enough, and I don't give a damn about any so-called Mafia connection. I really don't care who picks up the bill—I just want what I deserve." Dr. Ricin broke in, "Isaac! Let's get back to the point of this gathering. We have been called upon to provide an important service, and I am sure that we will be financially rewarded. Isn't that true Dr. Belcher?" Dr. Belcher indicated that Dr. Geldter should know the answer to that question. But Dr. Geldter was on another thought entirely, "And we can finally add that asshole Jared to the list. I have been trying to bring him down for years now, but he keeps popping up like the Goddamned battery bunny!" Dr. Ricin just looked at Dr. Belcher, who just shrugged his shoulders.

Dr. Belcher, who had been listening intently reverted back to his New York accent because a Mafia-sponsored hit was brought up. "I don't want to know about any of this directly! You have to do this in a way that draws no suspicion to me or my office." Dr. Geldter smiled and turned to Dr. Belcher, "Oh, shut up Francis! You know, I should be in your Goddamned administrative position." Dr. Belcher flashed a resentful look back to Dr. Geldter and whined, "You couldn't handle my position!" Dr. Geldter then indignantly retorted, "You don't seem to be handling *this* very well, already, Francis." Dr. Ricin interrupted the two, "Friends, Please! I know of a person that is an expert at biological agents that are virtually untraceable."

There was a pause, and everyone turned to Dr. Ricin. Dr. Geldter finally asked, "You mean, like the Russian Doll cocktail concept, . . . several components that alone are not lethal, but when hidden in a mixture produce a lethal combination. I know all about that bullshit. Hell, we were working on that when Amy and I were at Fort Detrick. Everyone thought that Nixon converted the place to cancer research." Everyone laughed at the reference to Nixon and the turning over of Fort Detrick to more 'peaceful' efforts to identify and destroy unusual diseases. Dr. Ricin now stated seriously, "This was attempted before, but for the life of me, I cannot understand why the McNichols survived that banquet." Dr. Geldter added indignantly, "Because you didn't do it right like I told you, that's why–dumkaupf!" Dr. Krappner thought back on Dr. Belcher's comments and then coldly stated, "One point that we have to consider, as Dr. Belcher mentioned, is just how dangerous Marie might become when she comes into her inheritance." But Amy quickly slipped back to her old behavior, "It's not fair! Just by a trick of birth some people inherit so much! Why should she get all that!" In a self-serving and whiny way Dr. Krappner continued, "I worked so hard for my degree and my position, and I did not have some money bags for a father."

Isaac turned to Amy. He was angry. "You moron! With your academic record, you wouldn't even be in your position if it wasn't for me!" Dr. Ricin appealed to the couple, "Stop it! Stop it! We cannot afford petty jealousies; you all seem incapable of clear-sighted judgment." Dr. Belcher agreed,

"Good! Finally we have something that we can agree on." Dr. Ricin stated firmly, "Let's focus! I did not make the trip here for petty arguments! I say we call this operation White Rose. I will contact the Mossad, and Isaac I'll give you the contact for the job of preparing the mixture." Dr. Geldter's scornful facial expression became unnaturally smug, and then he changed into his usual false smile. Dr. Belcher changed his tone and turned his head away while covering his ears, "I don't want to hear anything about this, this White Rose!" Dr. Ricin then continued and in a coldly calculating tone said, "I will contact my sources in the Kahane Ch'ai and get all of the information on Marie and Jared McNichols, but I must tell you, we have to avoid the IDF. For some reason the McNichols are held in high regard by the IDF– They even made Marie an honorary general." Dr. Geldter responded angrily, "I don't believe it! For what reason?" Dr. Ricin then stated, "The IDF considers the McNichols heroes. They claim that they helped them with IDF Special Forces and with the illnesses in Northern Israel after the Gulf War Iraqi missile attacks." Geldter responded, "That's a bunch of bullshit spread by our enemies! How can they be considered heroes by the Kuwaitis and also by the IDF? What kind of crap is this? That can't be right, already!"

Dr. Geldter then reminded the assembled group of the threat that the McNichols posed to the classified program in the M. K. Black Building. "They've been interfering way too much in our prison studies. Now they're involved with the people that live around the prisons where our studies are ongoing, already. Do you know how long it takes to complete one of these studies? Do you have any idea of the amount of time it takes to plan and execute a good clinical trial?" Dr. Ricin leaned over to Dr. Krappner, "Why don't you contact your friends in MI5." Dr. Krappner reacted irritated, "How did you know about MI5?" Dr. Ricin piped in arrogantly, "Because Israeli intelligence is the best. We will use factions in each of these agencies to supply information and operatives, and we will tell them only part of our mission." Dr. Geldter added, "Better let me do the planning here! Dr. Belcher doesn't want to be involved!" Dr. Belcher to Dr. Geldter, "I told you that I should not know the details of this mission! My office can't be involved!" Dr. Geldter replied with a sneer, "You mean *our* mission, Francis! Don't forget what Dr. Masters told us!" Dr. Ricin to Dr. Geldter, "I will help you with a new weaponized mycoplasma and you, Isaac, will prepare the asparaginase that you told me about." Dr. Belcher questioned the tactic, "I don't think that this particular approach worked the last time. But I still don't want to know about it." Dr. Geldter ignoring Dr. Belcher, "This is very important. I will supply you with the *best* macrophage inhibitors." Dr. Ricin said, "I hear from Isaac that Jared will be lecturing to a conference at Queens College in Cambridge." Dr. Geldter exploded, "What bullshit! I should be giving that lecture! Why would they invite him!"

Dr. Ricin continued to address the group as if he didn't hear Isaac, "We will random-drop each component to a central operative in Queen's College just before the meeting. This operative will then mix the cocktail and offer it in, say, a special dish or dessert, just for the 'special' American guests. We must be certain that they will eat it, so it has to be something Marie and Jared like." Dr. Geldter smirked, "Jared will eat anything." Dr. Ricin said, "I am not that worried about Jared McNichols." Dr. Geldter interrupted, "Oh yah, I can't wait to get rid of that sonofabitch! He always seems to be in my way. I would have had a Nobel by now if it wasn't for him!" Dr. Belcher was condescending, "Isaac, you're going to have to spend more productive time in your laboratory if you ever expect to get a Nobel! And you are going to have to stop those technicians and post-docs of yours from claiming that you fudge your data. I had to clean up some messy rumors because of your employees." Dr. Geldter replied angrily, "That's a lie, a lot of crap spread by my enemies! My techs never said that!" Dr. Belcher continued, "You better wake up, Isaac!" Dr. Krappner turned to Dr. Ricin who was trying to change the subject, "Don't listen to those alpha-males, Schlomo. At least I can see that you've done your homework."

Dr. Ricin indicated that an operative in some rogue faction of Israeli intelligence would help with the profiles of the McNichols, their personalities, likes and dislikes, and so on, but he needed some financial support. He was suggesting that he could recruit anyone if he had access to Texas-sized accounts like Isaac and Amy. Dr. Geldter ignored the comment about how much money he had access to and related to Schlomo, "I always tell people Marie's a gypsy." Dr. Ricin shot back, "Apparently not! My contacts have her heritage as Catholic Merrano and his as Scottish Protestant." Dr. Belcher finally added, "I thought that the Merranos were Jews who practiced Catholicism on the surface but Judaism behind closed doors during the Inquisition in Spain." He then almost lost his composure,

"But back to the main point, this whole thing is absurd! It's just ridiculous that we should be wasting our time plotting to eliminate, in my opinion, two rather insignificant scientists." Dr. Ricin responded, "By our standards they are anything but insignificant, especially if you consider the Las Vegas assets and the defense corporations that are probably part of Marie's inheritance." Dr. Krappner chewed on her lip nervously and added, "And if they found out about our special projects in the prison system." Dr. Geldter interrupted, "Do you have any idea how much effort we have put into the prison projects, Francis?" But Dr. Belcher did not want to know. Dr. Geldter continued, "You know, Francis, you don't seem to be cut out for this."

Then for no apparent reason Dr. Geldter went on a rampage. "I for one will relish being able to finally piss on their graves. Good riddance to both of them! I'm tired of hearing about the McNichols, already! Jared was even made the Editor of some bullshit cancer journal instead of me, and I want them out of my life forever!" Dr. Ricin tried to calm Isaac down, "Don't worry about that. It will all be taken care of. Listen my friends, this operation must be executed in a professional manner, and I repeat, no one should know why we are delivering the various cocktail components to Cambridge. My contact has already identified an operative who can be called upon for such a delicate operation. He goes by the code name Oozie." Dr. Belcher said again, "I told you I don't want to know any of these details!" He then repeated himself slowly, "I don't wanta know any of this!" Dr. Geldter ignored Dr. Belcher, pompously turned to Dr. Ricin and stated, "Schlomo, I congratulate you for orchestrating this! And, by the way, how did you know that you were being called for just this purpose. I did not mention the real reason when we spoke on the phone?" Dr. Ricin responded, "Like I said, no one is immune to us. Not even you. And besides, my compatriots make it a point to keep track of this situation."

Dr. Belcher was as nervous as ever, and he wanted to be a thousand miles away from this group. "This is so ruthless! I am still not convinced that they are such a threat that we need to . . ." Dr. Krappner then interrupted her boss, "Actually, it's a beautiful plan, and the best part is that we don't even have to be directly involved." Dr. Geldter added, "You know, Francis, I don't think you have the stomach for this. You are acting like the weak link in *our* chain." Dr. Belcher, who was still acting nervous as he thought to himself that he was in the midst of a bunch of sociopaths and he'd better hide his fear replied, "Don't be ridiculous! It's true, I am not in favor of your approach, but I am not stupid. You can count on my silence, but I still would rather stick to the professional character assassinations and ruining their careers. That's more up my alley, and I have certainly been successful at it in the past." Dr. Geldter added, "Yah, you're a real pro, Francis." Dr. Krappner laughed in a smug sort of way, "I can attest to that. I hope, Francis, that you like me, because technically you are my boss."

Amy had changed her tone again. She laughed, and Dr. Belcher managed a brief phony laugh, "Well, Amy you know what they say, all men seem to need a strong mother." Dr. Geldter interjected, "One minor problem, though, is that we are now going to have to put up with that obnoxious new Executive Vice President that Clement has hired, that pissant Clyde Bane." Dr. Geldter continued, "I don't think he knows how to zip his fly without help. He's just a piece of play-dough garbage, a giant idiotic . . . ." Amy interrupted, "Isaac, we can control him. Let's not get off on Clyde. We can neutralize his influence if we play our cards right. And besides he is small Mississippi potatoes!" Dr. Geldter thought about it and smiled.

Dr. Ricin wanted to get back to a more serious discussion. "Remember, the key to a successful operation of this nature is team-work. The operatives should only be given information on a need-to-know basis. We must be efficient. That Cambridge meeting begins in a few weeks." Dr. Geldter sarcastically added, "And to think that I worked overtime to have Jared McNichols thrown off the program. And now it plays right into our hands. No one would ever suspect me now! "Dr. Krappner added, "Well, let's not try to speculate. I prefer to think of them as some problems that need to be contained." Dr. Geldter turned to Dr. Belcher, "And that asshole Jared is in the way. Francis, once this is over, I want his department merged with mine immediately. Am I clear on that?" Dr. Belcher replied, "Don't try to second guess Dr. Masters, Isaac. You will get your just rewards, I am sure. And stop acting as if I can just increase your salary by 100%." Dr. Geldter was furious, "I bet that you can, if you tried hard enough!" Dr. Belcher replied, "I cannot even get my own salary raised!" Dr. Geldter shot back, "I would settle for 50% for me and 50% for Amy." Dr. Belcher ignored the last comment while Dr. Ricin continued, "It's best not to think of them as persons. Get used to thinking of them as targets, nothing more than a statistic in the universal scheme of things." Dr. Krappner cheerfully added, "Anyone want homemade whipped cream on their Crème Brulee?" Dr. Belcher now began to relax, "How gauche!" Soft chuckles were heard from all. It had been a good day in the Texas Hill Country.

Dr. Masters takes a personal interest

Dr. Masters had arranged a conference call with an ex-government official and some of his close administration and faculty that had been conscripted to orchestrate Marie's and Jared's professional and character assassinations, or worse. The meeting had been called at the request of Dr. Francis Belcher, who had indicated to Dr. Masters that a pep talk was necessary to convince certain faculty members that the underhanded actions against a senior faculty member and his wife were absolutely necessary and in line with Dr. Masters' administrative directives. Attending the meeting were: Drs. Clement Masters, Francis Belcher, Isaac Geldter, Amy Krappner, Martin Italiano, Roland Auchenhower, Laura Graham and James Ross. Dr. Masters also took this opportunity to introduce Dr. Clyde Bane, the new Executive Vice President for Hospital Administration. He was a flaccid looking individual of medium height with a pasty complexion. Although he just arrived at the Cancer Center, he already had detractors on the faculty, such as Dr. Isaac Geldter, who called him the Pillsbury Doughboy. Dr. Geldter was upset because of the salary that Dr. Bane made, and he took every opportunity to tell anyone who would listen that he deserved a higher salary. The meeting took place in Clement Masters' conference room. Dr. Schlomo Ricin, who visited Austin earlier but had not met Dr. Masters was to be connected by telephone to the conference. The atmosphere was very somber, but there was also a low-level exhilaration in the demeanor of some of the faculty who now realized that Dr. Belcher was not lying to them about the plans of the administration and Dr. Masters. They were almost proud to be invited into such an elite power group at the institution.

Dr. Masters came to his door to signal everyone that the meeting was about to start. He was in a jovial mood and wanted to continue the meeting in his own office in more comfortable surroundings rather than in the small conference room where his employees had been waiting. Dr. Masters motioned with his hands, "Come in. Make yourselves comfortable. There's fresh coffee and Eggs Benedict in a warmer over there on the table." Dr. Belcher asked sarcastically, "Am I dreaming. Has The D. O. Madison's kitchen actually gone gourmet?" Dr. Masters forced a chuckle, the kind of false chuckle that he was famous for, "I am afraid not, Francis. In view of the significance of the occasion, I told the office to have a catered breakfast ready." Dr. Italiano uttered in his slight New York accent, "My, God! Look at this spread." Dr. Geldter tried to be smug to show his colleagues that he does this often with Dr. Masters, "This is my kind of meeting." But Dr. Italiano continued, There's fresh strawberries and cream and even champagne to go with the fresh-squeezed orange juice!"

The faculty members were clearly impressed. They were not used to such amenities. Dr. Masters, who was always proud to show off his power and prestige to the faculty stated, "As I told you all, nothing but the best for my most loyal employees." Dr. Belcher was flabbergasted, because he had never been accorded such honor in the weekly senior administrative meetings with Dr. Masters. Dr. Auchenhower chuckled and then joked to Dr. Masters, "Dr. Masters, you have successfully bribed me with the aroma of that fresh brewed coffee." Dr. Amy Krappner hated early morning meetings, but she had been warned by Dr. Belcher not to miss the meeting. "It's not fair. I can't even think of food at this hour!" Dr. Geldter chided his wife, "Aw, come on Amy, I'm sure you can force down some of that champagne and orange juice and, look boob-a-lah, there's even some smoked salmon and bagels."

Dr. Masters was restless over his faculty fawning over the food instead of himself, and his mood changed. He began by speaking in a low friendly voice. "Dr. Geldter, I appreciate that you are fond of your wife, but let's refrain from the boobalah." Dr. Masters, who hailed from rural Mississippi actually hated Jews, but he had learned to hide it well over the years. Even he knew that academia was dominated by Jewish physicians, scientists and researchers, and he learned early on how to schmooze them into thinking that he actually liked and respected them. In fact, he did not like them–he despised them–but he needed them, and his Machiavellian sense of power required that he make them his allies.

Dr. Masters began pacing before the table in his office that had been set for the occasion, "I want to remind each of you of the significance of this meeting, but first I want to introduce Dr. Clyde Bane, our new Executive Vice President. Most of you already know Dr. Bane, so I don't need to go into a lengthy introduction. Let's just say that The D. O. Madison Cancer Center is blessed with talent, and your addition brings our faculty to a new level." Drs. Laura Graham and James Ross looked at each other with an expression that was a cross between uncomfortable and smug, as Ross pointedly glanced at the new administrative addition, Dr. Bane. When he thought no one was watching, he whispered to his wife Dr. Graham, "Bane stinks as a surgeon!" Dr. Masters then interjected after he gave Dr. Ross a sharp look of warning, "I want you all to be very supportive of Dr. Bane, since he is our new Executive Vice President for Hospital Administration." Dr. Belcher, who also didn't like to be outdone piped in, "Well, Clyde welcome aboard. Are you pleased to get out of Mississippi?" This was a major faux pas, since Dr. Bane left Mississippi many years ago. Everyone kept reminding Dr. Bane of Mississippi, but he hadn't been back to the state in years. Dr. Krappner then added, "I'm sure you will be a marvelous addition to an already splendid team of leadership." Dr. Masters beamed his approval, "Well put, Dr. Krappner." Dr. Geldter, who hated to be outdone by anyone, especially his wife who he claimed was less than competent without him, chimed in by pouring on the charm, "Welcome, Dr. Bane, I hope that you are finding us as delightful as we find you." Dr. Geldter did this at the same time that he made the effusive gesture of jumping up from his seat and going over to shake Dr. Bane's hand in a most rigorous fashion. Dr. Graham, who had a falsetto tone in her voice when she became nervous, as if years of elocution lessons to correct her speech pattern were of no avail, followed quickly with a large smile on her face, "It's a pleasure to finally meet you, Dr. Bane." She had a very insipid and artificial manner about her, and she wanted to shake hands with both of her hands instead of the usual one-handed shake. She was the epitome of insincerity, but she feared that he might have heard her husband's stupid remark. Finally, Dr. Ross found it necessary to add, "Well, at last I will have an opportunity to work with an outstanding surgeon. It's been so frustrating just passing you briefly at the National Surgical Society meetings." Dr. Bane looked at Ross and smiled, but he wouldn't make the same political mistake, especially in front of Dr. Masters, "I certainly know what you mean." He was a quick study in double-speak.

Dr. Bane then looked at everyone as he took his seat and said, "Thank you all so much for making me feel so welcome." There was a hint of sarcasm in his voice. Dr. Masters had not noticed, because he was looking at a note that was just handed to him by his secretary. He finally went to his seat at the head of the table, "I do want to keep this as brief as possible. I have a meeting in the Governor's office, and as you know we have to keep our channels with the Governor as open as possible."

Now that Dr. Masters had everyone's attention, he continued, "Now let's get down to business. We are scheduled to receive an important call to brief you on a vital mission concerning one of our faculty. Dr. Geldter has arranged for Dr. Schlomo Ricin, the premier expert on mycoplasmas to call at the same time." Dr. Masters was then interrupted by a buzz, indicating that a telephone call was coming through to his inner office. Turning, he proceeded to his desk where he faced away from the others to take the call. Meanwhile, Dr. Geldter who did not wait for Dr. Masters to return to the table replied to the group in a knowledgeable some might say, arrogant manner, "My sources indicate that our backers are powerful Las Vegas interests that own some of the largest defense companies in America." Dr. Ross interceded at this point, "May I interrupt and ask a question of Dr. Masters?" But Dr. Masters was still on his phone call, and he was also interrupted by his assistant and didn't hear the conversation. So Dr. Ross then turned to Isaac and asked, "Dr. Geldter, you seem to know more about this than the rest of us. What's this so-called Las Vegas financial group have to do with our meeting, and is there any organized crime element involved?" Dr. Italiano added, "I agree, what does a financial group that may have something to do with Las Vegas casino-organized crime families have to do with The D. O. Madison and our mission?" Dr. Ross spoke quietly, "I must tell you in confidence, Laura and I have done some extremely sensitive work for the CIA, and . . ." Dr. Graham interrupted her husband, "That's right. We were just up at Langley for a conference. And they've even sent us to the South of France on critical information procuring missions." Dr. Ross seemed irritated at being interrupted by his wife who was saying too much to the group, "To continue, if this financial group was so important, *we* would have known about it." Dr. Belcher sarcastically interrupted, "Well, now. The truth comes out, at last! I've been working with a couple of spooks that have risen in their occupations because of some spy-business. I always knew there had to be some explanation for the two of you to have advanced so far in this game. Dr. Graham became very irritated and stated, "How dare you, Dr. Belcher!" Dr. Geldter whispered to his wife Amy, "These two are such mediocrities." Dr. Graham turned directly to Dr. Geldter and continued, "How dare you imply that my work is not superlative!" Dr. Geldter sarcastically interjected, "Why did you think I was referring to you? Look at Amy here. She thinks that she's the best of the best!" Dr. Krappner arrogantly responded to her husband, "I believe that I am the best immunologist here at the D. O. Madison! Dr. Graham sneered at Dr. Krappner; she thought that Amy Krappner was a complete has-been, but she refused to tell her to her face.

Dr. Geldter did not try to change the subject and in a bombastic tone reiterated, "Dr. Belcher, I can't believe that you have the gall to be so self-righteous. You are not exactly a Fred Rosenberg or David Lipschitz!" Dr. Belcher was irritated to be compared to the two famous physician-scientists, "I'll have you know that when I was back in New York, our department *was* the *best* of the best!" Dr. Geldter replied, "Yeah, but I am the only one in this room with a citation classic! And I, not you Francis, should have more awards, already, and you should be supporting me more!" The meeting had clearly degenerated before it actually got started.

Dr. Masters, who was now off the phone, had been talking with his administrative assistant, taking notes and ignoring the group. Realizing that the meeting had deteriorated before it had even begun, he now returned to intercede in a fatherly manner. Dr. Masters liked to treat his faculty as if he were a father figure and they were children that needed more discipline. "Now boys, infighting will get us nowhere." Dr. Krappner became indignant and responded. "Sir, there *are* women here too. With all due respect, I for one would appreciate being properly addressed." Dr. Masters forever the politician replied, "Why yes, we have not forgotten about our esteemed female faculty members."

During the course of the brief meeting Dr. Bane wondered why he took a job with such bickering faculty members–He almost seemed out of place. He just sat back and observed; he did not feel a part of this group, but he considered himself probably the best politician in the room, with the exception of Dr. Masters, of course. Dr. Krappner quickly regained her composure and replied to Dr. Masters in her sweet voice, "I am sure that under your superb leadership we are all going to be given tremendous opportunities. Who knows what the successful completion of our mission will mean to our careers?" Drs. Auchenhower and Italiano had been quietly looking at each other, and the newcomer Dr. Clyde Bane finally broke his silence, "Dr. Masters, if I could interrupt. It seems to me that it serves no useful purpose for this esteemed group to disagree. Remember the old military adage of defeating an enemy by the strategy of divide and conquer. I am sure that under your leadership, we will accomplish whatever tasks you have in mind."

Dr. Clement Masters had turned again to his assistant and never heard the statement by Dr. Bane, but he finished and immediately interrupted without thinking about any of Dr. Bane's comments, or any of the other comments for that matter. "Good point, Dr. Bane! As I was saying, the principal financial backers of our project as well as the overall intelligence source for this delicate operation will for the moment remain anonymous and will only be known by me. Dr. Geldter's good friend Dr. Ricin is, shall I say, coordinating other individuals for our project. I am counting on Drs. Graham and Ross here to keep them informed with their 'sources.' In the rare event that the proposed task fails and certain people find out about it, we, and especially my office, must have full deniability. We do not want even the slightest possibility that certain people might find out about our classified programs with Belford College of Medicine."

Dr. Masters continued in an attempt to explain to the group why they had been convened. "You see, at the highest levels of power there are no loyalties or nationalities. No causes are peculiar to any one group or individual. Everyone in the power circles knows each other." Dr. Masters talked with authority as if he was a member of the 'power group' but in reality he was just a stooge being used like the rest of them. He continued, "However, this operation will be successful due to careful planning and execution by all of you. I am not going to ask you about the details, because this office must have complete deniability in this matter. I am sure you understand. I know that you will be successful. Dr. Belcher here will brief you, and you will all report to him on the progress, except for you, Dr. Bane, of course." Dr. Italiano finally stated, "I hope you are right, sir." Dr.

Auchenhower nodded his head in agreement with Dr. Italiano, and he continued Dr. Italiano's line of dialogue, "Dr. Italiano is just voicing his fears that none of us wants to be identified as part of this operation should, on the outside chance, it fails."

Dr. Masters frowned at the comment. He knew that each one of the participants, except for Dr. Bane, had been briefed by Dr. Belcher. "I do not like to hear such negative comments expressed by my staff, Dr. Auchenhower. You are all involved in this project, and have been from the start, and I suggest that you follow your instructions to the letter." Masters then smiled, looked around the table and said, "And that goes for everyone in this room." Dr. Masters now changed his demeanor to be more cheerful style and said, "Now Dr. Bane needs to be brought up to speed on our project. Dr. Belcher will be assigned to inform Dr. Bane of any necessary details. I should remind each of you that Dr. Bane comes to us with the highest recommendation. We are very fortunate to have him on our team."

Dr. Bane looked around the room at the smiling faces and wondered what he had gotten himself into. He was beginning to look very pale and was starting to act very uncomfortable when Dr. Geldter interceded. "Dr. Masters, I believe we all are aware of our critically important roles." Dr. Masters stated, "If anyone wants out and leaves this meeting now, I can't stop you, but I must warn you that I need to have team players at our institution." Dr. Masters did not like anyone else appearing to take control over the meeting, so he continued, "Dr. Geldter is absolutely correct. I am told by our Las Vegas financial source that he already knows each and every one of you, where you live and work and how you travel. They're a very well organized group, and they don't like excuses. Do you understand the situation?" Everyone nodded as if they all comprehend the ramifications in unison, but Dr. Bane appeared extremely uncomfortable. Actually he secretly wondered why he left his last position for this tempest.

Dr. Masters was now in complete control. "Good! I believe at last we have unity of purpose." A buzz was heard, and Clement Masters' administrator said through the intercom, "Dr. Masters. Your call is ready." Dr. Masters' countenance was delineated by a beaming smile, and most of the players were now smiling and silent. Dr. Masters began the call by saying, "Good morning, Sir!" The voice that came over the intercom sounded like a politician, "Same to you, Clement! I hope that this call isn't too early in the morning. Is your team assembled there?" Dr. Masters replied, "Assembled and ready, sir!" The former government official who was a National Security Advisor to a former President said, "Very good! Is the other contact on the line?" Schlomo Ricin responded, "Ricin here! Shalom from Jerusalem."

The former government official, Stephen V. Able, talked to Dr. Masters and his assembled co-conspirators over the speakerphone. "Good! I guess we're ready! Clement, could you have everyone introduce themselves." Dr. Masters replied, "With pleasure, Sir!" Dr. Geldter piped in first, "Good morning, Sir. I'm Dr. Isaac Geldter, and I have been working closely with Dr. Ricin on some critical projects. Mr. Able asked, "How are those Russian Dolls coming along?" Dr. Geldter was a bit taken aback but quickly recovered, "Near completion, sir. With my input we have perfected the macrophage inhibition component." Mr. Able said over the phone, "Good! You have been invaluable in helping us to achieve our ultimate goal!" Isaac Geldter acted very smug, looked around and smiled to the other participants as if he had scored a major triumph. Dr. Geldter then continued, "Sir, I'd like to introduce Dr. Amy Krappner, who has been essential in helping us design the necessary immunological experiments which complement the Russian Doll project." Dr. Krappner was giggling, "I'm so pleased to finally meet you, sir!" Mr. Able answered, "The feeling is mutual!" One by one Drs. Bane, Belcher, Italiano, Auchenhower, Graham and Ross introduced themselves by simply saying, "Good morning, and then they furnished their names. Even though they had the chance, it was not necessary for them to be so self-promoting in front of Dr. Masters.

Finally the real meeting began. Mr. Able said, "I am so glad that you all have agreed to assist us in this important operation. Before I start, I assume that Clement has cleared you with the secrecy aspects of this operation. Clement, here, has been working with us for some time on some very vital projects, projects that are essential to our 'National Security.' At this point Dr. Belcher muttered to himself so that Dr. Ross heard him, "National Security my ass, more like consummate greed." Dr. Masters, who was not quite within hearing range shot a look at Dr. Belcher and stated in an irritated voice, "Francis, do you have something to say that is so important that you must interrupt this discussion?" Dr. Belcher then answered, "No, sir. I'm sorry." Dr. Masters continued, "Oh just shut up, Francis!"

At this point everyone at the meeting was visibly nervous, but Dr. Masters was too self-absorbed to notice. Dr. Masters then continued in a conciliatory voice to the esteemed individual on the conference call, "I'm sorry, sir. Dr. Belcher here just has never been able to contain himself." Mr. Able just chuckled loud enough so that everyone could hear him to ease the tension and then stated, "That's all right, Dr. Belcher . . . I take it that Clement has briefed you on our current objective and explained to you why we consider the subjects to be a major threat to National Security." Dr. Geldter piped in, "Sir, we are all clear on the project and are in agreement on what has to be done. Dr. Masters has informed us that the initial attempts using Russian Doll cocktails failed for some reason, but I do not think that our new mix containing a weaponized Mycoplasma with Brucella and asparginase in combination with macrophage inhibitors will fail. With my extensive expertise in this area I suggested that the cocktail should also contain a component that should completely compromise the immune system. Through my own investigations I have found that one of our targets suffers from a violent allergy to asparagus. Well, it just so happens that I am the world's leading expert on asparaginase, an important enzyme in asparagus, and I have concluded that if we place asparaginase in the same cocktail, the mission will be successful. The immune system will have to contend with the asaparaginase and therefore will have nothing left for the other biologicals." Dr. Geldter sounded so smug during his explanation. He had achieved exactly what he wanted–the chance to completely upstage his colleagues.

Dr. Belcher just looked at Drs. Italiano and Auchenhower skeptically. They were stunned to be talking about murdering two of their colleagues. Dr. Bane was even more stunned. Although he had previously been at a university in Mississippi that was known for its work on biological warfare and testing biowarfare agents, it seemed as if this was completely out of his league. He felt as if he was in a living nightmare. He pondered the situation wondering if he was just imagining the thrust of this so-called executive meeting. Were these would-be criminals really his colleagues? He was beginning to regret his decision to join the D. O. Madison executive staff. Dr. Masters could not stop Dr. Geldter, but his look at the others encompassed a warning for them to keep their mouths shut and not to voice their scientific or moral opinions, which might be just the opposite to Isaac Geldter's.

Mr. Able finally responded to Dr. Geldter's comments. "This is great news, Clement!" Dr. Ricin then interjected, "Sir, my contacts have assembled a group of operatives who will each provide a component of the cocktail to be served to the targets at a conference in Cambridge." Dr. Geldter then piped in again, "Sir, to assure success, the cocktail has been designed so there will be no initial symptoms, and preferably no symptoms for a few days or so. In addition, Drs. Graham and Ross here have also agreed to include the asparaginase cocktail in some appetizers, which will be served at a party in honor of the graduation of one of Dr. Graham's students. Both targets were invited and should attend this party before they leave the U. S. After the targets receive their cocktails in Austin, the combination of the first dose and the stress of travel should prime them for a second more potent dose in Cambridge. The graduation party is scheduled the day before they leave, and they have both accepted the invitation. When the immune system encounters the second dose, the infection should be triggered to take off. And since the biologicals we are using in the second cocktail are slightly different from the first cocktail, they should be extremely susceptible." Dr. Krappner chirped in, even though she was warned not to, "Sir, it's analogous to a flu infection. People may have immunity to one strain, but when another strain appears that their immune system has not seen, they become ill. Even extremely healthy individuals are devastated from new strains of flu if they are first weakened!"

Mr. Able thought for a moment. "I see." In fact, he had no clue, but he did not bother to ask. He had learned over the years to let the doctors and spooks do the talking. If anything went wrong, he could deny everything. Dr. Masters then stated in his usual authoritative manner, "I believe we have everything under control." Mr. Able responded quickly, "I am very pleased to hear that! I would not want you to fail. A lot is depending on this mission. Now, make sure that your team is thorough in their professional activities. It would be better if the illness is perceived as psychological, and then no one will be surprised if a suicide occurs at a later date. We must deflect any suspicion that this was an organized mission and not some accidental occurrence. I know that your team will be successful. Be sure to keep my staff informed of any new information."

Dr. Masters sensed that the conference call was over. "Sir, it's been a pleasure talking to you. I promise we will keep you updated at every step." Mr. Able responded, "Thank you so much for meeting so early in the morning for this briefing. I have the utmost faith that I can count on each of you to make this a successful operation." Dr. Ricin interjected, "Before you sign off, Sir, would you have any objection if the code name for this operation is White Rose." Mr. Able quickly responded, "Good name. I like it. Kinda makes you think of a red rose that has the blood drained from it. You know what I mean. A modern House of York versus House of Tudor. Thanks, for your valuable assistance, Clement. Good luck to you all."

The conference call with the Mr. Able had been terminated, but Dr. Ricin was still on the phone. Dr. Ricin continued, "So, there we have it. Just leave the intricacies of the delivery to me. Dr. Geldter will keep me posted at every step of the project as it progresses. This operation must be properly orchestrated so that there is absolutely no room for error." Dr. Geldter replied, "Schlomo, this is Isaac, there won't be any error at this end." Dr. Ricin answered, "You're all an asset to the great state of Texas. Shalom, y'all!" The southern accent pun sounded ludicrous with Dr. Ricin's thick Israeli accent, but this time he got it right.

Chuckles were heard around the room. Dr. Masters even chuckled, and then got up out of his chair, "Well, ladies and gentlemen, I feel we are off to an excellent start. I don't need to remind you how important this project is to me. Don't fail! One final point, we have to infiltrate Jared McNichols' department. Francis, do you have any suggestions as to whom we could recruit in the department. Dr. Belcher proudly related to Dr. Masters, "I have that covered, Clement. Tom Domasovitch has been keeping close track of everything related to the McNichols. Domasovitch even had Jared's computers fixed so that they will make alias files of anything that the McNichols do on their computers. One of Jared's post-docs whom I recruited for the mission even helped with the programming." Dr. Masters asked, "Are they trustworthy?" Dr. Belcher responded, "Domasovitch will do anything to get ahead. These guys would kill their own mothers if it meant extra money or promotions, and, correct me if I'm wrong, Isaac, isn't that other faculty member Judah Nosan close to you." Dr. Geldter answered smiling, "Of course. Nosan looks up to me as an older brother, so he should be very easy to manipulate. I can have him eating out of my hand if I want." Dr. Belcher added, "Domasovitch is our man. He has limited talent as a researcher, and he has little character but I keep him around for certain purposes, under the condition that he be available for certain special jobs. Interestingly, he claims he was a Ranger in Vietnam, but I know differently. He was never a Ranger, and he abandoned his own men to save his own ass. I hold this over him, because I don't think anyone here knows the story." Dr. Krappner chortled, "Be serious, Dr. Belcher! We know the story, but it sounds like he's just the type you want." Dr. Masters was suddenly effusive and enthusiastic. He beamed and said, "Good! Francis, I want you to feel them out, and then, if it looks appropriate, arrange a meeting with the rest of us, so we can decide whether to bring them in on this critical mission."

Dr. Belcher stood up and gave Dr. Masters a mock salute. Dr. Belcher then said, "If you will excuse me, Dr. Masters, I am late for our scheduled meeting with The External Review Board." Dr. Masters then retorted as he did not want Dr. Belcher to think that his meeting was of more significance than the present gathering, "Remember, Francis, there will be extremely unpleasant consequences if you fail." Dr. Belcher replied, "I understand, Clement, but I think that depends on the rest of the group, not me! I am just the person coordinating the reporting for you. You can't expect me to accept any responsibility for the success or failure of this operation. I was not to be involved in any way." Dr. Masters stated firmly, "I expect all of you to accept responsibility for this operation and keep me informed of its progress, but not directly. You will report everything to Dr. Belcher here. I cannot be involved in any way." The rest of the group rose from their chairs and exited the room. Dr. Belcher remained behind to argue with Dr. Masters on who should take the responsibility if something went wrong. Neither of these top administrators wanted to take any responsibility if the mission failed, but they both wanted the accolades if everything worked out as planned.

In the hallway outside Dr. Masters' office Drs. Italiano and Auchenhower turned the corner and began walking to the elevator. Dr. Italiano looked over his shoulder to make sure no one was listening and spoke first, "I don't know about this, Roland. It's very scary." Dr. Auchenhower responded first, "What concerns me is the cold-blooded way our academic colleagues are orchestrating this. I really do not like the McNichols, and I don't mind screwing their careers, but I can't help thinking that this group could easily do the same thing to any one of us if we were in the same situation." Dr. Italiano said, "I find it hard to imagine that Marie McNichols is this heiress. Furthermore, I still don't understand why anyone in the government, if they are in the government, is so thoroughly convinced that Marie and Jared are such a threat to National Security. Someone always brings up some bullshit 'National Security' excuse to justify their actions." Dr. Auchenhower continued, "Dr. Masters did say that our high-level ex-government friend was once the National Security Advisor to the President, so he must have access to information about these two that we don't have." Dr. Italiano asked, "But suppose this ex-government guy has his own agenda? And what about this Las Vegas connection? What kind of bullshit is that? Are we all working for some Mafia-types in Las Vegas? Do you think that this has something to do with the involvement of The Madison in the prison testing that Isaac always brags about? What is this company, the Cornealyis Group, all about? Aren't they the company that was involved in some arms for drugs scandal in South America?"

After exiting the elevator Dr. Italiano mentioned to Dr. Auchenhower, "I hate to admit it, but Marie is developing an important technique for molecular biology." Dr. Auchenhower asked, "If you felt that way, why were you so zealous in your disruption of her seminar?" Dr. Italiano responded, "She's competition, even more than Jared! Come off it, Roland you had no problem heckling her at the seminar." Dr. Auchenhower answered, "I know. But I don't feel good about it; they're good scientists, and he won the faculty teaching award at the Medical School, but you're right. They're eventually competition, and there are just so many resources to go around, and I have to fight for my department." Dr. Italiano asked, "Could the fact that Jared was asked, not you, to take over the Cancer Biology Department have anything to do with your attitude? Weren't you previously in his department?" Dr. Auchenhower replied, "Yes, but I left the institution as he came on board. I only returned because they offered me another department chairmanship. Dr. Italiano then said, "I think I made my point, Roland. Wouldn't you like to merge your department with Jared's and take over all that space and money?" Dr. Auchenhower ignored the direction of the conversation and said, "Don't confuse me with Isaac Geldter!"

Dr. Auchenhower thought for a moment and continued the conversation after he lowered his voice. He did not want anyone to hear him. "By the way, what if this Las Vegas organization has some hidden agenda, and this is all just a smokescreen? I don't mind the ethics stuff and character assassination, but murder is way out of my depth, and I feel trapped. I don't want to go to jail as an accessory to murder. What if the FBI has been following these Las Vegas creeps, and they implicate us in their criminal activities? What's more, it's a very scary thought that Graham and Ross actually worked for some group in the CIA, and Geldter's zealous involvement in some highly questionable germ warfare experiments, not to mention his close relationship with this Ricin character. Well, it just does not sit well with me. This could be dangerous. I don't want to end my career in jail . . . . or worse."

Dr. Italiano whispered into Dr. Auchenhower's ear to avoid being overheard by the passing staff members. "But what can we do? We couldn't stop this operation even if we wanted to, and neither of us can afford to lose our jobs. Besides, they would just recruit someone else to do the dirty work. Look, they already recruited Domasovitch, and you know he will go along with anything that they want. He would do anything to advance his career. I wonder if they are recruiting someone in my own department to watch me! I don't know what to do. They may even be watching me now!"

Dr. Auchenhower looked back over his shoulder to see if he could recognize anyone from his department watching them in the hallway. They walked together down the hallway, and the two finally parted to go to their respective offices. Before they separated they both shook their heads not knowing how it would all end. They were not worried about the others–they would probably get what they deserved–their only thoughts were for their own careers and livelihoods. The thought of anyone, especially their own family members, finding out about their questionable activities was depressing to them. They had entered academia to pursue a noble cause, the acquisition of knowledge that could some day help people. Now they found themselves in a rat race that demanded for their own survival the very destruction of some of their own colleagues. Ironically, neither of them would ever warn the McNichols of the imminent threat to their health. They would go along with Dr. Masters and his plots.

CHAPTER 7

A Fateful Trip to Cambridge (1994)

The McNichols had to travel to Cambridge, England to attend a scientific conference at Queens' College. Jared had been invited as a major speaker at the conference, and Jared and Marie were both excited about the prospect of escaping from Austin for a week or so. They had been so busy that Marie forgot to contact Laura Graham about the invitation to attend her graduate student's graduation party. Two days before they were to leave she discussed the situation with Jared. "I really don't feel like going to Laura Graham's for this graduation party. If it were my own student, I wouldn't feel that I had a choice, but in this case I barely know the student." Jared responded, "I don't want to go either. It's just before we leave on a trans-Atlantic flight. Although I know the student, I don't feel responsible for making sure that her party is a success." Marie continued, "I am sick of doing obligatory socializing with the D. O. Madison staff. It's so phony! It's obvious how much the staff at The Madison hates me!" Jared agreed, "It's absurd! What's really ridiculous is the gossip at these social get-togethers. I hate it." Marie added, "I know what you mean!" Jared continued, "It seems everywhere we go people look at us sort of cockeyed. I hate being the subject of the gossip mill." Marie thinking back, "I've had it my entire life, and I still don't understand it!" Jared said after a sigh, "I'll have my secretary call Graham and make our apologies. We'll blame it on the trip." Marie then suggested, "I'll order some flowers, say roses, and send them to her student with a congratulations message." Jared thought about the situation and then agreed, "Good idea! I didn't want to go anyway."

The trip to Cambridge was tiring. Flying overnight from Houston to Gatwick Airport south of London, they then had to make their way to

Cambridge north of London. It was not the easiest pathway to their destination but what could they do. They had to take a train to Victoria Station, catch the Underground, which Marie hated, to North Euston Station and then hop a train north to Cambridge. By the time that they arrived, the quiet solitude of the Cambridge University Campus was soothing to Jared and Marie, who had been trying to put in eighteen-hour work days before they left Austin. They arrived by taxi from the rail station and checked into their accommodations at Queens' College. After finding their Spartan room upstairs, they decided to unpack and take a walk through the beautiful gardens near the Campus. The path wound its way along a canal or creek and then over the famous Mathematics Bridge. Jared told Marie that this was as far as he was going with her. After some protesting by Marie, he kissed her and rushed off to the conference site to register for the meeting. He would attend the conference for the both of them. Marie made her way back to the hotel room, but she was unhappy with Jared for just leaving her on the Mathematics Bridge and not bringing her back to the room.

The meeting with Professor Clever

The following day while Jared was attending the conference Marie visited with Professor Abraham Clever, a Nobel Prize winning physicist. She had not bothered to make an appointment because she wanted to confront him with her suspicions that he was blocking her scientific papers from being published. Marie wanted to know why Dr. Clever had taken such a dislike for her research.

Marie walked by herself to Dr. Clever's office. After a brief walk through the historic campus, she arrived at a beautiful old building on the Queens' College quad. The surroundings were so different from the tall, sterile buildings surrounded by concrete of the Austin medical center. She found her way up to Dr. Clever's office and determined that it was a typical office of a senior professor at Cambridge, one of the most prestigious universities in the world. Since the secretary that normally manned the empty desk in his outer office was not present, Marie hesitantly knocked on the inner office door. She heard Dr. Clever inside muttering, "Come in, please!" He had a very proper British accent, and his demeanor was even more condescending and uppity than when Marie first met him at the Meyerhoff Conference in Israel. He smacked of someone who would be extremely put out if he had to endure a meeting with a junior scientist.

Marie entered Dr. Clever's office with a smile and carefully studied her surroundings. The walls were covered with awards and mementos of his distinguished career. A photograph was featured behind his desk where he was receiving the Nobel Prize from the King of Sweden. He also had a sterling silver tea service on a small table and a fragment of a tapestry from Belgium. Next to the photograph of his receiving the Noble Prize was a primitive-style print with a theme from the story of King David of the Old Testament.

Dr. Clever's face showed a mixture of shock and disdain as Marie entered the room, as if he was extremely surprised to see her. In fact, he looked like he had seen a ghost. His shock imparted the suspicion that he never suspected to see Marie again. It was clear that Dr. Clever did not like Marie. Marie spoke first, "Professor Clever, I'm so happy to see you again! Do you remember me? I'm Marie McNichols, and I met you at the Meyerhoff Conference." Dr. Clever just nodded his head, probably hoping that Marie would just go away. She idolized Dr. Clever's mind and his distinguished contribution to the field of chromatin structure, and she was not about to be chased away so easily. Marie continued, "Dr. Clever, I want you to know that I have read all your papers, and I cannot express how much you have inspired and influenced me in designing my own experiments." Dr. Clever recovered quickly and impatiently said, "Yes! Yes! Right! Get on with it?" Marie asked, "Get on with what, sir?" Dr. Clever responded, "The reason for your visit, of course."

Dr. Clever continued the conversation in a very rude and abrupt manner. "I am foolishly disrupting my schedule, so get on with it." Marie was taken aback by his rude behavior, "Dr. Clever, I take it you are not as happy to see me as I am to see you?" Dr. Clever, "Frankly, Marie, I have no earthly idea as to why you should wish to see me." Marie responded, "Dr. Clever, I am here because you told me at the Meyerhoff conference that I should stick to my guns in testing my hypothesis on the Nucleoprotein Gene Tracking technique." She paused and looked at him directly, "You also informed me that you would do everything in your power to block my efforts in developing my research. I am here because I have the distinct suspicion that you are blocking my manuscripts that I submitted for publication." Dr. Clever answered in a sarcastic manner, "What a brilliant deduction, Marie!" Marie asked, "Why would a person of your stature take such pains to block the publication of my experiments? You know I find it bizarre that you would want to stop my career. Colleagues of mine have been implying that I shouldn't be allowed to publish and that I am unstable." Dr. Clever responded, "Perhaps you are!"

Marie did not let that comment pass without a fight. "Dr, Clever, quite frankly, I just do not see why individuals such as yourself should feel so threatened by my work that you would stoop to such lowly actions. And why is everyone so interested in me, and why does the interest take on such negative undertones." Dr. Clever responded, "I cannot speak for your colleagues, but you are acting as if you have delusions of grandeur. None of us really gives a damn about you or your career." Marie asked, "If that is the case, then why have certain people told me that you are gunning for me. So, Dr. Clever I am not imagining that you have a peculiar interest in my career." Dr. Clever abruptly and sarcastically responded, "Will you get to the point, Marie. I do not have all day to speculate if you are the victim of some conspiracy. You are, after all, merely a peon in the general scheme of things, and as far as leaving your personal mark on science, in my opinion, that is very unlikely as you obviously do not have the necessary talent."

Marie now became very angry. "How can you make such a blanket statement, sir, without even taking the time to study the manuscripts I have written?" Dr. Clever responded, "I don't want to read your manuscripts, nor do I want anything to do with you in any sense of the word!" Marie asked, "Pardon me, sir, but what have I done to you that you should feel such animosity towards me? I have always admired your work, and I cannot understand why you dislike me so when my work is merely an extension of your own. Why should I pose such a threat to you?" Dr. Clever asked, "Why would I be threatened by your work?" Marie responded, "That's what I would like to know! Your response has led me to conclude that you perceive my work to be a threat. From my standpoint, what else could it be?"

Dr. Clever suddenly had an enormous outburst. He jumped up from his seat behind his desk and said loudly at Marie, "I can not handle the fact that you exist! It is impossible for you to exist and yet here you are in apparent good health, standing before my very eyes." Marie was puzzled by his response, "I do not know what's wrong with you, Dr. Clever, and don't know why so many prominent scientists treat me as if I were some sort of ghost. I barely know you, and I cannot understand your irrational behavior and unwillingness to critique my science as you would any other student who coveted your opinion. And don't tell me I am imagining things, and that your rude behavior is not in some way connected to these unreasonable attitudes. I have seen this before."

Dr. Clever was speechless and looked stunned and uncomfortable as if he knew something, but he would not tell Marie. Marie continued, "I am not blind, but I have to be suspicious when my presence here is met with the same sort of scorn that I experienced at the Meyerhoff Conference. I know my work is good, and it's at least worthy of attention from scientists in the field. Granted, the work is in its early phases of development, but many senior scientists have urged me to continue to develop the Nucleoprotein Gene Tracking technique. They told me to ignore the negativity of the average scientist, and they have encouraged me by saying that throughout the history of science new ideas have been met with extreme resistance and ridicule."

Dr. Clever was unusually nervous, and he backed away from Marie and asked, "Why are you here?" Finally Marie had enough and said, "Dr. Clever I am at the end of my patience with you! You may have won the Nobel Prize, and everyone may kowtow to you. And you may be the director of the British Research Association, and a peer of the Order of the British Empire. But I'll tell you what you are not and what you do not have—You completely lack character, and I am younger than you. I will outlive you! No matter what it takes, I will publish my work. None of us is ever one hundred percent right or one hundred percent wrong and that includes you. Knowledge is an extension of the work of many, and if you continue to block my publications and persist in this idiotic blackballing, I can promise you that you will go down in history as a scientific fool. I, for one, will not be intimidated by your abrasive and rude manner, unlike others who you bully with your ridiculously crude tactics. You are not God!"

Marie turned quickly on her heal and headed toward the office door. "Good day, sir!" Marie then walked briskly out of the office. It was obvious that their altercation was overheard by Dr. Clever's administrator who had since arrived and now had a mixture of shock and outrage on her face. In spite of the drama of her encounter with Dr. Clever, Marie looked calmly and passively at Dr. Clever's administrator and said, "And Good day to you too, ma'am!"

The Conference at Queens' College

Marie was spending a lot of time sleeping in the McNichols' room in Queens' College while Jared was attending the conference. Although Jared had his detractors, most of the participants respected Jared and his research. The newer research of the McNichols on chronic illnesses associated with the Gulf War did not come up when he was in conversation with his European colleagues, and when it did come up, they were very supportive. In Europe most scientists and physicians did not trust the military's explanation for Gulf War Illnesses, and in Great Britain they had the same problems with their veterans. The veterans had been mislead so many times before that it had hardened them into not accepting anything that the British Ministry of Defence had to say on the topic, and the other Europeans were even more forthright. They flat out did not believe in what the Pentagon had to say about anything, which was sad indeed. Interestingly, they fully understood the problems in trying to assist the sick veterans of a war that was not popular in Europe, because they widely assumed that the U. S. Department of Defense played a role in starting the war by not restraining Iraq just before it invaded Kuwait. Now the DoD probably had much to hide, which was unfortunately true.

After two days at Queens' College, Marie and Jared were attending a cocktail and hors d'oeuvres party prior to the farewell banquet of the conference. There were about 100 people at the cocktail party engaged in chitchat or conversation relating to the scientific presentations of the meeting. Marie was dressed in a Blue silk evening dress and featured around her neck was a magnificent gold necklace with a large sapphire, a gift from her family. She had finally calmed down over the altercation with Professor Clever and was speaking to Jared about the encounter. She posed the hypothesis that the hostile actions of individuals such as Clever and those at D. O. Madison must have some common thread.

Some of Jared's colleagues then arrived and introduced themselves to Marie while Jared was talking to some young students. It was time to attend the banquet, and they offered to accompany Marie to the festivities. She was not accustomed to such nice treatment. The dining room at Queens' College where the banquet was held was a lovely room indeed. There were beautiful stained glass windows that reflected the early evening sunset light, and there were historical objects d'art placed strategically around the room. A string quartet was playing selections from Handel, Mozart, and Purcell.

Jared hurried over to the group after leaving the students who were not attending the banquet. He was dressed in a dark blue suit that complemented Marie's dress. Jared was drinking white wine and Marie, who didn't drink alcoholic beverages, was holding a soft drink. Marie was still thinking about her altercation with Professor Clever and said to Jared, "I cannot believe that Clever actually said he could not handle the fact that I exist!" She paused, "And he was incredibly hostile! I tell you Jared that this hostile behavior here in Europe and back in Austin must have been orchestrated. At least at the Meyerhoff conference the scientists completely ignored me, but here they love to play that British 'one-ups-manship' academic game that turned me off in college." Jared said, "Remember, all new ideas or observations are met with extreme resistance in science. At least you are getting some reaction." Marie responded, "I know, I know! My mentor in graduate school told me to throw myself into a controversy, and the controversy would act as a catalyst for my career. And he, too, told me about the extreme resistance to my being graduated. Controversy seems to follow me no matter what I do! But I tell you the attitude of Professor Clever and others is based upon something other than science. I have had to experience this weird and bizarre behavior all my life. I didn't understand it then, and I don't understand it now." She paused, "And I tell you, Jared, they act as if they wished I were dead, and they even seem surprised that I am alive."

Jared looked skeptically at Marie, "Are you sure that you're not overreacting?" Marie answered, "Why won't you believe me?" Jared continued, "I do, but I find this frustrating, and I do not know what to make of it." At just this moment Dr. Geoffrey Fence, a senior administrator at a major pharmaceutical company and an old friend of Jared's came up to the McNichols. Dr. Fence, who was about 6 feet 3 inches tall, was a distinguished looking man, with a devilish smile to match his blue eyes. Jared's face took on a genuine smile, "Geoff! It's good to see you! I completely enjoyed your presentation." As Jared spoke, the two men engaged in a hardy handshake. Geoff was British so he switched to his refined British accent, "Good to see you, old boy. Top flight presentation you gave, Jared." Then with a chuckle he continued, "No matter how good I think my latest studies are, yours always seem to be one step ahead." Jared smiled as if he knew a line when he heard it, "You're exaggerating again, Geoff, but I love it." Dr. Fence then turned his attention to Marie and with a puzzled expression but one full of affectation conveyed to her, "Bonjour, Marie!" Marie replied, "Bonjour to you, too!" Dr. Fence then took Marie's hand and gave it a continental kiss, "You're looking awfully fit and beautiful Marie! How do you feel?" Marie to Dr. Fence, "Quite well, thank you." Dr. Fence continued, "You appear to be completely recovered from that illness." Marie said, "I feel great now. I don't even have jet lag! But to be honest, Geoff, you don't look so well yourself. And you seem to be a bit shocked that I am well." Dr. Fence answered, "Now, Marie, that's absurd. It must be your jet lag that has prompted you to imagine such a thing. I happen to be thrilled that you have recovered and your beauty remains intact."

Dr. Fence had heard from his old friend Dr. Geldter about his attempts to kill Marie and Jared, and he did not agree with it. In fact, he rarely spoke to anyone in Austin now, so he was quite out of the loop. He did not know what to make of the hostility that was being directed at Jared and Marie in Austin, but it couldn't be simple academic politics. It had gone way too far for simple academic bickering. He said to Marie, "What a beautiful dress!" Marie replied, "Now, Geoff, you know that flattery will get you nowhere with me! How's Lynette?" Dr. Fence responded, "She's doing quite well. Unfortunately she could not accompany me to this meeting due to her work schedule." Marie said, "That's a shame. I would have loved to see her. Give her my best!" Dr. Fence asked, "Is that large pink sapphire around your neck real?" Marie responded as she held it up so that he could see it more closely, "As far as we know, it is. This is called the Cetta Darma Sapphire, and it is considered quite important to my European family." Dr. Fence exclaimed, "That's incredible! I have never seen a sapphire that size!"

At this point chimes were sounded, and everyone proceeded to file into the banquet room. Both Jared and Marie told Dr. Fence that their presence was required at the head table as Jared was the keynote speaker on that particular day of the meeting. Dr. Fence nodded and made a comment, "As I was saying Jared, you're still on top of your research. Do you wish that Isaac Geldter were here like in the old days?" Jared chuckled in a somewhat sarcastic way, "I didn't know you were nostalgic, Geoff. But no, I really don't want to look back, and I really don't want to see Dr. Geldter either. See you after the banquet."

As Marie and Jared turned and proceeded to the banquet head table, Geoff had a puzzled look on his face. No one noticed in the corner of the large room a man dressed in a black suit who whispered to another man, "Has the final component been combined?" The second man nodded. "Good, I will give it to our contact in the kitchen just before the dessert. Hopefully, it won't alter the taste." The second man said, "Only a person with a trained palette would notice any difference." The first man replied, "Let's hope so! I have to join the banquet now. Good hunting!" He saluted and hurried off to the kitchen.

In the banquet room, the time passed quickly, and the evening meal was enjoyed by the participants and friends alike. At the end of the evening the string quartet that had been playing during the dinner was replaced by a small orchestra that was playing "I'll be loving you always" in a waltz tempo. Marie looked at Jared with tears in her eyes. Jared asked, "What's wrong, baby?" Marie answered, "That's my song–it always chokes me up. It reminds me of my childhood." Jared said, "Maybe the song will trigger more memories that you have somehow blocked out. You know Marie, we will get to the bottom of who you are eventually." Marie replied, "I don't want to think about it! I'm just me!"

At that moment the chairman of the conference tapped on a microphone to get the attention of the audience in order to make a brief speech. "Right! I want to thank you all for being here, and I hope that you enjoyed the setting. This conference, I think you will all agree, has been a splendid success." He continued his brief presentation from a small platform that was installed for the banquet. At the end of his brief speech he said, "And I would like to present today's keynote speaker, Dr. Jared McNichols, with a small token of our appreciation for his marvelous presentation! Applause was heard and Jared walked up to receive a plaque.

Jared had to deliver a few comments at the microphone. "Thank you all so very much. My wife Marie and I are most pleased and privileged to be invited to this wonderful conference. We always love visiting the U.K. and especially meeting the young scientists with all their enthusiastic and brilliant ideas. These ideas and certainly the individuals are the future of our field. A meeting such as this is a rare opportunity to combine the enthusiasm of youth with the seasoned experience of some of the experts in our field. This continuity, I believe as your Queen would say, is the heart of promise for the future. Thank you again!" Jared returned to his seat after acknowledging the polite applause. As was usual at such conference banquets, most of the participants were engaged in scientific discussion and barely noticed the formalities. However, there was one person in the audience that was paying attention. Marie said to Jared as he sat down, "I'm so proud of you!"

The final course for the evening meal was being served during the brief presentations, and the tables had been readied for the dessert, Crème Brulee. Finally the waiters made their way to the last of the tables, except for the head table. A waiter offered the desserts to both Jared and Marie, and placed the dessert in front of them. The McNichols did not see the waiter's expression, but he briefly glanced at the man in the dark suit who was seated at a table off to the right of the banquet room. Jared was not particularly fond of Crème Brulee, because it was usually too sweet for his taste, but he took a small bite and told Marie, "I'm sorry, Marie, it's too rich for me! But I believe this is your favorite?" Marie answered, "Right you are!" She took a small bite and looked at Jared and said, "You know, Jared, it doesn't taste quite right." Jared told her, "Well, I didn't like it much either. So don't eat it!"

Marie and Jared continued to be engaged in quiet conversation while the rest of the table was involved in a typically British discussion of local politics. Marie to Jared, "You know, Jared, I know this is going to sound paranoid, but sometimes I think people are trying to hurt us." Jared replied, "That would depend on if we were important enough to harm. I doubt if I am, but to tell you the truth, Marie, the fact that you have the Cetta Dharma pink sapphire tells me that there is some kind of aristocracy or wealth in your background." Marie answered, "You could have fooled me. There were times when we could barely make ends meet." Jared asked, "Do you think you were placed with a family to hide you." Marie asked, "What do you mean?" Jared continued, "I mean that the secret to your identity may have put you at great risk, and someone may have taken great pains to put you in a place where no one would think to look. Furthermore, I think the lack of money in the family that raised you was part of the cover. You know, this sort of thing happened often in Europe during times of revolution and change."

Marie did not want to accept what Jared was saying to her, but in her heart she knew that there was something to it. "Jared, that's absurd." Jared then countered, "Marie, someday I want you to read the book 'Holy Blood, Holy Grail.' Marie asked, "What is that? I've never heard of it." Jared continued, "You know, you look French or Italian, not Eastern European. And there is something associated with you. I bet that this book will help you in your search. It's about the Merovingian dynasty, the precursor blood-line to all the European royals." Marie who felt that Jared's idea was absurd relented, "All right, I'll read the damn book. But now I'm tired and I want to leave this banquet and go right to bed." Jared smiled because he knew that he had finally made Marie confront what he felt was her aristocratic linage.

Jared and Marie were engaged in a final brief conversation with the other people at their table, and then they excused themselves and bid their farewells. Before leaving, they looked for the conference organizer to thank him. Jared said, "Thank you again for a such a lovely evening." The Cambridge man asked, "Leaving so soon?" Jared told him, "Marie is very tired, and we have a busy day tomorrow." The conference organizer said with an impish smile on his now rosy face from all the wine he had consumed, "You don't fool me a minute, Jared. You two lovebirds just want some privacy. Oh, by the way, I never did get a chance to congratulate you both." Marie responded, "Thank you very much." Jared said, "We plan to tour the Southeast." Marie added, "I am really excited, because I haven't been there yet." The organizer had a thought, "May I recommend that you drive down to Salisbury and have a look around. Then you should continue to Bournemouth by the sea. If you are lucky you'll have an excellent view of the Isle of Wight where Queen Victoria's beloved Osborne is situated."

Jared agreed, "Great idea!" Jared said to the organizer, "Thank you again for such a wonderful experience!" The organizer replied, "We hope to repeat this success in two years when the meeting will be moved to Edinburgh." Marie added, "I hope you keep us in mind for presentations." The organizer said, "Definitely!" Everyone then said their good-byes, "Good night!"

As Marie and Jared left the banquet room, they noticed Dr. Geoff Fence, who nodded and waved, and then they left. After they were outside the banquet hall, Jared turned to Marie, "You know, Geoff Fence was a lot nicer to us here in Britain than he was at that meeting in Houston. Don't you remember how he and Isaac Geldter were so horrible to us? I haven't forgotten, and I haven't felt quite the same about him since." Marie was quiet, unusual behavior for her, but she said as they left for their room, "I don't feel well, Jared!" Jared said, "I know what you mean, I don't feel especially well myself. Let's get some sleep. Perhaps we'll feel better in the morning."

Although Marie and Jared were given the poison cocktail at the dinner, neither of them ate enough to receive a lethal dose. However, Marie felt sick, and Jared had to get up in the night to vomit, which scared Marie. Jared also had night sweats and a roaring headache all night long. He had to get up early anyway and get ready for the morning session. Even though his stomach was still bothering him and the lack of sleep the night before was taking its toll, Jared dragged himself to the conference. However, he found it extremely difficult to concentrate when his stomach was still on fire. Marie spent the next day in bed in the room not eating anything and locking out the maids. Jared attended the final session of the conference after a bad night and a slow morning. He returned back to the room and found that Marie had finally risen and was showering. He waited for her so they could go together to the lunchroom in another building.

Marie and Jared finally felt up to eating a light lunch but neither of them felt very strong. On the way to the lunchroom Jared said, "I don't know what we ate last night, but it was pure poison. It did not agree with me at all." Marie added, "I tell you, it was that Crème Brulee. I know there was something wrong with it." Jared agreed, "I know what you mean, I didn't like it either. I had this sickly taste in my mouth the entire night. I hardly got any sleep." Marie asked, "What are we going to do? I think that we *were* poisoned!" Jared told her, "Don't panic, Marie, if anything was in the Crème Brulee, you didn't eat enough of it to kill you, at least today–I'm only kidding!" Marie abruptly stopped and said in an angry voice, "Stop making jokes about it. I tell you, something was wrong with it; I'm sure of it." Jared said, "Well, we took enough Pepto to thoroughly coat our stomachs–Your standard procedure." Marie continued, "No wonder we didn't feel well after that dessert!" Jared then said, "I think that we should watch it and be more careful but not panic. I still don't think that we had enough of it to do any lasting harm." Marie asked, "But what if you're wrong? What if we did eat enough?" Jared replied jokingly, "First, we're sick! Then we die!" Marie became mad and hit Jared, "Stop it Jared–You're scaring me! Why do you always make jokes about something so serious?" Jared just shrugged his shoulders. He was just trying to get Marie to lighten up and keep moving. If there was one thing that the McNichols had learned about poisonings, it was that you've got to keep moving so that you can metabolize the poison.

Jared held Marie's hand as they continued toward the lunchroom. He decided to change the subject. "You look like you're feeling better not worse than yesterday. That's a good sign–I don't think you're going to die. Perhaps this will all pass, and we can go on our merry way." As they found a table and sat down he said, "Here, take some of these immune enhancement products that I brought with me. These are very good at boosting your immune system against infections." Marie asked, "But what if it wasn't a contagion that they gave us?" Jared continued, "First, I don't think that either of us ate enough of anything last night to poison us, unless it was really exotic. If it was in the Crème Brulee, neither of us really consumed much of anything but a small taste. Second, if it was some poison, it would have to be very, very potent after all that Pepto we took. We probably couldn't absorb enough to do us much harm. Look! We're still here! Third, if it was something contagious, then the gastrointestinal route is a poor way to infect someone if they are taking immune enhancers to boost their immune system. And it would need some time to proliferate. We'll know in a few days." Marie was still upset, "What if you're not correct? What if we become really sick!" Jared responded, "Then we'll see in a few days." Marie said, "I don't like this! Why do you always joke about things like this?" Jared answered her. "I don't know. Probably because I have no control over them." But this time Jared *was* right, and they both would survive the next few days and not become sicker. They may not have felt as chipper as they should, but they were not completely incapacitated, and they continued on their trip about the English countryside.

An after conference trip in Southern England

Jared decided that they should leave Cambridge and drive to Salisbury and then to Bournemouth on the Southern coast. Since it was still noon, they decided to begin the drive to Salisbury, instead of staying another night in Cambridge. The conference was over, and everyone had to vacate their rooms anyway. Jared went downstairs, ordered up a car and had it delivered to Queens' College. After a good morning rest, Marie was feeling better and making comments about remembering to drive on the "wrong side of the road." Jared didn't appreciate the comments, because he was an old hand at driving in Great Britain.

Jared and Marie continued their drive South because Marie wanted to see the sea. Jared didn't dare add, " . . . see the sea before you die." Marie had grown wary of Jared's constant joking about poison and dying. He was just trying to make light of a bad situation, but Marie was right. Enough was enough.

Jared's plan was to avoid London. They would surely get caught in heavy traffic, so they took the M25 around London and headed directly south passing Gatwick Airport. Not that the M25 was any picnic—it was probably one of the busiest 'dual carriageways' in Great Britain. Eventually they did survive the M25, headed South past Gatwick Airport and eventually reached the outskirts of Bournemouth. Marie wanted to see the ocean, so Jared pressed on, and they arrived quite by chance at a lovely hotel by the sea. Marie was always nagging Jared to make sure that they had reservations, but Jared was becoming ever careful to avoid giving anyone their itinerary. Unknown to Marie, Jared was planning to make sure that no one knew in advance where she would be for the remainder of the trip.

They drove along the sea on a nice boulevard, finding that there were many rather small hotels that might be adequate. Finally, they found what they both wanted. The hotel that Jared was interested in was the Royal Bournemouth Hotel, and it was located right on the boulevard that was on the edge of a slight cliff above a rocky beach. It had an unobstructed view of the sea from most of its rooms. It was now quite late in the evening, and there was a full moon over the Isle of Wight off in the distance. Jared assured Marie that they would have no problem obtaining a room, although privately he was not so sure. There were other hotels by the sea in Bournemouth, perhaps not as grand as the Royal Bournemouth, but still very adequate for a brief stay. Jared parked in front of the hotel, left Marie in the car while he checked in, and he returned to face Marie, who was growing very uneasy waiting in the car alone. He was able to proudly tell Marie that they had a suite with an ocean view. Finally, Marie was excited about the place! They couldn't wait to see the room and the view.

After convincing the hotel night staff that the bumbling Americans who arrived late and missed dinner, were just late and not so bumbling, the staff took pity on Marie and Jared and fixed them tea and sandwiches. Everything seemed just right. They had a beautiful room, a magnificent view and a lovely warm bed. The sandwiches and tea came, and they were both quite happy eating with a magnificent moonlight view of the distant Isle of Wight. They were both exhausted and quickly fell asleep, but at about five in the morning Marie went through a brief episode of illness where all the symptoms she experienced during her long almost lethal illness suddenly appeared but for only a brief time. She woke up Jared to tell him, but he was so groggy that he couldn't concentrate on what she was saying. However, Jared also appeared to be sick, and the bed was wet with his perspiration.

About an hour later Marie woke up, and Jared was dripping in perspiration and had rashes all over his body. After first making sure that Jared would survive, Marie again speculated that they were poisoned and reiterated the strange behavior of some of the people at the conference. The wave of sickness passed from Marie by eight in the morning but Jared still had a problem, so they had some breakfast sent to their room. By noon Jared was feeling better, the maids were banging at the door to get in and clean the room, and so they decided to not miss the chance to visit the surrounding region. Jared, who was finally feeling better after a shower, packed up their luggage and told Marie, "I've repacked our stuff and loaded up the car. I can't believe how long that took me. I'm really not up to snuff. Have you finished changing into something more comfortable?" Marie answered, "I'm ready! I am so excited about seeing the South Coast of England! I've wanted to see Stonehenge since I was a little girl!"

While Marie was preparing to vacate the room, Jared hid from Marie and locked himself into the bathroom where he secretly vomited. He was sweating profusely, and he quietly leaned on the washbasin with his hands over his face. Marie finally realized that Jared had been in the bathroom a long time and knocked on the door. "Jared, are you O.K.? Jared shaking but coherent, "Couldn't be better! I'll be out in a bit. Just let me wash up." Marie knew that Jared had taken a shower only an hour ago, and she wondered what he was up to in the bathroom. "Are you sure that you're O.K." Jared washed his face, gained his composure and straightened up. "Yes I am. Can I have a little privacy here?" He did not want to let Marie know that he still had some problems from the cocktail that they received in Cambridge.

They finally left the room a full hour after check out time and made their way to the car park. As they approached the car, Marie automatically went to the right side of the car. Jared had to again remind Marie, "We're in England now. Remember, the passenger side is on the left and the driver sits to the right." Marie looked at Jared and flashed her eyes, "This is tough to get used to! Are you sure that you're not sick? You don't look right to me." Jared did not answer immediately, "You want to try driving here in England, Marie? You know, everything is reversed including the gear shift and the way it's operated." Jared knew that he'd got her—she wouldn't insist on driving in England.

After they entered the vehicle, Marie still had a worried look on her face. Jared tested the gearshift with the opposite orientation, "I have to really concentrate to get it right. Please don't nag me today." Marie looked at him in horror. She didn't really want to drive, so they had no choice. It was Jared or nothing. At last the couple began their drive along the coast, and Marie was still on the edge of her seat as Jared rushed through the round-abouts with the oncoming traffic. He tried to tell her, "If we don't keep up with the traffic, someone will run into us." Jared had to concentrate on the 'right of way' rules for round-abouts, but everything was just fine. Finally they were off, and they were not on the main M-motorways or even A-roads. She said, "Jared, I feel like I am plummeting into the side of the road, and it seems like you're going to hit those trees." Jared laughed,

"You'll get used to it." Marie screamed, "Oh my God! Here comes a truck!" Jared reminded her, "That's a lorry here in England."

Even Jared felt a bit uncomfortable as their vehicle crossed over a narrow stone bridge of the type often found on tertiary roads. As the lorry passed to the right of their car Marie let out a tiny scream. When the lorry had passed Marie said, "That was too close for comfort." Jared answered, "I must admit, even I was a little worried, but once we get onto the A-roads, everything will be just fine." Marie said, "You've forgotten that I've always had bad peripheral vision. And since the illness, it's gotten worse." Jared replied, "You've come a long way since the darkest days of the illness." Marie answered, "I think it was divine intervention that saved me." Jared agreed, "You may be right! It was horrible to see you wasting away before my very eyes, and I could do nothing." Marie added, "But I still feel weak on my left side and occasionally my vision is not quite right."

Marie had overall made a miraculous recovery from her near lethal illness. She related to Jared, "I do believe that I'm finally on the road to recovery, which I thank God for every day. I even have a new perspective on how the terminally ill must feel. Only in my case, by the grace of God, I have been given a second chance. I wonder why I was able to overcome the illness? And now you don't look so good!" Jared ignored the question, "I'm sure that one day, the true meaning of your experience will present itself. Until then, however, let's try to put this behind us and concentrate on happier and more productive pursuits . . . Deal?" Marie responded positively, "Deal!"

Marie and Jared spent the better part of the day exploring the little towns along the Southern coast. They were now driving by the sea, and Marie said, "Jared, it's beautiful here! But where are we going to stay?" Jared smiled, "It's a surprise! But we're almost there." Marie was not happy, "You know I hate surprises!" Jared pleaded, "It's just a little further." They entered a small town, and Marie felt a bit better about where they were going to stay. At least she had an idea of the town they would be staying in. Now she wanted to know about the accommodations. She asked, "Are we going to stay by the sea?" Jared answered, "That's just where we're headed."

Jared was turning and racing through the round-abouts like a native. The McNichols drove as far as they could, and eventually they went right up to where the sea met the cliffs. Jared turned left, and almost immediately he pulled into a small parking lot of a rather small hotel. Jared announced, "That was easier than I thought it would be. You wait here, and I'll go check on our reservation." However, Marie was suspicious, and this time she did not want to stay in the car. She knew that Jared couldn't have made a reservation and found the hotel so easily. Jared finally had to tell her, "Look, Marie, I don't know if I can just leave the car here unattended. Just stay in the car for a moment and watch the ocean while I make sure of our reservation." Marie was still suspicious, perhaps because she knew that there was no reservation. However, Jared was confident that he could find a room for them, reservation or no reservation, but he did not want to scare Marie by telling her the truth.

In a few minutes Jared came back out and told Marie, "Guess what? We're in luck! The hotel has even upgraded us to a suite!" Marie acted like she did not suspect a thing but it was just an act. "That's great! Jared, I've just remembered another incident from my early childhood." Jared said, "Good! We will talk about it once we're settled and have some tea."

The Victorian hotel by the sea

The McNichols struggled through the hotel lobby with their bags and into the elevator. They were getting onto the one very small elevator in the entire hotel, when Jared finally spoke. "See, that wasn't so bad?" Marie would not be convinced until she saw the room, however, so they made their way through a series of swinging fire doors and found their suite, which was very luxurious by English standards. It also had a spectacular view of the Isle of Wight. Jared was relieved, because he didn't fancy changing hotels at this point. They were in the Southeastern corner of the hotel. The room was furnished in elegant English country style with lovely antiques. Fragments from a demolished Christopher Wren facade of a building were mounted and featured over the canopied beds. The color scheme of the room was soft peach with emerald green accents. They were suddenly tired and decide to take a nap, which turned into a several hour deep sleep. It was dark when they finally woke up.

Marie and Jared finally got out of the bed, showered and changed into the special robes provided by the hotel. Marie looked out the window and marveled at the view. "Jared, look! The full moon is illuminating the water and the Isle of Wight. It's like a continuous mother of pearl glow accented by stars." Jared responded, "It's beautiful here, even better than the last hotel." They playfully kissed and teased each other, but it was clear from the way Jared was perspiring that something was still wrong. Marie finally said, "I'm hungry!" Jared was waiting for this moment. He knew it was coming. Like clockwork Marie would get hungry, and she had to be fed. This time he didn't argue with her, and he called room service. At least in this hotel he would not have to argue with the management to have some tea and sandwiches brought up to the room.

Later that night Marie woke up with some of the signs and symptoms of her near-fatal illness that she overcame. She turned to Jared, but he was not there. Marie was in a panic. She got up and noticed a light from under the bathroom door. She then heard the vomiting and became very scared. Marie was afraid of vomiting. Marie knocked on the door and called out, "Jared, are you sick?" He answered, "No, just give me a minute." But Marie was not buying his story, "Did you just vomit?" Jared lied to her, "No, go back to sleep." Marie irritated, "You're lying, Jared!" Jared did not answer but said, "Can I get some privacy here? I'll be out in a minute!" Marie quietly returned to the bed with a look of horror on her face, and she then covered herself with a pillow and began to weep. Marie was afraid of the vomiting. It was something from her childhood. She still remembered when her stepfather would go to the bathroom and vomit. It scared her then, and she never got over it. She found her little stuffed elephant 'Lucky' that she brought with her, and she held Lucky very tight against her chest. She did not want to hear the vomiting.

That night the suite in the little Victorian hotel was awash with moonlight, and the gentle breeze was rustling the lace curtains surrounding the window. It had been raining earlier, but the rain had stopped. Marie suddenly got up at four o'clock in the morning, which was very unusual for her. She sat up and shook her head while putting the palm of her hand to her forehead. She felt shaky and slightly nauseated. She nudged Jared awake, "Jared! I am having one of those spells again. Just like I had during the worst phase of the illness!" Jared was still half asleep, "What's wrong?" Marie was worried, "The illness has come back! I just know it has!"

Jared rolled over and turned on the light. "Marie, you're shaking." Marie cried, "Jared, my heart is pounding and I have tremendous pain all over my body! Look! I'm perspiring all over! Look at me!" Jared responded, "Damn, we don't have any antibiotics, and it's unlikely that we'll be able to get some on short notice. All we have is some Tylenol for your fever." Marie became panicky, "At least we have Benedryl and Pepto Bismol! Jared, if I have to take 100 milligrams of Benedryl, I'll be zonked tomorrow." Marie became more agitated, "Jared, I am sure that they poisoned us again! I told you something was wrong with the Creme Brulee!" Jared replied, "We should have thought about taking the Benedryl and Pepto earlier to prevent uptake." Jared retrieved the Benedryl and Pepto for Marie.

Marie's whole body was beginning to shake, and she had to force down the Benedryl and then the Pepto. After she swallowed the Pepto Bismol, Marie made a face and said, "Yeach! She was still shaking, however. Then she noticed that Jared had been sweating profusely and was beginning to shake just like Marie. Marie in a panic-stricken voice, "I tell you we've been poisoned! Look at you! I know you think I am paranoid, but did you see how Geoff Fence looked at us? When he looked at me, he acted as if he'd seen a ghost? I tell you somebody wants us dead! But why? What have we done? This is ludicrous! Those people are not even in my field. Not to mention the looks in Cambridge! This is very well-organized!"

Jared wiped off the sweat from his body with a towel. He was also shaking but trying to act stoic and hide his condition from Marie who was near panic. He also took the Benedryl and Pepto. After a few moments Jared began to speak again. He was obviously in pain but was trying to reassure Marie. He said, "I hate to admit it, Babe, but you're not overreacting. I saw the looks and heard the whispers. Believe me, as much as I love you, if I did not think you had the talent for science, I would have steered you in another direction. But the work is original, and it is not that difficult to see the potential applications." Marie was crying, "They don't want to see it! And they even blocked my non-tenure position!" Jared trying to reassure her said, "I know. And I'm certainly having my problems with the D. O. Madison administration, but let's please not get started on that tonight."

Marie's symptoms had begun to pass but Jared looked worse. After less than an hour Marie finally said, "You know what, Jared? I think it's beginning to pass. How do you feel?" Jared didn't answer. He was trying to hide his symptoms from Marie so as not to scare her. He turned away from

Marie and was shaking under the covers, and sweat was flowing down his face. "I'll be fine in the morning."

Marie's shaking began to abate, and she started to calm down. But then she became angry. She was not looking at Jared, so she didn't notice that he was sick too. He was trying to act as if nothing was wrong. Marie finally said, "I don't know why people have always tried to paint me as crazy, ever since I can remember! First it was my grandfather. Then when I was in college, I was contacted by my physician father, if he was my father. He always acted very cold to me, even though he tried to hide it. He was always telling me that he was going to close the book on me, because I was living a lie. Then, for no apparent reason, he called all my professors and told them I was crazy and didn't belong in college. Ultimately, the college took out a restraining order against him, and the head psychiatrist told me that for reasons he could not explain I was relatively well-balanced. He then went on to say that I had to forge a new life for myself due to the irrational behavior of my parents. He told me that he had never given such advice in his 45 years as a practicing psychiatrist. It has always been like this! People have always tried to make it seem like I was unbalanced. It's almost as if someone or something wants to drive me to despair . . . . and ultimately drive me to suicide!"

Jared tried to reassure Marie. "I don't know if we can jump to that conclusion, but I have to agree that there *is* a pattern of character assassination. I have never seen such an extreme attack on a young scientist. And I have been in this academic game for over 25 years." Marie said, "You know what?" Jared was trying to act O.K. "What?" Marie said, "Back at college when I talked to the head psychiatrist, I also told him that I thought I must be a paranoid schizophrenic, because I felt I was being watched and followed. I told him this as we walked across campus. He then told me that I did not fit the profile of a paranoid schizophrenic and that he had noticed that I was not mistaken. He said, "You are being watched! But why?" I told him that I didn't know why. I then asked him if he thought it had anything to do with the fact that I was training with physicists who worked on classified projects. He said he doubted it. It had to be something different." Jared added, "I've noticed it too! Remember Bryce Canyon? That French couple appeared to be following us. Everywhere we went, there they were." Marie said wearily, "Yes, I remember, but I don't understand why they were following us!" Jared noted, "One thing is clear. We are not going to figure it out tonight. But my guess is that it has to do with who you are. Who are you, Marie?" Marie gave her stock answer, "I'm me!" Jared then said in a much gentler tone, "Babe, I know that, but I'm suggesting that you may have another identity, a different heritage than you imagine. You know, you look and act nothing like anyone in your so-called family. You have none of their traits, and they don't seem to have any of yours. And they don't act like your parents."

Marie yawned. She was tired and wanted to change the subject. Jared asked, "How are you feeling?" Marie responded, "It's passed." Jared answered, "Good! I think we should go back to sleep. We can take our time tomorrow." Marie asked, "How are you feeling?" Jared lied to Marie, "I'm O.K. Maybe a little tired." Marie looking closer, "You don't look O.K. to me! You're sweating all over the place! . . . . You're shaking! Now it's happening to you! Why is this happening to us? Jared, I'm scared!" Jared paused and tried to reassure Marie, "I'll live. I've been taking enough Benedryl to put an elephant down. The analgesic should break the fever. We can sleep in tomorrow. You wanted to go back to Stonehenge; it's still not that far, if you want to go back there tomorrow."

Marie was finally becoming sleepy, and she lowered her head to the pillow. "Jared, I think I'm immune to whatever was in the Creme Brulee." Jared trying to reassure Marie, "If there was anything in the Creme Brulee." Marie whined, "Jared!" Marie was still talking in a somewhat whiny manner, as if she was exasperated with him for not enthusiastically supporting her in her suspicions. She was finally beginning to get very sleepy as the high dose of Benedryl took affect. Her voice became weaker and she closed her eyes and said, "Why don't you accept the truth about what is happening?" Jared quietly responded, "I know, the Creme Brulee didn't taste right! But why do you think it was poisoned?" Marie didn't answer, "I have just had an abbreviated episode . . . . I had most of the symptoms that I had during the illness. Something had to trigger it . . . . Jared, you know that I have very good instincts about these things . . . . You'll see . . . . One day we will find out that we were deliberately poisoned." Jared asked, "Do you think that you had a secondary immune response to something in the Creme Brulee?" Marie didn't answer. She was finally asleep.

As Marie fell asleep from exhaustion, Jared still appeared to be very sick but he had successfully hidden it from Marie. When he knew that Marie was completely asleep, Jared quietly went to the bathroom and kneeled down and put his head in the toilet and vomited. He was shaking all over his body, and sweat was flowing down his arms and chest. Jared quietly to himself, "What's wrong with me? Oh, Marie, you're right. They did it to us!"

On to Stonehenge and beyond

It was a new, rare bright day, and the hotel was bathed in sunlight. Jared and Marie were partaking of the buffet breakfast at the hotel dining room before they set out for Stonehenge. The day was much better than they experienced in the last week, and the sun was coming out strongly and penetrating into the dining room. Marie was feeling better, but Jared was perspiring heavily and was obviously still sick. The hotel restaurant had a typical British breakfast buffet. There was a large selection of eggs, grilled tomatoes, yogurts and fresh fruits accompanied by a centerpiece that was shaped in the form of a swan. The feathered part of the swan was hollowed out and an assortment of breads and muffins were meticulously arranged inside.

The view from the dining room was the ocean, and it was a spectacular day. As Marie and Jared selected their breakfast items from the buffet table Jared asked Marie, "How do you feel?" Marie answered, "I finally feel great! I have not felt this good in years!" Marie then asked, "But how do you feel?" Jared lied, "I'm O.K., I'll survive." Marie did not believe Jared, but she did not want to discuss the illness. She was afraid of the illness and changed the subject, "I always take 'Lucky Lucius' with me to protect me from bad things." Jared replied, "You're such a baby! I can't believe that you brought that stuffed elephant all this way!" Marie jokingly, "He's not just any stuffed elephant! He's 'Mr. Lucky Lucius.' I had him with me all night long, and you never noticed?" Jared trying to hide his condition, "I guess I was too tired to notice." Marie excited, "Let's hurry, I can't wait to go to Stonehenge!" She looked at Jared and finally said, "Jared, you do not look so well!" Jared responded, "As I told you, I'll survive."

Stonehenge could not be reached directly from where Jared and Marie were located. Therefore, they had to drive back to Bournemouth and then directly north to Stonehenge. As they were driving North from Bournemouth, Marie couldn't wait to get there. The previous day it was raining on and off and not good for sightseeing, but today was a beautiful bright day. Marie was excited about Stonehenge, and when it finally came into view she adopted a child-like demeanor, which was sometimes part of her personality.

Jared turned into a parking lot on the opposite side of the highway. Marie wanted to bolt across the highway toward the rock formations, but she was prevented from doing this by Jared and the fence that ran along the road. As he got out of the car, Jared said to Marie, "Hold it! Before you run off, I have to get the camera!" Marie and Jared then hurriedly crossed under the highway to Stonehenge through a pedestrian tunnel. It was a rare crystal blue day in Southern England. They paid the entrance fee and Jared observed, "The place is empty!" Marie said, "Maybe the tourist economy is bad. It's not a weekend." Jared continued, "But at the height of the season?" Marie said, "Places always seem to be empty when I visit them! Just look at how empty the Hotel was in Vienna at the height of the season, or remember the hotel in Montego Bay in Jamaica?" Jared agreed, "Yes, but I still don't think that all of these empty places have something to do with you!" Marie answered, "Maybe they do!" They both immediately forgot about their conversation, and they began to admire Stonehenge. There was something magical about the place.

Marie and Jared continued their excursion in Southern England for the remainder of the day, and then made their way back to Gatwick Airport where they had to stay overnight at a hotel not too far from the airport. They kept the car just to make their way back to the airport where they could turn it in the next morning. The stay in an airport hotel was uneventful and completely unlike the hotels on the Southern Coast. They were both exhausted and fell asleep without an evening meal. The next morning was difficult but they were both doing better. After a hearty English breakfast, they picked up their car and headed for Gatwick Airport and the car rental drop off. Then to the airport, which always seemed to be teaming with sleepy passengers waiting to board their aircraft for the long flights home or for some well-deserved vacation.

The McNichols overall had a delightful visit in England, except for the possibility of being poisoned in Cambridge, and now they must return to Texas and the troubles that they were in at the D. O. Madison. They were sitting together on the DC-10 to Houston, looking out the window and munching on snacks. In the tourist section there was not much room. Jared still looked sick and was sweating. Marie complained, "This food is not fit for human consumption! God, I hate these long flights. Turning to Jared she said, "You don't look so good!" Jared replied, "My legs are cramping!" Marie suggested, "Let's just get up and walk around!" Jared responded, "Good idea! My legs are killing me." Both Jared and Marie made their way over to the flight attendants' station. Jared asked a flight attendant, "Could I have a cup of coffee, please." The Flight attendant said, "Sure!" Marie asked, "And I'd like a coke!" The flight attendant, "Pepsi O.K.?" Marie nodded her head. The attendant prepared the coffee and handed Marie the Pepsi. Marie said, "Thank you." Marie told Jared, "I'm going back to my seat." Jared still wanted to stand, "At least you're small enough to actually fit in your seat."

CHAPTER 8

The Conspiracy Continues (1994)

Jared and Marie had come back from the Cambridge conference to the hostility of The D. O. Madison Cancer Center administration. Little did they know that they weren't supposed to come back at all. The unknown poison in the Crème Brulee did not work as advertised, and although they were weakened, they survived. When Jared returned to work, he noticed that Dr. Domasovitch was his old self. He had been left in control of the department during Jared's absence, and it almost seemed like he was moving into Jared's office. Not everyone was happy to see the McNichols, but the number of detractors in Jared's department seemed to have grown during his absence. Jared took this to mean that he must work harder to win the confidence of his faculty. On the other hand, Marie felt that it was a lost cause. She mainly stayed away from anyone except Jared's senior technician Bob Sonan, who always seemed to lift Marie's spirits with his expert work in the laboratory.

The D. O. Madison President has his way

President Clement Masters had called a meeting with Drs. Belcher, Krappner, Geldter, Ross and Graham. The meeting had gone over the expected time, and Dr. Bane was waiting in the outer office for the next meeting with Drs. Italiano, Auchenhower and Domasovitch. These latter faculty members were not entirely or completely in on the conspiracy to eliminate two members of the Department of Cancer Biology, but they were about to be roped into doing things that they never expected to do in their careers.

By the end of the first meeting Dr. Masters was on a rampage. He was pacing around his office in front of his desk as he talked on the phone. The cord was tangled, but Dr. Masters did not have the patience to straighten it out. The other people in his office looked sheepish–They didn't dare interrupt him this time. His face was red as he slammed the phone receiver down, turned and said, "Damn it! Why didn't the Russian Doll Cocktail work as advertised! Geldter! This is your fault!" Dr. Geldter who was hardly ever on the defensive said, "I can't understand it! I'm *never* wrong! I'm sure that adding the new variant strains of mycoplasma with the asparaginase would have done the job! *They* must have screwed up. It's not my fault, I swear to God, Dr. Masters, it's not *my* fault!" Dr. Masters was angry, and he didn't like excuses, especially from a blow-hard. He turned to the others in the room. "What about the Ross party?" Drs. Ross and Graham were quiet. Finally, Dr. Gelter answered again. "We were there for the party, already. I took care of that myself. Turning to Drs. Ross and Graham and pointing Isaac almost shouted, "What happened to the McNichols? They should have been there! This is *your* fault!" Dr. Belcher for once kept his mouth shut. He did not want to share the blame that was being passed out for the Crème Brulee debacle in Cambridge.

Drs. Ross and Graham were shocked to learn that Isaac Geldter blamed them for the no-shows at their student's party just before the McNichols left for Cambridge. Dr. Graham in a nervous, whiny voice responded, "We can't help it that the McNichols didn't show up for the graduation party. I tried very hard to get them there! Marie promised that they would both be there." Dr. Krappner, who adapted her most haughty way and insinuated from every gesture that she knew that she could lord it over the other couple since they had failed, but she wanted to manipulate them to be supportive of her own first wish and ambition, which was to be the next Vice President for Academic Affairs at the D. O. Madison. So she deflected Dr. Masters' criticisms by saying, "Let's not criticize Dr. Ross and Dr. Graham for things they could not control. They could not help it if the McNichols failed to show up to their student's party. In my opinion, Dr. Masters, I feel that we must use the asparaginase approach again. The anaphylaxis is a good sign that immunosuppression is occurring. Therefore, I feel that we must use Isaac's approach again." She was trying to help out her husband, but Dr. Masters was not going to let Geldter off the hook.

Dr. Masters looked at the assembled co-conspirators and shook his head. He could hardly believe what he had just heard from Amy. "What are you talking about? Isn't there anyone here who can do the simple task that was asked of them?" He was disgusted with them all and retorted into his intercom to his administrator, "Get Ricin on the line!" The secretary responded, "Yes, sir!" Dr. Ross, who felt out of his depth in the meeting, "I really do not want to know about this other stuff that you are doing. I'm not involved in that, and it sounds risky from a legal standpoint. Are you sure that the Government will protect us if this all goes South and we're found out?" Dr. Krappner replied in a proud tone, "At least the character assassination is working well. There is not a university on the planet that would offer Marie or Jared McNichols faculty positions or any other jobs for that matter. And we have shed so much doubt on their integrity and honesty that no one will ever believe them again." Dr. Belcher added, "Fortunately, their most powerful ally is so wrapped up in his own esoteric physics research he won't bother to come to their defense."

Dr. Masters was still angry, and nothing that anyone had said this morning could change that. "Let me make one thing clear. The character assassination is worthless!" He was truly ranting, "You were supposed to drive them to suicide! Now, how difficult can that be?" Dr. Belcher finally interrupted in his whiny voice, "I don't know about this approach, Clement. Perhaps Marie McNichols is not the suicidal type. I certainly don't think Jared would commit suicide. Besides, we had three suicides on our staff during the last year, and none of these people were really suicidal. Especially Fred McCarthy. Nobody seemed to buy his suicide, especially his family. I have heard that they want a formal police inquiry. People are starting to ask questions. The police are even asking why there are so many suicides on our faculty. And why are we involving ourselves in this business? Why doesn't the government take care of this problem? Why do we have to be involved in this at all? This Las Vegas thing smacks of organized crime, and I don't like it! I could be incarcerated for some of the things you've asked me to do! None of us was hired for this type of work!" Finally, Dr. Masters had heard enough, and he responded angrily, "Be quiet, Francis! You are not helping the situation! You don't know what pressures *I* am under. You are part of *my* team, and you're acting like just another useless faculty member." As Dr. Masters spit out his final words, he looked around the room at the frightened faculty members assembled in his office. He wondered how he had surrounded himself with such incompetence.

The intercom buzzed and interrupted Dr. Masters' thoughts, and he immediately turned his attention to the phone. The administrator said, "Dr. Ricin is on the line, sir!" Dr. Masters changed his mood completely. "Good! Finally!" He pressed the button on the speakerphone, and Dr. Ricin said, "Shalom!" Dr. Masters ignored his salutation–he didn't like Jews and especially Israelis, but he had learned to use them over the years, and he prided himself in knowing their weak points. Dr. Masters began with Dr. Ricin, "We were just talking here with Drs. Geldter and Krappner about your marvelous ideas." Dr. Ricin replied, "Sir, I don't think that they are my ideas or my plans." Dr. Masters' mood quickly changed as he sensed that Dr. Ricin was not going to take responsibility for the failure in Cambridge, and he angrily said into the speaker phone he had turned on, "Dr. Ricin, your Cocktail was a complete flop! They are apparently not showing anything in the way of symptoms!"

Dr. Ricin responded slowly to Dr. Masters. "Excuse me, Dr. Masters, that was *your* Cocktail not mine. They must have powerful immune systems to escape the Russian Doll." Dr. Masters replied, "We don't know for sure if they even received it. Now we are going to have to try something else. And Dr. Ross here assured me that the McNichols would be attending a party at their house. Now they too have failed me." Dr. Ross interrupted the conversation, "It wasn't our fault! They did not attend the graduation party, so we could not proceed as planned!" Dr. Belcher added in a whiny voice, "I hate to say I told you so, but I warned you that the addition of the asparaginase may have stimulated an immune response. Now they may have had a strong response to whatever you gave them." Dr. Ricin said, "Dr. Masters, my report is that they only took one small bite each of the material. That may not have been enough."

Dr. Graham, who was very uncomfortable at the dialog and the discussion of an apparent homicide attempt, interrupted in a sweet voice. "Dr. Masters, may I interrupt. I don't think that dwelling upon failure is going to change the situation. I think that we need another positive plan of action." She was so proud of herself. Dr. Graham naively thought that the group would now abandon the homicide approach, one that she and Dr. Ross felt particularly uncomfortable with, even if Drs. Geldter and

Krappner were all for it just to please Dr. Masters. Dr. Masters quickly grabbed at the thought, "Yes! That's what we need! A positive plan of action." Most of the attendees finally saw Dr. Masters for what he was, a dangerous, possibly insane, some might say evil buffoon who could not make a decision or plan anything without people around him urging him onward. He could not discern a good plan from a bad plan. He could only make the decision based on the arguments of his underlings. The strongest argument or strongest personality usually won out, even if it was completely absurd.

Dr. Masters got up from his desk and began pacing around his large office, "Yes! We are a can-do Texas institution. We're not going to dwell on failure. We need to have a more positive attitude!" Dr. Graham was so proud of her rare 'insight' that she could barely contain herself. Dr. Krappner was frowning. She couldn't stand to be out maneuvered by the younger female faculty member. Dr. Masters turned to the group in his office and looked directly at Dr. Graham and continued, "Perhaps we need someone of your talents more involved in this project." Dr. Graham became very nervous and said, "Sir, I didn't mean that I should be more involved. I do not do this sort of thing. I just meant that we need to think more positively about *any* project at our institution." Dr. Masters ignored the last part of her statement and forgot that Dr. Ricin was still on the phone, "Yes, I think that we need your talents and those of Dr. Ross." Dr. Ricin interrupted the group, "Dr. Masters, I believe that my part of your mission is complete. I would be very happy to assist you further, but I will wait for the agreed payment to my account. Shalom." Dr. Ricin was quickly cut off.

Dr. Masters did not bother to answer Dr. Ricin. He wouldn't get any money for such a debacle. Dr. Masters was planning his next move and didn't want to bother with Dr. Ricin, who was just another failure in a long line of failures that Dr. Geldter had introduced into the picture. Dr. Geldter always talked big but he couldn't ever seem to deliver, and Dr. Masters was growing wary of letting the Moroccan-born, ex-Israeli Dr. Geldter sell him another one of his 'used camels' as he often called Geldter's hair-brained ideas.

At one time several large pharmaceutical companies had courted Dr. Geldter and lavished money on his group to develop what some had called some very questionable science, but Isaac was so good at schmoozing them that they actually believed–or at least they desperately wanted to believe–his crack-pot theories and his data that appeared to support his proposals. Unfortunately, when they tried to transfer the science to their own facilities, it never worked as advertised. They could never reproduce Geldter's experiments in other laboratories. They should have contacted some of Geldter's competitors first, because it was widely known in the field that Geldter *selected* his data, taking only the data that *he* wanted because it confirmed *his* preconceived notions. Thus no one seemed to be able reproduce his results. Geldter was so good at selling himself that he actually began to believe his own hype and think that he could do anything and everything, but this was rarely the case for any scientist. In Geldter's case, he never credited his brother who was a partner in a major public relations firm as the one that taught Geldter how to be a master self-promoter. Most academics don't know how to hype their work like a Geldter, so they were never showered with money from the major pharmaceutical giants. It took a bombastic self-promoter to catch their attention, or a scientist who actually knew how to conduct first-rate research. One of the reasons that the giant pharmaceutical companies actually supported Geldter was that they knew that he was fully capable of eliminating the McNichols. The McNichols would eventually learn that the pharmaceutical giants had their own reasons for wanting them dead, particularly Marie. In addition to the defense industry, there were also intricate connections between the Las Vegas organized crime interests and their investments in the pharmaceutical industry.

Dr. Masters knew all too well the weaknesses of Dr. Geldter, especially his ability to over-sell himself, which was why Isaac would never go higher in Dr. Masters' administration. Not that academic excellence had anything to do with promotions in Dr. Masters' administration. Take, for example, Dr. Geldter's wife Dr. Amy Krappner, who was widely regarded as a scientific idiot–barely able to tie her own scientific shoes–but due to her political savvy, connections and a string of political successes she was considered a good bet to advance in Dr. Masters' administration. In addition, she was a woman, and she just happened to be the head of a group that recently hired a lobbyist to promote the hiring of more women in upper administrative positions at the University.

Dr. Masters was looking for *something* positive. There was nothing that Clement hated worse than failure. It did not matter whether an idea or plan was good or bad, he must win at all costs. He went to his desk and used the intercom to contact his administrator. "Send in Dr. Bane and his colleagues please." The administrator answered, "Yes sir." Dr. Masters was standing as Dr. Clyde Bane, the new Executive Vice President, and Dr. Domasovitch from Jared's Department along with Drs. Italiano and Auchenhower entered Dr. Masters office, which was now crowded with senior staff mostly in their white coats.

Dr. Masters' demeanor changed dramatically in front of the larger group, and he warmly walked over to shake their hands while he cheerfully said, "Good morning gentlemen. Thank you for coming to my office on such short notice. I assume that you know everyone here. Has my staff gotten you any coffee? Can we get you anything else?" Dr. Masters was holding out an open hand to the new participants, which he gently glided around in the air to indicate that the group should sit down in his section of couches, large chairs and tables. Dr. Masters always liked to put on a good show for anyone who entered his spectacular office. This let them immediately know who was in charge.

Dr. Masters had carefully chosen Dr. Bane, a very politically well-connected surgeon as his deputy for a reason. Many on the surgical staff were against the appointment, and in particular Dr. Ross, who firmly believed that Dr. Bane was a dangerous surgeon who shouldn't be practicing, because he didn't spend enough time in surgery to keep up his skills. Dr. Masters, however, needed a political animal like Dr. Bane to handle the academic problems as they came up at the D. O. Madison. Dr. Masters didn't want to be bothered with such trivial pursuits. He needed to be available for more strategic problems, and he prided himself on his connections at the State Capitol and in Washington. He felt that he was a complete political genius–capable of maneuvering around any political problem and turning it to his advantage.

Dr. Bane spoke first. "Dr. Masters, I have been introducing myself to Dr. Domasovitch. He has agreed to help with our project. And as you know, Drs. Italano and Auchenhower did an excellent job at a recent departmental seminar." Dr. Masters responded, "Good! We have to keep the pressure up from all directions!" Drs. Italiano and Auchenhower acted like they were very proud of what they had done. They actually wanted to believe that they were doing some patriotic duty for their country after the pep talk that Dr. Bane had given them, but in reality they knew exactly what was happening, and they were just going with the flow to insure their futures at the institution. Dr. Masters calmly turned to Dr. Bane, "Now Clyde, I also want you to take a more active role in this project." Dr. Bane, who was hesitant to be involved with the others said, "But Dr. Masters, I don't think that I . . ." Dr. Masters interrupting and smiling, "Nonsense! You have been brought on my team as my deputy, chosen by me personally, and I expect some excellent things from you. You know, I won't be in this position forever, and I need someone who is willing to take control at the proper time."

Dr. Masters was counting on Dr. Bane's ego and his ambitious streak, but Dr. Bane was actually hesitant to get involved in what he saw as Dr. Masters' potential legal problems. Dr. Bane really didn't believe in the direction that Dr. Masters was taking, probably because he still had a remnant of ethics left inside him. He said, "Dr. Masters, of course I support you completely, and I want to assist in any way possible, but . . ." Dr. Masters wouldn't let him finish and said, "Good!" He then turned to Drs. Italiano and Auchenhower, "What's this about you not fully committing to help Dr. Belcher?"

The two faculty members were becoming very nervous, and they looked at each other. They did not want to believe the story that Dr. Belcher used when he recruited them to harass Jared and Marie and drive them from the institution, but they fully accepted their roles. It's not like they hadn't done this before to remove an unpopular faculty member. But this was clearly something different involving much higher stakes.

Dr. Domasovitch from Jared's department was watching and listening. With the exception of Dr. Graham, he was more junior than the rest of the faculty present at the meeting, and he was feeling very superior to have been invited to an important gathering of such powerful people. He had been warned by Dr. Belcher not to be too assertive about his own ideas in front of Dr. Masters, who must have the first and final word. But Dr. Domasovitch spoke out anyway, "I believe that there must be some misunderstanding. Of course we are committed to assist you in any way possible Dr. Masters." Dr. Domasovitch was a complete scientific hack and was willing to do just about anything that was asked of him to get ahead, because he knew that he couldn't advance on his academic abilities alone. Dr. Masters quickly responded, "Good! It looks like we are finally all on the same page. Now where were we? "Most of the participants were too afraid to let Dr. Masters know that they felt that he must be going a bit daft. He couldn't seem to focus on anything long enough to determine what was real from what was fiction.

Dr. Geldter, who never agreed with the repeated suggestions from Dr. Belcher not to upstage Dr. Masters, finally couldn't contain himself. "Dr. Masters, let me return to the point I was making. In case immunity to the Russian Doll has been established, we need another tactic. I suggest that we try a more traditional approach like cyanide or arsenic?" Dr. Masters didn't want to be quoted as ever suggesting harm to anyone, so he turned to his staff for approval, "Well? What do you think of Dr. Geldter's proposal?" Dr. Belcher, the hematologist from Buffalo, New York, said in a whiny voice, "I don't know about that approach. That would be too easy to trace here in Texas. It would take a very bad pathologist not to recognize that type of poisoning. I don't like it."

The newer academic arrivals to the D. O. Madison, Drs. Graham, Ross and Bane, became very nervous during this discussion. They did not expect to hear what they just heard at a meeting with the President of the institution. Were they actually discussing possible approaches to murdering someone? And not just one person, they were discussing the elimination of an entire family. They had all heard the rumors about Dr. Cannon and the several suicides at the institution, but they never expected to hear what they just heard from Dr. Masters. Actually Dr. Masters was acting a bit desperate, and Dr. Belcher believed that Dr. Masters must be under intense pressure to successfully complete this mission. Drs. Graham and Ross felt that they should first get in touch with their intelligence contacts to determine their course of action.

On the other hand, Dr. Belcher just wanted to finish his career and retire, and he certainly didn't need the prospect of going to jail just to please Dr. Masters' ego. But he was also afraid of Dr. Masters, and he more than anyone else at the meeting knew that Dr. Masters was fully capable of having him murdered, if he became a threat. In fact, Dr. Belcher felt that Dr. Masters could easily order them all killed, if Masters felt it was necessary to protect himself. The better that Dr. Belcher knew Dr. Masters, the more he was sure that Masters was a complete psychopath.

Dr. Masters asked his Vice President, "Francis, are any foreign trips in the plans for Dr. McNichols in the near future?" Dr. Belcher responded, "Not in the immediate future, but I believe that Jared has been invited this year to be a visiting professor at the All Russian Cancer Center in Moscow, but to my knowledge he has not accepted. I have been lecturing him on your new foreign travel directive, and I fully expect that he won't go."

Dr. Masters thought for a moment. "Dr. Bane, didn't you have some contact with this center?" Dr. Bane responded, "Yes, that's true. And I have an idea that might be useful. As a part of my duties I am to go to Moscow to promote scientific and medical exchanges between our Cancer Association and the Russian Cancer Association. We could arrange to have both McNichols there and no one would be the wiser." Dr. Geldter interrupted, "Dr. Masters, I like it! I know a biochemist in Moscow who could be useful." Dr. Masters quickly said, "Good! Now I want Dr. Bane to arrange it."

Dr. Bane was still uncomfortable with Dr. Masters, because he did not want to be involved in such obviously illegal activities. He had to think of a way out. "Dr. Masters, I believe that Dr. Belcher should deal with this. He is Jared's superior." Dr. Masters quickly responded, "Nonsense! I think that you can handle this small task. Perhaps you were not in a position where you would know some details on our financial situation. We need the support of certain Las Vegas financial groups for my building program, and this problem is related to that support." Dr. Masters continued, "And I know that you all are not complete idiots. The Las Vegas financial group is heavily invested in the pharmaceutical industry, so if you expect research support from the pharmaceutical companies you better get with the program." Dr. Bane looked at everyone in the room to see if he could determine if they knew about this latest revelation from Dr. Masters, but their faces remained frozen with expressions that were almost clown-like. He then said in a mumble, "I heard that the surgeon founder of Belford actually operated on the Chicago crime boss Sam Giancanna in the mid-seventies." Dr. Masters, who had heard the comment, became impatient at this remark and barked back with sarcasm, "How well-informed you are Dr. Bane . . . but that has nothing to do with *my* building program."

Dr. Masters was referring to the largest building program in University history–*his* building program. He was extremely proud of the fact that he had pushed through the University System the unprecedented approval of four new buildings for the Cancer Center. He needed the backing of outside financial interests to complete the program, and the only backers who would touch the D. O. Madison, because it was already over-stretched financially, were Las Vegas organized crime interests. They could step in where conventional lenders would not enter. However, there was a down side to the unorthodox funding plan, and that was that the Las Vegas interests did not give their money cheaply. What Dr. Masters also left out was that Marie McNichols was an heiress to the very same financial empire that had been providing the funding for *his* building program. Of course, at the time none of this was known to any of the faculty at the D. O. Madison Cancer Center. It had been kept confidential by Dr. Masters and his most trusted associates, not that it would have mattered to most of the participants at the meeting.

The powerful Las Vegas organized crime interests and their investments, including several large defense contractors and the controlling interests in several of the large pharmaceutical corporations, wanted to prevent Marie from ever realizing her inheritance so that they could continue to use the assets of fifteen hotels and casinos left to Marie by her father and also the funds generated by several large international trusts. There was also a rogue faction in the CIA that was financially and politically connected to these powerful interests. In time, Marie would find out that powerful trustees, *her* trustees, actually controlled her assets, including the Five Star Trust, the Sterling Trust, the Century Trust and the Cetta Dharma Trust, the largest trusts in the world. These were the trusts that funded a major part of the Black Budget that supported the CIA and the Pentagon.

It was no wonder that some major politicians as well as organized crime families wanted Marie to disappear. Even a rogue faction of the CIA had been involved in attempts on Marie, and they played a major role in placing Dr. Ross and Dr. Graham at the D. O. Madison. In fact, Drs. Ross and Graham were considered valuable 'assets.' This rogue CIA faction also wanted Jared, but especially Marie, to disappear from the earth. Thus in addition to the McNichols bumbling onto the D. O. Madison-Belford illegal testing programs in the state prison system and inadvertently uncovering the Gulf War Syndrome fiasco, the other major motive in their demise was that Las Vegas organized crime-related financial interests and some rogue intelligence agents also wanted to see the McNichols gone forever.

Dr. Masters had 'reluctantly' taken on the mission of 'correcting' the problem to insure that *his* building program would continue unabated and of course to prevent some embarrassing disclosures about the joint clinical programs with Belford in the Texas prison system. These two issues drove Dr. Masters to complete his mission of either ridding the world of the McNichols or at a minimum forcing them to be someone else's problem.

Just as Dr. Masters was about to continue his staff meeting, he had an important call from the University System Administration that required the meeting to be interrupted. Dr. Masters pointed to his private conference room, and he told Dr. Bane to have the group assemble in his conference room. Dr. Bane immediately asked everyone to follow him, but it was obvious where they all should go. As they filed out of the President's office, Dr. Masters had to take yet another important phone call from some University System administrator, politician or shady financial backer.

Dr. Domasovitch and some of the others were very proud to have been asked to meet in the President's Office and rub elbows with the elite members of the institution. However, they privately wondered why Dr. Graham had been invited. Contrary to what she thought, the faculty in her own department felt that Dr. Graham was just some affirmative action political appointment that was arranged so that the Cancer Center could recruit her husband, Dr. Ross. They felt that no one would ever appoint such a marginal intellect to the position she received without extreme political pull, and they were completely correct. Dr. Graham made her reputation on discovering a new type of immune cell, but she didn't know that her colleagues knew all along that she actually stole the work from a nerd graduate student who had a crush on her.

Dr. Graham was only to be topped by Dr. Amy Krappner, who was the laughing stock of her entire field for her 'rat tanning salon' lectures. In a weaker moment when she was nominally friends with Marie, she even confessed that she was not well-liked by her peers in the immunology field, and she even shared with Marie a grant review that vilified Amy and placed in print that she tried very hard to get others to do her thinking for her, but it was obvious that Dr. Krappner could not think her way out of a paper bag. Dr. Krappner was barred from reviewing NIH grant applications because of allegations that she stole the ideas of young applicants and then later re-presented them as her own. The senior administrators at the NIH considered her to be a pariah who was dangerously devoid of any ethics, and they did not want her to ruin any more young scientists' careers.

One could easily see why this group had been carefully chosen from the faculty of The D. O. Madison. Their complete willingness to do anything that Dr. Masters asked to get ahead, or in the case of Drs. Bane and Ross for their political or intelligence connections, presented the perfect ruthless combination of ambition and lack of talent to foster criminal actions. When they assembled in the private conference room, Drs. Geldter and Belcher began to have an argument over who was better connected to the Mossad. Dr. Geldter felt that he knew everyone who was important in the Mossad, but Belcher felt just as strongly that Isaac only knew the obvious figureheads that everyone in Israel knew about. He told Geldter that he did not know that a rogue faction of the Mossad was actually controlled by a neo-Nazi group that escaped post-World War II Nuremberg Trials by posing as Jewish prisoners from the death camps, adopting their identities and subsequently immigrating to Israel. Dr. Geldter, who would never be outdone when it came to bragging about Israel said, "That can't be true. We have the best intelligence organization in the world!" Belcher sarcastically replied, "They have no idea that they have been infiltrated at every echelon of leadership." Dr. Geldter angrily responded, "You know, Dr. Belcher, that is just some Hollywood bullshit that you read somewhere!" Dr. Belcher replied, "You are straining my patience, Isaac. I happen to know that it is factual. I have excellent sources in the Spanish Royal family, and they know exactly what's going on!" Dr. Geldter angrily responded, "And what the hell do some Spanish royals have do with this, all ready! Francis, you've really flipped your lid!"

Dr. Bane interrupted the conversation. "Will you both please pay attention for a moment! Let's get back to the problem at hand." Dr. Domasovitch said, "Sir, if I could interrupt. I'd like to report that Marie McNichols has such influence over Jared, that some claim she is virtually running the Department. He is so concerned with her 'treatment' here that he is not acting professionally towards the rest of his faculty. He is demanding to know where we get our information about her, and he is suggesting to us that we are being used by the administration. Since he is suggesting that members of the administration might be involved, perhaps you should replace him with his Deputy." Dr. Belcher was skeptical, "That seems a bit farfetched, Thomas! I don't see any evidence for your statements. Jared has never complained to me that Marie has had unfair treatment, and to say that she is actually running the department. Come now! Could it be that you as Deputy Chairman just want to be the head of his department?" Dr. Domasovitch turned red and did not reply. His obviously self-serving statements were not immediately accepted by Dr. Belcher or anyone else, except for Dr. Geldter, who also wanted to take over Jared's department and make Dr. Domasovitch one of *his* deputies.

Dr. Geldter then proposed an old idea that he had proposed many times before to Dr. Masters. "Dr. Belcher, I have formally proposed that Jared Nichol's department be immediately merged into my department, and . . ." Dr. Belcher interrupted Isaac before he could finish. "With all the operatives and brilliant scientists and physicians here, I find it very hard to listen to the two of you sit here complaining like little girls about the chairmanship of one basic science department!" Dr. Bane added, "I'm sure that Marie's influence is just a bit distorted." Dr. Belcher continued, "I see no evidence of it." Just then Dr. Masters entered the private conference room.

Dr. Masters phone conversation was over, and he wanted to get back to the issues that were being discussed in his office. "Dr. Bane, Dr. Belcher, Let's get back to the important issues. Clyde, I thought about it, and I like the idea of a more conventional approach in Moscow. Get Jared McNichols on the phone and tell him we want him and that wife of his to represent the D. O. Madison in Moscow. And I want Isaac to contact Ricin again to see if he has any operatives there and inform him of this most crucial mission." Even though Dr. Geldter was in the room, Dr. Masters was addressing Dr. Bane and Dr. Belcher. He did not want to have anyone see him bypassing his deputies, at least to their face. Dr. Masters also wanted to put Dr. Geldter back in his place, because he really didn't like Jews and especially Israelis whom he considered crude and overly aggressive. "I want the rest of you to keep up the campaign and the blocking of Marie's and Jared's publications, grants, whatever! Dr. Domasovitch, I want weekly updates on the situation in your department. I want to know everything that's going on concerning these two individuals, their mail, telephone, email, and anything else that you consider important for us to know, and I don't want to know how you do it." Dr. Domasovitch responded quickly, "Yes, sir!"

Dr. Masters turned to Dr. Geldter and said, "Isaac, I want you to continue to work with Dr. Rook and let him update you on the vital work of our joint clinical programs with Belford." Dr. Belcher whispered to Dr. Bane, "Rook actually believes in the master race." Dr. Masters overheard the whispers of Belcher and turned to him, "Dr. Belcher, would you like to share with us what you just told Clyde?" Dr. Belcher nervously said, "Dr. Masters, I was telling Dr. Bane that I would like to have a comprehensive intelligence analysis of this so that we can once and for all clear up any doubts as to our mission in a global sense." Dr. Masters was visibly upset and said, "Dr. Belcher, I'm tired of your undermining of the leadership here at The D. O. Madison." Dr. Belcher responded, "But Dr. Masters, I am not undermining the leadership. I am just being cautious. After all, there are potential legal liabilities to these plans, and I am trying to protect you and the institution." Dr. Masters angrily told Dr. Belcher, "You are not paid to second guess my team, Dr. Belcher! I'll be the judge of our collaboration with any groups, which, in my opinion, are important to have in D. O. Madison's corner and any liabilities to my staff. Do you appreciate my point, Dr. Belcher?" Dr. Belcher answered in his usual whiny voice, "Of course, Clement."

Dr. Geldter added his own slant to the discussion. "Dr. Masters, these financial and defense groups, even the Las Vegas groups and their trusts don't concern me. I would like to see us get back to how this mission will result in adjustments to our salaries and positions." Dr. Masters replied sharply, "Later, Isaac! I told you not to bring that up now!" Dr. Masters then immediately changed his mood and chuckled, "Francis, I don't think I will ever get used to your sense of humor, and Isaac, as usual you have reduced the global scheme of things to reflect the balance in your bank account."

Dr. Masters paused to reflect on what he had said. "Remember, this is a team, *my* team, not a majority decision." Dr. Masters then turned his attention to Drs. Graham and Ross, who had been hiding in the corner hoping that Dr. Masters would forget about them. He didn't, and he said in his sweet Southern voice, "Dr. Ross, Dr. Graham, I want you to contact your people at Langley and ask them about a more conventional approach? Find out if they have any suggestions that will help us make this mission a success!" He then turned to Amy and said, "Dr. Krappner, I want you to do the same with your contacts. Once and for all, I expect this mission to be successful! Do not let me down a third time! Remember, all of you were chosen to join the staff here at D. O. Madison because you also had particular talents that we needed for our classified projects." Drs. Auchenhower and Italiano just looked at each other with a look of frustration. They were not involved in the classified projects, and they felt uncomfortable about discussing the murder of a fellow faculty member.

Dr. Masters' mood changed 180-degrees again, and he said, "Dr. Belcher, if you do not get with the program and stop your whining and complaining, I may be forced to look for another Vice President for Research. Do I make myself clear?" Everyone abruptly nodded their heads. Then Dr. Geldter spoke out, "Dr. Masters, I would like to . . . ." But Dr. Masters interrupted him before he could finish, "Not now, Dr. Geldter! I know what you are going to ask, and I think that Dr. Belcher is fully capable and committed to our team. Isn't that correct, Francis?" Dr. Belcher responded, "Clement, I think that we need to think about . . . ." Dr. Masters interrupted him again, "Now, it is my understanding that Dr. Bane here will be the liaison for this new operation in Moscow and the key man to contact if there are problems." Dr. Bane had tried not to be directly involved in Dr. Masters' scheming, but he was being sucked in by Dr. Masters. "But sir, I don't think that I have been here long enough to actually be involved in these sorts of things." Dr. Masters responded firmly, "Nonsense! We welcome your input on the team." Dr. Masters then got up and walked to the door, "I'm sorry, we have to end our little conversation. I have another meeting. You have your instructions. Good luck to you all!"

The faculty and administrators were left sitting in Dr. Masters' conference room just looking at each other, and they began to get up and leave. It was clear that they did not like each other in any way but have been forced to work together by Dr. Masters. Dr. Ross who was the last to go with Dr. Graham told her quietly, "Dr. Masters has gone completely mad. I'm not going to be a part of this and either should you." But Dr.

Graham responded, "But you heard what he said. We could be in trouble here if we don't go along with his directives." On the other hand, Dr. Domasovitch was quite proud of his performance. He had been invited into the inner circle of power at the institution, and he felt important and confident of his future. These faculty members would all do what they were told, and actually they would do it with gusto knowing that some future promotion or salary increase would be theirs some day after this little problem or two was finally resolved. Dr. Domasovitch also saw himself at the helm of a department and part of the new administrative blood of the institution. He also disagreed strongly with that pompous ass Isaac Geldter that *his* department must be merged with Geldter's department at the M. K. Black Building.

The McNichols attempt to fight back

Jared and Marie were relaxing at home in Queenswood before the day's work on the same morning that Dr. Masters and his underlings were conspiring against them. They sat together on a couch with Yin and Yang in the morning room with a marvelous view of the rolling hills behind the McNichols' home. Their modern house was made up mostly of wood and glass panels that faced the scrub and woodlands typical of the Texas Hill Country. The TV was on blearing a coffee commercial featuring Juan Valdez picking the Colombian coffee beans one-by-one, while Jared was reading a journal that he had just picked up. Jared sarcastically stated, "That's just how I feel, doing the work one bean at a time."

Marie was sipping juice and reading the daily newspaper. Jared said, "This journal has an interesting article on Mfi. You should read it. It probably has a lot to do with your illness." Jared was playing with the cats at the same time he was reading, and in a very intense manner started studying the research article. Suddenly Jared said to Marie, "This article describes a fatal illness that was caused by Mfi. It appears to be responsible for the deaths of some Armed Forces personnel in a study by our old friend Ming Lon along with Richard Armwhite at the U. S. Army Research Institute of Infectious Diseases at Fort Detrick. The signs and symptoms they described are almost identical to what you had, and I think that you might be interested in taking a look at this."

Marie put the newspaper down and looked at the article, while Jared read another journal. Finally after scanning the publication she said, "From the description, it sounds exactly like the illness I had. We knew that they were working on Mfi. I'm going to give Dr. Lon another call to see if we can learn more about this Mfi." Jared added, "According to the publication, they claim that Mfi is still a very rare type of infection. I don't see how this mycoplasma could have caused your health problems, unless it was deliberate. Nobody around you ever came down with this, except me, and that was later on after you were beginning to recover. You obviously didn't get it from me." Marie thought for a moment, "I have always believed that my illness was deliberate." Jared said, "The big question is how you could have come into contact with this thing. It doesn't seem very contagious." Marie stated from the publication, "Ming Lon indicates that it is only rarely found in healthy adults, but the infection may be particularly common in AIDS patients as a cofactor with the HIV-1 virus, but I didn't have contact with any AIDS patients. So I have to figure out who gave it to me . . . . and why?"

Jared did not want Marie to immediately assume that there was a conspiracy against her. "Let's not jump to conclusions about how you got the infection. We have to be consistent. Consistent behavior is the key." Marie shot back, "Jared, just stay open-minded! Remember how professor Clever and even Geoff Fence looked at me as if they had seen a ghost? And let's not forget the fake concern of Geldter and Krappner and the others in your department who are obviously unhappy that I am still here." Jared responded, "Some of them are obviously unhappy that I am still here too, but that doesn't mean that somebody is trying to eliminate me in order to take over my department. Besides, we don't have any proof. However, I tend to agree with you that there are lot of suspicious things going on around here, but we would need more evidence before we could say that foul play was involved." Marie became angry at Jared, "Damn it, Jared, this is like a guerrilla war operation. We may never get absolute proof, but there is one thing that I predict. Once the enemy presents itself, it's going to be too late! We're going to have to anticipate the enemy! I don't want to find you in your office some morning with a bullet in the back of your head?"

Marie had made her point, and Jared could not deny that some evidence was there for all to see. "O.K.! You've made your point. We'll try to be more anticipatory. And, by the way, I'd like to know who arranged those special privileges for you, like going inside the Stonehenge circle." Marie said, "I don't know. Who cares?" Jared said, "Things like that always seem to happen to you but not to ordinary people. I think it holds one of the keys to your identity. Once we learn of your real identity, then perhaps we will be able to figure out why this is happening to us, that is, besides stumbling onto some infections in the Gulf War veterans and prison guards. There has to be more to it than that. I think that the VIP treatment you often receive is essential to figuring out who you really are, and it will explain all the bullshit that has been hurled at us by our colleagues. I don't think that it's all about our Gulf War Illness work."

Marie did not want to continue the conversation. "O.K., let's change the subject!" Jared agreed, "Good idea! You know, something very strange happened to me yesterday. The new head of the hospital and clinics division, Clyde Bane, left me no alternative but to accept an invitation that we represent the D. O. Madison in Moscow at the All Russian Cancer Center. I was going to turn down the invitation because Francis Belcher was giving me a very hard time about my travel. He always approves Geldter's and Krappner's travel, but whenever I have a request, I get the third degree and lectures about being away from my duties. Now they *actually* want me travel to Moscow. You know, now we could have back-to-back overseas trips coming up." Marie responded, "I know you don't think I'm a world-class traveler, but I want to go with you. You say that I have to keep giving lectures, even if every position for me is blocked, just to prove I am still a recognized scientist." Jared responded, "It also proves that you cannot be blocked from invitations everywhere. Just keep doing the work, presenting it and publishing it, and in the end that's what will count. Everything else is bullshit, as Isaac Geldter would say!" Marie said, "Talk about bullshit! He's the biggest piece I've ever seen. I really need to get out of here, even for just a week."

Jared wanted to change the subject again. "Look, you think that you have all the problems. I just got a letter from Suzanne. She is having health problems again. She didn't even get a chance to finish flight school and get her wings. How would you like to spend a year in Saudi and Southern Iraq and then come home and prepare for your life's dream to be a pilot, and then you couldn't even finish flight school? Marie asked, "I hope that she is going to be O.K.? All that she and the others went through, and it looks now that it's still a mess over there." Jared added, "What you mean is it's still a bloody disaster! We could be at war all over again in a few years." Marie said, "God, I hope not! I don't think that the Iraqis are that stupid twice." Jared added, "Or are we that stupid twice!"

There was a pause in the conversation, and then Marie spoke again. "I'm still going to call Dr. Lon again and find out if he has finally detected Mfi in the Gulf War samples." Jared looked up from his reading, "Good idea. Let me know what he says, but I wouldn't hold your breath. I think that it's pretty clear that the Pentagon decided to cover this whole thing up and call all the veterans psycho cases." Marie was talking to herself, "I also have to call Bob Sonan to instruct him on some procedures for the next experiments. We are almost ready to write up the results on the organization of tumor supressor and oncogenes in metastatic lymphomas. I tell you, Jared, there is a definite pattern at the chromatin level that could give us clues on the nuclear differences in highly malignant cells." Jared answered, "That's great! We'll talk about this later. Don't forget, it looks like we now have to go to Moscow next month, so we have to get our research organized." Jared got up and the cats scattered. He told Marie, "I've got to run! I have a 10 AM meeting."

Later that day Marie was in Jared's laboratories talking to Bob Sonan as they looked over the raw data of the day. She told Bob that she was going to call Dr. Ming Lon about the unusual mycoplasma, Mfi, that they had found in the Gulf War veterans' blood samples. It was good for Marie to work with Bob, because he was a very mild-mannered, even-tempered, steady technician. Marie told him, "Bob, it's great to work with you. You are my one true-blue friend here at the Madison, and you are the only person I've worked with for any extended period of time and not had a fight with." Bob chuckled as Marie continued, "You know, Bob, I don't know what we would do without you. Don't think I don't know how you kept me from relapsing after my illness." Bob replied, "Please, Marie." It was obvious that Bob was getting embarrassed.

Marie then changed the subject. "Oh, by the way, have a look at this article Jared found in a pathology journal." She handed Bob the article. Marie continued, "The article describes the same unusual Mfi mycoplasma that Dr. Ming Lon at the U. S. Army Institute of Pathology Research found earlier." Marie turned the pages until she found the section in the article that she wanted to show Bob. "Look, the constellation of symptoms described by Lon fit those that I had during my illness and the illness survey forms that Jared has been getting back from the Airborne and Special Forces units. Blake Hall has been collecting the data for Jared." Bob scanned the article and replied, "I see what you mean. That's just like Jared described it on the board in his office!" Marie said, "Exactly! And it's like my own symptoms when I was sick. I'm going to give Dr. Lon a call and find out more about this Mfi, as well as his opinion on our Gulf War studies." Bob was curious, "I'd be interested to hear what he says. We all felt so helpless during your illness. You looked like a ghost." Marie said, "I know! I don't like to even think about it. Bob, I really believe that it was divine intervention that saved me." Bob replied, "I'm not as spiritual as you are, but I have to agree that something brought you through that illness." Marie said, "Well, Bob, keep up the fabulous work!" Bob replied cheerfully, "You can always count on me."

Marie waved and left Jared's laboratory, and as she walked down the hallway she encountered hostile looks from some of Dr. Nosan's laboratory workers. His laboratory was located on the opposite side of the hallway as she walked into her small office. Her office was at the end of a long hallway from Jared's office, and she felt that she was negotiating a minefield to get to Jared. Marie sat down at her desk and called a secretary on the intercom. Marie asked her friend Jane in the Department Office, "Jane, could you please get me the phone number of Dr. Ming Lon at the U. S. Army Institute of Pathology Research in Washington D.C.?" Jane answered, "Sure thing, call you right back, boss." Marie, "Thanks, Jane. But please don't call me boss. You can call Jared boss, but I am not your boss. Just call me Marie.

Marie took out a file and began analyzing some raw data, just as a young Asian student walked into her office with his laboratory notebook. The student was of medium height and of Taiwanese background. Marie said, "Hi, Steve. How are you progressing with the assays?" Steve replied, "I think I've found a genuine enzyme DNA cutter." Marie was excited, "Let me see the electrophoretic pattern." He handed her the data, and Marie's face lit up. She looked up, "Well, Steven, it looks like we were right! The enzyme complex has to be in a 'relaxed' structure to cut the DNA." She looked up at him from her desk, "You're doing great work, Steven!"

The elusive Dr. Lon

Marie was in her office as the intercom buzzed. She answered, "Yes?" The intercom voice of Jane was on the line, "Jane here, I have the number you requested." Marie said, "Thanks, Jane." She picked up the phone and dialed the U. S. Army Institute of Pathology Research so she could speak with Dr. Ming Lon. Dr. Ming Lon picked up the phone after the third ring. He was of Chinese extraction with dark black hair and wore very thick glasses. Dr. Lon answered, "Hello, Pathology lab." Marie replied, "This is Dr. Marie McNichols calling from Austin, Texas. I am trying to reach Dr. Ming Lon!" Dr. Lon replied, "Dr. Marie McNichols, do I know you?" Marie responded, "You might remember me, but I don't think so. We've talked before." Ming Lon then remembered Marie's voice, "Dr. McNichols, you're alive? Ah, I mean you're so fortunate to be . . ." Marie interrupted Dr. Lon, "Do you remember me? I called you once about *Mycoplasma fermentans incognitus.*" Dr. Lon continued, "I'm sorry, I was expecting another call, and I thought that you were someone else." Marie was puzzled but in an analytical way, "Are you sure that you're Dr. Ming Lon?" Dr. Lon replied, "I am sorry for the confusion. Yes, this is Dr. Lon." Marie said, "You may also know my husband, Dr. Jared McNichol. He found an article of yours that was just published in a pathology journal, and we were intrigued by the article." Dr. Lon replied, "Oh, Yes, the pathology paper." Marie continued, "This unusual mycoplasma, *Mycoplasma fermentans incognitus,* that you found associated with AIDS patients and responsible for the deaths of some Armed Forces personnel . . . ." Dr. Lon politely interrupted and went on, "Yes, *Mycoplasma fermentans incognitus* is a unique microorganism. At first I thought it was a large virus after visualizing its morphology by electron microscopy, but then it turned out to be more like a bacteria, and I was finally able to grow it out using special medium designed to allow mycoplasma growth. It grew very poorly. It appears to be quite pathogenic, but the concept of a lethal mycoplasma has not been acknowledged by the medical community since most mycoplasmas are relatively benign." Marie responded, "I am not an infectious disease expert, but I am curious about this particular mycoplasma, because we have found in it blood samples from some Gulf War veterans.

Dr. Lon suddenly changed his tone. "What? You must be wrong. I don't think that we found it in any Gulf War samples." Marie became suspicious, "That's funny, when I talked to you before, you said that you had also found it in some of the Gulf War veterans." Dr. Lon replied, "I did? I don't think so. You must have misunderstood me. We have gone back, and we can't confirm it in the Gulf War veterans' samples." Marie said, "That's funny. You were so sure about it when I spoke to you before. I also think I may have caught this particular mycoplasma. Several years ago I became very sick after a trip to the Middle East. The infection seemed to colonize every organ and tissue in my body, and some of my organs became inflamed and ultimately I developed meningitis and encephalitis. Initially, it started as a flu-like illness with aching joints, chronic fatigue, night sweats, gastrointestinal problems, vertigo, and other problems, and it also caused a kind of thyroiditis. My thyroid was swollen and my thyroid hormones were all over the place. I was nauseated for 13 months, my stomach felt like an inferno, and I was constantly dizzy and my weight dropped to 70 pounds. At one point I thought I had gotten HIV-1 from a blood transfusion that I received during surgery in 1983."

Dr. Lon reflected for a moment. "From what you've described, it sounds like you could have had an infection like the mycoplasma. How did you overcome it?" Marie, "Well, at first I went on ampicillin, and I got worse. Then, by process of elimination my husband determined that the antibiotic doxycycline might work. Within eight weeks of taking the antibiotic, my symptoms started to subside. I went on several more six-week courses of doxycycline, and then I began to get well enough to resume exercising with weights. All in all, though, it took about three years for me to fully regain my health." Dr. Lon explained, "You are a very lucky young lady. Most people in the medical community are skeptical about a highly pathogenic mycoplasma and probably would not have prescribed doxycycline. You were extremely lucky to have hit on doxycycline." Marie added, "You may laugh at me, but I am sure there was some type of divine intervention in my healing." Dr. Lon said, "I do not laugh at such things."

Marie continued the conversation with Dr. Lon. "You know, Dr. Lon, my husband is a department chairman here at the D. O. Madison Cancer Center, and he and I admire your work. I was wondering if perhaps you would be open to hearing about the Nucleoprotein Gene Tracking technique that we have been developing over the last decade. We have been using it to study some unusual genes associated with particular nucleoproteins." Dr. Lon responded, "That sounds interesting. Can you tell me more about it?" Marie continued, "My husband, Jared McNichols, is an expert on cancer metastasis, and initially we developed the technique to study cancer in terms of the chromatin organization of particular genes involved in the metastatic process. I am a believer that if you can find the pattern of particular phenomena, you can begin to understand more about the biochemical processes involved." Dr. Lon asked, "What are you driving at?" Marie said, "We are modifying the Gene Tracking technique to study the dynamics of HIV-1 virus infection in terms of integration of the virus' genes into the cell's chromatin. We have found that there is only a limited subset of controlling elements where the HIV genes can integrate into chromatin." Dr. Lon said, "That's intriguing. But I really do not understand the approach, and we did not find any evidence for a Mycoplasma in the Desert Storm veterans."

Marie disagreed with Dr. Lon but tried to be diplomatic. "I know it is difficult to grasp without the benefit of seeing the data. You know what? I have to give a seminar at Georgetown University in late November right before I travel to Europe. Perhaps I could come over to the Institute and present a seminar?" Dr. Lon was excited, "Would you really do that?" Marie responded, "Sure! I'll be in your neck of the woods anyway." Dr. Lon replied, "That would be great. I'll tell my colleagues General Armwhite and Dr. Deutschman. I'm sure they'll welcome the opportunity." Marie said, "O.K. That's settled."

As an afterthought Marie asked Dr. Lon another question. "By the way, where did you do your training?" Dr. Lon answered, "I did my undergraduate training at the National University in Taiwan." Marie asked, "I thought you were from Mainland China?" Dr. Lon replied nervously, "How did you know that? I am from Mainland China, but it was arranged for me to study in Taiwan. I completed my Ph.D., and then I did an M.D. at Belford College of Medicine in your city." Marie amazed, "Gee, I didn't know you had been at Belford." Dr. Lon replied, "I was on the faculty in microbiology there for a while. But I also spent some time at a small biotech company called Biox that was started out of the Microbiology Department." Marie replied, "That's amazing! I was a junior faculty member in the Micro

Department, and I don't remember running into you. I didn't know about Biox, but that doesn't really mean very much. I didn't keep track of the Belford faculty that had gone off campus to start biotech companies. What types of products are marketed by Biox?" Dr. Lon answered, "I don't know if they are actually selling anything yet. When I was at Biox, I was working on a variety of antibody-based tests against anthrax and related microorganisms." Marie asked, "Anthrax? Why on earth would anyone work on anthrax? It's so deadly that I recall that the government had to shut down a facility at Fort Detrick sometime in the late sixties due to an anthrax accident." Dr. Lon replied, "That's right, two people actually died during the accident. Moscow was heavily engaged in anthrax germ warfare during the Cold War, so we had no choice but to establish our own program." Marie asked, "My God! Are you saying that microbiology faculty at Belford were actually engaging in biological warfare research?"

Dr. Ming Lon did not answer Marie. He became extremely uneasy and nervous, and Marie could actually hear him fidget over the phone. But she continued, "You know, Dr. Lon, my department chairman at Belford asked me how I felt about germ warfare and if I would participate in Biological Warfare experiments just before I became sick in the late eighties. But I told him how asinine such research would be since we barely understand what makes us tick. He asked me if I would remain silent if I heard about any germ warfare research going on. I told him I wouldn't, and that such research was the height of scientific amorality. Of course, Dr. Lon I mean no disrespect to you." Dr. Lon replied, "I understand. You don't have to explain." Marie continued, "Anyway, two weeks later my position was eliminated!" Dr. Lon did not reply, so Marie continued, "Do you feel that the mycoplasma you found is a naturally-occurring microorganism, or do you feel it was altered?" Dr. Lon was nervous and said, "I cannot say. It's too sensitive!" Marie asked, "In other words, you don't know if it had been altered, or you can't say?" Dr. Lon, "You're going to have to draw your own conclusions." Marie said abruptly, "Oh well, I meant no offense." Dr. Lon answered, "I know." Marie finally said, "I look forward to meeting you." Dr. Lon had one more request, "Please send me your résumé. I'll be in touch with you about a seminar." Marie ended the conversation, "Nice talking to you." Dr. Lon replied, "It was a pleasure talking to you Dr. McNichols."

The U. S. Army Institute of Pathology Research

Later that same day Dr. Lon met with Dr. Deutschman and General Armwhite in a conference room at the U. S. Army Institute of Pathology Research. General Armwhite said angrily, "You actually invited Dr. Marie McNichols to give a seminar here? Are you crazy? Suppose she connects her illness to our programs." Dr. Lon replied, "I don't think that she will find out about our programs. I do not see why anyone would be trying to kill Dr. Marie. She seems to be a good scientist, and she is very personable." Dr. Deutschman countered, "It isn't personal, Dr. Lon. It's just that she comes from a powerful family, and she and her husband have stumbled onto some things that are best left alone." Dr. Lon asked, "Why? We could just ignore them, and let them find a way to treat the soldiers." General Armwhite replied, "What? Goddamnit, Ming! Don't you get it? You would think a person of your intelligence who was thrown in a work camp in China because of questionable political loyalties would see that we don't want them to let everyone know about the Day Lily. This is a classified project, and it will remain so until it's declassified. And that's not your decision. You are to follow orders and not question them. Is that clear!"

Dr. Lon was usually a more astute politician. "I was not thinking about the political aspects of this, sir. I was only thinking of the science." Dr. Deutschman continued, "I strongly urge you to wake up and see that our perspective is correct! Do-good people like the McNichols are a menace." General Armwhite added, "By the way, Dr. Lon, why didn't that Day Lily-Russian Doll Cocktail do its job? Our tests on the recruits all went quite well. We actually let you publish some of the data in that pathology journal, without any of the real details, of course." Dr. Lon asked, "You mean your people actually poisoned her?" Dr. Deutschman replied, "We didn't do anything of the kind. Our zealous colleagues in Austin were more than amenable to trying a little experiment. They didn't like the idea that this young scientist might have found out about their prison experiments. Dr. Lon shook his head and General Armwhite asked, "What's wrong with you, Dr. Lon? Don't you remember?" Dr. Lon replied, "Remember what, sir?" Dr. Deutschman interjected, "You helped design the cocktail for her." Dr. Ming Lon looked dazed and confused at General Armwhite's statement. He replied, "But I . . ." Dr. Deutschman interrupted and said to General

Armwhite, "Never mind! Dr. Lon here spent some time at the Montauk Point Intelligence Center for some mind rehabilitation." General Armwhite's smiled and his face lit up after Dr. Deutschman had explained. The Montauk Point Intelligence Center was a top secret facility for brainwashing, and personnel who had questionable loyalties were often sent for 're-programming' so they were less likely to reveal secrets that could embarrass the military or intelligence services.

General Armwhite returned to his previous thought. "Very well. Where was I?" Dr. Lon said, "You were telling us that you had an idea." General Armwhite continued, "Oh, yes! Since the Day Lily Russian Doll failed, perhaps we could exploit the McNichols' visit here. Is there some way that we could invite Jared McNichols as well?" Dr. Deutschman added, "We could arrange a dinner in honor of their visit after the seminar at some exclusive restaurant." General Armwhite said, "This time we better get it right, but I don't like the idea of the subjects being so close to home. We need to have the two of them together." Dr. Deutschman thought about some local sites, "I like that Romanian restaurant in Georgetown. The gypsy atmosphere with the violins is just the right touch. Don't you agree?" General Armwhite agreed, "I like that restaurant!" Dr. Deutschman added, "One of their colleagues at the D. O. Madison Cancer Center that is involved in our classified programs, a Dr. Geldter or something like that, might be of use."

Dr. Lon looked very uneasy as he watched the interchange between Dr. Deutschman and General Armwhite. General Armwhite picked up Ming's uneasiness and said, "Christ, Ming. Will you stop letting your sentimental emotions cloud your judgment. These McNichols are history . . . . because that's the reality of the situation. There's nothing we can do about it. By the way, Dr. Deutschman?" General Armwhite continued, "We should probably call that Clement Masters at the D. O. Madison. I understand Masters is very frustrated about the McNichols. He's apparently lost face. Dr. Deutschman agreed, "Indeed, it now looks like some other group will be on tap in Moscow when the McNichols go there later this month. We may not have to do anything but sit back and watch."

General Armwhite thought for a moment. "We just can't assume that the Moscow operation will be a success; we need a back-up plan. What better way to take care of someone, than after a professional seminar. It won't be expected." Dr. Deutschman disagreed, "That may or may not be true. I for one do not like the plan. It's too close to us." General Armwhite turned to Dr. Lon, "Ming, do you now understand the urgency and sensitivity of this issue?" Dr. Lon nodded sheepishly and replied, "Sir, may I be excused from this project?" General Armwhite was irritated, "Absolutely not!" Dr. Lon requested again, "Sir, I urge you not to have me become directly involved in this. Isn't there another way that this can be done? Can't we just threaten the McNichols so that they stop their research?" General Armwhite stated firmly, "I doubt if that would work." Dr. Deutschman added, "Don't worry Dr. Lon. We're going to have to take this to a higher level before anything is settled. For the moment, all you have to do is be friendly with the McNichols and find out what they know and who they have told. If they have written anything up, we need to get copies as soon as possible. Is that clear enough for you?" Dr. Lon nodded his approval. Dr. Deutschman finishing up said, "Good! Then let's get on with it then."

Dr. Masters has a plan

Dr. Masters had called a special meeting and was on the speakerphone with General Armwhite and Dr. Deutschman. Drs. Geldter, Krappner, Ross, and Graham were sitting in Dr. Masters' office, and Dr. Belcher had quietly but reluctantly just entered the office where the others were listening attentively to the important men from Washington. In contrast to the other D. O. Madison staff, Dr. Belcher did not like anything about Dr. Masters or his 'special' projects. He considered Dr. Masters to be a dangerous political hack, appointed to his position over the much better qualified and intellectually equipped surgeon Dr. Robert Hicks. However, pressure from certain financial interests in Las Vegas that Belcher thought were just organized crime bosses and their defense contractor investments were supporting Dr. Masters' and his obscene building program. Dr. Masters also had support from some ex-governmental officials like the ex-national security advisor to a former President, and these special interest groups forced the University System to place Dr. Masters into the leadership position at the Madison over the unanimous disapproval of the faculty search committee. He also thought that Dr. Masters had completely gone insane and was potentially dangerous to everyone on the staff at the Madison, including himself. In fact, Dr. Belcher was acutely afraid of Dr. Masters, who he considered to be fully capable of having him killed, just like Dr. Cannon and the rest, so he would go along with whatever Dr. Masters wanted. After all, he was close to retirement, and he was biding his time so that he could eventually leave all this behind. In his arrogance, however, Dr. Belcher did not realize that Dr. Masters really did not trust him, which is why Dr. Masters made sure that Dr. Belcher was thoroughly implicated in any plan that was concocted in his own office.

Dr. Masters smiled and motioned to Dr. Belcher to sit down. Dr. Masters was speaking to General Armwhite on the phone. "Well, General, it is fortuitous that your call coincides with our monthly Special Faculty Executive Meeting." Dr. Masters hesitated and said in a cynical voice, "All the key personnel on my team are present." General Armwhite was heard over the speakerphone, "I have Drs. Deutschman and Ming Lon connected from their respective offices. Let me start by saying that this McNichols situation has got to be handled once and for all. We simply cannot afford another failure." General Armwhite then asked Dr. Lon, "Ming, do you have any explanation as to why the Russian Doll mixtures that were given to the McNichols failed?" Dr. Lon answered, "We don't know why they failed. They may not have been given the correct dose. It could also be that the McNichols have excellent immune systems." Dr. Lon paused and then said, "And they were lucky to have stumbled upon the doxycyline as a treatment. Dr. Marie herself believes that there was divine intervention." General Armwhite interjected, "Can you believe such bull?" Dr. Masters scoffed, "That's just the sort of self-righteous comment I would expect from Marie McNichols." General Armwhite continued, "I have our coordinator Dr. Deutschman on the line as well. He has helped us in the past with foreign contacts and is an advisor to Dr. Geldter's and Dr. Rook's projects there in Austin." Dr. Deutschman then asked, "Can you all hear me?"

It was Dr. Masters who responded first. "You are loud and clear in Austin." General Armwhite said, "Roger here." Dr. Deutschman continued, "This is Deutschman here. Our people suggest that a more conventional approach might be useful in Moscow, because it is doubtful that an autopsy would be performed. As a back-up we will be capitalizing on a local seminar here. Dr. Marie McNichols has been invited to visit us. Of course, we would want her husband to accompany her as well. Can you arrange it?" Dr. Masters asked, "Why did you invite *her* to give a seminar?" General Armwhite replied, "That's our business, Dr. Masters, and you are in no position to question it." Dr. Masters quickly backed down, "I merely wanted to point out that every time Marie McNichols delivers a seminar at a prestigious institution, it lends credibility to her as a scientist. I am under pressure from our financial backers in Las Vegas to do everything possible to prevent acknowledgment of her work. They directed us to provide constant peer ridicule to drive them both to despair." Dr. Deutschman said, "Yes, that might be useful, but Dr. Masters, you do not appear to be very successful at carrying out your campaign. I don't see where you have succeeded."

Dr. Masters looked at his colleagues disdainfully. "It appears that I am surrounded by incompetence here." Dr. Geldter spoke out first, "Dr. Isaac Geldter here! If I may interject, already? We feel here that it is unlikely that the McNichols will ever return from Moscow. A more conventional approach will be used at a private dinner, which will be thrown by a 'friend.' The medical personnel and police authorities will be instructed not to look for certain things. It will be just be a matter of time, and it will all look quite natural. After all, people in Moscow die all the time of unusual things." Dr. Deutschman was not convinced, "That's a possible approach, one that we would have trouble implementing stateside with all of our shyster lawyers pouring over tests and documents, but if it fails, we have devised a back-up plan." General Armwhite interjected, "Of course, it's always better to execute an overseas plan. But just in case it does not go as we expect, I think it is imperative that we have an alternative approach." Dr. Deutschman added, "It's really only a matter of time, but we need to make sure this time."

Dr. Krappner interrupted the discussion. "Sir, this is Dr. Amy Krappner. I think we should also consider that it is imperative to have the immune system compromised in order to assure success with the conventional approach." Dr. Belcher then interjected sarcastically, "You obviously don't know what you're talking about, Amy. The immune system has nothing to do with this approach. And in addition, Dr. Krappner, how are you going to compromise the immune system? Remember, the last time you and Isaac suggested the asparaginase, which you were absolutely convinced would work, it appeared to boost the immune system, just like *I* predicted." Dr. Krappner quickly responded, "Dr. Belcher, we told you it was not our fault–it wasn't done correctly." Dr. Geldter added, "This time, we suggest the use of an organophosphate mixture." Dr. Krappner continued, "Remember, we want to make the subjects just sick enough so that they can travel but their immune systems will be compromised." Dr. Masters said sarcastically, "Good idea! I like your tenacity, Amy."

Dr. Belcher couldn't stand it any longer, and in his usual whiny voice he disagreed. "I don't know about your 'immunology' approach. It does not even sound sensible; I don't see any relationship between the approach being discussed and the immune system. I don't think any of you know what you're talking about." Dr. Geldter whispered to Amy, "God-willing this time it will work." Dr. Belcher said in a voice that he assumed would not be heard by their colleagues back East, "I find it odd Isaac that you don't consider you're breaking one of God's commandments." Dr. Belcher had been torn by the very nature of Dr. Masters' requests of him. On one hand he despised Dr. Masters and would just as soon turn him to the police for allegedly having Dr. Cannon murdered and attempting to murder other staff members at the Madison, if he had enough evidence so that he could escape the subsequent threat of being identified as a co-conspirator. On the other hand Dr. Belcher was terrified of being murdered by the very same people that he was meeting with this morning. It would be a dilemma that other faculty members also had but would never be resolved. Dr. Belcher and other faculty and administrators were drawn into the conspiracy in a way that they could not easily escape.

Dr. Masters waved his hands and apologized to the East Coast group. "Sorry about the interruptions. It seems we are having a disagreement here on the appropriate approach." He then quickly turned to Dr. Belcher and pointed, "You keep quiet, Francis." General Armwhite asked skeptically, "Let me get this straight. When would you use the organophosphates?" There was silence because Dr. Masters had no idea how to answer the question. So Dr. Krappner replied for him. "We could invite her to a women's faculty tea on the pretense that we are considering approval of a faculty appointment for her." Dr. Masters quickly added, "Good! I like that approach."

Dr. Deutschman the hack who questioned the wisdom of the D. O. Madison immunologists was still not convinced. "I think you would be better off administering aflatoxin rather than an organophosphate. It's more potent and the dehydration produced by vomiting and diarrhea should do the trick." Dr. Masters said as he turned to his faculty for support, "That's an idea. We need to consider that." Dr. Belcher added sarcastically, "I'm surprised no one has thought of the shellfish toxin cigaterra. It takes a full year to clear the body, if the individual actually survives." Dr. Masters then said, "Yes, good! Dr. Belcher, I see you're finally on board." But Dr. Belcher was simply being sarcastic. He really did not anticipate that they might actually consider his input. In this way he had thoroughly implicated himself in Masters' conspiracy.

Dr. Deutschman could easily sense that the entire meeting was unraveling, and he responded to the group. "If the cyanide and immunosuppression fail, we will take your suggestions into consideration. We don't want them to be so sick that they won't travel." Dr. Deutschman and Dr. Masters seemed to be finally on the same ridiculous bureaucratic wavelength. Now Dr. Graham, who did not want to be outdone by Dr. Krappner, interjected, "This is Dr. Graham, sir, I can assist at the women's faculty tea, and I am also an immunologist." General Armwhite was growing impatient with the antics in Austin. "This is getting a bit complicated, don't you think. I think that we will leave the details to Dr. Masters. Has anyone thought about how you are going to deal with Professor McNichols?" Dr. Masters replied, "Yes! That's right. I will get my team right on it!" Dr. Deutschman responded sarcastically, "Good! You do that! Remember Dr. Graham, and that goes for you Dr. Ross, since the last debacle you have a lot to prove." Dr. Ross responded, "But surely you realize that we had no control over whether they actually came to that graduation party." Dr. Deutschman who knew Dr. Ross well but didn't know anything about some stupid graduation party said, "Damnit Ross! Don't you give me any of your excuses. I know you too well."

Finally General Armwhite became impatient with the entire Austin group. "Dr. Deutschman and I are tired of your excuses too, Dr. Masters. You and your 'team' never seem to get anything right." Dr. Masters explained, "I disagree! True, we have had some minor difficulties but nothing that can't be corrected. Sir, my team is at your complete disposal. You can count on us." Dr. Masters looked around the room for help, "Does anyone else have any suggestions?" Dr. Geldter, who had been unusually quiet, was one never to be outdone or not have the final word. "Dr. Masters, I still think we should include a biological in the next operation." Dr. Masters vacillated, "That sounds like an excellent idea." General Armwhite was not convinced, "Why should we do that?" Dr. Masters hesitated and looked at Isaac for help. Dr. Geldter spoke first, "To weaken them, of course." He added, "A good dose of Epstein Barr virus could also do the trick." Dr. Masters had already forgotten what Isaac had just said, "Good! I knew Dr. Geldter would have a suggestion." There was silence from the East Coast participants.

Dr. Masters felt the need to regain control over the meeting by summarizing the various approaches. "Now let's review this morning's session. I believe that we decided to stick to the conventional approach and leave out the biologicals, at least for now." General Armwhite said, "I finally agree with that assessment. The rest is too hypothetical." Dr. Masters asked, "Do you have any additional comments?" He looked around the room trying to rally his troops. "Dr. Ross?" Dr. Ross nervously decided not to fall for the bait. "No. Not at the present, sir. But . . ." Dr. Masters interrupted and looked at Dr. Ross and Dr. Graham, "I am pleased that you two are joining my special team." Dr. Graham nodded and then blurted out, "I wonder why no one has thought of a lethal dose of radiation. It would be relatively easily to contaminate food with something radioactive to suppress the immune system and possibly induce a lethal cancer." Dr. Masters nodded his approval and said, "Yes, that is a possibility. What do the rest of you think?" There was silence around the room. Most thought the suggestion was completely idiotic but were afraid to make the situation worse.

Dr. Deutschman was more strained than ever and began to lose his patience. "That's food for thought, but we already considered that approach." He paused, "The problem is the long time period for the full effect, so to speak. At high doses radiation poisoning is way too obvious. But let's keep that idea in mind for future reference." General Armwhite added, "If all else fails, I suppose we could put a device on their plane.

Unfortunately, it's messy, and it can be traced. If we must use that approach, we have to get it authorized, and I feel that we've overused this tactic lately. This must not be traceable back to us."

Dr. Masters thought about the statement for a moment and wondered if one day these fiends would use that approach on him if something goes wrong. "Well, I agree, and I did, I believe, explain to my team that it also cannot be traced back to my office. Now, I think that we have a good game plan. If at first you don't succeed . . . ." Everyone forced a little laugh in Dr. Masters office but no one back East responded to the over-used comment. General Armwhite finally said, "We're signing off now Dr. Masters. Get your group and your game plan in order. Is that clear enough?" Dr. Masters responded, "We will be ready, sir. Signing off here in Austin." Dr. Masters pressed a button and disconnected the speakerphone. He looked around his office, but his hand picked team was just waiting for something to happen.

After they hung up the speakerphone in Austin General Armwhite started talking to himself. "What a clusterfuck! That Clement Masters has no clue about how to run an operation! No wonder they never succeed." Dr. Deutschman was still on the line, "We'll just have to make sure ourselves. We can't depend on those clowns." General Armwhite added, "God help us if we ever have to go to those losers in Austin. I think that Masters has flipped his lid. He has obviously lost touch with reality. I don't think we can depend on them to get anything right." Luckily for Marie and Jared General Armwhite would prove correct.

The McNichols prepare to leave for Moscow

Jared had received an invitation to become a visiting professor at the All Russian Cancer Center in Moscow, and to his amazement the D. O. Madison administration went out of their way to allow him to accept. Dr. Belcher even arranged to get Jared some travel funds for the trip, saying that it was an honor for the institution to receive such an invitation. As a friend of the Russian center, Dr. Bane had been arranging joint visits of some of faculty with the Moscow institution, so the invitation was not unusual. He told Jared that he was proud that the McNichols could represent the D. O. Madison in Russia and deliver lectures to the scientists and physicians at their sister institution in Moscow. Although Jared was suspicious and felt a bit uneasy about the change in attitude of the administration in Austin, he decided to go anyway and even take Marie with him to Moscow. He had been assured by Dr. Belcher that the D. O. Madison would look favorably on the trip because of the prestige of the appointment. That made Jared even more suspicious, and he wondered why Dr. Belcher or Dr. Geldter weren't representing the D. O. Madison instead.

One day before their trip to Moscow Jared was beginning to pack the bags for the trip. Marie could never seem to fit everything into one bag, and she usually waited until the last minute and then complained that she left something out. Jared insisted that they only take one large bag each with them so that they could handle their luggage themselves. He had learned over the years of foreign travel that you have to limit your baggage so you can be mobile, and mobility was often important in other countries where you may not speak the language. He said to Marie as one of his big black cats, Yang, jumped into the bag he was packing. "Yang doesn't want us to go to Moscow! He says there are bad people there!" Marie asked, "And there aren't bad people here? At least you've been to Moscow." Jared responded, "Yah, at the height of the Cold War. It was a pretty unfriendly place. Not that the scientists were unfriendly. They were actually very warm, but the bureaucrats were insufferable. I can't say that I enjoyed my trip that much, but it was interesting. I met some nice people there who really knew what they were doing."

Marie had fond memories of meeting Russian scientists at international meetings. "The Russians have always supported and admired my work, in contrast to the treatment I receive in this country. At that molecular genetics meeting in Greece they all stood up and gave me a standing ovation." Jared added, "That's because they understood what you were talking about with your nucleoprotein gene tracking experiments, *in contrast* to the likes of Krappner and Geldter, who couldn't think their way out of a paper bag." Marie said, "Actually it was Dr. Auchenhower who gave himself an award for his own presentation at the meeting, and all the Russians got up and yelled 'fix' and booed him. They all wanted me to win the award, and they gave me a standing ovation, but they said his talk was mediocre." Jared sarcastically said, "Why doesn't that surprise me! Did you ever think what it might take to give yourself an award in front of a hostile crowd for something that you didn't deserve? That takes some balls! . . . . What an asshole."

Marie pondered the thought of meeting her Russian colleagues again in Moscow. "I think it will be refreshing to talk to people who actually understand what we are doing in the lab. You know, some of the scientists in Moscow were actually translating their Russian publications for me so that I could see what they were doing. They were way ahead of us in chromatin research, but it's funny, no one in this country seemed to know about it." Jared responded, "That's because they only published in Russian language journals." Marie objected, "They didn't always publish in Russian journals, and even when they published in English language journals, their research was ignored." Jared asked, "Do you think that the Cold War had something to do with that?" Marie answered, "Yes, I do. We are so insular and arrogant here in the U. S. We think that everything we did is so great, and everything they did was mediocre." Jared added sarcastically, "And since during the Cold War we out-spent them into economic ruin, that proves it!" Marie answered, "Sort of, but not entirely. I think that it's more that the research in each country tends to be more controlled than we would like to admit." Jared agreed, "Well, I can certainly attest to that. Look what happened to my Outstanding Investigator Grant. A germ warfare guy who works on yeast genetics at Crystal Spring Harbor crashed the review committee meeting and immediately attacked me. He wasn't even a reviewer, but he did a complete hatchet job on my proposal, and it wasn't even his review assignment. Now who do you guess was behind that? Who directed him to go out of his way to trash my application? It's difficult enough to get a grant funded these days without having an 'asset' going after you!" Marie agreed, "I don't even bother anymore after they changed my NIH grant priority score from a 110 to a 310. The guy running the committee couldn't explain the change in my score, but at least he apologized to me. The committee chairman complained, but it didn't do any good." Jared sighed, "Yes, I know it well. The same thing happened to me with my Army grant application, and there was even an investigation by the Inspector General's Office but it didn't go anywhere. Some of the review committee members complained but in the end I never got the grant."

Marie felt that she and Jared had faced extreme hostility from their so-called colleagues. "You know, some day we are going to have to move to another country." Jared answered, "I know, but where? We can't just pick up and move overseas and end up right back in the same situation again. I have a feeling that we are going to have to fight this battle right here if we can ever expect to see any justice." Marie scoffed, "Don't hold your breath, Jared. We are not going to win anyone of importance over to our side here in Texas." Jared knew Marie was right. They would never see justice in Texas.

Marie then remembered something that she forgot to tell to Jared. "Oh, I forgot to tell you, Amy Krappner and Laura Graham invited me to a special women's faculty tea this afternoon." Jared laughed, "Oh, lovely. What in the hell is that all about? I can't see you sipping tea with those bitches." Marie said, "Maybe they are not as bad as you think. Perhaps I was too harsh in judging them. Amy Krappner said they wanted to discuss an appointment for me at the Madison." She continued, "I don't know if they are up to something in view of their past behavior."

Jared was completely skeptical. "Yah, they are nice and friendly, like stepping on sleeping rattlesnakes. They look all pretty and nice all coiled up, until they sink their fangs into your flesh, and the venom starts creeping up your leg." Marie responded, "Oh Jared, you just don't like women in science." Jared responded, "No, I love women in science–I married one, remember! I just don't like female blood-sucking parasites in science that have absolutely no talent. You know, they could be setting you up. Did you ever consider that, Marie?" She answered, "Yes, I did. I promise to be careful, *if* I decide to go." Jared said, "Let's ask Yang!" Yang, their male feline friend was still interfering in the packing process that was interrupted by the conversation between Jared and Marie. Jared picked up Yang and held him up to Marie while moving his paw as he spoke, "Yang says that we are on a negative thought loop, and we should think good thoughts!" Marie said, "Like, how exciting and historic it will be to see Moscow." Jared replied, "Right!" At this point Yang started to whine in a very Burmese way to tell them that it's time for his dinner. Both Marie and Jared started to laugh. Marie said, "Yang has given his paw of approval to a change of subject and activity!" Jared agreed, "You've got it!"

Jared and Marie were in the kitchen feeding Yin and Yang. Jared picked up Yang and held him up to Marie, "Yang says it's too close to our trip to Moscow, and why would you want to go to a tea with those two morons!"

Marie said, "Perhaps I'll just give Dr. Krappner a call and send my temporary regrets due to my tight schedule!" Jared answered, "That's a good idea! Keep the bitches guessing."

Marie then thought for a moment out loud. "I think I'll have Jane send both Krappner and Graham each a white rose as a gesture of regret." Jared asked, "White roses? Why would you waste the money?" Marie said, "It's my signature, remember?" She continued, "The white rose is the symbol of my new educational Foundation." Jared disagreed, "Why bother. They could construe a white rose as the kiss of death!" Marie laughed, "I prefer to think of it as a symbol of hope!" She continued, "I was often called Roses when I was growing up. It was my nickname." Jared asked, "Another clue to your real identity?" Marie replied, "Perhaps!" She continued, "You know, the rose is also a symbol of the Catholic Church." Jared asked, "It is? How did you know that?" Marie said, "Everyone knows that!" Jared disagreed, "No they don't!" Marie reflected, "When I got sick as a child I had a sort of godmother, Mary, who always went to the Vatican to pray for me! She said Novena for me every morning!" Jared asked, "But I thought that you grew up Jewish? Weren't you were brought up a Jewish home?" Marie answered, "Yes, but I was also very close to the Catholic Church. When I asked my grandmother why was it that every time I got sick, Mary went to Rome? She told me that I asked too many questions!" Jared was curious, "Go on, Marie." She continued, "Anyway, when she returned, she always had a little gift for me from the Pope. One time he sent me a wine decanter embellished with silver containing holy water from the Vatican. Another time he sent me beautiful hand-blown glass horses and an elephant! And she always brought me a rose with the gift, and she said the Pope sends his regards and wants me to have a rose! From then on, I was called Roses!" Jared asked, "Do you think you have some special connection to the Vatican?" Marie pondered the question, "I don't know. But I love to send roses to people! I even like to send roses better than receiving roses."

Jared indicated to Marie that what she has just told him would eventually help her find her true identity. "I believe you've hit upon an important clue. Keep thinking about what happened during the time when you were a little girl." Marie pondered what Jared told her and agreed that she would try to concentrate on her childhood to find additional keys to her identity.

The faculty tea

Later that morning Marie called Dr. Krappner on the phone from Queenswood. She was sitting on the bed petting one of the cats. The phone rang three times in Dr. Krappner's outer office, and her secretary picked up the phone. The secretary answered, "Good morning, Dr. Krappner's office." Marie said, "This is Dr. Marie McNichols. I'd like to speak with Dr. Krappner." The secretary answered, "One moment please." The secretary buzzed Amy Krappner, "Dr. Marie McNichols is on line two." Dr. Krappner responded, "Thank you. I'll take the call. Amy Krappner hesitated and looked around her office as she thought about how she would manipulate Marie. Her office was unusually opulent for a faculty member with rosewood office furniture and all sorts of antique pictures on the wall as well as pictures of Amy receiving various minor awards and posing with important people. Dr. Krappner finally picked up the phone and answered in a sweet voice, "Hi Marie." Her voice was liltingly false. Marie said, "Hello Dr. Krappner." Dr. Krappner tried to be friendly, "Call me Amy." Marie told her, "Amy, I'm afraid I won't be able to make it to the faculty tea. I have a schedule conflict, and the tea's awfully close to an overseas trip." Dr. Krappner responded sharply, "You can't do that to me! Isn't there any way that you could rearrange your schedule?" Marie answered, "I'm afraid not. Perhaps I could take a rain check?" Dr. Krappner continued, "Are you absolutely sure that you couldn't fit it in? It's not like it's a major commitment of your time, and I think that it could be especially important for your career. The other faculty members in our little group will be there, and I must say, we do wield some political power at our institution. We have been moving the University to hire more women at the upper administrative levels. Our academic institutions in Texas, you know, are quite behind in having women at the top positions." Marie said, "You don't say? I am sure that *you* will find a way to place more women into the upper echelons of power . . . . such as yourself." Dr. Krappner laughed, "This is not about me, Dr. McNichols, this is about equality and equal representation of women at all administrative levels in our public institutions." Marie replied sarcastically, "I see. Well, I am certainly gratified that you are working on this important problem."

Dr. Krappner was thrilled that Marie saw her side of the problem. "Why thank you! I have been working so hard on this, and I seem to get very little thanks from the other faculty. In fact, we have set up a fund to procure a lobbyist at the State Capitol to help correct the situation. Would you like to make a donation to a very important cause?" Marie responded, "I think that if I am allowed to actually join the faculty, that would be a possibility." Dr. Krappner disappointed, "Well, you don't move up with that kind of attitude, Marie. It seems that we have to fight harder for promotions than everyone else. Don't you agree?" Marie answered, "I wouldn't know, since every time I apply for a position at the D. O. Madison, it seems that it is blocked." Dr. Krappner seized the thought, "Yes! That is exactly what I mean, and this is why you need to make a donation to our group to insure the future of women in our academic institutions! Wouldn't you agree that this is a very worthy and important cause?" Marie answered, "Oh, yes, I do, but I don't think that I can be active in your group until I actually get a genuine offer to join the faculty." Dr. Krappner disagreed, "Nonsense, you can join our group at any time. We would be most pleased to have you." Dr. Krappner hesitated, "Marie, I would like to give you some friendly advice . . ." Marie was waiting patiently for Amy's lecture, "Yes?" Dr. Krappner continued, "There are people like me trying very hard to help you achieve your career goals, and I must say, we would like to see a bit more appreciation from you for our efforts." Marie responded, "I know that you are trying very hard to . . . to assist me, and I certainly appreciate it as a woman. I would very much like to attend your faculty tea, but I just do not have the time before we leave for Moscow. I am afraid that I will have to take a rain check on the tea, but I would like to attend a future meeting of the women faculty." Dr. Krappner became angry, "I am very disappointed in you, Marie . . . . To be honest with you, I thought that you were one of us, and we very much wanted to bring you into our group. You have to start working on your career, Marie, and this would be an excellent time to start–by coming to our tea and making a donation to our group."

Marie grew impatient with Dr. Krappner who would not take no for an answer. "I really would like to come, but it just isn't going to work for me this time. I have so little time to get ready for my trip. Perhaps next time." Dr. Krappner pleaded, "But there may not be a next time, Marie. I think that you are making a big mistake by rejecting our sincere offer. We may not be so willing next time to invite you into our group." Marie said, "Please don't misinterpret my comments, Dr. Krappner. I very much want to come to the faculty tea, but if we could make it next month after I return, it would be much better for me." Dr. Krappner said, "Marie, you are going to have to start thinking less about yourself and more about the bigger picture. We are trying to bring you onto the faculty here, and you do not seem to be responding to our efforts. After all the work that I have put in to help you, this is the thanks that I get!" Marie became impatient, "It's not as if I don't appreciate all that you have done for me, it's just that I don't have enough time before we leave for an exhausting overseas trip."

Dr. Krappner became mad and gave up on Marie. "Very well, but I am extremely disappointed in you. We will be having another tea next month . . . . perhaps you can join us then and make your donation at that itme." Marie said, "I'll certainly try to place this onto my schedule, but I do have back-to-back international trips." Dr. Krappner answered, "Well! I so wanted this tea to serve as a vehicle for your joining our faculty, but you don't seem to be very helpful. You know, there is still time to change your mind!" Marie said, "Thanks again, but it is highly unlikely that my attending a tea will alter Dr. Master's negative opinion of me." Dr. Krappner disagreed, "Nonsense! I happen to know that Dr. Masters has a great deal of respect for you." Marie responded, "Amy, somehow I doubt that. You know Dr. Krappner, I find it hard to believe that you would support me in view of the fact that we have had such a strained relationship in the past." Dr. Krappner had a slight falsetto laugh, "It was just a misunderstanding. I do not hold grudges. I believe that we need more faculty like you on our staff." Marie finally had all that she could take. "I am so sorry to disappoint you. Give my best to Dr. Geldter." Dr. Krappner said, "I know that Isaac will be disappointed that you will not be joining our tea. By hook or by crook I will get you aboard our faculty at The Madison." Marie said, "You can try, and I would appreciate that at least." She then said, "Good bye, Dr. Krappner. Thank you for all your wonderful support." Dr. Krappner said in an affected manner, "Ciao, Marie. And may you have a productive trip." She slammed the phone down angrily. "That bitch! She won't come to our tea!"

Amy thought for a moment and then dialed Dr. Masters' number. After reaching his office she said, "This is Dr. Krappner; I'd like to speak with Dr. Masters on an urgent issue, the faculty tea." Dr. Masters' receptionist responded, "One moment, please!" The receptionist buzzed Dr. Masters who was in his office. "Dr. Masters, Dr. Krappner is on line two with an urgent message." Dr. Masters asked, "What the hell does she want? I'm busy!" The receptionist said, "Sir, she said it was urgent." He replied, "Everything that these women faculty have to say is 'urgent.' Can't they wait their turn like the other faculty?" The receptionist, "She said it was something about a . . . . faculty tea." Dr. Masters almost shouted, "Well, why didn't you say so! O.K., I'll take the call and hold my other calls, please."

Dr. Masters pushed the button on the phone for line two, and his personality changed abruptly, "Amy, how good of you to call. I was just thinking about your faculty tea." Dr. Krappner said hesitantly, "Marie can't make the tea, and I won't be able to . . ." Dr. Masters interrupted before she could finish, "Goddamn it, Amy, we had a plan, and you were going to make sure that the plan was followed. And don't you ever talk about this issue on the phone. Just get your fat ass over here!" Dr. Krappner was taken aback, "Yes, sir!" He continued, "I am sick of all these obstacles threatening to ruin our mission." Dr. Krappner said, "I'll be right over!" Dr. Masters replied, "You do that!" He then slammed down the phone.

Within ten minutes Dr. Krappner was in Dr. Masters' office. He left instructions for his executive secretary to show her in immediately when she arrived. He was clearly in an agitated mood as he rose from his desk when Dr. Krappner entered his office. He waited for the door to close and then asked her, "Amy, why is it that none of you seem to be able to complete even the most minute part of the project that was assigned to you?" Dr. Masters was usually more refined, but his anger seemed to be getting the best of him. Dr. Krappner pleaded, "I can't control the fact that Marie turned down the invitation to attend our tea! I even personally called her today and pleaded with her to come to the tea. I don't understand it. Everything was going so well, and we were having such a good conversation." Dr. Masters, who was extremely angry, almost screamed, "Don't give me excuses like that insipid Graham. Am I surrounded by idiots? Why can't you ever seem to get it right and complete the most simple of tasks?" Dr. Krappner did not answer. He shook his head, "I don't know how you ever got so far in my organization." Dr. Krappner finally spoke out. "But sir, it wasn't my fault! Dr. Masters, you know I always try my best to do what you have asked!" He said angrily, "Oh, it's never your fault, Amy! Do you take me for an idiot? I suggest that we leave this to the operatives. It seems that no one around here can perform even the simplest things without screwing up. Let *them* worry about the problem." Dr. Krappner said, "You are absolutely right, sir, we can only do so much! We were never trained to do this kind of work."

Dr. Masters placed his hand to his head, looked out the window and said, "I may have to use other methods. I don't want to lose face with those Las Vegas boys and their Cornelyus Group." He looked out the window. He finally turned to Dr. Krappner and said, "Get out, Amy! Go back to your women's faculty tea!" Dr. Krappner was still pleading her case, "But, sir! I have always . . . ." He interrupted her by waving his hand, "Get out! I am sick of your excuses." Dr. Krappner started to cry, "I swear to God, it wasn't my fault! Can't you see that, Dr. Masters?" He said, "Stop your driveling in my office. Crying about what could have been is not going to solve the problem. I guess you're not ready for bigger things, Amy. I am very disappointed in you!" Dr. Krappner wiped the tears from her face. He said again, "Now out! Dr. Krappner pulled out a white handkerchief from her purse and began wiping her face. She turned quickly and ran out the office while the secretaries and receptionist stood to see what was wrong with Dr. Amy Krappner, who had once been the darling of the President of the D. O. Madison Cancer Center.

CHAPTER 9

A trip to Moscow (Late 1994)

The McNichols had to fly from Austin to Houston to Amsterdam to Moscow to reach their destination. It was a long trip, even longer with the layovers in Houston and Amsterdam. After an overnight flight, they arrived to gloomy whether* in Amsterdam. It was raining and cold compared to the boiling heat of Central Texas. After waiting for a flight to Moscow, there was another several hour flight.

The McNichols arrived in Moscow in the evening, and it had already been dark for six hours. In the beginning of winter the sun set at about 4 PM, but in the deep winter it can set around 3 PM in the afternoon. Marie had never been to Russia, so she was excited about arriving in Moscow. The airport was modern and busy, and as they were making their way through the Passport Control, Jared thought that it was curious that some rock song was playing in the background. He made some quip about the influx of capitalist tendencies, and they eventually found their luggage and cleared customs. Marie was wearing a rabbit fur coat and a Russian-style hat. She had on layers of clothing to brace herself against the Moscow cold. She was wearing none of this when they left Austin but was persuaded by Jared to prepare for a major contrast in weather.

The amusing Dr. Vassiloff

Marie and Jared were very tired from the trip, and it showed as they stumbled out of Customs with their bags. Now Marie realized why Jared insisted on only one checked bag each. They were lucky, however, as Dr. Yuri Vassiloff, a colleague of Jared's met them at the arrival hall. Dr. Vassiloff was a rather short, stocky, middle-aged Russian gentleman who had a very wise and jovial manner. He was a man full of life. He especially liked to make Jared laugh with his tales about Russian bureaucratic idiots, which he said were the bread for the masses in the old Soviet system. Jared saw Dr. Vassiloff first and yelled, "Yuri!" Dr. Vassiloff turned and responded, "Jared, my old friend! Welcome! Welcome to Mother Russia!"

Jared and Yuri got into a typical Russian bear hug. Yuri turned to Marie and asked, "Who is . . . beautiful young woman with you?" He spoke in a kind of broken English with a very strong Russian accent, but Jared and Marie had no trouble understanding his sincerity and warmth. Jared replied, "Why this is my beautiful wife, Marie." Dr. Vassiloff said, "Now I know why you did not want to leave . . . behind! She is so young . . . so pretty!" Marie said, "I just look a bit younger than I am, but thank you for the compliment." Dr. Vassiloff said, "Compliments . . . we have lots of . . . . especially for foreign visitors!" He laughed. "Remember last trip to Moscow in 81?" Jared responded, "Yes, it was horrible. There was no food in Moscow. I hope the situation has changed for the better." Dr. Vassiloff laughed and said, "It changed, but . . . . may not notice!" He laughed again. "At least we can complain and not go to KGB office." He laughed loudly, as this was something that no one would dare to say in public in the old Soviet days. Jared said, "Come on, Yuri!" Dr. Vassiloff laughed again and said, "In Russia we can change names, but everything still . . . . same!" He turned to Marie and said, "You see, we live to suffer in Mother Russia." He paused and asked, "You must be tired from journey?" Jared said, "We are." He paused, "But we will have time to rest up in Berlin on our way home." Marie added, "It has long been a dream of mine to finally visit the country that produced Rachmaninoff, Tschaikovsky, Doestoevsky, Tolstoy, Borodin . . . Your country is one of great passion!" Dr. Vassiloff laughed, "That is true!" He turned to Jared, "You married . . . . philosopher?" He paused, "I think, though, Russia best described as country built on *great* mistakes." Marie said, "Remember, if I may quote Pontius Pilate in the Movie Ben Hur, 'where there is greatness, error is often great!'" Yuri laughed, "Well, Mother Russia certainly is great and mistakes are great beyond description!" Yuri was on a roll, but when he got excited his English suffered a bit.

Turning back to Jared he finally became serious. "Did you bring supplies?" Jared smiled and answered, "Yes I did! Just like you requested." Dr. Vassiloff said, "Now we have vodka and then rest." Marie looked at Jared and said, "Not me. I'm going to sleep!" Jared said, "Perhaps we could visit together at the hotel so Marie can get some sleep. She never sleeps on the plane." Dr. Vassiloff said, "I don't either! I would like to not miss movies! And vodka!" Yuri then said, "I hope you will be patient with Yuri. My English . . . . not so good. Our system still in great flux, but not as bad as visit in '81." He continued, "Collapse of communists has produced much confusion, but average Muscovite at least has some food." He paused, "Even heat still rationed in some places. So, I'm afraid we cannot provide luxuries you treated me when I came to Texas." Jared said, "It looks like things have improved since our last visit. So life can't be so bad." Marie said, "We are here to see you and meet with our colleagues at the All Russian Cancer Center." Dr. Vassiloff smiled, "Still going to be a bit like returning to old Soviet state for you." Jared replied, "The luxuries are superficial. We won't be concerned about that." Marie asked, "Can I look forward to seeing some Russian kazatsky and throwing the vodka glass into the fireplace?" Dr. Vassiloff laughed, "I'm afraid vodka and glass breaking is Hollywood perception of our glorious Russia. Today, we don't waste one drop of vodka in fireplace. Is better to place in stomach!" Yuri rubbed his stomach, and Jared and Marie laughed. Marie said, "There is no way I can drink vodka!" Dr. Vassiloff turned to Jared, "I think we can provide Russian entertainment for Marie." She said, "I really want to see St. Basil's and the changing of the guard as well as Zagorsck and the Kremlin!" Yuri bowed slightly, "That is all arranged!" Jared laughed as they made their way out of the terminal building into the cold Moscow night.

They walked into the parking lot and it was dark, very dark. The small Russian vehicles were lined up and covered with frost. Marie turned and asked, "Where's the KGB?" Yuri laughed and said, "They're here–I assure you!" He continued, "Did they bother you at arrival?" Jared shook his head indicating they did not, while Marie said, "I am so happy to be here that the KGB can't possibly dent my joy!" Dr. Vassiloff said, "Tomorrow morning you rest; I then take you to Red Square and Kremlin. Then you give lectures at All Russian Cancer Center and later in week at Russian Institute for Molecular Biology." Jared nodded his approval.

They made their way to a small Russian car. Dr. Vassiloff apologized for the size of the car, "Is not like Texas cars, I think!" Jared responded, "It looks functional to me. Four good tires and I hope the engine runs." Dr. Vassiloff laughed and said, "Most of time! You know in Mother Russia, we have a saying . . ." Jared said to Marie who was falling asleep in the car, "Yuri always has a story about Mother Russia!" Dr. Vassiloff laughed and said, "But I haven't told story!" They all laughed. It was good to be in Moscow, even if it was freezing cold and as dark as a deep cave.

The All Russian Cancer Center Hotel

Yuri stopped the car in front of the Cancer Center's facilities and escorted the McNichols into a non-descript building and up to a worn reception desk. It was a sparsely decorated institutional hotel, and it still had some of the remnants of the old Soviet system. The old fat women, the 'Babushkas,' were still sitting at their desks at the elevators on each floor. In the old Soviet days, they had to take down the names and times of everyone that arrived or left on the old creaky elevators. As far as Marie and Jared knew, they were still taking the names and times down, just like the old days. Yuri was right. Some things never change.

After a rather long shouting match in Russian that neither Jared or Marie understood, Yuri turned and smiled as he calmed down, "Everything settled. Just Russian bureaucracy!" The clerk took Jared's and Marie's passports, and had Jared sign the register. Yuri smiled and helped Jared and Marie up to their room on the third floor. A very overweight Slavic woman who had a somewhat square build wearing a bubushka took charge of settling in the McNichols. She pointed out the samovar that had been provided for their tea. The woman said in broken English with a big smile, "Hope you . . . . be comfortable!" Marie and Jared smiled and nodded, Jared gave her some change, and after Yuri signaled that he would wait for them down stairs and closed the door, they proceeded to unpack. Marie looked at the Spartan surroundings and said, "This is really roughing it for me!" Jared added, "Hey, this is nothing! At least we have our own bath! And the bed looks O.K.!" Marie laughed when she looked at the antiquated

tub and small hose that could be used as a shower. She asked, "You call this
a shower?" Jared looked at the contraption and sighed, "It doesn't get any
easier does it? Are you sure you want to do this?" Marie said, "After that
trip I need a shower!" Jared made fun of Marie, "Even if it is just like using
a garden hose in the back yard?"

Jared left Marie trying to master the bath hose, and he decided to take
the stairs instead of the rickety elevator down to the reception area. There
he met with Yuri to discuss their joint experiments. They found some
over-stuffed chairs to relax in while they continued their scientific discussion.
Yuri was very happy to see Jared and receive the supplies that they needed
to complete their joint study. When Yuri visited Jared in Austin, he was
showered with laboratory supplies, office supplies, gifts of all sorts, and he
was a bit ashamed to not be in a position to return the favor. However,
these were difficult times for Russia, and scientists needed all of the help
that the West could muster. Jared had brought some expensive drugs,
antibodies, supplies and reagents to Moscow for Yuri's laboratory. It was
the least that they could do for their Russian colleagues. Fortunately, all of
the supplies fit in one rather small 'official-looking' box that Jared had
labeled 'medicine' and placed into his suitcase. Although it was opened, it
did not draw any attention to the custom agent who looked into Marie's
and Jared's bags at the airport. They were probably looking for other more
popular commercial items that were commonly smuggled into Russia.

The gathering in Red Square

The next morning Dr. Vassiloff would be picking up the McNichols at their
hotel located inside the All Russian Cancer Center. The McNichols made
their way down to the dining room for breakfast. It was bleak. Marie was
upset, because there was not much to eat with the exception of some
bread, flavored water, coffee and a hard-boiled egg. This was probably the
same exact breakfast that they had served for the last 50 years. After
breakfast and a brief rest in their room, Yuri arrived to take Marie and
Jared to Red Square.

It was extremely cold, and Marie and Jared were not used to the brutal
Moscow weather. Yuri's little Moscovite car had a good heater, and it was
cozy in the little car. The traffic was light as it was after the Moscow rush

hour, and they whizzed along the broad Moscow boulevards to the center of Moscow. They parked the car near the Square and made their way on foot. Marie had everything warm on that she owned, layer after layer, to keep out the Moscow cold. Jared didn't seem to mind the cold as they walked the two blocks or so to Red Square. The square was almost empty, except for a few brave souls walking around. St. Basil's Cathedral was at one end with its colorful turrets and towers that looked like an old-fashioned multi-colored candelabra. At the other end was a stark Stalinist building containing Lenin's tomb. There was still an honor guard at Lenin's tomb, and a small line of people were waiting to see his glass-encased body that had remained in state for many, many decades. Just behind the tomb and toward the middle of one side of the square was the massive grandstand where the Soviet leadership presided over dramatic May Day parades and special occasions.

Except for St. Basil's and another church, the architecture was of typical massive Soviet style. A group of soldiers then came onto the square. They were obviously recruits, young, shouting and playing with each other. They gathered in the middle of the square for a photograph. They could have been young recruits from any nation, laughing, joking and pushing each other. They immediately saw Marie, an obvious visitor. Marie wanting to be friendly said in broken Russian, "La yublu tebia!" The young soldiers laughed and surrounded Marie. They were all talking so fast it was difficult to know what they were saying, even if the McNichols understood Russian, but they were certainly friendly. They were talking so fast and laughing that one of them slipped and fell down. Everyone laughed at the young soldier, and he laughed too.

Yuri laughed and whispered into Jared's ear and told him that Marie had just asked the soldiers to make love to her! The young soldiers loved the attention that Marie was giving them, and they took turns posing for pictures with the American scientist visitor. Marie loved the attention too and didn't realize that she had asked the young soldiers to make love to her. They thought it was all great fun, for it was still rare to see such a pretty visitor who wanted to be friendly with the obviously lowly young recruits of the Russian Army. Since most of them were probably from Siberia or some other outpost of the Russian Federation, they likely had never spoken to a young, pretty woman from America. And they certainly had never had one ask them to make love right in Red Square!

The McNichols meet Dr. Luxembourg, the charming host

The following morning Marie and Jared were taken for a walk around Moscow by a Dr. Luxembourg, a rather non-descript man with a thick accent but rather good English, who worked at the Cancer Center. He greeted them at the hotel in the lobby where Marie and Jared were sitting in the overstuffed chairs. "Good morning Dr. and Dr. McNichols! I am Dr. Luxembourg, your tour host for today. I trust you have rested well?" Jared replied, "We fell asleep as soon as we hit the pillow." Dr. Luxembourg said, "Good! We will take the subway as you call it. Jared said, "Lead the way." As they walked in the cold Moscow morning, Marie noticed that her breath was freezing. Actually, the weather was well below freezing, but the Moscovites didn't even notice. Jared and Marie saw people eating ice cream and Marie asked, "How can they eat ice cream in this sub-zero weather." Dr. Luxembourg laughed, "It's a Moscow tradition. Our ice cream is the best in the world!" He continued, "And we are tough and used to the cold. Would you like to try some?" Marie answered, "Not this morning. We come from a very warm and humid climate, and I am not used to this cold. I swear I have become a lily-livered person." Dr. Luxembourg asked, "Lily-livered?" Jared explained, "An English term for spoiled and soft." Dr. Luxembourg looked at Marie, nodded his head and muttered, "Ah!" Marie, seeing a group of soldiers and remembering the previous day in Red Square, said to Jared, "Young soldiers again. Look at them. They're just boys!" Jared said, "So? You've seen young soldiers before, even yesterday." He smiled to warn Marie of her antics with the young soldiers of the previous day. Marie turned to Dr. Luxembourg, "We grew up with the propaganda of fear of the Red Army. But I personally was never afraid of the Russian people. The Russian literature and music were always my favorites because of the intensity of the emotion. And I was right!" Jared added, "Marie is still a naïve idealist at heart!" Marie continued, "I never could understand the hatred of war. Yet I know that the darker side of man exists." Dr. Luxembourg said, "You see, the scars of the Cold War are deep, and yet when you face your perceived enemy of childhood, you find that they are just boys." Marie said, "Dr. Luxembourg, I am so excited about being here that I feel as if I am 4 years old!" Dr. Luxembourg replied, "With your cheeks all rosy from the cold, you look like the vision of a young little Russian angel." Jared added, "You mean young little devil?" Marie playfully punched at Jared who feigned a blow. She didn't appreciate the comment. Jared apologized.

Dr. Luxembourg reminded them of their next stop on the tour of Moscow. "We are going to visit the oldest Church in Moscow before lunch and the cabin that belonged to Peter the Great." Marie asked, "Are you telling us that the Czar actually stayed in a cabin?" Dr. Luxembourg said, "That's right. The cabin was moved to Moscow as part of an effort to let the people know more about their past under the Czars." Marie continued, "I have always been fascinated by the religious art of the Russian Orthodox Church. It's so lovely." Jared asked, "Dr. Luxembourg, are you saying that most of the art typical of Czarist Russia is still in existence, even after the Bolshevik revolution and all the purges?" Dr. Luxembourg said, "Absolutely! It still exists. Our country did not perform destructive acts like those in China's Cultural Revolution." They were excited to be able to see the heritage of Mother Russia. It was something that Jared missed on his previous trips to the Soviet Union, because the trips were strictly on the business of science, and there was little time to socialize with the locals. In fact, it was frowned upon for Westerners to get too close to the Russian people. That had all changed.

At this point they all entered the old Moscow Church. The interior of the church was magnificent, and it was resplendent with candlelight, which was reflecting upon the gold of numerous icons and statues. You could hear the harmony of Gregorian chants, and the spiritual atmosphere was quite tangible. Marie whispered, "Are we intruding on a private ceremony?" Dr. Luxembourg answered, "The ceremony is private, but I assure you, you are most welcome."

Suddenly Jared and Marie realized that they have joined a funeral procession for six adults and two children. Several of the bodies were lying under shrouds on simple tables, and the Russian Orthodox Patriarch was swinging incense and praying over the dead. Their faces looked peaceful. Marie looked at Jared and said in a whisper, "No one is crying?" She then continued, "But the passion of the people is so apparent here." Jared whispered back, "As if the communist regime never really stamped out the Russian people's belief in God." Jared and Marie observed the ceremony, and they were unaware that they had become the object of curiosity of the families that had met to say goodbye to their loved ones. Marie leaned over to Dr. Luxembourg and whispered, "Don't you feel the intensity of the souls in this room." Dr. Luxembourg whispered back, "I do not really believe in God, so it's hard for me to be in a place like this."

Marie looked at Dr. Luxenbourg. "I think I understand, but to just listen to the Gregorian chants . . . The depth of the music reflects God more than any other place of worship I have ever seen and attended . . . . Dr. Luxembourg, you must see that this devotion did not spring up over night." Jared who had been listening from behind them whispered, "It just went underground after the revolution." Dr. Luxembourg appeared to be very uncomfortable, and he suddenly turned away from the couple and started to walk out of the church. The McNichols were not about to leave in the middle of the ceremony, because they felt that it might be disrespectful. Marie finally said to Jared, "I don't understand him?" Jared replied, "Don't even try to." Jared and Marie watched him as he left the church with a puzzled expression. He walked out into the cold Moscow air where he probably felt safer than in the old church.

Jared and Marie did not follow Dr. Luxembourg outside. Instead, they concentrated on the Gregorian chants that were still continuing in the beautiful chapel. Suddenly Marie began to cry. Everyone was looking at Marie and Jared. They knew that they were outsiders, tourists from the West who had somehow stumbled into their ceremony of death. Jared finally whispered to Marie when he saw that she was crying, "What's wrong now?" Marie answered, "Nothing's wrong. It's just that I feel the sorrow of the families here." Marie then began to sing but not in words with the people who were participating in the funeral service. She did not know the Russian words, but she simply followed the chants. Her high voice was easily heard above the chants.

The locals nodded their approval at these obvious tourists who had taken an interest in their loved ones who had passed. The head priest smiled at the McNichols, and the monks did the same as they passed in the orthodox procession at the end of the funeral ceremony. Finally, the families involved in the funeral released their emotions, and everyone had a good cry. The men, however, wiped their eyes but did not openly weep like the women. Jared gently pulled Marie away from the group and brought her to the front of the church where candles were burning in long rows. Just as he has done a hundred times for Marie, Jared picked up a candle from a stack, dropped some change in a box and gave the candle to Marie and then lit it for her in front of the alter. Some of the candles had burned down and had almost gone out. Marie placed the candle in a free holder and said a brief prayer. Then she and Jared crossed themselves like the Russians and left the church.

The McNichols finally caught up with Dr. Luxembourg on the Moscow street in front of the church. He had been pacing back and forth. Dr. Luxembourg finally turned and called to them. "I'm sorry to have been so abrupt with you." He paused, "It's just that I can not handle emotions too well. I really want to believe in God, but my life is so bleak . . . . and my family history is so turbulent. My father was in and out of the gulag for the political incorrectness of his scientific research." He thought for a moment and then continued, "Papa finally died in a Siberian work camp." Marie said, "I'm so sorry." There was a moment of silence, and Jared continued, "We can't begin to understand the depth of your experience growing up in the Soviet Union." There was silence for a moment.

Suddenly Dr. Luxembourg displayed a subtle unexpected hostility towards Marie and Jared. He turned to Marie and said, "With that capitalist father of yours, I imagine you were a most pampered person of the elite." Marie answered, "My father? He was a physician and true, the first seven years of my life were comfortable, but then he left, and it was hard to make ends meet. I suffered a great deal of ostracism because of my parent's divorce, which was a great stigma in the early sixties in the U. S. I may not know the hardship you have experienced, but I do know what it is to feel constant rejection and emotional humiliation for being different and not fitting into the established system." Jared cut in, "Who said life is perfect? There is no real fairness in life. As we say in the States, life is hard, then you die."

Marie ignored the flippant comments of Jared. She has heard this before, and she was now more serious. "I have always turned to prayer and the wisdom of the great philosophers to comfort me. And by the way, how did you ever hear of my father?" Luxembourg replied, "Not the physician-father, the father who killed everyone in his path and hoarded all the money for himself." Marie said, "Dr. Luxembourg, with all due respect, I think you are under some misimpression about my background.

The KGB has probably given you some disinformation for some unknown reason." Dr. Luxembourg stated, "I am most definitely not mistaken. It is you who are in the dark." Marie looked at Jared in a puzzled manner realizing that there were gaps in her background that she still didn't understand.

It was Jared who tried to break the apparent stalemate. "You know, my father was an engineer, and his father was an engineer. We grew up in relative comfort but nothing really fancy." He turned to Dr. Luxembourg and said, "I really don't think that we're going to resolve the world's problems on a street corner in Moscow." But Dr. Luxembourg continued in an abstract manner. "No one person should be entitled to so much!" Jared turned to Marie and asked, "What is he talking about?" Marie said, "Dr. Luxembourg, we are only in Moscow to share our work with our colleagues. It is true that we Americans have not endured the hardships you have, but I am not this spoiled heiress that you imagine." Jared asked, "What are *you* talking about?" She continued, "We want to help our Russian colleagues in any way we can. Why should political barriers continue to hinder our ability to work together in a cooperative way?"

Dr. Luxembourg walked silently with the McNichols for a minute or so and then began talking again. "People do not change so easily, Dr. McNichols, and I am sorry if I appeared hostile. Dr. McNichols . . ." Marie interrupted, "Please call me Marie." He continued, "You are so naive in some ways and yet so wise in others." Dr. Luxembourg finally stated, "Some bridges are never built!" Jared added, "And some bridges are built overnight! This bridge will be built if we are positive in our attitudes and put some effort into it." Dr. Luxembourg chuckled, "Well, perhaps you are right, the son of an engineer. And perhaps there is also a God." He hesitated for a moment and then continued, "And to prove to you that I am open-minded, would you do me the honor of sharing a dinner together with my family?" Marie said, "We'd be delighted!" Jared added, "Yes, it would be our pleasure!" Dr. Luxembourg replied, "Good, it is settled! No more deep philosophical conversations! Just a good time amongst new friends in traditional Muscovite style!"

Everyone finally felt at ease. As Marie and Jared turned to walk to the Cabin of Peter the Great, Dr. Luxembourg looked at the backs of the McNichols with a mixture of contempt and hatred. He muttered to himself,

"Certain ends justify the means." Jared turned to Dr. Luxembourg and asked, "Did you say something?" Dr. Luxembourg responded, "I was just mumbling to myself that certain means justify the end result." Marie looked puzzled. Jared said, "Machiavelli in Moscow?" Dr. Luxembourg shot back, "Something like that. We are a people whose country is a collection of mistakes, and we must work hard to build a future to merge with a world of free enterprise. But we, as a people, have no history of democracy whatsoever." Marie said, "If yee have faith as a mustard seed, nothing shall be impossible unto thee." Dr. Luxembourg thought for a moment and then retorted, "There we are back to the religious philosophical young lady." Marie laughed, "O.K., I'll keep my big mouth shut!" Jared added, "We are here to enjoy the Russian history not to lecture to you on religion or philosophy."

The unusual dinner at the Luxembourgs

The following day the McNichols had been invited to an intimate dinner at the apartment of Dr. Luxembourg. The apartment was only three blocks from the Cancer Center. Even though it was within walking distance, Dr. Luxembourg picked up Marie and Jared. It was much too cold for the McNichols to walk. After a quick ride from the hotel, the McNichols arrived at a group of Soviet-style apartment buildings. They looked exactly the same from the outside, bleak and plain. The buildings appeared to be equivalent to subsidized housing in the U. S., but they were more massively built in the Soviet style. Steam rose from the streets and buildings, indicating a central steam plant kept the buildings warm during the cold Moscow winters. They entered one of the buildings. The elevator was barely working, and there was trash scattered about. They made their way to the third floor. From the outside and the common areas, the building looked like a disaster. But when they entered the Luxembourg's apartment, they had a completely different opinion of the building. The apartment was extremely warm and cozy. It was furnished sparsely but comfortably, and there were personal items that gave it a homey appearance. There were cabinets and bookshelves that contained many very well-used books in all different languages. There was a photograph of Dr. Luxembourg as a young man with Khrushchev when he received an award for scholastic excellence. There were some typical 'worker era' works of art. Although the outside of the apartment showed no evidence of maintenance, inside the apartment it was spotless and showed the pride of its occupants. There was also an old piano along one wall. Jared was shocked to learn that the building was only six years old. Essentially no maintenance resulted in rapid deterioration of the apartment buildings in Moscow.

After a hearty welcome and introductions from Dr. Luxembourg's family, Mrs. Luxembourg, a non-descript looking woman of Slavic origin looked up and said, "Welcome, Welcome!" She had a thick Russian accent. Marie attempted to say, "I love you" or "Ya yublu tebia," the only words that she knew in Russian, but it didn't come out exactly right. Dr. Luxembourg said, "Not bad pronunciation!" He paused, "But in Russia we do not have the friendly equivalent of 'I love you' in our language." He chuckled, "In Russian it means, will you make love with *me*?" Jared laughed, "Yes, Marie found this out with some soldiers in Red Square!" Marie looked mortified and her face turned red as she said, "Do you realize that I went all over Moscow asking the young soldiers to make love to me! I just wanted to be friendly!" Jared added, "No wonder they were so anxious to have their picture taken with you!" Everyone laughed.

Marie wanted to apologize to Dr. Luxembourg for what happened the previous day, but in fact, there was really nothing to apologize for. "Dr. Luxembourg, I want to say again how sorry I am that I offended you yesterday in some way when we were visiting the church. But the beauty of the Gregorian chants and the glow of the icons made me feel as if I was touching God." Jared added, "Or some higher form of consciousness." Dr. Luxembourg replied, "You are quite the philosophers, Marie and Jared. And an amateur theologian, perhaps Marie?" Marie responded, "I understand that you must be thinking how spoiled I am to have the time to ponder the great mysteries of the universe or dwell upon the heritage of ancient scripture." He answered in an off-hand manner, "Not at all. I am sorry that I overreacted to what was obviously a cultural comment." Marie continued, "I cannot answer why I grew up in the relative comfort and prosperity of America, while you lived in a great but harsh country of turbulent ideologies, passions and poverty. I believe strongly that you and I are not that much different. As a matter of fact, I have a dear friend whose father was the former head of the Bulgarian KGB and was educated in Leningrad . . ." Dr. Luxembourg interrupted, "Now St. Petersburg again!" Marie continued, "And she finally defected to the U. S. Well, you might be surprised to know that I had more in common with this friend than the average American. We shared the same tastes in music, literature and art." Dr. Luxembourg answered, "Please do not take offense at my atheistic attitude. Believe me, I wish there was a God, or at least some supreme intelligence. I have just never seen it manifested in my country." Marie responded, "Dr. Luxembourg, I hope that one day you will open your eyes past the political structures of your country and look at some at the physical beauty of the magnificent pine forests surrounding Moscow. Just stop some day and notice the grace of the Bolshoi and the passion of Rachmaninoff. Perhaps that's the best that anyone can hope for, the experiences that transcend the ordinary."

Dr. Luxembourg smiled and turned to Jared. "I say again, Marie here is quite the passionate young philosopher!" Jared agreed, "You'll get used to it. She gets carried away in new, exciting places, and I think that she especially liked what she saw yesterday." Marie looked delightedly at the piano and asked, "May I?" Dr. Luxembourg said, "Be my guest!" Marie sat down and began the opening chords of the Rachmaninoff's 2nd Concerto. Dr. Luxembourg's wife then came out of the kitchen with a tray of typical Russian cold cuts and caviar. She seemed pleasantly surprised and marveled as Marie continued playing, "My, you are pianist!" Marie said as she played, "No, I am very much an amateur!" Luxembourg's wife said as Marie got up and interrupted her playing, "Would you care for caviar?" Marie replied, "Thank you!" Jared said, "You've gone to so much trouble for us!" Dr. Luxembourg answered, "It is a Russian tradition to share all we have with our guests." Jared stated, "You must let us take you out for a meal in downtown Moscow. I wish no offense, but at least we have come with some hard currency, knowing what a struggle you are all having with the economy here in Russia." When I visited in '81, we all noticed that it was particularly hard for our academic colleagues." Marie added, "We do not wish to offend your gesture of hospitality, but we are worried about the state of the Russian economy and how it is affecting our colleagues." Dr. Luxembourg was irritated, "Things have gotten better since then.

Dr. Luxembourg then became serious with the American visitors. "We will survive. We always have!" He then looked at his wife and said, "Ah!"

His wife gave a signal with her hands and said, "Dinner is ready! Please sit down!" They moved from the living room to the dining room, and Dr. Luxembourg motioned for Marie to sit next to him and pointed to the respective seats of the other guests. The Luxembourg's son had joined them for dinner. Vodka was offered to everyone, and Jared made a toast, "We want to thank all of you for making our visit to Moscow so unique and fulfilling. We are especially pleased to be here, and we hope that you are finally headed for better and happier times." Everyone agreed and drank the vodka except Marie. She held her glass up, and said, "I'm afraid I cannot drink vodka." Dr. Luxembourg said, "Nonsense! Everyone drinks vodka." Marie stated emphatically, "All it takes is one sip of wine and it goes completely to my legs." Dr. Luxembourg asked, "Legs, not head?" Marie replied, "That too! Can you imagine what vodka would do to me? Jared knows!" Dr. Luxembourg then stated, "You do not know what you are missing? But I will yield to your request. And we will even let you throw an empty glass into the fireplace in true Russian tradition." Marie laughed and Jared added, "That will not be necessary. Marie is just happy to be here as your guest."

The Luxembourg's son tried his English with the American visitors. "I will play balaleika! Important in Muscovite daily life." Dr. Luxembourg made a toast in Russian, which he then translated. "To life and friendship from Russia with love." Jared added, "May the politics of the Cold War cease to deter better understanding and cooperation between our Russian colleagues and the West!" Afterwards, Marie did throw an empty glass into the fireplace, and everyone shouted in Russian style. The Luxembourg's son again played the balaleika.

The dinner itself ran through several courses full of conversation and laughter, and then finally it was time for the dessert. Dr. Luxembourg's wife motioned for Dr. Luxembourg to come to the kitchen and to help her with the dishing out of Moscow's famous ice cream. In the kitchen Dr. Luxembourg's wife said to her husband in Russian while pointing to a small jar containing a white powder that he had brought home for this special event. "Are you going to add this to their dessert?" He answered, "Absolutely!" His wife said, "I do not feel right about this. They are very brilliant and sweet people! They do not deserve this." Dr. Luxembourg stated, "Do not think of them in a humanistic sense. They are spoiled people from America who are a threat to our way of life." His wife answered, "It is not their fault to be here? They are nice people. They mean us no harm." Dr. Luxembourg stated, "Fault is not a concern here, and they are not nice." He paused, "It is their destiny! And we are at a point in history where we must seize the moment. We must think in terms of what is good for the majority and the State. Do not be fooled by their many talents and compassions." Luxembourg's wife asked, "What if it were your children?" Dr. Luxembourg answered, "But they're not ours! They are Americans. Besides we do not even have a daughter." Luxembourg's wife shook her head and stated, "You are an evil person—I cannot watch!" Dr. Luxembourg sneered, "Just go back in the parlor and entertain the McNichols with your "Communist jokes!"

Mrs. Luxembourg returned to the parlor where Jared and Marie were sitting on a small couch and listening to the Luxembourg's son play the balaleika. They didn't notice the grim look on Mrs. Luxembourg's face. They clapped and laughed as he approached the end of a dramatic piece. Mrs. Luxembourg, who was actually quite a clown, calmed down and re-entered the parlor wearing an old Red Army General's hat, and she had put a Havana cigar in her mouth as a prop for her satirical jokes.

Jared and Marie didn't know exactly what to do at this point, but they decided that Mrs. Luxembourg would be doing some kind of Russian comedy act for them. Using the hat and then the cigar, she played a parody of a Soviet citizen and then a Soviet General. First without the hat but with the cigar, "Soviet worker! Pride of Mother Russia!" Then she put on the hat and affected the stern manner of a Soviet General, "Mother Russia does not see difference in sexes!" Then she removed the hat and the cigar and put her hands under her large breasts indicating that she was playing a mother, "Soviet mother, pride of Mother Russia!" She then put the hat back on and as the Soviet General said, "Well, all I see is baby bottle!" She then took off the props and said, "Love not important to Party!" She then put the props back on, and continuing as the General, "Changing diapers important!" She took off the props, "Sex?" She put the props back on and said as the affected General, "Sex—only two encounters per week—at most!" The General continued, "But for you, daughter, *never!*" The General then said, "In fact, I bring back . . . religion. Then I put you . . . . in convent!" She took off the props, "You are hypocrite!" She put the props back on, "A capitalist in reverse." She then paused, "It's secret, boobalah!" The General continued, "There is R in the U.S.S.R which stands for Republic! There is no R in U.S. of A." She took off the props, "So, U.S. of A. is really U.S.S.R. and vice versa!"

Mrs. Luxembourg then burst out laughing loudly, and Jared and Marie looked at each other and forced a laugh as well, but their laughs were not genuine. Their laughs were polite laughs while they looked at each other wondering what they had just seen. The joke was not completely clear to them. Perhaps something was lost in the translation? Dr. Luxembourg entered the room at the end of his wife's strange routine with a tray of ice cream. He said, "My wife is also quite the philosopher." He turned to Marie, "Just like you Marie!" Marie chuckled and said, "I must say that politics are not my strong suit. I am too strong in my opinions to be a good politician." Dr. Luxembourg's wife now said, "But once you see all political ideologies are same, it all becomes joke, a puppet show!" Marie asked, "Like the General and the worker?" The wife said, "Yes, like General of Soviet Army!"

Jared had already tasted the ice cream, and he didn't like it. It was too sweet for his taste. Usually when something was too sweet, he had a hard time eating it. At this point Marie took one bite of the ice cream and within moments she felt that something was wrong. She looked at Jared, indicating that she did not like the ice cream. It did not taste like the ice cream that they ate earlier in the day. The McNichols did not want to be bad guests, so they continued the conversation without eating much of the ice cream. Marie actually ate more than Jared, but she also stopped eating. Dr. Luxembourg asked, "Is there something wrong with our excellent Moscow ice cream? You ate some before today?" Jared smiled and answered, "Yes, but we usually don't eat such sweet desserts after dinner. We are just not used to it this late at night, and we are so full from all of the excellent courses." After a few minutes Marie was having problems, and she doubled over in pain." Jared asked Marie, "What's wrong?" She said, "My insides are burning up. I think it was something I ate." Dr. Luxembourg said, "Nonsense! I don't think it had anything to do with what you ate! Do you feel that we must get Marie to a hospital." Jared thought, "That won't be necessary!" Jared then said, "It's probably one of her food allergies." Marie turned and whispered to Jared, "I think it was in the ice cream. It tasted like bitter almonds." Dr. Luxembourg heard what Marie had said, "That's impossible! It was probably a bad almond. Sometimes various nuts, if they go stale, release a small amount of aflatoxin. It's nothing to be worried about. The ice cream is delicious. Look!" He took a big bite, but his wife looked worried and said, "We terribly sorry!" Marie replied, "I will be fine. I just want to change and go to bed! Could you please take us back to the hotel."

Jared told Dr. Luxembourg that they were very sorry, but they must return to their hotel room. "I am so sorry that we have to end such a lovely evening, but I think that we should get Marie back to the hotel." Dr. Luxembourg said, "You can't go so soon. You haven't finished your ice cream. It would be terrible to let it go to waste." Jared reiterated, "I am really sorry, but I think that we should get Marie back to the hotel." Dr. Luxembourg reluctantly agreed, "Very well, I will bring the car around and pick you up in front of the building. He stood up and left the room abruptly. Jared turned to Mrs. Luxembourg and said, "We've had a very lovely time, and I apologize for Marie. It's been a long day for us, and with the long trip to Russia, I think that Marie has just overdone it today." Mrs. Luxembourg looked very concerned that Marie did not feel well, "I understand. You go now. You did not like play?" Jared said, "Oh, we very much liked your play, and we are very grateful for the dinner and all the good fellowship. We are very pleased to be here in Moscow with such good friends and colleagues."

Jared stood and helped Marie stand up. She was a bit wobbly and needed support from Jared. Marie whispered to Jared, "I feel horrible. Please, I need to take some Benedryl and Zantac." Jared made his final good-byes and apologies to Mrs. Luxembourg, who told him that Dr. Luxenbourg should have the car ready in front of the building. Jared helped Marie down the stairs and out into the cold Moscow night. They did not try the creaking elevator, and the walking was actually better for Marie. As they walked into the freezing cold night Jared said, "I'm going to call Yuri as soon as we get to our room!" Marie pleaded, "I think there was something in the ice cream! And you know my body! If something's wrong with the food, my body rejects it as soon as it hits the salivary glands!" Jared agreed, "I didn't like it. It was not like the ice cream that we had earlier today, but I think that it was the chocolate sauce." Marie, "I have no tolerance for bad food."

Jared placed Marie into the small car, and Dr. Luxembourg drove them quickly to the hotel. Thankfully, it was only three blocks from the Luxembourg's building, and it took less than five minutes to reach the Cancer Center hotel. Jared said a quick good-bye to Dr. Luxembourg who didn't seem to be very concerned about Marie's health problems, and he helped Marie into the hotel and up in the elevator to their room. When they exited the elevator, even the old Bubushka was concerned and helped Marie and Jared to their room. Jared and Marie couldn't tell what she was saying, but Jared thanked her and closed the door. Jared, "She probably thinks that we're drunk!" He found the Benedryl and Zantac and put Marie immediately into the bed.

They both were finally in the bed and Marie told Jared, "I know there was something in the ice cream. It tasted like burnt almonds." Jared asked, "Cyanide? I better watch you closely tonight. I don't think you ate enough to hurt you, Marie, even if it was cyanide. I didn't eat as much as you did, and that's probably why I'm not feeling as sick as you are. But come to think of it, my insides *are* burning up too. I thought there was something wrong with the ice cream or the sauce. It was sickly sweet. Marie told Jared, "You take the Benedryl and Zantac right now. Don't argue with me this time. Jared got up and went to the bathroom.

Jared was not going to argue with Marie on this night. "Why would Dr. Luxembourg want to harm us?" Jared said from the bathroom, "I don't know if it was his fault. This is Moscow, you know. Bad food may be more common than you think." As Jared returned to bed, Marie grabbed him and said, "It's suspicious, and I don't feel well?" Jared replied, "They seemed O.K., but that Dr. Luxembourg gave me a creepy feeling. He was not at all concerned about your response to the ice cream. He even tried to say it was just a case of some bad almonds. That's pretty far-fetched." Marie to Jared, "I'm getting very tired. Let's go to sleep."

Back at the Luxembourg's apartment, after Marie and Jared had returned to their hotel, Dr. Luxembourg was trying explain to his wife what happened. He said, "I cannot understand it! The cyanide should have worked, but they did not have enough of it. This is not good." His wife said, "I do not know, but maybe there is a God that protected them. They did not deserve your ice cream. I am happy you failed. There is something about those people." Dr. Luxembourg said sarcastically, "Next you'll be telling me Marie is an angel on earth or some kind of Madonna!" He tried to laugh, but Mrs. Luxembourg said, "I don't care what you say, I liked them, and I am glad that they did not get sick." He paused, "I tell you she is more like a devil!" His wife disagreed, "Then you admit there is something spiritual about them, and therefore your atheist mind is confused?" At this point Dr. Luxembourg looked at his wife with hostility, and she returned the look. He muttered, "Capitalist bastards! They got what they deserved."

The Institute for Molecular Biology, Russian Academy of Sciences

The next part of the McNichols trip was a visit to the Institute for Molecular Biology of the Russian Academy of Sciences. It was the following morning, but Jared and Marie were not very comfortable. They woke up alive but not feeling well. They skipped the terrible breakfast at the Cancer Center hotel, and eventually Dr. Vassiloff called their room where they were resting to find out about their lectures at the Institute for Molecular Biology. Marie did not want to go visiting on this day, but Jared talked her into it because she was scheduled to give a lecture along with Jared. Jared felt that it was better to keep Marie moving around to metabolize any remaining toxins in her body. Also, he was afraid that if he let her sleep all day, he just might come back to find her incapacitated or worse.

So Marie and Jared showered, dressed and waited downstairs for Yuri to arrive in his small car. After about 30 minutes, Dr. Vassiloff finally arrived to take Jared and Marie to the Institute for Molecular Biology. He wanted to ask them about the dinner at the Luxembourgs, but Jared and Marie were in no mood to discuss the dinner or Dr. Luxembourg. Yuri did not press the issue. He had more important things to discuss with Jared about his own research project and the experiments that he had planned with the supplies that Jared brought with him to Moscow.

As they discussed their research, Yuri drove the McNichols to the Institute. It was located in an ornate, Stalinist style building near Moscow State University and was surrounded by a heavy fence and large gate. There were guardhouses at the entrance, but they were no longer occupied by military police. Yuri couldn't stay long. He had an important meeting back at the Cancer Center. Dr. Vassiloff turned into the car park and stopped his car right in front of the Institute entrance in a space marked with signs that probably indicated that he couldn't park there. Yuri ignored the signs (after all, what were they going to do about it?) and led the McNichols into the building to meet the Director. After making a brief call, he apologized that he must be at a meeting, so he said good-bye for the moment. The McNichols were brought to the Director's office by a staff member to meet the Director.

Dr. Gregori Gorgioff, Director of the Institute for Molecular Biology, Russian Academy of Sciences, met the McNichols just outside the Directors Office. After the introductions, Dr. Gorgioff brought the McNichols to his inner office to speak with Marie and Jared before their seminars were to be given in the main lecture hall of the Institute. Dr. Gorgioff's office had a high ceiling and was cluttered with papers and old desks and tables. The window was grimy and hadn't been cleaned in years. Looking through the grimy windows, one could see that it was beginning to snow outside.

Inside the Director's office the McNichols were engaged in a scientific conversation with Dr. Gorgioff, when Marie, who was not looking well began to get dizzy. Jared had just explained to Dr. Gorgioff that his department was working on several aspects of cancer genetics, including the new *MTA1* gene discovered by one of Jared's pathology fellows. Jared thought that the new gene that they had discovered was involved in the spread of cancer or metastasis and that it probably controlled important signaling pathways in cancer cells.

Dr. Gorgioff finally turned to Marie. "At the Institute we have followed your work with some interest. As you know, we have done much research in chromatin structure for some time, and some of the best studies on the subject have come from this Institute. Unfortunately, the Western countries seem to ignore our work." Jared said, "Marie and I certainly take your Institute's work extremely seriously. Marie has even examined your papers in Russian. Perhaps if you published more in Western European or American journals, it would have been more easily recognized in the West. Marie who normally couldn't ever be kept quiet finally spoke, "In fact, your publications in the Russian journals were an inspiration for our work and allowed us to develop the electrophoresis approach for the nucleoprotein separation. We based this on the research done right here in Moscow." Dr. Gorgioff said, "Thank you for those kind words. Most

Americans do not know our research well enough to cite the Russian journals.

Dr. Gorgioff looked at the clock on the wall in his office. "It is now almost time for the lectures. We must please have your slides for the projectionist." Turning to Marie he asked, "Are you feeling well?" Marie answered, "I don't know, I seem to be dizzy since the dinner at Dr. Luxemburg's last night." Jared reached over and grabbed Marie. "Are you sure you want to do this?" Marie tried to stand up, but she began to faint. Jared quickly moved behind her and caught her as she was falling back, and he placed her on the couch near the chairs they were sitting in. Marie quickly regained consciousness and asked for her slides. Jared was very worried about Marie. She was groggy and holding onto Jared. "Marie, are you sure you're feeling O.K.? You know, you don't have to do this. You can wait here, or we can have someone take you back to the hotel."

Dr. Gorgioff remained in his chair and did not seem to be very upset about Marie fainting in his office. He finally spoke in a matter-of-fact tone, "Marie does not seem to be feeling very well. Perhaps she should rest here in my office instead of giving her lecture." Marie finally seemed to be feeling better and said, "I have to get my slides!" Jared ordered her, "No you don't! How do you feel?" Marie responded slowly, "I'll be all right in a few minutes." Jared turned and told Dr. Gorgioff, "I think that we should get her back to our room at the Cancer Center as soon as possible. It was a long trip here, and Marie is exhausted. Since I made up the slides for her, I can give both lectures. Can we arrange for a taxi or a car to return Marie to the Cancer Center? If she needs help, the physicians at the Cancer Center will be able to assist her." Finally Dr. Gorgioff responded, "Yes, I can arrange for a car to the Cancer Center, if you feel that it will be necessary." Jared nodded indicating that he wanted Dr. Gorgioff to arrange for transportation for Marie.

Dr. Gorgioff picked up the phone and began yelling in Russian into the phone for what seemed like several minutes. Finally Dr. Gorgioff slammed down the phone and turned to the McNichols, "There, it is arranged. Professor McNichols, you will please give us both lectures now. May I have the slides?" Jared was a bit taken aback by Dr. Gorgioff's unsympathetic tone and said, "I want to make sure that Marie is safely on her way before we start the lectures." Dr. Gorgioff was irritated at Jared's comment and said in a very professional voice, "My staff will take care of everything. Please come with me now. The lectures are scheduled to start." Dr. Gorgioff stood and motioned for the slides and Jared to come with him to deliver the lectures. Jared handed over the slides, including Marie's, but he did not leave the office with Dr. Gorgioff, who took the slides to the outer office.

Instead of leaving with Dr. Gorgioff, Jared turned to Marie who was still lying down on the couch in the office and asked her, "Hey, kiddo, are you going to be all right? Marie answered, "I'm O.K., just a little dizzy and tired. It just suddenly hit me. My stomach has been on fire since the dinner last night, and I want to get my stomach medicine. Can I go back to the room now?" Jared answered, "Of course you can. Dr. Gorgioff has made arrangements to have you driven back to the Cancer Center." Marie whispered to Jared, "You know, Dr. Gorgioff is nothing like his letters. He seems very cold. I don't trust him." Jared said, "Marie, you just don't feel well. Professor Gorgioff is just a typical Soviet administrator. I will deliver your seminar for you. I want you to just go back and rest." Marie said, "I know that something is wrong here. I want you to go back to the room with me." Marie grabbed Jared and held him firmly, a good sign that she was not weak. Jared reassured Marie, "It will be O.K., Marie. I have to give the lectures, but I will ask them to get me back to the Cancer Center as soon as possible. Deal?" Marie was not happy but she agreed, "Deal! Just come as soon as you finish." Jared gave Marie a kiss. "Don't worry, I don't want to stay here any longer than necessary."

Jared now understood what Marie was trying to tell him. She didn't like the way that Dr. Gorgioff was acting toward them, and she didn't feel right about the Institute either. There was something very wrong going on here, and she sensed it as soon as they arrived that morning. It was the same feeling that Marie used to have about Belford College of Medicine and the D. O. Madison Cancer Center in Austin. They were up to no good here, and she could feel it in her bones. From the moment that they arrived, there were signs that this facility was more than just an academic Institute. The tall strong fence around the facility, the guardhouses, the security people at the desk in the entry hall, the attitude of Dr. Gorgioff—everything suggested that this facility was working for the Soviet 'defense' apparatus.

Dr. Gorgioff returned and motioned repeatedly for Jared to follow him to the lecture hall. Jared got up, turned, smiled and waved to Marie as he left the room. She was still lying on the couch when Jared turned into the long hallway to proceed to the lecture hall. After Jared and Dr. Gorgioff left his office, two very large Russian women helped Marie to her feet and to the car that would return her to the McNichols' hotel room. Jared didn't want to leave Marie in the hands of the two large women that he did not know, but he had little choice in the matter. His function in Moscow was to interact with the Russian academics and researchers, and right now he had to do his job.

Jared followed Dr. Gorgioff into the lecture hall. The lecture hall was an old large room with a very tall ceiling, and it had large windows that must have been two stories tall with long dark curtains that were being drawn to keep out the light, which was hardly necessary on this dreary day in Moscow. Dr. Gorgioff went down to the front of the lecture hall and delivered his lecture announcement and introduction of Jared in Russian. The introduction seemed to go on forever, and Jared could only think about Marie and the possibility that they had been poisoned the previous night at Dr. Luxembourg's flat. Finally it was time for Jared to deliver the two lectures, his lecture and Marie's lecture, to a lecture hall full of curious, polite Russian scientists. As he got up to approach the podium, Jared wondered about a possible relationship between Dr. Luxembourg and Dr. Gorgioff. Why were these scientists so passive-aggressive towards them, and especially towards Marie?

Jared delivered the two lectures without a break in between, except for a drink of water, and he answered all of the questions from the Russian audience with the help of Dr. Gorgioff. Much of the question and answer session required translation, which Dr. Gorgioff did from the front of the lecture hall. Jared was distracted by Marie's problems, and he tried to focus on the questions and his answers, but it was difficult. During any pause created by the discussion in Russian (Jared didn't understand it anyway) he thought about Marie and hoped that she was feeling O.K. and was safe back at the Cancer Center hotel.

After the lectures and the lengthy question and answer period, or about three hours later, Jared had to go for a late lunch with some of the academic staff of the Institute. However, he excused himself from the lunch at the Institute's private dining hall, explaining that his wife was sick and he had to leave immediately. Instead of spending more time at the

Institute, he requested to be returned to the Cancer Center as soon as possible. Dr. Gorgioff was quite disappointed that Jared was not staying longer at the Institute to meet more of the faculty and senior administrators, but after a discussion in the hallway, he finally agreed and arranged for a car to take Jared back to the hotel. Jared apologized profusely to Dr. Gorgioff, who seemed completely unsympathetic about Marie's apparent illness. He recovered his and Marie's slides and then left quickly to meet a waiting car. As he exited the front of the Stalinist style Institute buildings, a large black sedan was waiting near the entrance, the same car that had taken Marie back to the Cancer Center. Within moments he found himself in the back of the sedan on his way back to the hotel. Jared found out later that the sedan was assigned to Dr. Gorgioff by the State. He took one more look at the Institute as they drove away. It was obviously well protected with its high iron fence and guard posts. The driver said nothing during the entire trip, which didn't matter to Jared, since he was not in a mood to be diplomatic or discuss the Moscow weather.

The big black car finally turned into the entranceway in front of the Cancer Center hotel. Jared didn't wait for one of the creaky elevators, he dashed up the stairs, quickly bypassed the 'Babushkas,' and entered their room to see how Marie was doing. He didn't like what he found. Marie was in considerable pain and discomfort. There was blood all over the bed and sheets, and there was a trail of blood to the bathroom. Marie had a miscarriage from the poison that she received from the 'special' dinner the night before at Dr. Luxenbourg's flat. Jared immediately went over to Marie in the bed and whispered to her. She was weeping, and she grabbed onto Jared. Marie was very pale and looked terrible. The blood on the sheets was relatively fresh, and Jared was very nervous because he didn't know if she was still bleeding. He held her gently. Jared needed to find out more about her condition, but he didn't want to scare her and make it worse. He said gently, "How's my baby? .... Don't cry! .... Are you in pain? .... Are you bleeding?" Marie cried even harder as Jared asked each question. By the time that Jared was finished, Marie was balling uncontrollably and holding onto Jared very strongly, a good sign. Eventually her crying slowed enough to be able to say between gasping breaths, "Oh Jared .... I .... I had a .... miscarriage! .... It was awful! .... It was twins! .... I could tell .... One was a boy, ... and one was a little girl."

She started crying again, this time uncontrollably. "Oh, it was awful!" Jared finally said, "Baby, just don't try to talk, it's going to be all right." Marie still crying, "Oh, God! . . . . It was so painful! . . . . Please don't go to the bathroom! There may be blood on the floor!" Jared said, "I'm not going to worry about a little blood, but I have to know if you're still bleeding?" Marie told him between crying bouts, "I think it stopped." Jared tried to be cheerful but he felt terrible. "That's good, now where does it hurt?" Marie didn't answer. Finally she said, "I'm sorry, I couldn't get to the bathroom in time." Marie started crying again, uncontrollably. Jared tried to calm her, "Don't worry about the blood in the bathroom, I'll take care of it." Jared held Marie tightly in his arms while she released her sorrow and anguish.

Jared looked around the room while he held Marie. There was a trail of blood from the bed into the bathroom. Jared glanced through the door to the bathroom and saw that there was some blood on the floor. He was trying to calculate in his head how much blood Marie had lost. If she lost too much, he would have to take her to the hospital so they could provide intravenous fluid support and even blood, if necessary, and he was worried that Marie would refuse any efforts at hospitalization. She didn't like hospitals, and there was no doubt in Jared's mind that Marie would not like to be in a cancer hospital in Moscow.

Jared left Marie for a moment to assess the situation. Although Marie objected, he went to the bathroom, looked around, and then made his way back to the bed so that he could hold Marie in his arms again. He brushed his hand across her head and held her as close and as tight as he could without hurting her. There were now tears in his eyes too. Jared said as he rocked Marie gently in his arms, "Don't cry, baby. As long as you're O.K., everything will be all right . . . . Are you still bleeding?" Marie cried, "I don't know . . . . But I lost the twins! . . . . God, Jared, I lost the twins! . . . . And I missed my seminar!" Jared smiled and said, "Forget about the damn seminar!" Marie loudly said, "I didn't like that place!" Jared replied, "I didn't either. There was something very wrong going on there, and I didn't like Dr. Gorgioff that much." Marie added, "He was not at all like his letters!" She asked, "I am so thirsty. Can I have some water?" Jared quietly replied, "Of course."

Jared went into the bathroom and returned with a glass of water. Marie looked at the glass and said, "Not that water!" Jared smiled, "I see that you aren't completely out of it. I'll have to go out and get some bottled water. And I want you to be examined." Marie was crying again, "I don't want to be examined! I don't want them to touch me! Don't leave me! I'm scared!" Jared told her, "I promise that I won't leave you alone."

Jared returned to the bed and held Marie who was weeping again. He was trying to reassure her. "Marie, I know that you're upset about the babies. But we have to worry about you, now. Let's say a prayer for little Jared and little Marie. They didn't really have a chance in this cruel world." Marie asked, "You're not mad at me?" Jared smiling as he stroked Marie's head, "Why would I be mad at you?" Marie crying again, "But the twins! I lost the twins! You know that I have trouble carrying." Jared replied, "Marie, I am truly sorry that this had to happen, but you are the most important thing to me in the whole world. As long as you're O.K., everything will be all right." Marie was crying, "I didn't want to lose our babies. I thought that you would be mad at me for losing our babies." Jared said, "I'm not mad at you, Marie. I love you, and I want you to rest now." Marie was still sobbing, "O.K! .... You're sure .... you're not mad at me?" Jared reassured her, "I'm not mad at you. Now rest. I'll be in the other room. We'll say a prayer for the little babies; they're surely in heaven now." Marie sobbing, "I think I was poisoned! You were right! Cyanide ... You didn't eat much of the dessert with the almond sauce on it. I think it was poisoned. That Dr. Luxembourg!" Jared said, "I don't know .... It tasted too sweet ..." Marie interrupted, "I tell you, it was poisoned!" Jared told Marie, "I have to call Yuri. I'll just be at the phone in the other room.

Jared stood up from the bed and looked very worried at Marie. He then quietly left the bedroom and went to the only phone in the other room. He looked up a number that he wrote down and dialed Yuri's office. The phone rang and rang with no answer. Finally someone answered and Jared asked, "Dr. Vassiloff, please. After what seemed like over a minute, someone finally found Yuri and he was on the phone. "Yuri, this is Jared. Marie has just had a miscarriage, and I need someone to examine her as soon as possible." Yuri asked, "Is she bleeding? Is she in pain?" Jared responded, "She lost some blood, but .... No, she doesn't appear to be bleeding at the moment, but she is in pain." Dr. Vassiloff said, "I will have someone over to your hotel room immediately. Please stay with her!" Jared responded, "Don't worry, Yuri, I won't leave her." Marie yelled from the other room, "I don't want to go to the hospital! Don't let them take me! . . . Please, I don't want to . . ." Jared entered the bedroom and said, "Don't worry, baby, Dr. Vassiloff is having someone come by just to check you out and make sure that nothing's wrong. Are you still bleeding?" Marie was sobbing, "No." Jared replied, "That's a good sign. Everything will be all right. We will get through this and go on."

The McNichols return from a difficult trip

Professor McNichols completed the minimum requirements of their trip to Russia, lecturing at two other Moscow institutions, and he and Marie booked an early return to Austin. Since Jared had to give several lectures in the span of a few days, they had to forgo their trip to St. Petersburg that Marie was especially looking forward to in order to return a week early to the States. On the plane trip home Marie was still sobbing about the twins.

The McNichols had been poisoned and badgered so much by evil people that Marie would never be able to carry a full-term pregnancy. Thus they would never feel the joy of parenthood. It was the single most precious thing that they had to give up in seeking the truth and helping the veterans and the Texas prison employees. In their travels all over the world it was always immediately noticeable that the one thing that bound all people together was the love for their own offspring and children in general. Having children to carry on a family's traditions was as old as mankind. This was a universal joy that Jared and Marie would never have the luxury of experiencing. Unfortunately, they would never leave a living legacy, and no one would be left to carry on the McNichols name and traditions, so they must do what they could by themselves to leave something for mankind.

The vicious people that attacked the McNichols in Austin and elsewhere scoffed at the couple, because they knew that they had all of the resources, they had all the power, and they had all the financial backing to completely and utterly destroy Marie and Jared, and they almost succeeded. God must have been protecting them, Jared and Marie reasoned, because they would have been long dead and buried by now, and their scientific struggles would only have been a distant memory, not even a brief footnote in the history of science. They would have been relegated to the dustbin of academia. But Marie and Jared would rise from the ashes of their personal anguish to continue their quest for the truth. They would not let what they considered the forces of evil tear them down to nothingness and destroy all that they had created in their quest to help their fellow man. Jared comforted Marie on the long journey back to Austin, for they both knew down deep that the horror that they have endured wasn't over yet. In fact, it may have only begun.

CHAPTER 10

Back in Austin

Dr. Clement Masters received a phone call from his old friend, Stephen V. Able, the financial 'broker' for the Cornealyus Group and a former national security advisor to the White House. Mr. Able, a popular figure around Washington and staunch Catholic with ties to the Opus Dei, a New World Order group linked to the Illuminati and Vatican financial empires, was an advisor to several former presidents and cabinet members. He was also the lead financial advisor for a Las Vegas casino-based financial group with ties to organized crime that funded biotechnology and energy projects around the world, including some in Austin. In fact, Mr. Able and his colleagues were the financial geniuses that funded biotechnology-spin offs from several universities that conducted classified work for the Pentagon and CIA on unconventional weapons of mass destruction, for 'biological defense,' of course.

In the United States there were over 120 universities that had been involved in Biological Defense projects, most of them classified, and American universities turned out to be fertile ground for the technology necessary to create small biotech companies. Texas was considered a good place to troll for new technology to establish 'biological defense' spin-off enterprises, because the Texas universities had actually coveted such programs that brought corporate funds to their universities, and this provided a sizable subsidy for new programs. Also, the Texas institutions did not have to worry so much about what some of their leadership considered the bleeding-heart pacifist faculties that were concentrated on the East and West Coasts that could disrupt important classified research programs.

The small biotechnology spin-off companies usually had legitimate 'covers' to protect their secrecy, so that their real mission could be hidden from public view and scrutiny. Since they were all privately held companies, they did not have to divulge anything to the public about what they did, and they often paraded around the communities where they were located as humanitarian companies that provided jobs and income to the community and answers to complex medical and health problems. However, what went on behind their locked doors was often quite different from their public image, and probably none of the communities where they resided had any notion of the medical risks to their citizens if these companies' biological creations ever escaped the confines of their buildings. This was a very real possibility when you consider that most of these companies did not have adequate containment facilities for the microbes that they were working on. In fact, one of the few Level 4 containment facilities in the country was located at Fort Detrick, and this was available for their most dangerous work, but it was hardly used by the companies under contract with the DoD. The notion that only a few containment facilities existed so that few exotic microbes could be handled at any one time was simply faulty thinking. Such thinking probably could not prevent biological accidents from occurring at companies such as those that were located around the major cities of Texas.

Most of the spin-off biotech companies Boards of Directors were smart enough to make sure that they had a mix of classified and non-classified biomedical projects underway at any one time. Their diversified approach to the marketplace was championed by their private investors, who wanted to see quick profits for conducting biological defense work, while they waited for the long-term profits from the approval of new drugs and medicines. They often manipulated the system so that the Federal Government actually subsidized their private for-profit commercial projects and provided needed income during the early stages of corporate development. The classified biowarfare projects from the government contracts were so lucrative that even many established corporations, such as the pharmaceutical giants and large defense corporations like the Las Vegas-backed Cornealyus Group, also had their own 'Biological Defense' programs hidden behind their grand PR efforts that produced endless TV commercials and magazine adds about 'wonder' drugs and products that were so expensive that the average person could barely afford them. The subsidies offered by the Federal Government for 'Biological Defense' projects were also attractive in helping the 'bottom line' bean counters project healthy future profits and thus added value when and if they ever had a public stock offering. By the time they went 'public' the Biological Defense subsidies would have been long forgotten.

Mr. Able had contacted Dr. Masters, because he was particularly concerned about the noise coming from some academics in the Austin biomedical community about some whistle blowers who could cause some potential damage to Able's Las Vegas casino-organized crime investors, but his real concern was that somewhere down the road the whole ugly mess might become public and tarnish some very powerful political families. One of his pet projects in Austin was a company called Biox, Inc., a spin-off from Virgil Rook's Microbiology Department at Belford College of Medicine.

The chief scientists at Biox, including its president and founder Dr. Mary Ling and her husband Dr. Henry P. Ling, were experts in microbiology and biological warfare. They had recruited some of the best scientists from the Medical Center to work either full-time or part-time at Biox. One of Biox's contracts with the Pentagon was to test new 'medical techniques' and 'drugs' in the prison system using the expertise of Belford and D. O. Madison and their contacts in the prison system, especially the three retired Army Colonels who now ran the Texas prison health programs.

Mr. Able's foremost 'success' in the biological defense area was to arrange financing of a spin-off company from the highly classified MKNAOMI program of the research effort at Fort Detrick. The project that was spun-off to the civilian sector was called Project P2, named after the inner Masonic order of the Opus Dei. Project P2 was a highly secret testing program in Africa and other parts of the Third World for new biological defense discoveries that many in the academic community might rightfully regard as eugenic programs. The principals in Project P2 had been responsible for sending contaminated vaccines to Central Africa to test for and prevent important diseases that were endemic there, such as small pox.

Project P2 was secretly headed by Dr. Harry Koppla, an esteemed Philadelphia scientist. As a pathologist he was interested in the effects of the new pathogens on isolated communities, but he was also a fiend that found pleasure in seeing what the potent new biologicals could do to more 'primitive' societies. When members of his own laboratory objected to his 'experiments,' they either died under suspicious circumstances similar to what had happened at the Madison or became gravely ill and unable to work, just like Marie. As an important member of the U. S. Academy of Sciences, Dr. Koppla would never be suspected of spreading genocidal agents to the African continent under the guise of his specially designed 'humanitarian' vaccine projects. What the African countries receiving the vaccines did not know at the time, and still do not know, was that the vaccines were secretly contaminated with various candidate biowarfare viruses and bacteria that required 'field testing' to determine their effectiveness under 'real world' conditions.

Some academics had accused certain members of the American science community, such as Dr. Koppla, of advising and even directing this Third World program. The highly secret Project P2 had been suspected by some scientists as the principal mechanism for spreading hepatitis, smallpox, HIV-1 and other very dangerous pathogens to isolated regions of the Dark Continent for purposes of studying their community disease characteristics. An even more sinister role suggested by some scientists was that this project was part of a classified population reduction directive. As outlined in Henry Kissinger's now notorious National Security Study Memorandum 200, the document that promoted the 'National Security' justification for world population reduction by increasing the death rates in Third World countries, the long-term survival and the 'National Security' of the Western world and its culture was thought to depend upon reducing or limiting the world's population. One of the lead financial organizations, along with certain wealthy individuals and families, that provided funds for such insane eugenics research was the same Las Vegas organized crime-connected financial empire along with the European Illuminati, an empire that few understood who were not born into the organization. One of the principal sources of funding of the entire program was the giant multi-hundred billion dollar Cetta Dharma Trust, held off-ledger at a major bank in New York and whose trustees were some of the most prominent families and politicians in the world. It was also funded by an even larger multinational trust called the Five Star Trust.

Mr. Able was quite proud of his role helping the Las Vegas casino interests with their investments, which were also backed by the giant Cetta Dharma and Five Star Trusts. He was also involved with the government and financial networks that provided the technological seeds and financing for projects like Biox Incorporated. Thus he did not like to be told by his underlings that there were problems that could result in exposure, bad press and possibly even interruptions in the science of doom that had been conducted unabated in the United States since the early 1950s. Even though the United States was signatory to the 1972 Geneva Convention on Biological Warfare that prohibited the development of new offensive biological agents, their production, storage and testing, work on new biowarfare agents and their testing had continued unabated due to a clause in the treaty that permitted limited biological defense research. Important signatory countries to the treaty, such as the United States, China and the Soviet Union, had interpreted the treaty to mean that they could do just about anything that they wanted on biowarfare agents and their development. After all, it was quite difficult to ascertain the difference between defensive and offensive biological warfare research, and there were no provisions in the treaty for inspections of biological-capable countries to make sure that they were not cheating.

Some individuals had suggested that the downfall of Richard Nixon was caused, in part, by his attempt to shut down the massive United States biological defense program and convert its assets to more noble endeavors, such as the War on Cancer. Unfortunately, President Nixon was only partially successful in shutting down this program, resulting in only a minor blip in the covert science that supported the biological warfare programs of the United States. Mr. Able and his colleagues in the CIA and DoD were quite smug about their roles in circumventing this treaty by conducting 'biological defense experiments' that looked astonishingly like the prohibited offensive biological warfare mentioned in the treaty. After all, the other 'biological capable' countries around the world were doing the same thing, and we couldn't have a 'biological gap' like the famous and more public 'bomber gap' and later 'missile gap' between the Soviet Union and the United States of previous decades. The financial backers of this massive program, in particular, did not like public disclosure or discussion, because it could eventually come back to expose them as the public enemies that they were, rather than the humanitarian role models that had been projected by their own PR and by the American media.

Dr. Clement Masters was waiting for his call from Mr. Able when he was buzzed by his administrator, effectively jarring him out of his reverie of grandeur. He said forcefully but impatiently, "Yes! What is it?" The administrator answered, "Mr. Able is on line one." His demeanor instantly changed to a somewhat smug attitude as he pushed the button to place his phone in the speaker mode. He was, however, also nervous and was fidgeting with a paperweight. Dr. Masters had a lot to fidget about, because he was no longer held in the esteemed light that he thought he deserved by Mr. Able, who Dr. Masters considered just a financial lackey for some wealthy families, ex-Presidents and shady Las Vegas organized crime groups. While he fidgeted in his office he stared at a painting of the Texas bluebonnet flowers in full bloom under a mounted State of Texas Flag. Mr. Able finally broke his train of thought. "How are you Clement?" Dr. Masters responded, "How nice to hear from you, sir. How did the fishing go this year?

Mr. Able was in no mood to chat but he went along with the banter. "Clement, you know that I love Texas, but life does not get much better in New England than fishing off Maine. Sorry you were not here to join us this last summer. Listen, Clement, I hear that you have had some difficulty in handling that little problem of yours." Dr. Masters asked, "Are you referring to our projects with Belford and the prisons or the little problem with one of our faculty members? I think that we can handle them." Mr. Able responded, "That's not what I hear, Clement. I was told that you have dropped the ball!" Dr. Masters replied, "I respectively disagree, sir. I don't think we have dropped the ball. Perhaps we have had some problems, but nothing that we can't handle." Mr. Able said, "Those Doctors could make things embarrassing for us and the Pentagon. Not that they don't deserve it—the stupid and public way that they have been dealing with the veterans. Hell, even a moron could take care of the press with this Gulf War Syndrome thing, but the DoD and CIA seem to keep shooting themselves in the foot. We don't want to see this thing get out of hand, Clement. And then there's the question of Marie McNichols and the Trusts. We don't want her to find out that she is the principal heir to the Cetta Dharma and Five Star Trusts and the other trusts. That could cause some important families and politicians back here to be destabilized. They might eventually even have some financial problems as a consequence, and that goes for the government as well. I swear that her family is a blight on this planet. They and all their offspring should have been stamped out years ago."

Dr. Masters thought about what Mr. Able had said. "With all due respect, sir, I think you overestimate her and her family's influence. My contacts indicate that most of them have been eliminated. And I don't believe that I have failed entirely in my assignment. We have been very successful in completely discrediting her as well as her husband as people and as scientists. We have successfully blocked faculty appointments at the Medical Center, and we are in the process of removing her husband from his position. My deputies are overseeing a very effective character assassination campaign. We have made sure to blackball the two of them all over the country, and we have made sure that any invitations for them to speak, publish, you name it, have been blocked. It stands to reason that if her family was still so powerful, I could not do this." Mr. Able replied, "Well Clement, that's fine, but it's sophomore stuff. It's time to play hardball."

Dr. Masters became very nervous, because he thought that he *was* playing hardball with the McNichols. "Sir, I was thinking, and I would like to ask you if this ever occurred to you, that her family does not want her in science, and that we may possibly be playing into some agenda of theirs?" Mr. Able answered, "Dr. Masters, you're thinking again! I don't want you to think. Remember what I told you; I want you to do what you have been entrusted to do, and that's all. The rest is all academic crap! Is that perfectly clear?" Dr. Masters responded, "I believe that we are accomplishing our assignment as it was outlined to me." Mr. Able continued, "Clement, don't try to bullshit me; I am an old hand at bullshit tactics. You know exactly what I am interested in, and I want the situation corrected. Is that clear, Clement?"

Dr. Masters thought very carefully before he answered Mr. Able. "Yes, that's very clear." Mr. Able then asked, "Well then, what the hell happened in Moscow? What kind of games are you playing with us Clement?" Dr. Masters responded, "Sir, we're not playing games. In fact, we were just reviewing the circumstances around that trip and considering some alternative tactics. We are going to be successful—it's just a matter of time.

You will just have to give us a bit more time." Mr. Able responded, "Goddamn it Masters! Haven't you been listening to anything that I've been saying? For once I want to get it through that thick head of yours. No one here gives a damn about the science or the academic blackballing. We want to see some 'real' results. Am I clear on that? You're going to get off your ass and be more productive. Am I making myself perfectly clear, Clement?"

Dr. Masters was near panic, because he now believed that his fate could be the same as Dr. Cannon's if he failed. "What do you want me to do? Is there any way we can continue to assist you?" Mr. Able said, "You know what to do. People commit suicide all the time. I hear that you have had quite a few down your way in the last couple of years. I don't see anyone complaining that they are no longer at the Madison, even if they had a little help in the process. And I know that you have been helpful in this regard as well. But I have to tell you, Clement, that hit on the Colonel was crude, very messy. That didn't show me much in the way of sophistication, and it caused quite a bit of bad press."

Dr. Masters did not answer Mr. Able. There was silence for some time, and then Mr. Able continued, "Clement are you listening? If I can suggest a story; you probably know the story well by now. A talented young scientist is driven to despair by the rejection of her colleagues, so she commits suicide." Dr. Masters asked, "What about her husband? He is one of the most respected scientists on our staff? Mr. Able replied, "That's easy! Have you ever heard of the story about how a rumor campaign gets started about how he has lost it and goes nuts because his young wife committed suicide, and he ends up the same way? Or another story that is popular is that he kills his wife in a jealous rage and then turns the gun on himself. Come on, Clement. You know the stories; you've seen things like this before. As I recall, you know this angle very well indeed! I recall the hematologist at your place who got too close to the truth about some of our testing programs in your nursing homes South of San Antonio and had to be 'corrected.'

Mr. Able was referring to the nursing homes purchased by the D. O. Madison for the specific purpose of testing their biological creations on unknowing human victims. What better way to find out their effects on humans and mechanisms of action than to inject the exotic biological creations into senior citizens who had outlived their usefulness to society, at least that was what the director of this program, Dr. Joseph Reichsmann, reasoned. As a senior member of the faculty and department chairman, Dr. Joseph Reichsmann, ran the testing program from his department at the Cancer Center under the cover of a large drug development program. Dr. Reichsmann was a former Colonel in the Army Medical Corps and well acquainted with the use of military personnel for these types of experiments. In fact, he had been involved in this program even before Dr. Masters arrived at the Madison.

Dr. Masters sneered and responded to Mr. Able. "I am especially proud of that operation. The police immediately put it down as a suicide. The only slight problem was that we had to kill the rumors that he wasn't suicidal and was talking too much to his friends, but we took care of it." Mr. Able continued, "The former Air Force Colonel who was going all soft and was trying to blow the whistle on our germ warfare experiments in your place. I didn't like that approach. It's not my style–too messy. I want a cleaner operation this time, Clement. We need to get going on this, and I don't want to have to contact Las Vegas and have some of their people come in and fix some more of your mistakes. Is that clear?" Dr. Masters, "Yes sir, it is." Dr. Masters was petrified at the thought of some Las Vegas 'contractors' coming down to Austin to 'correct' the situation, because he could easily visualize himself as part of the problem that needed correction. He must take care of this himself or face the wrath of people like Mr. Able–or worse–his Las Vegas bosses.

While Dr. Masters was thinking of how he could escape Mr. Able's wrath, the former National Security Advisor to the President was reflecting on his own role in 'protecting' America. "Just think of the National Security aspects of this. While the goddamn commies were doing their anthrax experiments, we were just sitting on our asses. What in the hell were we supposed to do? Let Moscow get the better of us?" Dr. Masters replied subserviently, "No sir, I don't believe that we could afford to do that." Mr. Able responded, "Afford to do that! Hell, I get so damn sick of these bleeding hearts interfering in important matters that they know nothing about. Take your nursing home project. Who the hell cares if we get rid of a few sickly, old people who are nothing but a drain on our economy? And prisoners! I tell you, Hitler had a point! He just didn't go far enough. He didn't get them all." Dr. Masters looked out his window and became a bit abstracted. He weakly asked, "Sir?"

Dr. Masters' voice had a weak questioning tone. Mr. Able didn't like it, and he didn't let him finish his question. "Listen Clement. You will be doing a great service to your country and our Las Vegas interests by getting rid of that little bitch and her damned husband. In addition, they are interfering in our 'research' programs. Look, I hear you have an overcrowding problem down there in the prisons. What are a few prisoners, anyway? The way I see it, we are doing your State a favor by correcting their prison overcrowding problem. Clement, I don't hear the press screaming about the loss of a few condemned vermin."

Dr. Masters blurted out of nowhere, "I hate those Jews. They have polluted the planet, and even my own administration is full of them." Mr. Able answered, "Will you grow up Masters! This is not about Jews or Catholics or Muslims. This is about power and money and our survival! Our financial organization just uses the ethnic problem as a smokescreen to incite the old worn Biblical hatreds that keep our little Middle East armaments and oil markets going. You know, Clement? The concept of limited warfare to infuse a 'shot in the arm' to the global economy and keep prices and profits high. At the same time we can test our integrated warfare strategies." Dr. Masters replied, "Yes, Yes, I can see that." Mr. Able said sarcastically, "You can see that? Hell, it's potentially one hell of an investment, but we have to keep it going. And at the same time we can eliminate some undesirable elements from this planet. You know, Kissinger was right. We need to be concentrating more on controlling Third World populations."

Dr. Masters replied in a slightly puzzled way, "Sir, I really have not put enough thought into the more global issues." Dr. Masters was interrupted as he tried to continue by Mr. Able. "Why even some of the financiers of the so-called state of Israel don't give a flying fuck." The former White House National Security Advisor had a sarcastic tone to his voice. "Hell, these people even backed Hitler when it suited them. They just couldn't control him." Dr. Masters answered, "I feel the same way you do, sir." Mr. Able said, "Now you're finally listening, Clement. You won't disappoint me again, will you Clement?" Dr. Masters replied angrily, "By the time I finish with them they'll be dog meat." Mr. Able said again, "I still can't figure out why they survived Cambridge and then Moscow. It's a goddamn embarrassment, damn it! It would have been a good story. Scientist succumbs to exotic illness picked up while traveling. Damn, we even gave some others food poisoning at that conference to hide what you gave those two. I don't understand it. Clement, don't fail me again. I am running out of patience with everyone down there, and that includes you!"

Dr. Masters hesitated to bring up another important issue, at least to him and members of his staff. "Sir, there is one more minor issue, the financial aspects of . . ." Dr. Masters was interrupted before he could finish his sentence. "Of course, Clement, my friends are always well-compensated! We'll take care of it, as always. Now I want you to get off your ass! Do you get my drift?" Dr. Masters had perked up and was now with the program, "Sir, you can count on me!" Mr. Able said, "Good boy, Clement—remember, don't let me down again. Give my best to June and the kids." Dr. Masters said, "Please give my best to Lana and your family." Mr. Able had a final thought, "Good-bye and remember, don't disappoint me! A lot is riding on this." Dr. Masters said, "Again, sir. I will not fail—you can count on that."

Dr. Masters' last comments were not heard by Mr. Able. He had hung up on his end of the line before Dr. Masters could finish. Clement Masters slammed down the phone, thought for a moment about how he hated those East Coast know-it-alls who had unlimited entrée into the corridors of power and finance, and he took on the expression of a man who was scheming to be successful in his mission to 'correct' the deficiencies that had embarrassed him in the eyes of the power brokers. The McNichols had become a liability, and now an embarrassment. They were risking the good name of the D. O. Madison with their continued work with the veterans and now the prison employees. But it was the latter research that really concerned Dr. Masters, but he couldn't let on to his subordinates that he was worried about the situation. He didn't dare share his true feelings with them. He was proud of the way he could manipulate anyone in Austin to do what he wanted, but he was unsure of his abilities in the fast-paced world of Washington and New

York. There his down home Southern style was less than useless—it was considered 'hicksville.'

Dr. Masters started mumbling to himself again. Some of his close colleagues considered that he was psychotic, and talking out loud to himself was a frequent habit. "It's too bad you're such a pretty little bitch, Marie. It might have been fun to have a whirl with you." He sighed, "Ah, well, I am certain, my pretty little kiss of death, that my reward for 'correcting' you will far outweigh any pleasure fucking you would have given me. Hell, I don't even know who is behind this Las Vegas organized crime bullshit. But it seems like yours truly will hit the Vegas jackpot. At least I know that the Cetta Dharma Trust exists, and that is one hell of a lot of money." Dr. Masters then made a sinister sounding laugh to himself. "Do I use that blow-hard Isaac Geldter to assist in this mission, or do I use my local sources to put out a more professional contract on the McNichols. That could get expensive. That bastard Colonel cost me a pretty penny, but it was certainly a foolproof way to proceed. Now let's see, that prick Mr. Able doesn't want any more publicity. So let's use the blow-hard first. If he can't do it, I'll just have to go back to my tried and true sources, even if its going to be a pain in the ass to move some funds through my Madison accounts. I don't see why I should have to personally pay for this! That Israeli creep Ricin would do an assignment like this with relish."

Dr. Masters was considering his options. "Geldter can't stand it if Jared McNichols outshines him, so with this assignment he can kill two birds with one stone. Discredit and eliminate Jared and then that bitch Marie. I may even promise him Jared's department. That whiner Francis is against that, but he can be overruled. I will just proceed as if I am going through the usual legal procedures to remove McNichols from his position. That will be a good cover." He clasped his hands together and then ordered his administrator on his intercom to contact his Vice President of Research and Dr. Geldter to set up an emergency meeting as soon as possible. He also told her to get in contact with the Legal Department. "Ms. Broderick, get Isaac Geldter and Francis Belcher to meet me here in my office as soon as possible, and get Legal on the phone." Ms. Broderick answered, "Yes, sir."

Back in the laboratory progress is being made

One of the programs that Jared initiated was a Gulf War Illness information project that sent information packages to veterans and their families and a similar program for prison guards and their families. The packages informed them about Gulf War Illnesses and the unusual illnesses in the prison system, how to have them diagnosed and some possible treatments. Jared had to be especially careful about the last part of the information packages on treatment strategies, because this was where the administration could attack him and he was aware of this. He was careful to use only peer-reviewed publications for this part. Once the information had been published, it was in the public domain, and it was more difficult for the administration to go after him for simply giving out duplications of peer-reviewed, published research.

The D. O. Madison administration was particularly angry about Jared's information program, because they had been receiving calls from various people in Washington as well as locally from the State prison system and the VA to shut it down, because it was fostering too much publicity and questions in the community. Jared had been careful enough to use his own personal funds to pay for postage and copying, throttling an investigation initiated from Dr. Masters' office into misappropriation of State funds and resources in Jared's Department, which had become the most audited department in the Cancer Center.

Fortunately, Jared had some discretionary funds at his disposal that the President of the Cancer Center couldn't control, because they were from his endowed chair. The funds were to be used for whatever research project the recipient chose to use them for, and Jared had already survived a 'legal' challenge on this point from the Cancer Center's Legal Services Department. In fact, Dr. Masters and his henchmen even contacted the Dallas family that provided Jared's endowed chair to have their donation changed to a more restricted use at the Cancer Center. They also tried to have Jared removed from his own chair that the family had approved. After reviewing the situation, the family gave Jared a rousing letter of support that further infuriated Dr. Masters and the Madison administration.

In Jared's department this small operation was entirely in the hands of Blake Haley, a student in between high school and college that Marie and Jared had made one of their honorary godsons. Blake believed in what the McNichols were doing, so much so, in fact, that he cleverly resisted all of the pressures that the Madison administration put to bear to shut down Jared's little program. Blake had to do some maneuvering to avoid the department rats, such as Dr. Domasovitch and his staff, who were always snooping around trying to find some irregularity in hospital regulations or University Rules and Regulations to use against Jared. The scheming Dr. Domasovitch, who had benefited greatly from the support that Jared had given him over the years, even went so far as to have Blake's computer rigged with a silent 'alias' program so that he could retrieve everything that Blake had placed into his computer when the files were spooled for printing. He secretly did the same with Jared's computer, and each morning before six AM he used his secret master key provided by the administration to gain entry into Blake's and Jared's offices to make copies of what ever they were doing. Jared knew all about this from the few loyal people left in his office, and he laughed at such foolishness. He had offered to provide copies of anything that the Administration wanted from his computer, but Dr. Masters' weasels preferred to 'steal' the information, perhaps to gain favor with the higher-ups in the administration and prove their loyalty.

Jared once caught Dr. Domasovitch measuring his office as if to see how his own furniture would fit into a much more roomy space rather than his more cramped office quarters down the hall. Jared loved to play tricks on the rats by removing the alias programs and files from his computer or placing notes in the alias files telling them that he would be pleased to send them everything. Jared was sure that this infuriated Domasovitch. Since Jared's email was re-routed before it arrived in the Department, Domasovitch wasn't responsible for that type of electronic communication, but the faxes that came directly into the office were routinely intercepted by the office personnel and given to Domasovitch. Then he tried one morning to poison Jared's coffee. But since it tasted quite unusual Jared decided not drink it. Besides, it was hand-delivered by Dr. Domasovitch himself, and Jared immediately became suspicious and took only a sip before throwing it into a waste container.

There was also a cat and mouse game being played at the McNichols' home in Queenswood. Each morning after the mailman delivered the mail to the McNichols' large mailbox out on the street in front of their house, one of the faculty rats or one of Jared's postdoctoral students recruited by Domasovitch and who placed the alias programs in Jared's computer, were there to retrieve all of the mail for delivery to Dr. Masters' office for examination. Jared went so far as to complain to the U. S. Postal Service Inspectors about his and Marie's mail being stolen from their mailbox, but to no avail. In time the stolen mail would end up in a large pile in several boxes at a regional post office in North Austin. They were never able to recover their mail.

For sensitive materials Jared had to resort to a postal box at a local shopping center. He and Marie had given up on ever receiving any U. S. Mail on time, if they received it at all. They usually found that their mail was postmarked months before it actually arrived. The mail had more likely been intercepted by Dr. Masters' rats. Similarly, any faxed materials received at or sent to the Department office would be copied, and presumably all the telephone calls were monitored as well.

Dr. Masters was looking for something, anything that he could use against Jared and Marie. When Jared prepared a manuscript for publication, he had to be especially careful. If the department rats found out about the manuscript or where it was to be sent, the information was passed to Dr. Belcher or Dr. Geldter or one of the other faculty conspirators, who would then contact the journal to influence the editor that the data were tainted or faked. Since science and medicine were so competitive anyway, such an effort was usually disastrous to an individual's reputation. Journal editors had no way of determining who was telling the truth, so they usually avoided any controversy by returning the manuscript without any editorial decision. This was how Dr. Masters and his underlings slowly eroded the stature and prestige of Professor Jared McNichols, who had built his reputation over a 25-year period, only to see it quickly torn down. Colleagues stopped calling him or writing him letters, they removed invitations to speak at international meetings and conferences, and in general the campaign to paint Marie and Jared as over-the-edge scientists who had flipped their lids succeeded.

Drs. Geldter and Krappner played important roles in the discrediting process, and they spent much of their time on the phone during working hours to insure that Jared and Marie didn't have a chance to present their data at conferences and meetings. Even when Jared did receive important invitations, such as an invitation received by fax from Sweden to speak at a prestigious meeting, he never received it. The Department rats and the Madison administration had instructed the office personnel to keep such items from Jared, and they were given instead to Dr. Domasovitch for daily delivery to Dr. Masters' office. In this case, the organizer of the conference in Sweden sent a copy of the fax by regular mail, and Jared just happened to be in the outer office when it arrived, and he grabbed it before it was collected for forwarding to Dr. Masters.

Jared would never find out how many invitations and communications were intercepted and later destroyed. Fortunately, some of Jared's colleagues were wise to the ways of Dr. Masters and his underlings, who they considered sinister or even evil. There were even some acts of passive-aggressive behavior within Jared's faculty and staff by people who didn't like the way Jared and Marie were being treated. Most of the faculty that had been around the Medical Center for many years had seen this type of behavior before from Dr. Masters, the Madison and also Belford College of Medicine, and some of them even secretly attempted to warn Jared and even tried to thwart some of the more obvious acts against the couple.

The similarity of Gulf War Illness with the Wallsville Prison Illness

In the laboratory Bob Sonan had been assisting in the gathering of the data on the Gulf War veterans and the state prison guards and prison employees and their families. He had come to Jared's office to talk to Jared and Marie about the latest results. Bob said, "It's just like you said. About 45% of the veterans' samples are coming up positive for Mycoplasma, and about 80% of these are Mfi infections. And in the prison guards and other prison employees, more than 50% are coming up positive, and again more than 80% of these are also Mfi positive. Jared looked briefly at the results and returned to the board where a new table had been taking up space. Blake was also in the office, and he had been collecting the signs and symptoms data from the prison employees and their family members in the Wallsville area. After Jared had finished, he stood back and they examined the table.

Table 4

Comparison of signs and symptoms of Gulf War Illness, Wallsville Mystery Illness, Chronic Fatigue Syndrome and Marie's Illness.

Signs/ Symptoms	Gulf War Illness	Mystery Prison Illness	Chronic Fatigue Syndrome	Marie's Illness
chronic fatigue	+	+	+	+
joint pain/mobility	+	+	+	+
night sweats	+	+	+	+
muscle pain	+	+	+(not always)	+
fevers	+	+	+(not always)	+
headaches	+	+	+	+
skin rashes	+	+	+(not always)	+
memory loss	+	+	+	+
stomach pain	+(not always)	+	+(not always)	+
breathing problems	+(not always)	+(not always)	+(not always)	+
sleep problems	+	+	+	+
diarrhea	+(not always)	+(not always)	+(not always)	±
heart palpitations	+(not always)	+(not always)	+(not always)	+
vision problems	+	+	+	+
depression	+(not always)	+	+(not always)	+
hair loss	+(not always)	+	+(not always)	+
nausea	+(not always)	+(not always)	+(not always)	+
sinus problems	+(not always)	+(not always)	+(not always)	+
vertigo	+(not always)	+(not always)	+(not always)	+

Jared looked at the data. "They all look pretty much the same to me. And what's the common denominator, Mfi, at least for half of the patients." Bob asked, "What do you think the other one-half have?" Jared responded, "Either a similar type of chronic infection or something else. For example, we know that the Gulf War veterans were exposed to a variety of chemicals, so the illnesses in the patients who do not test positive for a Mycoplasmal infection could be from chemical exposures, or some other type of biological exposure. In the case of the prison system, a common infection that causes a lot of skin problems is Staphylococcus aureas. In fact, the Texas prisons have had a major problem with antibiotic-resistant *Staphylococcus aureas* infections or MRSA."

Although the Texas prison system had tried to cover up the presence of the MRSA epidemic over the years, it had now passed into the Texas population outside of the prison system. Jared continued, "Some patients have actually died from this infection when it became systemic, progressed and could not be treated with the usual antibiotics. Both the Mycoplasma and Staph infections could be related to the testing programs in the prison system, but the mere presence of these unusual infections did not prove that they were from testing programs." Some of the employees in the prison clinics indicated to Blake that Belford scientists and some scientists from a small biotech company with the ridiculous name Biox were testing vaccines and other biologicals at the Wallsville unit.

Marie perked up at the mention of Biox. "Biox was started out of my old department at Belford by the Lings, the husband and wife microbiologists. They seemed very interested in our Mycoplasma experiments. In fact, Mary Ling met me outside the building a few weeks ago and asked me why I was still alive? I asked her if she was involved in my poisoning, and she turned white and ran away. I thought that it was so bizarre that I didn't bother to mention it." Jared asked, "What else do you know about Biox?" Marie said, "Well, I know that Dr. Ming Lon was working there for approximately a year." Jared asked, "You mean the same Ming Lon of the Army Institute of Pathology Research?" Marie answered, "Yes, the very same. Did you know that his M.D. degree was from Belford?" Jared exclaimed, "No kidding! Do you think that Ming Lon was involved in Mfi experiments in the Wallsville prison?" Marie answered, "I'd say it was very likely, from what we have found in the sick prison guards and other employees. Some of them claim that Dr. Lon was even at the Wallsville Prison to collect blood." Jared said, "You know what this means, don't you?"

Jared asked for their attention so that they could discuss the unusual gene sequences found in the veterans' and prison guards' blood samples that tested positive for Mfi. "We almost forgot to discuss the most interesting result. I think that this is very significant. What you found is going to shake everything up and change the way we look at this problem. I am referring to the HIV-1 gene controls. The Mfi results also indicate the presence of a piece of or a complete HIV-1 gene in the same samples. Those HIV-1 gene sequences weren't supposed to be there! That a part of the *env* gene was found but not the *pol* or *rev* genes in the Gulf War veterans' samples indicates that this might be a gene modification in the mycoplasma, not co-infections of the HIV-1 virus in the veterans. And the fact that you found this in only the veterans' samples and not in the civilians with Chronic Fatigue Syndrome and *M. fermentans* strongly suggests that the veterans have a modified mycoplasma. But even more disturbing were the Texas prison results. There you found evidence for other HIV-1 genes but not in the same blood sample. The prison illnesses predate the Gulf War Illnesses by a few years, but they have the same overlapping signs and symptoms. The results are consistent with the notion that Texas prison employees might have been exposed to Mfi strains with different genetic modifications, whereas the veterans were exposed to Mfi with apparently only one modification, the *env* gene." Bob asked, "What do you think that means?" Jared replied, "I think that it indicates that by the Gulf War only a few or even one strain of Mfi infected the troops, but earlier other strains were apparent, as if the Gulf War strain was somehow *better* at causing disease or more virulent." Bob asked, "How would the HIV-1 *env* gene make the Mfi more virulent?" Jared answered, "I don't know, but it could make it better at invading cells by increasing its ability to attach to target cells. For example, it is thought that the envelope protein, the product of the *env* gene helps the HIV-1 virus invade into the brain. Also, the *env* gene product might interfere with immune cell signaling or cause immune suppression when presented to the right immune cells." Marie added, "In any case, if we can prove that the Mfi has been modified, then it might also prove that someone has been conducting illegal Biological Warfare experiments on the American people without their knowledge or permission."

They all stood looking at Jared, because he started the discussion. He waited for their complete attention and said, "I am afraid that we may have stumbled onto a massive biological testing program in the military and prison systems." Marie added, "I would say Biological Warfare testing program." Jared said, "Jeez, no wonder they have been after us. They were supposed to shut down the BW programs by the early '70s when Nixon converted Fort Detrick to civilian use in the late 1960s. Only the Army didn't convert all of Fort Detrick, just a portion, to cancer research and turned it over to NIH. Marie added, "Dr. Lon told me that he used to work at Fort Detrick before he received his appointment at the U. S. Army Institute for Pathology Research.

Jared thought about the implications of what they had found. "This could explain the hostility of the D. O. Madison Administration towards us and our research. We have stumbled onto their secret and highly illegal bioweapons programs." Marie asked, "And what do we do now?" Jared said, "I don't really know. I guess that we just keep this quiet for the moment. If we go public, Dr. Masters will destroy us." Marie responded, "I'd say he's doing a pretty good job of it right now. Jared you have got to wake up! We have to leave this place." Jared countered, "And go where?" Marie said, "Can't you go back to your old job at the University of California?" Jared said, "Masters would kill that in a second, if he hasn't already. I'm afraid that it's too late. We're going to have to stand our ground and win the battle here or die trying." Marie added, "That's comforting! You mean that we're going to continue being punching bags for Dr. Masters!"

Dr. Masters uses another approach

Near the end of the year Professor McNichols received a formal letter from the Department of Legal Services. Dr. Masters wanted to dismiss Jared McNichols outright for what he considered insubordination, since Jared had apparently refused to stop the Gulf War Illness project after he was given a direct order from Dr. Masters to do so. In fact, Jared considered the order, but since the research had received the approval at all of the usual Administrative levels, including Dr. Belcher' office, and the institution had even signed off on a grant application on the role of chronic infections in Gulf War Illnesses, he felt that he had all of the usual administrative approvals for the work to continue. Fortunately for Jared, the University attorneys agreed with him not Dr. Masters. This agitated Dr. Masters more than anything Jared could have ever done, precipitating a yelling match with the institutional attorney who counter-argued that Jared would have one hell of a legal case against the D. O. Madison if a tenured faculty member was removed from his position at the whim of the President without due process and without any evidence that University rules had been broken. Dr. Masters then ordered his deputy, Dr. Clyde Bane, to examine every possible rule that may or may not have been broken by Jared and to prepare a stern letter of warning that would be edited by

Legal Services to insure that Dr. Masters was complying with University regulations. Eventually Dr. Masters relented in firing Jared *at this time*, but he was still furious that the university lawyers refused to let him dismiss Dr. McNichols on the spot. But he did manage to get the university lawyers to agree that if Jared failed to comply completely with the stipulations in the 'warning letter,'" then Dr. Masters could have his way. Jared knew he was in trouble when he received the letter from Dr. Masters.

December 7, 1994

LEGAL SERVICES

Professor Jared McNichols
Chairman, Department of Cancer Biology
The D. O. Madison Cancer Center
Austin, Texas

Dear Professor McNichols;

You are no doubt aware that the Cancer Center has received numerous inquiries related to some statements you have made concerning your research on the microorganism *Mycoplasma fermentans*. I have discussed the matter with Dr. Clyde Bane, Executive Vice President for Health Affairs and Dr. Francis Belcher, Vice President for Research, as well as several other vice presidents and administrative and legal officials at our institution. We share a common concern that scientific support for your statements must be reviewed by officials of the institution to protect both your reputation as a scientist and the Cancer Center's good name as an internationally renowned center of excellence. I have the following directives that I expect to be followed, effective immediately.

1. **Administrative Approvals.** We have no institutional record of any administrative approval of the research from your

laboratory on this field of investigation, nor do we have any formal data to substantiate your claims concerning the subject.

2. **Biohazzard Approvals**. We can find no approvals that would permit experimentation with a dangerous and communicable pathogen of this nature within the institution.

3. **Relationship to Mission of the Institution.** We find no relationship between this issue and cancer, and we can find no relationship of this research to the mission of the institution.

4. **Administrative Authorization to Use Facilities**. We have found no authorization for the use or the application of institutional facilities, resources or faculty reputation in this area.

I have made arrangements for you to meet with Drs. Bane and Belcher and I as soon as possible to review the pertinent information that forms the basis of your statements and publications. I am appointing an expert review panel of impartial specialists to help clarify and resolve these serious allegations. In the meantime, you will cease all research in this area and refrain from making any public statements until all of the issues surrounding *Mycoplasma fermentans* have been resolved.

Given your reputation as a productive and conscientious scientist, I am certain that you recognize your special responsibilities in the area of scientific rigor and scholarly integrity. It is imperative and I am prepared to take appropriate action to fulfill our institution's responsibilities to the public.

Sincerely,

Clement A. Masters, M.D.
President

Jared had only a few days to reply to the formal letter from the Department of Legal Services signed by Dr. Masters. He did his best to reply quickly, and actually he beat Dr. Masters' deadline. If he had not answered Dr. Masters' letter within the allowed time, he would have been immediately dismissed. Jared realized that Dr. Masters was after him and especially Marie, and Dr. Masters had a reputation for always getting his way, especially when he wanted to fire someone. Once Dr. Masters had it in for one of the breast cancer oncologists at The Madison, and he had one of his henchmen watch his clinic to see if any hospital rules were ever violated. The oncologist slipped one night and left patients in his service waiting to be seen. Dr. Masters was immediately notified, and he went directly to the clinic and made arrangements on the spot to fire the tenured oncologist the next day.

Jared knew that it might only be a matter of time before one of his department rats found something, even minor, and the ax would fall. His only hope was that Dr. Masters, who would have to retire on or before August 31, 1996, would go first and go quietly. Therefore, he decided to work a bit harder to see that he would not be leaving the Cancer Center before Dr. Masters, knowing full well that he was holding a very poor hand of cards compared to the powerful and egotistical Dr. Masters, who held all the aces and always got his way. The key would be to draw out the game and keep Dr. Masters off balance.

December 10, 1994

Clement A. Masters, M.D.
President
The D. O. Madison Cancer Center
Austin, Texas

Dear Dr. Masters,

Concerning the comments in your recent letter of December 7, 1994 and the meeting that you have scheduled in your office, I have the following statements.

1. **Administrative Approvals.** *We have no institutional record of any administrative approval of the research from your laboratory on*

this field of investigation, nor do we have any formal data to substantiate your claims concerning the subject. As to the point that a registered research project does not appear on institutional administrative records, this policy was abandoned two years ago in favor of departmental records, and of course, this does appear on our department records as a legitimate research project.

2. **Biohazzard Approvals**. *We can find no approvals that would permit experimentation with a dangerous and communicable pathogen of this nature within the institution.* This project involves the proper handling of patient samples, and it conforms to our existing institutional requirements of registration of patient blood and blood products. Furthermore, the project received approval from the Biohazzard Office at our institution. We have ample experience in dealing with the biohazards associated with the handling of blood, and we take the same precautions with every sample of blood that is analyzed in our department. In addition, we are not nor have we ever attempted to culture any infectious agent from patient blood samples. Once we complete the development of a commercially useful diagnostic test for Mycoplasma fermentans incognitus, large-scale testing or clinical trials will not be done at our institution.

3. **Relationship to Mission of the Institution.** *We find no relationship between this issue and cancer, and we can find no relationship of this research to the mission of the institution.* I find the comment that the research does not have any relationship to the mission of our institution interesting. We have several ongoing projects at our institution in several clinical and basic research departments on infectious microorganisms. In fact, the old Virology Department was merged into my own department, and several faculty members work on infectious microorganisms in this and other departments. One only has to read the recent Annual Research Report of the D. O. Madison Cancer Center to see the wide variety of infectious agents that are being examined by our staff as well as new approaches in the clinical management of such infections in our patients. Thus an important part of the

mission of our institution is to investigate infections that could be transmitted to cancer patients who often have compromised immune systems. This is why our institution has a separate clinical unit just for the identification and treatment of infectious microorganisms.

4. Administrative Authorization to Use Facilities. *We have found no authorization for the use or the application of institutional facilities, resources or faculty reputation in this area.* I find this comment interesting, since we do have administrative approval. The Vice President of Research approved of the research with his signature on a Federal grant application of mine on the very same subject. By his signature on this grant application, the institution has formally approved of the research and agrees to accept a grant in the subject area if it is awarded. In addition, the research had departmental approval, and funding was made available from my own endowed chair. No new facilities, resources or funding was requested from the administration, and the research complies with all safety and biohazard regulations. As to the comment about my reputation, I remind you that I have 25+ years of scientific experience, have published over 400 scientific papers and edited 12 books, am one of the 100 most-cited scientists in the world in the biomedical sciences, serve as Editor or Associate Editor on 15 medical and scientific journals and enjoy a scientific reputation that is matched by few at our institution. As I mentioned above, we are also collaborating with some of the most renowned scientists in the world in Mycoplasma research.

There have been very few statements made to the public or press concerning the Desert Storm Illness and the possible involvement of a pathogenic mycoplasma in this illness. Our data form the basis of three peer-reviewed publications on the subject in academic journals. The statement that seemed to trouble the Administration of the D. O. Madison Cancer Center was that we have obtained preliminary evidence that unusual gene sequences might be in a pathogenic mycoplasma found in patients with this disorder. While admittedly preliminary, that is exactly how it was presented. This statement is strengthened by published data on other unusual, inserted sequences found in this mycoplasma by the U. S. Army Institute for Pathology Research. In addition, it is strengthened by preliminary data from the laboratory of Professor Gerald Brookman, a leading expert on this type of microorganism, in the University's Medical School Microbiology Department. You have my assurances that any future statements will be carefully drafted to insure that they are backed up by sound laboratory and clinical data.

Concerning the review of our research by the Cancer Center, I doubt that we have anyone on our staff who is an expert in this area and can do this in a fair and unbiased manner. Therefore, I suggest if you need assistance in the evaluation of our data that individuals who are experts in the area, such as the professor indicated above, be called in to examine our data. I believe that it is hardly necessary to establish a local committee to oversee and screen our research. In fact, there is no precedent at the Cancer Center for such action, and it smacks of political control over our academic right to conduct research that has the chance to benefit many patients who are currently being denied care and treatment.

I assure you that the utmost care will be taken to ensure that accurate, critical data will emerge from our studies, and these will be subject to critical peer-review, as were three of our publications on this subject in respected medical publications during the last year. At the appropriate time, our techniques and procedures will be transferred to another institution that deals more exclusively with these and other types of infections, so that a suitable clinical trial can be initiated. I hope that this letter adequately addresses your concerns.

Sincerely,

Jared McNichol, Ph.D.
Samual Burker Chair in Cancer Research
Professor and Chairman

Jared never heard directly from Dr. Masters or the Legal Services Office concerning his letter of response to Dr. Masters' letter. He decided to not press his luck, so he tried as much as possible to take a low-key approach by refusing the many press interviews and refusing to go on local TV. He was, however, asked by the National Security Committee of the House of Representatives to testify on his research, and he was also asked to present his case to the President's Commission on Gulf War Veterans' Illnesses in Washington DC. These and other formal requests for expert testimony could not be ignored, and his travel requests could not be blocked by the Administration because Jared received formal notice from the United States Government for his expert testimony, the equivalent of a legal summons.

As time went on Jared became more and more disillusioned with the faculty at the D. O. Madison Cancer Center. He assumed that at least some of the faculty would come to his defense, but in reality very few ever did. Most of the faculty, at least those that were recruited for the purpose of driving the McNichols from the institution, were quite content to take the perks that the Administration was offering to go after him, even the faculty in his own department that were originally recruited and nurtured by Jared. The most disappointing of the faculty 'rats' were the ones that Jared had actually helped the most in terms of their own careers. They turned on him like hyenas on a dying animal—without one hint of remorse or regret. Perhaps they thought that tearing down Jared would leave them with higher salaries, more lab space, higher positions and additional perks but, of course, the administration rarely came through with their promises. Perhaps the administration felt that it didn't have to fulfill its promises, and to do so might even smack of academic manipulation and actually give credence to the allegation that the administration was orchestrating a smear campaign against Jared to drive him from the institution.

Dr. Masters did, however, ultimately reward a few of the faculty members in Jared's department. One of these was Dr. Domasovitch, Jared's first academic appointment and a disappointment as a researcher, who was elevated to an administrative position in the Department of Educational Affairs where he could sit all day in his office and play around with the teaching programs of the institution, making graduate course A into course B, and vice versa. Since he was considered a mediocre scientist, the administration had to find something to elevate his pay status. Marie had warned Jared that most of the faculty in his department had no character and would not come to his defense. Jared felt otherwise, but Marie turned out to be completely correct about Drs. Nosan, Domasovitch and an immunologist, Bill Costerman. Jared had fought hard to get tenure for Dr. Costerman at the Cancer Center. Jared had recruited Dr. Costerman from the Midwest where he had been a postdoctoral fellow in the laboratory of one of Jared's friends and colleagues. Jared actually considered Bill Costerman a friend, or at least Jared thought he was a friend, but Jared would learn the hard way that some of the young faculty that he advised and aided along their career paths would do just about anything to get ahead. In this case Dr. Costerman was either a very insincere person or he was so ambitious that destroying Jared to get ahead at the institution was of no particular concern to him. Dr. Costerman was the department's representative to the Faculty Senate, and in this position he was able to bring information to the Senate that was potentially damaging to Jared. At one point the Senate was strongly considering sanctioning Jared, and the administration was pushing for just such action, and it was Costerman who would provide the necessary faculty 'corroboration' for the attack.

The chairman of the Faculty Senate was none other than Dr. Joseph Reichsmann, the senior faculty member who was responsible for running the biological testing program in the nursing homes South of San Antonio purchased by the Madison to test biological cocktails on human subjects without their consent or knowledge. Dr. Reichsmann hated Jared and Marie for interference in programs that were not their concern. He was pleased, indeed, to have Dr. Costerman provide information on Jared for the Faculty Senate from within Jared's own department. This added credence to the allegations sent secretly to the Senate from Dr. Masters through Dr. Clyde Bane to Dr. Reichsmann that Jared was acting in ways that they considered unethical or not in the best interests of the D. O. Madison. Unknown to Jared, Dr. Reichsmann was coordinating a secret Faculty Senate 'investigation' of Jared's activities, including his research on Gulf War Illness patients and the prison guards and their families. The function of the 'secret' Faculty Senate committee was to consider the unsubstantiated allegations made against Jared and to make recommendations to the administration on what to do with their wayward faculty member. The committee was being pushed by Dr. Reichsmann to recommend termination of Jared; however, when it came time for the committee to consider exactly which University rules and regulations that Jared had violated, there was intense disagreement on the committee as to whether Jared had in fact violated any University rules and regulations. On one side was Dr. Reichsmann, aided by Dr. Costerman from Jared's department, and on the other side were faculty members who could see that it was a set-up to stifle Dr. McNichols' research. They probably could see themselves in a similar situation if they dared some day to conduct research that was considered politically incorrect by the administration.

The faculty members in Jared's department, and in fact the entire institution, were divided into three camps when it came to Jared McNichols—those who jumped at the chance to ingratiate themselves to the D. O. Madison Administration at any cost, those who remained completely neutral and refused to take sides at all in the debate, and those that actually defended Jared and fought with the faculty that were easily recruited by the Madison administration for their dirty work. As one might expect, the weakest faculty in terms of their abilities and academic prowess were the ones who most eagerly signed on to the McNichols' harassment and defamation programs. Only the academically strongest faculty came to Jared's defense, but they couldn't fight the D. O. Madison administration and all the other faculty members who wanted to ingratiate themselves to the administration at any cost. Even the D. O. Madison administration wasn't monolithic when it came to Jared McNichols, however, and there were some members of Dr. Masters' own administration that disagreed strongly with his attempts to terminate Jared.

CHAPTER 11

The Veterans and Prison
Guards ask for Help (1995)

During the time that the controversy raged in Austin the McNichols became lifelong friends with Sandy Maitland and her husband Clayman, the couple from Wallsville, the prison town struck with the 'Wallsville Mystery Illness.' Their daughter Jenny who was diagnosed with Lou Gehrig's Disease or ALS at the Belford College of Medicine, slowly began to recover from her 'terminal' condition on the antibiotic doxycycline, as did other residents struck down with unusual degenerative neurological diseases in Wallsville. If their daughter really had ALS, an antibiotic like doxycycline would have had little effect on her condition. The neurologists at Belford were mad at Marie and Jared for interfering with their East Texas ALS patients, but of course, Jared and Marie really had nothing to do with the Belford neurological patients, other than to test some of them to see if they had chronic bacterial infections. If they found chronic infections in these patients, they were provided with Jared's published information on how the infections could be treated.

Although the D. O. Madison was angry with the McNichols for interacting with patients that came to them for help, they couldn't easily interfere with people who freely called or wrote to a tenured faculty member to ask for advice. Jared was careful not to openly contact patients—they did not advertise or recruit any patients from area physicians or claim in any way that they treated patients or accepted patients for any clinical studies. The patients that came to the McNichols were strictly word-of-mouth referrals. Somehow they found the McNichols, and the only reason that they flocked to the Austin laboratory was that they were not receiving the assistance that they needed to overcome their illnesses. The McNichols were wary enough to leave the diagnosis and treatment of diseases like ALS, MS and other neurological disorders to neurologists, and they did not get directly involved in their initial work-ups or treatments in any way, even though some patients pleaded with them for assistance with laboratory studies on chronic infections.

Jared made sure that no one interfered with any physician's diagnosis or treatments, and they would only consider assisting patients that had exhausted all of the traditional medical services available to them. Sometimes the McNichols did get involved in certain patients' programs, if they considered that the patients had been treated unfairly or that their initial diagnoses were obviously wrong or their treatments generally ineffective. For example, they did not consider patients like Jenny Maitland to be classical ALS patients, notwithstanding the original diagnosis by a qualified neurologist. Jared had been trying to get the Belford neurologists to listen to his argument about *Mycoplasma fermentans* and neurodegenerative diseases, but they would not budge from their positions, even though they could offer their patients essentially nothing in the way of effective treatments. These neurologists all too easily sacrificed their patients rather than admit that they did not have all of the answers to the treatment of neurodegenerative diseases.

Most if not all neurologists did not believe in nor were they open-minded enough to consider an infectious basis for most neurodegenerative diseases, even if infections were indirect factors in the process or suspected co-factors for diseases like ALS, MS, Lupus and other diseases. They also refused to listen to Jared as a scientist when he agreed with them that it was unlikely for neurodegenerative diseases to be solely caused by mycoplasmal or other infections. But Jared argued that the Mycoplasmas in combination with other infections, genetic propensity and other factors might be important in neurodegenerative diseases. After all, weren't viral infections of the central nervous system an important neurological problem? Thus the McNichols found that certain infections might be important co-factors that did not cause the disease on their own but could play a role in its progression or in its inception. Thus chronic infections might be more important than realized in diseases like Alzheimer's, Parkinson's, Pick's, and various forms of dementia. In fact, there was already some evidence in the literature indicating the presence of certain nervous system infections in these diseases.

The mindset of most physicians was that if an infection was causing a particular clinical problem, then everyone with that specific infection should come down with exactly the *same* disease. It was the old warn-out 'single agent' cause and effect argument, such as poliovirus caused *only* polio, and that was it. This was certainly not the case for chronic infections, such as Mfi. This type of infection and probably other chronic bacterial and viral infections seemed to be implicated in a variety of diseases and illnesses *but* not in every clinical case. These illnesses were quite diverse, and the observation that every patient did not have the same type(s) of chronic infection(s) had been used over the years to completely dismiss any relationship between illnesses and chronic infections. The fact was that certain syndromes, such as fatiguing illnesses (chronic fatigue syndrome, fibromyalgia syndrome, Gulf War Illnesses), rheumatic diseases (rheumatiod arthritis, ankylosing spondylitis, Lupus, Reiter's), respiratory diseases (asthma, chronic bronchitis, emphysema), vascular diseases (atherosclerosis, vasculitis, endocarditis, myocarditis), gastrointestinal disorders (inflammatory bowel disease, pancreatitis, ulcers) and other conditions, showed very high rates of chronic infections. Even more interesting were patients, whose chronic infections were successfully treated, that subsequently recovered from their illnesses. Thus it seemed ridiculous to dismiss the role of chronic infections out of hand in these illnesses. But this was exactly what most physicians were trained to do.

The notion that chronic infections potentially played a role in so many clinical conditions seemed to fly in the face of conventional medicine. In fact, one of the neurologists who had a lot to hide because of his involvement with the deadly Belford experiments in the prison system complained to Dr. Clyde Bane at The Madison that Jared was interfering with the treatment of his patients. Jared was concerned that this would cause him more problems with Dr. Masters, who was just looking for an excuse to fire him. The neurologist was mainly upset, however, that patients were considering other neurology services rather than Belford's Neurology Department. Fortunately, he really didn't care about any blood tests that the McNichols were performing on the patients that came to his practice. He was just upset at losing patients to other services or other practices. Jared argued that he would have lost the patients anyway, because he had nothing to offer them in the way of effective treatments.

Finally, the Belford neurologists decided that the presence of infections in their patients was all coincidence, and the chronic system-wide infections like *Mycoplasma fermentans* were not in their medical domain, so they simply ignored the obvious findings. Ironically, the neurologists at Belford had never successfully treated an ALS patient to recovery in the history of the Neurology Department, so they should have been at least somewhat interested in the apparent slow but complete recovery of an ALS patient diagnosed by *their* neurology service on Jared's antibiotic and immune enhancement protocols. Not so! In fact, it was just the opposite. They were also very angry that in the future their neurology patients might decide to leave the 'specialist' care given by neurologists and go to a general practitioner, which was exactly what was happening with some of the ALS patients who never went back to Belford. With the slow recovery of Jenny from her 'terminal' disease, the angry Maitlands agreed to be the contact point in Wallsville for the prison guards and employees and their families who became sick with unusual illnesses and neurological diseases that could not be diagnosed by local physicians.

The Maitlands received so many calls that Sandy was tied up most of the day with the problems of the prison employees and their families. Sandy turned out to be quite the social worker, barefoot physician, psychologist and marriage counselor all rolled up in one. She also read everything that she could get her hands on to the castigation of the prison doctors who had been ducking the question of illnesses in the Wallsville Prison, among its employees and in the surrounding community. In fact, the prisons wouldn't comment at all about the illnesses in the community, as they claimed that it was out of their jurisdiction, even if most of the illnesses were localized in prison employees' families.

The local physicians in the Wallsville area didn't know what to do with all the people who were coming down with the Wallsville 'Mystery Illness.' They had no idea how to treat it or even determine what it was. Could it be severe Chronic Fatigue Syndrome? Rheumatoid Arthritis? MS? Lupus? Also, they received little or no assistance from the State prison system, even though most of the sick people in the community were prison employees or their family members. Since a link with the Texas Department of Corrections (TDC) prisons, the largest employers of Wallsville residents, and the 'Mystery Illness' was undeniable, rumors in the community were rampant about the origin of the Disease–it was obviously originating from the Wallsville Prison and other TDC facilities in the area.

People in Wallsville respected Sandy Maitland because of her innate intelligence and the fact that her husband was the Assistant Warden of the Wallsville prison, so Sandy and especially Clayman were in a position to know what was happening in the prison. Unfortunately, they did know. There were lots of prisoners with the 'Mystery Illness' in the prison, so much so, in fact, that the prison hospital was full, and sick prisoners were being transferred to other institutions where hospital beds were available. Clayman was in a difficult position because he was the Assistant Warden of the prison, so he let his outgoing wife Sandy handle all the calls about the health problems that the local people brought to the family.

Sandy Maitland brought some important news and information to the McNichols. She and her comrade-in-arms (some would claim co-conspirator) Cindy Black had found some documents in Austin from the TDC Prison Board Minutes that could be important in determining why there were so many sick citizens in Wallsville. Together with the information that they had received from Freedom of Information (FOI) inquiries, they pieced together a reasonable scenario for what happened in the prisons. It seemed that the TDC Prison Board approved a number of clinical trials at Wallsville and other Texas prisons, including some involving dangerous contagious pathogens and experimental vaccines during the 1970s and 1980s. Some of the clinical trials were sponsored by the DoD or pharmaceutical companies, and most were administered by Marie's old colleague, Dr. Virgil Rook and the Belford College of Medicine. Some were joint trials between Belford and the D. O. Madison.

Sandy also had the results of the State Health Department report on the Trinity River Region. These two items peaked the interest of Jared, who immediately asked Sandy about what she had found. First, they discussed the Texas Environmental Resources Department, which did an environmental study on the water in the Trinity River and surrounding areas and produced a report on their findings. The report was quite extensive and studied several possibilities, but it only focused on the water and water sources, such as wells in the area. The negative results were reported in the local paper with much fanfare.

The report also included the original complaint, which did not even mention the water at all as a possible source for the illnesses. In fact, the complaint named the Wallsville Prison and other prisons in the area as the most logical source, but this was apparently ignored by the Department of Environmental Resources. Sandy was mystified, but Jared mentioned a possible reason. "You know, the Environmental Resources Department is not going to investigate another State Department, especially one as insular as the TDC. What probably happened is that the TDC told them to lay off their departmental area and go do their study elsewhere. Since they could easily access the water supplies in the area, they concentrated on what they could access. This is like the story of the drunk who lost a dime from his pocket at night, but the only place he looked was under a lamp post down the street because that was the only place where there was enough light to see anything. Of course, he never found the dime!"

Sandy immediately understood the analogy. "Exactly! This was our main complaint about the study. They didn't follow up on the most logical source." Sandy continued, "But we did manage to find some interesting documents in the TDC Board of Minutes. As a footnote in the Board minutes, three or four recently retired colonels had replaced the entire upper level medical management staff at the TDC during the late 1970s to mid-1980s. These colonels were from the U. S. Army Medical Corps. Jared thought that was particularly interesting and wondered if any of them had ever been posted at Fort Detrick or other facilities where biological warfare research had been conducted.

The newly hired ex-Army colonels immediately revved up the TDC's clinical prison research programs and the testing of new biologicals and vaccines with Belford and to a lesser degree D. O. Madison and other Texas universities. Sandy was very proud of her find. "The information was right in the TDC Board of Directors minutes." Marie said, "No wonder Dr. Rook was so interested in what was going on in the prison system. I always thought that he was volunteering his time at the prisons to help the prisoners. What hypocrisy! I knew that he was running clinical trials at the prisons, but I had no idea exactly what these trials were all about. Other faculty members in his department, such as Dr. Richard Chair, head of the

Virus Program at Belford, were also heavily involved in the prison trials. So were the Drs. Ling." Sandy perked up and said, "There was a Dr. Ling listed in the minutes, along with a funny sounding company with an X in its name." Marie exclaimed, "Biox?" Sandy answered, "That could be it. That sounds familiar. It was a very peculiar name, and it didn't say exactly what they were going to do with Belford and D. O. Madison, except that they were going to use Mycoplasmas and viruses to stimulate immunity, whatever that means."

Jared placed his hand on Sandy's shoulder. "I think that you just hit the jackpot. Remember, I asked you about Dr. Ming Lon and what he was doing?" Sandy replied as she was going through the stack of papers, "Yes, and I found him along with the . . . . here it is, Biox Incoporated.' Marie said, "Bingo! That's it, Biox! Ming Lon was coming down to Texas from Washington to do research on mycoplasmas in the Texas prison system *and* at Biox, a spin-off from his and my old department at Belford!" Sandy continued, "It gets better. Although the mycoplasma and virus projects that were approved included Belford and the Biox company, I know from my contacts that Dr. Lon and the company scientists conducted these specific experiments at only a few of the Texas prisons, and one of these was Wallsville!" Jared asked, "Were there any cases of unusual or 'Mystery Illnesses' in the communities around the *other* prisons that weren't part of the clinical trials involving Belford, D. O. Madison, Biox or Dr. Lon?" Sandy paused for a moment, looked at her notes and replied, "Not to my knowledge!" Jared said, "That has got to be it! Do you have a list of the types of clinical trials that were being conducted by name, principal investigator and institution?" Sandy said, "You betcha!" Marie added, "You just know that this is all going to fit with the illnesses at Wallsville and the other units where chronic illnesses were reported!" Sandy finally said, "I'm sure it will, and from what data I collected—it all fits!"

Jared raised his fist into the air and punched an imaginary target. "Well Sandy, you have certainly done your homework! This *is* going to be useful! By the way, did Dr. Lon ever test any of the people who lived in Wallsville and had the 'Mystery Illness?' You know, in Dr. Lon's patent entitled 'Pathogenic Mycoplasma,' which was a patent on the detection of *Mycoplasma fermentans* in various illnesses, he indicated that this particular Mycoplasma species was implicated in Chronic Fatigue Syndrome and other autoimmune and neurodegenerative diseases, either as a cause or co-factor." Sandy said, "You know, that's real interesting. We sent more than 100 blood samples from our support group to Dr. Lon, and I know many more were sent from the prison, but Dr. Lon indicated that the community samples were destroyed or went bad and could not be analyzed. He would never tell us anything about the prison samples. So another 20 blood samples were sent to Dr. Lon from the community, but apparently only five could be analyzed, and all of the samples tested positive for Mycoplasma infections. Dr. Lon claimed that only two were *Mycoplasma fermentans*." Marie stated, "That's very suspicious that most of the samples were lost." Jared added, "It sounds just like what the soldiers told us about Dr. Lon. They actually found that he was allowing the veterans' blood samples to sit on the lab bench in his laboratory for weeks before analyzing them. Of course, by then they would all have been negative. We know that blood samples degrade within a few days at room temperature. We have the control experiments to prove it."

After examining the information on the 'Mystery Illness,' which looked less and less like a real mystery with time, the news spread throughout the community. Sandy and Clayman, who were themselves victims of the prison system experiments, would be the focus of continuing attacks from the TDC and the county administrations. These attacks were like those that the McNichols faced and were likely meant to discredit them and keep them from probing further. It became more and more difficult for Sandy to continue to assist the McNichols in gathering information in East Texas on the TDC experiments, and Clayman was under fire to rein in his pesky wife.

Eventually Clayman retired from the TDC, and the Maitlands decided that it was better to leave Texas than continue the fight, and they were right. It would not have ended with Clayman's retirement, and their safety could not be assured. So they eventually moved to Kansas where they had a much quieter life away from Texas and its health and political problems. Unfortunately, no one will ever know how many prisoners died or suffered needlessly under the unethical TDC medical testing programs. Marie said, "We might as well be back in Auschwitz and have Dr. Mengele running the prison hospitals." In fact, unknown to most Americans Dr. Mengele had been a consultant to certain U. S. Government agencies after World War II while he was hiding from other agencies that sought his arrest on an international warrant for crimes against humanity and genocide.

The McNichols were also contacted by a former resident of Wallsville, Cindy Black, who had moved from Wallsville to College Station with her ill son. Her son was eventually diagnosed with a parvovirus B19 infection, but he also had a mycoplasmal infection as well. Cindy felt quite strongly that the Belford study in the prison system with viruses and mycoplasmas resulted in illnesses in several of her neighbors who worked in the Wallsville Prison. Their family physician placed Cindy's son on an immune suppressing protocol using steroids and non-steroidal anti-inflammatory drugs, the standard protocol at the time along with gamma globulin for the treatment of B19 infections, but this actually made her son worse not better. When Cindy contacted Jared, her son was showing most of the signs and symptoms of the Wallsville 'Mystery Illness.' He suffered from severe headaches, gastrointestinal problems, blurred vision, throat spasms, rashes that would come and go, vomiting, knee pain episodes, esophagus spasms, chest pains, fevers that would come and go, incontinence, extreme fatigue, dental problems, among others. And this was not a complete list. The key piece of information that eventually led Cindy to consider Mycoplasmas and contact the McNichols was that she had read that steroid immune suppression actually makes mycoplasmal infections worse not better, and so she suspected that her son also had a mycoplasmal infection along with the B19 parvovirus infection. Consistent with this hypothesis was the result that doxycycline actually made Cindy's son feel better, and his signs and symptoms began to abate but only when he was on the antibiotic.

As her son was beginning to recover from his infections on doxycycline, Cindy made contact with Sandy Maitland, and together they began to sift through information from the minutes of the monthly meetings of the TDC Board of Directors to see what they could find. These TDC documents were a matter of public record, so they sent Freedom of Information requests to the State and went to the State Capitol to begin their hunt for information. Unfortunately, they were told that all of the records had been ordered destroyed. However, whoever gave the order forgot about one copy that was hidden away in an old State building in Austin where ancient records were kept. There they found the old TDC Board minutes that indicated that the Board had approved the Belford-D.

O. Madison clinical study using mycoplasmas and viruses. Some of the more interesting information that they found was that there were also experiments in the prison system using dogs and insect vectors that could spread pathogenic infections through their blood meals. The TDC dogs were affectionately called the 'Belford Dogs' around the prison system, and they were kept in a special unit on the prison grounds.

What was interesting about the TDC Board minutes was that they found evidence of clinical trials that were approved for undescribed species of Mycoplasmas or they were approved for *Mycoplasma pneumoniae* not *Mycoplasma fermentans*. When Jared and Marie analyzed blood samples from the Wallsville community and in particular from the prison employees, they found predominantly *M. fermentans* not *M. pneumoniae*. Marie's old colleagues at Belford (or Biox and Dr. Lon) had probably switched the Mycoplasma samples to the more pathogenic *M. fermentans*! Cindy was convinced that Dr. Lon had substituted *M. fermentans*. She did not trust Dr. Lon, and she considered him dishonest because he published a brief note in a medical journal with some prominent physicians who worked on Chronic Fatigue Syndrome that said that antibodies against mycoplasmas could not be detected in these patients.

At the same time Dr. Lon's own patent that was issued on Mfi indicated that antibodies against Mfi couldn't be detected in nonhuman primates until they were near death from the infection, long after they started showing symptoms. Thus Dr. Lon was caught in a dilemma. If you couldn't detect antibodies in patients, this could have been due to the fact that antibodies were not being made against the mycoplasmas hiding inside cells and tissues, not that the patients did not have the infection. Antibodies could only be detected at later stages of the disease. Marie remembered that Dr. Lon first told her that the Gulf War veterans tested positive for Mfi, and then later he changed his story. Was he under pressure to deny that Mfi was involved in the prisoners' and veterans' illnesses? Since Dr. Lon was acting so suspicious, it seemed likely that he was trying to satisfy his handlers, rather than seek the truth.

Interestingly, Marie's old department chairman, Dr. Virgil Rook, was the principal investigator on most of these TDC prison studies, and some of the studies also contained the name of Dr. Ming Lon. Dr. Rook would not speak with Cindy, and Cindy's conversations with Dr. Lon were less than satisfactory. She considered Dr. Lon a very deceptive person, fully capable of lying about his results to reflect the official stance that Mfi and other mycoplasmas were not involved in human diseases, notwithstanding his own patents and publications on the topic. Perhaps because of the growing flap about the Gulf War veterans and prison experiments, Dr. Lon was under increasing pressure to deny that Mfi could be involved in any human disease. Cindy was never able to obtain a straightforward answer about Mfi and disease from Dr. Lon. Perhaps he was under the constant threat of death, if he dared to tell the American people the truth about Mfi?

In the meantime, Sandy and Cindy were passing out the information packets that Jared had made up for the TDC prison employees. Cindy later told Jared over the phone and in a letter, "When I carried your documents and those that we dug up on the prison testing programs to some of my son's physicians, one stated, *"Maybe they didn't realize what they were releasing."* Another stated, *"Now I know why we have so many rare illnesses in this area."* Cindy told Jared, "This is not what I wanted to hear. I wanted them to tell me there was nothing to it. Instead, they confirmed what Sandy and I had concluded. These dangerous pathogens had been released in our community with complete lack of regard for the inmates, the guards who worked at the prisons and the guards' families. Now they have brought it home to the community at large."

Cindy was beginning to feel the heat from the TDC prison officials. Jared said to Cindy, "What you and Sandy have found was completely consistent with our studies on the prison employees and their family members. We could come to no other conclusion than the prisons must have been used by Belford, the D. O. Madison and companies like Biox for the testing of dangerous biological agents." Jared and Marie found out over the years that one of the most important reasons that the institutions in the Medical Center went after them so vigorously and brutally was to discredit and discourage them, and to drive them out of Texas (or eliminate them) in order to keep their unethical, amoral and illegal medical experiments from ever being exposed to public scrutiny.

Cindy eventually went back to school in Central Texas and entered a graduate public health program, and she did her masters thesis on the clinical research programs in the State prison system. Although her thesis committee was originally enthusiastic about the entire scope of her thesis, the authorities and graduate school administrators eventually found out about her thesis topic and got into the act. Her committee then decided that most of her thesis would have to be deleted from the final version before they could approve it. Cindy had found out the hard way the types of 'dirty tricks' the system can use to silence its critics. Cindy, Sandy and Jared and Marie would find that whistle blowers were not appreciated, and they usually ended up broke, jobless and outcasts of the very system that they were trying to save. Sometimes even worse things could happen to them. In Texas too often the whistle blowers died under inexplicable circumstances, as was the case for several of the McNichols' colleagues.

The third member of what Jared was calling "The Three Moms" (as they later liked to call themselves) was Beth Mowgall of College Station, Texas. Beth, who had a daughter who had been sick with a mysterious illness, had attended a conference on rheumatic illnesses that Jared was speaking at, and she met Marie who was inadvertently sitting in front of her in the audience. Marie and Beth struck up a conversation, and Marie mentioned during a break that she should contact Sandy Maitland of Wallsville and Cindy Black of College Station. Beth indicated that she used to live in Wallsville, and she eventually called Sandy and Cindy to share notes on the Wallsville Mystery Illnesses.

Thus a new friendship began, and even though this alliance would become strained over the years because of the pressure atmosphere and politics surrounding the Wallsville 'Mystery illness,' the 'Three Moms' had a lot in common because of the illnesses in their families. Eventually Beth met with Cindy and Sandy, and it was Sandy who usually drove to College Station in her trusted Chevy Suburban. Sandy always seemed perfectly willing to travel anywhere, just as long as it was within the range of her Chevy Suburban. The massive size of the vehicle alone probably proved valuable, since they could cart around massive amounts of boxed documents, and it was hard to harm them with some kind of phony, orchestrated accidents that some unknown persons had tried repeatedly on Marie.

The Three Moms shared boxes of information on that first trip, too much to digest, in fact, for the next several months, but eventually everything began to come together. Beth was well known in the area of Central Texas for running a patient support group for chronic illnesses. Her group was named, in part, for the alterations in health caused by chronic fungal, viral and bacterial infections. The reason that Beth was so interested in infections like Mfi was that she suspected that her daughter became sick when they lived next to the Wallsville Prison that they later found out was involved in vaccine experiments using Mycoplasmas and viruses. Could the illness in her child be related to the same 'Mystery Illness' of Wallsville, which in turn was related to experimental testing programs on prisoners using mycoplasmas and viruses? Beth followed this story for many years and even wrote about it in her newsletter, which she distributed free of charge to anyone who asked for a copy. Beth was particularly disappointed in Dr. Lon and his responses to her questions about Mfi, the prison illnesses and the illnesses in the communities around the prisons. Dr. Lon was probably directed by his superiors at the U. S. Army Institute of Pathology Research not to talk to civilians about Mfi or any testing programs in the prison system, and he dutifully followed his orders. In general, he refused to discuss the topic with the Three Moms, with the exception of a brief conversation with Cindy. Thus using her newsletter Beth began to take aim at Dr. Lon and his involvement in the TDC testing programs. Although never widely distributed, Beth did raise a major regional stink in her newsletter that still hasn't been settled in the Great State of Texas.

One aspect of the TDC-Belford-Madison clinical trials at the Wallsville Prison and other State prisons that was rarely discussed was what happened to the prisoners who died during the experiments? This was a question that no one in the prison system dared to ask, because they were told not to reveal anything about the ongoing clinical trials at the prisons. At least most of them didn't end up like one of Jared's students, a pathologist named Samuel Pen. Dr. Pen was studying with Jared when he discovered a new gene involved in the spread or metastasis of breast cancer. After completing his studies with Jared and passing his research project on to two visiting physician-scientists from Japan who were also studying with Jared, Dr. Pen was appointed to the pathology faculty at the State medical school in Galveston, Texas. Since this medical school had a proud history and was the first medical school in the state, it was by Texas law directed to be responsible for the autopsies on prisoners who died while in custody at TDC prisons.

During the time that Jared and Marie were finding that the 'Mystery Illness' of Wallsville was linked to mycoplasmal and possibly other infections in the Wallsville Prison run by the TDC, Clayman Maitland quietly indicated to Jared and Marie that at the height of the prison testing programs they were losing a few prisoners per week at the Wallsville unit alone. What he meant was that the prison 'Mystery Illnesses' were fatal to perhaps hundreds of prisoners at that one TDC facility alone each year. Since there were several TDC prisons involved in the testing programs, there could have been several hundreds or even thousands of prisoners dying each year in the State prison system of unknown and unusual illnesses related to the clinical testing programs run by Belford and other institutions.

Since the three ex-Army colonels took over the Medical Division of the TDC, information on prison fatalities was no longer available to the public, and so it was difficult to find any information on the deaths of prisoners at TDC facilities. After Dr. Pen was appointed Assistant Director of the Autopsy Service at the State University medical school in Galveston, he tried to look into this after a long conversation with Jared. Dr. Pen became suspicious, because the prison fatalities were not being sent to his service for autopsy as dictated by State law. What Dr. Pen found when he dug deeper was that the prisoners who died under unusual circumstances at the Wallsville unit and other prison units within the TDC were being sent to a U. S. Army base outside of San Antonio for autopsy, instead of the medical school at Galveston where by law they should have been sent. This was also confirmed by at least one of the prison guards at Wallsville during a visit to Austin to see the McNichols to get help for his own 'Mystery Illness.' Jared and Marie found Mfi in this guard, who related to them in a subsequent visit that he was responsible for transporting the bodies from the Wallsville unit and other TDC prisons to the Army base outside of San Antonio. When the Army was finished with the bodies, he was called and then ordered to take them to a private crematorium built for just this purpose on a large private tract of land in Central Texas. There the dead prisoners and their medical records were reduced to ashes.

The prison cremation program was all very secret and carefully hidden from public view and scrutiny. The guard also told Jared that all of the medical records were copied by the Army before being sent to the private crematorium. If any medical records were missing and later found, it was the guard's responsibility to bring them directly to the Army base after they were found at the Wallsville unit and other prisons. After the Army was finished with the records, he was instructed to take them to the secret crematorium for destruction. He didn't know if the prisoners' ashes were ever given to relatives who requested them, but few probably went through the cumbersome procedures to receive their relative's ashes.

Unfortunately for Dr. Pen, raising the issue of the missing prisoners' bodies may have ultimately resulted in his premature death, of questionable natural causes. Dr. Pen died in his mid-40s, but his death was never thoroughly investigated. His family was told that he had a possible heart defect, but Jared and Marie found that explanation somewhat weak since he was a physician himself, and he never mentioned the problem while he was with Jared in Austin. Was he given Mfi or some other infection or drug that weakened his heart? The answer to this will probably never be known for sure, but one of the organ systems attacked by Mfi is the heart, and victims of Mfi infections often complain of heart problems and then later die of heart attacks due to endocarditis or myocarditis, infections of the heart. Over the years several of Jared's protégés would die under mysterious circumstances.

Jared felt strongly that one of the reasons for a fatal Mfi infection was weakening of the heart valves and coagulation problems from vasculitis, resulting in thrombosis, blood clots and blockage of the heart arteries. Vasculitis, or inflammation of the vascular system, probably occurred when Mfi or other infections invaded the endothelial cells lining the blood vessel walls. When this happens, the endothelial cells release substances that cause increased coagulation of the blood, and eventually this results in the formation of blood clots that could clog the heart blood vessels and other arteries and small blood vessels of other organs.

When Jared learned of Dr. Pen's untimely death, he was angry and wanted the State District Attorney's Office to launch an investigation. But since the TDC and the DA were ultimately under the same criminal justice system in Texas, it was fruitless to dig any further into what really happened to Dr. Pen. It was reminiscent of the tragedy of Dr. Cannon. The issue of the dead TDC prisoners was never resolved, and an analogy with the Nazi testing programs of the Third Reich in the death camps and prisons of Eastern Europe of 50 years prior was never far from the thoughts of

Marie, Jared or The Three Moms. They often asked themselves how this could happen in a 'free' and 'democratic' America? They all considered themselves patriotic and strong supporters of the United States and the American way of life, but the events in Texas had shaken their belief systems.

The U. S. Navy SEALs thank the McNichols

One Sunday afternoon Marie and Jared received a call from Dale DeJon, the Navy Lt. Commander and SEAL that Marie and Jared had rescued from losing his eyesight. He was going through Houston with his family on a brief visit and wanted to bring his wife and children to Austin to visit the McNichols. They agreed on a time and place to meet near Queenswood, because Jared did not want to agitate Dr. Masters who might be informed by the rats in his department of the visit of a Navy SEAL officer. The U. S. Navy SEALs are such an elite Special Forces unit that this would certainly draw the attention of the D. O. Madison administration. Also, the fact that the SEALs had problems with Gulf War Illnesses might strain the widely publicized myth that the ill veterans from the Gulf War were malingers and malcontents who were prone to psychological problems. The very nature of SEAL training precluded such psycho-mumbo-jumbo explanations. Most of these sick SEAL veterans had been to war before and not suffered the chronic illnesses, and they were not unstable or prone to psychological problems.

On the day of the visit the McNichols were waiting for Dale and his family to arrive at their home in Queenswood. The McNichols decided to take the DeJons to their country club, the Queenswood Country Club, for a mid-day meal to discuss Dale's bout with Gulf War Illness. While they waited for the DeJons to arrive, Marie was teary-eyed as she began talking to Jared. She had just received an anonymous letter with no return address. It was post-marked Austin in the area of the Medical Center. Marie said, "This letter is awful! Listen to it! She read parts of the letter to Jared. *"What was that nonsense you delivered at your so-called seminar!" "How dare you disgrace the good name of The D. O. Madison." "It is common knowledge that the only way you got into the D. O. Madison was by sleeping with Jared McNichols." "The fact that he is using his position here at The Madison to house a madwoman in his department shows me he has no ethics!" "It is a complete conflict of interest! Let's keep the bedrooms separate from the laboratories and act like upright citizens."* It was signed *'Concerned.'* Jared asked, "Who do you think wrote it?" Marie answered, "I don't think! I know! It was written by Clement Masters–just look at the phrasing. 'How dare you disgrace the good name of The D. O. Madison.' That is strictly Clement Masters. I have friends in the FBI and they can lift a finger print off this and have it analyzed." Jared said, "If it is Masters, it does not bode too well for us here! Of course, the style is completely consistent with his more formal letters to me." Marie continued, "Masters is so influenced by Drs Geldter, Krappner and Belcher! These people hate me!" Jared said, "It doesn't sound like he needs those three to stoke his hatred. If it is him, and I think you're right about the letter, he is even more over the edge than I thought." Dr. Masters was over the edge, and in fact, he was probably an outright psychopath. Even his administrators at the Madison knew this and feared him.

Marie was distraught about the letter. "The irony is that I don't know any of them! Masters and the rest never took the time to check out my résumé. They have no idea that I earned perhaps one of the toughest Ph.D.s in the world. They have architected a smear campaign against me and have blocked my chances of a faculty position anywhere!" She said, "I'll never forget how Dr. Blair told me that there were serious accusations against me, but then he refused to tell me what they were!" She continued, "He told me I have powerful enemies!" She tried to talk between sobs, "And that he, for one, was not interested in being responsible for my career. I have been accused of everything under the sun and of being a whore! I tell you Jared, all my life people have been conducting whisper campaigns against me and I don't know why!"

Marie started sobbing. Once she regained her composure she continued. "The odd part is that ever since my phony uncle visited here, I hear exactly the same lies that he screamed at me when I was nine years old, only now it's coming from the Madison faculty! And look at how people like Dr. Clever and others have looked at me since I recovered from my near fatal illness. They were not happy to see me survive, I tell you, and something beyond my science is involved." Jared told Marie, "I don't think that you are who you think you are, Marie." She replied, "Look, I'm me! I've always been me!" Jared said, "I've noticed that people of power and position always seem to act deferential toward you. And you have had some highly unusual experiences that ordinary people don't have." Marie finally stopped crying and said, "You can sure say that again. But do you think I deserve this kind of treatment or have in some way engendered this hatred?" As Marie wiped her eyes, Jared said, "No! Absolutely not! This is deranged! And I don't understand it. It really defies reason. But whatever it is, some of the hatred is now directed at me too." She said, "I'm sorry!" Jared continued, "It's not your fault, Marie." She responded, "I have always played by the rules in my academic career, and I am sick of everyone questioning my integrity and my competence as a scientist!"

Jared tried to give Marie some advice and build back her self-esteem. "There are those who truly respect you. Just don't conclude from the rat-pack in my department that no one respects you. Remember what I have always told you. Don't expect to be liked for being the best. Remember how many of your supporters warned you that professional jealousy can reach untold heights, especially when someone who is pretty like you makes a significant finding or breakthrough." Marie countered, "You may think I am pretty, but I am only pretty in terms of the other female scientists." Jared continued, "Whatever! You're unusual, and that's why I love you! And I know you are a sweet and caring person." Marie said as she wiped her last tears, "Thanks! . . . . I love you too!" Jared said, "Sooner or later we will get to the bottom of the mystery about you!"

The DeJons arrive to visit the McNichols

There was a knock on the door, and both Marie and Jared turned their attention to their visitors and headed for the front door. As Jared opened the door Dale, who was on a brief leave before deploying to Haiti, was standing there in his battle fatigues with his wife Lorraine and two little girls of age less than six that were dressed in very pretty dresses. Dale had some leave time before he left, and he wanted to visit the McNichols and personally thank them for the help they had given him and his SEAL Team. After meeting at the McNicols home in Queenswood, the two parties departed for the Country Club, about a half-dozen blocks away. Dale, still in his battle fatigues, wondered if his attire would cause a problem at the fancy Country Club, but Marie and Jared convinced him that the people at the Country Club were very patriotic and would be very pleased to see him and his family visit the club. During Desert Storm the Country Club flew American Flags and yellow ribbons all over the facility to indicate their support for the troops, so Dale was assured that he and his family would receive a warm welcome.

They arrived at the Country Club in two cars, because the DeJons had to leave directly after the meal and drive back to Houston. The main dining facility at the Country Club was a large, single story structure with a high roof. It was an elegant place inside, and the decor was done in a variety of shades of greens to blend in with the wooded area where the McNichols lived. Dale was escorted to the table with his wife Lorraine and their two little girls and the McNichols. Dale said as they sat down, "We are so glad to be able to come to the Country Club with you." Marie answered, "Why thank you. We're thrilled that you are feeling better and that your vision has improved. I was horrified that you were actually going blind, and the details of your illness in your letter made me cry!" Dale replied, "Well, I've come here with my family to thank you both personally for saving my life and the lives of my Team. We are forever thankful–the SEALs won't ever forget what you two have done, and if there is anything that we can do for you, just say the word!" Jared joked, "Well, we both may need jobs!"

Jared laughed but he then noticed that Dale was looking very serious at the two of them across the table. Jared said, "I was just kidding." Unfortunately, Jared was not kidding, but he was certainly not going to ruin the festivities to discuss the McNichols' problems. Dale said, "You know, the antibiotic worked almost immediately! Before long my vision started to return, and I no longer had the fevers, night sweats and joint pain." Lorraine added, "I believe Christ put you two here for a very special purpose, and you will always be in our family's prayers." Marie replied, "Thank you Lorraine; Dale's recovery has given me the will to continue." Jared said, "To be honest with you, Marie and I have received a lot of flack and ridicule for our work on Gulf War Illnesses." Dale responded, "I am truly sorry for that. My commanding officer and most of my fellow Delta One colleagues think of you both as heroes. In fact, we are going to make you honorary U. S. Navy SEALs. You two will be the first honorary SEALs in the history of the Navy." Jared smiled, "That's quite an honor, Dale, and one that Marie and I will cherish. You don't have any idea how resistant the DoD has been to our work."

Dale then became somber. He waited until Lorraine and the girls had gone to the bathroom before telling the McNichols the message he had brought from Fort Bragg and Delta One Headquarters. "I have been asked to warn you that your lives are in jeopardy if you continue to come forward to help the veterans." Marie responded first, "But Dale, we must continue! There are other Dales out there, some who are not soldiers, marines or SEALs, some who are innocent children who may be victimized by the infections that we found." She continued, "And I gave my word to God that I would help those who were similarly afflicted when he allowed me to survive my near fatal illness." Jared tried to lighten up the atmosphere by saying, "There you have it, Dale! We are not going to stop as long as we can help families like yours." The discussion continued, and Jared and Marie explained their laboratory results with the veterans' blood samples and how they found the unusual Mfi that Dr. Lon discovered at the U. S. Army Institute of Pathology Research. Dale seemed particularly interested in what they had found in the laboratory with the veterans' blood samples.

At this point Lorraine, who had returned from the bathroom with her girls, came within hearing range, stopped and had begun to cry. Dale stood up, and he excused himself to go for a brief walk with Lorraine and the girls. Lorraine did not want to hear such serious talk after Dale recovered from his illness. Dale then returned in a few minutes, but Lorraine continued on with the girls. After they left, Dale spoke, "Since Loraine has gone for a walk, I can tell you more. I don't want Lorraine to worry, and it is against orders to share the secrets of our missions with our families." He continued, but you two are family, and I already consider you SEALs. Aside from your Gulf War Syndrome research, the work that has placed you both at some risk, Marie is at additional risk because of who she is."

Marie was a bit taken aback by Dale's last comment. "What do you mean by that? All my life people have been asking me who I am? As if they know something that I don't know." Dale said, "I can't divulge all the information, but the near-fatal illness that you had while you were working at Belford College of Medicine was no accident, and we know that you have been poisoned on several occasions, especially when you were both out of the country." Jared responded, "Well, we know all about this, because we had to live through it, but how did you know about it?" Dale answered, "Through our contacts in the intelligence community." He continued in a soft voice so that no one at another table could hear him. "And I'm almost embarrassed to say, some of my colleagues were actually ordered to eliminate you at one point." Marie asked, "I don't understand?" Dale explained, "We are a 'special operations' unit." He continued, "I probably shouldn't even be telling you this, but we do special assignments for the Government, like the assassination of Pablo Escobar." He paused, "My own unit is part of the Presidential Assassination Squad, and we perform some very special duties on occasion."

Jared smiled while Marie took a deep breath. "I see!" Marie turned to Jared and said, "You see, Jared, I told you that my near fatal illness was no accident! Dale, I told Jared that it was not in my imagination the way certain scientists looked at me when I recovered my health and began lecturing again. They were not happy to see me recover, but I don't know these people that well, so I didn't understand their hatred." She paused, "Particularly the hatred of Dr. Clement Masters, the President of the D. O. Madison." Dale said, "I am not at liberty to tell you everything, but I urge you to watch what you eat and drink and where you go. Always ask to see the bottle or can when you order soft drinks and open it yourself! Change your routine, and don't accept invitations from people you don't know or trust. Don't sit near windows, and don't accept gifts from people you don't completely trust." He continued, "And be especially careful when the two of you leave the country. We have sent your picture to all the military bases and Special Forces units around the world. They all know who you are. We will do our best to protect you." Marie said, "Thank you, Dale, for warning us!"

Jared wanted to know why there was such a mystery surrounding Marie. "We're trying to deduce why Marie is such a target for harassment and this cloak and dagger game. I don't have all the answers, but I do know that numerous attempts have been made on Marie over many years. It can't be just for our work on veterans' illnesses." Dale added, "In fact she holds the record for more attempts on a U. S. citizen and civilian than any other person in U. S. history." Jared said, "Sooner or later we will unravel the mystery of Marie's identity, but it probably didn't help matters getting involved in the Gulf War Illness problem."

At this point Lorraine and the two girls returned to the table. Lorraine sat down and made sure that the two girls were seated properly and said, "Marie, you and Jared are always in our prayers. But I think that you need to stop your work with the veterans, for your own safety." Marie answered, "Well Loraine, when I had my near death experience I was told that I had to come forward if I heard of anyone in the future who was sick like I was, and I had to promise to help others who were ill. Even if it meant setting myself up for extreme danger and ridicule. I am just following those divine orders!" Dale added, "Thank God for people like you two! You two scientists are truly courageous and compassionate."

Marie wanted to leave Dale with one more thought. "Dale, I have to tell you one more thing and then I say let's enjoy this dinner and fellowship." Dale answered, "Shoot!" Marie said, "I am convinced that a powerful and influential economic machine is responsible for this horror. In fact, I concur with a friend of mine who is the Director of Special Investigations at the Justice Department in Washington. His specialty is to flush out eugenics proponents. He has been following the collusion between the organized crime groups and the defense industry. Both Jared and I feel that there seems to be a link between some Las Vegas-based group and small, and perhaps even large, biotechnology companies that do defense work." Dale then interrupted Marie. "I have to tell you that you two have stumbled into a major hornet's nest. Just watch your back! Be very careful!"

Then Dale shook his head. He wanted to change the subject with Lorraine and the girls present, so he became instantly jovial. "I can't get over it. To me you still look like a little high school cheerleader!" Marie laughed, "But I was a cheerleader!" Jared interrupted and smiled at the two young girls, "I say we go to the buffet table and check it out." The girls smiled back, and they all seemed to be in agreement with Jared's suggestion. Marie and Jared would not forget the warning that Dale gave to them that day in Queenswood. They would try to be more careful, but they would not abandon the veterans and the prison guards and their families, no matter what the cost.

The Veterans and their family problems

One of the many families that the McNichols helped during the course of their research was the family of Capt. Richard Hamlin, who fought with the 101ˢᵗ Airborne Division in Southern Iraq during the Gulf War. Capt. Hamlin, his wife Julie and their young daughter Linda would all become victims of the war. When the Hamlins contacted the McNichols, the entire family was sick with unknown illnesses that at the time Capt. Hamlin thought was directly related his service in the Gulf War.

This was a pattern that Jared and Marie would see over and over, and it would eventually lead to a medical publication on the sick family members of the Gulf War veterans. The VA and DoD hated the McNichols for this study, because it directly contradicted their own statements and pronouncements that the families were not getting sick when the veterans returned from the Gulf War and slowly became ill. To this day any illnesses in the family members of Gulf War veterans as a consequence of transmission of chronic infections from the ill veterans to their immediate family members had been completely and utterly denied, and the VA had even gone so far as to fund a purposely flawed study that was skewed in an attempt to 'prove' that there was no such thing as illness transmission from Gulf War Illness patients to their immediate family members. In fact, just the opposite was true, and the VA knew it. They were purposely lying to the American people, possibly to prevent criticism and fear in the communities where military bases were located.

Jared was receiving many calls a week from family members of sick veterans who had themselves become slowly sick after the veterans presented with unknown chronic illnesses or Gulf War Illness. One of those families was the Hamlins. When Capt. Richard Hamlin returned from the Gulf, he even burned his combat fatigues and anything else he brought back so that nothing could be transferred to his family from the Persian Gulf. However, within six months after he returned he became sick with severe flu-like symptoms that would not pass, including chronic fatigue, skin rashes, diarrhea, severe headaches, memory loss and other signs and symptoms. Then his wife came down with similar problems, including gynecological problems and severe uterine swelling and bloating. She also had thyroid problems. Then their five year-old daughter began to show the same problems and was unable to keep awake at school where she had behavioral problems. She had severe fatigue, rashes and bloody diarrhea and her teeth were falling out.

The Hamlins met with and found that other families were having exactly the same medical problems. When they tried to get help from the Army, it was all denied—the official policy was that the illnesses could not be related. The family members were told that they weren't sick or that their problems were not related to the Gulf War or to veterans. The families found out about the antibiotic treatments for Gulf War Illness that the McNichols were advising, and the Hamlins even attempted to get the Army Medical Center in Washington DC to put them on the appropriate antibiotics, such as doxycycline. Their military doctor told them, *"That's interesting, we will be putting everyone on doxycycline soon."* However two days later this same doctor recanted and said, *"I wasn't supposed to say that just yet."* Later he said, *"What antibiotics? I didn't say anything about antibiotics!"* Capt. Hamlin concluded that his superiors in the Medical Corps had told him to shut up about the possibility of infections and antibiotic treatment.

It was clear to the Hamlins that the Army wasn't going to admit that there was any biological cause for their illnesses, and they weren't even going to admit that spouses and children could come down with illnesses similar to Gulf War Illness. Thus they did not want to admit that an infection might be involved. It was a blatant pattern of lies that would be repeated thousands of times all over the country by the DoD and the VA. The Hamlins told the McNichols that the Army refused to give them the appropriate medicines for their illnesses. "We don't know why the Army is refusing to help the soldiers and their families." Fortunately, the Hamlins managed to get antibiotics from sympathetic civilian physicians, and the entire family eventually recovered. They wrote to the McNichols to say *"We believe that it is a small group of doctors who are bad, because any of the military doctors who tried to help us were reassigned or frightened, or were left out of the loop. We have given up on the system at this point. We thank you, Jared and Marie, for having the courage and the compassion to help us."* In another letter Julie Hamlin stated *"The military lied about Agent Orange, they lied about radiation poisoning, and today they are lying about Gulf War Illness, and they are getting away with it."* Julie should know, because before she married Richard she was a noncommissioned officer in an Army intelligence unit based at Fort Meade, the top-secret headquarters of the National Security Agency.

The McNichols meet the Hamlins at Fort Meade

After their occasional telephone calls, mostly about Gulf War Illness and its treatment and the harassment that the Hamlins were receiving at the hands of the Army Medical Corps, the McNichols decided to visit the Hamlins on one of their trips to the Washington area. Capt. Hamlin was posted at Fort Meade, Maryland, home of the National Security Agency (NSA) and the Defense Intelligence Agency (DIA). As a part of Echelon, the NSA's top-secret electronic intelligence gathering program, it was probably the most important 'signals' intelligence base in the U. S. It was responsible for monitoring all telephone, fax, radio and internet traffic world-wide. The civilian and military intelligence experts at Fort Meade were by far the best in the world at electronic intelligence.

The McNichols would be entering the grounds of Fort Meade but only as far as base housing. Fort Meade was situated along the Washington-Baltimore Parkway in the gently rolling Maryland hills between Washington DC and Baltimore. The U. S. Army fort itself was named for a famous Civil War general who was considered too conservative by Lincoln and was later replaced. The McNichols would not go into the super-secret part of the base, but they would enter the area containing base housing. As they drove down the military streets with their military names past groups of housing duplexes, they ended up on a street where Capt. Hamlin's duplex, which looked just like all of the other duplexes, was situated on a small hill. As Marie and Jared got out of their rental car, they heard the Hamlin's two Dalmatians notifying the Hamlins that the McNichols had arrived.

The McNichols were greeted at the door by Capt. Hamlin, an Army officer in his mid-30s, his pretty wife Julie, who was formally in the Army and stationed at Fort Meade before they started a family, and Linda, a shy, pretty dark haired seven year-old in a flowered dress and, of course, their two rambunctious Dalmatians. The Hamlins were very happy to see that the McNichols had survived the onslaught in Austin due to their research on Gulf War Illnesses. After they met and hugged each other, they had a long discussion that covered a number of topics. Capt. Hamlin, who had a sly grin then retrieved a bag which contained the symbols for the surprise he had for the McNichols. He was proud to pull out Army fatigue caps with the eagle insignia of a full Colonel on each one. He told them, "Well, you know that you were approved by the commanding general of the post and by the Special Forces to be Honorary Colonels, so we are just trying to make you feel at home here at Fort Meade." He looked inside each cap to inspect that the names were correctly spelled. Each one had either COL M. McNichols or COL J. McNichols printed on the identity flap. Marie and Jared were pleasantly surprised to receive such a warm welcome at the base, and they were especially pleased to be recognized by the officers who were present as honorary fellow officers with the rank of Colonel. As it turned out they were two of only six civilians to ever be appointed to this honorary rank in the U. S. Army. The significance to the McNichols was that although most of the medical officers did not support them, at least the line officers and the fighting soldiers were behind them. Capt. Hamlin chuckled and kept reminding them that a Special Forces Colonel was worth at least two Medical Corps Colonels. The McNichols laughed and enjoyed the camaraderie with the other officers.

For the remainder of the McNichols' visit that day, they didn't take off their caps, and they received salutes from the other officers who had come by to visit with the McNichols. Each one of the soldiers began by saluting and then thanking the McNichols for their help in regaining their health and the health of their family members. It turned out to be the highlight of a very bad year for the McNichols. Jared in particular was quite conscious of the fact that immediate family members could come down with Gulf War Illness, since he had been comparing the types of infections in sick family members to the sick veterans.

Jared found that for the most part when the military family members got sick, it was only after a veteran returned from the Gulf War, and their signs and symptoms were similar to the sick veteran in the family. However, there were some interesting differences. For example, many of the children that were less than 10 years old were diagnosed with autism, a behavioral disorder characterized by communication and speech problems and impaired social skills. Repetitive and obsessive behavior and even self-injury or aggression often appeared in these patients. In the case of Linda, she had changed from a very extroverted, top student to a very withdrawn student with near failing grades. She no longer wanted to interact with the other students in her classes, she was tired all the time, and she exhibited repetitive behavior and short-term memory loss. But she was not a classic autistic child. She felt very bad all of the time with aches and pains but would only talk to her mother about her symptoms. Julie still showed some of the excessive abdominal swelling that made people think that she was pregnant, and the whole family still had some chronic fatigue and other problems, even after almost a year on and off doxycycline. At least now they were showing the signs of recovery. Richard could even run again after having reached a point where he felt that he couldn't even lift his legs.

After getting the run-around for some time at the U. S. Army Medical Center in Washington, the Hamlins decided to contact the McNichols about their health problems. Their military physicians were denying that the family illnesses had anything to do with Richard's service in the Gulf War, even though all three had many signs and symptoms in common. So they were extremely happy that the McNichols had come to their base this day, and it gave everyone the opportunity to have a one-on-one conversation with the couple. The Hamlins had prepared a Bar-B-Q dinner for everyone in honor of the McNichols visit, and the neighbors also brought special dishes just for the McNichols. Everyone had a grand time, and Jared and Marie were busy answering question after question about Gulf War Illnesses. Obviously, the Army kept its officers and veterans in the dark about the condition and its treatment. The sad point brought out at the Bar-B-Q was that the DoD was still trying to diagnose Gulf War Illness as PTSD, and there were a number of jokes at the dinner about the base psychiatrist who kept diagnosing every Gulf War veteran with PTSD. As it turned out, he really didn't believe in the diagnosis for the Gulf War veterans, but he went along with his commanding officer because he and his CO did not want to make waves. It would take years for the McNichols to uncover the ugly politics and the reasons for the continual denial, and their search for the truth would evolve into a dangerous quest. It was a quest that would eventually uncover some of the hidden reasons for the terrorism that was now directed at the United States and its allies.

After the food and drink were gone and the Hamlins' friends and neighbors had finally left, the McNichols sat down with the Hamlins for a more serious discussion. Julie said, "We found something interesting in our neighbor's trash that we would like to share with you." Julie noticed the expression on Jared's face, laughed and quickly explained. "My neighbor is an officer in one of the Intel units here at Fort Meade, and his wife is a third-year medical student at the Uniform Services Health Sciences University at the Naval Medical Center in Washington. She ran out of storage room because our little bungalows don't have much space as you can see, and she was throwing away her second-year notes and syllabuses from the various medical school lecturers. I was curious and found these pathology notes and the course syllabuses and thought that you might be interested." Jared was quite familiar with this technique of teaching medical students, since he had done this for years in the Pathology Block at the Medical School in Austin. He immediately picked up the book entitled Pathology Syllabus VI from the pile of similar books on different blocks that medical students must memorize. The lecturers' notes had been bound in the different syllabuses with different colored covers signifying the various blocks or subjects. Julie continued, "I see you're interested in the Pathology Syllabus. As Jared went to the red tab placed carefully in the syllabus, Julie said, "A Navy Commander named Ellen Martins working at the U. S. Army Institute of Pathology Research lectured on *Mycoplasma fermentans incognitus,* and a summary of her lecture on the mycoplasma is in the syllabus." As Jared opened the syllabus and began scanning the material for a few seconds he remarked, "That's interesting, I didn't think that the military publicly acknowledged Mfi." Julie responded, "Well, from what my neighbor said when I asked her, they don't, but this is *their* medical school, the only medical school for active duty military personnel. Since it's their experts and their materials, I assume that they don't publicly spread these books around. What I found interesting, and I think that you and Marie will also find this interesting, is that although they deny it now, they knew all along that Mfi was a dangerous infection." Julie immediately showed Jared where to look in the Pathology Syllabus VI from 1994. It was the section on *M. fermentans* by Commander Ellen Martins of the U. S. Navy. It read as follows:

Mycoplasma fermentans

The most serious presentation of *M. fermentans* infection is that of a fulminating systemic disease that begins as a flu-like illness. Patients rapidly deteriorate developing severe complications, including adult respiratory distress syndrome, disseminated intravascular coagulation, and/or multiple organ failure.

The organs of patients with fulminant *M. fermentans* infections exhibit extensive necrosis. Necrosis is most pronounced in lung, liver, spleen, lymph nodes, adrenal glands, heart and brain. *M. fermentans* is identified in areas of necrosis, particularly in the advancing margin of necrosis, by the immunohisto-chemistry using specific anti-*M. fermentans* and *M. fermentans incognitus* antibiody and/or by in situ hybridization assays using cloned *incognitus* strain DNA. Mycoplasma-like particles are found intracellularly and extracellularly by electron microscopy.

After reading the above introduction to *M. fermentans,* Jared read the remainder of the section and then the student's notes. Suddenly he was not feeling so well. When he got to the section on the treatment of Mfi, there was a doxycycline protocol, almost exactly the same dose and treatment schedule as Jared had been recommending. The military had obviously known all along that Mfi was a dangerous infection that could lead to a fatal disease *and* that could be successfully treated with doxycycline. Jared suddenly felt a pain in the pit of his stomach, as if someone had poked him with a sharp stick. While this was going on, Marie and Richard were laughing and playing with the Hamlin's two Dalmations that were running around the room and licking Marie's face.

Jared decided not to spoil Marie's fun, because she would just get upset at seeing the summary on Mfi. The syllabus indicated that the DoD knew all along about the dangers of Mfi. Jared said to Julie, "Not only did they know all about Mfi, but they also knew how to effectively treat it! You know, if these military physicians were out of the Army and in private practice, they would all be sued for malpractice!" Julie said, "It gets worse. Not only did they know all about Mfi. They knew how to treat it, and they purposely ignored their own directives on how to identify it and care for patients. They ignored our pleas to test for Mfi, and they even ignored these sections of the Pathology Syllabus from *their own medical school.*"

In the less than the five minutes that it took to examine the Pathology Syllabus section on Mfi and the student's notes Jared became sick, but it also strengthened his resolve. Jared tried very hard for the rest of the visit to be upbeat and interactive, but he could not shake the feeling that he had in his gut about what the military had done to their own veterans. After

Jared and Marie had thanked the Hamlins, made their good-byes and wished the Hamlins well, they made their way off the base and back onto the Parkway for the trip back to Washington DC. About half way back to Washington, Jared got the courage to tell Marie about the exchange with Julie and the Pathology Syllabus. He was afraid that she would blow-up and become very angry, but instead of becoming angry or crying or having an emotional outburst as Jared expected, Marie just said to him angrily, "What did you expect? I tell you, the United States is gone, it's history. When I see how America has treated its own military families, I tell you, there is no country on the planet that can do this and ultimately survive." She continued, "Unless these criminal factions in the government's scientific and medical sectors are rooted out and exposed, I see nothing but terror and destruction in our future."

After thinking about her comment for a moment Jared answered Marie. "I know that I have resisted your thinking on this, but I am afraid you're right. It's a sad day to realize that your own government may be behind this entire mess along with organized crime and their defense investments." The following year the Pentagon ordered the removal of the section on *M. fermentans* from the Pathology Syllabus VI. They would never explain why the section written by Dr. Ellen Martins was quietly removed from the medical curriculum at the DoD's own medical school. It was too late, however, the cat was out of the bag, and it was right there in official print, and they could not take it back no matter how hard they tried. There were a million excuses for the military medical school's description of Mfi as a dangerous pathogen and the instructions on how to treat its infections, but the most effective tactic was to just pretend that it never happened, which was exactly what they did—*and they got away with it completely.*

The U. S. Air Force Reserve nurse

One of the more interesting people that Jared and Marie met in Austin was Janet Riles, a former Air Force nurse and reserve officer in the Air Force. Although Captain Riles never fought in the Gulf War, she was activated and assigned to one of the C-130 Hercules air evacuation units that returned wounded soldiers from the Gulf. She had received all of her vaccinations and was preparing to deploy to the Persian Gulf when the war ended.

After the war, she was deactivated and returned to her hospital job, when she slowly came down with Gulf War Illness. As a nurse, Capt. Riles had contact with ill soldiers and marines that were returning from the Gulf, but she never actually went to the theater of operations.

Marie and Jared met Capt. Riles in Austin where she ran a weekly radio show for nurses called Nurse Talk Radio. In civilian life Capt. Riles was an ER nurse, and her radio show reflected that perspective, but she also developed a strong interest in Gulf War Illnesses because of her own health problems and those of other Air Force personnel and other veterans. Janet contacted the McNichols because of her interest in finding out about her own illness, but she also knew from her colleagues still in the Air Force that many veterans were slowly becoming sick and leaving their active duty positions because they could no longer perform their duties.

In time Capt. Riles became a strong advocate for the Gulf War veterans and their medical problems. In fact, she would often travel around the country delivering her lectures on the Gulf War and Weapons of Mass Destruction, concentrating on the little known fact at the time that certain companies in the United States sold Weapons of Mass Destruction to Iraq before the war with the blessings of the U. S. Department of Commerce. Among those weapons were a variety of 'dual-use' pathogenic bacteria and viruses that could be used as Biological Warfare agents.

Nurse Janet was a charming, eloquent lady who felt strongly about the way veterans had been treated after the Gulf War. The DoD had been attacking her for her outspoken views, but she had her supporters, and now among them, the McNichols. Jared and Marie agreed to be on one of Capt. Riles' radio shows, so they drove to a small commercial building complex in South Austin where Janet had access to a small radio studio. Although her radio program was local, she was in the process of trying to have her show go national. There was some interest but only by the patriot radio networks that have non-stop talk shows that deal with various conspiracy theories and other topics of ultra-conservative nature. Jared and Marie enjoyed their session with Janet on the air, and between the three of them, they raised some tough questions and issues that needed discussion on a wider scale.

Janet had become more and more submerged in the entire conspiracy surrounding the Gulf War Illnesses issue. This just stimulated her to find more information about the illnesses and why the U. S. military seemed to be ignoring the issue and not offering treatments beyond antidepressants and pain medications. Capt. Riles was especially mad about the PTSD debacle. When she started digging for information from completely legitimate sources, she usually ran into a stonewall. But she kept digging and digging, and finally she found enough material from the Congressional Record, publications, government archives and other sources to back up the theory that the United States had been working on biological weapons of mass destruction long after signing the 1972 treaty banning such efforts.

The most damaging information that Capt. Riles found or at least made more visible was, in fact, published in the U. S. Congressional Record a few years earlier. There for all to see were the reports from the Senate Banking Committee on Iraq's WMD. These reports documented the transfer of 'dual use' chemical and biological agents from the United States to Iraq during the Iran-Iraq war. In fact, this U. S. Senate committee under Senator Don Riegle found that the Commerce Department gave its blessing to the transfer of these dangerous weapons to Iraq's Atomic energy Commission and various universities in Baghdad and Basra in the 1980s during the Reagan administration, and this should have been a major embarrassment. But no one seemed to care that the United States and its allies armed Iraq with the very weapons that might now be playing a role in the deteriorating health of American, British, Canadian, Australian, Dutch, Danish and other veterans of the Gulf War.

Eventually Capt. Riles left Texas for a new home in Missouri, the "Show-Me' state, and she married and settled down. But she still continued the fight for veterans' rights on a new syndicated radio show with her new husband. With her U. S. documents in hand, Janet decided to change her life from a part-time veterans' advocate to a full-time radio talk show host with her husband and lecturer on unpopular topics like how our veterans were wounded by our own chemical and biological weapons and were then betrayed by their own country to hide the truth from the American people. She also formed a new Gulf War veterans' organization where she could continue the fight for veterans' rights from her new home in Missouri, far away from the depressing environment of Texas. It seemed ironic that many of the individuals that raised questions about veterans' health care had come from academic institutions or from the veterans community in

Project Day Lily 365

Texas, the same state that was at the center of the controversy on the origin of these same problems.

A doctor in the VA needs help

Although the VA Medical Centers were generally hostile to patients with Gulf War Illnesses, moving them mostly to psychiatrists so that they could receive a diagnosis of PTSD, there were some VA physicians who realized early on that the Gulf War Illnesses were medical not psychiatric illnesses. This especially hit home when the physicians themselves started to display similar signs and symptoms to their patients, and in some cases they even brought the condition home to their families, just like the veterans who brought Gulf War Illness to their spouses and children.

A VA physician in Oklahoma named Dr. Harry Moss contacted Jared McNichols because he began to show flu-like symptoms that progressed to a mild form of Gulf War Illness that was treatable with antibiotics, but then his wife started to show similar signs and symptoms. In fact, his wife was virtually incapacitated with the severe problems similar to what Dr. Moss had seen in his VA Gulf War referral clinic.

Since Dr. Moss was not a full time VA physician, he was less susceptible to the political pressure that was placed on the full-time VA medical staff, and he was more open to what was actually going on in his service. Dr. Moss tried to investigate Gulf War Illnesses as a medical problem, and treat his patients accordingly. In other words, he was actually trying to help the veterans solve their health problems, instead of just pushing them off onto psychiatrists who would then diagnose them with PTSD and stuff them full of antidepressants. The psychiatrists probably felt that they were just doing their job to diagnose psychiatric disorders and follow the directives of the VA.

Dr. Moss had noticed that the signs and symptoms of the Gulf War veterans with chronic illnesses did not fit with PTSD, but his pleadings were quickly dismissed by his colleagues because he was not a board-certified psychiatrist. Dr. Moss liked to call himself just a 'country doctor,' and how in heaven's name would this 'country doctor' know anything about a complex, stress-associated condition? In other words, how would he know that the veterans were not suffering from PTSD? But Dr. Moss was not satisfied to just send his patients to the psychiatrists for their PTSD diagnoses when he knew in his gut that it was not right. So he began to fight back when he noticed that both he and especially his wife were coming down with the same signs and symptoms as his patients.

His wife became progressively sicker and more incapacitated, but he could not ascertain what was wrong with her medically. Dr. Moss realized that it couldn't be PTSD—his wife was never in the Armed Forces or anywhere near Iraq—so he started to read everything he could get his hands on about the illnesses associated with service in the Gulf War. At the time there wasn't much to read about, but he became convinced that his wife's condition was caused by contact with him, and in turn, was likely caused by contact with the veterans, suggesting transmission of a biological exposure, an infection.

The VA just laughed and wrote off Dr. Moss' notions off as ridiculous. Then he heard from one of his patients that a husband-wife research group in Texas had found infections in Gulf War veterans. This was the type of information that he wanted to follow up on, because the spread of the illness to himself and especially his wife indicated an infectious process. Unfortunately, at the time the transmission of Gulf War Illnesses to spouses was hotly denied by the VA and the DoD, so Dr. Moss was bucking the system when he decided to follow up on this clue.

Dr. Moss tracked down Jared in Austin and called him on the telephone. Dr. Moss began by asking Jared what he and Marie had found in the Gulf War veterans that could explain their illnesses. Dr. Moss eventually told Jared, "I'm just a simple country doctor from Oklahoma trying to help the local VA with their Gulf War cases, but it seems to me that there is something being transmitted here, and one of my patients brought in some of your information. It looks very interesting." Jared replied, "That's funny, you don't sound to me like a simple country doctor." Dr. Moss continued, "Well I am. And I don't believe for one minute the bull that the VA is giving these veterans!" Jared responded, "That would be a reasonable conclusion. I don't believe them either, especially after they went out after me and my wife for making a simple suggestion, one that is helping the veterans." Dr. Moss asked, "What have you found down there in Austin?" Jared answered, "We found that approximately one-half of the sick veterans had an unusual chronic bacterial infection called *Mycoplasma fermentans.* But it can be treated with doxycycline along with immune and dietary support." Dr. Moss said,

"Well hell, that makes a lot of sense from your papers I have here. Does this bug cause a lot of different signs and symptoms in your patients?" Jared replied, "Oh, I would say so. Some of the vets with this infection have over forty different signs and symptoms. The most prominent ones are chronic fatigue, joint and muscle pain, headaches, cognitive problems and memory loss, gastrointestinal problems, skin rashes, heart problems, vision problems and a lot more." Dr. Moss said, "I see. How about the female patients? Do they show a lot of female problems with their periods, bloating and such?" Jared responded, "They sure do. We were just visiting with the wife of a Gulf War veteran from the 101st Airborne, and she looked almost pregnant because of bloating. She also had major problems with her periods, PMS and vaginal infections."

Then Dr. Moss got down to a critical question. He asked, "How is it spread?" Jared continued, "It appears to be an airborne infection, but I think that it can also be passed to spouses by sexual contact. When children come down with it, they usually present after the adults, and they often have unusual problems such as autistic behavior." Dr. Moss said, "I think this may be bigger than you think, and I believe that you are onto something important. Does the VA have a contract with you for testing?" Jared laughed, "Are you kidding? They would like to see us shut down for good!" Dr. Moss replied, "Damned them, if they do succeed in shutting you down!"

Dr. Moss was not surprised to hear what Jared had just told him. He told Jared, "I think I am beginning to see why you hit a nerve. You know, I'm just a country doctor, but some things are so obvious that even a simple doctor like me can't avoid seeing them. You said it could be successfully treated with doxycycline?" Jared responded, "Yes, that's right, 200 milligrams per day plus some supplements." Dr. Moss replied, "To me that sounds simple enough. I appreciate what you're doing, and so do my patients. My wife is showing the illness, and I am going to try your protocol on both of us. I know that some other physicians here are having the same problem, but I don't know if they are going to be smart enough to contact you." Jared said, "Well, we're used to that. Some people just want to avoid the obvious if it involves some painful truth that they would rather forget." Dr. Moss said, "I want to keep in contact with you, if it's all right. We may need your assistance again here in Oklahoma." Jared responded, "No problem. We'll be here for you."

CHAPTER 12

The Trips to Washington DC (1995)

Marie had previously applied for a faculty position in a clinical department at the D. O. Madison Cancer Center. On the basis of this application, now almost a year old, Dr. Augustus Blair, the chairman of the Department of Pediatrics had offered Marie a faculty position. For reasons that had more to do with the direction of research that Dr. Blair wanted in his department, Marie had put off making a decision on whether to join his department. Although he had not contacted Marie since that time, and she had not followed up on the offer, Marie had become desperate for a faculty position in Austin. Also, the position had been advertised recently in a professional journal, so she decided to press the issue. Jared had warned her that it was now unlikely that she still had a chance at the position, but since the position was recently advertised and was still open, she decided to contact Dr. Blair to see if he was still interested in hiring her. Marie might as well find out herself about the dirty politics of the institution when it came to hiring new staff. She made an appointment with Dr. Blair, and to her surprise, she was told that she could see Dr. Blair the next day in his office.

The following day at the Cancer Center Marie found herself in the office of Professor Blair, Chairman of the prestigious Pediatrics Department, in which Marie was to have received an entry faculty position after a compulsory seminar. Dr. Blair was a very short man of very nondescript appearance, and he had very small but kind eyes for his size. He loved children and his personality fit quite well with his patients, but it also betrayed him as a 'suck-up' artist. He did, however, give off an air that he truly cared for his young patients. He was not an especially brilliant man compared to his D. O. Madison colleagues, but he was a good physician, and he was well-liked by his colleagues and the families that flocked to the Cancer Center, usually as a last resort for their terminally sick children.

Dr. Blair's office was furnished in the vivid colors of a childhood nursery. There were lots of stuffed animals on display, even some vintage stuffed animals, which Marie suspected belonged to Dr. Blair himself, possibly reminders of his own childhood. The wall was covered with awards that Dr. Blair had received in recognition of his crusade to discover new treatments for childhood cancers. The furniture was typical office furniture, nothing too opulent. He had probably not been to Dr. Geldter's office and seen the expensive rosewood furniture that cost hundreds of thousands of dollars and caused the Cancer Center quite a scandal in the press.

Marie had entered Dr. Blair's office while he was on the phone, and he signaled for Marie to take a seat. After several minutes, he eventually hung up the phone and immediately turned to Marie. "Dr. McNichols, you have powerful enemies! And their attitude towards you is very deep-seeded." Marie replied, "I guess that means that my possible appointment to the faculty in your department has been blocked." Dr. Blair in a very cold way said, "Well, at The Madison we don't block faculty appointments, but if I were you I would seriously consider doing something else with your life. It is unlikely that you will find employment in Austin. According to my sources, your candidacy here has been seriously compromised." Marie answered Dr. Blair by looking him directly in the eyes, "I am aware of the blackball here at The Madison, but I do not know why. I was trained by some of the top scientists in the world in the hard sciences, and although my personality is not exactly like those of my colleagues, I am not that much different in demeanor from other beginning faculty."

Marie finally got to the point. "Do you have an explanation for this, Dr. Blair?" Dr. Blair became nervous and very uncomfortable before he answered, "No, not really. Marie, remember, I am relatively new to The D. O. Madison. Prior to coming here I had never heard of Drs. Geldter or Krapner. But it seems that these people are not your supporters. Even worse is your apparent conflict with the upper administration. I have to assume that you have contributed in some way to cause their current attitude." Marie replied, "They're not in my field. I don't even really know these people!" Dr. Blair responded, "Even if you haven't ever met them or don't know them well, why do you think that they are so forcefully against your candidacy? There must be some reason?"

Dr. Blair reflected for a moment and then became more direct with Marie. "I honestly could not be responsible for the career of someone with any controversy surrounding them, and I have heard what you and your husband are doing with that Gulf War Syndrome patients. You have to understand my position. I have to be very careful whom I hire into the Department. And I have to cooperate fully with the Administration. This puts me in a very difficult position, and you wouldn't want that, I'm sure."

Marie looked directly at Dr. Blair. "Did it ever occur to you, Dr. Blair, that there are always two sides to a story?" Dr. Blair responded, "Well yes, Dr. McNichols, it has occurred to me. But I do not have the time for any controversy, nor the inclination to cause problems for my Department." Marie said, "Dr. Blair, answer one question for me. Why would the President of The D. O. Madison be interested in a peon such as myself. You know I am just an entry level faculty candidate, and chief executive officers seldom even know the names of the people at my level." Dr. Blair answered, "Which is why there must be some basis for this, and there must be some truth to what people say about you. Marie, let me be frank with you. There are serious accusations against you and your husband." Marie asked, "Well, what are they?" Dr. Blair said, "I can't tell you."

Marie sarcastically responded to Dr. Blair's comments. "Well, that's just perfect! People whom I do not even know are levying serious accusations, as you call it, against me, which have in essence, halted my academic career. But I am not allowed to know what these accusations are. It's as if I am being treated as a criminal with no means to defend myself. At least criminals get to have a fair trial." Dr. Blair consoled Marie, "You should not take it personally." She continued, "Dr. Blair. I am sure if the shoe were on the other foot, you would take it personally." He nodded his head and Marie said, "Are you aware that I studied with some of the top physicists of this century. One of them, a former President of the National Academy of Sciences, thought I was one of the best students he had seen in his entire career, which spanned half a century. It's right there in my reference letters. I will not dignify this discussion by going into a long explanation of my achievements. I know, they say that we cheat and fudge our data on the Gulf War veterans' results. Dr. Blair was beginning to get uncomfortable,

"This is very embarrassing, Marie." She asked, "For whom, Dr. Blair? What else? Oh, I know, I slept my way into D. O. Madison by bewitching my husband, Jared. You can stop me, Dr. Blair, but I have heard it all. Yes, it is true that I slept with my husband. But I was never promiscuous, nor would I stoop to such behavior to procure some inconsequential faculty position. Dr. Blair, did it ever occur to you that those people who have branded me have sex not their jobs on their minds? If they were truly devoted to doing their jobs, they would not spend time in such guttural gossip. Perhaps these people view me in some sexual manner themselves?" Dr. Blair answered, "You have a point." Marie said, "Thank you, Dr. Blair."

He finally became uneasy at continuing the conversation. "Well! That was interesting. I'm glad that we had this little conversation." Marie said, "All these things are just unsubstantiated rumors, and I have one last statement. I am not a petty or vindictive person, but you have to agree that I have been treated very badly by the system here." Dr. Blair looked visibly relieved that the conversation was about to end. "So Marie, are we all going to be O.K.?" Marie responded, "If you have done nothing wrong, than you have nothing to fear." Blair began to look nervous again.

Marie was now toying with Dr. Blair because of the intense hurt and anger she felt from her treatment at the hands of the D. O. Madison administration and faculty. Dr. Blair continued, "You said you were not a vindictive person." Marie answered, "That's true. But I cannot account for the behavior of my godfather who is very protective of me. My family may perceive this whole episode as an incredible blight upon my honor, even if he has mixed emotions about my having a career in science. You see, he's a very old-fashioned gentleman, very aristocratic, actually! But don't worry, I'll put in a good word for you." Marie paused and said, "There's no point for everyone to suffer due to the vicious pettiness of some administrators. But you just better pray that my godfather and I are far more reasonable in our dealings towards you and your colleagues than D. O. Madison's administration has been to me." Dr. Blair then exclaimed, "You know what? I feel better about you as a person now that we have had this little talk, and I think it's a tragedy that you have been treated this way. Unfortunately, my hands are tied with respect to the appointment. I am truly sorry, there is nothing I can do!" Marie responded, "You know what, Dr. Blair, I don't feel better about you as a person, because you base your opinions on hearsay. A good leader bases his or her decisions on facts not hearsay. I believe that you have clearly failed to do that in my case, and I doubt I would be happy in a department whose director is so malleable. With all due respect, sir, you are a typical yes-man. I am sorry if I have offended you with my comments, but this episode does not portend well for the long-term viability of this institution. Businesses whose leaders make decisions based purely on emotion rarely succeed, and today's economic trends are not conducive to running a large operation like this hospital according to the Texas good ole' boy system. No, Dr. Blair, I predict that D. O. Madison's leadership will ultimately force this institution to bankruptcy."

Dr. Blair was now visibly irritated. "That's impossible! This institution can always call upon the Permanent University fund." Marie said, "Don't be so sure. Even the Roman empire fell." Little did Marie know at the time that it was her own massive inheritance that backed up the Permanent University Fund. Dr. Blair then said, "I'm truly sorry, Marie, about this whole episode, and I wish I could make amends. But it is just impossible. I wish you luck, however, in your endeavors, and as a remembrance of our division I have decided to present you with our special children's bear." He handed the bear to Marie. She held her temper in check and tried not to view the act as the ultimate insult. She somewhat sarcastically said, "Oh, thank you, Dr. Blair I just love stuffed animals. I will cherish this bear always. Good luck to you!" As Marie left the room with her bear, leaving Dr. Blair to just shake his head and wonder what went wrong with the meeting.

After the disastrous meeting with Dr. Blair, Marie found her way to Jared's office carrying the stuffed bear. People stopped her in the hallway to comment on the bear. It seemed that everyone liked the bear, or at least it was a point of conversation. Marie made her way past the office personnel and walked right into Jared's office. He was on the phone, and Marie sat down and waited until he finished his conversation before a tear showed up on her face. Jared got up and came over to Marie. He asked her, "That bad?" Marie replied, "Worse! I should have listened to you. I should have never gone to Dr. Blair's office. It was a complete waste of time." Jared said, "Well, it looks like you got a nice bear from the interview. Was that your booby prize?" Jared did not want to make Marie feel worse than she did already, but he succeeded. He apologized, "Marie, I'm really very sorry. I didn't want you to go to see Dr. Blair. You knew that it was a waste of time, but you went anyway. You look nice though. I love you for your tenacity." Marie responded, "At least I got something out of it." Jared said, "Yes, you did. It's a nice bear. At least he has some good taste in something, *the little maggot!*" Marie paused and said, "It seems from Blair's comments that the entire administration is terrified of my elusive family." Jared just shook his head and thought to himself that once again Marie was touching on the issue that she was probably someone else, possibly an heiress from some elusive European family. Could Marie be somehow linked to the financial web that was entangled in the Medical Center finances? Jared kept this thought to himself.

Marie jumped up and said, "Well, are you taking me to lunch or what?" Jared answered, "It looks like I am." He took off his lab coat, and they left the office together holding hands. Jared said to the officer personnel as they left, "Jane, I am taking my beautiful wife here to lunch. I don't know when I'll be back. Please take messages for me."

The Department of Defense goes after the McNichols

One of the patients that contacted Jared and Marie was an Air Force cargo handler who worked at Dover Air Force Base in Delaware. His name was Master Sergeant Albright Letterman. Sergeant Letterman had actually been out of the Air Force for some time, but he was involved in unloading Iraqi tanks, armored vehicles and other equipment from giant C-5A cargo planes at Dover AFB after the war. These trophies of war were brought back undamaged for examination by the Army at the Aberdeen Proving Grounds and later for possible use in training Marine and Army armored units in the California desert. MSGT Letterman was not deployed to the Gulf during the war. The only contact he had with the Gulf War was his involvement in unloading Iraqi equipment after the war and his receipt of the anthrax vaccine and other vaccines that the deployed airmen received.

Some of the vehicles and other equipment came home completely wrapped and sealed in plastic, but the cargo handlers were never told why. After his contact with the war trophies, MSGT Letterman slowly came down with a chronic illness that was undistinguishable from Gulf War Illness. Unfortunately for him, he left the Air Force after a long career, and the VA wouldn't accept that he had any illnesses related to the Gulf War. Perhaps it was just as well, for they didn't try to send him to the psychiatrists for a PTSD diagnosis. Even the VA wasn't that stupid. But MSGT Letterman wouldn't accept that his illness was not work related. He began getting sick before retiring from the Air Force where he was forced to take the anthrax vaccine, and his signs and symptoms matched those veterans who did serve in the Gulf War. Was it the vaccines or the Iraqi equipment that caused his illness?

Sergeant Letterman was concerned that he might have been exposed to chemical and biological agents carried back on Iraqi equipment from the Gulf or something in the anthrax or other vaccines that he was forced to take while in the Air Force. After getting the run-around from the Air Force and the VA, he decided to write his Senator, William Roth of Delaware, who promptly forwarded his letter to the Assistant Secretary of Defense for Health Affairs, Dr. Joseph Johns. Dr. Johns in return sent a formal letter of reply to Senator Roth and other members of Congress on this general issue. It was clear that he had apparently used similar letters on a number of occasions.

In the letter to Congress Dr. Johns forcefully stated that *"there is no scientific or medical evidence that either chemical or biological agents were deployed at any level during the Gulf War,"* nor he argued in his letter were there any exposures of U. S. service members to chemical or biological warfare agents. Furthermore, he stated that any chemical alarms that sounded during the Gulf War were caused by dust particles. Of course, he didn't bother to mention that biological detectors were not even present in the theater of operations, so how could there be any evidence of non-exposure to biological agents when there were no detectors anywhere near the Gulf? Also, there was ample evidence that chemical alarms only sounded during not before or after the war.

At the same time that Dr. John's letter was circulating to members of Congress, in one of their own Congressional Committee hearings an Army chemical/biological weapons officer testified under oath that there were over 14,000 chemical alarms that sounded during but not before or after the conflict. Presumably there was dust before, during and after the war. The fact that chemical alarms sounded during but not before or after the war was conveniently hidden from the public until this Army Nuclear Biological Chemical Warfare specialist testified to Congress under oath about the number and type of chemical detections during the war. Unfortunately when Congress asked for the chemical logs to substantiate his testimony, none could be subsequently found! They had been lost or destroyed after the war. Nor did Dr. Johns bother to mention that a defense contractor detected chemical warfare agents using infrared detectors located in satellites in stationary orbits over Iraq.

Of interest to the McNichols was a statement in Dr. Johns' letter that was a complete lie. Dr. Johns had stated in his letter that mycoplasmas could not be causing the illnesses, because *Mycoplasma fermentans* had not been shown to cause disease in man. When Jared was sent a copy of the letter written by Undersecretary Johns, he was furious. Notwithstanding the U.S. patent awarded to Army pathologist Dr. Lon on *Mycoplasama fermentans* entitled 'Pathogenic Mycoplasma' and the publications from the U. S. Army demonstrating the pathogenic properties of this microorganism and the teaching manuals in the military's own medical school on its pathogenic properties, there was considerable evidence published by the DoD itself indicating that *M. fermentans* could cause a fatal disease in Armed Forces personnel as well as healthy non-human primates that had been injected with the microorganism. Since the military taught their medical students at the Naval Medical Center that *M. fermentans* was pathogenic, Dr. Johns must not have received his medical training in the military. He should have found out what his own military medical school instructors were teaching their students before spreading such rubbish in formal letters to Congress. Jared wondered if the laws governing Congressional perjury applied to letters sent to Senators from Pentagon big-wigs. He would have loved to see Dr. Johns convicted of lying to Congress.

In a telephone conversation with Sergeant Letterman Jared was still furious. "So an undersecretary deliberately lied about *M. fermentans* in a formal letter to Congress? What else is new?" Jared discussed the situation, "They have been lying for years to Congress. It looks like you got tanked by that liar Dr. Johns!" Sergeant Letterman said, "You told me this was going to happen, and you were right. Now I have to convince Senator Roth's office that Dr. Joseph Johns is a liar, and that won't be easy. This is the same guy that testified to Senator Roth's committee on Pentagon budgets and health matters. The Senator thinks he's a 'nice' guy." Jared replied, "I think he a fiend! I don't think that it would be difficult to show that Dr. Johns is a liar, and he is not a 'nice guy' to the veterans. After all, most of the research that demonstrates that *M. fermentans* is pathogenic comes from the Army itself, and he probably knows all about it. Anyway, what is the penalty for lying to Congress?" Letterman replied, "I have no idea. I didn't know we had fallen so far to have our leading Pentagon physicians behave this way."

Sergeant Letterman thought for a moment. "I think this explains why Dr. Johns essentially called you a charlatan on a TV interview last week. He went out of his way to paint you and Marie as opportunistic, know-nothing jerks that prey on the veterans with your wild ideas." Jared laughed, "Well, we both know who the charlatan is, and we both know who is preying on the veterans! I would like to see him pass a lie detector test on the subject to find out what he knows but won't tell to the American public. But this does bring up an interesting question. Why would the DoD go to such lengths to hide the truth about the mycoplasma? What's the big deal about this Mfi infection? Is it some kind of biowarfare agent that got loose and they don't dare to admit it to the public? You know, like another Lyme Disease that got loose from Plum Island?" Sergeant Letterman said, "Affirmative! And then they sent it to Saddam!"

Sergeant Letterman was not far off base in his last comment. Congressional records showed that very dangerous chemical and biological agents were actually sent to Iraq from the United States before the war with the blessing of the U. S. Commerce Department. But did the Iraqis get Mfi from the United States or some other nation willing to sell it for the right price? And what about the vaccines given to deployed Armed Forces personnel? Most deployed personnel received 20-30 different vaccines within a few days during deployment. Any immunologist knows that this is very suppressive to your immune system. If there were even some minor contaminants in any of the vaccines, the vaccinated servicemen and servicewomen might have been especially susceptible because their immune systems were compromised.

The Pentagon spokesperson and his traveling circus

Another person that went after the McNichols was a spokesperson for the DoD in the Office of Gulf War Illnesses, Dr. Roger Rott. Actually, Dr. Rott did not have a scientific or medical degree, but the press called him Dr. Rott anyway, and he did nothing to correct their mistake. It would take some time for the press to actually find out that Dr. Rott had a degree in education and was poorly qualified to make serious comments on medical conditions or treatments. Nonetheless, Dr. Rott was constantly going after physicians and scientists who dared to buck the Pentagon on the issue of Gulf War Illnesses. Thus, if anyone disagreed with the DoD and their PTSD bandwagon, they became a potential target, and that certainly included the McNichols. After all, everyone knew that the illnesses from the Gulf War, if there were any, were all caused by stress!

Mr. Rott was spending most of his time defending the position of the DoD with respect to the 'psychiatric' casualties from the Gulf War. In fact, he took his show on the road, and his traveling bandwagon, some would claim traveling circus, was scheduled to visit various communities where large military bases existed to convince active duty Armed Services personnel, veterans of the war, their relatives and the local press that everything was under control with respect to Gulf War Illnesses. In fact, just the opposite was the case, and it was Mr. Rott's 'spin-job' to 'keep a lid on it' so that the situation did not get out of hand and cause further embarrassment to the DoD.

In the process of leading the Pentagon cheering section on the traveling show around the country, Mr. Rott was often greeted with hostile questions about the veterans' possible exposures to chemical and biological agents. The veterans and their families were concerned, and the major purpose of the traveling show was to bring 'peace of mind and clarity' to the veterans and to the public. Unfortunately, it rarely accomplished either. In fact, some of the traveling shows become somewhat rowdy when the participants felt quite rightly that they were being lied to by the spokesperson from the Pentagon. This often happened when Mr. Rott repeated over and over again that there was no evidence that the veterans of the Gulf War were exposed to chemical or biological agents. However, the veterans seem to have known otherwise, mostly from a handful of websites that were established by the veterans themselves. Some of these proudly displayed the documents indicating the complete opposite of the 'snake oil' that Mr. Rott had been selling on his traveling shows.

When the questions inevitably came up during the traveling shows about possible biological exposures during the Gulf War, one of the popular targets of Mr. Rott were the McNichols. He delighted in telling the crowds about Dr. Lon's failure to confirm the McNichols' findings on Mfi in the veterans' blood and the bogus statement that the infection did not even cause disease. Mr. Rott knew exactly what he was doing, which was to cast doubt on any findings which went against the Pentagon line. In fact, the traveling PR show continued on for some time, but the DoD was eventually forced to change its position in a number of areas, in response to the increasing criticism that it was being less than forthright with the veterans and the American public.

Thus the traveling PR show of Mr. Rott probably didn't yield the outcome that the DoD expected. For example, there was a flap over the exposures of U. S. Forces to the toxic clouds from the destruction of Iraqi bunkers at Khamisiyah immediately after the Gulf War. At first, the Pentagon denied that *anyone* could have been exposed to anything toxic from the blowing up of bunkers and munitions after the war, until it was made public that some of the bunkers actually contained chemical and biological weapons. A CIA analyst blew the whistle on the DoD when he determined that a toxic cloud likely spread from Southern Iraq to the Gulf and could have exposed U. S. and other forces on the ground to low-level chemical and biological agents that were stored in the bunkers that were blown. Even the Pentagon's own Deputy Director of Policy in the Command and Control had written a treatise entitled *"A matter of national integrity,"* which addressed the issue of low-level exposures. He expected to be fired over the article, but to his amazement he was actually promoted and would become a life-long friend of the McNichols and give them hope that the Pentagon leadership still had some integrity.

In another embarrassing moment for the Pentagon, a soldier in one of the engineering units assigned to blow up the bunkers had taken home movies with his own VCR of the munitions in some of the bunkers at Khamisiyah. The videotape clearly showed that there were chemical and biological weapons stored at Kamisiyah. Interestingly, his video also showed that some of the cases of weapons had the U. S. Interstate Commerce Hazmat or hazardous materials stickers still on the cases, indicating that some of the weapons were of American manufacture and were shipped from the United States to Iraq.

Thus the DoD was forced to keep changing its official position on the possible exposures of U. S. Armed Forces personnel to toxic materials in the air. From the initial position that no soldiers were exposed to only a handful of troops were potentially exposed to thousands and finally hundreds of thousands of veterans were potentially exposed. The Pentagon did not dare admit that civilians were exposed, even though the McNichols knew otherwise from their communications from colleagues in the Middle East who reported the existence of unusual increases in undiagnosed chronic illnesses and cancer cases in the region.

Throughout this entire flap, Mr. Rott was completely unflappable. He had become the artful dodger, cleverly avoiding criticism and giving the press and the public any ammunition that could be used to challenge the Pentagon's official line. His ultimate reward for such unsavory behavior was not a ticket out of town but an appointment as an Undersecretary in the Department of Defense. Thus the protectors of the 'truth' (according to the Pentagon) were handsomely rewarded for their service in deflecting any criticism from the 'barbarian' public and especially the 'traitorous' press.

Mr. Rott was often accompanied on his 'control and containment' missions by a Navy Captain, Dr. Charles Murphy, a non-descript Naval medical officer who wore his Navy 'whites' for all such occasions. What few in the veterans' community, the general public and especially the press knew was that Capt. Murphy was an infectious disease expert who had been involved with Biological Warfare defense during his career. He was there to handle the questions about potential biological warfare agents *("there were none released in the Gulf War and there was no evidence of exposure")*, chronic infections *("there is no evidence for chronic infections in the Gulf War veterans")* to the illnesses themselves *("all the evidence points to a stress-related cause")*. But there was more to Dr. Murphy than it seemed, and he was carefully chosen for his position as medical flak catcher for Mr. Rott.

As it turns out, Capt. Murphy was in addition to a biological warfare expert, a former commander who was in charge of a unit in the Navy that had illegally experimented with dangerous biological agents on Marine recruits. He was also the former head of a special biological warfare laboratory in Egypt that specialized in tropical diseases. In fact, one of his victims, former U. S. Marine Michael James, came to Jared for help when he found out that there were actually some civilians who would help in such cases.

Michael James was a young Marine rifleman just out of basic training at the Marine Recruit Depot, San Diego, when he first met Dr. Murphy at Camp Pendleton in North San Diego County. Dr. Murphy was then a young Navy Lt. Commander and director of a unit at Balboa Naval Hospital that apparently performed horrific experiments on unwitting Marine guinea pigs. Michael James was one of Dr. Murphy's Marine guinea pigs that had been 'volunteered' to be part of the Navy's biological warfare experiments. In fact, his entire platoon was 'volunteered' without any pretense of informed consent, and most of them apparently died during 'the experiment' that James was involved with and never made it out of Balboa Naval Hospital alive. At least when PVT James woke up from one of his delirious episodes in the hospital and asked the orderlies about his platoon buddies, he was told that they didn't make it.

Michael James was one of the 'lucky' Marines that survived. After a partial recovery and quick medical discharge from the Marines, it took the former Marine rifleman years to recover from Dr. Murphy's horrific experiment. When confronted by the former Marine, Dr. Murphy hotly denied the entire story, including the part where he was the Marine's attending doctor. That was until Mr. James was able to recover his medical records from the Marine Corps. The records from Balboa Naval Hospital clearly had Dr. Murphy's signature on records that also bore the secret codes for a biological warfare experiment. Finding his medical records and determining what the 'codes' actually meant turned out to be no small feat, since at first the Marine Corps denied that Mr. James had ever even served in the Marines, and then later the Marine Corps denied that he was ever hospitalized at Balboa Naval Hospital. With the assistance of his Congressman, Mr. James eventually recovered his Marine Corps hospital records with Dr. Murphy's signatures on various pages as the physician-in-charge of an experimental unit at Balboa Naval Hospital. It seems that it was no accident that Dr. Murphy, the biological warfare expert, was chosen as Mr. Rott's deputy in the Gulf War Illness section at the Pentagon, and it was certainly no accident that Dr. Murphy was chosen as the medical back-up on the Pentagon's Gulf War Illnesses traveling circus. After all, anyone with the rank of a Navy Captain commanded and received great respect from the veterans who, of course, had no idea of Dr. Murphy's background in biological warfare.

The government spin-doctors had to control the situation at all costs. They had even gone so far as to enlist a few right-wing journalists to write articles on how Gulf War Syndrome was nothing but a made-up psychosomatic condition due to the *'neurotic nature of the journalists who had convinced the veterans that they were sick because they ought to be sick from the war.'* The rationale for this neurotic condition was that it wasn't their experience in the Gulf War that was haunting them, but rather what they were seeing on TV shows, what they were reading in newspapers, what they were hearing from congressional demagogues and from activists, and what they had heard from their fellow veterans. In other words, the veterans were simply being bombarded by the press that kept telling them that they were sick, and they were succumbing ('media shock' instead of 'shell shock?') to the message that they *ought* to be sick. Since they were so gullible and malleable by the press, they simply became psychologically sick in response to the media assault on their health!

One of these writers, who was actually an attorney by profession, had published in a magazine that Gulf War Syndrome was caused by some sort of *'epidemic of hysteria'* created by the media and certain politicians. Even the term *'epidemic hysteria'* that was used so freely in the article by this self-proclaimed 'medical expert' was demeaning to the veterans. And where did this term come from? It turned out to be a 'mental condition' invented by a woman English professor who felt that journalists and politicians had played a significant role in escalating the veterans' 'anxieties' to the point that they apparently caused some sort of *mass hysteria because of too much information from politicians and the news media.* Jared laughed and told Marie that if this were the case, one might expect that a rather large fraction of the population in the Washington D.C. area would have been suffering for decades from 'epidemic hysteria' after being bombarded by too many politicians and Washington journalists! As if the veterans were so gullible, and of course, their family members were also so gullible, as to believe everything that the press had written and the politicians had discussed about Gulf War Syndrome was just completely ludicrous. The thought of blaming sick infants for being gullible about politicians and news reporters and thus becoming chronically ill was especially appalling to Jared. How could they stoop so low?

Of course, the McNichols were in the crosshairs of such 'assets.' In their articles on what they called the *Phony Gulf War Syndrome* they were quick to attack the McNichols with completely bogus information, or they produced pure hearsay about their research and attributed ridiculous comments in their articles to the McNichols themselves, without ever interviewing them. Compared to the other insults and real threats to their health and safety, this seemed like child's play to the McNichols, but it was irritating and insulting.

Some medical scientists take on the Veterans' Administration

Jared and Marie had met Dr. Jack Baumgardner at a meeting on Gulf War Illnesses organized by a veterans' organization. They hit it off immediately, and a wonderful friendship developed. Dr. Baumgardner was the head of Neurology at the Los Angeles VA Medical Center, and he was trained as a psychiatrist as well as a neurologist. With his distinguished background, Dr. Baumgardner was particularly well equipped to determine if the veterans were suffering from PTSD or instead some organic medical problem.

Dr. Baumgardner always smiled or laughed when discussing the issue of PTSD and the Gulf War veterans. His superiors wanted the Gulf War veterans that came to the VA Medical Center in Los Angeles to be diagnosed with PTSD and placed on antidepressants, but Dr. Baumgardner resisted, mainly because he felt quite strongly that the veterans might have been exposed to multiple toxins in the Gulf that caused many problems that couldn't be explained by stress alone. In fact, since he was a neurologist, Dr. Baumgardner had been interested in the neurological aspects of Gulf War Illnesses and what might have caused the memory loss, headaches, cognitive deficits and problems with hearing, vision and other senses in the veterans. Since he was also a Board-Certified psychiatrist, he was amply qualified to determine if there were any psychiatric reasons for the illnesses.

The medical problems of the Gulf War veterans suggested that actual damage could have occurred to their brains. Thus Dr. Baumgardner set out to test his hypothesis by performing brain scans on the Gulf War veterans. Using an imaging technique that measured metabolic differences in brain tissues Dr. Baumgardner found that the ill Gulf War veterans showed multiple lesions of differing metabolic activity in their brains that could have been the result of multiple toxic insults. Such lesions could not have been caused by stress or PTSD, and there was no evidence in the neurological literature indicating that stress caused similar multiple lesions. Since there was no history of PTSD causing such dramatic brain lesions, Dr. Baumgardner concluded that it was not stress that was causing the veterans' chronic illnesses, it was exposure to unknown toxic substances, such as chemicals and biological agents that can penetrate into the central nervous system and cause focal damage to brain tissue.

For his efforts, the VA amply rewarded Dr. Baumgardner by closing his department and sending him packing from the VA. Before his department was closed down for good and he and his employees released from their duties, Dr. Baumgardner was actually forbidden to speak about his brain scan results at scientific meetings and especially to the press. The Veterans' Administration was very sensitive to the issue that pathological damage may have occurred in the veterans, because it flew in the face of their psychiatric diagnoses and solutions to the problem. Their final solution was: *kill the messenger.*

Dr. Baumgardner was forced to leave the VA, so he went into private practice in Los Angeles. Unfortunately, without the expensive brain scanning equipment left behind gathering dust at the VA in his now closed department, he could not complete his study for publication. He wanted to publish his research in a highly ranked medical journal, but since he no longer had access to the equipment he needed to finish his studies, it couldn't be done. He did eventually publish some of his findings, but he was never able to publish his work in a top ranked medical journal. Eventually he retired for health reasons. He was too ill to continue the battle, and his eyesight was failing. Marie and Jared wondered if Dr. Baumgardner picked up Mfi from his patients and, like SEAL Commander Dale DeJon, was losing his sight because of the infection.

Dr. Baumgardner's research on the Gulf War veterans was eventually continued, and even expanded upon, by a research group in Dallas that eventually landed some Federal funding for the project. The Dallas group completed and published a Gulf War Illnesses brain lesion research project that demonstrated that Gulf War Illness patients did have unusual lesions in their brains that showed dramatic differences in metabolic states. The VA and DoD response to the brain lesion research, however, was more ridicule and disbelief. In an attempt to discredit Dr. Baumgardner and the Dallas group that followed him, the VA and Pentagon claimed that there was absolutely no evidence to control for the possibility that the veterans may have had the lesions before they left for the Gulf or that the lesions did not have any relationship to Gulf War Illnesses.

It was the usual strategy of *'delay and deny'* that had plagued virtually any and all researchers who had attempted to do any non-psychiatric research on the Gulf War veterans. Even though the Dallas group was actually financially supported by the DoD and published their results on brain lesions in the Gulf War veterans in excellent medical journals, the Pentagon continued their refusal to believe in the validity of the research. If they accepted that the brain lesions in the veterans were real, then their PTSD charade was over. So, they didn't accept the brain lesion reports.

Dr. Cathy Workman looks at sand

Another VA physician who took an unpopular stand on Gulf War Illnesses was Dr. Cathy Workman, an infectious disease specialist at a regional VA Medical Center in Central Pennsylvania. Dr. Workman, as the head of a Gulf War Illness referral center, noticed that the signs and symptoms of the Gulf War veterans were consistent with an unusual chronic infection, and she initiated her own studies in an attempt to find out what was causing the chronic condition. However, the VA administration was very unforgiving to its physicians who dared to challenge the system, and in the case of Dr. Workman, it eventually resulted in her release from the VA for going against the PTSD stampede.

Dr. Workman had the gall to recommend that some of the sick Gulf War veterans be given antibiotics. In her studies on the veterans, Dr. Workman found that their condition was best described as an unusual, sand-associated infection that could be transmitted. An interesting aspect of the Gulf War that had been kept out of the mainstream press was the deployment of Iraqi biological weapons sprayers just before and during the war. In fact, the Marine and Army units that invaded through Southern Iraq and Kuwait found over 60 mobile Italian-made biological weapons sprayers fully deployed during the war. The sprayers were usually mounted on heavy trucks and were used to spray biological weapons onto the sand to create 'biological minefields.'

Some of the types of weapons that could have been deployed in the biological sprayers were: anthrax or *Bacillus anthracis* spores, *Brucella* species which causes brucellosis, *Yersinia pestis* which causes pneumonic plague, *Coxiella burnetii* which causes Q fever, *Francisella tularensis* which causes tularemia, and of course, mycoplasmal infections caused by Mfi.

Were biological weapons sprayed onto the sand in Southern Iraq? Only the DoD knew for certain, and they had refused to discuss the Italian biological weapons sprayers found in the Gulf. In fact, what was found in the sprayers has remained classified, and it was difficult to find anyone who could discuss what happened in Iraq and Kuwait with the biological weapons sprayers and what they sprayed onto the sand.

Eventually a Colonel from Fort Baker in California decided to go public about the bioweapons sprayers and the absence of any biological detection equipment deployment to the Gulf. He came out with this information just before his retirement from the Army, but for some reason, the mainstream press dismissed the declaration of this full Colonel and biological warfare expert. After all, the DoD stated that there were no biological weapons released in the Gulf War! How did they know that if there were *no* detectors deployed to the Gulf to monitor the release of biological weapons? This question had never been answered, and to this day it has not been answered. The Army did take some biological samples from Iraq, and it sent them to a top secret laboratory in Egypt. What did they find in the sand? What was loaded into the Iraqi biological sprayers? Jared said to Marie, "We will probably have to wait until hell freezes over to get the answers to these questions. I guess the Pentagon has too much to hide to be forthright about the biological weapons sprayers. They will just classify this information and keep it secret for the next 50 years."

Dr. Workman had collaborated with the McNichols on a few publications, mainly letters to editors and brief notes, on the medical aspects of Gulf War Illnesses. A few of these publications even took on government scientists and administrators that they felt strongly had skewed and manipulated their data to support the Pentagon's stance on PTSD, infections, hospitalization and death rates, among other issues, and Gulf War Illnesses. Since Dr. Workman was a VA physician and infectious disease specialist, her work actually added credence to Jared's and Marie's hypothesis that there were medical reasons for the illnesses, such as infections and chemical exposures, rather than stress-related psychological reasons that explained the illnesses found in the Gulf War veterans.

Here was a Harvard Medical School trained infectious disease specialist, the head of a Gulf War Illnesses Referral Center in the VA, agreeing with the McNichols about the presence of infections in Gulf War veterans. However, Dr. Workman's bureaucratic bosses in the VA were not pleased with her because of Dr. Workman's forthright attitude about the medical aspects of Gulf War Illnesses and her conviction that many of these veterans had chronic infections not PTSD. This was not a conviction based on pronouncements that came down from above in the VA chain of command, it was entirely based on Dr. Workman's medical examinations and evaluations of her patients in her VA referral center. Her conviction about the medical explanations for Gulf War Illnesses would cost Dr. Workman her VA job as an infectious disease specialist. The VA and the DoD were very unforgiving to its physicians that did not go along with the dogma on the stress-related cause for Gulf War Illnesses.

After being forced out of the VA and establishing herself in private practice in environmental and travel medicine in Central Pennsylvania, Dr. Workman continued to collaborate with the McNichols. Now she was free to publish what *she* decided was important not the VA administrators who had previously overseen the work in her Gulf War Illness Referral Center. Dr. Workman had dared to go up against the bureaucratic establishment on a principle that was as old as organized medicine itself, the ethical treatment of patients. From what Dr. Workman personally saw in her clinic, she did not believe in what Washington was proclaiming on the subject of Gulf War Illnesses, and she felt that it was jeopardizing the abilities of her patients to receive appropriate treatments for their conditions. Since the VA and DoD had often used the fact that the McNichols were researchers not physicians, and therefore didn't know what they were doing in context with the veterans' health problems, Dr. Workman was a wonderful addition as a collaborator.

Jared McNichols goes to Washington

Even with the Madison's efforts to stop the McNichols' manuscripts from ever being reviewed let alone published, Jared was committed as ever to publishing their laboratory results, if they could get by the D. O. Madison's administrators and Jared's own department faculty rats. The Cancer Center's administration had even gone so far as to attempt to place Jared's laboratory under a faculty committee that would oversee his and Marie's research. However, Dr. Belcher was against this, mainly because it would have set a bad precedent at the Center. Also, it would have been difficult to find faculty members that were willing to openly go directly up against Jared and his reputation, and possibly because they would then have to worry that the same tactic might some day be used against themselves if they fell from grace with Dr. Masters and the Madison administration.

As the McNichols began to publish their research on the comparisons of the signs and symptoms in Gulf War Illness patients and mycoplasmal infections in Gulf War veterans, a Dr. Thomas Granite, director of the VA's clinical research programs at the VA headquarters in Washington DC, contacted Jared about coming to Washington to deliver a lecture to the VA and DoD about their research on Gulf War Illnesses. Dr. Granite *seemed* like a reasonable person, and Jared and Marie were relieved that they might have found someone at the VA in Washington who appeared to be open-minded and reasonable about what they had found. Dr. Granite had been speaking to some of the physicians within the VA system who were actually having some success using Jared's protocol for the treatment of Gulf War Illnesses using antibiotics and immune enhancement supplements. For the most part, these VA physicians were foreign trained and more open to the fact that infections might be involved in Gulf War Illnesses. But they also had to buck the system to get their patients treated properly. In some cases this required that they give their patients other diagnoses in order to get around the PTSD problem in the VA. For example, one VA physician in one of the New England VA regional centers was diagnosing his Gulf War patients with sinusitis so that he could prescribe antibiotics like doxycycline, the antibiotic that Jared was recommending for treatment of the mycoplamal infections found in Gulf War Illness patients.

The Washington invitation came after some epidemiologists in the VA Environmental Medicine Section viciously attacked the McNichols the previous year for proposing that a subset of the Gulf War veterans had chronic infections. The VA epidemiologists didn't apparently know anything about the scientific approaches that Jared and Marie had taken with respect to chronic illnesses in the Gulf War veterans, and they had never even bothered to talk to Jared or Marie about their data. The McNichols were skeptical that this group of government scientists and physicians could have an intelligent, unbiased discussion because of the questionable political agenda that drove them. The McNichols learned that they were poorly trained in molecular medicine and didn't have the scientific and research backgrounds to understand what Jared and Marie had found. They had simply attacked the McNichols because their research didn't fit with the plans of the VA and DoD to ascribe PTSD as *'the'* cause of Gulf War Illnesses.

The Federal epidemiologists that worked at the VA had produced questionable research on Gulf War veterans' health problems, primarily because it appeared that they were selecting their data to reinforce the political decisions that had been made concerning Gulf War veterans' illnesses. Thus they were either complete frauds who had been ordered to 'cook' their books to produce what the VA wanted the public to know, or they had been fed bogus data about the health problems of the veterans. It was clear that they knew more than they were willing to discuss with the McNichols or anyone else for that matter. They wouldn't discuss the VA's and DoD's own results on *M. fermentans,* and they dismissed out of hand the results of other laboratories that were just beginning to obtain similar results to the McNichols' with Gulf War Illness patients. These epidemiologists usually tried to frame their questions in such a narrow way that they ended up ignoring the obvious.

There was something very unreal about the VA and their approach to the problem of Gulf War Illnesses. First, they went along with the Pentagon and denied that the illnesses existed, and they allocated little or no resources to helping Gulf War veterans with their problems. This was done mainly because the DoD indicated that there was no such thing as Gulf War Syndrome or later Gulf War Illnesses or any chronic illnesses related to the Gulf War. Then the VA followed the Pentagon in deciding that Gulf War Illness was primarily a psychiatric condition, PTSD. So the VA did not do much more than send Gulf War veterans to VA psychiatrists, just like the DoD did after the war with active duty personnel. When the pressure on the VA from Congress and the veterans themselves eventually required them to respond to a growing crisis, mainly caused by the growing complaints from veterans and the lack of any measurable clinical responses to the antidepressants given to them, they established a few specialized Gulf War Illness Referral Units at some regional VA Medical Centers to deal with the increasing numbers of casualties from the Gulf War. Since the DoD and VA had always denied that veterans could transmit their illnesses to immediate family members, veterans' families were excluded from such assistance.

The VA seemed to be particularly hostile to the notion that many of the veterans might have chronic infections that could be transmitted to immediate family members. In one case, they actually went so far as to design a narrow study to 'disprove' that veterans' family members were coming down with illnesses similar to the veterans. However, even the U. S. Senate Committee on Banking, Housing and Urban Affairs reported to Congress as early as 1994 that approximately 77% of spouses and 65% of children of Gulf War Illness patients were showing signs and symptoms similar to the ill veterans. Unfortunately, this was completely discounted by the VA, because the data were not collected by their own scientists and physicians. Moreover, the VA units that were established to deal with the increasing health problems of Gulf War veterans, especially any psychiatric problems, did little more than evaluate the Gulf War veterans and forward the data to the DoD. Thus little was offered in the way of meaningful treatment for Gulf War Illnesses.

What the VA did in the face of this crisis was to prescribe antidepressants and other mood-altering drugs that tended to lessen the complaints of veterans. But these drugs were of dubious long-term benefit to the veterans, even with a PTSD diagnosis. Naturally the veterans were less inclined to complain when they were doped up on Zoloft and other mood-altering drugs, and perhaps that was the purpose of the exercise. If the VA and DoD were doing the right thing for the veterans, why were so many veterans complaining about the lack of assistance for their health problems? Why were so many of them still sick and not getting any better?

Little did the McNichols know at the time that Jared's invitation to visit the VA Headquarters in Washington DC was a complete set-up designed to discredit the McNichols in front of senior VA and DoD scientists and physicians. Basically the VA and Pentagon had already decided that there was little to the results that the McNichols were publishing, and perhaps this husband and wife research team were getting a bit too close to the DoD's own classified programs. Because Jared McNichols was a prominent scientist who had been asked to testify to Congressional committees and to the President's Commission on Gulf War Illnesses, they decided that they should show their 'neutrality' on the issue and give the McNichols' ideas a 'vigorous' examination. What this really meant was that the McNichols' research needed to be debunked, and they needed to be exposed as scientific charlatans, which had already been described to the press by Undersecretary of Defense Dr. Johns. For some reason Dr. Granite was apparently left out of the loop about this set-up, or at least he did not come across as obviously hostile, the usual indicator for the government cover-up artists who were 'quick with a knife' to attack any new non-psychiatric notions on Gulf War Illnesses.

Dr. Granite did not seem to fit the typical VA mold, and as far as Jared could tell, he was basically sincere and genuine. After a few discussions with Dr. Granite over the phone, Jared made his arrangements to go to Washington to deliver a lecture on the chronic infections in the ill Gulf War veterans. He was about to learn another lesson about Washington that Marie would learn separately in her own way. Once a decision had been made at the upper levels of the Federal bureaucracy, there was no easy method of reversing it. This was true for Agent Orange exposures in Vietnam veterans, and it was true for the chemical and biological exposures in Gulf War veterans.

The trip to Washington DC was relatively uneventful for Jared. He flew in from Austin on an early morning flight to Washington National Airport and immediately caught a cab to downtown Washington. When he arrived at the new VA Headquarters near the Capitol Mall, he was immediately taken up-stairs to Dr. Granite's office, dragging his suitcase along with him. There was nothing special about Dr. Granite's office, but he did have a good view of the Capitol out of his window. Papers were piled high on Dr. Granite's desk just like Jared's desk! Dr. Granite was a pleasant, even mannered physician in his 40s who Jared felt might have been a bit over his head on the Gulf War Illnesses issue, even though he was the director of VA clinical research programs. It was his job to oversee the design of clinical trials within the VA system, and as far as Jared could tell he was competent at his job. Jared had the feeling that Dr. Granite wanted to do the right thing for the veterans, but he was against a very rock-hard wall, and that was his superior, Dr. Jack Fuysen, who was the Director of Clinical Programs for the VA system. Dr. Fuysen came to the VA from Utah by way of the Navy Medical Corps as a conservative physician-researcher who was well acquainted with the use of military recruits for human experimentation on new weapons of mass destruction.

Jared had already bucked heads with Dr. Fuysen, who he basically considered a closet fiend, easily capable of killing hundreds of thousands of veterans for his own power and glory or to protect his own administrative skin. Dr. Fuysen had close contacts with the military physicians who were running the office in the Pentagon that dealt with Gulf War Illnesses, especially Mr. Rott and Dr. Murphy, and he loathed scientists like Jared and Marie for making public statements on how the veterans were being treated, some would say mistreated, by the VA. In fact, Dr. Fuysen took great pleasure in running the McNichols into the ground every chance he got in private and even in public, because he felt that Jared, in particular, had demeaned the VA with his comments on how poorly the Gulf War veterans had been treated within the VA system. Actually, Jared and Marie felt quite strongly that the VA had a very poor record, in general, in protecting the health of American veterans, and they thought that the VA had a lot to prove to earn the McNichols' respect.

Historically the VA had been involved in some of the most medically questionable clinical trials ever conducted in the history of the United States, such as the purposeful irradiation of veterans just to find out how much radiation they could tolerate. Such information might have been marginally useful for the DoD during the Cold War when the chance of nuclear conflagration with the Soviets was real, but it really wasn't the job of the VA to destroy their own patients to gather research information for the Pentagon.

Dr. Fuysen fit in quite nicely with the mentality of the Pentagon medical sector when it came to the use of veterans as research subjects or human guinea pigs. He really didn't give a damn about their welfare, and in general, he had promoted subordinates who felt exactly the same way. Dr. Granite appeared to be the exception. Dr. Fuysen had gone after anyone who dared to produce data that showed that Gulf War Illness was not a psychiatric condition. After some run-ins with Dr. Fuysen, Jared wanted desperately to accept that Dr. Granite was the exception to the 'Fuysen rule' at the VA. However, this was not the case with some of the other players around VA headquarters.

One VA epidemiologist that was particularly in the mold of Dr. Fuysen was Dr. Fiona Mathews. Dr. Mathews would have actually been considered a rather good-looking lady with long dark hair in her late thirties, if she didn't wear a full-time sneer on her face. She had cold, beady dark eyes and a robotic stare, and Jared considered her a nasty piece of work. It was Dr. Mathews, the VA epidemiologist in charge of Gulf War Illness studies, who actually did the most damage to veterans' lives by her reports that claimed that Gulf War Illness patients were not more likely to be sick than the general public at large. She also claimed that Gulf War veterans had not been hospitalized or had not died at higher rates than other service personnel. Of course, such studies were aimed entirely at hiding the real truth. For example, Gulf War veterans had chronic illness rates that were far, far higher than those of Vietnam or Korean War veterans and certainly much higher than non-deployed personnel. The VA epidemiologists, however, were becoming famous for being able to twist the truth by creative data selection and management. For example, the VA acted quickly to 'adjust' the data to 'demonstrate' that there was not a higher rate of illness in Gulf War veterans, but eventually the documented numbers of veterans with VA-accepted disability cases indicated exactly the opposite, and the difference was so obvious that the hole could not be easily plugged, even by the explanation that the VA had 'relaxed' the rules to allow more veterans to receive compensation than usual. The VA hospitalization rate data comparisons were criticized because the VA excluded without explanation from their calculations hospitalizations in civilian and military hospitals. In fact, Dr. Cathy Workman and Jared had published a letter to the editor of an environmental medical journal that was critical of the VA data published in the same journal on the subject. In addition, the VA itself possessed information that indicated that the death rate of Gulf War veterans was far higher than expected when compared to non-deployed personnel, but they had kept this data secret from the academics that studied such things, and they especially had kept it secret from the American people.

Not everyone at VA Headquarters agreed with the program of Dr. Fuysen to hide the truth from the American public. At one point a two-foot high stack of official raw VA data was secretly sent to Jared by an intermediate-level VA employee in the epidemiology section. This 'deep throat' would supply additional data to the McNichols until the packages abruptly stopped, and they never heard from him again. Jared and Marie always wondered what had happened to the VA whistleblower. Did the VA find out and fire him? Did they have him killed? For years the VA would only admit that the accident and suicide rates among Gulf War veterans were higher than expected, and from this we were urged to accept their explanation that the death rates of Gulf War veterans were not higher than expected. However, the data that the McNichols received secretly indicated just the opposite from what the VA was telling the press and the American people. Jared was particularly interested in the cancer rates, which were skyrocketing among the Gulf War veterans compared to their non-deployed colleagues. Among these were unusual brain and brainstem cancers and especially skin tumors that were being found at unusually high rates in Gulf War veterans. None of this was ever made public. Jared felt that he could not use the data, however, because he would have been immediately attacked by the VA because of its dubious source. All that the VA had to do was claim that the data was bogus or manufactured by the McNichols, and Jared would have no way to prove otherwise.

It was in this hostile environment that Jared had agreed to deliver a lecture to the VA and DoD staffs on chronic infections in Gulf War illnesses. Usually when a lecturer visits an institution, a schedule is drawn up so that they can meet with individuals with similar interests. However, the only VA staff member on Jared's schedule was Dr. Granite. Jared thought about the VA scientists that had sent him data in the past, but it would not have been prudent to ask for appointments to visit them, and in fact, it might even cast suspicion on them and their loyalty. The data that had been secretly sent to the McNichols came with a warning not to divulge the 'messenger.' From what Jared knew about the VA, that was probably a prudent suggestion. Neither Jared or Marie ever divulged the sources of their information from inside the VA headquarters, but eventually these sources dried up because of internal transfers, retirements or even possibly premature releases from the department or worse.

When the time came for Jared's lecture, Dr. Granite took him down to the lecture hall. Approaching the lecture hall with Dr. Granite, Jared could feel the animosity and hatred of some of the people who would be in attendance at his lecture, but he tried to ignore their stares. The next hint that there was something wrong was that just before Jared and Dr. Granite approached the lecture hall, Jared was told that his seminar would be closed to the general public. What that meant was not clear until Jared was met immediately outside the door to the lecture hall by several veterans, some in uniform as active duty military officers. They were not being allowed to enter the seminar room. Jared did not consider these Gulf War veterans 'the general public' but his pleas for their admittance fell on the deaf ears of the VA. Some officers in uniform of intermediate rank did manage to slip into the seminar, possibly because the VA may have been hesitant to bar them or they just thought that they were part of the audience. Some officers up to rank of major general were in the audience, and most of these officers were from places like Fort Detrick and the U. S. Army Institute of Pathology Research.

There was nothing that Jared could do as a visitor to help the veterans attend his seminar. He had to go into the seminar hall and wait for his own fate. Before the seminar started, it was common for the speaker's host to introduce the speaker and the subject. As Jared's host, Dr. Granite did a marvelous job at introducing the topic and the lecturer from Texas, and Jared was relieved that at least he was treated fairly by Dr. Granite.

Jared had planned his talk to be nonpolitical, so he could focus just on the science. Jared tried to deliver his seminar in a very low-key fashion so as to not fan the flames, because there had been some bad blood between the McNichols and the VA administration on the issue of the treatment of Gulf

War veterans. When he completed his seminar, he answered questions for approximately thirty minutes. Most of the questions were of technical nature, and the VA bureaucrats and senior military officers were finding it hard to stay awake. Standing at the side of the lecture hall the entire time was the zombie witch Dr. Fiona Mathews, who was staring at Jared with her usual fixed sneer. She didn't ask any questions. Dr. Fuysen didn't even bother to attend the seminar. Perhaps he felt that if he attended, he might lend some credence to the McNichols research, which he certainly didn't want to do.

By and large the audience at Jared's seminar was respectful, but Jared had no way of knowing that the VA or DoD had brought in some 'hired guns' for the occasion—scientists on the payroll of the DoD or active duty officers from Fort Dietrick, biowarfare scientists and experts on chronic infections. Some of these had been brought in from as far away as Alabama and Texas to take on Jared. They were not invited all the way to Washington and paid as consultants by the VA to celebrate the joys of scientific inquiry. They were brought in to debunk the McNichols work, and Jared felt that they were having a hard time doing it. Although he never received any feedback from his lecture at VA Headquarters that day, just the fact that there was little or no explosive fallout was probably all that could be expected. Jared would later wonder why the D. O. Madison administration never reacted adversely to his VA seminar invitation in Washington DC. Perhaps they were in on it all along.

Dr. Lon from the U. S. Army Institute for Pathology Research was at the seminar, but he didn't really say very much, except to introduce himself to Jared before the seminar and ask one question after the seminar. Dr. Lon looked very professional in a dark suit, white shirt and dark tie with his signature black-rimmed glasses. He could almost pass as one of the VA bureaucrats, except that he was Chinese. He was respectful, made one comment at the end of the seminar, briefly nodded at Jared and left the lecture hall. Jared never got a chance to discuss his research with him or ask Dr. Lon any questions. Dr. Lon was obviously a bit nervous around the assembled group, especially when Jared praised his work on *Mycoplasma fermentans*. Dr. Lon did not expect to be praised by Jared, and it made him very uneasy, especially when a few members of the audience turned and stared at Dr. Lon.

Even with the polite but antagonistic audience, Jared guessed that he held his own, which under the circumstances was an accomplishment. It was very clear that he was not there to win the hearts and minds of the VA or the DoD. He was there to be cannon fodder. The first question after the seminar was actually a comment made by Dr. Lon. He mentioned that he could not find *M. fermentans* in the veterans but he did not use the same procedures as the McNichols. With that comment he covered his scientific tracks, but he made it clear to the audience that the official DoD position was that there were no infections in the veterans that could explain their signs and symptoms. In fact, Jared remembered that Marie had told him about a conversation she had with one of the VA scientists who amazingly stated to her *"There are no such things as mycoplasmas in the Middle East."* It was this ridiculous, stubborn and ignorant attitude that typified the unswerving and unspoken tone of the audience.

The next few questions were all about the pathogenic properties of *M. fermentans*. Jared could not identify the persons asking the questions, and in contrast to the DoD and VA personnel introduced to him just before his seminar, they did not identify themselves. Jared wondered whether they were DoD contractors, or more spooks from the CIA or DIA.

Jared went to the black board to the right of the screen to answer the questions about the pathogenic properties of the mycoplasma that they had found in the Gulf War veterans. He began by making a list of properties that *M. fermentans* should have if it were to be considered pathogenic. Jared said, "According to the literature, a mycoplasma species should fulfill most if not all of the following list of criteria in order to be considered pathogenic and involved in human illness." Jared wrote the following on the board:

(1) *The mycoplasma should be found at higher concentration and prevalence in ill patients compared to normal subjects.* Jared added, "This is exactly what we have found, and I reported on it today. In addition two other groups have similar results to ours.

(2)   *More of the mycoplasma should be recovered from diseased patients than from controls.* "Although *M. fermentans* is extremely difficult to recover, this appears to be the case."

(3)   *An antibody response should be found in symptomatic patients.* "According to Dr. Lon, as specifically outlined in his patent and publications, *M. fermentans* does not elicit an antibody response until an infected subject is near death, so we would not expect this particular item to be useful in determining whether *M. fermentans* is pathogenic."

(4)   *A clinical response should be accompanied by suppression of the mycoplasma.* "This is exactly what we have found with antibiotic treatment, and I reported on this today."

(5)   *Clinical responses should be differential, depending on the antibiotic.* "In fact, only certain antibiotics are effective in alleviating signs and symptoms, other are not, and this is completely consistent with the response of *M. fermentans* to antibiotics, as I reported today and from the literature."

(6)   *The mycoplasma should cause a similar illness in animals.* "This is actually quite dramatic and well documented in several publications. *M. fermentans* causes illnesses in mice, rats, hamsters, sheep, and even monkeys that is similar to that found in humans. In these non-human species, the infection causes a chronic illness that eventually progresses to organ failure and death, just like the studies of Dr. Lon with Armed Forces personnel."

(7)   *The mycoplasma must cause a similar disease in man after inoculating human volunteers.* "Since this type of experiment is no longer considered ethical, I know of no way to answer this question."

(8)   *A specific anti-mycoplasma reagent or immune response protects subjects from the disease.* "I don't know if this has, in fact, been done or not.

Jared continued his explanation of the pathogenesis of the mycoplasma, "Thus most of the requirements of pathogenicity have been met, and from this I would conclude that *M. fermentans* is pathogenic. From his publication on the subject in a pathology journal, I am sure that Dr. Lon would agree with me. He found this infection and only this infection in Armed Service personnel that later died of their infection." There were some questions about the lack of detectable antibodies against the mycoplasma in patients, but Jared kept referring to Dr. Lon's patent, which was quite clear on this issue. Dr. Lon had only found antibodies at the late stages of the disease process, and this was confirmed by his primate studies where antibodies were only found when the animals were near death.

After the seminar Jared met informally with some of his detractors. Dr. Mathews left immediately after a final sneer and a cold stare with her dark beady eyes, and Dr. Armwhite was there. When Jared met him, he didn't identify himself as an officer from Fort Detrick. Although Jared recognized him instantly as a Major General from the two stars on his epaulets, Jared wrongly thought that he had come over from the Pentagon. General Armwhite was not particularly happy about Jared's seminar, but this was not the time or place to dress down Jared. There was also a certain military respect for your enemies, even if Jared did not consider himself General Armwhite's enemy. Another officer that Jared met was an Air Force Colonel who was also apparently assigned to Fort Detrick. He was a nasty piece of work, but he at least kept up the veneer of appropriate behavior. All of these detractors were acting very professional in the semi-public environment of the seminar hall, but Jared wondered if they would have been as polite if he had met with them in private at Fort Detrick.

After answering a few more questions, Jared noticed probably the only friendly face in the crowd, Capt. Hamlin from Fort Meade, who had managed to sneak into the seminar. Capt. Hamlin was in full uniform and towered over the wimpy DoD scientists and VA administrators who were left in the room. He came right up to Jared, held his hand out and said loudly to the dismay of the remaining participants, "Colonel McNichols, that was an *outstanding* seminar! You have done a great service to the veterans of the Gulf War! You and Mrs. Dr. McNichols saved my life and probably my wife's as well. And our daughter would probably be crippled if it weren't for you two brave scientists."

Jared smiled and thought that Capt. Hamlin was overdoing it a bit, but he had his reasons. After all, he was stationed at Fort Meade, the nerve center of the NSA and the military's electronic intelligence units. He was obviously getting healthier than even the last time that Marie and Jared saw him at Fort Meade, and he must have felt a sense of amusement by loudly calling Jared 'Colonel,' even though Jared and Marie were only honorary colonels. This was his way, Jared assumed, of throwing a little dig at the administrative military officers and DoD biowarfare scientists who were mostly nerds who would never have the respect of the Special Forces. When they turned to examine Capt. Hamlin's credentials, which were worn proudly on his uniform, they quickly identified him as an Army intelligence officer. Besides, he could probably whip any two of them in hand-to-hand combat with one arm tied behind him. They were not going to take on Capt. Hamlin, not now and not anywhere!

Jared mentioned to the small group that Capt. Hamlin was an example of successful antibiotic treatment of Gulf War Illness. Most of the small group that was left after Jared's lecture didn't seem particularly pleased to see Capt. Hamlin say that the McNichols had probably saved his life and those of his family. In fact, they looked just as glum and hostile as they had before the lecture. Jared could only guess at what most of the audience did for a living, because most were in civilian clothes and looked suspiciously like scientists not bureaucrats. For the most part, they were likely biological warfare mavens from the DoD and outside biological warfare contractors along with a few middle level VA bureaucrats. All of the recognizable VA administrators left immediately after Jared's seminar, including Dr. Granite, or they didn't attend at all like Dr. Fuysen. Jared was left to fend on his own, but now, of course, with Capt. Hamlin's support it turned into a welcome respite from the seething atmosphere surrounding the prelude and aftermath of his seminar. Later Jared would wryly think to himself that etiquette and protocol seemed to be in short shrift at VA Headquarters that day.

Finally, the last remaining die-hards departed, and Jared was left with Capt. Hamlin to find his way from the now quiet seminar hall and out of the building. After picking up his slides and his overnight bag left in the back of the room by some unknown messenger at the now quiet and blacked-out projector, Jared and Capt. Hamlin made their way down the nearest stairs and exited directly onto the street. It was good to be out of VA Headquarters, Jared thought to himself, as they basked in the bright sunlight of a fine autumn afternoon. Capt. Hamlin, who drove his own car to Washington to be there when Jared lectured to the VA, had to excuse himself to get back to Fort Meade. He was given only a few hours leave by his commanding officer to attend Jared's seminar, and he had to immediately return to Fort Meade.

When they were about a block away from the VA headquarters, Capt. Hamlin turned to Jared and asked, "What did those Air Force pukes want? I don't trust them." Jared smiled and said, "They're just part of the biowarfare scum from Fort Detrick. They would rather see you and your family die than lift a finger to help. They were probably concerned that their little anthill may have been penetrated. You know, they would rather see their mother die than give up the antidotes to their weapons. I don't know what to think of them. Scum like that shadow us whenever we go to present our data in public." Capt. Hamlin said, "Don't let those pukes get you down. You have a lot of support from the line officers. They're just a bunch of desk-jockeys. They've never been in a real war. They just think that they're real smart, but I'd like to give them a M-16 and put'em in the front line!" Jared laughed, "I don't take them too seriously. As you said, they're nothing but a bunch of pukes!" Capt. Hamlin continued, "Don't trust that Dr. Lon either. He gave us the run around about testing for the mycoplasma. He told us that none of his Gulf War samples turned up positive, and then we found out from another soldier that he let the samples sit on the lab bench for a few weeks before testing them. I'd like to run that goddamn 'chink' out of here and send him back to Red China." Jared calmly said, "Yes, I've heard the story before. I can't seem to pin him down on the mycoplasma. He just won't commit in public to finding anything, but just after the war he told some officers from the 3st Armored Division that they were positive for Mfi, and then he later denied it and said that the tests were all wrong." Capt. Hamlin said, "I want to get my hands around his skinny neck. I just want to crush his windpipe." Jared laughed, "Look, it wouldn't take much. But the more important question is who is telling him to shut up, and why? Is this their bioweapon? Is it too embarrassing to admit that publicly?" Capt. Hamlin agreed, "It's got to be something like that. I'm going to do some looking into this. Too many good people are dying for some pukes who are playing around with germs. It's just a game to them. Jared added, "A dangerous game at that. Be careful, Captain, and keep a close eye on your family." Capt. Hamlin said, "Yes, sir! That I will, sir!" Jared thought to himself that those 'pukes' were not just endangering the lives of military personnel, but they were also toying with the lives of the general public by denying the infectious nature of the microbes spread by their reckless and illegal activities. Later Jared and Marie would publish a paper stressing the dangerous precedent for the nation to not acknowledge such infections, because terrorists might consider that they had free reign to use biological weapons against America without the slightest chance that they would be acknowledged, until it was too late. Something had to be done, but he and Marie were very much isolated because of their quest to help the veterans and their family members who had become sick after the Gulf War.

After a firm handshake, some verbal encouragement and another pat on the back, Capt. Hamlin stiffened up to attention and gave Jared a snappy salute as he said, "Colonel, Sir!" He turned on his heal, and walked away sharply. Jared didn't have time to return the salute. He was holding his briefcase and bag, and he felt a little uneasy about saluting in his civilian clothes anyway, because it wasn't proper protocol and he wasn't a real colonel. But at this point, who cared? He called to Capt. Hamlin, and as he turned around, Jared dropped his bag, saluted and said, "Airborne!" Capt. Hamlin returned his salute and answered back, "Airborne! Sir!" Although Capt. Hamlin served in the 101st Airborne Division, which is now technically an air assault force not a paratrooper unit, Jared thought he might appreciate the historical perspective. The 101st had a rich history from the paratroopers who jumped during the Normandy invasion on through Korea, Vietnam and now the Gulf War, and Capt. Hamlin *was* a qualified paratrooper, meaning that he had been through Army 'jump school' in Georgia.

Capt. Hamlin was gone in a hurry. Jared watched the tall, straight Army officer walk briskly down the street for a moment, and then after he was finally satisfied that Capt. Hamlin was truly recovered from his ordeal with Gulf War Illness, Jared turned and started walking in the opposite direction to find a cab. Eventually he waved down a cab to take him to National Airport. The taxi driver was glad to take the obviously out-of-towner to Washington National Airport. He was an Afghan, and he didn't speak much English but knew how to get to National Airport.

In the cab on the way to the airport Jared had some time to think about what had happened at VA Headquarters. The VA obviously knew much more about what the McNichols were doing than the McNichols knew about what the VA was doing, and perhaps that was by design. Washington was such an insular 'need-to-know' place, and Jared could not help feeling that he and Marie were crashing their private party. The 'them-versus-us' attitude was quite obvious to Jared, and this was probably why the VA did not want any outsiders at his seminar, *especially* any reporters. Jared did not have any contact with reporters on this trip, and it was just as well, because he would have to face the D. O. Madison administration if anything appeared in print about the seminar at VA Headquarters.

The VA had been stung recently by some sharp reporters and critical newspaper articles. No matter how much they tried to push off Gulf War Illnesses as psychiatric illnesses, after talking to individual veterans, the press for the most part was not buying it. Jared had a feeling that the administrators in Washington didn't like to be bothered by provincials from the heartland, especially those that might bring a message to Washington that they didn't want to hear. Jared had managed to survive his trip to Washington with relatively minor 'injuries,' mostly to his ego, although Marie would find it more difficult with the group at the U. S. Army Institute for Pathology Research. They were much closer to the unethical agenda that Marie and Jared were now convinced permeated the whole Gulf War Illnesses issue.

It was much later on that Jared learned that his lecture had been secretly summarized in an unflattering way by one of the Pentagon attendees and provided to an Assistant Secretary of Defense, Dr. Joseph Johns. If this summary had been balanced, Jared probably would not have cared one way or another, but it was completely unfair and biased against the McNichols and their research. Dr. Johns had already slandered Marie and Jared with his letter to Senator Roth, and the attacks would continue.

Jared arrived back in Austin and was picked up at the airport by Marie. He said to Marie after giving her a kiss and a smile, "You know, I thought about it, and I've come to the conclusion that I really hate Washington." Marie didn't acknowledge his little joke and smile, and she said very seriously, "I have been telling you that. Now maybe you will listen. We have to get out of this country. They are killing everyone, and they don't give a damn about any of us." Jared was now sorry that he had set off Marie at the airport. "Can we talk about this later at home?" Unfortunately, Marie had been ignited, and she wouldn't quit so easily, "You're the one who wants to stay here and fight it out! I say we leave. It's a lost cause. Can't you see it?" Jared was now very sorry that he brought it up in the first place. He said, "You agreed with me when we started this whole thing, and you were the one who told the SEALs that we would go on because there were more Dales out there." Marie indicated, "Well, I was wrong!" Jared stopped, grabbed Marie and hugged her tightly. He could feel her squirming in his grasp trying to escape his hold on her. She was mad at Jared for continuing the quest, which she felt was like tilting against windmills. Sometimes Jared conceded that she was right and he was wrong to continue the battle. After all, they had helped their own get better and overcome the illness, so why continue to buck City Hall? You just knew that you couldn't win; they held all the cards. And the system was so corrupt that it seemed like no one was listening, even though the failure to act could have the most extreme consequences to the nation.

It would take over a decade for Marie and Jared to learn that it would be the checks and balances in the system that would eventually begin to overcome this dangerous faction, a faction of killers, with no loyalty to anyone or anything. It was a faction that hid in the inner recesses of the massive government bureaucracy. In fact, one Lt. General who served as an Undersecretary of Defense under four presidents would say to the McNichols, "This is dangerous . . . This is scary . . . . It will take the divine to navigate the jungle created by this vicious group of defense scientists and physicians."

Jared and Marie had learned that no one liked whistle blowers, and this was how they were treated, even by the few friends that they had left in Austin and elsewhere. Most of their fair weather friends, it turned out, turned on them in a microsecond, especially most of their faculty colleagues at the D. O. Madison Cancer Center. Even Jared could not defend their despicable behavior, and he no longer tried to rationalize to Marie why they acted the way they did toward the McNichols. Jared concluded that it was so competitive out there that your professional colleagues thought nothing about slitting your professional throat, if they thought that they could have your lab, your technicians, your students, your office, your department and your position. That was the way it was in academia, at least from Jared's perspective.

Marie McNichols goes to see Dr. Lon

Jared wasn't the only one to 'do his duty' and visit Washington. It was only a couple of days after Jared returned from Washington when Marie decided to call Dr. Lon. She had cooled down about the treatment that Jared received at the hands of the VA and DoD. Jared had not been treated that badly at VA Headquarters, and he had told her over and over that the Washington administrators were not important in the long run, only the truth was important, and they couldn't hide it forever. Deep inside Marie knew this, but she still resented the way the McNichols were being treated in Austin and Washington, just because they stumbled onto some chronic infections in the veterans and prison guards that a small number of people wanted to keep secret from the American people. Who would have thought that the authorities would not be pleased to have a reasonable explanation for a large group of the sick veterans, and a viable treatment protocol. The truth was that once egocentric people had made up their minds, they couldn't easily accept that their pre-conceived notions could possibly be wrong.

Jared told Marie that not everyone was an egomaniac and a jerk in Washington. Jared had mentioned to her that Dr. Lon had been polite and basically passive during his seminar at VA Headquarters, and he had no problems with Dr. Granite. He was not as hostile as the other VA administrators and epidemiologists. Marie felt that Dr. Lon might even be helpful to the McNichols, even if he was constrained by the politics of Washington and the Pentagon. After all, the McNichols were only confirming Dr. Lon's own theories about the role of Mfi in chronic illnesses. He couldn't be all that bad. He might even welcome support for his own theories from outside the beltway.

Jared had to remind Marie that the road to hell was paved with good intentions. He felt that Dr. Lon had not been completely forthright with them on the role of *his* Mfi mycoplasma in Gulf War Illnesses and other conditions. But the McNichols had no idea of the pressures that Dr. Lon might be under to protect the secrets about Mfi.

Marie finally decided to call Dr. Lon. She asked Jared what he thought about it, and he just shrugged his shoulders. He obviously thought that it was a waste of time, but Marie thought otherwise. Although Marie had quite a temper and blew quite easily, she actually had more faith in mankind than Jared, who was becoming more and more pessimistic as time went on. Although Jared had to spend more time fending off the barbarians at the gate who wanted to take everything from the McNichols that they had worked so hard to build over the years, he had not suffered as long as Marie. Marie had a temper, but she was also quick to reconsider her position. Jared was more true to his brooding Scottish heritage. Once he made up his mind, that was it. There was no turning back.

Marie found Dr. Ming Lon's telephone number that she saved from a few years ago, and the following morning she dialed Dr. Lon's number at the U. S. Army Institute of Pathology Research. She was amazed when Dr. Ming Lon picked up the phone after the third ring, "Hello, Pathology lab." She said, "This is Dr. Marie McNichols calling from Austin, Texas. I am trying to reach Dr. Ming Lon." Dr. Lon replied, "Dr. McNichols, how are you!" Dr. Lon was pleasantly surprised because he had been recruited to call Marie anyway, and this was much more natural. "Your husband just gave a seminar over at the VA a week ago." Marie said, "Yes. Actually the reason that I'm calling is that I was intrigued by an article you published recently on *Mycoplasma fermentans*." Dr. Lon replied, "Oh? Yes, the recent article where we isolated the mycoplasma." She continued, "The unusual mycoplasma, we call it Mfi, that you found associated with AIDS patients and also responsible for the deaths of some Armed Forces personnel." Dr. Lon continued, "Yes, *Mycoplasma fermentans* incognitus is a unique microorganism. It can be quite pathogenic. But the concept of a highly pathogenic mycoplasma has not been acknowledged by everyone in the medical and science communities." Marie continued, "I am not an infectious disease expert, but I am curious about *this* particular mycoplasma, because I think that I may have caught it somewhere, and as you know from Jared's lecture we have been finding it in the Gulf War veterans but more recently in some prison guards down here in Texas." Dr. Lon asked, "What?" He had not heard the prison guard story, because Jared left it out of his seminar so as to not stimulate the subsequent wrath of Dr. Masters. Marie repeated herself, "I said, I think I caught this mycoplasma in the late 80s. I became very sick after a trip to the Middle East. It seemed to infect every organ and tissue in my body, and some of my organs became inflamed and ultimately I developed meningitis and encephalitis. Initially, it started as a flu-like illness with aching joints, chronic fatigue, night sweats, gastrointestinal problems, skin rashes, vertigo, and then it progressed into a kind of thyroiditis, and finally it became meningitis. My thyroid was swollen and my thyroid hormones were all over the place. I was nauseated for thirteen months, my stomach felt like an inferno, and I was constantly dizzy. I had problems with my vision and hearing."

Marie continued her conversation with Dr. Lon. "At one point I thought I had gotten HIV from a blood transfusion I had during surgery in 1983, and my weight dropped to 70 pounds." Dr. Lon said, "From what you've described, it sounds like you could have had a severe infection like this mycoplasma can cause. How did you overcome the illness? Was it similar to the protocol you and your husband have been suggesting to the veterans?" Marie continued, "Well, at first I went on ampicillin, and I got worse. Then, by process of elimination my husband and I empirically tried the antibiotic doxycycline. Within several weeks of taking the antibiotic, my symptoms started to slowly subside. I went on four six-week courses of doxycycline, and then I began to be well enough to resume exercising with weights. All in all, though, it took about three years on and off again antibiotics for me to fully regain my health." Dr. Lon continued, "As I think I told you before, you are a very lucky young lady. Most people in the medical community are skeptical about a highly pathogenic mycoplasma and probably would not have prescribed doxycycline. You were extremely lucky to have hit upon doxycycline." Marie said, "You may laugh at me, but I am sure there was divine intervention in my healing." Dr. Lon responded, "I do not laugh at such things." Marie was secretly testing Dr. Lon's memory about their previous conversation to determine and gauge his attitude towards her. She still suspected that Dr. Lon might have been involved in her illness, which she now felt was deliberate. She said, "You know, Dr. Lon, you met my husband who is a department chairman here at the D. O. Madison Cancer Center, and we admire your work. I was wondering if perhaps you would be open to hearing about the Nucleoprotein Gene Tracking technique we have been developing over the last decade."

Dr. Lon couldn't believe what he was hearing from Marie. It was his chance to invite her to visit the Institute without the McNichols becoming suspicious about his motives. He said, "I heard your husband's seminar at the VA recently, and it sounds very interesting. Can you tell me more about it, say in person here in Washington?" Marie replied, "Actually that was the purpose of my calling you today. As it turns out I have to be in the area, and I thought that it might be possible to visit your Institute." Dr. Lon responded, "That's intriguing. I would really like to learn more about the technique that you have developed. I do not understand the approach that well, and your husband really spent more time explaining why the Gulf War veterans' illnesses were related to chronic infections than on the techniques that you two used to find them. I am interested in this problem, because to be frank with you Dr. McNichols, we have not found this particular mycoplasma in the veterans. Would you be willing to come here and show us your detailed data?" Marie replied, "I know it is difficult to grasp without the benefit of seeing the data. But since I have to give a seminar at Georgetown in December, perhaps I could come over to the Institute and present a seminar?" Dr. Lon said, "We would appreciate that. I'll tell my department staff, and I'm sure they'll welcome the opportunity to have you visit." Marie said, "Then it's settled . . . . By the way, I think I asked you this before, but where did you do your training?" Dr. Lon replied, "I did my undergraduate training at the National University in Taiwan." Marie was testing Dr. Lon when she asked, "I thought you were from Mainland China?" Dr. Lon continued, "I am, but it was arranged for me to study in Taiwan. I completed my Ph.D., and then I did an M.D. degree at Belford College of Medicine in your city." Marie said, "Gee, I didn't know you had been at Belford. I was on the faculty there for a few years." Dr. Lon said, "After I finished my M.D., I went to work temporarily at a small Belford biotech company called "Biox."

The word 'Biox' sent a jolt through Marie, but she tried to hide her response. Marie said without giving herself away, "I've heard of it. I believe it was started by the Lings, who were from my old Department. What kinds of products are being marketed by Biox?" Dr. Lon replied, "I don't know if they are actually selling anything yet. When I was at Biox, I was working on a variety of antibody-based tests against anthrax and related microorganisms." Marie asked, "Anthrax? Why on earth would Biox work on anthrax? It's so deadly that I recall that the government had to shut down a facility at Fort Detrick sometime in the seventies due to an anthrax accident." Dr. Lon said, "That's right! Moscow was heavily engaged in anthrax germ warfare during the Cold War, so we had no choice but to establish our own program. I was actually interested in some of the contaminants in the cultures." Marie asked, "Are you saying that scientists at Belford were actually engaging in anthrax experimentation?"

Dr. Lon did not answer Marie's question, and Marie could tell from his hesitation that he was becoming extremely uneasy about the direction of the conversation. She immediately changed the subject, "You know Dr. Lon, my department chairman at Belford asked me how I felt about germ warfare and if I would participate in experiments just before I became sick in the late eighties. I told him how asinine such research would be, since we barely understand what makes us tick. He asked me if I would remain silent if I had heard about any germ warfare research going on in the department. I told him I wouldn't, and that such research was the height of scientific amorality. Of course, Dr. Lon, I meant no disrespect to you." Dr. Lon quickly replied, "I understand."

Marie changed the subject again—she was trying to get more information out of Dr. Lon, "Do you feel that the mycoplasma you found, Mfi, is a naturally-occurring microorganism or do you feel it was altered in some way?" Dr. Lon became very uneasy and hesitated, "I cannot say. It's too sensitive!" Marie asked again, "In other words, you don't know if it was altered?" Dr. Lon replied, "You're going to have to draw your own conclusions." Marie spoke abruptly, "Oh well, I meant no offense. You probably know that we found some unusual gene sequences in the Mfi in the soldiers and the prison guards, but we really haven't found the same sequences in some civilians with Chronic Fatigue Syndrome." Dr. Lon said, "I know you have looked at Chronic Fatigue Syndrome and Fibromyalgia Syndrome from your husband's lecture." Marie finally said, "Well Dr. Lon, I look forward to meeting you and discussing this further." Dr. Lon had one more request, "Please send me your résumé. I'll be in touch with you

about your seminar." Marie added, "Nice talking to you Dr. Lon." He
finally said, "It was a pleasure talking to you Dr. McNichols."

After the conversation, Marie thought about what Jared told her about
Dr. Lon. Jared considered him a shifty character who wouldn't admit that
he had also found *Mycoplasma fermentans* in the veterans and in some of the
civilians with Chronic Fatigue Syndrome, and he did not trust Dr. Lon. But
Marie felt more comfortable about Dr. Lon, who she felt might have been
trapped by circumstance into working on biological warfare agents, if that
was what the Mfi strain of the mycoplasma was, and Dr. Lon could not
admit it to Marie. She also thought that Dr. Lon couldn't admit that the
veterans had mycoplasmal infections without endangering his himself or
his family. Marie told Jared that Dr. Lon had probably been threatened,
and he couldn't tell the truth about his results with the Gulf War Illness or
Chronic Fatigue Syndrome patients. As usual, Marie would turn out to be
correct.

Dr. Lon notified his department head of the intent to invite Dr. Marie
McNichols to deliver a seminar the U. S. Army Institute of Pathology
Research. The request was forwarded up to the administration. Dr. Lon
was then notified he had to meet with General Armwhite and Dr.
Deutschman. A few days later Dr. Lon was told when and where to meet
with his superiors. As he entered a small conference room at the Institute,
they were both standing in the room discussing something in hushed
conversation. General Armwhite was obviously distracted. Without even
saying hello, General Armwhite turned to Dr. Lon and said, "Ming, you
were actually able to bring Marie McNichols here to give a seminar? Dr.
Lon replied, "Yes." He added an afterthought, "I do not see why anyone
would be trying to kill Dr. Marie McNichols. She is an excellent scientist
and very personable." Dr. Deutschman trying to be more diplomatic said,
"It isn't personal, Dr. Lon, it's just that she comes from a powerful family,
and it is simply too dangerous to let one bleeding heart scientist inherit so
much money and at the same time know so much about our programs." Dr.
Lon who didn't know that Marie was an heiress asked, "Why is she
considered an heiress? Why haven't I heard about this?" General Armwhite
replied, "Goddamnit, Ming. Don't you get it? You would think a person of
your intelligence who was thrown in a work camp in China because of
questionable political loyalties would not want to see some little bitch with

so much money." Dr. Lon said, "I was not thinking about her in terms of money, sir! I was only thinking of the science." Dr. Deutschman said, "I strongly urge you to wake up and see that our perspective is correct. People like Marie and Jared McNichols are a menace, and we certainly don't want to see them have any financial resources to continue their probing into *our* business."

The discussion of the McNichols was about to get worse. General Armwhite was growing impatient and asked, "Why did that Day Lily Russian Doll Cocktail fail?" Dr. Lon who didn't know that Marie's illness might have been induced asked, "You mean you people actually poisoned her with a Day Lily Cocktail?" Dr. Armwhite said, "What's wrong with you, Ming? Don't you remember?" He asked again, "Remember what sir?" Dr. Deutschman said, "You helped design the cocktail for the McNichols!" Ming looked dazed and confused at Armwhite's statement. He tried to answer, "But I . . ." Dr. Deutschman interrupted and said to General Armwhite, "Never mind, General. Dr. Lon here spent some time at the Monarch Point Intelligence Center in New York for some mind rehabilitation." Dr. Armwhite nodded and then asked, "Very well! Where was I?" Dr. Lon said sheepishly, "You were telling us that you had an idea." General Armwhite said forcefully, "Oh, yes! I have decided that we can exploit the McNichols' visit. Is this clear, Dr. Lon? Can you get the both of them here?" Dr. Lon replied, "I don't know. Marie McNichols will come for sure, but I don't know about Professor McNichols, since he was just here at the VA. She did not indicate that he would be coming with her." Dr. Deutschman said, "Make sure that he comes along. This time we better do it right, but I don't like the idea of this being so close to home. We could arrange a dinner in honor of their visit after the seminar at some restaurant." General Armwhite was calming down, "I like that Romanian restaurant in Georgetown. The gypsy atmosphere with the violins is just about the right touch. Don't you agree?" Dr. Deutschman replied, "Yes, I like it! One of Marie's colleagues at the D. O. Madison Cancer Center, a Dr. Geldter, who has done some work for us, even if it turned out to be shit, refers to her as a gypsy." General Armwhite commented, "You are up on her profile." Dr. Deutschman continued, "I have to be! We can't let these things get out of hand."

Dr. Lon was very uneasy about the entire meeting, and while he watched the interchange between Deutschman and Armwhite, he started fidgeting with his glasses. General Armwhite picked up on Dr. Lon's uneasiness and said while he waved his arm, "Christ, Ming! Will you stop letting your sentimental emotions cloud your judgment. The McNichols are history, because that's an order. There's nothing we can do about it. Is that clear?" He then turned to Dr. Deutschman, "We should probably call that pompous ass Clement Masters at The Madison Cancer Center so that we can coordinate this better. I understand Masters is very frustrated about the McNichols. He's lost face with Washington and is trying to get rid of them. Dr. Deutschman replied, "He and Kenneth Able recruited some group in Moscow when the McNichols went there a month or so ago, but they completely blew it." General Armwhite sneered, "What goddamned amateurs! We just should have assumed that the Moscow operation would be a screw-up, and we should have had a decent back-up plan. Oh well, what better way to whack someone, then after a professional seminar? It won't be expected. And we should get Ellen Martins involved. Marie will like her–just like two peas in a pod." Turning to Dr. Lon he said, "Ming, do you now understand the sensitivity of this issue?" Dr. Lon nodded sheepishly and asked, "Sir, may I be excused from this project?" General Armwhite became instantly angry, "Absolutely not!" Dr. Lon again, "Can I ask what you're going to do to them?" General Armwhite replied, "No!" Dr. Deutschman added, "You don't want to know."

Back in Austin Marie discussed the upcoming trip to Washington with Jared, who was against her going and couldn't go with her because Dr. Belcher would not approve his travel request. Since Jared was not the invited speaker at the Army Institute of Pathology Research, Dr. Belcher was not about to approve his travel and face the wrath of Dr. Masters. Besides, Dr. Masters was trying desperately to find anything that he could use to fire Jared, but he had to proceed very carefully since Jared was a tenured faculty member. Dr. Belcher just wanted to harass Jared to the point where he would throw in the towel and leave without having to go the administratively difficult process of removing him from his tenured position.

The removal of a tenured faculty member from the staff for their research directions would likely trigger a nasty lawsuit. It could cost them some bad PR if the truth came out that Jared was fired for his research on the Gulf War veterans' illnesses, and it could end up a messy case in court. Not that the threat of a lawsuit had ever stopped Dr. Masters before. The Madison was currently being sued by other former faculty members, including one that blew the whistle on the D. O. Madison Radiology Clinic for purposely damaging patients with radiation without their full informed consent in a government-sponsored research project on the effects of radiation on tissue damage. Dr. Masters had been trying desperately to buy off the Judge in that case. In Texas most of the judges went to the University Law School, so they were not at all sympathetic to any faculty member who actually had the gall to sue their alma mater.

No matter how much Dr. Masters claimed that he could handle the courts and the press, Dr. Belcher knew that Masters' ego wouldn't let him even be a devil's advocate and raise the issue that they were not in a favorable position with respect to Jared McNichols. He had actually gotten The D. O. Madison some good press over the last year or so, and he would have an extremely strong lawsuit if they tried to fire him. The whole spectacle of forcing out a senior faculty member because of his research direction was disturbing to Dr. Belcher, even though he would go along with the program if Masters ordered it. Dr. Belcher often spoke about academic freedom, especially when it came to himself. Dr. Belcher still feared Dr. Masters, however, and he would do what he was told, even if he didn't believe in it himself.

Due to a breakdown in communication the wishes of General Armwhite that Jared accompany Marie McNichols was not passed on through the proper channels to Austin, and so the administration at The Madison did not realize that Jared should accompany Marie on this particular trip. His request for participation in the visit to the U. S. Army Institute of Pathology Research was denied, and Marie must now travel alone to meet her fate. Jared tried to talk Marie out of going to Washington, but Marie was stubborn and would not listen to his arguments. She wanted to visit with Dr. Lon, and she felt that this was the only way to get more accurate information from him on Mfi.

A few weeks later it was time for Marie's trip to Washington DC, and Marie and Jared left Queenswood and drove to the airport. Jared parked the car in the short term parking area next to the terminal and recovered Marie's bag from the trunk. Marie wanted to wait in the airline club before her departure, so Jared took her to the Continental Airlines President's Club in the terminal. As they were about to enter the small Club, Marie had second thoughts about the trip, on the very day on which she was about to embark. After discussing the situation with Jared, she decided to go. She had to visit Georgetown as well as the Pathology Institute, and she did not want to miss her Georgetown seminar by canceling her trip at the last minute. Although she felt uneasy about going on her own to visit Dr. Lon, she decided that it was going to be O.K. But as the time grew nearer to departure, Marie was obviously nervous about the trip, and Jared was even more nervous about her safety.

As Marie and Jared entered the President's Club, they found that the attendants were wearing Texas accessories with their uniforms in honor of 'Go Texans Day.' Even the musak was gently playing Mitch Miller's rendition of 'The Yellow Rose of Texas.' Beautiful Yellow Roses were displayed in bouquet arrangements, and the McNichols received greetings from the Club's attendants, as they were frequent fliers who were known in the club. Marie handed her ticket to an attendant. "Drs. McNichols! Good to see you both again! Today's a proud to be a Texan day!" Jared said solemnly, "We're not natives." The attendant replied, "Neither am I, but I'll bet you have the Texas spirit!" Marie said, "We do, but we wish our colleagues did too." The receptionist then said "Well then, howdy to ya'all!" Marie said, "You too!" Jared didn't bother answering, and he certainly wasn't going to ya'll back. He no longer felt the Texas spirit; he felt that Texas and the real Texans who stood for truth and honesty, if they still existed, had let him and Marie down.

The receptionist checked Marie's ticket and pronounced, "You're all set, and I've upgraded you." The receptionist turned her attention to Jared and asked, "Not traveling today?" Jared answered, "That's right. I'm just going to play house husband for a change." Marie then looked at Jared and said, "You know, I always wanted to be like you, go on the lecture circuit and be recognized for my work." She continued, "But you know what? This isn't much fun."

As they walked away from the desk, Jared turned his attention to Marie and asked, "How about a coke?" Marie spoke to Jared as she nodded her head and they heard 'The Yellow Rose of Texas' playing in the background. "You know, when I was a little girl of about three years-old I loved that song. I couldn't pronounce the word yellow so I always sang it as 'lello.' I told my grandmother, "When I grow up, I'm going to be a cowgirl and live in Texas!" She continued, "And now look what happened! I made it to Texas only to be crucified." She continued, "I have never hated a place as much as The Madison!"

Trying to calm Marie down before her trip was proving to be difficult. Jared said, "There are lots of good people there. It's not as bad as you think." He was also trying to talk himself into feeling better about the situation that they found themselves in, but he really wasn't too convincing. Marie said, "As far as I'm concerned the good people here have no backbone. They didn't defend us—they jumped on the bandwagon. I thought there was some pioneer spirit down here, a good place to do innovative research, but what I found instead was a bunch of backward, prejudiced and evil people." Jared chided her, "Come on Marie, you are in a negative thought loop again!" Marie replied, "I don't care!" Jared tried to get Marie off the subject of the D. O. Madison, "You met and snared me here, didn't you?" She finally agreed, "I guess in a backwards way I actually owe my happiness to Dr. Masters. After all, didn't he personally recruit you?" Jared replied, "Yes, and it was probably the biggest mistake of my entire life to accept his offer. I would never have come to the Madison if I had known. But we will persist, and sooner or later the truth will come out. The truth is our best weapon." Marie said, "You always say that! But will it ever come out? You have more trust in your fellow man than I do."

Marie turned away from Jared and sat down. After several seconds, she continued, "Sometimes it's easier to believe a lie than the truth!" Jared asked her again, "Are you sure that you don't want a coke? Marie finally agreed, "O.K." Jared said as he went to get Marie a drink, "You've got to get a more positive attitude in preparation for your lectures." Marie was feeling very negative about the upcoming trip. Jared was too, but he didn't want to let Marie know. He returned with the coke and sat down with Marie. She was quite fidgety. He said, "Now, Marie don't go and get yourself paranoid just because of Dale's warning. It's probably some sort of a mind game. You know, psychological warfare." Marie stated, "Better paranoid and safe than dead." Jared was trying to calm Marie down, but he wasn't having any luck, "Look, I know you will do just fine, and your seminars will be a big hit." She asked, "Even at the Institute of Pathology Research? Remember, I will be going face-to-face with Ming Lon, Mr. Mfi himself!" She continued, "You know, I found out that he was also an anthrax expert. He sure acted odd when I talked to him about my illness. It was if he already knew of it." Jared said, "Look, we're having a rough time, and I know that there have been attempts on us, but we have to stay calm and somewhat collected. Remember, when we watch those B-rated horror flicks, and they play the victim game." Marie laughed slightly. It was a nervous laugh. He pointed to Marie and said, "Victim! Victim! As the heroine stupidly puts herself in harm's way and invites the perp to do her in . . . ." Jared stopped making jokes and became serious, "Marie, you're a survivor! Don't be a victim. But be very careful."

Jared remembered to tell Marie that she would have friends with her at the seminar. "Remember, Louis and Melinda will be with you for the seminar at Ming Lon's place." She added, "I can't understand why Lou with his busy schedule would cancel all his important meetings at NIH to hear my seminar." Jared said, "Because he respects your work." Marie said, "I tell you, there was something fishy about that Commander Ellen Martins' offer for me to stay at her place." Jared said, "Since you don't even know her, let me fill you in. I went on the website of the Institute, and she is the Director of Infectious Disease Research. Furthermore, remember the lecture notes from the medical school pathology block at the Naval Hospital that the Hamlins gave us. There was a Commander E. Martins that lectured on Mfi. I think that it's the same person, and I wouldn't trust her for a second. Why would she invite you to stay with her? She doesn't even know you." Marie said, "You're right! I have to be really leery of anyone who tries to worm their way into my life. She loved our research almost too much. It's as if she wanted to ingratiate herself to me intellectually for some reason. Compared to the constant criticism that I receive here in Austin, it just sounded fishy." Jared added, "Because it was fishy! Just be prudent, and you'll be all right. Don't give her anything and watch yourself, especially what you eat and drink."

Jared gave Marie some last minute instructions as her flight was called, and they stood up to get Marie in line with the other passengers. "Remember, I have faith in you—but please be careful. And give Larry my regards when you see him at Georgetown. We need his microbiology expertise and input with our Mycoplasma studies. And be sure to give a big hug to Lou and Melinda." Marie said, "I will. But I have never lectured at Georgetown, it has me a bit scared. Hopefully they won't throw spitballs at me like they did down here." Jared reassured her, "Forget about the D. O. Madison." After a few seconds he said, "Oh, I forgot to ask you if I should hire a limousine so that Lou and Melinda don't have to go out of their way to pick you up at the airport." Marie commented, "That's O.K. I already hired a car to take me to their home. They made plans to pick me up at the airport, but I didn't want to bother them with the airport traffic." Jared said, "Good. Lou is always so busy." Jared gave Marie a kiss, "You'll do great! I love you!" Marie said, "Me too!" She turned and disappeared in the crowd boarding the flight to Washington National.

The flight to Houston was short, and the connection to Washington was uneventful for Marie. Fortunately, she had plenty of room on the Washington National flight, and she spent most of her time reading magazines and a book that Jared had bought for her. Three and one-half hours after she took off from Houston Marie arrived at Washington National Airport. She disembarked from the plane, picked up her bag from the crowded arrival area and headed for the exit to find her waiting limousine. Outside the terminal Marie noticed a black limo parked at the curb.

The driver immediately got out of the car and identified himself as Marie's ride and reached for her baggage. He said, "Dr. McNichols?" Marie answered, "The one and only!" He smiled and then opened the door for Marie. She sat down in the back seat and waited for the driver to finish loading her bag and situating himself in the driver's seat. Marie then said, "I hope your agency informed you that I need to be driven to Potomac." The driver turned around to face her and unexpectedly said, "You know, everyone in Washington wants you dead." Marie was startled, but she hid her expression and replied, "So are you going to kill me or drive me to my destination!" She paused, "Or do I get another driver?" The driver then said in a sheepish voice, "Oh, I'm sorry. I was just supposed to say that to scare you. But obviously you don't scare so easily." Marie said, "Don't tell me, are you another agent sent to warn me off or whatever!" He replied, "In a manner of speaking." Marie then said, "You and your fellow spooks, operatives and mechanics can play all the spy games you want, but sooner or later you will all have to realize that your spy games are only second on the idiocy scale to the politics behind the cover-up of the biological and chemical weapons used in Desert Storm."

The driver was completely caught off guard and actually embarrassed. "I was not expecting such a young lady . . . ." His voice trailed off. After exiting Washington National Airport, they drove by the Pentagon on the George Washington Parkway and made their way along the Potomac River. Marie stared for a moment at the massive structure along the Potomac. In a few seconds she said, "When will you spooks ever learn that you cannot contain a germ. Sooner or later you will all have to realize that everyone is at risk!" She paused and then said, "Oh, and by the way, your threats don't scare me; they only serve to make me feel more secure. It's when I can't see you that's actually more scary, because then I wouldn't have a chance. There would be a bullet coming from nowhere and my light would be turned out forever." The driver responded, "I am really sorry, Dr. McNichols. You seem like such a nice young lady, and may I say beautiful as well." Marie said, "Flattery gets you nowhere with me! Go tell your bosses to stop their idiotic psychological war games with me. Our only concern has been for the soldiers' health, and that should be the concern of Washington. It's ludicrous that all of us should have to pay for some amoral agenda of a few high officials." She continued, "It's as if we have some sort of fascist agenda in the heart of our government!"

As Marie was being driven to the Washington D.C. suburb of Potomac, Maryland, the D.C. skyline with the Washington Monument in the foreground flashed by to the right. Then they were driving in a forest high above the Potomac River. Marie remembered driving the same route with Jared, who loves driving the G.W., as he calls it. Marie looked pensive and said to her driver, "You know, looking at the majesty of Washington, I am reminded of ancient Rome. The driver asked in an abstract manner, "What do you mean?' Marie answered, "It's the grandeur of the façade . . . . Like Rome." She paused, "A magnificent facade that completely masks the amoral and barbaric corruption lurking beneath the grandeur." He said, "You're too philosophical for me, ma'am!" Marie answered a bit sarcastically, "No doubt considering that you were willing to play along with tactics to scare me." He answered, "I said I was sorry!" Marie continued, "Sorry is not good enough, sir! You should assess who the real enemy is! Remember germs do not discriminate! They attack everyone in their paths!" The driver said, "Paths? Germs?" Marie asked, "Don't you get it? By attacking my husband and me, you are in fact attacking yourself!" The driver said, "I don't understand!" Marie tried to tell him, "Well, let me summarize it for you! There are not many people out there who give a damn about the average G. I. Joe in the military or on the streets. Who do you think has the background scientifically to figure out how to stop the biological weapons that were released in the Gulf War?" The driver asked, "Why would these biologicals, if they were even released, affect me?"

Marie decided that the driver needed a brief history lesson. She somewhat impatiently said, "Look it's like the flu. There was the Spanish flu, the Russian flu, the Asian flu and then the Hong Kong flu. These bugs all made it to the U.S., and they killed millions of people. So why wouldn't biological agents from the Gulf War reach here? After all, the soldiers came back, and now their families are getting sick!" She continued, "And then there are always businessmen traveling in and out of the Middle East. The world has grown smaller, and airborne contagions are now a reality everywhere." The driver was finally beginning to understand, "Gee, I never thought of that!" Marie continued, "I know you didn't think about it. I don't think you and your spook friends think at all!" She paused, "Unfortunately for my husband and I, we happen to care about guys like you! You kill us, and who is going to bail you out? Although I have to tell you, it has been a really dangerous and thankless job. I ask myself why the hell should I risk myself for people when 99% of the time, they just grow to resent our help. My husband is back in Austin right now fighting for his job, our livelihood, just because we helped people like you." The driver asked, "Why do you go on?" Marie said, "Because I was given a direct order from the divine to not let anyone suffer who can be helped." The driver said, "I never met anyone like you! Your husband is a very lucky guy." He continued, "You're like an angel on earth!" Marie laughed, "That's what a Dr. Luxembourg said in Moscow! And then he promptly poisoned us when we had dinner at his home. I lost our twin babies the next day, and now I don't think I can ever have children." Marie continued, "But believe me, I'm no angel!" She mused, "I'm just a fool!" The driver said, "I really feel awful about scaring you!" Marie told him, "Well, stop feeling awful! Do something constructive, like informing your fellow operatives and bosses that they too are at risk!"

The driver continued up the Potomac River on the G.W. Parkway until they reached I-495. The driver took the Washington Beltway across the Potomac River, and he finally turned off the freeway and headed south to Potomac. The driver asked Marie, "Do you have a card?" Marie nodded her head and said, "I'll give one to you when I get there." The driver added, "We're almost there. According to the address, the house should be just up ahead." He then spotted the house, "There it is."

The car pulled into the driveway, the driver got out of the limo and ran around to open the door for Marie. At this point the door to the house opened and Lou and Melinda Leone came out to greet Marie. They all gave each other hugs. The driver waved as he got back into the limo. Marie shouted to him, "Wait, here's my card, and how do I pay you?" The driver said to Marie as she handed him her card, "Forget about the trip. It's on me. I'm real sorry for everything." Marie replied, "Apology accepted. Just get the word out." He answered, "Sure thing!" He then quickly drove off.

The Leone's were curious about the interaction with the limo driver. Lou asked, "What was that all about?" Marie said, "Just another spook sent to scare us off the Desert Storm project. He had a change of heart after I set him straight." Melinda asked, "Spook?" Marie said, "That's intelligence operative." Lou looked as if he didn't understand, and Marie wondered why Lou, who has been at NIH for many years, didn't know much about the DIA and the CIA.

Lou picked up Marie's bag and they all entered the Leone's house. It was a nice home in a nice neighborhood. Marie imagined that when it snowed, it must look beautiful with the woods and roofs covered in white snow. It was so different from Central Texas. Melinda asked, "Why were they trying to scare you and Jared?" Marie said, "They're hiding something about the release of biological agents during Operation Desert Storm. Some of our soldiers who fought in the war have been getting sick and so are their families. Jared and I are trying to help the vets and their families." Lou said, "We'll talk about this over dinner." He said, "I'll put Marie's bag in her room." Melinda mentioned, "I've made dinner for us, and you're just in time." Marie said, "Great! Am I hungry!" Melinda asked, "I hope you like Cornish hens?" Marie answered, "It's one of my favorites."

After Lou returned, it was time for dinner. Melinda motioned for Marie to sit to the right of Lou. Lou and Marie sat down as Melinda returned to the kitchen to get the appetizer. Once Melinda had left the room Lou asked, "What's going on with your work?" Marie said, "Jared and I have been having a very rough time since we began our pilot study on the Desert Storm Illnesses after our step-daughter returned from the Gulf and became sick." Lou asked, "How is she doing?" Marie said, "She's recovered but she had to leave the Army, even though she was accepted for flight training because she was too fatigued to keep up with the training." Lou asked, "What do you and Jared think is wrong with the veterans?" Marie said, "We feel that some of them, perhaps almost half, have an invasive mycoplasmal infection. The species that we found seems to have some genetic alteration. And Jared has been working with the Special Forces and has found that the antibiotic doxycycline is very effective against this microorganism. We feel that there are probably other biological and chemical agents involved in the illnesses, in keeping with Soviet Warfare Doctrine concept." Lou asked, "What's that?" Melinda had just entered the room as Marie said, "Soviet Warfare Doctrine is the use of multiple agents, both biological and chemical, in combination with conventional weapons."

Melinda asked, "I heard you talking about the Gulf War. Do you think germ warfare materials were released during the Gulf War?" Marie said, "I think so. How else can we explain the fact the veterans' families are getting sick as well as the veterans?" Melinda shook her head and said, "I tell you Marie, we have lost our country! The U. S. is gone!" Lou said, "Now honey, don't exaggerate!" Melinda said, "Lou, you of all people should know that something is very wrong in our government. Just look at all the hush-hush stuff at the NIH." Melinda turned to Marie, "Do you know that Lou was ordered not to do a project, because it was politically incorrect!" Marie commented, "Sounds familiar. Jared and I are having the same problem at The D. O. Madison, and to me political correctness is just another word for communism. If I was living in the Soviet Union of 10 years ago, we probably would have been thrown in the gulag system for what Jared and I have done at the lab bench." Lou chimed in, "It's ominous, but I have faith it will all work out." Marie and Melinda looked at each other skeptically, "You mean how it worked out for our neighbor, Vince Foster?" There was silence for over a minute.

The dinner conversation continued but with mainly small talk. Everyone was enjoying Melinda's cooking, so it was hard to be negative. At the end of the fine dinner Lou wanted to continue their earlier conversation but with a more positive focus, so he summarized the earlier comments. "Getting back to Marie's and Jared's studies . . . . Look at the positive side, the Desert Storm Illnesses project appears to be productive, and they will have a chance to present their case to the Institute of Pathology Research. I don't think that they can ignore the work." Marie added, "Thanks again for taking the time to come to my lecture tomorrow." He said, "The Pathology Institute is a funny place." Marie asked, "What do you mean?" He continued, "It is not exactly the friendliest atmosphere to give a seminar, so I thought I'd come and give you some moral support." Marie was thankful, "That would be great! Right after the Pathology Institute lecture, I have to lecture at Georgetown in Larry Rosen's Department." Lou said, "I don't think I can make that lecture. We'll have to make it another time. If you get a chance, please give my regards to Larry."

While Melinda was out of the room making the dessert, a soufflé, Lou said to Marie. "I am so sorry that you and Jared are having so much trouble just because of your research. It isn't right." Marie said, "It's not just those asses Geldter and Krappner." Lou responded, "You know, everyone in the field has their number. They have been playing dirty tricks on everyone for years now. One of the pathology fellows that I trained claims that they are pure evil. In my almost thirty years in science, I have never seen such a vicious attack as the one Isaac and Amy have done on you and Jared. What have you and Jared done to deserve their venom?" Marie told Lou, "Jared says that it is not just the mycoplasma and the Gulf War Illness work and the fact that Isaac has always wanted to take over Jared's department and merge it into his own and demote Jared in the process. Jared says that it has something to do with my true identity." Lou asked, "Do you agree?" Marie responded, "Yes, it has to be something like that. Why would this continue for so long?" Lou asked, "Who do you think you are?" She answered, "Jared thinks that I must be from a European Illuminati family, because there appears to be a great deal of power and money involved. When I was

9 years old I was given a 65 ct pink sapphire, and I was told that it was the Cetta Dharma Sapphire from India or what is now Pakistan. Recently we found out, again from Jared's digging, that this stone identifies me as the heiress of the Cetta Dharma Trust, one of the largest trusts in the world. Although from my standpoint, I have never benefited from my background. In fact, there were times when my adopted family could barely make ends meet. Jared thinks that the financial difficulties in my adolescence were all part of the cover for my real identity. I'm just beginning to find out about my real family." Lou said, "God, it's so complicated. You know, Marie, you will always have our moral support." Marie responded, "Thanks Lou! That means a great deal to me, especially now that we are under attack. It seems to come from everywhere. I respect you tremendously as a scientist, and people like you and Melinda are the best!" Lou broke out into a smile and continued. "Thank you! But I only wish I could do more. One thing I can try to do is neutralize those idiots in Austin. You know, they are not welcome at NIH. Amy Krappner in particular was told not to come back here after she showed some disgraceful behavior on a NIH review committee. Perhaps my fellow was right. They are just evil people."

At this moment Melinda entered the room with the soufflé. Marie exclaimed, "It's a work of art! Just like your beautiful paintings." Marie then said after Melinda handed her a portion and she took a bite, "This is scrumptious! It makes me feel as if I have died and went to heaven." Melinda said, "I heard from the kitchen part of what Lou and you were discussing. Frankly, we would really rather have you here on earth." Marie said, "Sometimes I get so battle weary from the constant character assassinations that we have endured—all because we wanted to help people." Lou said supportively, "Don't give up the fight!" Marie replied, "We won't!" After Marie ate most of her soufflé, she turned to Lou and asked, "Would you mind if I give Jared a call to say I arrived safely?" Melinda told Marie, "Why not use the phone in the kitchen so Lou could chat with Jared?" Lou added, "I need to ask Jared about the upcoming program for the Metastasis Research Society." Marie said, "Sure!"

Marie was led into the kitchen, which was visible to the dining room via a serving window. She dialed Jared who picked up the phone in Austin and stated, "Hello, McNichols residence." Marie answered, "It's me! I arrived in one piece and have just had the most divine home-cooked meal, Cornish hen and chocolate soufflé." Jared answered, "Gees, I'm sorry I missed that. You remember Captain Hamlin? He called from Fort Meade. He wanted to know if he could attend your seminar at Georgetown?" Marie replied, "I'll have to ask Larry. You know Larry; he's petrified of any political controversy. I'll call you back and let you know sometime tomorrow." Jared continued, "Also a Cory Lovell, who was a member of an Army Graves Registration Unit during the war called, and she wants to attend. She's is in a wheel chair and requires oxygen but she wants to be there." Marie asked, "What's a Graves Registration Unit?" Jared told her, "It's a unit that recovers dead soldiers or buries enemy combatants." Marie asked, "She might have been exposed to chemicals and biologicals when she came in contact with the dead bodies." Jared answered, "Possibly. She is really sick. I don't know if they have the facilities if something goes wrong with her." Marie said, "I promised Larry I would stick to science, but I don't think he would mind if some of the veterans were there. At least he will see that there is a great need for this research, and maybe he will even be inspired to really help us with his expertise. Jared, I'm still scared about my talk at the Pathology Institute. I really respect Ming Lon, but I feel that he can't communicate to me in a free sense, and he has clammed up on me since the war." Jared said, "You'll do just fine, and Lou will be there to keep things in check should they get out of hand. But I don't trust Ming Lon. He has lied too much about the possible role of Mfi in chronic illnesses. I have heard now from two different people that he leaves his Gulf War blood samples sitting on the lab bench for weeks before examining them. You know what that means." Marie replied, "Yes, he lets them degrade on purpose so he can get negative results. Why do you think he does that? He didn't seem like a dishonest person over the phone." Jared said, "Neither does Mr. Rott from the Pentagon, but he's a lying bastard! You watch yourself, Marie, and be especially careful with those creeps, and don't eat or drink anything at the Pathology Institute." Marie said, "O.K. I promise." Lou then came into the kitchen while Marie said to Jared, "I love you!" Jared answered, "Me too!" Marie then added, "Lou wants to talk to you about the upcoming Society meeting." The two researchers who were long-time friends and colleagues continued the conversation while Marie slipped back into her own conversation with Melinda. Melinda told Marie that she would drive her to the U. S. Army Institute of Pathology Research, and Lou would meet them there. Marie was suddenly very tired from the prospect of going to the Pathology Institute in the morning. She asked Melinda if she could be excused to get some sleep.

The next morning Melinda was dressed and ready and was warming up the Land Rover while Marie was still finishing her hair. Marie was not a morning person, and it was good to have Melinda to move things along. Finally Marie was ready. She checked her slides again, wishing that Jared had been there to make sure they were in proper order, grabbed her purse and went out to the Land Rover. Melinda had been at the wheel waiting patiently for Marie. She then said to Marie as she climbed into the vehicle, "I feel like I am acting as your unofficial body guard." Marie quipped, "You probably are! Thanks for packing a lunch for us. I know this sounds paranoid, but I promised Jared that I would not eat or drink at the Institute. To be honest with you, I really do not like to eat at any scientific functions anymore. Jared and I have been sick one too many times at a variety of banquets that we have attended. And we did receive confirmation from an officer of Delta One that there have been attempts on our lives. He told us to watch our backs, vary our routines, be careful what we eat and never accept a drink unless we can have the can or bottle and open it ourselves." Melinda said as she drove, "This is horrible! But you know what, I am worried about Lou too!"

Melinda continued the conversation after a moment of driving. "Lately there has been a very negative atmosphere at the NIH, and there have been some suspicious incidents." Marie asked, "Like what?" Melinda said, "Several weeks ago, a young postdoctoral student came forward about her suspicions of having been poisoned in her lab." Marie added, "We know that there were poisoning incidents at one of the Rockefeller University labs." Melinda said, "You know Marie, the United States has changed!" Marie agreed, "I know. It's scary! But I have always sensed some underlying agenda from the time I was in college. I didn't really understand it then, and now I am just starting to put the pieces of the puzzle together. I have to be honest with you. It's not a pretty story. In fact, I wish that I was really just paranoid, and then I would not have to deal with the fact that all that I have experienced is true." Melinda added, "No one wants to deal with the idea of a conspiracy. Look at what the press does to anyone who even suggests that there is some kind of conspiracy going on. They are crucified."

Marie said, "You have to be an idiot not to see the collusion of special interests in a global sense." Marie then became pensive. "You know what? Melinda, five years ago I watched a 20/20 show that dealt with the unexplained deaths of 12 physicists in Great Britain. I have always wondered what really happened to those scientists. Colleagues of mine in the physics community, one who was a Nobelist, were also poisoned."

Marie continued with her thoughts to Melinda. "You have to wonder. It's almost as if someone or something has targeted the scientists for elimination who happen to be humanitarians." Melinda asked, "How do you figure that? Why would anyone do such a thing?" Marie says, "It's only speculation at this point. But I do see a pattern, and so do others." Melinda said, "I guess time will tell."

After a few minutes of silence while Melinda was threading her Land Rover through heavy traffic, she exclaimed, "We're here!" Marie commented, "The Institute is sure not a welcoming looking place! It looks like it was built to withstand a nuclear blast." Melinda said, "That's one reason why Lou wanted to be here to support you during the seminar." Melinda turned the Land Rover into a guarded parking lot. She leaned out the window to tell the guard that Marie was here to give a seminar at the Institute. The guard asked their names and checked a list on a clipboard. He finally waved them through. Marie said, "This is making me nervous!" Melinda replied, "So am I!"

Melinda parked the SUV, and they entered a forbidding building that was actually encased by several thick walls. There were no windows anywhere. Melinda said, "Why is this building so ominous looking?" Marie replied, "Probably because it houses some of the most horrible chemical and biological weapons known to mankind, and its directors want the building to be completely contained." Melinda asked, "Why do you think they invited you to give a seminar here? You don't seem the type to come to a building like this?" Marie said as they walked through the building and approached a security desk, "I am sure they have some hidden agenda, but I'm just going to play it straight and be open—just like Jared told me to do." An officer was on the phone, and she motioned the women to wait for her to finish. Melinda turned to Marie and stated, "They probably can't handle a straightforward approach." Marie answered, "Exactly!" She added, "and we have a higher power on our side!" Melinda was not so sure, "I don't know if my faith can withstand this!" Marie said, "I know what you mean!" She then chuckled "Let's go! Remember, David slew Goliath! It's just a question of discerning their Achilles heel." Melinda asked, "Which is?" Marie answered, "Their overconfidence." Melinda said, "I don't know about this!!" Marie whispered to Melinda, "It's like guerrilla warfare!" Marie masked her discomfort better than Melinda, but both women were hesitant about the visit to the Institute of Pathology Research.

The officer manning the security desk, a middle aged black woman, was in charge. Marie said to the officer after she finished her phone conversation, "I am Dr. Marie McNichols, and I'm here to give a seminar in Dr. Ellen Martins' Department at the request of Dr. Ming Lon." She continued, "This is Mrs. Melinda Leone, who has graciously accompanied me to the seminar and provided my transportation." The black woman officer who was surprisingly friendly motioned as she looked at her clipboard, "Dr. Marie McNichols, yes, I have you right here. I don't have a Melinda Leone on my list, but I am sure that you can go in." She hesitated, "But just to the seminar room with the doctor here. You both have to sign in, and I have to issue you temporary visitor passes. These will only allow you to go directly to and from the seminar room. You can't visit any other parts of the building. Do you understand?" Marie responded, "Yes! Thank you." She was relieved that Melinda could accompany her to the seminar room, and she then said to the officer, "You know, you are a ray of sunshine in this almost dungeon-like atmosphere." The black woman responded, "I try to be, and I know what you mean—sometimes this place even gives me the spooks!" The black officer laughed, "But the pay and benefits are worth it." Melinda added, "I am sure they are."

The black officer then picked up a microphone for the building's paging system, and then spoke into it. "Dr. Ellen Martins, please come to the front desk." She turned back to Marie and smiled, and then repeated into the microphone, "Dr. Martins! Your seminar speaker is here." The black woman officer then told Marie and Melinda, "She should be here in a couple of minutes. Just make yourself comfortable." Marie said, "We'll try." The black officer chuckled and said as she waved her hand down, "Now girl, it's not that bad!"

While they were waiting for Dr. Martins, Marie turned around and noticed a plaque on the wall. She was glancing at the building's dedication plaque with Melinda as Dr. Ellen Martins appeared. Dr. Martins was about the same height as Marie and was surprisingly very pretty. In fact, she almost looked like she could be Marie's sister. She was in her Navy Commander's uniform and was wearing her long dark hair tied up in a severe chignon. She approached Marie holding her hand out to greet her, "I'm so glad you could make it. I'm Commander Ellen Martins, but you can call me Ellen." She continued, "We weren't sure that you would be able to make it." Marie asked, "Why not?" Dr. Martins replied, "We knew you had a tight schedule, and well, we heard about your bout of illness in Moscow." Marie asked, "You did? How, may I ask did you know about that?" Dr. Martins was a bit uncomfortable at the question. "You might know that Dr. Bane and Dr. Masters from your hospital called us after you returned and told me that your husband Jared had mentioned the episode to them." Marie said, "I didn't know The D. O. Madison kept such close tabs on my schedule. I am really only a consultant there." Commander Martins answered, "I see. It was just a passing comment. The Institute of Pathology Research tries to keep abreast of the major research exchange programs involving cancer centers, such as The D. O. Madison, particularly in view of the changing political climate of Russia. Besides, you yourself told me that you had just recovered from your trip to Moscow." Marie asked, "Did I?" Melinda said, "I don't mean to interrupt, but my husband Lou should be here from the NIH at any moment. I would like to make sure that he could join us." Dr. Martins said, "Don't worry, he'll be in time and will have no problem getting a pass. By the way, please call me Ellen." Marie said, "You know Ellen, for some reason, looking at us, we could be sisters." Ellen laughed, "We kind of look alike, don't we?" In fact, Melinda noticed that the two women did look like sisters. They were approximately the same height and weight, same coloring and same looks.

Dr. Martins continued the conversation as they walked through the building. "I was disappointed that you didn't take me up on my offer to stay with us at our new house." Marie said, "I'm terribly sorry, but I didn't want to offend the Leones." Melinda added, "We would have been hurt if Marie had not stayed with us! My husband Lou and Jared have been friends for years." Dr. Martins said, "I understand." Marie added, "Perhaps another time. I must say I am not accustomed to anyone in the scientific or medical communities being so positive towards my work, and I might add, as nice as you have been." Dr. Martins asked, "Why not?" Marie answered, "Quite frankly, my interactions with other professionals have been rather negative since college. Sometimes I wonder what it is about me that is such a turn-off. And I've come to the conclusion that something in my background threatens a lot of people." Dr. Martins said, "That doesn't really make sense." Marie responded in a sarcastic manner, "I know it doesn't seem to make sense, so it must be my ditsy coloratura personality." Dr. Martins looked puzzled and asked, "Do you sing Opera?" Marie responded, "I do, and perhaps I should switch to it as a profession. Life is too short." Dr. Martins said, "I am sorry you are having such a rough time." Marie asked, "Are you?" Dr. Martins answered, "Yes, I am truly sorry."

Melinda who had been quietly following the curious conversation looked at Marie. Marie winked back at Melinda as if to give her a signal that she knew that Commander Ellen Martins was insincere. Marie then said, "I think I will take you at face value." Dr. Martins asked, "What do you mean?" Marie answered, "You must know that everyone, particularly in your area, has a whole array of hidden agendas?" Dr. Martins answered quickly, almost too quickly, "I try not to think about that!" She then became surprisingly candid. "You know, Marie, my family was on Castro's hit list when we escaped to the U. S. from Cuba in 1959. I know what it feels like to be stalked and hunted for no apparent reason other than your background." Marie then said, "Please keep your own experience in mind when you are dealing with me, and perhaps you will appreciate that I definitely perceive a danger here similar to the one you probably experienced when you were a little girl." Marie paused and then continued, "Only in my case the danger has never departed." Commander Martins looked uncomfortable now. She hurriedly turned and said, "I'm going to find Dr. Lon. He's probably in his office."

They then turned to enter the administrative offices where the seminar room was located, and Dr. Martins introduced Marie to the Office Manager and said, "Clara, could you call audiovisual and make sure that the seminar room is ready?" Marie said, "I have my slides arranged in a standard carousel." Dr. Martins answered, "I'm sure it will be complimentary with our equipment." Commander Martins then indicated, "I'll be right back." Clara buzzed audiovisual, and Melinda looked at Marie in an uncomfortable manner. Marie then said, "It's only ten minutes until the seminar begins."

Melinda asked, "Are you ready?" Marie answered, "As ready as I'll ever be!" They both laughed nervously as the audiovisual man came into the office and took Marie's carousel. Marie said to the man, "I made sure that the slides were in the correct orientation, but would you mind just checking them out for me again before the seminar." The man replied, "No problem, Ma'am." Marie said, "I have this innate fear of all my slides being upside down." The man chuckled as he turned away with the slide carousel.

Commander Martins then reappeared walking down the hall with Dr. Ming Lon, who was just as Jared described him. He was wearing a beaming smile, and he immediately told Marie how much he respected her and Jared's work. Marie told Dr. Lon that the feeling was mutual. Dr. Martins said, "You know Dr. Lon discovered *Mycoplasma incognitus.*" Marie said, "Yes, and I'm so glad to finally meet you. My husband and I have been intrigued by your research, and in particular your data that showed that the mycoplasma penetrates into the nucleus." Dr. Lon answered, "I am happy to finally meet someone who understands the importance of this finding. But we are having a problem correlating good sound molecular biology to our confocal microscopy analyses. The microscopy clearly shows the mycoplasma penetrates into the nucleus, but the molecular biology using PCR was not able to confirm this result." Marie asked, "Have you considered that the chromatin structure of the nucleus in conjunction with the nucleoprotein of the mycoplasma itself might interfere with the PCR reaction because of complexing?" Dr. Lon looked puzzled. Marie continued, "If you cannot get at the mycoplasma DNA once it penetrates the nucleus, your PCR reaction might be a false-negative. Perhaps the mycoplasma DNA integrates and associates with the insoluble portion of the cell nucleus, just like we found for the HIV-1 genes. We could design experiments to probe for it, and in fact, we have already found the mycoplasma gene sequences are associated with the insoluble chromatin fractions." Lon said, "It might certainly be worth a pilot study." Marie said, "Think about it after you have heard the particulars of the Gene Tracking technique. Dr. Lon asked, "Would you collaborate with me on such a project?" Marie responded, "I'd be delighted to, but wait until you see the rationale for the technique, and then you tell me if you think it's a worthwhile approach." Dr. Lon replied, "I must say we have not really explored the chromatin complexing angle."

It was now approaching the time scheduled for the seminar. Dr. Martins said, "They're ready for the seminar now." She paused as she noticed Dr. Leone, "Oh, Dr. Leone has arrived and is seated in the front row. Melinda, will you be attending the seminar?" Melinda said, "Yes, if it's O.K. with you? I am not a scientist, but I believe I will be able to grasp some of Marie's concepts." Dr. Martins asked, "Really?" Melinda added. "Marie gave me a special presentation tailored for a lay person, and I thought that the concepts were fairly clear." Dr. Martins said, "Then, come on in! We have to get seated, so we can stick to the schedule." Melinda sat down next to Lou, and Ellen and Marie went up on the stage. The audience was made up mainly of military scientists. It was a somber group. There was little of the usual scientific chatting that Marie was used to at the university lectures that she normally attended.

Commander Martins introduced Marie by saying, "We are happy to have Dr. Marie McNichols with us today. She is going to tell us about a new technique that she and her husband developed called Nucleoprotein Gene Tracking and its applications to understanding infections such as HIV-1 in terms of chromatin organization. We all hope that she will explain to us how the technique might be used to study *Mycoplasma incognitus* and other intracellular infections in an effort to reconcile the discrepancies between molecular biology and microscopy analyses." Dr. Martins then went into Marie's background, and then finally she said in a jesting manner, "The show is all yours!" Marie then took the podium and said, "I am very happy to be here today." She continued with the seminar, and the audience was quite polite, and they did not interrupt like the staff in Austin.

Marie's seminar went very smoothly, and after about 50 minutes, Marie's formal presentation was over, and she answered questions. Dr Lon stood up first and stated, "I think you may have hit upon a unique approach to understanding invasive infections. Dr. Martins asked, "So you think that we can use this Gene Tracking approach for *Mycoplasma incognitus?*" Marie answered, "I do, provided that your laboratories can assist me with the proper oligonucleotide probes."

There was another man in the audience, actually he was a general in the Army but he was not in uniform. General Armwhite stood up and identified himself. "I am Major General Armwhite, and I am in charge of some of the programs at Fort Detrick." He continued, "Are you aware of the fact that you and your husband have opened up the worst political can of worms in the history of the United States?" Marie was completely flabbergasted at the comment. "I don't understand what you mean by your statement, sir? I have never paid much attention to politics." General Armwhite said, "It shows!" Marie continued, "Well sir, I have no idea of the politics of these issues, but I really think that we can help Dr. Lon reconcile some of the discrepancies he has found in locating his mycoplasma inside the cell nucleus." General Armwhite asked, "Why would you want to work on this particular mycoplasma?" Marie answered, "Well sir, I myself was very sick with a peculiar illness six years ago that resembled the illness of our stepdaughter who served in the Gulf War. We both responded to doxycycline, and we both slowly recovered. She had Gulf War Illness, and my husband has studied the signs and symptoms in over 650 veterans with Gulf War Illnesses and compared them to civilians with Chronic Fatigue Syndrome. We have concluded that Chronic Fatigue Syndrome is the civilian counterpart of Gulf War Illness." General Armwhite said, "That does not prove anything!"

At this point Dr. Deutschman introduced himself. "I am Dr. Deutschman, and I am from the Department of Defense, but I was trained as a physical chemist." Marie suddenly remembered Dr. Deutschman, "Didn't I meet you at the Meyerhoff conference in Israel? I believe you sat next to me at a banquet where I passed out and subsequently had to be medically evacuated from Israel." Deutschman looked very uncomfortable at her statement but he coolly replied, "I can't remember if I was at that particular conference." Marie said, "Never mind about the conference, what point were you trying to make, sir?" He said, "I am trying to deduce why you are so interested in this particular mycoplasma? And why you are trying to connect this questionable Gulf War Syndrome to this mycoplasma?" Marie replied, "Sir, I believe that my husband, Professor Jared McNichols, just lectured recently at the VA here in Washington DC on a proposed link between the *Mycoplasma fermentans* and a subset of patients with Gulf War Illnesses. I suggest that you contact him for more information. The connection is just speculative, and is based upon an observation of ours, if you will, that started because of my illness and that of my stepdaughter. My husband has more detailed information on diagnosis and treatment of Gulf War Illnesses, the results of clinical testing for *M. fermentans* in these patients, and the possible role of *Mycoplasma fermentans* in chronic illnesses and their response to antibiotics. I have been more concerned with learning more about invasive, intracellular infections in general and how they might be tracked to the nucleus and why they seem to complex with the nuclear proteins.

Major General Black then stood up and identified himself. He stated, "I am the chief medical officer at Army Medical Center next door to the Institute of Pathology Research, and I would like to state for the record that we have excellent antibody-based tests for *Mycoplasma fermentans*, and our results using the sera of various soldiers from Desert Storm have all been negative. Would you care to comment on this?" Marie answered, "General Black and General Armwhite, sirs, I have the highest respect for the military and your expertise. With all due respect, sir, antibody-based tests are often poor indicators for infections that arise from poorly immunogenic intracellular microorganisms such as *Mycoplasma fermentans incognitus*. As Dr. Lon himself has stated in his own patent, this mycoplasma does not elicit antibiodies until near death. It stands to reason that a penetrating microorganism such as this mycoplasma may hide inside cells making it difficult for the host's immune system to see the invader. Furthermore, if one looks only at sera, the risk of false negative results are very high because, in general, this kind of mycoplasma tends to be sequestered in the white blood cells, not in the sera or plasma."

Dr. Lon stood up and actually supported the McNichols' findings when he stated, "Dr. Marie here and her husband's findings certainly compliment my own. I feel that they are worthy of further investigation." General Armwhite then turned to Dr. Lon, "Dr. Lon, all you ever think about is your own egotistical suppositions." Marie could see the question and answer session slipping away. Marie concluded, "I believe that further discussion of our studies may not be productive, and I would like to summarize by saying that our laboratory would welcome the opportunity to collaborate with Dr. Lon's laboratory. Thank you again for having me here today. The experience has truly been enlightening." There was a hint of sarcasm in Marie's voice.

After the seminar and question period were over, Lou walked up to Marie and said, "Great talk, Marie, but I have to get back to work." Marie replied, "Thanks for coming, Lou. I know you are very busy. I hope to see you later." Melinda said to Lou, "Bye, Honey. See you this evening. Don't forget that Marie and I are going out to dinner with Ellen Martins tonight! I've left a stew in the refrigerator for you!" Lou said as he was leaving, "Thanks! Love you!" Dr. Lon came up to Marie and said, "I really believe that your technique could help to reconcile some of our research problems." Marie replied, "I'm glad I if can be of help! Call me when you get a chance so we can coordinate any collaboration. Also, could you send me your reprints?" Dr. Lon answered, "I would be delighted." Marie said, "Thanks, I appreciate it." Almost all of the attendees had left the room when Dr. Martins then said to Marie as Melinda listened intently, "I can't talk now because of 'dust-to-dust' and 'ashes-to-ashes'." Marie and Melinda exchanged looks of puzzlement. Dr. Martins continued, "You will understand that it all hinges on the private island in the Caribbean." Marie then asked, "I take it you're talking in some kind of code that you expect me to crack?" Dr. Martins said, "Something like that."

Commander Martins' expression changed abruptly, and she then continued on a lighter note. "Don't forget, we are going to meet at Romanov's for dinner. It has a sort of gypsy atmosphere and fabulous Romanian and Hungarian cuisine." Marie asked, "Would it be all right if Melinda joins us? And I thought you might like to meet Larry Rosen; he's the microbiologist at Georgetown who invited me to give a lecture tomorrow. You probably have a lot of research interests in common, since you are both infectious disease experts." Dr. Martins replied, "That would be great. I have been concentrating principally on the study of leprosy, but it has occurred to me that Dr. Lon's *Mycoplasma fermentans* could act in a synergistic manner with the leprosy bacterium." Marie said, "I find that a very scary thought. Why don't you and Larry brainstorm on this tonight?" Dr. Martins replied, "I think that's an idea for a productive evening." Dr. Martins then looked at Melinda, "Are you sure that you won't be bored listening to us talk about our respective research interests." Melinda chuckled, "I'm married to a scientist, and he lectures to me all the time. I have sort of learned to understand some science by osmosis." Dr. Martins said, "Then I look forward to seeing you both and Dr. Rosen this evening around six. Marie, if you have a number for Larry, I can fax him directions." Marie rummaged through her briefcase and handed the number to Dr. Martins, who said, "Thanks. Melinda, do you know how to get to Romanov's?" Melinda replied,

"Yes, it's right off Chevy Chase Avenue on the corner of Cherry Blossom Lane." Dr. Martins exclaimed, "Good! You won't need directions. I've really got to get back to the lab." Commander Martins smiled to Marie and Melinda, and quickly left the small group and walked smartly down the hall.

At this point the audiovisual man returned with Marie's slides and told her, "I'll help you find your way back out of this place." Everyone had set off in different directions, and as she was walking away Dr. Martins whispered to herself, "I'll be damned if I'm going to poison someone who looks so much like me! We could almost pass for sisters. I'll have to come up with some explanation as to why this won't work on Marie."

Marie and Melinda walked out of the U. S. Army Institute of Pathology Research and entered the parking lot next to the Institute. Marie said to Melinda, "Wasn't that a weird place for a seminar? And the bizarre behavior of everyone." Melinda responded, "I couldn't believe that General Armwhite with his 'political can of worms' that you and Jared supposedly opened up." Marie said, "And that Dr. Deutschman–I would say they were quite hostile in a friendly sort of way–don't you think?" Melinda said, "What an understatement!" Marie chuckled, "Believe me, they were absolute angels compared to the people at the D. O. Madison when I gave a seminar recently." Marie continued, "They actually threw spitballs at me!" Melinda said, "Lou told me about it and said that nothing surprises him when it comes to your institution."

As they stopped to get into Melinda's Land Rover, the discussion became more serious. Marie asked, "Tell me, I didn't imagine that Commander Martins talked to me in code about some 'dust-to-dust', 'ashes-to-ashes' nonsense." Melinda added, "Don't forget the private island in the Caribbean." Marie said. "Right! I wonder if the dust-to-dust refers to some kind of plague. I am surprised she did not sing *Ring around the rosy, a pocket full of poesy, ashes, ashes, we all fall down!*" Melinda said, "Pardon?" Marie continued. "The old nursery rhyme referring to the bubonic plague of the Middle Ages." Melinda said, "I didn't know that!" Marie thought out loud, "I'll bet Commander Martins was alluding to some sort of biological weapon. Only I am not sure what the private island in the Caribbean means. Do you think it has something to do with organized crime? They often purchase islands for their drug shipments." Marie paused and then stated, "I am so sick of this spy bullshit!

Marie thought for a moment as Melinda navigated the Land Rover out of the parking lot and into the streets of Washington D.C. "During the last several years I have met several individuals who refer to 'the private island in the Caribbean.' It has gotten so that I feel like I am living in a grade B spy movie. The intelligence services must spend a fortune on these mind games and discrediting campaigns. They are experts at taking a perfectly honest and sane person and making them look dishonest and insane. I am sick and tired of all the agents and their code antics. Why don't they just come and ask me what it is they want to know, and tell me why they are so threatened that contracts have been taken out on my and Jared's lives?"

After about one-half hour driving North into Maryland, mostly on Wisconsin Boulevard until they crossed the Maryland border, and then along the Potomac River until they arrived in the small community of Potomac. Melinda finally said as she pulled into her street, "We're almost home! I am so drained from all of this that the only way that I will be able to make it to this evening's dinner is to take a nap." Marie agreed, "What a great idea!" Melinda turned into the driveway, and then they both got out of the Land Rover and entered the Leone home. Then Marie asked, "Do you think I could call Jared to tell him about the strange things at my seminar?" Melinda responded, "Go ahead!" Marie asked another question, "Would you mind if you got on the line to corroborate to Jared about the strange code spoken by that Commander Ellen Martins?" Melinda laughed, "I'd be glad to!" Marie said, "Thanks Melinda. At last I have a reliable eye witness for Jared to prove that I did not imagine these things."

Marie dialed the number for Jared's office and Jane answered, "Cancer Biology." Marie said, "It's me Jane." She answered, "Well, hi there! How goes it?" Marie replied, "Don't ask!" Jane said, "That bad huh? Marie continued, "Let us just say that I feel like I am living in a grade B spy movie." Jane laughed, "Why don't you tell me about it when you return." Marie said, "I will! Jane, could you get Jared on the line for me?" Jane said, "Sure thing. I'll transfer you to Jared. After a few moments Jared was on the phone line, "Hi, Babe! How did it go?" Marie said, "It went O.K., but I can't say if it was all that good." Jared asked. "Was it that bad?" Marie said, "It was after the seminar that things got really weird. Would you believe that Commander Martins, my host, began talking to me in code; something she couldn't talk about because of 'dust-to-dust' and 'ashes-to-ashes' and some ubiquitous 'private island in the Caribbean.' Melinda was there and heard it, so at last I have a witness to prove that I did not imagine these things." Jared replied, "I know you're not imagining these things. I have to tell you that Defense Intelligence is an oxymoron." Marie asked, "Meaning?" He said, "It's obvious that they are not as smart as they think they are. I am sure that the intelligence agencies are keeping close tabs on you. I know it's weird, but we will eventually sort all this out." Melinda picked up an extension and said, "Jared this is Melinda, and I have to tell you that I am exhausted from the undertones and nonsensical code in the conversations after Marie's seminar." Jared asked, "Did Lou hear the code too?" Melinda said, "No, he had to get back to work, and besides, he does not like to think of anything that might implicate the government in, shall we say, peculiar dealings." Jared said, "I'm sorry I couldn't be there, but I appreciate that you and Lou are looking after my baby." Melinda said, "It has been a pleasure, and tonight I am her unofficial body guard for a dinner at the Romanov Restaurant with Ellen Martins and Larry Rosen." Jared exclaimed, "Thanks for the assistance! Remember to be cognizant of what you eat and drink." Melinda said, "Marie has filled me in on the precautions." She continued, "Look, I have got to lie down. I am simply drained. I'm signing off now and am looking forward to when you are both here for the Society meetings." Jared then replied, "Take care and give my best to Lou."

Jared then began speaking to Marie again. "Listen Babe, all these weird goings-on and your lecture schedule convinces me that you should put off your trip to Europe for at least six months. I am not telling you to cancel the trip, I just want you to reschedule the trip in conjunction with my visiting professorship in Egypt." Marie replied, "I guess you are right about Europe. I am sort of tired, and I still have to lecture at Georgetown before the Dallas meeting." Jared said, "I knew you'd see it my way. There is no sense in making yourself sick from too hectic a schedule."

Marie was tired, but she didn't want Jared to know. "You know what Jared? It isn't so much fun being like you after all." Jared chuckled, "Don't forget to ask Larry at dinner if the Hamlins and Cory Lovell can attend your talk tomorrow." Marie answered, "I won't, and I'll tell him that I promise to leave out the politics." Jared added, "That will help. But actually it's good for the veterans' morale to see us in action. They need to know that we do more then just pay lip service to their problems, but we don't want to get Larry in any trouble either, and I especially don't want to see you in trouble." Marie then said, "I love you!" Jared said, "Me, too! Come back soon, ya' hear!" Marie knew that he was being sarcastic and said, "I'll see you tomorrow evening! Don't forget to pick me up at the airport."

The dinner at the Romanian restaurant and the following day at Georgetown was a blur for Marie. Commander Martins decided that Marie could easily be her own sister by her looks and personality, so that night she actually watched what Marie ate and drank very closely. She didn't leave Cuba to come to the United States to grow up and become a Naval Officer to poison a young scientist who could have been her sister! This is not why she pledged her loyalty to the United States of America–to kill its citizens for trying to help Gulf War veterans that were exposed to weapons that she didn't even understand. Dr. Martins would have to take the flak from General Armwhite and Dr. Deutschman for not going along with their plan, but she had an out. She told them in a telephone conversation later after the dinner that Marie was suspicious of the dinner and would not eat. Therefore, the plans could not be implemented as they designed. Commander Martins would find out just as Marie and Jared had learned the hard way. The system was not forgiving to young aspiring professionals who go against the orders of its criminal leadership who had a lot to hide. In fact, Commander Martins would be reassigned to a position in Africa, and she would have to give up on the thought of ever being promoted to a Navy Captain.

The following day at Georgetown Marie was scheduled to give a seminar in the Microbiology Department on the HIV-1 genes that are incorporated into nucleoprotein complexes in the nucleus of human cells of infected individuals. Marie was quite excited about the chance to speak at an academic department outside of Austin where the scientists and physicians were actually open-minded and fair.

That morning Professor Larry Rosen met Marie at the entrance to the Georgetown Medical School. After greeting Marie and leading her through a maze of hallways and buildings, they finally arrived at the Microbiology Department and the AIDS Research Institute. As the Director of the AIDS Research Institute, Larry had been very supportive of the McNichols' research efforts. As they continued down the hall of the Institute, Larry reminded Marie to be careful about what she said to the staff, "You know Marie, you're scaring everyone with your germ warfare comments." Marie asked, "What do you mean?" Larry responded quietly, "Well, we're all petrified for one thing. You just don't discuss these things in public."

For some reason Larry's comment set off an explosion in Marie's head. She had been under pressure ever since she had arrived in Washington, and the cab driver said that everyone wanted her dead. Marie replied in an impassioned voice, "Larry, if the scientific community does not stand up to the murderers within our ranks, who will make the world a better place for future generations? I am really sick and tired of the apathy and lack of responsibility for horrific experiments by the global scientific community! In my opinion they are nothing but a bunch of spineless wimps!" Larry then retorted, "Whoa there! That's not true!" Marie fired back, "Isn't it?" Marie was in one of her provocative states. She would not keep quiet, even though Larry had placed his finger over his lips indicating that she should be quiet. But Marie continued to speak, "We have never taken responsibility for our ill-advised Cold War experiments, releasing all sorts of biological agents in over 200 open air tests on the American people."

Larry was dumbfounded but Marie could not be stopped, "Don't tell me that you didn't know that Licio Gelli and his physician Dr. Leon Gauci stole funds from the Vatican Bank to fund the development of immunosuppressive agents in their amoral eugenics program. And they had help from the Mafia." Larry was speechless. There was nothing he could do to stop the passionate young scientist from venting her anger right in the middle of his Department. Marie continued, "Larry, isn't it obvious that organized crime is mixed up with the funding of biological warfare through their pharmaceutical investments?" Larry responded, "Actually, I've never heard of this, and I doubt if any of my colleagues have either. Are you sure that you're correct about this?" Marie answered, "The Mafia are not the jokers you see on TV shows. They're a sophisticated money laundering and financing organization that has penetrated into our science community. And to make matters worse for me, I think that my elusive father was one of them, and he was probably the boss." Marie was nearly crying when she spit out her last statement. Larry was still dumbfounded at Marie's tirade. He did not know exactly what to make of

Marie's revelation that she was related to some Mafia boss. He tried to brush it off as some ridiculous comment made in a heated moment, but he changed his mind later that day when the black limos showed up in front of the building where Marie gave her seminar. He decided not to press her on the issue, and besides it was close to seminar time, and Larry did not want to make the afternoon any more complicated than it was at the moment.

Larry tried to calm down Marie so that she could go on and deliver her lecture to his department. He looked at Marie with a mixture of genuine concern and admiration and said, "Let's just concentrate on your seminar, O.K.?" Larry had heard that the McNichols were under tremendous pressure to abandon their research, and he had also heard that Jared McNichols was in danger of being fired for their work on Gulf War Illnesses. Isaac Geldter and others in the Austin Medical Center had gone all over the scientific community telling anyone who would listen that Jared was in the process of being fired for fabricating the McNichols' results on Gulf War veterans' infections. Personally Larry did not believe any of the rumors, but there were many, even at his own institution, that accepted what Geldter and others had been saying. After all, why would Geldter and the others go out of their way to make such outlandish statements if there wasn't some element of truth in what they were saying? Larry turned to the visibly upset Marie and asked her, "Is this going to be a normal day, Marie? Is this going to be just a routine seminar?"

Marie finally regained her composure and told Larry something that she had neglected to tell him last night. She said, "I think that it is going to be a normal day, but I did invite some soldiers at Fort Meade to attend my seminar. Is this going to be all right?" Larry thought for a moment and then answered, "Why not. After what you told me about the Army Institute of Pathology Research, I think that we can cut you a little slack." With that comment Marie relaxed a bit and told Larry, "I think I'm ready now. Please forgive me for lashing out in your department." Larry replied, "Don't give it a thought. I have some idea of the pressures that you and Jared are under at the moment. I want you to know that I am behind both of you in your efforts." Larry then took Marie to the seminar room for her lecture.

The seminar went smoothly but what happened after the seminar was anything but normal. After the seminar Larry decided to take Marie and some of the faculty members in his department to lunch at the faculty club.

As they exited the Research Building, Marie pointed to the black limos. Larry said, "We sometimes have visiting dignitaries. It's probably some VIP." Just as he spoke a tall distinguished looking man in a dark suit got out of one of the limos and asked Marie, "Is everything O.K.?" Marie stared back at him and asked, "Who are you?" The man replied, "Come on Marie, you know that I'm always here to protect you." Marie turned away from the man standing by one of the limos and refused to acknowledge his question. As the group of faculty walked on, Larry asked Marie, "Who was that?" Marie replied, "I'm not sure. But now at least you have seen it too." Larry decided not to press Marie further about the limos and the strange tall man. Marie was trying to suppress some painful truth about her background.

As the group approached the Faculty Club where the dining hall was located, they noticed that there must have been some sort of meeting of Naval officers at the University. They noticed many officers in dress whites and some in more casual dress coming out of the building. Turning to one of the officers Larry asked, "What's going on here?" The officer replied, "Bomb scare. We were told to leave the building." Larry turned to the small group of faculty and just shrugged his shoulders and made a face to indicate that he didn't know what was going on in the building. The group decided to wait a few minutes before deciding on a change of plans, and some of the faculty got into a discussion with Marie about her seminar. No one seemed to be concerned about the bomb scare. After a few minutes the building was opened, and a man told the assembled group of faculty, friends and Navy personnel that everything was O.K., just a false alarm.

The groups of people began to line up to re-enter the building when two Naval officers came up to Marie and saluted to Marie. One was an admiral who patted Marie on her behind as he passed. He told the group as he passed, "We feel confident that you can now dine. You will find our calling card at your table. Carry on!" Larry smiled and asked the admiral, "Hey, that's sexual harassment." The officers smiled but did not reply. After they had entered the building, Marie suddenly remembered that she had seen one of the officers before. It was Commander Dale DeJon! What was he doing at the Georgetown Medical School?

The faculty group from the Microbiology Department found their table. It was the only one with two Navy officer dress white caps on the place settings. One of the caps contained extensive gold braiding indicating the rank of a Vice Admiral, and the other was for a Navy Commander. It must have been the Admiral who greeted Marie just before they entered the building. The faculty members with their visitor from Texas continued their lunch without incident. Marie would never learn whether she was at any risk that day at the Faculty Club in Washington. After she returned from the trip and related the story to Jared, he just smiled and told Marie that Commander DeJon and the admiral were probably just emphasizing to her that they were there to protect her. That was the kind of support that made the McNichols feel more secure and more positive about the trials and tribulations that they were going through. It meant a lot to know that the line officers in the Armed Forces were behind them, even if the Medical Corps had repeatedly tried to tear them down.

CHAPTER 13

Dr. Masters Becomes Impatient (1996)

Jared opened his internal mail one morning to find that he had received an invitation to speak in the internal seminar series of the Department of Laboratory Services on molecular biology and Gulf War Illnesses. Although he was somewhat surprised to receive the invitation from Dr. Jose Gonsalez, the head of the department and a world-renowned pathologist and expert on head and neck cancers, he shouldn't have, because Dr. Gonsalez was a friend and colleague of many of the younger department chairmen at the Cancer Center. But he was also a close friend of Dr. Belcher's, and unbeknownst to Jared, he had already been in heated discussions with Dr. Belcher at the way Jared and Marie were being treated by the D. O. Madison administration. Dr. Gonsalez was essentially out of the loop when it came to the administration's actions against the McNichols, and he didn't have any idea why Dr. Masters was acting so nasty against what he considered were good young academics. Dr. Gonsalez was from a noble Spanish family, and he could trace his roots back to the first Kings of Spain. He was also above all, a most polite and polished individual who was extremely well-liked by his faculty and colleagues. He was also held in very high regard among the other institutions in the Medical Center. Jared was lucky indeed to have a clinician of Dr. Gonsalez's stature on his side. When Marie went on a rampage against the faculty of the Cancer Center, which was happening more and more often, Dr. Gonsalez was one of the examples that Jared used to counter her argument that every one of the chairmen at the D. O. Madison was corrupt and against them.

Dr. Gonsalez wasn't the only department chairman that supported the McNichols against the D. O. Madison administration, but he was probably the most influential, along with some of the other clinical department chairmen that supported Jared. This was especially true of various departments that covered medical oncology, surgical oncology, neurooncology and radiology. Without the support of other department chairmen, Jared would have been steam-rolled by the administration long ago. There were usually some checks and balances in any large organization, and the clinical department chairmen plus the few Vice Presidents who were not in Dr. Masters' pocket and the Legal Services Department were the only administrative checks against the overwhelming power of Dr. Masters. And of course, the State System administration that was just beginning to take a closer look at the D. O. Madison administrators. Unfortunately, with the untimely murder of Dr. Cannon, the State System would not be proceeding against Dr. Masters, so for the moment he had free reign over the Cancer Center as his personal fiefdom.

Since Jared had been ordered by Dr. Masters not to speak on Gulf War Illnesses, except for official testimony to U. S. Congressional and other government committees and panels, he arranged for Marie to receive the invitation instead to give the seminar in the Department of Laboratory Services. This department was responsible for all clinical laboratory testing at the D. O. Madison Cancer Center, and the deputy chairman, Dr. Richards, was interested in the data that Jared and Marie had been collecting on the Gulf War veterans. Since Marie was a consultant on Jared's grants and no longer on the staff as a paid employee of the Cancer Center, Dr. Masters couldn't order her not to give an invited seminar in one of the clinical departments. Since she was a consultant on an active Federal grant, he couldn't stop her from entering the facility, because she must have first-hand access to the research being conducted under the grant. Jared thought that he had all the bases covered when he suggested that Marie give the seminar the Department of Laboratory Services instead of himself but, in fact, he was testing the limits of power of a megalomaniac, and that was not a smart thing to do.

The important part was the timing. Marie was speaking as an invited guest of the department on short notice, and Jared hoped that Dr. Masters or even Drs. Belcher or Bane would not have time to intervene and prevent the lecture, or they might not even notice it. Even with the distinction of Marie not being officially on staff and immune to the orders of the

Administration, Jared was concerned that Dr. Masters would place pressure on or retaliate against Laboratory Services or his own department for letting Marie lecture on Gulf War Illnesses at The D. O. Madison. Jared had always wondered why Dr. Masters had focused so much on Marie. Dr. Masters was obsessed with Marie and had given orders to his Administration that Marie was never to receive any salary or consultancy fees, even if she had been approved as a consultant on one of Jared's NIH grants.

Although Jared thought that the invitation to speak at an internal Madison seminar was under the radar screen of the administration, he didn't realize that Dr. Masters was closely shadowing his every move and had already tried to have the department withdraw its invitation to the McNichols to present their data. However, Dr. Gonsalez regarded Dr. Masters' order as only a 'suggestion' to his department, not an order. After carefully considering the administration's 'suggestion' to pull the invitation, the department decided to proceed anyway. They just didn't see the need to cancel the seminar because the topic might be politically embarrassing for the administration. After all, the seminar was an internal affair, even though it was advertised through the pathology community in the Medical Center. Dr. Gonsalez was a strong supporter of Jared and Marie, and he previously had urged them to continue their important work.

Usually Dr. Belcher would have stepped in to control the research information of the Cancer Center as its Vice President for Research, but since Dr. Belcher owed his appointment to the European Academy of Science to the political influence of Dr. Gonsalez with the Academy, he was hesitant to criticize Dr. Gonsalez and interfere in his department affairs. Dr. Bane was also hesitant to step in, because Dr. Gonsalez was not a man to cross swords with. He had an elegant manner about him, some would claim arrogant, and he could be very forceful with his polite but convincing European style. Jared very much liked and respected Dr. Gonsalez, and the feeling was mutual. Unfortunately, Dr. Gonsalez had just been diagnosed with prostate cancer, and his political effectiveness would in the future be limited because of the therapy he would now have to undergo. However, that did not stop Dr. Gonsalez from working on the McNichols' behalf behind the scenes at the Medical Center. Therefore, the seminar remained on the books as scheduled, and the preparations were made to have Marie speak in one of the larger conference rooms at the Cancer Center on the topics of molecular biology and Gulf War Illnesses.

On the day of the seminar Jared and Marie walked down a hallway in the hospital to the conference room where Marie would deliver a lecture on the research that she and Jared were conducting on Gulf War Illnesses and on her own molecular biology studies. The conference room was typical of any conference room at the Cancer Center, and it had capacity seating for approximately 200 people. They entered the conference room before most of the attendees had arrived, and Marie whispered to Jared, "Do you think I should mention how Suzanne is doing since her return from the Gulf?" Jared answered, "I just spoke to her early this morning, and she said she is feeling much better." Marie responded, "That's great! Can I mention it today?" Jared replied, "You should probably stay away from personal stories, and please don't editorialize or make any inflammatory comments. Just keep to the data that we have collected. They can't defame us about the data, but Masters' dupes will be here, and you don't want to give them any ammunition. I don't want to have us both up in Masters office for violating his orders, even if they are illegal."

Marie hesitated and then became very somber. "You know, I hate giving seminars here. I don't know why we even bother to continue at this place. I wonder if they'll heckle me again and throw spitballs?" Jared reassured her, "Don't worry, I will be here to control the situation, and you are talking in a department that is very supportive of our work. Dr. Gonsalez is one of our strongest supporters. He must know something about what's happening in the prisons. He's very close to Belcher, and Belcher needs him to prop up his international academic standing." Marie fired back, "What standing? Without people like Dr. Gonsalez, nobody would even give Belcher a second thought."

After a few seconds at most Marie turned around and looked at the growing audience. "I see that Dr. Domasovitch is here, and you know he really hates me. Look at that sneer on his face when he looks at me!" Jared said, "I doubt that he hates you or me; in fact, he probably likes us. Isn't he always smiling around us? He's just taking advantage of the situation. Masters or Belcher probably bribed him to give us a hard time. I expect him to move up the ladder and eventually receive some kind of 'reward' from Belcher. I wouldn't be surprised if they offered him a promotion in the Education Department as an Assistant Vice President if he can get us to leave, which he really can't do if we decide to stay. When he could no longer get any political help from me, he just jumped ship." She continued, "Yah, after you loyally supported him for the last ten years. I tell you, he hates me, and he would slit your throat to get ahead, and you know I'm right. Look at how quickly he turned on you." Marie continued, "I have instincts for these things. Look at Dr. Nosan, he is not the type to give presents, and yet he was always bringing presents to me. Don't you find that suspicious?" Jared just shrugged his shoulders and said, "Well, I guess we are going to have to start checking those presents for unusual properties, although I doubt that he would go that far." Marie continued, "It's certainly not a romantic gesture, so he must feel guilty, or he is trying to stay in my good graces–or your good graces." Jared said, "Basically he is just taking advantage of the situation. He probably thinks that Masters is going to make him the next chairman of the department. It's funny how Nosan, Domasovitch, Geldter and who knows who else thinks that they are going to be handed the department. I wonder how many people were promised my position by Masters?" Jared shook his head and tried to chuckle as they took their seats in front of the conference room. Marie whispered to Jared, "To me Masters is capable of murder. I just know that they are all in on it with him." Jared just shook his head. He knew in his heart that Marie was probably correct. He felt the same way, but there was nothing that either one of them could do about the situation.

Just before the McNichols sat down at the front of the lecture room, Marie asked Jared about her slides. "Will you set up my slides?" Jared replied as they sat down, "I am the highest paid slide-maker in the business, and I will gladly assist you." Marie said, "Stop teasing me!" She hesitated and whispered to Jared, "I really hate these lectures." Marie then stood to meet the department deputy chairman, Dr. Martin Richards, who came to the front of the room. Jared considered Dr. Richards a nice person and a quality faculty member. He wouldn't let the seminar degenerate into a free-for-all, especially if outsiders 'crash' the talk with the intent of trashing Marie. Jared warned Dr. Richards that some people might try to disrupt the seminar, recalling what happened in his own department, and Dr. Richards assured Jared that it couldn't happen today.

Jared was relieved that the seminar couldn't be easily disrupted by some of Masters' dupes. At that same time a bit of a commotion transpired outside the lecture hall, and all heads turned to the door as the Maitlands and Cassie Mayer with a cameraman walked into the conference room. All eyes seemed to follow Cassie Mayer and the cameraman, and in fact many in the audience immediately recognized Cassie because she did the local medical segments on Eyewitness News. Jared quietly said to Marie, "Oh, no! They actually came. I hope this is not going to turn into a circus!" Marie replied, "It's already a circus!" Jared assumed that Marie was just being polite when she invited Sandra Maitland and her reporter friend Cassie Mayer to her seminar, but here they were at the seminar, just as Sandy promised. Jared secretly prayed that Cassie checked in with the administration first and had permission to be at the seminar. If they hadn't, then Jared and even the Clinical Services Department could be in big trouble with Dr. Masters.

Marie noticed that Jared didn't look too well, but she knew why, as she too noticed the TV reporter and cameraman. She whispered quietly, "And like I said this morning, think of The D. O. Madison as Funeral Parlor City." Jared tried to make light of the situation, "Are you thinking of my untimely immediate future, or didn't you call your home in South Florida by that same name?" Marie continued, "I tell you the place is a giant front for something sinister." Jared tried to calm down Marie before her seminar, "Please get out of your negative thought loop and sarcastic mood." He said, "There are some very nice people here and top notch professionals too. You would have never been invited to this department if they were all jerks." Marie said, "See, I'm smiling!" As Jared frowned, she continued, "But in general the faculty here have no backbone, and even the best here do not measure up to the intellectual prowess of the Institute where I trained." Jared looked at Marie and said, "Now be professional, Marie." She answered, "Aren't I always?" Jared never answered her.

Sandy Maitland saw the McNichols and came immediately over to introduce Cassie Mayer to Marie and Jared. The McNichols stood to meet the TV reporter and her cameraman. Marie said, "I'm glad to see you all again." Sandy introduced the visitors, "Marie, Jared, this is Cassie. She's an investigative reporter with the Eyewitness News team, and she has been following our story of the Wallsville 'Mystery Iilness'." Cassie said, "Pleased to finally meet you, Dr. and Dr. McNichols." Cassie turned to Marie and said, "Now that I recall, I believe I did an interview on your husband a few years back on his breast cancer research." Jared had not remembered but he went along. "That's right. I almost forgot, and I was impressed with the piece that you did on the subject." Cassie responded, "Well, thanks! We reporters rarely get any credit for what we do." Jared asked the reporter, "Cassie, I hope you cleared this with our Public Affairs Office?" Cassie replied, "Why, I always do that, Dr. McNichols. I know the rules around here." She briefly laughed, indicating that she thought that all the academic formalities were unnecessary. She was probably right, but not this time.

Actually Jared agreed with Cassie Mayer, but he couldn't take the chance that a reporter might come to Marie's seminar without clearing it first with the Madison administration. Cassie turned to Jared and became more serious and asked, "Tell me something, do you think there is a connection between the Gulf War Syndrome and the Wallsville 'Mystery Illness'?" Jared responded, "When you look carefully at their signs and symptoms, they are very, very similar, and when we used our laboratory tests we found the same chronic infections in both of these groups of patients." Marie added, "So far, in our preliminary investigation, which I'll explain during the lecture, the patterns that we are finding in the Wallsville 'Mystery Illness' victims and approximately 50% of the Gulf War veterans indicate exactly the same agent, and the results show the presence of an invasive mycoplasma, *Mycoplasma fermentans incognitus,* in both groups of patients. I'll explain what a mycoplasma is during the seminar, but basically it's a very primitive type of bacteria."

Marie continued the discussion with the reporter in an area that Jared did not want her to discuss. "Surprisingly, when we were conducting controls for the experiments, we found the presence of one of the HIV-1 viral genes. The HIV-1 virus is the virus that causes AIDS. In some of the patients from Wallsville and some of those who served in Operation Desert Storm we were able to find certain HIV-1 genes or parts of genes."

Marie tried to qualify her remarks, but it was too late. The cat was out of the bag, and Jared could only wonder about the consequences. "But I have to caution you, our results are only preliminary. In the end I think, as my husband will explain, we will find that multiple agents are involved in both instances." Jared stiffened and hoped that the reporter would forget about the mention of the HIV-1 gene. Cassie asked, *"Agents?"* She had focused on *'agents'* instead of on the HIV-1 genes. Marie continued without thinking of the consequence of what she had just said to the reporter. "We hypothesize that the Persian Gulf War veterans were exposed to biological and chemical *'agents'* in accordance with Soviet Warfare Doctrine." Marie continued, "And from what I gather from Sandy and her family, there is the possibility of exposure of the Wallsville residents to a variety of *'agents'* in the prison system.

Jared tried to quickly repair the situation and play down the discussion of chemical and biological *'agents.'* The use of this term suggested that the McNichols had found chemical or biological *weapons* in the veterans and in prison guards as well. Jared tried to casually extend what Marie had told Cassie. "In short, Cassie, the Wallsville situation may mimic some of the conditions that were found in the Gulf War, especially the exposure to certain chemicals and certain infections, such as the mycoplasma that we found in the veterans' blood." The problem was that Cassie could not discern the difference between a *natural* exposure and exposure to a *war agent.* Jared was very concerned that she would report that the McNichols had found biological weapons in the patients that they examined. That would certainly trigger a very negative response from the administration, even if it was likely to be the truth.

But it was entirely too late–the cat was out of the bag. Especially when Marie said, "Off the record, I am beginning to conclude that Operation Desert Storm was one gigantic Soviet War Doctrine experiment and that some of the same biological *agents* were tested well before the war on the Wallsville prisoners. Like the Tuskegee syphilis experiments where prisoners were exposed to syphilis and then just watched to see what would happen if the infection went untreated." Not to be stopped, Marie continued even as she was being gently kicked by Jared, "And I strongly suspect that some high level government officials might have profited from the sale of the biological weapons to Saddam Hussein, which means that the U. S. may have violated the 1972 Geneva Convention, the international treaty that banned the manufacture, sale, use and dissemination of biological agents." Jared was having a brief coronary while Cassie looked puzzled, so Jared gently added, "Marie sometimes becomes a bit too emotional about what we have found. There are a few gaps in the story, and this isn't the final word, so please don't quote us on Marie's last few comments. We have some more work to do in the lab to put this on more solid ground. And please don't quote her on the comments about the treaty."

Marie, however, could not be stopped by Jared, who was trying to keep the local reporter from reporting on their preliminary laboratory results and bringing down the wrath of the administration. Marie however said, "How can I not get emotional? I am just stating the truth. Remember, just because I am passionate does not mean that I am not objective about my science." Jared said, "O.K., I know. But in your lecture, just stick to the facts, please!" Cassie was, unfortunately, beginning to understand the ramifications of what Marie had just told her. "I believe that this is an ugly story that needs to be told. When Sandy mentioned to me what you found and what has happened in the prison system, I decided that the people of Texas deserve to know what is going on in their communities, especially those with prison facilities. But I also understand that this could have very negative repercussions in certain places."

Jared's heart was beating very rapidly, but he, in fact, was being told by Cassie, the reporter out for a good story, that she would try to be careful and objective. This was reassuring, and then finally Marie began to respond to the worried look on Jared's face, which she knew meant that Jared was worried about the internal political consequences of her comments. So Marie changed her tone, "But if you can approach the story in a positive way . . . ." Cassie asked, "How?" Jared intervened, "We have a brief publication in the *Journal of the American Medical Association* that summarizes our work with the veterans who used the antibiotic doxycycline to overcome Gulf War Illness. And we have another publication in a British medical journal explaining the medical as well as the political aspects of our findings. I will make sure that you have copies of these articles. They should help explain what Marie has just summarized, and then you can quote the published work rather than quoting us directly." Cassie did not really know the significant difference between quoting a 'source' and quoting a peer-reviewed published paper. The former can be attacked directly but the latter invites criticism of the publication and perhaps the review and editorial process that resulted in the publication. Also, Jared knew he could defend his publications better than a direct quote, and Dr. Masters would have a hard time firing him for his comments taken from a peer-reviewed publication. After all, he would just be quoting published material that had passed the critical test of peer review.

Although Jared was trying desperately to have everyone sit down so he could start the seminar, Marie continued speaking to Cassie, the reporter. "We are tying to complete the circle of evidence. You know, the old Roger Bacon line of investigation of observation and experimentation. But in the case of the veterans and the prison employees, we had to do something or let them suffer or even die. So, we had to quietly tell some of the patients to try the antibiotic to see if it worked." Jared added, "We really need to get the seminar started here! I am sure that the Administration is very concerned with the safety of patients, and this is why they are being so cautious." Cassie responded, "I hope you're right about that, but I have to be candid with you Dr. McNichols, most of the time I have found that administrators are more interested in protecting their backsides than they are in protecting the public." Sandy said, "We sure feel a hell of a lot better since we began the antibiotics, and Julie's so-called Lou Gehrig's Disease symptoms are going away." Jared had to explain, so Cassie would not incorrectly conclude that infections solely cause neurodegenerative diseases. "Which means she likely did not have classical ALS, which is a rare neurodegenerative disease. She may have had an infection that caused the death of the same nerve cells that are affected in ALS." Sandy added, "Four people on our block alone who are not related were diagnosed with Lou Gehrig's disease, and our neurologist told us that it was impossible!" Clayman, who rarely interrupted anyone also got into the act, "And many of those diagnosed with MS are already responding to the doxycycline, just like the McNichols predicted!" Jared tried desperately to explain, "We feel that these infections can mimic a variety of autoimmune-like illnesses besides MS and neurodegenerative diseases like ALS." Marie added, "They're the great imposters because they can invade so many places in your body."

Jared tried to take control so the seminar could start. He faced the audience and waved his arms downward in an attempt to tell the audience to sit down. Dr. Richards, who had come to the front of the room finally said, "Please, everyone, the room is almost full, and we're ready to begin the seminar." Everyone finally took his or her seats. Even Marie sat down, and Jared who had been asked by Dr. Richards to give the introduction went to the podium. As he walked up to the podium, Jared wondered if he had been asked to deliver the introduction in order to keep the faculty from Laboratory Services from being in trouble with Dr. Masters. He decided that it was probably better for him to do it. After all, he was in trouble anyway, and this introduction was unlikely to make the situation any worse for him than it was already.

Jared said to the audience, "Good morning!" As the audience calmed down, he continued. "I am Jared McNichols, and Dr. Richards has asked me to give the introduction. I hope that you do not mind that Eyewitness News, which has been cleared by our Administration to record parts of the seminar, will be here today. The seminar will be given by my wife, Dr. Marie McNichols, who is a consultant to the Cancer Center. Marie will cover the topic of Nucleoprotein Gene Tracking and its use in an attempt to understand the role of invasive infections, such as viral and mycoplasmal infections, in chronic illnesses. In some cases, these illnesses are associated with Persian Gulf War Syndrome or what we call Gulf War Illnesses and the outbreaks in the Texas prison system at certain units that have even been reported on Eyewitness News." Jared continued, "We realize the topic is controversial, but let me remind you that here at The D. O. Madison cancer patients are often immunosuppressed, and they would be prime candidates to contract some of the invasive infections that will be discussed this morning. In fact, the issue of opportunistic infections in patients undergoing cytotoxic therapy is an important one that cannot be easily dismissed, because it is one of the most common problems facing us today in cancer therapy." Jared continued the introduction by introducing Marie's professional background and the research that they had done together in the Department of Cancer Biology.

Marie stood up, approached the front of the lecture hall and began her lecture by focusing on the use of the Nucleoprotein Gene Tracking technique to study various scientific problems. The lecture then moved forward with Marie showing many of the slides that Jared prepared for her on the data that they had gathered to support their hypothesis that chronic infections might be the cause or at least part of the cause of various unusual clinical conditions, such as those found after the Gulf War and in the Texas prison system.

After Marie presented the data that she and Jared had used to support their hypothesis, she began to summarize her seminar. Since some in the audience were not scientists or clinicians, she decided to add a few editorial comments. "To know the pattern of an enemy is to overcome the enemy, and the techniques described today have enabled us to locate DNA sequences from invasive microorganisms that have penetrated deeply into the cell and even into the cell nucleus." She continued, "I often tell soldiers when I lecture that the microorganisms are like guerilla warfare elements. They're insidious and invisible and almost impossible to detect." Marie was at the end of her lecture, and she decided to editorialize a bit, even though Jared had warned her not to provoke Dr. Masters, who presumably had many spies in the audience. Marie said, "I believe that we as American citizens have all been betrayed. There are over 120 universities in the U. S. alone that have been involved in chemical and biological warfare defense, and in some cases this has resulted in research that could be conceived as 'offensive' in nature. This was supposed to stop in 1972 with the signing of the Geneva Convention on Biological Weapons." She continued, "These weapons were even put together into mixtures called Russian doll or Metroushka doll cocktails, which are mixtures of various components that by themselves are relatively harmless or incapable of causing lethal illnesses, but when combined produce deadly combinations of components, which remain for the most part hidden. These cocktails are also designed to create immune suppression.

Finally, Marie ended her seminar with some political statements. "I didn't become a scientist to harm people. Nor am I standing in judgment of Cold War policies that may have resulted in a secret biological weapons race. But the onus for the waves of illnesses that we see affecting significant numbers in the general population could be the fault of the global science and medical communities who should have known better. For once the scientific community should be called on the carpet for concentrating on the dark side of their wonderful new discoveries. These horrible new weapons cannot be controlled. Think about it! Why did you become physicians and scientists? Didn't you want to help mankind? Or have you forgotten the teachings of Maimonides that state that it is our duty to care for our fellow human beings! Why should a few mediocrities that cannot make it on their talent alone benefit by performing amoral experiments? They're amongst you! Don't let them win!"

Marie received a rousing ovation from some members of the audience for her unusual lecture, but it was very clear that not all of the participants were pleased with the seminar. Only a consultant could have given such a talk, because an employee of the Cancer Center would have to face Dr. Masters and his henchmen for daring to buck the system. Jared looked around the audience and noticed that Drs. Nosan, Domasovitch and Auchenhower, among others were not applauding. In fact, they were leaving the room as quickly as possible. Jared thought that they must be headed for the nearest phone booth to report to the administration that Marie may have defamed over one hundred universities! He secretly laughed knowing that when they review the tapes of the seminar, they won't find a 'smoking' gun. The McNichols had survived to live another day. Marie did as Jared told her to do—she did not defame the D. O. Madison. Dr. Masters would not have his way on the basis of this seminar.

Carrie was quick to take advantage of the situation, and she had her cameraman set up outside the conference room. The first person that they interviewed was Dr. Richards. He would be badgered that night by the administration for letting Marie and Jared go astray and present some political points in their department seminar series. Jared was doing some damage control with the other faculty members of the department. Sandy Maitland went up to tell Marie, "Girl that took guts!" Marie asked, "For what? I was just trying to tell the truth." Clayman then added, "That's a rare commodity these days." The room finally cleared out and Jared returned and said, "Well Marie, your lecture was splendid, but I can predict that I will be receiving a great deal of harassment from the administration over your lecture today."

Finally, Carrie came back into the conference room to have a final word with the McNichols. Jared was concerned that Dr. Masters would use Marie's lecture against him and the department that sponsored her seminar, so he decided not to be interviewed by Eyewitness News. After all, Dr. Masters told him that he did not want to see any more publicity without the approval of the Public Affairs Department. Carrie again assured Jared that she had the approval of Department of Public Affairs before she could bring a cameraman into the Cancer Center. Jared was still concerned about repercussions, regardless of whether the Eyewitness News crew was approved or not to film the lecture and conduct interviews after the seminar.

Jared was right. The segment appeared on the evening news, but Jared escaped any TV exposure. Not so with Marie. Even if the Eyewitness News crew had the approval of the administration, Jared felt uncomfortable. He had a feeling that they have not seen the last of The D. O. Madison administration when it came to the seminar. He was right.

Dr. Masters always gets his way

The next day after Marie's seminar in the Department of Laboratory Services, Jared was contacted by Dr. Belcher. Jared returned his call to find out what he had called about, but in reality he knew. He had a sickly feeling in the pit of his stomach. It must be about Marie's seminar. He reached Dr. Belcher in his office. Jared asked Dr. Belcher, "Francis, I think I know why you called me this morning." Dr. Belcher said, "I thought that you might. Jared, I thought that we had an agreement that you would not drag this Gulf War Syndrome thing out in the press." Jared responded, "Dr. Belcher, I did not publicly speak on that subject. I think you might be referring to Marie who gave an invited seminar yesterday in the Department of Laboratory Services. And if you are referring to the segment on Eyewitness News, I was not a part of that segment as you must know by now, and the TV crew was approved by the Public Affairs Department."

There was a moment of silence on the line. That in itself was quite unusual for Dr. Belcher. He then responded in a fatherly manner, "Jared, let me give you some friendly advice. It doesn't matter if you were or were not on TV or in the newspapers. What matters is that Dr. Masters feels that the good name of the institution has been dragged through the mud by your direct actions. And I don't think that anyone can change his mind on that point." Jared asked, "How can he come to that conclusion? The segment on TV was very positive for our image in the community." Dr. Belcher who was not angry but sounded resigned said, "It doesn't matter what you or I think. Because that is the conclusion that he has come to, and there is nothing that I can do about it. You were warned not to speak in public about this, and you were told to shut down this research. You violated that trust, and I must now tell you that Dr. Masters will be taking some punitive action against you because of it." Jared asked, "What kind of action?" Dr. Belcher answered, "I believe that you will be removed from your chairmanship, effective immediately. You serve at his pleasure, and I must say, you have just about burned all your bridges with the administration here. And there may be more, but I am trying to get Dr. Masters to listen to some reason."

Jared thought about what he had built in the Department and what his laboratory had accomplished in the last decade, and he became angry at what he had just heard. "Dr. Belcher, you know that I have done nothing wrong, and you know that I have not broken any rules or regulations. You and Dr. Masters are acting like I am some criminal that needs to be punished. All that we have done is help the veterans and help the prison guards from an illness that is spreading in the military and in the communities where State prisons are located. We have been very careful about the science that we have done, and I believe that we are correct in our assessment of the chronic infections in these patients. The patients that we have helped have recovered or are beginning to recover from their illness, and we have published our results in peer-reviewed journals. I thought that is what we were hired to do at our institution—help those with illnesses recover from their health problems. I didn't think that we were here to turn our backs on problems when they arose in the community, especially if we could help them, just for political reasons. And if I am removed from my position because of that reporter yesterday, I must conclude that this is some sort of aberrant institution and I rue the day that I ever came here." He paused and stated, "Besides, Cassie Meyer had the approval of the Administration to be at that lecture."

Dr. Belcher was in no mood to listen to Jared. He said in his whiny voice, "Listen Jared, don't get self-righteous with me. It doesn't matter a damn that you've helped someone or what you've published your data or who had approval to be at the seminar yesterday. You were directed to shut down this line of investigation, and you chose not to. Now you have to pay the piper and face the consequences. Dr. Masters might have left you alone if you had just stopped throwing this whole thing back in his face. Now he won't stop until you are dismissed from the institution. Am I making myself clear, Jared. You have gone too far, and I don't think that anyone can help you, not even the Governor. My advice is to find a new position somewhere else, if you are dead set in continuing this line of research. I would be amazed, however, if you could find any place that will have you. I don't even know that if you stopped this entire mess right now that it would matter at this point. Once Clement has made up his mind to fire someone, he always gets his way."

Jared was stunned. He thought that he could survive until Masters retired in about eight months time. Now it looked like he might not make it to September. Jared said, "Thanks for your help, Dr. Belcher. I don't know exactly what I am going to do, but I will be looking for another position, I can promise you that. Hopefully someone here will support my applications. When a tenured faculty member is told that his research is politically incorrect and that he must shut down his laboratory just because of some bullshit secret programs that inadvertently were stumbled upon, it is a sad day for the University."

Dr. Belcher became irritated and told Jared, "You had better keep your opinions to yourself, Dr. McNichols, because what you just said could be considered slander by the administration. Dr. Masters could have your job for that one comment alone." Jared thought about what he had told Dr. Belcher and said, "O.K. Dr. Belcher, that's between you and me, even if it's the truth. But you know that I have served this institution with hard work and distinction, and *you have stated that yourself in writing in my annual evaluations.* All of my annual evaluations have been superlative at this institution, and that is a matter of record. I have done everything that has been asked of me, and more."

Dr. Belcher was becoming impatient with Jared, because he felt that Jared had not listened to him earlier when he advised him to stop the Gulf War veterans' research and the other research projects that could have political repercussions. Dr. Belcher responded, "You know that it all doesn't mean a thing when Dr. Masters has made up his mind. And he has made up his mind. I don't think that I can do anything for you. The only thing that might help you is that the University attorneys are holding Dr. Masters back for the moment, but you know that it is only a matter of time. Dr. Masters will get his way; he always does. I will be glad to help you find another position. I don't want you to leave us with a bad feeling." Jared sarcastically said, "I'm sure you don't, Dr. Belcher. Let me think carefully about your offer." Dr. Belcher replied, "Don't wait too long, or I may not be able to assist you. I am not even sure that I can even help you. You know Dr. Masters will find out where you have applied for positions, and he will make sure that it be difficult for you." Jared said, "That's what I have heard. Thanks again for your offer. Let me get back to you." Jared hung up the phone. He thought that Dr. Belcher was just trying to get him to over-react and resign his position and leave immediately. That would make it easier on him and the administration. He would just have to try to tough it out until Dr. Masters retires and hope that the next President would not be cut from the same mold. Jared did not feel good about the conversation with Dr. Belcher. His feeling was correct because the next day he received another letter from Dr. Masters.

January 11, 1996

LEGAL SERVICES

Professor Jared McNichol
Chairman, Department of Cancer Biology
The D. O. Madison Cancer Center
Austin, Texas

Dear Professor McNichol;

Previously I discussed in a letter to you some deficiencies in your conduct and related activities and provided written guidelines regarding your future as a senior tenured faculty member at this institution. You responded in a memo dated December 10, 1994. Since that time, additional issues have surfaced that must be addressed or severe consequences will follow if they are not immediately addressed. Some senior faculty members have expressed serious concerns about your department leadership and administrative judgment in institutional matters, and others have made allegations about your research that can no longer be ignored. For example, I recently received a memo from the Faculty Executive Committee listing several allegations on your research into Gulf War Syndrome. I agree with the faculty that these allegations must be immediately addressed, and I have incorporated these into this formal letter of warning to you.

Because of the serious nature of the matter, I am compelled to take the extraordinary measure of communicating directly to you through our Legal Services Department about these allegations so that they are fully informed of the situation. In addition, I have provided you with specific directives that define my expectations of your conduct within the established framework of the Cancer Center and the University.

I want to make clear to you that the consequences of not complying completely and immediately with my directives which are extremely serious. You are required to abide completely by the Regents' Rules and Regulations and institutional Handbook of Operating Procedures. You must also abide by my directives or risk termination of your faculty tenure and position at our institution. Because of the concerns that follow, I directed the Vice President for Academic Affairs to withhold your annual faculty appointment contract, pending a thorough review of your response and actions.

It is regrettable that your actions have caused the following events to have reached the present state. I sincerely hope that by complying fully and immediately with all of my directives, you will allay some of the concerns of the administration and your peers, so that we can address this important matter in a way that is satisfactory for all concerned. Please provide me with all of the information requested in my directives within the next ten days. Failure to do so will constitute gross insubordination and result in my proceeding immediately with your termination.

1. **You have discussed your research results in the public press that have not been published or passed by an**

appropriate peer review body. It is my understanding that your advocacy of antibiotics as a treatment for the Desert Storm Syndrome is based only on empiric observations, rather than on reproducible scientific evidence obtained in an appropriate, approved and controlled clinical trial. Furthermore, to my knowledge your work in this area has not been published in peer-reviewed journals that the senior faculty would deem appropriate for the subject matter. Directive: Provide me with the results of any peer reviewed research in the area of this subject matter. This will be evaluated by a institutional committee that has been assigned to oversee and direct your research in this area. You will abide by any and all of the decisions and directions of this committee; failure to do so will be considered insubordination and will result in your immediate termination. You will not make any public statements without prior approval of the institutional committee and my office.

2. **You have advised medication in the absence of acceptable published research.** We have information that you have advised patients with symptoms attributed to "Gulf War Syndrome" to take antibiotics on the basis of one of your publications that has not been evaluated by our senior faculty, which creates the perception that you are providing medical advice. I find no evidence that you are a board-certified infectious disease physician, and providing treatment advice could constitute practicing medicine without a license. I warn you that this constitutes violation of the Medical Practices Act, and penalties could be severe and include termination and criminal indictment. Directive: You will immediately cease making any medical statements, and you are prohibited from making recommendations directly or indirectly to patients on Gulf War Syndrome or related illnesses.

3. **You have offered medical tests without necessary agency approval.** You have made an unsolicited offer to one cancer

patient to perform a new diagnostic test to determine if cancer has spread or metastasized. Your offer implies that the test is only available through your laboratory, and this might result in violations of our institution's certification or accreditation. Any test that could be performed must have the approval of the administration, or this could constitute misuse of State resources. Directive: You must immediately cease making unsolicited offers to perform any diagnostic test through your laboratory. Any tests that are developed must be evaluated by the institutional committee that I have assigned, and the interpretation of such tests must be made by a physician assigned by the committee for this purpose.

4. **You have conducted laboratory research on recombinant DNA material without the required approval.** You have apparently conducted research involving pathogenic DNA material; however, there is no administrative record with the Biosafety Department or Department of Research of such research. Directive: You must have the appropriate approvals in order to conduct such research. Failure to have such approvals constitutes a grave violation of institutional regulations. If you conduct any research without such approvals, you can be terminated.

5. **You have used departmental resources to the detriment of other faculty members for purposes outside of the mission of the department and the institution.** State law prohibits the use of State-funded support services, equipment, materials, personnel and facilities for private purposes that do not relate to the mission of the institution. In addition, you have identified yourself as a faculty member of the University and have used the institution's and University's name for what I consider to be a private purpose outside the mission of the institution. Directive: If I find that you are misusing or have misused State or University resources or facilities, you will be immediately recommended for termination.

6. **You have expressed political views in the press.** You have continued to appear on radio talk shows and have been interviewed by the press about the Gulf War Syndrome, even though you were warned by me not to do so. Directive: If you make any additional public statements about the Gulf War Syndrome, and if you identify yourself as a faculty member of this institution, you will be subject to termination for insubordination.

7. **You have alleged that you are paying certain technicians from private funds or your endowed chair.** This raises several concerns. All employees at our institution must be approved and processed through the Office of Academic Affairs or Office of Human Resources to insure that they meet the qualifications necessary to perform their duties. If any technicians are present on institutional grounds without going through the usual approval process, they will be immediately barred from institutional facilities. Directive: You must provide me with a list of all personnel that are being paid by non-institutional funds. Even if these individuals have gone though the appropriate institutional procedures and have been approved, the institutional committee will determine if these individuals are qualified and competent to perform the duties that you have assigned them. If the committee determines that they are not qualified for the tasks that have been assigned, they must be immediately barred from performing any work in your laboratory.

8. **You have used volunteer labor in an unauthorized fashion for purposes other than the mission of the institution.** Persons performing volunteer service must be authorized by the institution. Directive: You must provide me with the names of volunteers, their duties and their qualifications. The institutional committee will determine if these volunteers have the necessary qualifications to perform the duties that you have assigned to

them. If the committee determines that they are not qualified for the tasks that have been assigned or they are conducting unauthorized work, they must be immediately barred from performing any work in your laboratory.

These directives must be remedied quickly or you will face termination. I remind you that you must respond to me in writing within ten (10) days. The institutional committee and I will review your response and determine if it is adequate.

Since it has become apparent that you have failed in your administrative responsibilities, I am removing you effectively immediately from your position as Chairman of the Department of Cancer Biology. An acting Chairman will be appointed to the department to insure that all of the rules and regulations of the University are closely followed.

Sincerely,

Clement A. Masters, M.D.
President

Jared read the letter from Dr. Masters, and it made him extremely angry. It was a travesty of false allegations and misrepresentations of the truth. After all Jared had done to serve the institution, he had been removed from his chairmanship and warned that he would essentially be stripped of his endowed professorship and his tenure and banished from the institution on the basis of completely false information. Dr. Belcher had been absolutely correct about Legal Services restraining Dr. Masters, but he had warned Jared that Dr. Masters could take away his position just about any time he wanted *"for a simple comment alone,"* and it was *"only a matter of time"* before Dr. Masters *"would have his way."*

The attorneys in the Department of Legal Services were at the institution mainly to protect the University and Dr. Masters from litigation and guide the administration by providing their legal advice. They were not in place to protect a faculty member who stumbled on illegal and immoral activities, fell out of grace with the administration and was now the target of a megalomaniac leader of the institution. Nor were the lawyers in Legal Services there to protect the public and the employees of the institution, although they claimed otherwise. Actually all that the university attorneys did was foster the criminal and amoral activities of Dr. Masters by protecting him and providing him with justification for just about anything that he wanted. After all, the attorneys were not independent counselors; they were administratively under Dr. Masters. They were *his* employees just like every faculty member and employee at the institution.

Dr. Masters had decided to terminate Jared and get rid of Marie in the process, and it was only a matter of time. It didn't matter that the so-called 'facts' were twisted or completely false, they were nonetheless used to support Dr. Masters' notion that Jared was unfit to continue in his position. It didn't matter that the allegations were untrue and not supportable by evidence. The Department of Legal Services could only restrain Masters for so long, and then he would *"get his way."* After all, didn't Dr. Belcher tell him that Dr. Masters always got his way when it came to firing staff members.

Jared thought about what had happened over the last few years at the D. O. Madison and said to himself in a matter of fact manner, "O.K., it looks like I need a new job." He was tired of fighting for his survival while at the same time struggling to maintain his cancer and chronic illness research programs, editorial positions, department administrative duties, teaching assignments, training responsibilities and trying to keep ahead on his grants and manuscripts. As it was, Jared was working an eighteen hour-per-day seven day-per-week schedule, with only a couple hours off for volleyball league each week and a few hours for his family life. Add to that the numerous detractors going all over the world defaming his and Marie's personal and professional reputations and circumventing every thing that they had tried to accomplish.

It would not be easy overcoming Dr. Masters' and his rats and at the same time finding a suitable position elsewhere. As soon as Jared applied for an academic position at another institution, the administration seemed to find out about it, and Jared felt that his applications suddenly were not taken seriously. In addition, Dr. Masters' henchmen had convinced many in the academic community that Jared had gone insane and flipped his lid over the veterans' illnesses. He was now thought to be unstable and incapable of holding an academic position. Jared was told that his applications had been placed on hold or that someone else was more likely to be appointed to the positions. Universities that tried to recruit Jared previously were suddenly not interested, and in some cases they did not even bother to return his phone calls or letters. Even when Jared knew someone at the universities where he applied, he was told that all of a sudden his status had changed from a desirable faculty recruit to a leper. It seemed that no one wanted to hire a 'whistle blower' or someone who had been painted as possibly insane by his own institution, and that was what Jared had become in the eyes of his colleagues at other institutions. Unbeknownst to Jared, many of the institutions that he applied to for a position also had their own secret classified research programs, and thus Jared was considered *persona non grata*. Within two short years Jared became an academic leper in the eyes of the science and academic community after 30 dedicated years of research, teaching and service.

Jared knew that he had to answer Dr. Masters' letter within the allowed ten days, because to not address the issues raised in the letter, no matter how ridiculous they were, would result in his immediate termination by Dr. Masters. Jared needed to keep working, not only to pay the bills, but to continue the research efforts on behalf of the veterans and the prison employees and their families. Jared wondered whether he would be thrown out of his office and his laboratories now that someone else was chairman of the Department. To think that the weasel Dr. Domasovitch might be appointed the new acting chairman of the department that Jared built from scratch in 1980 made Jared feel sick to his stomach. No wonder he was measuring Jared's office to see how much space he would have in *his* new surroundings. Some of the office personnel quietly told Jared that Dr. Domasovitch had been secretly going into Jared's office to sit in his chair and work on Jared's computer. Jared had shrugged it off as just another faculty chairman 'wantabe,' but Marie warned him that Domasovitch among others in his department were after Jared's job. There was blood in the water, and the sharks were gathering. Now Jared had begun to take the big hits on his career that had taken over 30 years to build. But he knew that he had to first answer Dr. Masters, if he were to even be employed at the Cancer Center and not out on the street within a few days.

January 19, 1996

Clement A. Masters, M.D.
President
The D. O. Madison Cancer Center
Austin, Texas

Dear Dr. Masters,

Concerning your recent letter of January 11, 1996 and the contents therein, I have the following responses and statements. I appreciate the chance to respond to the apparently confidential Faculty Executive Committee comments. If you had not contacted me about these allegations, I would not have known about the confidential memo that contains several unproven allegations from unknown sources. Since you mentioned it in your letter, I have made a formal request and to examine a copy of this memo. I have been informed that I cannot see the original memo or know the authors, nor can I request a copy of this memo. Since I have not been allowed to even see a copy of the allegations that have been made or know the identities of the individuals that have made them, I have not been allowed a minimum amount of fairness and due process expected for a faculty member at our institution. The undocumented allegations made by unknown person(s) are completely false, as I will detail below:

1. You have discussed your research results in the public press that have not been published or passed by an appropriate peer review body. We have published three peer-reviewed papers on the subject in internationally recognized academic medical and scientific journals. Furthermore, I have been invited to testify under oath to the President's Commission on Gulf War Veterans'

Illnesses in Washington DC on this issue, and I previously furnished a copy of my sworn testimony to the Vice President of Research. I have also been formally asked to testify to a committee of the U.S. House of Representatives. Furthermore, I have given three formal lectures at U.S. Government institutions: The U. S. Army Institute of Pathology Research, the Army Medical Center and at the request of the Deputy Secretary of the Department of Veterans' Affairs, to the Central Headquarters of the Department of Veterans' Affairs in Washington DC. My travel for the purpose of delivering testimony or lectures at these institutions was approved by the Vice President of Research. Furthermore, with the approval of the Vice President of Research, I have contacted the U.S. Army to submit a grant application in the area of question, and this was approved for submission by the Office of the Surgeon General of the U. S. Army. The application was prepared along with all necessary institutional approvals, including Biohazard, Recombinant DNA, and other approvals, and the application was signed by the Vice President of Research as the authorized individual for approval at this institution. This constitutes the usual process of administrative approval at our institution. Furthermore, my co-investigator is a department chairman at Belford College of Medicine, and that institution has administratively approved the application for submission to the U. S. Army. The grant is currently in the review process. Any other process, such as prior approval by a local committee that I am not even allowed to know the membership, is not a part of the usual approval process at our institution that every other faculty member uses. As to my discussing any of my research without prior administrative approval, I know of no other faculty member who is required to submit requests from the press to a secret committee that I am not allowed to know the membership of for prior approval before being allowed to talk to the press. Thus I am not receiving fair and equal treatment expected for a faculty member at our institution. I am being singled out because of some research that we conducted on Gulf War veterans that apparently displeases the administration.

2. You have advised medication in the absence of acceptable published research. We have not recommended treatments to patients, nor have we made any medical care pronouncements. We have, however, discussed our peer-reviewed published research with primary care providers. It is their decision completely on how to use this information and solely to evaluate and decide on their patients' medical care. We certainly do not intervene in this process. We have never provided any medications to patients. We have received requests from physicians, such as those in the Joint Special Operations Units at Fort Bragg, and we have tried to provide information to these physicians at this as well as other bases that have requested our assistance.

3. You have offered medical tests without necessary agency approval. We have never provided any patient with unauthorized tests, nor have we ever offered to perform any test that was not a part of an approved clinical laboratory protocol. I challenge the secret informer to provide evidence of such an act. All physicians who request diagnostic testing must fill out a request form and an informed consent form, and any test request must fit one of our approved laboratory protocols.

4. You have conducted laboratory research on recombinant DNA material without the required approval. This is not correct. We have the necessary approvals from the Biosafety Office and the Committee on Recombinant DNA.

5. You have used departmental resources to the detriment of other faculty members for purposes outside of the mission of the department and the institution. I know of no misuse of State or other resources or funds in my department, nor am I utilizing resources to the detriment of other departmental faculty. In fact, analysis of the space allocations based on grant and contract funding shows that I have the most outside funding and lowest amount of space per dollar of funding or of state resources, such

as technical assistance, of any faculty member in my department. My research grants and contracts actually subsidize research in my department conducted by other faculty. To my knowledge all of the research conducted in the department is within the missions of the institution.

6. You have expressed political views in the press. To my knowledge I have not expressed any political views in the press as an employee of this institution, and if I ever do express political views, this will be done as an individual not a member or representative of the faculty or institution. I have been asked to make comments to the press about our research, and in fact, our institution's Press Office has sent TV crews and members of the press over to my office for information that they could not provide. I agreed previously to have all press interviews approved by the Public Affairs Office, and I am amazed that the administration does not know of this arrangement, since the Office of Public Affairs is a part of the Administration.

7. You have alleged that you are paying certain technicians from private funds or your endowed chair. There is no secret about this, because all employees must receive approval before they can work in our department. As to whether a secret local committee can assess the credentials and work of technicians in our department and actually direct them without identifying themselves is unlikely, and I ask them to come forward, identify themselves and come to our department to see what each technician is doing on a daily basis. We have nothing to hide, nor do our technicians.

8. You have used volunteer labor in an unauthorized fashion for purposes other than the mission of the institution. I know of no unauthorized use of volunteer labor in our department. All employees must receive approval, volunteer or paid employee, before they can work in our department. I ask that the secret committee to come forward and visit our department to see firsthand what each member is doing.

Finally, I am appalled that for apparently the first time in the history of our institution a 'secret' committee has been appointed to oversee a senior faculty member, who is one of the most productive, internationally known and visible members of our faculty. Recommending severe and punitive administrative action without due process and even a chance to rebut unsubstantiated allegations or even receive copies of secret memos containing such allegations does not bode well for our institution. I remind each of you if you receive a copy of this memo that you could find yourself in exactly the same situation, and you should consider whether this is an appropriate precedent for our institution.

Sincerely,

Jared McNichol, Ph.D.
Samual Burker Chair in Cancer Research
Professor

At this point Jared was not sure that his response would be adequate to buy him some time to find a new position elsewhere. Certainly he could not apply for a faculty position anywhere in the State of Texas, but he was unsure about other universities as well. After discussing the situation with Marie, who was very negative about Jared finding a job any time soon because of the blackball that Jared's colleagues had gone along with, Jared decided to contact the recently retired Executive Vice President of the institution, Dr. Richard Hicks. Dr. Hicks, a crusty old surgeon with a strong wit, had always been a strong supporter of Jared and Marie. In fact, it was probably Dr. Hicks that prevented Dr. Masters from firing Jared approximately one year ago when the issue of his research first surfaced. Jared called Dr. Hicks to make an appointment to see him in his office, which had been moved to a new administrative building away from the hospital. Dr. Hicks actually sounded pleased that Jared had called to make an appointment, and he told Jared to come right over. Jared decided to go immediately to Dr. Hicks' new office.

Jared made his way to Dr. Hicks' office by foot. He had been moved to a recently renovated building down the street from the Medical Center. As Jared walked to the building he thought about what had happened to him and Marie. His recent recurring nightmare and utmost fear was that Dr. Masters and his henchmen could show up at any moment in his Department, and in front of Jared's assembled faculty and staff Dr. Masters would rip off Jared's name badge and pin of excellence given to him earlier by Dr. Masters himself and drum him out of the institution under armed guard. In fact, Dr. Masters had done this before, at least the armed guard part, so it was not out of the question. Not withstanding the fact that both he and Marie had been made honorary full colonels in the U. S. Army Special Forces and the fact that they were made the only honorary Navy SEALs in the history of the U. S. Navy, Jared had the recurring dream that Dr. Masters would disgrace him in front of his assembled faculty for disobeying Dr. Masters' orders to shut down the Gulf War Illness research. Jared and Marie had been on a mission, and it was one that had become physically and economically dangerous.

Jared finally made his way into the office building, the newest addition to the Cancer Center. The building had been owned by a large insurance company, and its style was different from the other buildings in the Medical Center. After Jared found his way up the elevator to one of the floors near the top of the building and down a long hall to Dr. Hick's office, he noticed that the environment was a far cry from the fancy setting that Dr. Hicks had on the top floor of the busy Cancer Center hospital. The building looked sterile, almost empty, and Jared could not find a human being in the entire hallway. Jared found the office and knocked on the door. In his crusty voice Dr. Hicks called for Jared to come in.

Dr. Hicks' new office had rather average furnishings, although it was still large by the usual faculty standards. Dr. Hicks had journals and papers piled high on several tables, and he apologized to Jared for the state of his office, but Jared did not mind at all. He was not there on a social visit. He was visiting Dr. Hicks for advice on how he might be able to save his job, at least for enough time to find a new job. Jared did not consider that he had done anything wrong or broken any University rules or regulations, and it was as if he was being treated like a disgraced cavalry officer whose only crime was to challenge the wisdom of his commanding officer.

Dr. Hicks was an interesting contrast to Dr. Masters. Actually, the Board of Regents had unanimously chosen Dr. Hicks to become the president of the institution over Dr. Masters, but Dr. Masters' friends in the government and some Las Vegas interests intervened and the Board was overruled. The Board of Regents knew that Dr. Masters was unfit to serve as president of The D. O. Madison. He had previously been removed from an administrative position for gross misappropriation of funds, so Jared felt it was ironic that Dr. Masters was trying to remove him for exactly the same reason, only in Jared's case it was not justified by the facts, and Dr. Masters and his henchmen knew it. They would have to find something else.

As it turned out Dr. Hicks knew Jared's and Marie's plight quite well, and in fact he had been trying behind the scenes to circumvent some of Dr. Masters attempts to fire Jared because he felt that it was not justified. The University attorneys also did not agree with Dr. Masters, and Dr. Hicks told Jared that he was trying to save Jared's job, but there was only so much that he could do now that he was retired. Jared explained to Dr. Hicks the situation that he had found himself in, and he showed him the letters that Dr. Masters had sent through Legal Services and the responses to Dr. Masters' letters. Jared immediately had the feeling that Dr. Hicks had seen these letters before. After a several minute wait while Dr. Hicks quickly scanned the letters, he finally turned and said in a fatherly tone to Jared, "I don't know if I can help you here, but I will try. Have you been applying for positions outside the Medical Center?" Jared responded, "Only outside of Texas." Dr. Hicks smiled and answered, "That would be prudent!" Jared said, "I don't know if it will make any difference in the long run, because it seems that every potential job offer has been withdrawn or tabled." Dr. Hicks said, "I know the routine quite well. You don't get to be my age without knowing something about people. No one wants any controversy these days. It seems that administrators will listen to anyone when it comes to something negative, but they will only accept positive information from only the most distinguished sources."

In addition to finding another job, Jared had another major concern. "I'm sure that I can find a job if I have enough time, but it seems that Dr.

Masters wants to fire me before he retires this August. Maybe after he goes, the heat will be off somewhat." Dr. Hicks reminded him, "Don't hold your breath on that. And I mean for either of those possibilities. I know Dr. Masters extremely well, and he always gets his way, one way or another. Even after he retires, he will be pulling the strings for some time at this institution. Clement just likes to fire people, and he particularly likes doing it face-to-face. He really enjoys calling them in early in the morning and making them sit down in his office in front of his legal and administrative people and firing them on the spot and then having them taken away by the University Police and escorted from the institution. Sometimes they are allowed with a police escort to remove their personal effects, but usually they aren't even allowed to go back to their offices."

Jared was not feeling too well after hearing what his fate might be at the Madison. It *was* just as bad as his worse nightmare. Somehow the thought of being killed in one of Masters' hits did not strike as much fear in Jared as the humiliation that he might have to endure in front of the faculty and staff of the institution. Jared felt that Dr. Masters knew his fear. Dr. Masters usually tried to extract as much public pain as possible from his victims before cutting off their heads.

Dr. Hicks continued the conversation in a fatherly and friendly way. He told Jared, "I will do what I can for you, but you have to be realistic about your chances here. I suggest that you find another job as soon as possible." Jared said, "I know that your advice is right. I don't consider that I have much of a future here. I'm just trying to buy some time so that I can find a job without it blowing up in my face each and every time." Dr. Hicks confided, "That is going to be a problem that you will have to deal with. Remember, Clement takes great pride and joy in firing people publicly. Don't leave yourself exposed for too long. You might live to regret it." Jared responded, "I'm beginning to regret ever coming down here to the D. O. Madison. Things would have been different if you had been made President." Dr. Hicks smiled and said, "I seem to hear that comment just about every day. You know, there just might be something to it." Jared said, "Believe it, Dr. Hicks! If you had been made President of the institution, I don't think that we would be in the mess that we are in today with all of the State budget cuts, a building program that doesn't seem to end and the bad press." Dr. Hicks said, "Well, I don't know about that, but at least we would not have all of these secret committees and firing of our best staff, and I'm not just referring to your case. But I promise you that I will do what I can. I still know a few people around this place who might be of some help. But it is best that you don't ask about it. Just continue what you are doing with the veterans, and I will do what I can to help on the inside. There are enough veterans on our staff that will be willing to assist you behind the scenes."

Jared had not even considered that the veterans on the Madison staff might come to his aid. Most of these veterans were in the Cancer Center administration in various jobs from the men that worked in maintenance to the people that staffed the various white-collar positions required by a large institution. Jared had no idea that these veterans even knew about his struggles with Dr. Masters and the administration, but they did know because of the local publicity that Marie and Jared had received from reporters like Cassie Mayer for their work with the veterans and prison guards.

Jared thanked Dr. Hicks for his support and left to go back to his own office. During the walk back Jared wondered when he would be kicked out of *his* office, just like Dr. Hicks. The difference was that Dr. Hicks retired with honor. Jared was going to be run out of town or murdered by the maniac Dr. Clement Masters, and no one was going to do anything about it. Some of the staff members were petrified of Dr. Masters and would do whatever he wanted, at least to his face, so that Masters would not have them replaced or killed like Dr. Frank Cannon. Alternatively, some would like to see Jared and Marie eliminated because they were in the way of some administrative aspirations, such as Dr. Geldter or Dr. Domasovitch. The most insidious of all were the outside forces that wanted them dead because Marie could some day inherit a fortune that was currently controlled by her trustees, who were criminals in the defense industry or in Las Vegas organized crime circles, the secret financial backers of Dr. Masters and his massive building program.

CHAPTER 14

The Attacks Continue (1996)

Jared had been invited over a year ago to be the first speaker at a small, prestigious scientific conference to be held in a small town in Germany. The topic of the conference was angiogenesis or the formation of new blood vessels, and its importance to cancer. Jared had been interested in this research area, and he actually held a research grant from the American Cancer Society on the topic. Some of Jared's graduate students had been among the first to isolate and grow endothelial cells, the cells that form the lining of each and every blood vessel in our bodies. Jared's group had learned to grow endothelial cells from various organs in tissue culture, and these organ-specific endothelial cells were being used in various experiments to understand why certain cancer cells metastasize or spread to certain organs and not others. For years now, Jared's laboratory had accumulated data supporting the theories of a British pathologist who proposed that metastatic cells spread non-randomly to certain sites because of their own properties and ability to recognize certain organ sites and because of the unique properties of the organ site. The theory was called the 'seed and soil' theory of cancer metastasis, and one of the important properties of the 'seeds' or cancer cells was how they recognized the endothelial cells in various organs and lodged at specific sites as they traveled in the bloodstream. This had been Jared's topic in his award lecture at the British Society of Medicine in London just as the Gulf War broke out in 1991.

Jared's students had collected data over the years indicating that specific cancer cell 'seeds' could recognize unique organ endothelial cells (from the specific 'soil') and bind to them. Once they bound to the endothelial cells through molecular receptors on their surfaces, they then stimulated the endothelial cells to retract or pull back and open a space so that the cancer cells could exit the bloodstream and invade into the organ. This was how the process of cancer cell invasion and metastasis to distant sites was accomplished after the cancer cells found their way to the organ site through the blood stream. The various steps in the entire process had been documented previously by Jared and his group using light and electron microscopy, and some of the molecules and enzymes involved in cancer cell attachment to endothelial cells and subsequent invasion had been isolated and identified. Jared's group had also found that the organ endothelial cells released certain invasion or motility factors that stimulated the movement of the cancer cells into the organ and specific growth factors that triggered the growth of the cancer cells in their new organ environment.

The topic of organ endothelial cells and the motility and growth factors that they made and released was why Jared was invited to be the first speaker at the conference, because the chairman of the conference thought that Jared's research would be a good introduction to the meeting. Because of his problems with the D. O. Madison administration, Jared decided to put off the request to attend this conference in Germany, because he was afraid that it would be denied, even though all expenses were being paid by the conference and the Cancer Center would not have to pay anything for Jared's attendance. Normally such invitations are considered prestigious, and it was usually considered an honor for a faculty member to represent his or her institution and bring back important new research information. However, in Jared's case, such invitations were considered in a negative not a positive way, because the administration did not want Jared or Marie to receive any invitations that might suggest that they were still first-rate scientists. This was especially true of international invitations.

Jared knew that attending the conference was going to be a problem, and he did not want to have to go to Dr. Domasovitch, his new boss in the department, for the first approval in a long chain of approvals in order to go to Germany. Dr. Domasovitch was at the moment basking in the glory of being the new acting chairman of the Department. He relished attending the various meetings that were usually attended by the department chairmen, such as the promotions committees, research committees and the other administrative meetings, and signing off on practically everything going out of the Department. Jared thought that as one of his first decisions

Dr. Domasovitch would kick Jared out of his office. But Dr. Domasovitch did not immediately kick Jared out of his office and confiscate his laboratories as Jared thought he might do if he was made acting chairman. Jared had to thank Dr. Belcher for allowing him to stay, at least temporarily, in his office and laboratories. If it were up to Dr. Domasovitch, Jared would have been moved to the building down the street where Dr. Hicks was sent after he retired. But the institution had made space commitments to the funding agencies that supported Jared's research. This meant that the institution had committed the use of Jared's laboratories for Jared's research projects not for other uses. It was Dr. Belcher who would restrain Dr. Domasovitch from abusing Jared and humiliating him further.

To obtain permission to attend the conference in Germany, however, required that Jared make an end run around Dr. Domasovitch and use Dr. Belcher's pride in having his faculty represented at important international meetings. Jared had warned Dr. Belcher that it would not look good for the D. O. Madison to deny Jared the chance to present his data because of political reasons, and Dr. Belcher eventually agreed to sign his travel requisition. He only did this after he realized that he couldn't get Dr. Geldtner to substitute for Jared, because Jared made a good case that Isaac didn't really know anything about this particular line of research and it would be an embarrassment to send a substitute who didn't know the subject or wasn't involved in the research. Besides, it wouldn't look good if the administration sent Dr. Geldtner instead of Dr. McNichols, who was the only one in the Medical Center that received an invitation. It would give some credibility to the complaints that Jared was making about his problems with the 'political correctness' of the D. O. Madison Cancer Center.

So Jared was cleared by Dr. Belcher to attend the conference. Jared was looking forward to going to the conference, which would take place at a small town in the Black Forest region of Germany. Dr. Belcher kept quiet about the conference so as to not incite Dr. Masters, who might fly into a rage if he knew that Belcher had actually approved the trip request. By the time the department rats notified Dr. Masters that Jared was traveling overseas to a scientific conference, it would be too late to call him back. That was the plan, anyway. What Jared did not know at the time, and not even Dr. Belcher knew, was that Dr. Masters had been informed through

Dr. Geldter that Jared would be attending the meeting in Germany. Dr. Masters would have a little surprise for Jared.

The conference in the Black Forest of Germany

When Marie found out that Jared was attending a conference in the Black Forest, she wanted to go along, but that was out of the question considering the current circumstances and their tenuous situation with their research projects at the Madison. But Marie did not want Jared to fly to Germany alone, and Jared did not want to return and find his laboratory closed by Dr. Domasovitch. So it was decided that Marie must mind the store while Jared was in Germany. Marie was also afraid that Dr. Masters might try something in Jared's absence, especially since he was furious that Dr. Belcher approved Jared's travel request. They would just have to try to have some sort of normal scientific life, if that were ever possible.

Jared was excited about the program at the conference in Germany, but Marie was still not very happy to see Jared fly overseas when they were having such a difficult time in Austin. At home in Queenswood a few days before Jared was scheduled to leave, Marie was finally told that the trip was on and that Jared would be leaving in a few days. Actually, she knew about the trip when Jared first received the invitation about ten months prior, but she never considered that the administration would ever let him attend the conference. Marie was mad at Jared for not telling her sooner about the trip. She told him, "Why didn't you tell me your trip to Europe was approved?" Jared replied defensively, "I did. You just forgot about it." Marie said, "You can't go now! We are in a war here, and you are just running away!" Jared responded, "I'm not running away! I have an invitation to be the first speaker at a very prestigious meeting in Germany. If I don't go, then they will just send Isaac Geldter instead! And it's my work, not his! How would you like it if the Cancer Center sent Amy Krappner somewhere to give *your* invited lecture?" Marie replied, "I would hate it. You're right. But you can't leave now. We are just about to finish the project with the Special Forces samples. I need you here, not in Germany!" Jared said, "I know, Babe, but I have to do this. I can't let them bury me just because we decided to do some veterans' research project or help some prison guards and their families. If I am ever able to get another academic position, it will be because I have maintained my international reputation. If I sit at home and sulk, we will never be able to recover. They are burying us now, and we have to save our academic reputations." Marie answered, "They already buried mine, two-times over!" Jared replied, "Which is exactly why we can't let them ruin mine as well. We are going to have to find faculty positions somewhere, and to do that I have to somehow maintain my stature." Little did Jared know at the time, but his reputation and stature had already taken a big hit from the intense campaign of Masters' henchmen. Yang, Jared's favorite feline friend of all time, was again jumping onto Jared's briefcase and scratching it as if he knew that Jared would be leaving town again. He had an amazing knack of knowing when Jared was about to leave on a trip, and he always acted up when he thought that Jared was leaving town. As it turned out, Jared should have paid more attention to Yang's concerns about the conference in Germany.

The conference was held in Titisee in the middle of the Black Forest. Jared had to fly to Frankfurt, catch a train to Heidelberg and beyond. Finally, he had to travel by small bus to his final destination. Titisee was located in a remote region of the Black Forest, if one can find any remote region in Europe. Actually, even the legendary Black Forest was quite populated, and there were numerous resorts that catered mostly to Germans, but also some other visitors who found their way there as well. The little resort that Jared was going to was located in a hilly region of the forest by a lake. It was quite quaint, and the entire village was reminiscent of the old German style. The signs were all carved in wood, and the shops and houses looked as if they hadn't changed in the last few hundred years. The small hotel where the conference was to take place was also in the same quaint gingerbread style, as if it also hadn't changed in hundreds of years. But inside the hotel, it was modern and run with German efficiency.

After a long and tiring trip, Jared checked in and was taken to his room. The room was quite small by American standards, but he considered that the room size probably hadn't changed over the years. Only the addition of a bathroom, telephone, TV and other amenities made the room look different from what it was probably like over one hundred years ago. Although Jared was quite tired from the trip, he turned on the TV and thought back over the warning that he received when he stopped at the train station in Heidelberg. The U. S. Army has a major intelligence facility in Heidelberg, and while Jared was waiting for his connecting train he was approached by a young man who looked military and who told Jared in a very Southern accent, "Dr. McNichols. I have been told by your friends in the Special Forces to give you a warning. Be very careful while you are in Germany. Be especially careful about who you eat with." As soon as he appeared, the man was gone. Jared was a bit taken aback, but by now he and Marie have become used to the Special Forces warning them of dangers ahead. They usually sent someone or contacted them by phone when they least expected it. Jared decided to take the warning seriously. After all, who would bother sending someone to give such a stupid warning. But if he did heed the warning, there was likely no place to eat in the small village. The only other alternative to the hotel was to go to the small shops and stores in the little village. There was a small café, but it was only open for a few hours a day when the tourists were around. Jared was tired and hungry. He listened to the German TV for about an hour, and although he understood some Deutsch, it was tedious because of the rapid rate of delivery of the German commentators.

Jared decided to try the village for some food. Unfortunately, it was after the tourists had left for the day, and nothing was open. He was left with the small hotel. Although Jared received a tangible warning that he might be poisoned during his trip, he decided that he was too hungry to resist. He took a chance and ordered something in the small bar by the entrance to the hotel. Jared reasoned if anyone was interested in him, they would not know who he was until he actually paid for the meal. If he ordered a meal from his room, they would know immediately who ordered the food. Thankfully, the food finally came, a German cold plate with fresh bread and local beer, and Jared consumed it without a second thought. That was easy, Jared thought. But it would be more difficult the next day. Fortunately, he was the first speaker of the conference. So Jared retired to his room to go over his slides for his presentation the following morning.

A buffet breakfast was the usual European fare in the morning, and Jared grabbed everything that he could get his hands on from the buffet bar, knowing that it was unlikely that anyone could try anything using a buffet setting. After he had consumed his fill with some friends from Ghent, Belgium, the conference was about to start. Jared had been discussing their Gulf War Illness results with Dr. Marcus DeMerrel of Ghent. He was gratified to learn from Marcus that most European scientists did not believe the American military's explanation that Gulf War Illness was mostly caused by stress. To Europeans it did not make sense that stress was causing the complex signs and symptoms found in Gulf War Illness patients, and they were very supportive of McNichols' research. Their discussion was interrupted by the ring of a small bell carried into the breakfast room by one of the conference chairmen. As the conferees made their way into the conference room, Jared made sure that he found a seat near the front of the room.

Jared was delighted to be the first presenter at the conference. It was like speaking to his friends, since he knew practically everyone who had been invited to the conference, with the exception of some young German scientists. The chairman of the conference was from the German Cancer Center at the University of Heidelberg, and he introduced Jared and the conference. The only person that Jared felt he had to stay away from was Dr. Michael Klinger from Ottawa. Dr. Klinger was a very short, nasty piece of work, and he was a close friend of Isaac Geldter's. He had the appearance of a bulldog, but his demeanor in public was that of a friendly, jovial sort of person who tried to joke his way into a conversation. However, most professionals who knew him well stayed far away from Dr. Klinger, because he was known to be a real back-stabber who would stick it to anyone who was in his way.

When Dr. Klinger was at Western Ontario University, he had quite a reputation among his colleagues for being completely two-faced, a scientist to avoid whenever possible. Fortunately for Jared, Dr. Klinger was located in Ottawa not Austin. But Jared couldn't be worried about every friend of Isaac Geldter's, because they were probably just as untrustworthy as Isaac and would turn on anyone, even Isaac, to get ahead. Jared would learn the hard way not to ignore the little bulldog.

As the first speaker, Jared introduced the conference and presented his data that had been gathered over the last few years in his laboratory that showed that cancer cells that metastasize preferentially to certain organs had unique properties. The example that Jared liked to use for such lectures was a tumor model that Jared's laboratory had developed for studying brain metastasis. Jared considered this topic quite important, because few patients ever survived from brain metastases, and it would take some heavy-duty research on the subject to find new therapeutic approaches for brain metastases.

At the mid-morning break, Dr. Klinger came up to Jared and to Jared's amazement, he was actually quite nice and complimentary. Dr. Klinger, whose own colleagues in Canada reckoned that he had never had an original idea in his entire career, liked to schmooze his colleagues and then steal their ideas, repackage them as 'new' ideas and then present them as his own. Jared was not worried about the concepts from his own talk–they were already in the scientific literature. Jared just filed away the information that Klinger was acting suspicious, but he didn't think much else about it as he entered into an intense discussion with colleagues from The Netherlands who worked on similar topics to the one that Jared discussed in his lecture.

At the lunch break the audience filed into an adjoining room where the lunch was to be served. Unfortunately for Jared, there was little he could do to escape the ubiquitous conference meals. As Jared was involved in an intense discussion with the Dutch group, he did not notice that Dr. Klinger had sat down right next to him and had joined the discussion. Jared should have realized that although this was completely normal behavior for the affable Dr. Klinger, he was not to be trusted. But Jared was distracted and not always able to watch Dr. Klinger, who was sitting to his immediate right, but still mostly in his peripheral vision.

As the lunch proceeded and as each new course was delivered from salad to main meal to dessert, Jared decided to not eat or drink much, and it was lucky for him that he didn't eat much because he almost paid for his lack of attention to what he had eaten with his life. Although he never actually saw Dr. Klinger place anything in or onto his food, he did remember later that Dr. Klinger had been caught a few years back trying to shake something from an unusual container onto Marie's food at a restaurant in Milan. That was also at a conference meal for invited speakers, and Marie would never forget the incident. At the meeting in Milan Jared and Dr. Klinger were also on the same program, and as Jared's wife, Marie was invited to the dinner at a nearby Milanese restaurant. Dr. Klinger had been exceptionally charming that evening to Marie, and as he was being especially complimentary about her science he sat down right next to her and Jared at the dinner table. During the festivities Dr. Klinger had placed something onto Marie's meal while she was distracted, but one of the waiters was immediately behind Dr. Klinger, and he saw exactly what was happening. The waiter quickly removed Marie's dish from her place setting before she could take a bite. Thus as Marie was about to dig into her pasta, it was replaced with another dish.

The McNichols never found out what Dr. Klinger was up to at the restaurant in Milan, but they do remember vividly that the owner of the restaurant had two Dobermans, and they instinctively hated Dr. Klinger and tried to bite him, causing quite a stir. Jared always felt that these two dogs that bared their teeth at Dr. Klinger and lunged at him had excellent instincts, because they didn't trust the little bulldog from Ottawa with the red face.

Later that evening in his hotel room in Titisee Jared became deathly sick. In fact, he was so sick that he could barely call the front desk to tell them that he needed medical attention. He had been vomiting non-stop for three hours, and dehydration was now a problem. Jared could not take in enough fluids to replace the fluid he was losing. As soon as he tried to drink anything, he vomited. He was also running a high temperature, and sweat was pouring out onto the sheets in his bed. The paramedics were called by the hotel desk personnel, and when they arrived and saw Jared lying in a sweat-saturated bed with a very high temperature, they immediately started an i.v. They then decided to transport Jared to a nearby clinic. Jared tried to tell them in Deutsch that he didn't need to go to the clinic, but they wouldn't listen to him. So off he went.

The head of the conference came to Jared's hotel room just as he was being wheeled to the waiting ambulance in a wheel chair. He reassured Jared that he was to be taken to a good clinic where he could be checked out. So Jared was taken for what seemed like a rather long ride to an emergency room for observation. Jared didn't remember much about the night at the emergency room and later the clinic, but he remembered the attempt to check himself out of the clinic the next morning to return to his room in Titisee. That day Jared felt very weak but he was alive, and he was strong enough to argue for thirty minutes with the attending physician and then the clinic administrator to be returned to his hotel room. Eventually the clinic director became irritated with the feisty American who would not cooperate, so they returned him by taxi to the hotel.

For the next two days Jared was recovering from what he suspected was another attempt to poison the McNichols. Although he was still very weak and dehydrated from the non-stop vomiting, Jared insisted on going down to the meeting room to the final afternoon session to face Dr. Klinger, who was a bit taken aback to see Jared still at the meeting after being absent for two days. This was exactly what Jared wanted to see. He wanted to know if the little bulldog with the red face was upset to see him ambulatory. Jared tried to make the most out of the end of the conference, and he again was able to discuss the research of his laboratory with his colleagues from Ghent. Even with the episode of the 'food poisoning' Jared enjoyed meeting with his colleagues and the discussions of recent laboratory results.

At the end of the conference Jared had an interesting conversation with the conference chairman, who was from Heidelberg. Jared told him of the warning at the train station, and the German scientist did not seem surprised to hear that there was another attempt on Jared. He confided to Jared that some European scientists had known about the attempts on the lives of the McNichols, and they were very much appalled by the behavior. Such a thing could have only happened in Europe during the Cold War because of State secrets, but now there was no place for such activities among European academics.

Late that night, after the last day of the meeting, Jared called Marie in the hope that she was home. It was still early in the afternoon in Austin, but Marie happened to be home, and she answered the phone, "Hello!" Jared was relieved to hear Marie's voice, and he said trying to be upbeat, "Hay Babe, how are you doing?" Marie quickly answered, "Jared, where were you? I was worried to death when I couldn't get you on the phone. I almost took the next flight to Germany to find you. Where did you go?" Jared tried to reassure Marie, "Well, I had a little problem . . . . but I'm much better now." Marie did not buy Jared's story—she knew him too well, "Jared, you're lying to me. What happened to you?" Jared decided to come clean to Marie to keep her from flying to Europe on a ticket that they couldn't afford. He said, "Please don't get mad at me, Babe, but do you remember that little ugly spud Dr. Klinger from Ottawa?" Marie was still mad, "You mean the little ugly bastard who tried to poison me in Milan?" Jared replied, "Yep, the very same one—the little bulldog with the red face. Well, I think that he almost got me, but not to worry, I'm glad to report that he didn't succeed." Marie yelled into the phone, "I'm going to fly over tomorrow! Don't go anywhere! Will you wait for me?" Jared replied, "Now Marie, I'm on my way home tomorrow. Why would you want to fly over here–I won't even be around by the time you arrive!" Marie still mad at Jared yelled, "I hate you! Why did you go to that damned conference? You belong here! I need you! You could have been killed!" Jared tried to sound calm, "I know you want to be supportive and nice to me, and I *am* on my way home. Please wait for me. Don't go off and do something stupid." There was silence for some time on the phone, and then Marie said, "O.K. But I'm still mad at you! And you're a stupid idiot for not listening to me!" Jared replied, "I know, I screwed up Babe, but I'm still here, and I will be home before you know it. Are you going to wait for me?" Marie answered, "Damn you, Jared!" He replied, "I'll take that for a yes. You take care, and I will be home before you know it. I love you. Bye Babe!" Marie said, "Damn you, Jared!" Jared had hung up on Marie, and she was still mad but at the same time relieved to know that he would be flying home in the upper cabin and not shipped home in the cargo hold in a box.

The next morning Jared was still weak but he was better than the previous day. On the way out of the hotel at four AM he ran into one of the German organizers of the conference who was upset that Jared had taken sick at the conference. Unlike his colleague from Heidelberg, he didn't understand what happened, and the hotel was even more upset because this had never happened before in little Titisee in die Schwartzwald. Jared was offered a private car and driver from the hotel, which he gladly accepted. This time the car took him all the way to Frankfurt and to the airport. Although it was a long ride to Frankfurt, Jared was actually relieved. He was not looking forward to the train ride back to the airport. The thought of dragging his luggage around the train station and changing trains again in Heidelberg didn't appeal to him at this point. The trip to Frankfurt was uneventful but tiring for Jared. He slept most of the way.

Jared didn't remember much about the flight home, but when he arrived at Houston Intercontinental from Frankfurt, Marie was waiting for him outside U. S. Customs. As Jared exited customs and looked around to get his bearings and find his plane to Austin, Marie ran up to him yelling, "Jared, Jared! Look at you! I am so mad at you!" Jared smiled and hugged Marie, "It's nice to see you too, Marie."

They embraced and Marie started crying. She was elated and mad at the same time. She asked Jared, "What happened to you? I was so scared when they couldn't find you at the hotel and said that you went to a clinic. I couldn't get in touch with you. I thought you were dead!" Jared brushed her hair back and said, "I missed you, Marie." She asked, "Dammit Jared, what happened?" Jared said, "I just had a little problem. Do you remember that ugly little spud Dr. Klinger from Ottawa?" Marie replied, "You said something about him on the phone. What did he do to you?" Jared said, "You mean what did he try to do to me? Well, I really can't prove anything, but he is a close friend of Isaac Geldter." Marie said, "Don't get cute with me, Jared, I'm still mad at you!" Jared answered, "Well, I see you were mad enough to meet me in Houston. Now you're going to have to drive me home." Marie was mad but not that mad, "But you know I don't like to drive." Jared responded, "Does this mean that you're no longer mad at me?" Marie pouted and turned away. She was wiping tears from her face. Jared said, "I take it that you actually missed me?" Marie said to him, "Jared, aren't you ever serious?" Jared replied, "Only when I have to be. Come on, I'll drive you home. Where did you park?" Marie said, "I don't know, someplace in the parking structure at Terminal C." Jared said, "You've got to be kidding. You parked in Terminal C?"

The international flights arrive in Houston at the International Terminal not Terminal C. Jared and Marie would have to make their way back to another terminal and find Marie's car. After a half-hour search, they found Marie's car, and Jared and Marie started the long drive back to Austin from Houston Intercontinental Airport. Although Jared was tired from the flight, he was also happy to be with Marie and safely on his way home to Queenswood and his feline friends who were waiting for him as usual in the window.

The laboratory freezers are Target Number One.

While Jared was in Germany, he learned that some of the equipment in his laboratory had been the target of sabotage. In particular, the freezer where they stored the Gulf War veterans' blood samples was being unplugged at night when no one was around the laboratory. Jared had ordered the locks changed on his laboratory to prevent someone from entering the lab while no one was there at night, but it apparently did not help. Dr. Domasovitch had a master key anyway. Fortunately, this particular freezer was well insulated, and it took almost a full day for it to come to temperatures above freezing. Since Bob Sonan came in very early in the morning, his job was now to first check out all the equipment before anything else. Not only had the freezer been unplugged, but the alarm was also defeated, which could be done by turning off the alarm switch. Thus it was not an accident. Since this sort of thing continued to happen, Jared ordered the freezers hard-wired to their electrical outlets with flexible exterior electrical cable, and new locks were installed on the freezer door. This stopped the problem completely.

Other equipment in the lab was also sabotaged. Jared had the other equipment fixed, but he was getting tired of the silly pranks designed he reasoned to disrupt their research and send them a message. Since he was getting tired of the dirty tricks being played on them, he complained to the University Police Department that persons unknown were entering his lab and trying to destroy his equipment. Unfortunately, this was eventually reported to the Cancer Center administration, and ultimately to the President's Office. Dr. Masters' response was to accuse Jared of inappropriate use of State equipment. It took almost a month of letting Drs. Hicks, Belcher and other staff members talk some sense into Dr. Masters, but that was the last time that Jared ever complained to the police. He should have known that since they worked for Dr. Masters, they would do what they were told. As far as Jared knew, the police themselves were behind the problems, but that seemed extremely unlikely. Most of the University policemen were veterans, and they secretly supported Jared and Marie, in spite of Dr. Masters' opinions. They were probably also suspicious of Dr. Masters ever since the hit on Dr. Cannon. After all, Dr. Masters was probably still a suspect in that unsolved capital crime. Indeed, Dr. Masters was no stranger to the police. He was a prime suspect in the murder case of a colleague who was poisoned at his previous institution, but no one in Austin seemed to know about this incident.

At the same time as the freezer problems, the Texas Department of Corrections had begun an investigation of Jared's and Marie's activities with the prisons and the prison employees. They were very sensitive to the bad press that they had been receiving over the Wallsville 'Mystery Illness,' and some of the prison system administrators wanted to blame Jared and Marie for the problem. Notwithstanding that the prison administrators were the likely perpetrators who created the problem in the first place, the TDC sent an investigator to interview Jared about the allegations that some sort of 'illegal' clinical testing program was going on in the State prison facilities.

Jared had previously discussed on the phone what his laboratory had found with TDC investigators. He tried to reassure them that no one in his laboratory had any contact with TDC prisoners, nor had anyone from his laboratory ever been inside a TDC facility. He told them that he had no knowledge of what happened or what is happening in the prison units in Wallsville or other Texas cities. What he did tell the TDC was that they obviously had a problem, because the employees themselves came to his laboratory to ask for assistance with their health problems. It was the prison employees that told the McNichols stories about the testing programs in the prison system. Jared decided not to report this to the investigators.

Jared asked one of the investigators if he was ever a prison guard. His answer was that all of the current investigators started their careers as prison guards or police officers. Jared then told them what if they were still prison guards and were sick and no one would help them because the TDC wanted to keep something secret. Who would they turn to for assistance? Would they later crucify the only people who offered to help them?

The tactic apparently worked. Jared and Marie later guessed that the prison administrators would have killed the 'messengers' to keep the entire mess in the Texas prisons quiet, and they had to convince the TDC that they were not the messengers. They had never been to a TDC facility, in contrast to Dr. Lon and his colleagues who had spent considerable time in prison facilities with their experiments on prisoners.

A few weeks later Jared received a telephone call from one of the detectives who worked for the prison system. He told Jared that unless Jared agreed to a taped interview with TDC investigators, they would push to have Jared arrested. Jared agreed to be interviewed on tape, but he insisted that his attorney be present for the interview. The only problem was that Jared didn't have an attorney that could handle anything remotely related to criminal law. Although Jared was sure that he and Marie had not violated any criminal statutes, the last thing that he needed was to have the investigators tell the D. O. Madison administration that they are going to arrest Jared to force an interview with him. That would be all the ammunition that Dr. Masters needed to fire Jared on the spot, so this was something that Jared couldn't easily dismiss. Even if Jared was interviewed and nothing came of the interview, that might be sufficient to allow Dr. Masters to claim that Jared was a suspect in a criminal investigation and as such was *persona non grata* at the Cancer Center. Of course, Dr. Masters himself was a suspect in a murder investigation, the unsolved murder of Dr. Frank Cannon, but that did not count at the Madison where the rules were made by those in power.

Jared decided to delay the interview, claiming that he had a right to proper legal representation at the interview. The ploy bought some time, and the interview was put off until Jared could engage legal counsel. In the mean time, Jared and Marie used their influence with the veterans and especially with the Special Forces and SEALs to find out who was pushing for the interview and why? This tactic worked, and the interview was not scheduled until Jared had secured adequate counsel. Jared guessed that the only reason for this was that the detectives that worked for the TDC were probably veterans themselves, and they were probably former prison guards too. They probably didn't like some administrator covering his ass by going after the McNichols, claiming that the prison problem was all their fault.

Jared never heard from the TDC again. Perhaps they decided that it might be better to let the whole episode just fade into the sunset rather than drag it out into the public domain. Besides, an interview could go two ways. Jared wanted to ask the investigators about some incidents in the prisons that the prison guards had related to the McNichols. Jared also wanted to know about their private crematorium and the relationship between the prison system and the U. S. Army. Of course, they wouldn't be inclined to answer any of Jared's questions, but it would let them know that they were opening up Pandora's Box with their interview.

It was a relief to know that there might be some justice in the world. Actually, the TDC did not stop their harassment as Jared and Marie thought, but the maneuvering continued on behind the scenes and never made its way to the surface, and the McNichols would never have to face a formal investigation. The McNichols found out later that the TDC actually claimed at one point to the Wallsville newspaper that Jared was a former prison doctor who worked part-time in the Wallsville Unit. Thus he should have direct knowledge of the prison testing programs and was possibly involved in the programs. Jared thought that this was completely ludicrous. Marie would write a letter to the local Wallsville newspaper to debunk the misinformation spread by the TDC. Perhaps it was a set-up or at least a justification to come after the McNichols by claiming that they broke confidentiality by speaking about the medical programs and patient records. The TDC was obviously incompetent because Jared had never even been in a TDC facility, let alone ever was a prison doctor!

The driving 'accidents' and scary people became a problem

One of the ongoing problems that Marie and Jared had with commuting to the D. O. Madison Cancer Center from Queenswood was that at least once a week or so since the beginning of the year someone would try to get one or both of them into a car crash. At first this was directed at Marie who drove a small car. They usually used large pick-up trucks or heavy SUV type vehicles with blacked out windows. They would hit Marie's car from behind or try to force her into a ditch that usually lined the rural roads in Texas. On the major expressways or freeways this was usually not a problem, possibly because there were other vehicles around, but on secondary roads this was often a problem. It was if they knew exactly when and where to 'hit' Marie or Jared to cause maximum damage.

The problems on the highways became worse just as Jared was facing the most difficult time of his career at the Madison. Marie had been driven off the road on several occasions, and at one point she was chased by a large truck into the park just outside the Medical Center. She escaped by going off the road, and her front wheel drive vehicle was able to move on the park grass while the heavier vehicle behind her bogged down in the soft soil. She was lucky. The large truck probably didn't have four-wheel drive, or it would have kept on coming. Jared also had his problems, but it was not so easy to drive Jared off the road in his large Dodge truck with 4-wheel drive and five-speed overdrive transmission with the largest engine available. He could just leave the road at any time and leave them in the dust, which is exactly what he did on a few occasions. That, however, did not stop someone who really wanted to shoot Jared. At one point Jared had to have his windshield replaced, because a bullet hole in the front window on the driver's side caused so much noise at high speed that it was bothering him. This went on for about six months when finally whoever was involved gave up. Marie and Jared always thought that it was Dr. Masters who recruited people to stage these accidents. They did not have the flavor of professional hits, and it would be just like Dr. Masters to try to convince Marie and Jared to throw in the towel and leave the Cancer Center.

Early in 1996 when the harassment of Jared and Marie was at its maximum, there was one incident that stood out. Marie and Jared were working late on a Thursday evening when they noticed some strange men wearing sunglasses walking by in the hall outside their laboratory. Marie was the first to notice that they were walking by the lab and looking in to see who was present. It wasn't just a one-time event; they kept on doing it. In the evening the night cleaning crew was usually working the halls, offices and labs, so the McNichols didn't think much about the strange men until the janitors went on their break. Jared exited his laboratory and noticed that the cleaning crew had left their floor buffers in the hall, but the strange men were still down the hall waiting and now looking at him. He immediately went into his office, called Marie on the phone and told her to drop everything that she was doing and come immediately to the office. A few minutes later Marie entered the office, and Jared told her, "Did you notice those guys down the hall? What's that all about?" Marie answered, "I don't know. I didn't recognize any of them, and they are acting very nervous. Jared, I don't like this!" Jared replied, "I don't like it either. I think that we better get the hell out of here pronto!"

Jared went to the outer office door and looked down the hall. At that point he decided that it was time to be prudent about the situation and live another day. He grabbed Marie and they left his office, but as they turned the corner to head down the main hallway that they needed to take in order to leave the building, they noticed that instead of two men that they didn't know, there were now three men. They didn't recognize any of the men. They didn't belong in the Research Building, and they turned when they saw the McNichols. Without speaking to one another, they were now coming down the long hall directly towards the McNichols. Jared grabbed Marie's hand and told her, "Not that way!" He turned around and practically dragged Marie back towards his office. Jared knew that just before his office was a stairway that led down to the lower floors. As they reached the end of the hall, it made an abrupt turn to the right but then it ended in a conference room. Jared knew the floor plan well, because he helped design the layout for the building. As it turned out, Jared was the only faculty member at the Cancer Center that had a degree in engineering, his first degree as an undergraduate student. This proved useful when new research or other buildings were planned, and Jared had become a kind of unofficial advisor to Dr. Belcher on building planning and construction. It would prove useful tonight because Jared knew the entire floor plan of the research building.

After pulling Marie down the stairwell to the floor below, Jared and Marie ran down to the next available stairwell. Jared then checked it to make sure that the men had not split up and headed for all of the stairwells in the building and pulled Marie down another flight of stairs. They exited quickly with Marie complaining, "Jared, what are you doing? I can't keep up with you. You're going too fast for me." Jared told her not so politely, "Marie, you're going to have to keep up. I don't trust those guys, and I don't think that we should be in this building alone at night." Marie said, "Since you put it that way, let's go!" Marie was now running down the hall with or even ahead of Jared. They took a turn to the left and down another hall to another elevator. Jared asked Marie, "Do you think we can trust this elevator?" Marie said, "What choice do we have?" Jared replied, "We could run down the six flights or take the elevator. I'll tell you what, if the elevator comes from a higher floor, we take the next stairway. If it comes from a lower floor, we take it." Marie said hesitantly, "O.K."

Marie and Jared were waiting for the elevator for what seemed like minutes, but in fact, it was just a few seconds. Jared looked up at the floor indicator above the elevator doorframe, "It looks like it's coming from below. Let's take it!" The elevator came from a lower floor, but Marie and Jared were nervous when the door opened. If one of the men was on the elevator, they were trapped. Fortunately, there was no one on the elevator. It was late, and there shouldn't be anyone on the elevator, but the hospital never slept, so it wasn't out of the question. Marie and Jared rushed into the elevator, and Jared punched the button for the first floor. The ground floor would not get them out of the building, because it was in the animal facility and required a special card to gain entry. So they had to get off on the first floor and find their way out by the library or through the library.

As the elevator stopped on the first floor, Marie and Jared held their breath as the elevator stopped. The door opened slowly, and it was very quiet. No strange men. Jared slowly stuck his head out of the elevator and looked around while he pushed the 'door open' button. Nothing. He reached back and grabbed for Marie's hand and pulled her out of the elevator. They then made a run for the library as the elevator started going up again. Jared stopped, turned and noticed that the elevator indicator indicated that the elevator was going to a higher floor, near the top of the building. Jared did not wait to find out which floor the elevator was going to. With Marie in tow, Jared ran to the library. He checked the door. It was usually locked at this time of night, but it wasn't locked. The cleaning crews were probably inside and they had left the door open. Jared and Marie decided to use the library as the exit point from the building.

They could exit the building from back of the library where the men wouldn't expect to see them, and then make their way across the street and into the parking structure where Jared had parked his truck. They made their way to the back of the library. No one seemed to be in the library, but it wasn't locked, so they couldn't be sure. The McNichols didn't wait around to determine why the library door was not locked. There must have been someone in the library after hours. Jared and Marie made their way through the library to the back stairwell. Jared tried the door. No one was on the other side. He leaned into the stairwell to see if he could spot anyone above or below the first floor. Nothing. He said to Marie, "Only one floor, let's go!" The McNichols ran down the stairs, and exited the building on its north side. There was no one around when they ran out of the building.

The cold night air was refreshing as they made their way across the street. They then had to back track to get to the parking structure, and Jared decided that they would take the open stairs instead of the elevator. They would be able to see if anyone entered the stairwell from below while they were climbing the stairs. His truck was parked on the forth floor, so it was not much of a hike up to the forth level. Fortunately, his truck was parked near the stairs, so it took only a few seconds to reach the safety of the truck. He quickly started the big Dodge engine, and they roared down the parking structure at speeds that Jared would never attempt during the day.

Outside of the structure, Jared turned back into the Medical Center instead of out of the Center and into the park to the West of the Medical Center. As they drove off Marie noticed one of the men in dark glasses with what appeared to be a gun in his hand. It was too late–the McNichols were moving too quickly. Marie asked Jared what was he thinking, but Jared was just trying to be unpredictable. He decided that they needed to have some dinner, so he drove to the other side of the Medical Center and exited there and onto a busy boulevard where they could find somewhere to eat. Jared finally explained to Marie that they needed to be less predictable in everything that they did from now on. They never found out whether the strange men in the Research Building were there to kill them or protect them.

Eventually Jared found an open Ihop restaurant where they could get a bite to eat. The place was full of medical and nursing students studying for their exams and having a late meal with their fellow students. Eventually Jared and Marie made their way home, the back way, after going on the freeway part of the way to Queenswood. Their cats, Yin and Yang, were waiting up for them in the window as usual, and Yang in particular was making himself known as they entered the house from the garage. Yin and Yang had been at the window all evening waiting for Jared and Marie. Now that they were all safe, Yang demanded to go out outside on cat patrol, but Marie would have nothing of it. She did not want to lose one of the family members to some strange people who had been shadowing the McNichols.

The legal and criminal assaults continue

Dr. Masters was close to retirement, but not close enough for Jared and Marie to feel comfortable. One day Jared was again contacted by the Department of Legal Services. This time they wanted to interview Jared to make sure that no University rules or regulations had been violated. Jared was already the most scrutinized member of the Cancer Center's faculty. He had several financial audits of his department (at least when he was still the chairman), examination of his personnel file (unfortunately for Dr. Masters, Jared's file was exemplary), examination of his grants and contracts (to see if anything was amiss or if any funds were not used appropriately) and even his personal life (nothing there either). The Legal Services Department was apparently working with the Texas Department of Corrections, because the wording in the letter was suspiciously oriented toward the work with the prison guards and employees.

Jared began to tire of the many attempts to find something that could be used against him so that he could be brought up to Dr. Masters' office and fired by Dr. Masters in front of his staff before he retired. Jared began to feel that Dr. Belcher was right, and Dr. Masters would not give up until he had brought Jared in under armed guard and fired him in front of his assembled staff. To Jared and Marie Dr. Masters seemed obsessed with expelling them from the D. O. Madison and shutting down their research on chronic infections. Jared felt strongly that he must have competent legal advice, so he and Marie started looking for an attorney with a track record against the Cancer Center. Fortunately, they didn't have to look far. It seemed that the University, and the Cancer Center in particular, was being sued by a number of people: ex-patients, former employees, former faculty members and even organizations that were unknown to Jared and Marie.

After scanning the county court records on line, the McNichols noticed that one attorney stood out. His name was Melvin Neeman. This was the type of attorney that probably sent the anti-Semite Clement Masters up the wall. As it turned out, Mr. Neeman was a conservative Jewish attorney with an excellent record against Masters and the University, and so Jared and Marie considered that he must be the one. The only problem was that he was very, very expensive. The first meeting with Mr. Neeman was quite reasonable, as expected, and Mr. Neeman just listened to their story. But at the second meeting, he dropped the bomb. Jared and Marie had to turn over the deed to their home and any other assets to Mr. Neeman if the legal assault translated into major litigation with the University. Jared was not about to give up his home that he built in 1980 when he moved to Austin just for the privilege of suing Dr. Masters and the University. So Jared and Marie decided to delay the aggressive Mr. Neeman until they could determine whether a lawsuit was even necessary. Besides, Jared and Marie did not want to stay in Austin fighting the

University for the next ten years in the courts, especially in front of judges that were mostly trained as attorneys in the University's law school. Jared just wanted to leave The D. O. Madison with dignity and not be thrown out for doing nothing more than helping the veterans and prison guards with their health problems, something that the Cancer Center should have been doing anyway.

It was during one of these meetings with the attorney that Jared received a page from the security company that monitored the McNichols' home in Queenswood. He immediately asked to use the phone to call the security company. It seemed that there had been a break-in at the McNichols' residence, and the meeting had to be aborted.

When Marie and Jared finally arrived home, they found one of the security company's trucks in their driveway but no one was in sight. After looking around the outside of the house, which was in a wooded area on about an acre of land, they found one of the security men looking at a ladder hidden in the brush near the house. After identifying themselves and showing the security man their drivers' licenses, they were asked about the ladder but Jared didn't identify it as one belonging to the McNichols. There was no evidence of a break-in around the perimeter of the house, so the security men eventually left after filling out a report. However, Jared was not convinced that the security people had covered everything, so he retrieved his own ladder from the garage and brought it around to the back of the house. In spite of Marie's protests, Jared decided to take a look on the roof.

Once Jared was on the roof, it took him about two seconds to find something interesting. There was a large hole that had been hacked into the McNichols' roof directly above the master bathroom. In this area there was a false ceiling and attic area that eventually led to a drop-down ladder in the hallway that was used to access the attic. There was even a black plastic tarp covering the hole to keep the rain out, and possibly to allow multiple entries. Without touching anything, Jared yelled to Marie to call the security people and the police. This was why the security system was triggered. The perps didn't know that Jared had installed motion detectors in all of the halls of their home as a back-up system. Jared hypothesized that when they tried to use the drop ladder in the hall, the motion sensor went off.

This would explain why none of the exterior windows or doors showed any evidence of tampering. The McNichols were fortunate. Nothing of any value was missing from their home, nor could they find any documents missing. Was this just a break-in by local burglars? Jared and Marie immediately dismissed this, because why would the perps place black plastic tarp over the hole they meticulously cut through the roof? It looked like someone wanted access into the McNichols' home, and they wanted access more than once. Was this like the disappearing mail and the suspicious people that the McNichols had noticed around their home? Who needed the possible documents that the McNichols kept at home to stage such an elaborate break-in?

Both Jared and Marie came to the same conclusion at almost the same time, Clement Masters. He probably heard that the McNichols were meeting with his old nemesis Melvin Neeman, and he just couldn't stand not knowing what was going on and whether the McNichols were going to sue him and the Cancer Center. Alternatively, since the McNichols were not leaving their data in the laboratory, someone might have been interested in looking at the McNichols' lab books and results from the tests they were conducting on the veterans and prison guards and their family members. Eventually Jared found unusual wiring in the attic that was attached to the telephone system and led to a small black box placed under the insulation in the attic. This was probably an electronic bugging system, and Jared reported it to the local police who didn't seem a bit concerned about the break-in or electronic monitoring equipment. The police also ignored a report by one of the McNihcols' neighbors who noticed that there were strange men on the McNichols' roof. All of this was very discouraging and disturbing to the McNichols.

Jared knows the new President of the D. O. Madison

During the spring before Dr. Masters was retiring a replacement was found for the President of the D. O. Madison Cancer Center. As it turned out, the next president of The D. O. Madison Cancer Center was an old friend of Jared's, or so he thought. When Jared was a beginning faculty member in San Diego at the Salk Institute, he met and even interacted with an oncologist, Dr. Kevin Morningstone, who was later to become one of the leading oncologists at the prestigious Mayo Clinic. Dr. Morningstone was a prime candidate to replace the retiring Clement Masters, and Jared had even met with him on one of his recruiting trips to Austin. The Administration and faculty were in unanimous agreement that Dr. Morningstone not Dr. Bane would be the best candidate to replace the soon-to-be retiring Dr. Clement Masters.

Dr. Bane had so alienated the faculty at The D. O. Madison Cancer Center that the faculty committee that had been organized to screen candidates for Dr. Masters' position eliminated Dr. Bane in the first cut of possible candidates. There were two surgeons on the committee, and this probably sunk Dr. Bane's candidacy. Although Dr. Bane was a well-known surgeon in academic circles, he was unanimously disliked by the other surgeons at the Cancer Center, and they were not about to recommend him as the next president. Dr. Morningstone had made several trips to Austin during the Spring to meet with the faculty committee that made recommendations on senior staff appointments. In fact, during one of these trips to Austin, Dr. Morningstone and Jared had lunch together at the same Italian restaurant that Marie, Jared and the Maitlands often ate when the Maitlands visited the Medical Center. The lunch was friendly, and Jared and Dr. Morningstone shared memories of their academic days in San Diego.

Jared felt good about contacting Dr. Morningstone concerning his own situation with Clement Masters and the Cancer Center. Because of a past relationship, Jared thought that he could negotiate with Dr. Morningstone. He turned out to be dead wrong. Dr. Morningstone had changed dramatically. He refused to even discuss Jared's situation with him or even take his telephone calls. This was a major set-back, because Jared felt that he had some sort of professional relationship with Dr. Morningstone, and they had a delightful lunch together just a few weeks prior to Jared making the phone calls. Someone must have gotten to Dr. Morningstone about the problems with the McNichols, and that someone was likely Clement Masters. So Jared could not expect much help from his so-called friend from long ago. He now expected absolutely no help from Dr. Morningstone. Marie often badgered Jared for expecting too much from his scientist and physician friends, who Marie felt were never sincere and completely driven by their own egotistical career goals.

Marie always felt strongly that academics like Dr. Morningstone and most of the faculty at the Madison would sell their mothers for the right price, and they would turn on Jared like hungry jackals. Although Jared had tried on many occasions to change Marie's mind on this subject, recent history unfortunately proved her correct. Jared defended his faculty as caught between a rock and a hard place where he was concerned, but he could not defend the actions of rats like Dr. Domasovitch, who seemed to go out of his way to undermine Jared at every opportunity. Between Drs. Domasovitch, Nosan and Costerman everything that Jared and Marie did in the Department was monitored for the administration: computer, mail, faxes, telephone calls and visitors to the Department, and especially their research was all carefully monitored and reports sent up to Dr. Masters office.

These department faculty members would also be used to gather any possible useful information that they found to present to the Faculty Senate and the secret committee that had been established to monitor Jared McNichols. The Faculty Senate at the D. O. Madison was originally constituted to be a buffer between the faculty and the Administration. Jared had no idea that the Faculty Senate could actually be used as a tool of the Administration to go after him. But the head of the Faculty Senate was none other than Dr. Reichsmann, who just happened to be the Clinical Director of the classified offsite patient testing programs in the five nursing homes outside of San Antonio that were used to test some of the lethal Russian Doll weapons developed by Virgil Rook at Belford and Isaac Geldter and his colleagues in the 'secret' M. K. Black Building facility. Using its Cancer Center Foundation as a cover The D. O. Madison purchased the five rest homes outside of San Antonio for the sole purpose of testing the lethal Russian Doll mixtures. In other words, the illegal testing of bioweapons on helpless civilians was very much a part of the D. O. Madison's classified collaboration with rogue scientists working at other facilities like Fort Detrick. The rest homes were also near U. S. Army facilities that were conducting the autopsies on the prisoners who died from other bioweapons experiments in TDC facilities. The subjects that died in the rest home experiments were probably also sent to the same Army base for autopsies.

To say that Dr. Reichsmann was an enemy of Jared and Marie would be a mild statement. In fact, after a chance encounter in an elevator with Jared and some of his graduate students Jared made the mistake of making a joke about Dr. Reichsmann's work in the nursing homes. Dr. Reichsmann himself then initiated disciplinary action against Jared through the Faculty Senate. Jared had no idea what the Faculty Senate was doing against him, because it was all done in secret. However, a member of the governing committee of the Senate approached Jared in the Faculty Dining Room to warn him that Dr. Reichsmann was trying to trump up some kind of charges against Jared and his research. Among other allegations, Dr. Reichsmann attempted to present to the Faculty Senate Executive Committee that Jared had been illegally advising patients about medications and had been conducting experiments in his laboratory without proper administrative and safety approvals. These were exactly the same bogus allegations that Dr. Masters had advanced in formal letters to Jared, and Jared just assumed that the administration had spoon fed the same allegations to the Faculty Senate to build up their case for firing Jared.

Dr. Bane was the main contact point for Dr. Reichsmann in the D. O. Madison Administration, and it was Dr. Bane who was Masters' right hand man when it came to faculty personnel problems. So Jared assumed that Dr. Bane was the person who urged Dr. Reichsmann to move against Jared. Dr. Bane probably recycled the same letter that Dr. Masters had sent through the Department of Legal Services to Jared, ignoring that fact that all of the items in the letter had been answered and debunked by Jared. This was a way to bypass the Department of Legal Services and have the secret Faculty Senate committee investigate the allegations. They might come to a completely different conclusion than the University's attorneys, and if they did, Dr. Masters could use that conclusion to become self-righteous and remove Jared from his position at the recommendation of the Faculty Senate, an elected body of the faculty.

The two players that Jared knew were serving on the secret Senate Faculty committee on the subject of Jared McNichols were, of course, its Chairman, Dr. Reichsmann, and the representative from Jared's department, Dr. Costerman. Jared had no idea who the rest of the committee members were because the membership was confidential. To find out what was transpiring in the committee Jared called Dr. Costerman to his office, but Dr. Costerman refused to discuss anything about the secret committee or the Faculty Senate Executive Committee. He coldly told Jared that the

Faculty Senate disciplinary hearings were confidential and he could not tell Jared anything about them or even that he was the subject of disciplinary proceedings. Interestingly, Faculty Senate deliberations were not confidential, according to the bylaws of the Senate, and if he wanted Jared could show up at the meetings to defend himself against the unproven allegations. However, the Executive Committee meetings of the Faculty Senate were now confidential, at least in Jared's case, and they prevented Jared from attending any of the meetings to defend himself against the untrue allegations passed to the Executive Committee from the secret committee set up just to screw him. It was impossible under these conditions for Jared to receive due process and a fair hearing on the bogus allegations, so he directed the Faculty Senate to send all communications directly to his attorney. Jared now had nothing but disdain for the so-called Faculty Senate, whose members were apparently just lackeys for Dr. Masters, Dr. Bane and the classified programs of The Madison. Dr. Masters often told his subordinates *"we must protect the good name of the Cancer Center."* Jared and Marie often reminded each other that the "good name of the Cancer Center" wouldn't be so 'good' if the general public actually knew what was really going on.

The University Police show up in Jared's office

One of the tools that Dr. Masters had available was his own police department. The chief of the University Police, Chief Costa, didn't technically answer directly to Dr. Masters, but you wouldn't know it from the way Dr. Masters used the police to do his dirty work. As Dr. Hicks once related to Jared, Clement Masters likes to use *his* Police Department to bring employees to his office so that he can fire them publicly and have the policemen immediately escort them out of the D. O. Madison. Jared joked to Marie that Clement probably told the policemen to bring their 'night sticks' just to show everyone who's the boss.

One morning a detective and a uniformed officer showed up in Jared's office without an appointment. Jared let them into his office fearing that this was his last hour at the D. O. Madison Cancer Center. But instead of bringing Jared up to Dr. Masters' office for his public firing, they were there to discuss other incidents that had taken place in front of the main entrance to the hospital that dominated the D. O. Madison Cancer Center. As it turned out, there had been demonstrations in front of the Cancer Center by Gulf War veterans, complete with veterans in their uniforms carrying signs and passing out leaflets stating that the Cancer Center was unfairly trying to prevent the Drs. McNichols from continuing their research on Gulf War Illnesses. Sometimes there were even TV cameras. Although Jared had heard about the possibility of demonstrations and had even talked to one of the organizers, he never thought that they would actually go through with it. Approximately one week before in the morning when he was walking from the parking lot to the hospital he actually saw the demonstrators and even a TV news crew, and there was Dr. Domasovitch taking notes from the side of the assembly. The University Police were there as well to maintain order, but it didn't appear to be a violent demonstration. Jared thought that it was curious that Domasovitch was there to take notes, possibly for Dr. Masters or Dr. Belcher, and he wondered at the time if this would also be used against him. Jared decided not to wander into the crowd, and it was a good thing that he decided not to go near the disturbance.

The detective and the policeman were now in his office asking some very direct questions about Jared's possible involvement in organizing the demonstration. Jared could rightfully claim that he knew nothing about the demonstration, and since no one had evidence that he was ever involved in the demonstration, there was nothing that the police could do about it. It was Dr. Hicks that eventually told Jared that Dr. Masters was furious about the demonstrations by the veterans in front of the Cancer Center. But since Jared was not involved in the demonstrations, Dr. Masters could not fire Jared for the incidents, even though he tried. Jared expected the detective and the policemen to be antagonistic, but they were just the opposite. Since Dr. Masters used the University Police as his personal Gestapo, Jared did not really expect them to be supportive of him and Marie, but as it turned out both the detective and the policeman were veterans, and they both thought that what Jared and Marie were doing for the veterans was wonderful. Although they could not officially support what Jared and Marie were doing, they did offer their assistance in finding out who was sabotaging Jared's laboratory. Jared ended the meeting by giving the police copies of his publications and reports on the infections in Gulf War veterans. They were actually well received by the Police Department, because Jared assumed that there were many veterans on the force, and as it turned out that they didn't like Clement Masters any more than Jared and Marie.

One of the tactics that Dr. Masters used against his faculty to keep them in line was to order a complete review of their activities. This was usually done under the guise of obtaining budgetary information for the State so that the Administration could decide whether to expand, contract or even eliminate certain units at the Cancer Center. It was completely within Dr. Masters' prerogative to order such reviews, and normally they were used judiciously but not in Jared's case. The review could be financial, scientific, medical, administrative, or it could cover resources, faculty and even future plans. When requested, the preparation of materials needed for the reviews usually fell on the shoulders of the relevant department chairman, but Jared had recently been removed from his chairmanship by Dr. Masters and replaced by Dr. Domasovitch. Thus Dr. Domasovitch would have to be the point person for any administrative review ordered by Dr. Masters.

All of the review areas were fair game when it came to Jared McNichols. The task of the actual reviews and who would do the reviewing for the science staff usually fell on Dr. Belcher, since he was the Vice President for Research. So Dr. Belcher delegated this task to subordinates in his office who began by contacting Jared for information on all sorts of things. Actually it required Jared to fill up an entire table with stacks of papers. In parallel with the Office of Research's review Dr. Bane also initiated a similar review by the Faculty Senate through Dr. Reichsmann using some of faculty in Jared's own department, presumably Dr. Costerman, to be part of the review process. Dr. Bane had even gone so far as to claim that it was the faculty in Jared's department who initiated the Faculty Senate review because of their complaints about Jared and Marie. With the exception of Drs. Nosan, Domasovitch, Costerman and perhaps one other faculty member, Jared didn't think that any of the remaining dozen faculty members had complained. At least they indicated to Jared that they were going to support him, not help the administration bury him. Unfortunately all it would take was for Dr. Domasovitch or Dr. Costerman to complain to Dr. Reichsmann that Jared had diverted valuable Department resources to his own use without consulting the Department faculty during his chairmanship, and it would be all over for Jared at the D. O. Madison.

Jared had to take valuable time away from his own research to assist in the reviews. He considered it curious that he had to be so intimately involved in the process, since he was no longer the chairman of the Department, and it was the chairman who usually defended the Department turf. Unfortunately, Jared could expect no such assistance from Dr. Domasovitch, and he began to despise his new acting chairman who always smiled at Jared as if he knew that Jared would be the next victim of Dr. Masters. Dr. Domasovitch was acting like a jerk towards Jared, and Jared considered it ridiculous since he always treated Dr. Domasovitch with respect when Jared was the chairman and Dr. Domasovitch was his deputy. On the other hand, Marie never liked him. She always considered him a complete hack who was incapable of doing any good science but was such a suck-up artist that he could always find something to do for the Administration to gain favor. At least Jared still had his office, thanks to Dr. Belcher.

During the review process, which was expanded to include the entire Department probably to head off any notion that Jared was being singled out for his research interests, rumors were going around that the department was being split-up, with one-half of the faculty and resources going to Dr. Geldter and the rest going to Dr. Krappner and their respective departments. No one ever seriously considered that Jared would survive the break-up of the Department and be assigned to either Geldter's or Krappner's department, and it was widely assumed that it was only a matter of time before Dr. Masters fired Jared. Actually, none of the faculty in Jared's department wanted to be under the thumb of either of the two blood-suckers Geldter or Krappner, and unbeknownst to the McNichols there was a concerted effort to convince Dr. Belcher and Dr. Masters that it would be a grave mistake to split-up the department and especially to merge it with Dr. Geldter's department. These were no longer concerns of Jared's, however, because he was fighting just to survive at the moment.

Jared's detractors, including Drs. Geldter and Krappner and most of the administration of the D. O. Madison, had been provided information on prospective faculty offers for Jared, possibly from the snooping of Dr. Domasovitch and some of the people in the Department office, and they had managed to block any possible offers for a faculty position at other institutions around the country. So Jared and Marie had to consider where they would move and what they would do for the rest of their careers.

Marie wanted to move to Europe, but Jared would have nothing of the kind. They didn't have positions at any European institutions, and such offers even if they did eventually materialize were unlikely to come in time to save their home and possessions or academic careers. Jared had been telling Marie that European institutions favor Europeans not Americans, so the chance that they might receive an offer or two from European academic institutions was extremely unlikely, especially with the discrediting campaign that was underway against them. In this case Jared was right, and they did not receive any offers from Europe or elsewhere for that matter. Although Jared had applied for positions at other universities, his applications had been placed on hold, probably because other universities did not want what they considered whistle blowers like the McNichols.

The committee to oversee the McNichols' research

Dr. Masters warned Jared that he would establish a 'local' or 'institutional' committee to oversee Jared's research and decide what he could work on in his own laboratory. Such a committee was to be constituted from the Faculty Senate or some other source and might take some time to organize and go over the evidence, or so Jared thought. It might also be unpredictable and not give Dr. Masters what he wanted most, Jared's head. Instead, Dr. Masters ordered Jared to appear before his own administrative committee made up of the D. O. Madison Vice Presidents plus Dr. Reichsmann as the Faculty Senate representative. The committee was to be chaired by Dr. Masters, so it could be quite predictable. The role of the Vice Presidents was unclear, since Dr. Masters had the authority that he needed to do what he felt was necessary. After all, Dr. Masters was the President of the institution and had clear administrative authority to do just about anything he wanted at the Cancer Center, and he knew it. Jared just assumed that Dr. Masters had ordered his Vice Presidents to be at the meeting to spread the liability around if Jared ever sued the University. The President of the Cancer Center could self-righteously claim that the unanimous decisions of his Vice Presidents guided him in making his decisions.

One day Jared received a hand-delivered memo to attend a 'mandatory' meeting with Dr. Masters and his Vice Presidents to discuss various faculty complaints made against Jared. With only a day or two to decide what to do, Jared and Marie discussed Dr. Masters' meeting. Jared could demand that his attorney be present, but Jared and Marie did not have the funds to retain Mr. Neeman, who wanted a large retainer. Jared was worried about the large retainer required by Mr. Neeman, because he wanted only to proceed on a large lawsuit, and Jared only wanted to use Mr. Neeman sparingly. The last thing that Jared needed was to be locked into a multi-year lawsuit, because he needed to leave Texas and not return repeatedly to Austin to be present for depositions and courtroom proceedings. So Jared decided to attend the meeting without counsel. This was taking a chance, but Jared felt at the time that he had no choice.

The morning of the meeting as Jared made his way to the President's Conference Room where the meeting was to take place he ran into Dr. Bane. Dr. Bane was friendly enough, but when Jared casually asked Dr. Bane about the meeting, he became very evasive and didn't want to discuss it. Dr. Bane acted as if he really didn't know anything about the meeting, but Jared suspected that he was just acting and was sent to bring Jared into the meeting at the appropriate time after the members had been briefed by Dr. Masters. Like Dr. Masters, Dr. Bane thought that everyone liked him personally at the D. O. Madison, and he tried to use this to his own benefit. Of course, egomaniacs like Masters and Bane never realized that discerning individuals might be suspicious of their overly friendly manner and smiling faces. They thought that they could fool everyone, but in reality they fooled only themselves.

With a big smile on his face, Dr. Bane shook Jared's hand, produced some small talk as if to placate Jared and then brought him into the meeting at the appropriate time. Jared tried not to appear nervous in front of all of the D. O. Madison Vice Presidents. He wished that Dr. Hicks was still the Executive Vice President, but that was wishful thinking. The group was very somber except for a few jovial individuals who Jared suspected wanted his head on a platter to please Dr. Masters. There was, of course, Dr. Masters now with a sly smile on his face as he sat at the head of the conference table like a king presiding over his realm. To his left was Dr. Belcher, who didn't look like he really wanted to be present, then Dr. Reichsmann, who always seemed to have a large smile on his face. Jared thought that Dr. Reichsmann reminded him of Reichsmarshall Herman Goering, and finally there were the remainder of Dr. Masters' Vice

Presidents who were the ones that were not smiling. Of course, there was also the smiling Dr. Bane, who led Jared to the chair facing down the conference table to Dr. Masters, and then he took his seat to the right of his boss.

Dr. Masters began the meeting by stating, "Dr. McNichols, I want to thank you for agreeing to attend this meeting without an attorney. I have had to call this meeting because of the unpleasant situation created by your activities in the Department of Cancer Biology. I must remind the committee that Dr. McNichols was removed as the Chairman of this Department because of reports from other faculty members in the Department that he was abusing his position and not conducting himself in a manner befitting a faculty member at our institution. In fact, reports have been received in my office but also in the offices of Dr. Bane and Dr. Belcher that Dr. McNichols has betrayed the trust of his faculty by favoring his wife over their resource needs and assigning her laboratory space, even though she is not on the faculty or even an employee of the Cancer Center. I will have the Department of Legal Services look into this aspect of the situation to see if any State laws against nepotism have been broken. I have also received reports that Dr. McNichols has been conducting research without the usual administrative and biosafety approvals, and other necessary approvals. Some of this so-called research has made its way into the press, and I find it necessary to protect the good name of the Cancer Center by preventing the premature disclosure of preliminary and unconfirmed research that, I believe, falsely raises the expectations of the general public and also falsely directs criticism at our Armed Forces. There are also serious issues that have been raised that Dr. McNichols has been advising patients on what drugs to take and has been offering unproven and unlicensed tests to veterans and the general public. These are just some of the points that have been raised by faculty at our institution, and I take these criticisms very seriously. In fact, I have asked all of you to be here to question Dr. McNichols about these and other events so that we can come to an understanding about exactly what has happened and how the administrative controls have failed to protect the good name of the institution."

As Dr. Masters droned on in his monolog, trying to be extremely serious about the situation, Jared thought to himself that this sounded just like the administrative letters that he had received from Masters' office. He was just repeating the same worn out allegations that Jared had carefully answered previously. Jared was waiting for the punch line–something new and startling that he hadn't heard before, but to his astonishment the only thing that was new was that allegation that Jared was actually organizing demonstrations against the Cancer Center, an unprecedented move for a tenured faculty member. Dr. Masters then allowed Jared to answer the charges that had been made against him by unknown accusers in his Department. Jared began by saying, "Dr. Masters, I take these proceedings very seriously, and I will try to answer each of the unproven allegations that you have brought before your committee. First, I would like to pass out my written responses to your last legal letter to me so that the committee can see that I addressed each and every one of the allegations that you have made today." Dr. Masters interrupted Jared to say, "That won't be necessary. I want you to answer my specific questions and those of the committee." Jared responded, "Yes sir, I will, but I believe that each of my responses has been documented in my letter of response to you, and I would like the committee to see my responses in writing."

Jared had already passed out copies of the letter while he responded to Dr. Masters, and this seemed to cause Dr. Masters tremendous irritation. He said, "Dr. McNichols, I just stated that I want you to answer the criticisms brought by the committee, not provide a copy of a letter that you sent to me previously." Jared repeated his statement, "Yes sir, I will respond to each of your allegations. First, I believe I documented in my letter that I actually have less research space allocated on a grant dollar basis than any other faculty in the Department, so I disagree that I allocated more space to myself than to other faculty based on need. This was actually the formula that Dr. Belcher had attempted to apply to our Center in order to determine space needs." Dr. Masters turned to Dr. Belcher and asked, "Is this true, Dr. Belcher?" Dr. Belcher responded, "Yes, Clement you approved of this approach yourself to evaluate research space at our institution, and according to the figures provided by Dr. McNichols, which my office has not yet confirmed, it appears that Dr. McNichols has the grant funds to justify the space allocation for his research. It also appears that he has not favored himself over his faculty in terms of space allocation."

Dr. Masters looked stunned. He wasn't expecting his own Vice President for Research to back Jared over *his* position. Dr. Masters said, "Dr. Belcher, I expect you to give me a written report on this later today. I want these figures confirmed by your office." Dr. Belcher replied, "I believe that we can furnish your office with a space evaluation of the Department later today." Dr. Masters replied, "Good! Now I would like to move on to the criticism that nepotism rules have been violated at our institution." Jared responded, "Sir, my wife is a highly qualified Ph.D. researcher who has been approved as a consultant on my grants. As a consultant, her role is to help in the evaluation of research, which she does on almost a daily basis. She does not perform the research herself. The actual laboratory research is performed by a technician who is an employee of the institution." Dr. Masters interrupted, "And how is this technician being paid? What account is this technician being paid from?" Jared responded, "The technicians under my direction are supported mainly from my grants and contracts. The only technical assistance that isn't supported by grants and contracts is for general laboratory assistance. I do have some technical help supported by my endowed chair." Dr. Masters turned again to Dr. Belcher, "Is this true, Francis?" Dr. Belcher replied, "According to the information provided to the Office of Research, this is correct, just as it is spelled out in Dr. McNichols' letter." Dr. Masters said, "We are not discussing this letter today, and I have asked Dr. McNichols to answer my questions. Do you think that Dr. McNichols has answered my question?" Dr. Belcher replied, "Clement, we have looked into this, and my office can't find any violations in personnel use, biosafety approvals or violations in the conduct of research by Dr. McNichols."

Dr. Masters again looked stunned. He didn't expect his own Vice President to contradict him on these important issues. He said, "Dr. Belcher, I expect you to be more respectful of my position and provide any information that you have on the subject." Dr. Belcher replied, "But Clement, I provided your office with a thorough analysis of these allegations. I just don't see any violations." Dr. Masters became angry and said, "Dr. Belcher, I want you to go back and re-analyze this again. Is that clear?" Dr. Belcher replied, "Yes, I believe that we can do that." Dr. Masters said, "And I want you to report back to the committee." Dr. Belcher again, "Yes, I understand." Dr. Masters then said, "Well, where were we?" Dr. Reichsmann piped up, "I believe that we were to discuss administrative approvals for Dr. McNichols' research." Dr. Masters said, "Yes, that's it! Dr. McNichols, I do not see where I have approved your research. Isn't it true that you have conducted your research on the veterans without my approval?" Jared responded, "Sir, I don't know of any instance where your approval is specifically required on any of the research conducted in the Department. As for approval of the veterans' research project, I obtained the approval of the Office of Research, and the signature of Dr. Belcher on my grant applications indicates the usual administrative approval required at our institution for research projects. Is there something else that I am not aware of?" Dr. Masters smugly said, "You didn't get my approval for your research, did you? Do you admit here in front of the Committee that you did not get my direct approval for this research?" Jared responded, "Dr. Masters, I obtained the proper signatures necessary according to the directives from the Office of Research. I know of no research projects at our institution that require your direct approval or signature. They do require the signature of Dr. Belcher, and I believe that we have his signature on the appropriate forms." Dr. Masters turned again to his Vice President for Research, "Is this true, Francis?" Dr. Belcher replied, "According to the written directives that you yourself approved two years ago, I believe that Dr. McNichols is compliant with our regulations on research."

That was not what Dr. Masters wanted to hear from his Vice President for Research. Dr. Masters' face began to redden. He had forgotten completely about the directives on research, which were implemented to save the President of the institution from having to go through hundreds of research projects that he knew nothing about. The authority for approving research was given to the Vice President for Research. He continued, "We will discuss this point again in conference. I don't think that you are correct in your assumptions, Dr. Belcher, and I will need more than your assumptions in this case. I think that we should move to the next item. Where were we?" Dr. Reichsmann replied, "Dr. Masters, I believe that an important criticism that we must address is that Dr. McNichols has been advising patients illegally on what drugs to take for their undiagnosed conditions, and my reports say that he has actually given patients certain antibiotics. This is a grave violation of State laws." Jared responded forcefully, "Dr. Reichsmann, I can assure you that I haven't ever given a patient any drug, and I would like to know the evidence that shows otherwise. I have advised physicians who have called me about what we have found in our studies, and I believe that it is our duty to respond to the community with information if we can provide it on health matters. It is presented to them as ongoing, preliminary research. In fact, I have done nothing more than relate what is printed in our peer-reviewed publications on the subject. And I might add, that this advice was published in some of the most widely read medical journals in the world, and it is just advice. It is the responsibility of individual physicians to evaluate the medical needs of their patients and act accordingly. We do not interfere in the physician-patient process, and we do not provide patients with anything other than information that they can take to their own physicians for evaluation. We do not see patients in our Department, and we do not perform any test that is not covered by our research protocol that was approved by the Office of Research and Biosafety Office."

Dr. Reichsmann was still smiling as he turned to Dr. Masters. After a few moments, Dr. Masters who had stopped smiling said, "Did you take part in a demonstration in front of the hospital?" Jared responded, "No sir. I did not. Nor did I know anything specific about any demonstration." Dr. Masters turned to Dr. Bane. Dr. Bane believing that he should respond said, "We are having Chief Costa and the Police Department look into this." Dr. Masters pulled a paper out of a file and said, "It says right here in this press clipping that you have tested veterans and have found an unusual mycoplasma that you claim has been modified. What do you say to that?"

Jared didn't know quite how to respond to Dr. Masters' question, so he just said, "We believe that part of the statement in the press account is correct, sir, but it is incomplete. And I did not make that particular statement to the press." Dr. Masters held up the newspaper article and said, "It says differently right here!" Jared responded, "Sir, if you will look carefully at the article, it attributes that quote to Dr. Marie McNichols not to me." Dr. Masters' face became red and he stated, "Frankly, I don't care if it's your mother. You have defamed the good name of the institution by your comments in this news article!" Jared responded, "Actually, the article that you're holding up was very complimentary of the Cancer Center. It was not critical. It actually shows the D. O. Madison helping patients, and I don't believe that you will find any quotes by me in that article that could be considered damaging to the institution." Dr. Masters replied, "I don't accept your explanation. I will be the judge of whether you have violated my directives. You say it does not defame the institution. Well, I believe that it does. I believe that any of our faculty here would conclude that such press reports are defaming the good name of the institution. Didn't you agree not to give any press releases without the strict approval of my office? Isn't that true?" Jared said, "Sir, I didn't hand out any press reports or releases. I have never handed out press reports without the approval of the Office of Public Affairs. In fact, I haven't made any press reports in the last two years, and the last report that I sent to the Public Affairs Office was on the new breast cancer gene that we discovered. These were reporters that contacted me after seeking approval through your Public Affairs Office. I have no control over what they actually write in their articles." Dr. Masters turned to his Vice Presidents and said, "We have got to have control over the press! We can't have our faculty going to some reporter over their preliminary research without our approval." Jared responded, "Dr. Masters, I did not go to any reporter. Some reporters have come to me after going through the Office of Public Affairs. It was *your* Public Affairs Office that sent them to me. I thought that this was the standard procedure at our institution?" Dr. Masters said, "I don't want you talking to any reporters without *my* personal approval. Is that clear?" Jared nodded his head, even though he knew that this was not the University's policy.

After a few more questions from Dr. Reichsmann, who seemed to be trying to find something, anything, to pin on Jared, the meeting ended abruptly. Dr. Masters spoke to Jared, "Thank you Dr. McNichols for appearing this morning. We will be going into executive session to discuss the matter more fully, and you will not be needed again this morning. However, I am going to ask you to be available to answer any other questions as they come up during our discussions." Jared asked, "Could that be by phone, sir?" Dr. Masters looked at Dr. Bane who nodded, "That will be sufficient for the time being, but I want you to be available all day today to come back to the committee, if necessary." Jared responded, "Dr. Masters, I will be available to answer any and all questions from your committee. Thank you gentlemen for your patience."

Jared stood up abruptly, spun on his heal and made a quick exit from the meeting. At the door to the outer office, Jared ran into one of Masters'

Vice Presidents who was late for the meeting. He looked serious and asked Jared, "How did it go in there?" Jared responded, "Oh, you mean the witch-hunt? I didn't exactly get burned at the stake, but they tried." Jared then added, "Good luck in finding anything. I'm innocent of all these bogus allegations, and they know it." The Vice President replied, "I certainly hope you're correct. It's not good for the institution." Jared decided not to ask whether he was referring to Dr. Masters. He waved his hand and bolted down the hallway. It was now less than four months until Clement Masters must retire. Jared wondered if he could make it, or would Dr. Masters have his scalp on his pole along side the other victims of this petty but very dangerous bureaucrat.

CHAPTER 15

The McNichols Decide to Leave (1996)

Jared and Marie finally decided on a move that would take them away from their Texas nightmare. Since they had been completely blocked in finding suitable faculty positions around the country by the concerted efforts of the administration and a few of the usual faculty 'suspects' at the D. O. Madison, the McNichols decided to form a small, non-profit research institute in California. Jared was from California, and he was previously a full professor at one of the University of California campuses. In addition, Jared and Marie had purchased a cozy condo overlooking the Pacific Ocean in Laguna Beach in 1986 as a vacation flat. It was a location that the McNichols both loved, and it was near Jared's parents, making it especially convenient for Jared to monitor his parents' health problems. Thus they would not have to wait to sell their home in Queenswood before they moved, and in fact, they could move quickly to their condo, if necessary. Since the housing market in Queenswood was in free-fall in 1996, and there was no assurance that they could even sell their house in a reasonable period of time, it was a good choice.

The McNichols had much to do before they left Texas, and the move would be contingent on Jared managing to get his four active grants released by the D. O. Madison administration. Without the four grants, Jared and Marie would not have the resources to start even a small foundation. The D. O. Madison didn't have to release Jared's grants if they could assign a suitable Principal Investigator from the Madison faculty to replace Jared on the grants. Jared would find that moving his grants was not as easy as it first appeared, since it would require administrative approval. Jared reasoned that this would be difficult, if Dr. Masters found out what he was trying to do with his grants. The trick would be to move the grants while Masters was tied up with his retirement and training his replacement, Dr. Morningstone. Only Dr. Belcher was required to sign the administrative release of Jared's grants, so Jared felt that they had a fighting chance to keep and move the grants.

Jared hoped that Dr. Belcher was feeling just a bit guilty over what had happened during the last few years at the Madison, and he might be willing to help Jared since he too was near retirement. Jared was aware that the Administration could assign Dr. Geldter or Dr. Domasovitch to be the replacement Principal Investigator on his grants, so Jared was trying to find ways to warn them in advance not to cross him on moving his grants, or they would have an enemy forever. Academia was a small world, and Jared reminded them that he knew exactly what they had been doing to him and his career, and he would now make it widely known what they had done. Jared also set up a meeting with Dr. Belcher, who now did not want to be involved in taking Jared's grants. It was one thing for Dr. Belcher to secretly block Jared's grant applications when they were being reviewed, whereas it was entirely something else to arrange a take-over of an existing, active grant. In the latter case it would have been very apparent to the academic community that Dr. Belcher was tampering with Jared's grants, and Jared could easily prove in a court of law that he was discriminated against by the D. O. Madison and was denied due process because of the unpopularity of his research on veterans' illnesses.

Dr. Belcher decided that he didn't want any part of a discriminatory action requested by Dr. Masters. If Jared decided to seek legal remedies, Dr. Belcher would have been defendant number two on a long list of defendants. After some delay, probably because Dr. Masters was close to retirement, Dr. Belcher finally agreed that Jared could move his grants. Actually Dr. Belcher did not like and actually feared Clement Masters, who he considered a psychopath fully capable of killing anyone in his path. But he also knew that once Dr. Masters retired, his bite would be just about non-existent without access to the University accounts, or so he reasoned. Dr. Belcher would never do anything that might jeopardize his own retirement or his own physical health. Dr. Masters was removed from his previous University position for misallocation of funds, so Dr. Belcher knew that Masters would think nothing of contracting a hit on him and charging it to some University account. However, once Dr. Masters retired, it would be much less likely, if a possibility at all, that he would allocate any of his own money to go after one of his former Vice Presidents. He might need all of his tidy retirement funds to fight the numerous pending lawsuits that he elicited while President of The D. O. Madison Cancer Center.

In order to move Jared's grants, a new institution had to be established, so Jared and Marie formed the Molecular Medicine Institute and incorporated it in Nevada. It was easier to form a corporation in Nevada and then qualify it in California or any other state for that matter. Of course, it was not so easy to form a tax-exempt, non-profit corporation, but the McNichols were assisted by a former senior IRS attorney that they had attended church with in Austin. The Austin attorney was formally the director of litigation of the IRS district covering the Mid-Atlantic States, and he was still well-known and respected around the IRS. The McNichols were lucky to have found the attorney, and they were able to establish the Molecular Medicine Institute as a nonprofit organization under the tax laws in near record time.

Jared and Marie had no idea why they were being helped in establishing a new nonprofit research organization so quickly. As it turned out there were always some former soldiers and other veterans around to assist them, and the McNichols' reputation for helping veterans paved the way. With the approval of the new Molecular Medicine Institute as a nonprofit organization, Jared was able to initiate the transfer of his grants to the new Institute to be established in California. Before that could be done a physical presence had to be established in California, and so Jared and Marie decided to establish a small laboratory in Southern California for the new Molecular Medicine Institute.

Dr. Morningstone is in charge?

The day finally came for Dr. Masters to step down as the President of the D. O. Madison Cancer Center, and by some miracle Jared was still on the faculty, at least for the moment. On June 1st Dr. Morningstone was officially placed in charge of the Cancer Center, but Dr. Masters was still around for three months until he formally retired. Jared and Marie celebrated the end of the horror they had endured under the tyrannical psychopath Dr. Masters, but as it turned out their joyous observance was short lived.

The following morning Jared received a message from Dr. Masters' office indicating that the Cancer Center would be moving to terminate him from his position for 'insubordination.' Jared immediately called his attorney, Mr. Neeman, who had ample experience dealing with the ravings of Dr. Masters. According to Mr. Neeman, and also the published University Rules and Regulations, there was no provision for terminating an employee for insubordination, nor was insubordination even mentioned in any of the University handbooks or regulations. It was so typical of Dr. Masters to 'invent' a university rule so that he could do what he wanted–in this case have Jared terminated.

Jared decided immediately to contact Dr. Belcher's office. After all, Dr. Belcher actually supported Jared in a back-handed way during the 'interrogation' in Dr. Masters office with his Vice Presidents. Dr. Belcher was a tragic figure, torn between what he knew was right and the reality of dealing with a totally corrupt system, and Jared actually felt sorry for the position he was in because he actually liked Dr. Belcher and accepted all his faults. Dr. Belcher may have wanted to help Jared and Marie, but he probably feared Dr. Masters' wrath to the point where he felt paralyzed. Dr. Belcher agreed to see Jared on short notice.

As Jared entered Dr. Belcher's office, he was directed to sit down while Dr. Belcher talked to someone back East on the phone. Finally when Dr. Belcher was free, he hung up the phone and looked at Jared for a moment and stated, "Well, Dr. McNichols you have certainly done it now. Dr. Masters is on the warpath again, and as you know he usually gets what he wants . . . and he wants your head." Jared asked, "What have I done now? I've been keeping a very low profile. I haven't talked to the press; I haven't been on TV; I haven't testified to Congress lately. I have been minding my own business and trying to find a job outside of Texas. I even turned in my resignation letter. He knows I'm leaving. Why doesn't he just let me leave the Cancer Center with some dignity? Why does he have to drag my bloody, decapitated body through the dirt. Hasn't he done enough to destroy my career . . . . my life?" Dr. Belcher said, "Now Jared, don't get emotional about this. You decided to work on the veterans' project against my better judgment. You could have stopped that project at any time, and you would have probably been brought back into the fold." Jared asked, "And let thousands of veterans die? What kind of a choice is that?"

Jared looked at Dr. Belcher and asked him without a hint of emotion, "What would you have done if your daughter had come back sick from a war, and no one would acknowledge it, or help in any way, and all that anyone would tell you was that it was all in her head?" Dr. Belcher responded, "I know that you think that you may have done the right thing, but everything in life is about choices and consequences." Jared asked, "And so for helping the veterans I loose my job? . . . . or my life?" Jared was angry and said, "Dr. Belcher, you know that this is pure bullshit. Marie told me to think of this entire nightmare as another agenda connected to her inheritance." Dr. Belcher shook his head and responded forcefully, "This is not about you losing your job for some frivolous reason or about you being targeted because Marie is some heiress, if that is what you believe, this is about throwing a gauntlet in Dr. Masters' face." Jared said, "I never threw a gauntlet in Dr. Masters' face. All that I was trying to do was my research, and Dr. Masters got this burr up his ass to shut down my laboratory because of what we found." Dr. Belcher responded, "You didn't exactly act in a professional manner with your results." Jared became angry and continued, "I submitted our results to professional, peer-reviewed journals. I was asked to testify to the President's Commission on Gulf War Illnesses in Washington. I communicated what we found to the Department of Defense and Department of Veterans' Affairs, and Marie and I lectured at their facilities in Washington on the subject. I was asked to testify to Congress under oath." Dr. Belcher countered, "And you threw the whole thing in Masters' face by going to the press and making him look like a fool." Jared said, "Frankly, he is a fool, and you know it, Dr. Belcher! And I didn't go to the press, they came to me!" Dr. Belcher shot back, "Now Jared, don't split hairs with me! You must have known the consequences of your actions." Jared said, "No I did not! We sincerely thought that we were helping people, and I mistakenly thought that this was what we should be doing at the D. O. Madison, helping people with undiagnosed illnesses!"

Dr. Belcher thought for a moment and then became fatherly. "Jared, one of the problems that you don't seem to grasp is that there are forces beyond our control that do not want this information widely known." Jared asked, "What do you mean? The fact that this bug might be from a U.

S. Government laboratory?" Dr. Belcher responded, "That kind of thinking will get you no where. All it will do is get you in trouble . . . . real trouble!" Jared said, "You mean, like I am in now?" Jared continued, "You know, when Marie and I had lunch with Dr. Bowman before he retired, he told us that during World War II he worked on Biological Warfare for the Army. He said that what we found was consistent with what he knew about the programs that were underway in the Army after the war. You know, if Dr. Bowman had not retired, I probably wouldn't be in the fix that I'm in now."

Dr. Belcher's voice became whiny as he said in his New York accent, "That is supposition and guessing. It was a long time ago. It's better not to speculate about such things. It could get you in a lot of trouble." Jared said, "We as a nation are in a lot of trouble if we turn our backs on these problems just because it might embarrass someone or expose some stupid illegal program that should have never been done in the first place." Dr. Belcher cautioned Jared and said, "Let me say again . . . . that kind of thinking will get you in a lot of trouble. It's not our place to second-guess what happened during the Cold War. There were a lot of mistakes. We need to bury them and forget about it." Jared said, "Like we're burying veterans from the Gulf War . . . . by the thousands! Is that your idea of burying your mistakes?" Dr. Belcher admonished Jared, "Don't get sanctimonious with me, Dr. McNichols. I served in the Navy. I know the risks when you put on a uniform." Jared said, "You told me that you worked in a pathology lab at some stateside Navy hospital on a research project! You never were deployed overseas." Dr. Belcher became embarrassed and said, "Never mind, Dr. McNichols. No wonder Dr. Masters has such a problem with you. You're a smartass." Jared responded, "Well, at least I'm honest." Dr. Belcher pointed to Jared and said in a jovial manner, "You're an honest smartass! Now get out of here, so I can get some work done!" Jared stood up and smiled as he headed toward the door, "O.K., boss. Thanks for the support, anyway. I never did get to thank you for coming to my defense during my 'interrogation' by all of the Vice Presidents."

At over 6 feet tall, Jared towered over the very short Dr. Belcher when he finally stood up, which is why Dr. Belcher always had his visitors sit down while he stood and paced in front of them. Jared knew Dr. Belcher's weak points but he was able to overlook them because of some semblance of ethical support against Dr. Masters. With all his faults, Jared respected Dr. Belcher's intellect, and he did try to help Jared in his own way, just like Jared tried to help his own faculty. In the end Dr. Belcher turned out not to be such a bad person after all. He was weak for sure, but he also had his good points, and it was rare to find anyone of administrative rank at the Madison who had any semblance of ethics and honor. It seemed that the Vice Presidents that Jared respected the most had either retired, left or were murdered.

Jared and Marie were now complete outcasts in Jared's own department. In fact, Dr. Masters had issued an order that Marie was to be arrested on sight and escorted out of the D. O. Madison Cancer Center if she entered the complex. Although Marie and Jared knew that this was completely illegal, since Marie was an approved consultant on some of Jared's grants, and it was completely within her rights to visit the institution as an approved member of Jared's research team, they decided not to test the egomaniac Clement Masters and his phony order. Also, they remembered the vicious hate note sent to Marie that they thought was from Dr. Masters. It was quite obvious that whoever wrote the note was obsessed where she was concerned. Also, there was some question as to whether Dr. Masters still had the authority to order anyone around at the Cancer Center. Dr. Morningstone was now the President, and Dr. Masters had been relegated formally to President Emeritus status. Jared had thought that he was finally safe from the wrath of Dr. Masters, but again, he was wrong to underestimate the evil psychopath Dr. Clement Masters.

It was naive for Jared to think that with the formal changing of the guard at the Madison that anything had really changed. Dr. Masters was still around, and he had a lot more time on his hands to complete some unfinished business before he formally retired. Jared and Marie were not the only targets of Masters' wrath, but they certainly felt like it. Jared could not get any assistance from Dr. Morningstone, who had now long forgotten that he and Jared were once friends in California. Dr. Morningstone had much to do to learn the ropes in his new position, and he didn't want to be bothered by a faculty member who was soon to be an ex-faculty member, one way or another.

There was one rare bright spot, however, in Jared's academic life during the last year he was in Austin. Jared also had an appointment as Professor of Internal Medicine at the University Medical School in Austin, and the Department Chairman did not approve of the way that Jared and Marie had been treated at their sister institution, The D. O. Madison Cancer Center. Jared actually considered transferring to the Medical School faculty but after careful thought, he and Marie decided that the academic environment had been irreversibly poisoned for them in Austin by Dr. Masters and his henchmen. It would have been a very difficult move anyway, because Dr Masters had the authority to continue his bludgeoning of Jared, even if he were across the street at the Medical School. It was the same University, and Dr. Masters was a senior administrator at that university but at another branch.

After considering all of the alternatives, Jared and Marie decided to leave, and they wanted to leave Austin and never return as far as they were concerned. Jared and Marie also decided that she would remain at home until they had finally left Texas, both for her own safety and to keep the move low key. Around the Department Jared was hardly seen by the other faculty, but he was in daily contact with his own laboratory personnel. He stopped attending Department meetings because he couldn't stand the gloating of Dr. Domasovitch, the acting chairman, and he rarely went to the Faculty Club for lunch because he no longer wanted to explain to other faculty what happened to his once promising career that was now relegated to the toilet. Jared sometimes attended seminars but he avoided other faculty members, most of whom were uncomfortable around Jared anyway because of his leper status. He had to keep up certain appearances for the morale of his laboratory personnel, but it was clear that many of these technicians and post-doctoral fellows just wanted to now leave as soon as possible so their careers would not be tainted. Some actually thought that some bad stink might be transferred to them if they remained any longer in Jared's laboratory. The disinformation campaign of Isaac Geldter and Amy Krappner and now other Cancer Center faculty was bearing bountiful fruit, and Jared was no longer invited to speak at important meetings or nominated for any awards.

Jared found out the hard way about Dr. Masters' reach when he applied for faculty positions around the country. He could have ten supporters, but if one detractor came forward and vigorously attacked Jared, his chances of receiving a faculty offer were nil. As the faculty rats found out about

Jared's applications, he found that he had little hope for a fair hearing to defend himself. Universities did not want any controversy, and they would try hard to avoid hiring a controversial faculty member. Dr. Masters had even sent Dr. Geldter to California to speak to administrators to poison Jared's chances of returning to any of the University of California campuses. Jared had mistakenly thought that his former university knew him well enough to withstand the disinformation. Even old friends from his former department in California now shunned or advised him to forget about coming back to his old position. His leper status was now national in addition to local. At least it still did not extend to Europe, Asia and other locations.

Jared decided that this was the price that they must pay for taking on the Pentagon and the State of Texas. It was a forgone conclusion that they would lose—it was no match. They had lost before they had even started. Now the price must be paid. Jared did not want Dr. Masters to find out about Dr. Belcher approving the transfer of his grants and equipment to the new Institute that he and Marie had formed in California, so he mislead his colleagues around the Department that the McNichols did not know exactly when they would be leaving the institution or where they would be going. In fact, the paperwork on his resignation and the transfer of his grants and equipment were in Dr. Belchers' office. As a last favor to Jared, Dr. Belcher kept the information to himself and forwarded the necessary paperwork through the usual administrative channels without Dr. Masters' knowledge. Jared felt that it was a passive aggressive act on Dr. Belcher's part, but in fact, Dr. Belcher did not agree with Dr. Masters' criminal assaults on the McNichols. He had decided that he would do what he could to help Jared and Marie without risking his own career or perhaps even his life. For that Jared was eternally grateful. It was rare indeed to find an administrator around the D. O. Madison who had any semblance of honor and a sense of fair play. All of the administrators who could have helped Jared and Marie had now retired or left the institution.

For the McNichols the summer of 1996 in Austin was probably the worst summer of their lives. Jared was treated like a leper in his own department that he founded and built from nothing in 1980, and Marie was not even allowed entry into the institution on threat of eviction and even arrest. Jared was fearful on every morning that he hesitantly entered the D. O Madison Cancer Center that he would be immediately accosted by the University Police, dragged up to Dr. Masters' office and placed in front of the administrative 'firing squad' without a modicum of due process or any possibility of appeal. There was absolutely no pity for the plight that the McNichols were in, because most people thought exactly as Dr. Belcher related to Jared in his office that one morning–the McNichols had brought it entirely upon themselves.

The McNichols reflect on their future

At home in the evening Jared and Marie had a chance to reflect on how their professional and personal lives had taken a steep decline but at the same time they may have unlocked a key that could help millions of people with chronic illnesses. Because of their work on Gulf War Illnesses thousands of veterans lives have been saved, and now the follow-on to their research on the Gulf War veterans showed that other chronic conditions, most with unknown etiologies, such as chronic fatigue syndrome, fibromyalgia syndrome, autoimmune diseases like rheumatoid arthritis, ankylosing spondylitis, lupus and multiple sclerosis, irritable bowel syndrome, atypical heart and kidney infections, respiratory conditions like asthma, chronic bronchitis and atypical pneumonias, craniofacial and maxillofacial pain from chronic infections, among other illnesses and conditions. These all appeared to involve the types of intracellular chronic bacterial infections that Marie and Jared had found in the Gulf War Illness patients and their symptomatic family members. The infections that the McNichols and now other laboratories were also finding in chronic illnesses were not always related to the primitive mycoplasmas. They were also related to other intracellular bacterial infections like those caused by *Chlamydia pneumoniae*, often associated with chronic pain, arteriosclerosis and heart disease, and *Borrelia burgdorferi*, the bacteria that caused Lyme disease (along with mycoplasmas and other bacteria) and other infections. These bacterial infections were also found commonly with certain viral infections, such as Human Herpesvirus-6 (HHV-6), cytomegalovirus (CMV) and other viruses, and together the multiple bacterial and viral infections were found in most chronic illness patients. These bacterial and viral infections appeared to play a major role in determining the severity and types of signs and symptoms found in these patients, and in some cases they probably even caused many of these illnesses along with other toxic exposures and genetic susceptibilities. The stumbling of Jared and Marie onto a path that may open an avenue of treatment for millions of patients with chronic illnesses was exciting, and this was probably the only thing that kept them going and optimistic about their futures. Thus they made plans to pursue this new and exciting line of investigation in California at the new Institute. It was the one bright spot in their lives.

Another topic that Marie and Jared frequently discussed at home was Marie's inheritance. After all, this could be used to fund the new Institute, if she could just unlock it. Marie should have received part of her inheritance, but the trustees of the Cetta Dharma Trust and the other trusts had prevented her from accessing the information needed to claim her inheritance. They wanted to continue using the trusts for their own projects and personal needs, and they did not seem at all interested in following the terms of the Trusts that stated that Marie was the sole heir. Marie and Jared decided that it was the trustees of the Cetta Dharma Trust, Five Star Trust, Sterling Trust, Century Tust and the other trusts along with the Las Vegas criminals that had been at work against them in the background all along using institutions like the D. O. Madison Cancer Center, because this institution was hundreds of millions of dollars in debt to the trusts and Las Vegas for its massive building program. No wonder Dr. Masters focused on Marie the moment that she arrived in Austin. This also explained the efforts to ruin Marie's career and drive her to despair. If the trustees and Las Vegas interests could kill or permanently incapacitate Marie or drive her to insanity or suicide, then they could continue to use the trusts and Marie's Las Vegas assets for their own purposes, without the meddling of some heiress to interfere with their plans.

Interestingly, the more that Marie found out about her trusts and Las Vegas interests left by her notorious and wealthy father, the more that Marie and Jared came to the conclusion that at least one of the massive trusts, The Cetta Dharma Trust established in 1930 and held off-ledger by the Morgan-Chase Bank in Manhattan, New York, had been the major funding vehicle for Black Budget Operations by the Federal Government. In fact, it now appeared that the Cetta Dharma Trust, Century Trust and Sterling Trust were the principal instruments that funded the Manhattan Project that developed the atomic bomb during World War II. This was probably why the project was called the 'Manhattan Project.' More recently the Cetta Dharma Trust was used to fund the Manhattan II Project, a massive unconventional weapons of mass destruction development program started during the Cold War to counter the Soviet Union's large research and development programs in unconventional weapons. Thus the Cetta Dharma Trust was probably the main source of funds for the MKULTRA, MKNAIOMI and other infamous programs that developed new weapons of mass destruction based on chemical, biological, radiological and electromagnetic weapons.

The McNichols also found out that the Cetta Dharma Trust and the other trusts had been used to advance population control measures like those expressed in National Security Memorandum 200 by funding the development of new biological agents that caused new lethal diseases after their release in the Third World. Marie and Jared discussed how ironic it was that Marie, who was the sole heiress to the Cetta Dharma and the other trusts, was involved in discovering one of the microorganisms that was likely an incapacitating Biological Weapon whose development and testing in the military and in the Texas prison system was funded by the very trusts that she would one day inherit! In fact, upon further investigation Marie and Jared found out that several very prominent American families and politicians, had used the trusts as collateral for loans on their own industrial projects, mainly defense and biomedical projects.

It was no accident that even small biotechnology companies like Biox, Inc. were directly or indirectly supported by Marie's trusts. Indeed, the same people who were trustees on the Cetta Dharma Trust and other trusts were listed as the primary owners of companies like Biox. The money that founded these companies either came from Marie's trusts or from loans backed by the trusts. By piecing together information from various sources, including information from officers in the Joint Special Operations Command, intelligence agencies and veterans of the Gulf War that Marie and Jared had assisted, the corporations and institutions that were funded and controlled by the trustees of the Cetta Dharma and other trusts became clearer. Some of the most prominent defense corporations and institutions in America had received funds from the trusts. It was actually a relief to Marie and Jared that they could finally learn the names of some of the companies funded by Marie's trusts, because the McNichols had no explanation as to why certain corporations and institutions had gone after them to ruin them professionally and drive them into bankruptcy. Now it was all becoming clear. The evil trustees of the Cetta Dharma Trust and the other trusts did not want Marie to survive to claim her inheritance, or at the very least they did not want her to be in any financial condition to make her rightful claim on any of the trusts, a process that could involve lengthy and expensive court battles.

No wonder Marie had so many near-death episodes during her lifetime where she almost died from various accidents, illnesses and other disasters that one hundred people would not have collectively experienced during their lifetimes. It was all traced back to the trusts and the greedy trustees and Las Vegas criminals who would have Marie killed in a heartbeat if they thought she would present a problem to their investments. Even Jared's and Marie's problems with the D. O. Madison Cancer Center were traced back to the trusts as well as Las Vegas crime interests. The massive building program of the Cancer Center was, in fact, funded by the trusts, or at least the loans required for the building program were collateralized by the trusts, and as it turned out many of the major universities in the United States had used the trusts to collateralize their loans or finance questionable programs. Dr. Masters knew this, and he was just doing the bidding for the trustees in destroying Marie. He was also doing the bidding of the Las Vegas organized crime interests that were trying to keep Marie from making any claims on her Las Vegas casinos and other properties that were rightfully hers.

Dr. Masters' replacement, Dr. Morningstone, was brought into the criminal conspiracy and now knew the truth about Marie's inheritance and the role of her trusts in funding the building and other programs in the Medical Center. Thus Dr. Morningside quickly replaced Dr. Masters as the source of major problems for Jared and Marie if they remained in Austin. This explained why Dr. Morningside shunned his old friend Jared and refused to meet with him or even return his telephone calls.

It was quite clear why the McNichols had to leave Austin, and leave as soon as possible. They had no choice. Marie could not fight her trustees from a position of financial weakness. She and Jared had to make new lives out from under the control of the trusts and the Las Vegas crime interests, if they could. Thus the thought of a small independent nonprofit research organization became more and more attractive, because most of the major universities were linked either directly or indirectly to the Cetta Dharma Trust and Marie's other trusts through their capital building programs or even their assets. This had to be the explanation that Marie and Jared were seeking. They felt all along that there must be something else besides the mycoplasma research that justified the treatment that they received from the D. O. Madison Cancer Center and now other academic institutions as well.

The financial influence of Marie's massive trusts and Las Vegas interests also explained why Jared had to watch everything in their personal finances for sabotage and dirty tricks. Along with all the professional problems and attempts on their lives, the McNichols had also been the victims of bank fraud, credit card fraud, mortgage fraud, insurance fraud, consumer fraud, and the list went on and on. Before the McNichols moved to California Jared was spending an increasing amount of time dealing with the financial problems related to various schemes directed at the McNichols from normally reliable institutions. It was a good thing that Jared and Marie had made a few loyal friends in Austin, among them their banker, Mike Trane, and their broker, John Portz. Trane and Portz would help them repeatedly though the difficult times in Austin, and even after they left Austin for Southern California.

One evening Jared had just about reached the end of his financial rope because of all the sabotage directed at them. He had always handled the financial duties for the family, and the stress of continual sabotage was taking its toll. Jared said to Marie, "I don't know whether I can take any more of this financial mess we always seem to be in! Why does everything always turn to shit for us! We've had nothing but problems with even the most trivial things. Yesterday I found out that our mortgage company purposely lost our mortgage payments by placing them into another account. Then they attempted to foreclose on us for not making our payments, even after I furnished the cancelled checks proving that we had made the payments. Meanwhile they contacted the credit bureaus and indicated to them that we didn't make our mortgage payments and were months behind and had defaulted on our mortgage. And that was just one creditor. The same thing is happening with several creditors simultaneously, and at the same time our credit cards have been used to run up thousands of dollars in debt that we didn't have anything to do with! We can't possibly pay for all this, fight the fraud and at the same time fight Masters, now Morningstone and their cretins at the D. O. Madison. Marie, I am just about finished. I'm completely spent fighting every day for our survival and at the same time keeping up with everything that I have to do in a normal day." Marie responded, "Jared, you're going to have to be stronger to withstand the evil that we have found ourselves surrounded by here in Austin." Marie paused and then said, "When I fist moved to Texas, I was so excited about going to such a dynamic place where just about anything could be done." Jared responded sarcastically, "Yes, you found out that just about anything could be done, only you found out that it was being done against you, and you couldn't do anything about it!" Marie responded, "Oh Jared, why do you always have a sarcastic answer for everything?" Jared replied, "Probably because that is the only way I can keep my sanity. It would be easy to go completely nuts around here with everyone coming at you day after day." Marie calmly related to Jared, "I have had this treatment in one way or another since 1962, the year my notorious father died. I am actually relieved that I did not imagine the unusual and cruel persecution that I have experienced. Jared, we will prevail! We are stronger than they think!"

CHAPTER 16

The Move to California (1996)

As the time drew near for the McNichols to leave Austin forever and never go back, the now ex-President of the D. O. Madison, Dr. Clement Masters, tried one more time to fire Jared for 'insubordination.' Even though Dr. Morningstone had assumed his duties as the new President of the Cancer Center, Dr. Masters still had considerable influence at the Cancer Center. In fact, it was hard to tell that Dr. Masters was no longer the President! He was still issuing orders from his office as if he was still the CEO. Jared reasoned that it must be very confusing to the executive staff of the D. O. Madison to receive two sets of orders each morning, one set from the new President and one set from the ex-President. It was not very funny, however, if you happened to be on the wrong end of the stick and Dr. Masters was trying his damnest to beat you to death with it.

Dr. Masters was giving it one last try to fire Jared, even though it was not clear at all if he even had the authority any longer to actually go through with terminating a tenured faculty member. Jared returned to his office one afternoon late in the summer of 1996 to find an administrator waiting for him. Jared had seen this tactic before. When Dr. Masters wanted to deliver what he felt was something very important, he had a runner from his office make sure that the document or envelope was hand delivered. Usually the document was stamped "hand delivered" on the top to stress its importance. Jared tore open the letter and excused the 'runner' from Dr. Masters' office so that Dr. Masters would not even learn of Jared's immediate response to his letter.

The letter was quite a bit shorter than the usual letters from Dr. Masters that detailed Jared's alleged deficiencies or articulated the failure in Dr.

Masters' mind of Jared to follow the rules and regulations of the University. Those types of letters were actually quite laughable, because they were so easy to answer with simple facts. Since every administrator that surrounded the egomaniac Dr. Masters was a 'yes person' that would always agree with Dr. Masters or tell Dr. Masters exactly what he wanted to hear, Jared reasoned that Dr. Masters would rant and rave about something, and everyone would agree with him whether it was true or not. They were simply there to receive the wisdom of the President and translate it into a letter, fax or memo, which could then be signed by Dr. Masters. He even had a signature machine so he did not have to waste valuable time in proofreading the pontifications before they were sent out of his office.

The letter that Jared received was basically ridiculous. It claimed that Jared had been 'insubordinate' to the President of the D. O. Madison. The nature of this 'insubordination' was that Jared did not immediately stop his research on the Gulf War Illness patients and Texas prison guards at the whim of Dr. Masters and his henchmen. The letter basically went on to describe Jared's and Marie's research as violating the bounds of decency and trust that were expected of a tenured faculty member of the University. Jared had heard all this before, and it was nonsensical. The research that Jared and Marie were conducting had been approved by the Office of Research, which was the usual procedure at the University for obtaining approval for a research project. The Office of Research had the responsibility to make sure that all other required approvals had been obtained, such as biohazard, recombinate DNA, radioactivity use, etc. If everything was in order, then the project could be approved for outside funding, if an organization could be found to fund the project. Jared had this approval and a signature on the approval sheet. The signature was Dr. Belcher's, Clement Masters' hand-picked Vice President for Research. Therefore, Jared had not been 'insubordinate' when he determined that he had all of the necessary approvals to continue the research project.

After some thought Jared decided that he would respond with a letter answering Dr. Masters allegations to Dr. Moringstone not Dr. Masters, since Dr. Morningstone was the new President of the D. O. Madison Cancer Center, not Dr. Masters. Since Dr. Morningstone had not had the privilege of seeing the previous letters sent by Dr. Masters to Jared, he was planning to include a few of these and his written responses as well. Also, Jared thought that it might be important to have his attorney, Mr. Neeman, send the letter to Dr. Morningstone with a copy to the University attorneys. Thus Jared contacted Mr. Neeman with the letter from Dr. Masters and his responses to the allegations of 'insubordination.'

This time Jared's attorney made it very clear to the University Counsel and Dr. Morningstone that Dr. Masters did not have the authority to fire Jared, because he was no longer the President of the D. O. Madison Cancer Center. In addition, his allegations of 'insubordination' were not listed as justification for removal of tenured faculty members in the Regents Rules and Regulations for faculty at the University. As usual, Dr. Masters was trying to invent some new rule in an effort to fire Jared McNicols without due process or a chance to rebut his allegations. The response of Dr. Morningstone to the 'fight' between Dr. Masters and Jared McNichols was to ignore it completely. In fact, Jared never heard from Dr. Morningstone again.

Since the 'letter of termination' of Dr. Masters to Jared failed, Dr. Masters then attempted to make Jared appear in his office without his attorney, but Jared instead contacted his lawyer and he, in turn, contacted the University Counsel to stop the bogus proceedings. The attorneys for the University probably did not want another lawsuit, and they knew that Jared had many reasons for filing a massive lawsuit against the University and against Dr. Masters and other administrators and faculty members of the Cancer Center.

Just for the tampering of Jared's U. S. Mail alone, certain administrators and faculty could go to prison, and although it might be difficult to prove beyond a reasonable doubt in a criminal court that certain individuals were directly involved and following the orders of Dr. Masters, the same charges in civil court do not have to proved to the standards used in criminal court. The murder attempts on Marie and Jared were likely to be even more difficult to prove without a costly investigation. Several of Jared's colleagues died under mysterious circumstances after taking on Dr. Masters, and Marie and Jared believed strongly that Dr. Masters was a murderer and more, but it would be difficult to prove in a court of law, especially in Texas. Jared even thought about filing a discrimination case in Federal Court, because the State courts in Texas were populated by judges that could be easily manipulated by the University. Jared was constantly reminding Marie that most of the judges in Texas were graduates of the University, so filing a lawsuit in a Texas State court would be a costly mistake.

The McNichols begin the move from Texas

Instead of focusing on the negative experiences that Marie and Jared had lived through in Austin, including the murder attempts and academic and economic harassment that Marie and Jared had endured, Jared wanted them to look forward to their move, hopefully to a new life. They both realized that the Las Vegas organized crime interests and the trustees of the Cetta Dharma Trust and Marie's other trusts would never leave them alone, even after they moved to another state, but it could take them some time to get their fangs into the McNichols as deep as they had in Texas. For some reason the 'can do' and 'anything goes' attitude of the native and transplanted Texans made it easy for financial interests to penetrate into the highest offices in the University. Usually there were checks and balances that prevent such obvious misuse of University administrative structures, but in Texas everything and anything seemed to be fair game. Most 'real' Texans, such as the offspring of the original pioneer families that first colonized Tejas would have been appalled to learn what had happened to the McNichols in Austin.

Since Jared was from California and had family and friends there, it would be more difficult for the trustees, many of them Texans, to attack the McNichols in their new environment. Also, Marie and Jared thought that the Las Vegas boys would find it harder to bribe local officials to harass them. Thus they felt that they had a few years to enjoy their freedom before the trustees and Las Vegas interests caught up with them. They were wrong to assume this, but it did keep their spirits up before their move from Austin.

There were still some important matters to deal with before the actual move from Austin, including Dr. Masters, who had found out that Jared had obtained permission to move his grants and equipment out of the Cancer Center. Fortunately for Jared, Dr. Masters placed the complete blame on Dr. Belcher for the oversight, but in reality there was now nothing that Dr. Masters could do. He no longer had the authority to stop Jared from leaving or to fire him in his office in front of his staff. Dr. Morningstone was apparently finally listening to the University attorneys, and he decided not to intervene to fire Jared on Dr. Masters' behalf.

The McNichols were finally allowed to leave Austin with some dignity and with Jared's grants and equipment. So during their last summer in Austin, Jared and Marie spent more time at home than at the Cancer Center completing the research reports that would eventually translate into several publications on Gulf War Illnesses, chronic infections, cancer and other topics. Along the way Marie and Jared had learned the techniques that spies used to avoid tampering with their mail, such as the dead drop where mail is taken to some random mailbox or Post Office and multiple mail pick-up points, including friends and neighbors. Any mail that came to their residence was re-routed to other locations, and Jared now picked up all his mail at the Post Office to avoid the Department rats that were still working for Dr. Masters. By routing most telephone calls, faxes and other communications to their home in Queenswood, the McNichols avoided most of the problems that they had at the Cancer Center. Marie seemed to enjoy having Jared at home more, even if he spent too much of his time playing with his favorite feline friend, Yang.

Jared and Marie even agreed to do some radio programs from their home, most of which were on the Gulf War Illnesses and other chronic illnesses that seemed to be taking an ever increasing toll on America. If the Cancer Center had found out about these radio interviews, they would have certainly attempted to block them, just as they had been attempting to block Jared's grant applications, publications and invitations to professional meetings.

The Molecular Medicine Institute

Jared and Marie were taking an increasing number of trips to California to set up the newly formed Molecular Medicine Institute, and they found a former Navy and American Airlines pilot that would become the first President and Business Manager. Mr. Beckham was hired mainly on a promise, since the only funds available to start the Institute were Jared's grants and personal funds of the McNichols. During the honeymoon period of the Molecular Medicine Institute the new President Mr. Charles Beckham proved to be capable and a good worker. Although Mr. Beckham would later succumb to the grasp of Marie's trustees and Las Vegas crime interests and turn on the McNichols, at this point in time he was an enthusiastic partner in the new venture. A building was found that was formally used by a large scientific instrument company as a small R & D facility, and this proved to be the ideal size for a small, new research institute. There was even a treasure trove of equipment left behind by the scientific instrument company, and some of the heavy, expensive items like chemical fume hoods, laminar flow biological cabinets and laboratory benches were purchased for a small fraction of their replacement costs. Jared often traveled back and forth between Austin and Southern California, and Marie was also spending more time in their ocean condo.

When the time came for the move from Austin, there would be a facility ready to receive the equipment and supplies that Jared had accumulated over the years. Some of Jared's post-doctoral fellows would also be making the move to California, so there would be some staff available to continue the progress made in Austin. Although any move can be disruptive, the McNichols looked forward to the time when they could actually conduct their research free of interference and harassment.

Since Jared was generally prevented from talking to the press while in Austin, there were numerous reporters who wanted interviews with the McNichols to learn about their progress with Gulf War Illnesses. Also, Marie and Jared testified to Congress, the House of Representatives Committee on Government Reform and Oversight, and Jared testified to the President's Commission on Gulf War Veterans' Illnesses, and they had lectured to the Department of Defense and Department of Veterans' Affairs. Thus various reporters had heard about or had seen some of these presentations and now wanted to write articles on the McNichols' research.

The new Institute welcomed the press, because it served as a vehicle to obtain donations to continue the research begun in Austin. In fact, the Institute received many small donations from veterans and their family members, prison employees and even ex-prisoners who wanted to help in the efforts to expose the questionable programs instituted by the U. S. Government to test weapons that were developed secretly and financed directly or indirectly by the Cetta Dharma Trust, the Sterling Trust, Five Start Trust and other trusts. But the Institute did not receive the major financial support that the McNichols expected.

Over the years a few individuals had contacted the McNichols with proposals for funding. Most of these proved to be completely bogus, and Jared and Marie thought that they just wanted to learn exactly what the McNichols had found out in their investigations on Gulf War Illnesses and other topics, such as the infections found in prison guards. However, some of these financial people seemed legitimate, and they indicated that once the nonprofit Molecular Medicine Institute was formed, its status would allow entry into the world of high-yield investment programs. Financial people who one way or another made contact with the McNichols stressed that the nature of what the McNichols were doing for the general public and the military and the nonprofit status of their Institute under the Federal Tax Laws would enable them to find partners who would put up the funds necessary to enter the high-yield investment programs controlled by the Federal Reserve and the Treasury Department. Such programs were very attractive to the McNichols and their Institute, and Marie and Jared spent an unbelievable amount of time trying to arrange for the Institute to be a part of the high-yield investment programs. However, in the end for one reason or another usually related to the Cetta Dharma Trust and the other trusts and their evil trustees, they were prevented at the last minute from any financial benefits from the investment programs. The Institute would have to survive on grants and contracts and some small donations. Stable funding for the Institute was at the moment out of the question, but the Institute did manage to survive and continue its important work.

At the Texas border

Jared barely survived in his position to see the end of Dr. Masters and his era of fear and brutality at the D. O. Madison Cancer Center, and Clement Masters was finally formally retired with much fan-fare and celebrations. However, the McNichols did not attend any of the festivities, nor did many of the other dozens of faculty members that had been ruined or even destroyed by Dr. Masters. The evil master had finally been deposed, but Jared and Marie did not plan to wait around in Austin to see if justice would finally be served. They were leaving Texas for good, finally to be rid of the horror that they were subjected to by the University and the Trusts that virtually owned the Cancer Center due to their loans to the University for Dr. Masters' obscene building program.

The McNichols' saga would not end with their departure from Texas, but it was the end of a very unpleasant chapter in their lives, one that they would rather forget than dwell upon. By giving up his endowed chair and tenured professorship, Jared lost millions of dollars in salary, retirement and other benefits from the incident, but at least they would be free, or so they thought. Lurking behind the scenes were Marie's trustees and the Las Vegas organized crime interests, and they would not rest until the McNichols were destroyed once and for all. But for the time being Marie and Jared were quite happy to be leaving Texas and the unpleasant memories of their struggles against a university that was bent on destroying them.

When the time came to pack up their belongings and head West, Marie and Jared left most of their move to the professionals who specialize in such things. They filled up Jared's truck with some of their personal effects and with Ying and Yang jumping around the cab of the pick-up, they took off for El Paso and the Texas border. It was early, well before sunrise when they reached I-10 and headed West. With the cover on the back of the pick-up flapping in the wind, Jared and Marie continued through a dozen towns with names like Ozona, Fort Stockton, Van Horn and finally El Paso. As they passed through El Paso with the rail yards and finally the Rio Grande River to their left, they continued on to the New Mexico border. Then they saw it, the Texas border loomed just ahead. As Jared, Marie, Yin and Yang passed over the border, Jared let out a whoop. They had survived the last several years and lived to tell their tale. Jared pulled into the New Mexico tourist bureau center along I-10. Leaving Yin and Yang in the truck, Marie and Jared jumped and hugged each other and finally embraced in a long kiss. Jared swung Marie around just like the day he proposed to her in Queenswood some years back. They had survived their Texas ordeal to fight another day. And that day would come sooner than they thought, but at least for now they rejoiced in the little victory of survival that day at the Texas border.

EPILOGUE

The Struggle Continues

After the McNichols left the D. O. Madison Cancer Center at the end of August 1996, Jared's department was indeed split up and the faculty scattered. Instead of giving half of the department to Dr. Isaac Geldter and half to Dr. Amy Krappner, as was planned by Dr. Masters, Dr. Moringstone decided to elevate Dr. Krappner to Vice President for Academic Affairs and allow a few of Jared's former faculty to form a new department around the molecular biology of cancer. Dr. Hong, who refused to be assigned to a department under Dr. Geldter's control, would be the new chairman of this department, which would remain physically in the same location and have some the best and brightest young Madison faculty as its new members. Interestingly, the members of Jared's old department that worked so hard to see Jared removed from his chairmanship now had the tyrant Isaac Geldter as their new chairman, and they found themselves in a much worse political situation than they ever were in under Jared's departmental administration. Most of these faculty and staff would be forced to move to the M. K. Black Building away from the main Cancer Center facilities. Jared noted that these were just rewards for some of his former faculty.

As for Dr. Krappner becoming Vice President for Academic Affairs, Jared just laughed when he discussed the topic with Marie, but Marie did not laugh at all. Any institution that would elevate a mediocre scientist like Dr. Krappner to a Vice President in charge of evaluating academic credentials deserved to go down. Dr. Krappner, who was prevented by the prestigious NIH from serving on any of their committees because of improprieties while she was a reviewer for NIH, was exactly the wrong type of person to be the head academic at the largest cancer center in the world. Although Dr. Krappner had been agitating the State and the University for years to elevate more women to senior positions at The D. O. Madison, no one ever considered *her* academic credentials noteworthy or indicative of an appropriate candidate for Vice President for Academic Affairs. Dr. Krappner was just another example of the Peter Principal at work.

Other faculty members at the Madison also benefited from Dr. Masters' regime. Dr. Domasovitch received his reward from the institution and was made an Assistant Vice President for Education at a much higher salary. His dormant laboratory was closed, and he moved to the Administration Building. He now worked directly under Dr. Krappner, mainly shuffling paperwork and organizing educational courses and committees for the graduate school. Dr. Nosan received a promotion to Assistant Vice President for Cancer Prevention, a newly created position that apparently had little or no administrative responsibilities but came with a nice salary increase. Dr. Belcher decided to retire as did several other Vice Presidents at the Cancer Center, and they joined Dr. Clement Masters as emeritus members of the faculty with fat retirement packages.

With Dr. Masters' power and influence in rapid decline, he eventually left the Cancer Center and Austin to become a more normal retiree. Interestingly, he was rarely seen or heard of at the Medical Center after his retirement. When Dr. Masters was at his zenith of power, he was one of the most feared administers in Austin. Without his powerbase, Dr. Masters was nothing but a pathetic ex-President who rarely dared to show his face among the faculty that he had terrorized.

The murder of Dr. Fred Cannon was never solved. Nor were the deaths of other five colleagues of the McNichols that died under mysterious circumstances at the D. O. Madison Cancer Center. They were the casualties of a secret war waged against the American people by a small handful of dangerous scientists and bureaucrats who would stop at nothing, including cold-blooded murder, to hide their traitorous acts.

Marie and Jared continued their battle for veterans' health and benefit rights. However, they were thwarted at every turn by an unmovable government bureaucracy. Various Senators and Congressmen were sympathetic to their efforts, and they continued testifying to various Congressional Committees on veterans' health issues and Gulf War Illnesses, and they also continued publishing on the bacterial agents found in veterans' blood. However, they could not seem to move the Department of Defense or Department of Veterans' Affairs. The same people that started the problem in the first place were still in control in these huge bureaucracies, and they resisted any efforts to change or reform the system. In fact, some of the worst individuals who were involved in the illegal experimentation on military recruits and prisoners were placed in control of programs that were established to help the veterans. Although the DoD along with the VA actually conducted a clinical trial based on Jared's and Marie's work with the Gulf War veterans, they then sabotaged the clinical trial after the initial results looked too promising (and embarrassing). Marie and Jared decided that they could not work with the Government on these issues, at least for the time being, because they had too much to hide from the public, and they were prone to go after any scientist or physician that dared to disagree with them.

One small consolation was that the McNichols did receive the endorsement of many members of the U. S. Congress and the Commanding General of Allied forces in the Gulf War. Despite all the sabotage, the website of the Molecular Medicine Institute became the number one site in the world for inquiries about molecular medicine and chronic illnesses. Retired three star generals and active members of the Pentagon's Command and Control Center would join their advisory staff.

The main source of Marie's and Jared's problems remained the trustees of the Cetta Dharma Trust, the Sterling Trust, the Century Trust, the Five Star Trust and several other trusts that were being held off-ledger at major banks and illegally kept from Marie as well as the criminal elements in Las Vegas that also held onto Marie's assets. Even though they had moved to California, which removed the McNichols, so they thought, from the grip of the Texas trustees, the long hand of the trustees and the Las Vegas interests still plagued the McNichols. The trustees and especially the Las Vegas organized crime interests and their armaments and weapons companies had promised to kill Marie if she made a claim on her inheritance, but it was only a matter of time until Marie would learn to make use of U. S. Government agencies to confront the trustees and the crime bosses in Las Vegas. Even with the backing of the U. S. Government, the McNichols still found that the vicious scientists and bureaucrats that went after them and were still going after them were all financed by Marie's trusts or by the Las Vegas crime interests.

With the passage of the Patriot Act it was now possible to penetrate the trusts, because the assets could no longer be used without the consent of the true owner of the funds. The trusts were to have been turned over to Marie according to her father's will, and although Marie was still unable to access the trusts, the trustees and their legions of unethical attorneys had failed to break the terms of the trusts. Of course, none of these trustees thought that Marie would ever survive to actually claim her trusts. Until Marie with the assistance of the U. S. Government can claim her rightful inheritance in its entirety, the illegal and immoral programs that had been financed by Marie's trusts and by Las Vegas financial interests will continue to take their toll on the American people. The illegal use of Marie's assets also had inadvertently paved the way for terrorists' justifications in attacking the United States, and Marie and Jared would eventually find out that these terrorist groups had actually used some of Marie's trust funds and Las Vegas assets to finance global terrorism. Marie learned that she must work with the U. S. Government, at least the parts of the government that could not be bought off by her trustees, to insure that her massive empire would be used for humanitarian purposes and to the benefit of the people of the world and never again used to finance terrorism like the deeds of September 11th and unconventional weapons development and testing.

APPENDIX 1

ABOUT THE AUTHORS

Garth L. Nicolson, Ph.D.

Professor Garth L. Nicolson is the President, Chief Scientific Officer and Research Professor at the Institute for Molecular Medicine in Huntington Beach, California. Born in 1943 in Los Angeles, Dr. Nicolson received his B.S. in Chemistry from University of California at Los Angeles in 1965 and his Ph.D. in Biochemistry and Cell Biology from the University of California at San Diego in 1970. He is currently Professor of Integrative Medicine at Capitol University of Integrative Medicine and a Conjoint Professor at the University of Newcastle (Australia). He was formally the David Bruton Jr. Chair in Cancer Research and Professor and Chairman of the Department of Tumor Biology at the University of Texas M. D. Anderson Cancer Center in Houston, and he was Professor of Internal Medicine and Professor of Pathology and Laboratory Medicine at the University of Texas Medical School at Houston. He was also Professor of Comparative Pathology at Texas A & M University. Among the most cited scientists in the world, Professor Nicolson has published over 550 medical and scientific papers (including 3 *Current Contents* Citation Classics), edited 14 books, served on the Editorial Boards of 20 medical and scientific journals and is currently serving as Editor of two (*Clinical & Experimental Metastasis* and the *Journal of Cellular Biochemistry*). Professor Nicolson has received peer-reviewed research grants from the U. S. Army, National Cancer Institute, National Institutes of Health, American Cancer Society and the National Foundation for Cancer Research. Dr. Garth Nicolson has won many awards, such as the Burroughs Wellcome Medal of the Royal Society of Medicine (United

Kingdom), Stephen Paget Award of the Metastasis Research Society, the U. S. National Cancer Institute Outstanding Investigator Award, and the Innovative Medicine Award of Canada. He is also a Colonel (Honorary) of the U. S. Army Special Forces and a U. S. Navy SEAL (Honorary) for his work on Armed Forces and veterans' illnesses.

Nancy L. Nicolson, Ph.D.

Nancy L. Nicolson is the Chairman of the Board and Chief Executive Officer of The Institute for Molecular Medicine in Huntington Beach, California. She is also the President of the Rhodon Foundation for Biomedical Research, Inc. Dr. Nancy Nicolson was born in New York in 1953 and received her B.A. in Physics from Johns Hopkins University in 1975 and her Ph.D. in Molecular Biophysics from the Institute of Molecular Biophysics at Florida State University in 1982. She was formerly on the faculty at the Baylor College of Medicine in Houston, Texas and is currently a Conjoint Lecturer at the University of Newcastle (Australia). Dr. Nicolson has published over 50 medical and scientific papers, and she has delivered over 60 international and national scientific presentations. Dr. Nancy Nicolson won the Harold Lampart Award from the Biophysical Society and was the Who's Who in the World International Women of the Year for 1996-97. In 2000 she was named in the Wall Street Journal as Businesswomen of the Year, and in 2003 she was awarded the U.S. Congressional Business Medal of Honor. She was also named the Up and Coming CEO in Who's Who in American Executives, and she was chosen as among the 500 Most Notable Women of Twentieth Century. Recently Dr. Nicolson was appointed the Secretary General of the United Nations Cultural Convention. She is also a Colonel (Honorary) of the U. S. Army Special Forces and a U. S. Navy SEAL (Honorary) for her work on Armed Forces and veterans' illnesses. Dr. Nicolson is currently working with the U. S. Government to recover her assets and trusts that have been held and used illegally.

APPENDIX 2

WRITTEN TESTIMONY OF
Dr. Garth L. Nicolson
COMMITTEE ON VETERANS' AFFAIRS
Subcommittee on Health
UNITED STATES HOUSE OF REPRESENTATIVES

January 24, 2002

Dr. Garth Nicolson is currently the President, Chief Scientific Officer and Research Professor at the Institute for Molecular Medicine in Huntington Beach, California. He was formally the David Bruton Jr. Chair in Cancer Research, Professor and Chairman at the University of Texas M. D. Anderson Cancer Center in Houston, and Professor of Internal Medicine and Professor of Pathology and Laboratory Medicine at the University of Texas Medical School at Houston. He was also Adjunct Professor of Comparative Medicine at Texas A & M University. Among the most cited scientists in the world, having published over 520 medical and scientific papers, edited 14 books, served on the Editorial Boards of 20 medical and scientific journals, including the *Journal of Chronic Fatigue Syndrome*, and currently serving as Editor of two (*Clinical & Experimental Metastasis* and the *Journal of Cellular Biochemistry*), Professor Nicolson has held numerous peer-reviewed research grants. He was a recipient of the Burroughs Wellcome Medal of the Royal Society of Medicine, Stephen Paget Award of the Metastasis Research Society and the U. S. National Cancer Institute Outstanding Investigator Award.

The most important question that this committee must ask is whether the United States military health system failed in its important mission of Force

Protection before, during and after the Gulf War. I believe strongly that it did, and the reason for this failure must be determined in order to better treat the chronic illnesses displayed by over 100,000 U.S. veterans of the Gulf War, including in some cases their immediate family members [1,2], and to prevent history from repeating itself.

First, there is the issue of the initial denial the Gulf War veterans were ill in numbers more than expected for a deployed population of approximately 600,000 men and women. This has now been conclusively shown, and the data indicate that there are much higher prevalence rates of Gulf War Illnesses (GWI) in deployed than in non-deployed forces [2-4]. Case control studies of Gulf War veterans showed higher symptom prevalence in deployed than in non-deployed personnel from the same units [5,6]. For certain signs and symptoms, this difference was dramatic (some over 13-times greater than in the non-deployed group [6]). Steele [7] showed that in three studies, Gulf War-deployed forces had excess rates of GWI symptom patterns, indicating beyond a doubt that GWI is associated with deployment to the Gulf War.

Second, since it is now clear that the Gulf War produced casualties beyond those expected, it is important to determine what caused these casualties so that preventive measures can be employed to prevent this from occurring in future conflicts. An important corollary of this is that illnesses that occur in deployed personnel must be prevented from spreading to civilians [7]. We believe that GWI is caused by accumulated toxic insults (chemical, biological and in some cases radiological [1-4,8]) that result in chronic illnesses with relatively nonspecific signs and symptoms [2-8,10]. Unfortunately, some of these illnesses are apparently transmittable and can be passed to family members [9,10] and possibly to the general public.

Post-Traumatic Stress Disorder and Obtaining a Diagnosis of GWI

For years the Departments of Defense (DoD) and Veterans' affairs (DVA) promoted the notion that Post-Traumatic Stress Disorder (PTSD) was a major factor in GWI [11]. Most researchers doubt that stress is a major cause of GWI [5,7-10], and it certainly does not explain how some immediate family members presented after the war with the same signs and symptoms

[9,12]. Psychiatrists who have studied GWI do not believe that most GWI is explainable as PTSD [13], and researchers studying GWI find that it differs from PTSD, depression, somatoform disorder and malingering [8-10,14]. Although most GWI patients do not appear to have PTSD, they are often placed in this diagnosis category by DoD and DVA physicians. GWI can be diagnosed within ICD-10-coded diagnosis categories, such as fatiguing illness (G93.3), but they often receive a diagnosis of 'unknown illness.' This, unfortunately, results in their receiving reduced disability assessments and benefits and essentially little or no effective treatments because they don't fit within the military's or DVA's diagnosis systems. In addition, many active-duty members of the Armed Forces are hesitant to admit that they have GWI, because they feel strongly that it will hurt their careers or result in their being medically discharged. Officers that we have assisted eventually retired or resigned their commissions because of imposed limits to their careers [9].

In the absence of contrary laboratory findings, some physicians feel that GWI is a somatoform disorder caused by stress, instead of organic or medical problems that can be treated with medicines or treatments not used for PTSD or other somatoform disorders [9,14]. The evidence offered as proof that stress or PTSD is the source of most GWI is the assumption that veterans were in a stressful environment during the Gulf War [9,10]. However, most GWI patients feel that PTSD is not an accurate diagnosis of their illnesses, and testimony to the House of Representatives questions the notion that stress is the major cause of GWI [15,16]. The GAO has concluded that while stress can induce some physical illness, it is not established as a major cause of GWI [17]. Although stress can exacerbate chronic illnesses and suppress immune systems, most officers that we interviewed indicated that the Gulf War was not a particularly stressful war, and they strongly disagreed that stress was the origin of their illnesses [18]. However, in the absence of physical or laboratory tests that can identify possible origins of GWI, many physicians accept that stress is the cause [15,16]. The arthralgias, fatigue, memory loss, rashes and diarrhea found in GWI patients are nonspecific and often apparently lack a physical cause [19], but this may simply be the result of inadequate workup and lack of availability of routine tests that could define the underlying organic etiologies [4-9].

We have been trying for years to get the DoD and DVA to acknowledge that different exposures can result in quite different illnesses, even though signs and symptoms profiles may overlap [14,18]. Illness clusters similar to GWI can be found in non-Gulf War veterans deployed to Bosnia [7]. Although such epidemiological analyses have been criticized on the basis of self-reporting and self-selection [19], it remains important to characterize signs and symptoms and identify exposures of Gulf War veterans in order to find effective treatments for specific subsets of GWI patients [14,15,18,20]. Our contention is that GWI patients that suffer from chemical, biological or radiological exposures should receive different treatments based on their exposures [2,4,8,10].

Patients with GWI can have 20-40 or more chronic signs and symptoms [1-6,8]. Civilian patients with similar signs and symptoms are usually diagnosed with Chronic Fatigue Syndrome (CFS), Fibromyalgia Syndrome (FMS) or Multiple Chemical Sensitivity Syndrome (MCS) [9,10]. Although clear-cut laboratory tests on GWI, CFS and FMS are not yet available, some tests that have been used in recent years for GWI are not consistent with a psychiatric origin for GWI [20-26]. These results argue against a purely somatoform disorder.

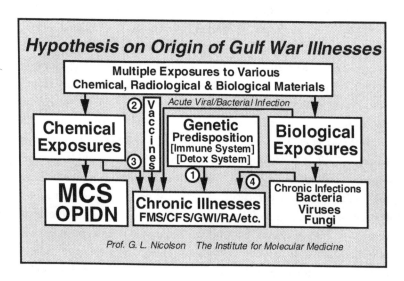

Figure 1. Hypothesis on how multiple toxic exposures, including multiple vaccines (2), chemical (3), radiological and biological (4) exposures, may have resulted in GWI in predisposed, susceptible individuals (1) (modified from Nicolson *et al.* [10]).

Chemical Exposures During the Gulf War

During the Gulf War personnel may have been exposed to chemical substances that could be the underlying causes of their illnesses [2,4,9,10]. Gulf War veterans were exposed to a variety of chemicals, including insecticides, such as the insect repellent N,N-dimethyl-m-toluamide, the insecticide permethrin and other organophosphates, fumes and smoke from burning oil wells, the anti-nerve agent pyridostigmine bromide, solvents used to clean equipment and a variety of other chemicals, including in some cases, possible exposures to low levels of Chemical Warfare (CW) agents [6-8]. Some CW exposure may have occurred because of destruction of CW stores in factories and storage bunkers during and after the war as well as possible offensive use of CW agents [27]. Although some former DoD physicians feel that there was no credible evidence for CW exposure [19], many veterans have been notified by the DoD of possible CW exposures.

Exposures to mixtures of toxic chemicals can result in chronic illnesses, even if the exposures were at low-levels [20,21,28,29]. Such exposures can cause a wide variety of signs and symptoms, including chronic neurotoxicity and immune supression. Combinations of pyridostigmine bromide, N,N-dimethyl-m-toluamide and permethrin produce neurotoxicity, diarrhea, salivation, shortness of breath, locomotor dysfunctions, tremors, and other impairments in healthy adult hens [28]. Although low levels of individual organophosphate chemicals may not cause signs and symptoms in exposed, non-deployed civilian workers [30], this does not negate a causal role of multiple chemical exposures in causing chronic illnesses such as GWI. Organophosphate-Induced Delayed Neurotoxicity (OPIDN) [31] is an example of chronic illness that may be caused by multiple, low level chemical exposures (Figure 1) [10]. Multiple Chemical Sensitivity Syndrome (MCS) has also been proposed to result from multiple low level chemical exposures [32]. These syndromes can present with many of the signs and symptoms found in GWI patients, and many GWI cases may eventually be explained by complex chemical exposures.

In chemically exposed GWI patients, memory loss, headaches, cognitive problems, severe depression, loss of concentration, vision and balance problems and chemical sensitivities, among others, typify the types of signs and symptoms characteristic of organophosphate exposures. Arguments have been advanced by former military physicians that such exposures do not explain GWI, or that they may only be useful for a small subset of GWI patients [19]. These arguments for the most part are based on the effects of single agent exposures, not the multiple, complex exposures that were encountered by Gulf War veterans [33]. The onset of signs and symptoms of GWI for most patients was between six months and two years or more after the end of the war. Such slow onset of clinical signs and symptoms in chemically exposed individuals is not unusual for OPIDN [34]. Since low-level exposure to organophosphates was common in U.S. veterans, the appearance of delayed, chronic signs and symptoms similar to OPIDN could have been caused by multiple low-level exposures to pesticides, nerve agents, anti-nerve agents and/or other organophosphates, especially in certain subsets of GWI patients.

Radiological Exposures and GWI

Depleted uranium (DU) was used extensively in the Gulf War, and it remains an important battlefield contaminant. When a DU penetrator hits an armored target, it ignites, and between 10% and 70% of the shell aerosolizes, forming uranium oxide particles [35]. The particles that form are usually small (less than 5 µm in diameter) and due to their high density settle quickly onto vehicles, bunkers and the surrounding sand, where they can be easily inhaled, ingested or re-aerosolized. Following contamination, the organs where DU can be found include the lungs and regional lymph nodes, kidney and bone. However, the Armed Forces Radiological Research Institute (AFRRI) also found DU in blood, liver, spleen and brain of rats injected with DU pellets [36]. Studies on DU carriage should be initiated as soon as possible to determine the prevalence of contamination, and extent of body stores of uranium and other radioactive heavy metals [10]. Procedures have been developed for analysis of DU metal fragments [37] and DU in urine [38]. However, urine testing does not detect uranium in all body sites [36]. So far, analysis of DU-contaminated Gulf War veterans has not shown them to have severe signs and symptoms of GWI [38], but few Gulf War veterans have been studied for DU contamination.

Other Environmental Exposures and GWI

In addition to chemical exposures, soldiers were exposed to burning oil well fires and ruptured petroleum pipelines as well as fine, blowing sand. The small size of sand particles (much less than 0.1 mm) and the relatively constant winds in the region probably resulted in some sand inhalation. The presence of small sand particles deep in the lungs can produce a pulmonary inflammatory disorder that can progress to pneumonitis or Al-Eskan Disease [39]. Al-Eskan disease, characterized by reactive airways, usually presents as a pneumonitis that can eventually progress to pulmonary fibrosis, and possibly immunosuppression followed by opportunistic infections. Although it is doubtful that many GWI patients have Al-Eskan Disease, the presence of silica-induced immune suppression in some soldiers could have contributed to persisting opportunistic infections in these patients.

Biological Exposures and GWI

The variable incubation times, ranging from months to years after presumed exposure, the cyclic nature of the relapsing fevers and other signs and symptoms, and the types of signs and symptoms of GWI are consistent with diseases caused by combinations of biological and/or chemical or radiological agents (Figure 1) [1,10]. System-wide or systemic chemical insults and/or chronic infections that can penetrate various tissues and organs, including the Central and Peripheral Nervous Systems, are important in GWI [1-5,10]. When such infections occur, they can cause the complex signs and symptoms seen in CFS, FMS and GWI, including immune dysfunction. Changes in environmental responses as well as increased titers to various endogenous viruses that are commonly expressed in these patients have been seen in CFS, FMS and GWI. Few infections can produce the complex chronic signs and symptoms found in these patients; however, the types of infection caused by *Mycoplasma* and *Brucella* species that have been found in GWI patients, can cause complex problems found in GWI [reviews: 23,40,41]. These microorganisms are now considered important emerging pathogens in causing chronic diseases as well as being important cofactors in some illnesses, including AIDS and other immune dysfunctional conditions [23,40,41].

Evidence for infectious agents has been found in GWI patients' urine [4] and blood [12,24,41-44]. We [12,24,41-43] and others [44] have found that most of the signs and symptoms in a large subset of GWI patients can be explained by chronic pathogenic bacterial infections, such as *Mycoplasma* and *Brucella* infections. In studies of over 1,500 U. S. and British veterans with GWI, approximately 40-50% of GWI patients have PCR evidence of such infections, compared to 6-9% in the non-deployed, healthy population [review: 23]. This has been confirmed in a large study of 1,600 veterans at over 30 DVA and DoD medical centers (VA Cooperative Clinical Study Program #475). Historically, mycoplasmal infections were thought to produce relatively mild diseases limited to particular tissues or organs, such as urinary tract or respiratory system [23,40,41]. However, the mycoplasmas detected in GWI patients with molecular techniques are highly virulent, colonize a wide variety of organs and tissues, and are difficult to treat [23,45,46]. The mycoplasma most commonly detected in GWI, *Mycoplasma fermentans* (found in >80% of those GWI patients positive for any mycoplasma), is found intracellularly. It is unlikely that this type of infection will result in a strong antibody response, which may explain the DoD's lack of serologic evidence for these types of intracellular infections [47].

When civilian patients with CSF or FMS were similarly examined for systemic mycoplasmal infections 50-60% of these patients were positive, indicating another link between these disorders and GWI [23]. In contrast to GWI, however, several species of mycoplasmas other than *M. fermentans* were found in higher percentages of CSF/ME and FMS patients [48,49].

GWI can Spread to Immediate Family Members

During the last year we have documented the spread of GWI infections to immediate family members [12]. According to one U. S. Senate study [50], GWI has spread to family members, and it is likely that it has also spread in the workplace [18]. Although the official position of the DoD/

DVA is that family members have not contracted GWI, these studies [12,50] indicate that at least a subset of GWI patients have a transmittable illness. Laboratory tests revealed that GWI family members have the same chronic infections [12] that have been found in ~40% of the ill veterans [42-44]. We examined military families (149 patients; 42 veterans, 40 spouses, 32 other relatives and 35 children) with at least one family complaint of illness) selected from a group of 110 veterans with GWI who tested positive (~41% overall) for mycoplasmal infections. Consistent with previous results, over 80% of GWI patients who were positive for blood mycoplasmal infections had only one *Mycoplasma* species, *M. fermentans*. In healthy control subjects the incidence of mycoplasmal infection was 7%, several mycoplasma species were found, and none were found to have multiple mycoplasmal species ($P<0.001$). In 107 family members of GWI patients with a positive test for mycoplasma, there were 57 patients (53%) that had essentially the same signs and symptoms as the veterans and were diagnosed with CFS or FMS. Most of these patients also had mycoplasmal infections compared to non-symptomatic family members ($P<0.001$). The most common species found in CFS patients in the same families as GWI patients was *M. fermentans*, the same infection found in the GWI patients. The most likely conclusion is that certain subsets of GWI can transmit their illness and airborne infections to immediate family members [12].

As chronic illnesses like GWI (and in some cases CFS and FMS) progress, there are a number of accompanying clinical problems, particularly autoimmune signs/symptoms, such as those seen in Multiple Sclerosis (MS), Amyotrophic Lateral Sclerosis (ALS or Lew Gehrig's Disease, see below), Lupus, Graves' Disease, Arthritis and other complex autoimmune diseases mycoplasmal infections can penetrate into nerve cells, synovial cells and other cell types [40,41]. The autoimmune signs and symptoms can be caused when intracellular pathogens, such as mycoplasmas, escape from cellular compartments and stimulate the host's immune system. Microorganisms like mycoplasmas can incorporate into their own structures pieces of host cell membranes that contain important host membrane antigens that can trigger autoimmune responses or their surface antigens may be similar to normal cell surface antigens. Thus patients with such infections may have unusual autoimmune signs and symptoms.

Involvement of Infections in Gulf War Veterans with ALS

Amyotrophic Lateral Sclerosis (ALS) is an adult-onset, idopathic, progressive degenerative disease affecting both central and peripheral motor neurons. Patients with ALS show gradual progressive weakness and paralysis of muscles due to destruction of upper motor neurons in the motor cortex and lower motor neurons in the brain stem and spinal cord, ultimately resulting in death, usually by respiratory failure [51]. Gulf War veterans show at least twice the expected incidence of ALS.

We have recently investigated the presence of systemic mycoplasmal infections in the blood of Gulf War veterans and civilians with ALS [52]. Almost all ALS patients (~83%, including 100% of Gulf War veterans with ALS) showed evidence of *Mycoplasma* species in blood samples. All Gulf War veterans with ALS were positive for *M. fermentans*, except one that was positive for *M. genitalium*. In contrast, the 22/28 civilians with detectable mycoplasmal infections had *M. fermentans* (59%) as well as other *Mycoplasama* species in their blood, and two of the civilian ALS patients had multiple mycoplasma species. Of the few control patients that were positive, only two patients (2.8%) were positive for *M. fermentans* (*P*<0.001). The results support the suggestion that infectious agents may play a role in the pathogenesis and/or progression of ALS, or alternatively ALS patients are extremely susceptible to systemic mycoplasmal infections [52]. In the GWI patients mycoplasmal infections may have increased their susceptibility to ALS, which may explain the recent VA studies showing that there is an increased risk of ALS in Gulf War veterans.

Successful Treatment of GWI Mycoplasmal Infections

We have found that mycoplasmal infections in GWI, CFS, FMS and RA can be successfully treated with multiple courses of specific antibiotics, such as doxycycline, ciprofloxacin, azithromycin, clarithromycin or minocycline [45,46,53-55], along with other nutritional recommendations. Multiple treatment cycles are required, and patients relapse often after the first few cycles, but subsequent relapses are milder and most patients eventually recover [42,43]. GWI patients who recovered from their illness after several (3-7) 6-week cycles of antibiotic therapy were retested for mycoplasmal infection and were found to have reverted to a mycoplasma-negative phenotype [42,43]. The therapy takes a long time because of the microorganisms involved are slow-growing and are localized deep inside cells in tissues, where it is more difficult to achieve proper antibiotic therapeutic concentrations. Although anti-inflammatory drugs can alleviate some of the signs and symptoms of GWI, they quickly return after discontinuing drug use. If the effect was due to an anti-inflammatory action of the antibiotics, then the antibiotics would have to be continuously applied and they would be expected to eliminate only some of the signs and symptoms of GWI. In addition, not all antibiotics, even those that have anti-inflammatory effects, appear to work. Only the types of antibiotics that are known to be effective against mycoplasmas are effective; most have no effect at all, and some antibiotics make the condition worse. Thus the antibiotic therapy does not appear to be a placebo effect, because only a few types of antibiotics are effective and some, like penicillin, make the condition worse. We also believe that this type of infection is immune-suppressing and can lead to other opportunistic infections by viruses and other microorganisms or increases in endogenous virus titers. We have also found *Brucella* infections in GWI patients but we have not examined enough patients to establish a prevalence rate among veterans with GWI.

The true percentage of mycoplasma-positive GWI patients overall is likely to be somewhat lower than found in our studies (41-45%) [12,42,43] and those published by others (~50%) [44]. This is reasonable, since GWI patients that have come to us for assistance are probably more advanced patients (with more progressed disease) than the average patient. Our diagnostic results have been confirmed in a large study DVA/DoD study (~40% positive for mycoplasmal infections, VA Cooperative Clinical Study Program #475). This DVA study is a controlled clinical trial that will test the usefulness of antibiotic treatment of mycoplasma-positive GWI patients. This clinical trial is based completely on our research and publications on the diagnosis and treatment of chronic infections in GWI patients [42,43,53-55]. This clinical trial is complete but the treatment results have not yet been analyzed. There is a major concern that the DoD/DVA will not be forthcoming about this trial.

Vaccines Given During Deployment and GWI

A possible source for immune disturbances and chronic infections found in GWI patients is the multiple vaccines that were administered close together around the time of deployment to the Gulf War. Unwin et al. [5] and Cherry et al. [56] found a strong association between GWI and the multiple vaccines that were administered to British Gulf War veterans. Unwin et al. [5] and Goss Gilroy [57] also noted an association specifically with anthrax vaccine and GWI symptoms in British and Canadian veterans. Steele [7] found a three-fold increased incidence of GWI in *nondeployed* veterans from Kansas who had been vaccinated in preparation for deployment, compared to non-deployed, non-vaccinated veterans. Finally, Mahan et al. [58] found a two-fold increased incidence of GWI symptoms in U.S. veterans who recalled they had received anthrax vaccinations at the time of the Gulf War, versus those who thought they had not. These studies associate GWI with the multiple vaccines given during deployment, and they may explain the high prevalence rates of chronic infections in GWI patients [59,60].

GWI signs and symptoms have developed in Armed Forces personnel who recently received the anthrax vaccine. On some military bases this has resulted in chronic illnesses in as many as 7-10% of personnel receiving the vaccine [60]. The chronic signs and symptoms associated with anthrax vaccination are similar, if not identical, to those found in GWI patients, suggesting that at least some of the chronic illnesses suffered by veterans of the Gulf War were caused by military vaccines [59,60]. Undetectable microorganism contaminants in vaccines could have resulted in illness, and may have been more likely to do so in those with compromised immune systems. This could include individuals with DU or chemical exposures, or personnel who received multiple vaccines in a short period of time. Since contamination with mycoplasmas has been found in commercial vaccines [61], the vaccines used in the Gulf War should be considered as a possible source of the chronic infections found in GWI. Some of these vaccines, such as the filtered, cold-stored anthrax vaccine are prime suspects in GWI, because they could be easily contaminated with mycoplasmal infections and other microorganisms [62].

Inadequate Responses of the DoD and DVA to GWI

In general, the response of the DoD and DVA to the GWI problem has been inadequate, and it continues to be inadequate. This response started with denial that there were illnesses associated with service in the Gulf War, it has continued with denial that what we (biological exposures) and others (chemical exposures) have found in GWI patients are important in the diagnosis and treatment of GWI, and it continues today with the denial that military vaccines could be a major source of GWI. For example, in response to our publications and formal lectures at the DoD (1994 and 1996) and DVA (1995), the DoD stated in letters to various members of Congress and to the press that *M. fermentans* infections are commonly found, not dangerous and not even a human pathogen, and our results have not been duplicated by other laboratories. These statements were completely false. The Uniformed Services University of the Health Sciences taught its medical students for years that this type of infection is very dangerous and can progress to system-wide organ failure and death [63]. In addition, the Armed Forces Institute of Pathology (AFIP) has been publishing for years that this type of infection can result in death in nonhuman primates [64] and in man [65]. The AFIP has also suggested treating patients with this type of infection with doxycycline [66], which is one of the antibiotics that we have recommended [53-55]. Interestingly, DoD pathologist Dr. Shih-Ching Lo holds the U. S. Patent on *M. fermentans* ("Pathogenic Mycoplasma"[67]), and this may be the real reason that in their original response to our work on *M. fermentans* infections in GWI, the DoD/DVA issued guidelines stating that GWI patients should *not* be treated with antibiotics like doxycycline, even though in a significant number of patients it had been shown to be beneficial. The DoD and DVA have also stated that we have not cooperated with them or the CDC in studying this problem. This is also not true. We have done everything possible to cooperate with the DoD, DVA and CDC on this problem, and we even published a letter in the Washington Post on 25 January 1997 indicating that we have done everything possible to cooperate with government agencies on GWI issues, including inviting DoD and DVA scientists and physicians to the Institute for Molecular Medicine to learn our diagnostic procedures on 23 December

1996 at a meeting convened at Walter Reed AMC. We have been and are fully prepared to share our data and procedures with government scientists and physicians. The DVA has responded with the establishment of VA Cooperative Clinical Study Program #475, but many Gulf War Referral Centers at VA Medical Centers continue to be hostile to non-psychiatric treatment of GWI. The DoD and DVA continue to deny that family members of Gulf War veterans could contract the illness or that there could be an infectious basis to GWI.

DoD/DVA Scorecard on GWI from Previous Testimony

In my previous testimony to the U. S. Congress in 1998 [15,18], some suggestions were made to correct for the apparent lack of appropriate response to GWI and the chronic infections found in GWI patients. It seems appropriate to go back and revisit these suggestions to see if any of these were taken seriously or corrected independently (*Updates in italics*).

1. We must stop the denial that immediate family members do not have GWI or illnesses from the Gulf War. Denial that this has occurred has only angered veterans and their families and created a serious public health problem, including spread of the illness to the civilian population and contamination of our blood supply. *This item has still not been taken seriously by the DoD. The DVA has initiated a study to see if veterans' family members have increased illnesses; however, they have decided to group GWI patients together independent of the possible origins of their illness. Since veterans who have their illness primarily due to chemical or environmental exposures that are not transmittable will be grouped with veterans who have transmittable chronic infections, it is unlikely that studying family members of both groups together will yield significant data. Whether intentional or not, this DVA study has apparently been designed to fail. Potential problems with the nation's blood and organ tissue supply due to contamination by chronic infections in GWI and CFS patients are considered significant [68,69], but no U.S. government agency has apparently taken this seriously.*

2. The ICD-9-coded diagnosis system used by the DoD and DVA to determine illness diagnosis must be overhauled. The categories in this system have not kept pace with new medical discoveries in the diagnosis and treatment of chronic illnesses. This has resulted in large numbers of patients from the Gulf War with 'undiagnosed' illnesses who cannot obtain treatment or benefits for their medical conditions. *The DoD and DVA should be using the ICD-10 diagnosis system where a category exists for chronic fatiguing illnesses. Apparently little progress in this area has been made by the DoD or DVA.*

3. Denying claims and benefits by assigning partial disabilities due to PTSD should not be continued in patients that have organic (medical) causes for their illnesses. For example, patients with chronic infections that can take up to or over a year to successfully treat should be allowed benefits. *The DVA has recently shown some flexibility in this area. For example, Gulf War veterans with ALS will receive disability without having to prove that their disease was deployment-related. Similarly, GWI patients with M. fermentans infections (and also their symptomatic family members with the same infection) should receive disabilities. Thus far there has been no attempt to extend disability to GWI-associated infectious diseases. Instead of waiting for years or decades for the research to catch up to the problem, the DoD and DVA should simply accept that many of the chronic illnesses found in Gulf War veterans are deployment related and deserving of treatment and compensation.*

4. Research efforts must be increased in the area of chronic illnesses. Unfortunately, federal funding for such illnesses is often rebudgeted or funds removed. For example, Dr. William Reeves of the CDC in Atlanta sought protection under the 'Federal Whistle Blower's Act' after he exposed misappropriation of funds allocated for CFS at the CDC. It is estimated that over 3% of the adult U.S. population suffers from chronic fatiguing illnesses similar to GWI, yet there are few federal dollars available for research on the diagnosis and treatment of these chronic illnesses, even though each year Congress allocates such funds. *There has been some progress at NIH on this issue, but in general little has changed. The DoD and DVA have spent most of the hundreds of millions of*

dollars allocated for GWI research on psychiatric research. Most of these funds have been spent on studies that have had negligible effect on veterans' health.

5. Past and present senior DoD and DVA administrative personnel must be held accountable for the utter mismanagement of the entire GWI problem. This has been especially apparent in the continuing denial that chronic infections could play a role in GWI and the denial that immediate family members could have contracted their illnesses from veterans with GWI. This has resulted in sick spouses and children being turned away from DoD and DVA facilities without diagnoses or treatments. The responsibility for these civilians must ultimately be borne by the DoD and DVA. I believe that it is now accountability time. The files must be opened so the American public has a better idea how many veterans and civilians have died from illness associated with service in the Gulf War and how many have become sick because of an inadequate response to this health crisis. *Unfortunately, little or no progress has been made on these items for the last decade or more, and the situation has not changed significantly since my last testimony in 1998.*

References and Notes Cited

1. Nicolson GL. Gulf War Illnesses–their causes and treatment. *Armed Forces Med. Dev.* 2001; **2**:41-44.
   <http://www.immed.org/publications/gulf_war_illness/AFMD-Nicolson2001.htm>

2. Nicolson GL, Nasralla M, Haier J, Nicolson NL. Gulf War Illnesses: Role of chemical, radiological and biological exposures. In: *War and Health*, H. Tapanainen, ed., Zed Press, Helinsiki, 2001; 431-446.
   <http://www.immed.org/publications/gulf_war_illness/whc.html>

3. Nicolson GL, Nicolson NL. Chronic Fatigue Illness and Operation Desert Storm. *J. Occup. Environ. Med.* 1996; **38**:14-16.
   <http://www.immed.org/publications/gulf_war_illness/JOEM.html>

4. Nicolson GL, Hyman E, Korényi-Both A, Lopez DA, Nicolson NL, Rea W, Urnovitz H. Progress on Persian Gulf War Illnesses: reality and hypotheses. *Intern. J. Occup. Med. Tox.* 1995; 4:365-370.

5. Unwin C, Blatchley N, Coker W, *et al.* Health of UK servicemen who served in the Persian Gulf War. *Lancet* 1999; 353:169-178.

6. Kizer KW, Joseph S, Rankin JT. Kizer KW, Joseph S, Rankin JT. Unexplained illness among Persian Gulf War vetrans in an Air National Guard unit: preliminary report–August 1990-March 1995. *Morbid. Mortal. Week. Rep.* 1995; 44:443-447.

7. Steele L. Prevalence and patterns of Gulf War Illness in Kansas veterans: association of symptoms with characteristics of person, place and time of military service. *Am. J. Epidemiol.* 2000; 152:992-1002.

8. Murray-Leisure K, Daniels MO, Sees J, Suguitan E, Zangwill B, Bagheri S, Brinser E, Kimber R, Kurban R. Greene, W.H. Mucocutaneous-Intestinal-Rheumatic Desert Syndrome (MIRDS). Definition, histopathology, incubation period, clinical course and association with desert sand exposure. *Intern. J. Med.* 1998; 1:47-72.

9. Nicolson GL. Written testimony to the Subcommittee on National Security, Veterans' Affairs and International Relations, Committee on Government Reform, U. S. House of Representatives, January 24, 2002. <http://www.immed.org/testimony/gulf_war_illness/ct102.html>

10. Nicolson GL, Berns P, Nasralla M, Haier J, Nicolson NL, Nass M. Gulf War Illnesses: chemical, radiological and biological exposures resulting in chronic fatiguing illnesses can be identified and treated. *J. Chronic Fatigue Syndr.* 2003; 11(1):135-154. <http://www.immed.org/publications/gulf_war_illness/netaGWI_JCFS.html>

11. Engel CC Jr, Ursano R, Magruder C, et al. Psychological conditions diagnosed among veterans seeking Department

of Defense care for Gulf War-related health concerns. *J. Occup. Environ. Med.* 1999; **41**:384-392.

12. Nicolson GL, Nasralla M, Nicolson NL, Haier J. High prevalence of mycoplasmal infections in symptomatic (Chronic Fatigue Syndrome) family members of mycoplasma-positive Gulf War Illness patients. *J. Chronic Fatigue Syndr.* 2003; **11**(2): 21-36.

13. Lange G, Tiersky L, DeLuca J, et al. Psychiatric diagnoses in Gulf War veterans with fatiguing illnesses. *Psychiat. Res.* 1999; **89**:39-48.

14. Haley RW, Kurt TL, Hom J. Is there a Gulf War Syndrome? Searching for syndromes by factor analysis of symptoms. *JAMA* 1997; **277**:215-222.

15. Nicolson GL. Written testimony to the Subcommittee on Benefits, Committee on Veterans' Affairs, U. S. House of Representatives, July 16, 1998. <http://www.immed.org/testimony/gulf_war_illness/ct98.html>

16. U. S. Congress, House Committee on Government Reform and Oversight, Gulf War veterans': DOD continue to resist strong evidence linking toxic causes to chronic health effects, 105th Congress, 1st Session, Report 105-388, 1997.

17. U. S. General Accounting Office, Gulf War Illnesses: improved monitoring of clinical progress and reexamination of research emphasis are needed. Report GAO/SNIAD-97-163, 1997.

18. Nicolson GL. Written testimony to the Special Oversight Board for Department of Defense Investigations on Gulf War Chemical and Biological Incidents, U. S. Senate, November 19, 1998. <http://www.immed.org/testimony/gulf_war_illness/ct1198.html>

19. Sartin JS. Gulf War Illnesses: causes and controversies. *Mayo Clinic Proc.* 2000; **75**:811-819.

20. Baumzweiger WE, Grove R. Brainstem-Limbic immune dysregulation in 111 Gulf War veterans: a clinical evaluation

of its etiology, diagnosis and response to headache treatment. *Intern. J. Med.* 1998; **1**:129-143.

21. Haley RW, Fleckenstein JL, Marshall WW, *et al.* Effect of basal ganglia injury on central dopamine activity in Gulf War Syndrome: correlation of proton magnetic resonance spectroscopy and plasma homovanillic acid levels. *Arch. Neurol.* 2000; **280**:981-988.

22. Magill AJ, Grogl M, Fasser RA, *et al.* Viscerotropic leishmaniasis caused by *Leishmania tropica* in soldiers returning from Operation Desert Storm. (1993) *N. Engl. J. Med.* 1993; **328**:1383-1387.

23. Nicolson GL, Nasralla M, Franco AR, *et al.* Mycoplasmal infections in fatigue illnesses: Chronic Fatigue and Fibromyalgia Syndromes, Gulf War Illness and Rheumatoid Arthritis. *J. Chronic Fatigue Syndr.* 2000; **6**(3):23-39. <http://www.immed.org

24. Urnovitz HB, Tuite JJ, Higashida JM *et al.* RNAs in the sera of Persian Gulf War veterans have segments homologous to chromosome 22q11.2 *Clin. Diagn. Lab. Immunol.* 1999; **6**:330-335.

25. Hannan KL, Berg DE, Baumzweiger W, *et al.* Activation of the coagulation system in Gulf War Illnesses: a potential pathophysiologic link with chronic fatigue syndrome, a laboratory approach to diagnosis. *Blood Coag. Fibrinol.* 2000; **7**:673-678.

26. Nicolson GL, Nasralla M, Hier J, Nicolson NL. Diagnosis and treatment of chronic mycoplasmal infections in Fibromyalgia Syndrome and Chronic Fatigue Syndrome: relationship to Gulf War Illness. *Biomed. Therapy* 1998; **16**: 266-271.

27. Nicolson GL, Nicolson NL. Gulf War Illnesses: complex medical, scientific and political paradox. *Med. Confl. Surviv.* 1998; **14**:74-83.

28. Abou-Donia MB, Wilmarth KR. Neurotoxicity resulting from coexposure to pyridostigmine bromide, DEET and permethrin: Implications of Gulf War exposures. *J. Tox. Environ. Health* 1996; **48**:35-56.

29. Moss JL. Synergism of toxicity of *N,N*-dimethyl-*m*-toluamide to German cockroaches (*Othopiera blattellidae*) by hydrolytic enzyme inhibitors. *J. Econ. Entomol.* 1996; **89**:1151-1155.

30. Baker DJ, Sedgwick EM. Single fibre electromyographic changes in man after organophosphate exposure. *Hum. Expl. Toxicol.* 1996; **15**:369-375.

31. Jamal GA. Gulf War syndrome-a model for the complexity of biological and environmental interactions with human health. *Adver. Drug React. Tox. Rev.* 1997; **16**:133-170.

32. Miller CS, Prihoda TJ. The Environmental and Exposure and Sensitivity Inventory (EESI): a standardized approach for quantifying symptoms and intolerances for research and clinical applications. *Tox. Ind. Health* 1999; **15**:386-397.

33. Haley RW, Kurt TL. Self-reported exposure to neurotoxic chemical combinations in the Gulf War. A cross-sectional epidemiologic study. *JAMA* 1997; **277**:231-237.

34. Gordon JJ, Inns RH, Johnson MK *et al.* The delayed neuropathic effects of nerve agents and some other organophosphorus compounds. *Arch. Toxicol.* 1983; **52**:71-82.

35. Briefing Note 03/2001. Depleted Uranium Munitions. European Parliament Directorate General for Research-Directorate A. Scientific and Technological Options Assessment. January, 2001.

36. U. S. Congress, House Subcommittee on Human Resources, Committee on Government Reform and Oversight. Status of efforts to identify Gulf War Syndrome: Multiple Toxic Exposures. June 26, 1997 hearing. Washington DC: U.S. Government Printing Office, 1998.

37. Kalinich JF, Ramakrishnan N, McClain DE. A procedure for the rapid detection of depleted uranium in metal shrapnel fragments. *Mil. Med.* 2000; **165**:626-629.

38. Hooper FJ, Squibb KS, Siegel EL, *et al.* Elevated uranium excretion by soldiers with retained uranium shrapnel. *Health Phys.* 1999; **77**:512-519.

39. Korényi-Both AL, Molnar AC, Korényi-Both AL, *et al.* Al Eskan disease: Desert Storm pneumonitis. *Mil. Med.* 1992; **157**:452-462.

40. Baseman JB, Tully JG. Mycoplasmas: Sophisticated, reemerging, and burdened by their notoriety. *Emerg. Infect. Dis.* 1997; **3**:21-32.

41. Nicolson GL, Nasralla M, Haier J, *et al.* Mycoplasmal infections in chronic illnesses: Fibromyalgia and Chronic Fatigue Syndromes, Gulf War Illness, HIV-AIDS and Rheumatoid Arthritis. *Med. Sentinel* 1999; **4**:172-176.

42. Nicolson GL, Nicolson NL. Diagnosis and treatment of mycoplasmal infections in Gulf War Illness-CFIDS patients. *Intern. J. Occup. Med. Immunol. Tox.* 1996; **5**:69-78. <http://www.immed.org/publications/gulf_war_illness/pub4.html>

43. Nicolson GL, Nicolson NL, Nasralla M. Mycoplasmal infections and Chronic Fatigue Illness (Gulf War Illness) associated with deployment to Operation Desert Storm. *Intern. J. Med.* 1997; **1**:80-92. <http://www.immed.org/publications/gulf_war_illness/pub5.html>

44. Vojdani A, Franco AR. Multiplex PCR for the detection of *Mycoplasma fermentans, M. hominis* and *M. penetrans* in patients with Chronic Fatigue Syndrome, Fibromyalgia, Rheumatoid Arthritis and Gulf War Illness. *J. Chronic Fatigue Syndr.* 1999; **5**:187-197.

45. Nicolson GL, Nasralla M, Nicolson NL. The pathogenesis and treatment of mycoplasmal infections. *Antimicrob. Infect. Dis. Newsl.* 1999; **17**:81-88. <http://www.immed.org/publications

46. Nicolson GL, Nasralla M, Franco AR, *et al.* Diagnosis and integrative treatment of intracellular bacterial infections in Chronic Fatigue and Fibromyalgia Syndromes, Gulf War Illness, Rheumatoid Arthritis and other chronic illnesses. *Clin. Pract. Alt. Med.* 2000; **1**:92-102. <http://www.immed.org/publications/treatment_considerations/pub2.html>

47.   Gray GC, Kaiser KS, Hawksworth AW, *et al*. No serologic evidence of an association found between Gulf War service and *Mycoplasma fermentans* infection. *Am. J. Trop. Med. Hyg.* 1999; **60**:752-757.

48.   Choppa PC, Vojdani A, Tagle C, Andrin R, Magtoto L. Multiplex PCR for the detection of Mycoplasma fermentans, M. hominis and M. penetrans in cell cultures and blood samples of patients with Chronic Fatigue Syndrome. *Mol. Cell Probes* 1998; **12**:301-308.

49.   Nasralla M, Haier J, Nicolson GL. Multiple mycoplasmal infections detected in blood of Chronic Fatigue and Fibromyalgia Syndrome patients. *Eur. J. Clin. Microbiol. Infect. Dis.* 1999; **18**:859-865.
       <http://www.immed.org/publications/

50.   U. S. Congress, Senate Committee on Banking, Housing and Urban Affairs, U. S. chemical and biological warfare-related dual use exports to Iraq and their possible impact on the health consequences of the Persian Gulf War, 103rd Congress, 2nd Session, Report May 25, 1994.

51.   Walling AD. Amyotrophic Lateral Sclerosis: Lou Gehrig's Disease. *Amer. Fam. Physician* 1999; **59**:1489-1496.

52.   Nicolson GL, Nasralla M, Haier J, Pomfret J. High frequency of systemic mycoplasmal infections in Gulf War veterans and civilians with Amytrophic Lateral Sclerosis (ALS). *J. Clin. Neurosci.* 2002; **9**:525-529.
       <http://www.immed.org/publications/treatment_considerations/pub2.html>

53.   Nicolson GL, Nicolson NL. Doxycycline treatment and Desert Storm. *JAMA* 1995; **273**:618-619.

54.   Nicolson GL. Mycoplasmal infections–Diagnosis and treatment of Gulf War Syndrome/CFIDS. *CFIDS Chronicle* 1996; **9**(3): 66-69.
       <http://www.immed.org/publications/gulf_war_illness

55.   Nicolson GL. Considerations when undergoing treatment for chronic infections found in Chronic Fatigue Syndrome, Fibromyalgia Syndrome and Gulf War Illnesses. (Part 1).

Antibiotics Recommended when indicated for treatment of Gulf War Illness/CFIDS/FMS (Part 2). *Intern. J. Med.* 1998; **1**:115-117, 123-128.
<http://www.immed.org/publications/treatment_considerations/pub1.html>

56.   Cherry N, Creed F, Silman A, et al. Health and exposures of United Kingdom Gulf war veterans. Part II: The relation of health to exposure. *J. Occup. Environ. Med.* 2001; **58**:299-306.

57.   Goss Gilroy Inc. Health Study of Canadian Forces Personnel Involved in the 1991 Conflict in the Persian Gulf Volume I. Prepared for Gulf War Illness Advisory Committee. Ottawa: Department of National Defense. April 20, 1998.
<www.dnd.ca/menu/press/Reports/Health/health_study_eng_1.htm>

58.   Mahan CM, Kang HK, Ishii EK et al. Anthrax vaccination and self-reported symptoms, functional status and medical conditions in the national health survey of Gulf War era veterans and their families. Presented to the Conference on Illnesses among Gulf War Veterans: A Decade of Scientific Research. Military and Veterans Health Coordinating Board, Research Working Group. Alexandria, VA: January 24-26, 2001.

59.   Nicolson GL, Nass M, Nicolson NL. Anthrax vaccine: controversy over safety and efficacy. *Antimicrob. Infect. Dis. Newsl.* 2000; **18**(1):1-6.
<http://www.immed.org/publications/gulf_war_illness/anthrax3-18-00.html>

60.   Nicolson GL, Nass M, Nicolson NL. The anthrax vaccine controversy. Questions about its efficacy, safety and strategy. *Med. Sentinel* 2000; **5**:97-101.
<http://www.immed.org/publications/gulf_war_illness/anthrax2-18-00.html>

61.   Thornton D. A survey of mycoplasma detection in vaccines. *Vaccine* 1986; **4**:237-240.

62. Nass M. Anthrax vaccine linked to Gulf War Syndrome. Report to the Institute of Molecular Medicine, October 2, 2001. <http://www.immed.org/publications/gulf_war_illness/GWIanthraxvacc01.10.2H.html>

63. Uniformed Services University of the Health Sciences, Pathology Workbook VI, 1993.

64. Lo S-C, Wear DJ, Shih W-K, Wang RY-H, Newton PB, Rodriguez JF. Fatal systemic infections of nonhuman primates by Mycoplasma fermentans (incognitus strain). Clin. Infect. Dis. 1993; 17(Suppl 1):S283-S288.

65. Lo S-C, Dawson MS, Newton PB, et al. Association of the virus-like infectious agent originally reported in patients with AIDS with acute fatal disease in previously healthy non-AIDS patients. Amer. J. Trop. Med. Hyg. 1989; 41:364-376.

66. Lo S-C, Buchholz CL, Wear DJ, Hohm RC, Marty AM. Histopathology and doxycycline treatment in a previously healthy non-AIDS patient systemically infected by Mycoplasma fermentans (incognitus strain). Mod. Pathol. 1991; 6:750-754.

67. Lo S-C. Pathogenic mycoplasma. U.S. Patent 5,242,820. Issued September 7, 1993.

68. Hinshaw C. American Academy of Environmental Medicine, Personal Communication, 1997.

69. Gass R, Fisher J, Badesch D, et al. Donor-to-host transmission of Mycoplasma hominis in lung allograft recipients. Clin. Infect. Dis. 1996; 22:567-568.

Under penalty of perjury, I swear that the statements above are true and correct to the best of my knowledge, information and belief.

Garth L. Nicolson, Ph.D.
President, Chief Scientific Officer and Research Professor
The Institute for Molecular Medicine (www.immed.org)
Professor of Integrative Medicine

Appendix 3

Sworn Testimony to the U. S. Congress and Presidential Commissions

Testimony of Garth L. Nicolson, House Committee on Government Reform, Subcommittee on National Security, Veterans' Affairs and International Relations, United States House of Representatives, January 24, 2002.

Testimony of Garth L. Nicolson, House Committee on Veterans' Affairs, Subcommittee on Health, United States House of Representatives, January 24, 2002.

Testimony of Garth L. Nicolson, Special Oversight Board for Department of Defense Investigations of Gulf War Chemical and Biological Incidents, U. S. Senate Hart Office Building, November 19, 1998.

Testimony of Garth L. Nicolson, House Committee on Veterans' Affairs, Subcommittee on Benefits, United States House of Representatives, July 16, 1998.

Testimony of Garth L. Nicolson and Nancy L. Nicolson, House Committee on Government Reform and Oversight, Subcommittee on Human Resource and Intergovernmental Relations, United States House of Representatives, June 26, 1997.

Testimony of Garth L. Nicolson and Dr. Nancy L. Nicolson, House Committee on Government Reform and Oversight, Subcommittee on Human Resource and Intergovernmental Relations, United States House of Representatives, April 2, 1996.

Testimony of Garth Nicolson and Nancy L. Nicolson, Mycoplasmal Infections in Gulf War Illnesses, President's Advisory Panel on Gulf War Veterans' Illnesses, Washington D.C., August 14-16, 1995.

CPSIA information can be obtained
at www.ICGtesting.com
Printed in the USA
BVHW031319190520
579963BV00003B/8/J